One woman in love with two men.
Why choose, when she wants them both?

Samantha is in love with her roommates, Geoff and Chris, and she's sure they feel the same way. She's also pretty sure Geoff is a sexual Dominant who wants to claim both her and Chris for his own. Yet the two men have been best friends since childhood, and that friendship keeps them frustratingly hands-off toward her and each other.

She wants to respect their code of honor, but she craves deeper, more primitive reactions from them. Driven by her own submissive desires, she'll tease Geoff's Dominant side to life to see if her naughtiest wishes can become the love of a lifetime, with the two men who are everything her heart desires.

NAUGHTY WISHES

The Complete Novel

JOEY W. HILL

FOREWORD

Naughty Wishes was released by the original publisher as a four-part serial. Since the installments were released a month apart, some refresher points were included in Parts II through IV that may feel a bit redundant in the compilation. We hope this won't interfere with our readers' enjoyment of Geoff, Chris and Samantha's story.

To honor the story's original form, we have attempted to keep the new edition content essentially unchanged, except for the unavoidable obsessive tweaking and polishing by the author.

BODY

Part 1

*D*ivide and conquer.

For the past several days, it had been her mantra, a rallying call to summon her courage. Today Samantha Beth Gerard was going to act on it.

A storm had hit the Gulf, so Chris and the landscaping company that employed him were in Mississippi for the next few days, picking up as much work as they could. Which left her and Geoff alone in the rental house the three of them shared.

She sat in their backyard, inside the flying aviary Chris had built to nurse and rehabilitate birds and other animals he rescued during the course of his job. Ron, Hermione and Harry, the three permanent inhabitants, flew from branch to branch, chirping. Sam drew her knees up on the edge of the wooden Adirondack chair, curling her bare toes in the wooden slats. Turning her head, she rested it on her knees and looked through the picture window of their small house.

Geoff was working at the dining room table they'd found at a secondhand store. His laptop was open and there were two file boxes on the table. Papers were arranged on the table like a neatly landscaped garden in multiple shades of white. As usual, he was working on a case. A young attorney working his way up the ladder of a corporate firm, he put in a lot of hours. She had no doubt he'd be offered a partnership within his specified timetable and then split off to form his own office. He typically ended up as the lead on any project he was

1

assigned, even if it didn't start that way. He embraced responsibility, control.

According to her friend Flo, men like that would sometimes crave submission in the bedroom, needing the release of not being in control, but that wasn't the vibe Sam got from Geoff. Not in the least. Sam suspected Geoff was a Dom, one who was self-aware but who'd never truly embraced it.

After meeting him over a couple of dinners, Flo had concurred. "Oh yeah. That one wants to be in charge. He needs it like you need chocolate. Once he decides he's ready to explore his Dominant side, he'll be a storm that sweeps you off your feet. In a good way, if he has his shit together."

Flo was a teller at the bank where Sam worked. An attractive, delicately fox-featured woman in her fifties, she had shrewd brown eyes and short hair dyed a bird's-wing brown with golden highlights. Though there were nearly thirty years' difference in their ages, she and Flo had gravitated toward each other in the usual way that coworkers became friends. Day-to-day interactions, the occasional lunch, then slipping on their athletic shoes for lunchtime walks in the downtown Charlotte area where they worked.

As Sam started opening up about her feelings for Chris and Geoff, Florence had listened attentively. Friendship turned into confidences, and one day Flo told Sam she was a Domme, a Mistress.

"Being Dominant or submissive can be an orientation, like being gay and straight," she'd explained. "Some women might take charge in the bedroom on occasion to spice things up, purely for fun, but for me, it runs deeper than that. The men I'm with need to surrender, to submit, to help them find pleasure and release, and I need to control and dominate, feed off that exchange and surrender, to be satisfied."

Between Flo taking her to several private parties, where Sam could see what a sexual Dominant was in context, and studying Florence at the bank, Sam started to understand even more. There was a sharp directness to how Flo dealt with everyone, a firmness that made coworkers and customers alike respond to her with respect. All the tellers knew if a customer was causing a problem, Flo was the one who could step in, defuse the situation and restore balance.

Those nuances and vibes . . . they were different versions of Geoff.

When she first confided that to Flo, wondering if she was crazy, her friend had given her a blunt look.

"You see it because you're his mirror, Sam. You're a sub, and that defines how you operate in a relationship. That first night you went with me to a party, I saw you watching the male Doms. You were like a kid outside a candy store, a kid who loves candy but only wants her favorite kind. The kind waiting for her at home." The woman's lips curved. "Geoff is easy to define. Chris will be your wild card. It'll be interesting to see where he falls in all of this. But to get anything started, you're going to have to get Geoff on board first."

Nothing had technically ever happened between Sam, Geoff and Chris, but over time it had become clear, at least to Sam, that something had been happening all along. Subtle things, small moments that had drawn them closer, the seeds of desire and need taking root. But she'd come to the same conclusion Flo had: Geoff was the key.

Flo made it sound like a wonderful adventure was just waiting for her, which had made waiting for the right moment even worse. Sam's initially vague fantasies were now in hi-def, digging so deeply into her they could make her heart pound and ache whenever she was around the two men.

While she valued their friendship more than anything, and was terrified she might be about to screw that up, her sex drive and emotional compulsions were overriding every caution. Her daily exposure to two hot men she loved made it at least partially their fault that she'd reached this reckless point. She wanted them both.

No time like the present to start making that clear.

Flo had compared Geoff to a storm. Sam thought of him as the forked lightning that split open the darkness of a room, revealing every corner, everything hidden in the shadows. As she imagined being touched by that lightning, she quivered deep inside, her fingers tightening on her coffee cup.

Courage, Samantha Beth. You can do this.

Rising from her chair, she slipped out of the aviary, secured the door and padded back into the house, letting the screen door in the kitchen close behind her with a small *squeak*. The sunlight made her feel warm and ambitious. Optimistic. Geoff wasn't the only one who could be goal-oriented.

She paused at the door, letting herself savor the sight of him. He had dark blond hair, the strands of lighter and darker colors tangled in an artful, rakish mix he kept longer over his brow, severe on the sides and the nape. Geoff had to be conscious of his appearance, since his law firm was one of the city's best. He honed his looks as he did any other skill, until looking urbane, professional and devastating were second nature, not an affectation. For the days he would be in court, he wore crisp white dress shirts, slim silk ties and one of his two Hugo Boss suits. Despite the suits' formidable cost when he'd bought them, he'd considered them investments. One was dark charcoal, the other the color of creek rock that picked up the golden tones of his hazel eyes. Currently those eyes were trained on what he was studying while he typed notes one-handed.

When Geoff won his first solo trial, she and Chris had put their money together and bought him silver cuff links. Since he liked the Marvel movies and they teased him about being a legal super hero, the cuff links were the Avengers emblem, an *A* with one leg longer than the other. Buying anything fashion-related for Geoff was a risk, but even if he only kept them in a drawer, she figured he'd enjoy the sentiment of looking at them on occasion. Instead, he wore them every time he went to court. He said they were his good-luck pieces.

Today he was in casual weekend wear, a worn *Just Do It* Nike T-shirt and jeans. While she loved the look of him in a suit and had all sorts of Dom/sub fantasies about that, usually with him fully dressed in the suit and her in nothing but a pair of heels and pearls, kneeling before him, she liked his casual look as well. It was a reminder that he was home, and that she was part of what he considered home.

She stopped behind his chair, inhaled. He showered and shaved every morning, a personal gift to her whether he knew it or not, because the scent of his aftershave on his warm skin kept her world balanced and pleasantly tilted at once. Like the smell of sunshine and cut grass on Chris after he took care of their small lawn.

She and Chris were so used to Geoff working, respecting his space and train of thought, he wouldn't expect her to talk to him, wouldn't think her silence rude. But she wondered how long it would take him to notice her standing behind him. Did he have a heightened awareness of her, the way she had of him? She thought about sinking to her knees next to his chair, waiting for his notice, for a command. Would he laugh at her? Ask her what she was doing down there? Or worse, would she see that sharp awareness in his eyes that told her he knew exactly, but he'd shutter that look and play dumb?

Stop overthinking this. Setting aside the coffee, she laid her hands on his shoulders, leaning over one so her long, straight hair fell over her fingers, spilling onto his chest. "Do you want me to get you another cup of coffee?" she murmured in his ear. She let her thumbs slide along his neck. A close-up inhale of his aftershave and warm flesh made her almost dizzy. Honest to God, she trembled when she touched him, because she wanted something only he could provide.

He tilted his head. His serious eyes could make Sam lose her train of thought when they focused on her the way they did now. The starburst of brown around the pupil interlaced with gold, those two colors melting into a forest mix of green.

"If you're making some more for yourself."

"No." She paused. "I want to make some for you. May I?"

He stilled under her touch. She almost drew back, but instead she let gravity take her fingertips beneath the ribbed collar of his T-shirt to savor the rough friction of his chest hair, the smooth bump of his collarbone beneath her thumb. He reached up, closed his hand on her wrist. He was studying her, weighing her actions.

Figure it out, she thought. *Don't make me be more blatant about it, or I might chicken out.*

"You must be lonely for Chris," he decided. "The two of you usually keep each other company when I'm having to do this crap." His look was calculated. "Done your exercises yet?"

She almost groaned and pulled her hand away. Yes, she was lonely for Chris, but that wasn't why she was seeking Geoff out now. He couldn't really be thinking of things to occupy her, like she was some kind of bored child. But then a thought crossed her mind and, rather than snarling, she shrugged. "I hate doing them."

"I know you do. But you hate that needle even more."

Because of the hours she spent at the computer as an assistant bank manager, she occasionally suffered a frozen shoulder that had to be loosened up with a steroid shot and a few weeks of agonizing rehab. After it happened the third time, she did resistance band exercises regularly to maintain range of motion.

"Okay." She slipped her hands off him reluctantly, but before she went to get the PT aid, she put another K-cup in the coffeemaker and

5

made his coffee, adding the dollop of skim milk he liked. Geoff preferred sugar cubes to sweetener or spooned sugar. Lifting the small lid off the glass jar full of neat, glittering squares, she plucked out four to add to his coffee.

While waiting for his breakfast sandwich to heat in the microwave, Chris would sometimes pull out a handful and make faces or small pyramids out of them. Geoff would grumble, but Sam noticed he'd always snag his requisite four out of the formation Chris had left. They had so many daily rituals like that, evidence of the intimate friendship that existed between the three of them.

Bringing the fresh cup to Geoff, she set it down by his elbow and took the opportunity to touch him again, letting her hand drift over his biceps, his forearm. Chris was brawny, the kind of build that suggested football player or human tank. Geoff had a runner's physique, but he added bulk with strength training. As a result, the body under her hand was leaner than Chris's but just as tough. Chris simply had more mass.

She smiled at the thought. If Geoff was the lightning, Chris was the mountain. A mountain that smelled of forest and earth, with rock-hard muscles, steady brown eyes, tanned skin and callused hands. Whose laughter was like sunlight reflecting in a moving creek.

She left the kitchen to retrieve the resistance band, came back and hooked it over the kitchen doorknob. She did the warm-up reps, conscious of the riffle of papers as Geoff looked for something, the tapping of his pen as he read through what he'd found. As her heart tripped a little faster, anticipating what she was about to do, she comforted herself with the thought that, if she was about to make a fool of herself, he might not even notice. She reminded herself of the things Flo had told her to fortify her for this moment.

"You already feel his Dominant side, Sam, and you respond to it. I think you're right, that he hasn't actively embraced it yet, which isn't unusual, even if he didn't have his insane workload. A man, vanilla or kinky, has to get through those fumbling high school and college years to develop a baseline sexual confidence. If he manages that, one with Dom cravings then has to get past a load of politically correct bullshit that tells him he's an abuser if he wants to dominate a partner. When he finally emerges from that quagmire, he has to find an environment in which he can explore his Dom side. Or the right sub to inspire him to it." Flo had winked at her. "It's just exhausting. Must be why the best Doms are in their forties or older. My opinion, of course."

Well, if Geoff had never deeply explored that side of himself, Sam was standing at the front of the line, volunteering. But getting the ball rolling was making her stomach quake.

In the middle of that discussion, Flo had gripped Sam's hand. The woman was spare with physical affection, so it emphasized the importance of her point. "Having to take the lead to convince him of what you want is pretty much the antithesis of a submissive's makeup," she'd said seriously. "But any Dom will tell you, the submissive is usually the braver of the two of them. To surrender control, to truly trust another person to that level, takes a special kind of courage."

Okay. *Sis boom bah, Sam. Go, team, go.* Turning her back to the kitchen door, Sam clasped the two ends of the band she had hooked around the knob. She stepped forward until her arms started to straighten behind her, her shoulders drawing down and back. She knew when Geoff started noticing, because the tapping of the pen stopped, and in the corner of her eye she saw his head lift.

"Can you count it off for me when I'm fully extended?" she asked casually. "Twenty seconds. I always rush to get it over with, and I know you won't. You're such a sadist."

She added that with an absent smile. Then she dared to glance his way.

She nearly choked on a ball of air when she saw how fully she'd captured his attention. His gaze was practically etching out the effect of her arms being drawn back, and marking how the resistance band wrapped over her wrists. She was still wearing the baby tee she'd worn to bed and her pajama bottoms. No bra, so her nipples were straining against the jersey fabric, and the T-shirt was short enough she felt the flow of air over her abdomen, the tingle against her navel piercing. His attention slid down over that, the heat of it like the trail of a fingertip over her exposed hipbone. She swallowed. "Geoff? Are you counting?"

"Yes. Do you want me to count aloud?" Normally he would smile when he teased her like that, asking the obvious, but instead his eyes met hers with a simmering intensity.

"It's harder for me when you don't count aloud," she managed. "I have to wait for you to tell me when you've reached twenty."

7

"Yes. That's true." And still he just looked at her.

She bit her lip, realizing the exercise was more difficult when she was breathless. She was a total nature girl when it came to keeping herself in shape, preferring hiking, biking or swimming to a gym or calisthenics. She considered exercises like this pure torture. But at least the element of sensual torment kept it from being tedious. When he rose from the chair, her heart pounded faster, enough that she worried she'd underestimated the strength of her reaction. If she passed out, it would likely ruin any progress she might be making with him.

He came around the table and stood in front of her. Reaching out, he toyed with a strand of her hair, following it down. Her hair was hanging loose, away from her body, but close enough that she could feel the layer of air compress between his hand and her tingling nipple.

"You can hold out another ten seconds."

She shook her head. "I don't think so."

"No?" He tugged on the strand of her hair and feathered his knuckles over her nipple. "Even if I do that?"

Her gaze lifted to his, and she moistened her lips. "Do what?"

His mouth curved, but it wasn't with humor. "Stay where you are, Samantha Beth. Don't close your eyes. Tell me when your shoulders start to hurt."

He was the only one who occasionally called her by her first and middle names. She wondered why he thought she'd close her eyes, but then he brushed both palms over the tips of her breasts. Once, twice . . . Sensation speared between her legs, to the base of her spine, up into her throat and through her aching shoulders. She found herself straining toward him, lifting her chest. Whether intended or not, he'd made sure she was doing a very good stretch. But it also pushed her into the red zone.

"Geoff . . . it's starting to hurt."

"Eighteen . . . nineteen . . ." He teased her nipples once more and moved his hands to her shoulders, holding them and easing her back so she didn't hurt herself trying to relieve the pressure too quickly. "Twenty. You should probably do some of the exercises that work those muscles out another way. You really pushed it on that one."

He returned to his chair and started working again. As if nothing had happened. Seriously? Was he playing some kind of Dom game with her? No, that was the counting thing, and he'd been getting into it, she could tell. Then he'd withdrawn.

She tried not to scream. Ever since she'd become determined to actualize this thing between them, she kept hitting this wall, with both men. She'd come to the conclusion they were restrained by the belief that it was an either/or situation: that she was going to choose one or the other. Though the three of them had met in college and been roommates ever since, Geoff and Chris had been friends since childhood, so neither would step over that line and jeopardize the chances of the other man.

Yet if she truly were in love with only one of them, she would have denied herself and moved out, because she would never drive a wedge between Geoff and Chris. However, she'd always sensed something percolating between the two as strong as what she felt for them. It was buried in the shadows of their deep friendship, but she could feel it waiting. If she was brave enough, she might just be the bridge for all of them. If the stubborn cluelessness of the two men didn't make her brain explode.

She'd thought about trying to have a meaningful conversation about it, but any attempts to get them to talk about feelings resulted in withdrawal plus shutdown. Or they'd just listen to her, nod, and things would continue the same as always. God had a sick sense of humor when it came to communication between the sexes.

She did a few more exercises and coiled up the resistance band. As she passed behind Geoff again, her gaze slid over what he was doing. She'd seen him print out the document under his left hand, and he hadn't written any notes on it. The work documents and notes that had to be preserved were to his right, perched on a couple of law books. His laptop was in a safe space. Should she . . . *Oh, the hell with it.* She eased forward. "Geoff, do you think—"

It was ridiculously easy to tip the coffee mug, as less than a fourth of the contents were left. A finger of fluid swept across his printout as she drew in a breath. "Oh, I'm so sorry." She hurried to get a paper towel and started to mop it up. "That was really clumsy."

"Yes, it was."

His tone was torn between exasperation and something else. She tried to hide a smile that was part mischief and all nerves, both fueled by something more urgent than either one. She really couldn't get more contrived. Her face was flushed, she was sure. When he closed his fingers around her wrist, she jerked, not to get away, but a twitch of response.

"Take off your shirt, Sam."

The unexpected command sent a thrill right down to her toes. Especially when she raised her lashes to meet his hazel eyes and saw exactly the look she'd been hoping to inspire. "I can't . . . unless you release my wrist."

"Ask me to do that."

Did he feel like she did, a foreigner who'd suddenly found someone who spoke her language, making it impossible not to speak straight from her heart?

"I don't want you to let go of me. I like how it feels, you holding me like that."

His gaze flickered, his jaw tightening. He loosened his grip, but only enough to guide her arm across her body. With her wrist still resting in his hold, she was able to use that hand to free her other arm from the sleeve and pull the shirt over her head. The shirt slid down and draped on the connection between them. He let go of her to pull the shirt off, then recaptured her wrist. He sat at eye level with her breasts, studying the quivering curves.

"Skin like milk and snow. That's what Chris says. He's always worried about you going out without sunscreen." Geoff cupped one of her breasts in his free hand and she made a whimpering sound in her throat as he held it firmly, passing his thumb over the nipple until it beaded further. Her pale skin felt too tight for her body. She wanted to be released to fly, only she wanted to fly right to him. When he lifted his gaze to her face, the look in his eyes arrested her. So often she'd seen thrilling hints of what she'd suspected was there, and his even, cool expression sent a hot flush through her. So much was happening behind those eyes, things that simultaneously scared her and unleashed the cravings she'd kept wrapped up for far too long.

If he truly hadn't explored his Dom side, they could be about to crest the first big hill of this roller coaster together. That was scary, but it didn't scare her, if that made sense. She'd seen things at the private parties with Flo that had scared her, things she wasn't sure she wanted to do. Florence had helped her with that, too.

"A Master or Mistress doesn't dominate with ropes or pain. They do it with a word, a look, a simple touch. The rest is just fun and play. The root of what you desire will come from his lips, his hands upon you, the way he looks at you. Dom/sub relationships are ninety percent about the mind."

Now she understood exactly what Flo meant, because when Geoff was wearing that expression, she was a morass of confused desires and a still heart, waiting for a word from him to begin beating.

"You knocked over my coffee on purpose," he said thoughtfully. He had a mesmerizing voice. Regardless of whether he spoke softly or in his court voice, it drew attention, making a woman strain her ears to hear what he said. "Did those exercises to tease me."

"Yes." She lifted her chin. "That day we went to Naughty Bits . . . we didn't get to talk like you said we would. I'm tired of waiting."

About a week ago, she'd coaxed them into an erotica shop, Naughty Bits, thinking that would be the best way to send them the message that it didn't have to be either/or, that she wanted both of them. The intuitive owner, Madison Fine, had drawn Geoff over to the Dungeon Room. Barely breathing, Sam had watched out of the corner of her eye as Geoff fingered floggers and rope, studying the things Madison showed him.

When Sam had darted a glance toward Chris, she'd found him staring at Geoff with an unfathomable expression, until he noticed her watching. He started teasing her about the role-playing costumes the two of them had been left to examine.

They hadn't bought anything that day. Madison had suggested they go to a local bagel shop, discuss their desires and come back after they decided. They'd headed off to do just that. Then Geoff got a call from work about some kind of affidavit crisis. Twenty-four hours later, Esteban was ringing Chris's cell about the trip to Mississippi.

"Hmm." Geoff had precisely sculpted features, a far more masculine version of the male beauty often depicted in the sensual Abercrombie & Fitch ads. Though he was a corporate attorney, when his expression became more uncompromising, as it did now, she imagined him as a criminal prosecutor, bringing a hostile witness in line. Or making a point to the jury the way a judge did when admonishing them or giving them instruction.

"I'm tired of bad girls who interrupt my work," he said in just that tone. "I'm going to spank you."

Oh God. Yes, please. He must have registered her reaction, for his lips quirked, though his gaze remained steady, flat. He stroked his long fingers over her throat, making her lift her chin, then his grasp on her wrist increased. She wondered how he was going to proceed, how she needed to cooperate or react so they both didn't end up feeling foolish, but he took all those concerns away. In one decisive pull, he yanked her down over his lap.

Strong as she knew he was, feeling it firsthand stirred up a whole hive of bees in her lower belly. He steadied her before she could even start to flail, uncertain of her position. Bracing a hand on her ass, he took a nice solid grip on one cheek through her flannel pajama bottoms.

He wasn't tentative about it, which made suspicion bloom. He'd done this before. Or maybe he was like her, thinking about the same kind of thing so often that he'd switched from theory to practice without a blink. She'd told herself she'd have to have courage to go down this road, but what if she couldn't handle the reality of it? She was about to find out. Maybe that was why he'd decided to finally act. Not because she'd pushed it, but to see if he could scare her back into her corner.

No. A sadist he might be, but cruel he wasn't. He wouldn't humiliate her with no purpose, or he wasn't the friend she felt she knew, inside and out. But still, anticipating his Dom side for so long, imagining what it would be like, was very different from being so abruptly immersed in it.

Hooking his thumb under her waistband, he dragged her pajamas to her thighs, exposing her ass. Once committed, he didn't believe in half measures. She bit back an unexpected moan, not wanting to do anything to change his mind. Geoff had her over his lap, her backside exposed, and was going to spank her. She was shaking a little, no matter that she was trying to hide it.

"Milk and snow here as well," he mused. "I've thought about making this gorgeous ass red plenty of times. Especially when you parade around in front of me and Chris in these tiny T-shirts and low-riding pajama bottoms like we're your brothers or some shit like that."

He sounded almost mean. She wet her lips. "I didn't mean—not at first."

"I know. But you still need to be taught better manners. Now be quiet. I'm going to count in my head again, and you'll just have to guess how high I'm going to go. Spread your thighs. I want to see your cunt get wet from this."

She'd never thought of such words coming from Geoff's mouth. She'd imagined some things, but she'd shied from the rougher stuff, not sure of herself. Yet when she heard the primitive word fall from his cultured lips, anticipation leaped in her chest. She adjusted her thighs.

"Nice," he said, in a low voice that had gone thick with lust. "Christ, Sam. You're going to kill me."

"But . . ."

Whap!

She jumped at the first swat. It was more surprising than painful, but the sensation stopped the words in her throat, so that his subsequent admonition wasn't necessary.

"I told you to be quiet. No talking. You can moan or plead all you want, though. I'd like to hear that."

That outrageous statement came with a surge of confusing response. Sam wasn't sure whether she was supposed to be insulted or . . . quiet. She found she wasn't capable of either.

He kept a restraining hand clamped on one buttock as he worked on the other, and it was a crazy feeling, the grip of his fingers on her flesh as his palm cracked against the opposite cheek in a series of blows that warmed her skin, making it tingle. Then it began to burn and sting. He switched, worked on the other side, then adjusted his hold to the center of her back to spank the full heart-shaped area.

"I've wanted to do this for so long . . . Your pussy's all slick and smells like heaven. I'd like to tie you up. Chris and I would take turns eating you for hours."

Oh God. He *understood*.

It was the first time either of them had acknowledged or suggested sharing her in any way. It made her so glad and hopeful, the words pulled another whimper from her. He'd gone still again, as if waiting to see what her reaction would be. He chuckled, a dangerous sound.

"Careful what you wish for, little girl."

He started spanking her again. Hard swats that came up from below, hitting the widest part of her ass, making both buttocks wobble, followed by straight down, flat cracks of his palm against the sides and tops of her cheeks. She was lifting up for more, pleading, moaning. Her arousal dampened the pockets of her thighs, slid over her clit, tickling it. When she pressed her mound against his leg, the resulting reaction sent her into a near-climactic haze. A harder swat made her yelp.

"You won't be rubbing your pussy against me, Samantha Beth. I decide if you get to come, and you've been very bad."

She swallowed another moan as he continued her punishment. Her ass was throbbing, and the blows were coming hard and fast enough to be painful, but she couldn't stop wanting more. The only reason she wanted him to stop was to put her over the table, fuck her while she laid on his papers, marking everything that belonged to him with her scent. She wanted his cock inside her, wanted him to completely claim her, make her his.

Flo had warned her about this flood of crazy. *When you finally let yourself have a submissive experience, it's going to crash over you like a tidal wave, like a drug you'll never get enough of. Make sure you're with someone who knows how to handle that.*

She wasn't sure if Geoff knew how, but both of them seemed caught in the unrelenting grip of the moment. Geoff's breath was rasping in his throat. His cock pressed against her belly, a steel bar under his jeans that made her pussy twinge with longing to have it shoving inside, joining their bodies.

"Geoff, please . . ."

He stopped so abruptly, she wobbled on his lap. He steadied her again. The way he made slow, teasing circles over her backside with his palm, it was as if he was calming himself, all while he aroused her past her ability to control herself. She needed to come. She couldn't think beyond that.

"Do it," he muttered. "Rub yourself against me now. Ask me to come when you're ready for it. Beg me."

He wrapped his hand in her hair, tight, and kept his other hand on her ass, kneading, pressing her down against his thighs. She spread hers farther, adjusting, and he helped. The firm muscle of his thigh flexed right where she needed it as she strained against him. She couldn't think about how this must look, this humping against his leg, but his reaction to it made her impossibly more aroused. He wanted her in this awkward pose, wanted to see just how hot and wanton he'd made her, shameless in her need to come.

The orgasm vibrated through her. "Geoff . . . please. I want to come. Please . . ."

He stayed silent, as if waiting to see what she would do if he said nothing, held back. She fought the climax, tried to stay on the razor's edge, waiting, needing to hear him say it. "Please . . . Geoff." Her voice broke in desperation. "I don't . . . want to go . . . until you say . . ."

"Come, then. Come for me."

She bucked against his leg, rubbed furiously and uttered tiny, frustrated cries because contact was hit or miss, denying her the full strength of the orgasm without diluting its drawn-out intensity. But when he started to spank her again, her reaction jumped to the level of screaming ecstasy, causing him to curse reverently under his breath. He left off spanking her long enough to capture a nipple in a thumb and forefinger, pinching hard and sending pain shooting through her. Yet it gave the climax another bump, a shard of incredible sensation rippling right behind the pain.

"God . . . oh God . . ." It was gone too soon, ebbing off of her like a rushing tide, leaving her vibrating body braced for another onslaught. She wanted more. More, more, more.

~

Instead, Geoff's cell rang. He barked another curse, this one not reverent in the least. "It's Mr. Cade," he said, referencing his boss. "Christ, Sam, I'm sorry."

He righted her so she was sitting on his knee. Holding her in the curve of his arm, he picked up his hands-free piece, stuffed it in his ear. "Yes sir?" He cleared his throat. As he listened to the senior partner, he typed a note on his laptop screen, drawing her eyes to it with a short gesture.

Go get dressed, bad girl. We'll talk about this later.

He lifted her to her feet, not giving her a choice. He helped adjust her pajama bottoms and panties, pressed her shirt into her hand and sent her toward the hallway with a firm squeeze of her smarting ass. But her legs were trembling, and she felt dizzy, disoriented. The hallway was moving off to the left while she moved off to the right, the wall suddenly in front of her face. She stopped, swaying, just as she heard a chair scrape. A breath later, Geoff's hands were on her, his body giving her a stable place to lean.

"Yes sir. I can have that ready by Monday without a problem. I've already started on it."

Though she had friends who bitched about boyfriends who ignored them when they were on the phone, she found she had no complaints with Geoff's attentiveness in that regard. The rhythm of his speech remained as smooth as ever, yet he turned her toward him, bent and scooped her up in one easy movement, carrying her into her bedroom. He'd never carried her before. She'd jumped on Chris's back when they were roughhousing in the fall leaves and he'd dumped her in a big pile of them, but that was as close as she'd gotten to this.

She hadn't imagined literally being swept off her feet, but she wasn't objecting in the least.

Geoff put her down on the bed. She shouldn't play with him when he was on the phone with the man responsible for his paychecks, but she wasn't playing. She couldn't release his neck and shoulders. She pressed her face in his neck, needing him to hold her.

He gave in to her, continuing the conversation with one knee pressed on the bed, him leaning over her. He slid his arms around her, warm and tight, his breath teasing her cheek as he responded to whatever questions were being asked on the other end of the line. He did that for a few full moments, steadying her before he at last gave her a firm squeeze and slid free, standing by the bed and looking down at her. She hadn't put the T-shirt back on, so she was spread before him half naked. His gaze returned to her breasts to caress her bare flesh with merely a look.

Reaching out, she trailed her fingers over his thigh. He was still blatantly aroused, such that she licked her lips at the sight. She wanted to touch him. She wouldn't, of course, wouldn't distract him further, but he obviously wasn't as sure of that as she was. Closing his hand over hers, he held it. She gave him an impish smile and he narrowed his eyes at her, though his mouth twitched.

"Yes sir. I'll be in within the hour."

She bit back a curse of her own. She and Chris both knew the demands of Geoff's job. He wasn't high enough on the totem pole to secure many work-free weekends, though it had improved since his first few years with the firm. He still worked long hours, but he could do more of it at home, and there were brief periods where they could spend the day together, or watch a movie and have dinner in the evening. Or, true bliss, they could take a three-day weekend in Asheville or Myrtle Beach, a getaway. She thought of the last time they'd done that, her stretched out on the beach between the two of them, the sun baking their skin like a coating of molasses. They'd bodysurfed and played in the waves together.

For the past several years, it had never occurred to any of them to take a vacation on their own, or with different friends. The three of them were a unit, whether they'd made it official or not. And Geoff had finally acknowledged it with those delicious words.

"Chris and I would take turns eating you for hours."

Geoff clicked off and looked down at her. Stretching out her fingers, she teased the firm muscle of his thigh despite his hold on her hand. "I know you have to go, but I don't want you to."

"I know. Stay here and rest a few minutes while I get dressed. I mean it. Don't get up until I come back and make sure you're fine on your feet."

"It was just an orgasm, not a blood sugar crash." Though the feeling was similar. She'd seen Flo give aftercare to her subs. Sometimes she held them just the way Sam had needed Geoff to hold her. The Mistress said that the psychological journey a Dom and sub took during a session could put the sub into what she called subspace, a disoriented euphoria that impaired physical and mental judgment. Sam wasn't sure she'd gone that far, but she was knocked off her axis, for sure.

"I know you have to go, but would you mind lying with me, just a minute? I won't get all wild and crazy on you. Promise."

Usually she thought these things over before blurting them out, but maybe that was part of what the subspace thing did. She felt like she could say anything, trust her Dom with all her thoughts and feelings.

Geoff smiled but put the earpiece on the side table and stretched his long body out next to her. She gravitated to him like a magnet, burrowing against him as he wrapped his arms around her. Their legs twined together, his thigh over hers, her leg bent and resting between his so their bodies could be pressed together from thigh to chest. He put his head over hers, kissing her hair. "Did I hurt you?"

"Yes. I liked it. I liked all of it. I want to do more. Please."

That stillness gripped him again. Stroking her hair from her cheek, he kept his lips pressed to her temple. When she would have said more, he made a quelling noise and shook his head. She subsided, vaguely dissatisfied, but he was holding her, and that made up for a lot. After a few minutes, he kissed her forehead again and drew away to retrieve her T-shirt. She didn't want to wear it, liking how his eyes rested on her in her half-dressed state, but he didn't give her a choice. After he guided her arms back into the sleeves and pulled the shirt down to just above her midriff, he lowered her back onto the pillows and rose. "I'll get dressed and come back. Stay put," he reminded her.

Maybe if she were a sub-for-spice-only kind of girl, she would have teased him with an *Or what?* flirty taunt. But she wasn't. Evolving or not, he wasn't that kind of Dom, either. She wanted to show him she could obey, to please him. He studied her an extra moment, as if reading all that from her face, then he nodded and left her.

She listened to him move down the hall and heard the snap of the light switch in his room. Her and Chris's bedrooms were on one side of the hall, while Geoff had the master bedroom across from them. He had a king-sized bed, and since that room was the only one that could accommodate its size, neither she nor Chris had disputed him having the master. They probably wouldn't have even if he'd had a twin bed. It was just one of many ways they acknowledged his alpha rank in their trio. Or at least she did. Chris perhaps wouldn't have given it any thought for different reasons.

He didn't have a bed at all, not technically. Chris had a mattress on the floor and a hammock strung between two supporting studs above it, like a modified form of bunk beds. Sometimes he slept on one, sometimes on the other. He had both sleeping options up against the opposite side of the wall where her headboard was, so sometimes before they went to sleep at night, he'd knock on the wall and play Name That Tune with her. She could tell if he was in the hammock or on the mattress by where the taps happened. Since the very first night they'd started living here, he'd always tapped "Itsy Bitsy Spider" up and down the wall as his signoff and her bedtime song, to help send her off to sleep.

She tapped it out now for herself, up between the slats of her headboard. When she heard Geoff returning, she turned on her side toward the door, eager to see him. He didn't wear a suit to the office on the weekends, but he still dressed professionally: golf shirt and slacks, sleek belt and polished loafers. "I don't know how long he'll keep me."

She bit back a sigh. He had that look, the one that said he thought they needed to ease back, reevaluate. Maybe even pretend it hadn't happened. If he did that, she might just kill him.

Watching her with thoughtful eyes, he bent and kissed her lightly. He'd done that plenty of times, a sign of their "friendship." However, this time he coupled the casual gesture with something else. Bending over her abdomen, he pushed back the hem of her shirt and put his lips to her navel piercing, a little pewter bear with tiny rhinestones for eyes. She shuddered at the moist heat of his mouth, a tingle running through her as he tugged on it with his teeth, the tip of his tongue caressing her before he straightened. Squeezing her hand, he gave her a hard look.

"I did hear what you said, Sam. What we did wasn't wrong, but I want to process it. Let's just leave it there for a while and both think about it. Chris will be back in a couple of days."

"Did you like it? What we did?" Her heart thudded as she sought any trace of regret.

"You know I did." He touched her face. "Leave it alone for now. You feel okay? Steadier?"

She nodded, but that didn't satisfy him. When she teased him by getting up and doing a twirl, he shook his head and moved to the doorway.

"You know where I'll be. Call me if you need me."

She needed him. God, how she needed him. She wanted to take all of this as a good sign, but she already sensed she was going to have to keep pushing. She didn't want to disrespect his feelings on the matter, but she just couldn't wait for Chris's return. If she did that, they'd do the damn male solidarity thing, resisting together what she now knew for certain they should all be embracing. She couldn't tolerate another minute of them watching her with eyes that said how much more they wanted, all while they stayed behind the perimeter of their convictions, the push-pull of those ties keeping them all close, but held at a certain distance at the same time.

She heard the dead bolt turn as he left through the kitchen door. He always did that when she was here by herself. If he worked late and Chris was out of town, he'd call her at dinner and before bedtime, making sure she'd set the security alarm both times. But it wasn't a double standard. When he or Chris was running late and didn't call, one of the other two would track the missing person down via text, email or phone, to verify all was well. They watched out for one another.

She turned onto her other side, curled up into a ball and wrapped her arms around her pillow, imagining Geoff holding her again. The protective care had been there from the beginning, hadn't it? She'd been attending State for her business degree when she'd had the misfortune of getting involved with Anthony Williams. Flo had told her that submissives were sometimes prone to getting involved with alpha males who put off the Dom vibes, but who in reality were just overbearing assholes.

"Not all Doms are obvious alpha males, and many alpha males are *not* Doms," she'd said emphatically.

Anthony didn't like hearing the word *no*. When she broke off the relationship, he told her she was the first woman who thought herself not good enough for him. Then he started calling her twenty times in the middle of the night and confronting her at unexpected places: the coffee shop, coming out of her yoga class. His harassment built up so gradually that it wasn't until she'd lost ten pounds, was having trouble maintaining her grades and jumped at every noise outside her apartment that she realized she had a problem. At which point she discovered the harsh truth every woman who'd ever had a stalker or abuser faced. Everyone's hands were tied unless he actually did something to her. Anthony was a law student and knew far too well how to skirt the edges of such rules.

So she worked on ways to protect herself. She moved to an apartment complex off campus. For a short time things improved, since she did all she could to make sure he didn't know where she lived. Then one night, she'd pulled out her key to unlock her door and suddenly there he was, behind her. He was drunk, belligerent and on a rant about how she didn't know what she was walking away from.

She wasn't a fool. Instead of opening her door, which would give him the chance to push her inside, she'd thrown the key as far from them as she could and tried to get away. When he grabbed her arm, any reservations about being overly dramatic vanished. She screamed her goddamned lungs out.

He hit her, probably to shut her up, but then his rage spilled over. She hit the wall on the next punch. As she slid down it, trying to cover her face with her hands, he started kicking her, his fists continuing to rain down on her head and shoulders.

Just when the terror of realizing he could kill her before anyone could stop him was closing over her, he was gone. She'd opened her eyes to see a man built like Thor—the Chris Hemsworth version—pluck Anthony clean off his feet and slam him against the entryway wall so hard the siding cracked. Her rescuer wore a T-shirt and jeans stained with dirt, while another man, this one dressed like he'd just come from an office, crouched over her. Despite the differences in their appearances, she had no doubt from the well-dressed man's hard expression and taut body that he was more than capable of protecting her from a follow-up attack if Anthony got loose. Just as she was pretty sure nothing was getting free of that other male once he had it in his large fists.

The police were called. Anthony was charged with assault and released on bail. A first-time offender with a high-priced attorney, he was sentenced to six months of community service and anger management classes. In the meantime, Chris Montague and Geoff Tywin told her they had an extra bedroom and could use a third tenant to share rent costs. She couldn't explain why she trusted them so immediately, or how she'd known they'd get along so well, but she moved in with them the same day they offered. The two of them ferried her small amount of furniture to their apartment and had her settled in a couple of hours, after which they shared their first pizza together on the floor of the living room. The local pizza place offered a vegan pie option, and they gallantly each tried a slice before returning to their own hamburger and pork sausage blend.

She smiled at the memory. They teased her about her dietary choice, but the two of them had never been mean about it. When they were in charge of the grocery list, both were careful to double-check ingredients for shared dishes. In turn, she respected their choice to eat meat—mostly—but had gradually migrated them to organic and humanely raised options.

Her move into their apartment was originally couched as a temporary situation, since she was only a few months from graduation, like Geoff. Then Geoff was offered a position in a Charlotte firm. Chris, working for a local Raleigh landscaping company, was ready to make a change, so he decided to tag along. Since Sam had interned with a Charlotte bank and the job opportunities for her were best in that city, they'd found their current rental house together, and that was where they'd been for the past several years.

It had taken her a while to reclaim confidence in her judgment and restore herself mentally and physically. She was amused and touched by how her new roommates became involved in that. Chris brought her vegan cupcakes to help her regain weight and Geoff coaxed her out with him on his daily runs. They were decent, good men.

At first, because of Geoff and Chris's close rapport, she'd assumed they were gay. Geoff was handsome and a snappy dresser, after all, and there were a reason stereotypes existed—they were often true. Chris wasn't a snappy dresser, but he had a certain vibe toward Geoff.

Over time, she learned enough of their dating history to know they appreciated women. However, whenever they talked about dating, it was always double dating, and nothing had panned out for either of them into any meaningful relationships. Though she couldn't point to Geoff making any direct mentions of dating men, she deduced fairly quickly that Geoff was comfortably bisexual. Chris . . . as far as men went, there only seemed to be one toward whom he exhibited that level of interest: Geoff. Yet they seemed solidly based in a platonic relationship, on the surface at least.

If she'd nursed any idea that they were in denial about their feelings toward one another, the longer she spent with them, the more she realized it wasn't denied as much as it was . . . dormant? Waiting for something?

Around the time she accepted that conclusion, she also realized they were noticing her in a definitely heterosexual way. Though they took care not to ever make such subtle cues uncomfortable for her, she'd grown more conscious of that regard every day.

So here they were. Maybe they were like three plants who'd needed one another's proximity to flourish and grow, twine together and become one. She sensed they were pretty close to the twining part; she just wondered if there was a fertilizer to speed the process.

Grinning at the thought, she rolled out of bed. Chris was their green thumb. Maybe she should ask him that question. She could just imagine what his reaction would be.

∼

Geoff's text came in later that day, telling her he'd be working late, well past her normal bedtime. Disappointing, but certainly not unexpected. She occupied herself in the usual ways: watching TV, playing on Pinterest, reading in the backyard. In the evening, she texted to tell him she'd set the alarm, punctuating it with a smiley face and several heart emoticons, sap that she was. He sent her a brief okay, though the heart emoticon he included made her smile.

Waking Monday morning, she wasn't sure he'd even been home. A text telling her he'd sacked out in his small office for a short three hours before his morning meeting confirmed it. With a sigh, she showered and got ready for work. As she was heading out the door, she received a text from Chris, saying he anticipated being home later in the week. He'd attached some pictures of seabirds and other scenery from Gulfport.

When he got home, what should she tell him about what had happened? Or would Geoff do it? Tonight, Geoff would likely be home. Did she keep pursuing this with him, trying to get him fully on board before Chris's return, or should she listen to Geoff, wait until Chris got back and then try to talk it out with them again?

Though that seemed the safest route, her instincts told her differently. She needed to make sure she and Geoff were a little further along. She needed to make sure he was pushed to the point she was— not content to let things stay as they were. She ignored the little voice that suggested it was more her OCD nature than her instincts pushing her in that direction.

She almost didn't talk to Flo about it at lunch, afraid her friend might disagree and sway her on it. But as they were hoofing it through downtown on their lunch walk, it all came spilling out, in enough detail she was sort of appalled at herself. But she pressed forward with her questions.

"I don't want to wait for Chris to get back. I want to do something else to throw this in Geoff's face, make him react. What kind of sub does that? Am I being too pushy? I'm afraid I'm too revved up over it all, not using good judgment. Flo, what happens if I do the wrong thing and ruin our friendship?"

Keeping it all percolating through the morning had obviously turned her into a teakettle about to blow. Flo linked arms with her and kept them moving forward.

"First off, breathe. Second, you need to think about something pretty significant. Yes, you're friends, but you stopped being only friends some time ago." She ticked off the points on her long nails. "When was the last time any one of you had a date? Or didn't spend most your free social time with each other? You're lovers, even if you're not sharing a bed. You've already crossed that line."

"I've dated. I've . . ." Sam trailed off. "Okay, a year ago."

"You're a good-looking twenty-five-year-old woman, and you last had a date a year ago. How many have you turned down?"

"A few. But they weren't really right for me. Sometimes I've worried that was because of Anthony. I don't really trust anyone like I trust Geoff and Chris. Am I using them as a crutch?"

"Only you can answer that. Didn't Mark from Records ask you to join us at that new bar this week? In kind of a *Let's see how we like each other in a group* way?"

"Yes."

Florence shrugged. "Well, that seems a safe way to resolve that question in your mind, but I honestly think you're just frustrated that Geoff hasn't jumped in with both feet. And, honey, I can tell you this. You can't push a seasoned Dom into anything, so the fact he might be new to it but is being so careful with you makes me have good feelings about what kind of Master he'll be, even if it's driving you batshit."

Sam rolled her eyes. "Great. Dom bonding. Want to stand in as his proxy and let me slap you upside your stubborn-ass head?"

"Only if you want to draw back a stump." Flo smiled serenely. "As far as you not taking risks because of Anthony, it seems to me your relationship with Chris and Geoff has strengthened your confidence in yourself, your sense of your own sexuality and what you truly want out of a relationship. So stop worrying so much. Don't you think your relationship with Chris and Geoff can handle a few strains on it, especially if it helps it grow?"

At Sam's uncertain look, Flo shook her head. "Let me put it this way. Can you live with it staying how it is? The three of you just 'friends' who are fantasizing about one another but not doing anything about it?"

"No," Sam said resolutely. "Hell no. I'm done with that."

Flo pinched her arm. "All right, then. Go home tonight and give him that additional push."

"Isn't trying to manipulate him wrong? I thought you just said Doms can't be pushed into anything."

"They can't, and if I felt you were trying to manipulate him in the wrong way, I'd be the first to suggest you need to pull back. But Geoff seems like a big boy who can figure out what's driving you. And in your situation, it might help Geoff to know just how much his submissive wants and needs what he has to offer." She lifted a shoulder. "If he's pretty close to being ready and you yank his chain the right way, you'll get a response for sure. Like you did this weekend."

Sam remembered how he put her over his lap so decisively, pulling her pajama bottoms out of his way, his palm clapping against her tender flesh. She shuddered a little, a smile playing on her lips. Flo gave her a knowing look.

"Should we take a poll from that homeless guy over there about whether or not you should go home and try to get Geoff to slap that ass again?"

Sam pushed at her playfully. "Stop it. You're terrible."

"And you're blushing. It's adorable."

"Shut up."

Flo linked arms with her again. "I know I'm giving you some conflicting messages, but I trust your judgment. You're a smart woman, Sam, and you have a loving heart. I can also tell these two guys think the world of you, so no matter what happens, I know you'll watch out for one another. But on that note, I am going to say one thing to you that's really important, okay?"

Florence brought her to a halt, faced her, her expression now serious. "If Geoff's as new to this as you are, it's all the more important that you communicate with him. I believe he'd cut off his arm before ever hurting you, so if you go down a road where you're uncomfortable or afraid, you talk to him. A good Dom wants to know if what he's doing is mutually pleasurable. Nothing pisses us off like a sub enduring the wrong kind of pain or, worse, risking harm because they're afraid speaking up or using a safe word will make us end the session altogether."

"But at this point, I *am* afraid of that."

"I know. That's why I'm telling you. If you want to be his submissive, then you trust him to know the right call to make if something doesn't feel right. All right? You nod or say yes to me, young lady."

Sam tried to laugh, but Flo's expression was the one she had when dealing with her own submissives. Sam couldn't help but squirm. While she didn't respond to Flo as a Mistress, she felt the weight of Flo's friendship and concern behind that mien. "Yes. I'll try. I really will."

Flo scrutinized her for an intent moment, then nodded once. "In the words of Yoda, 'Do. Or do not. There is no try.' Else I'll kick your ass myself."

～

Once Sam arrived home, she found herself at loose ends with her restless thoughts. Since she worked from eight to three and Geoff worked from eight to nightfall most days, she was home well before him.

Usually she changed into her yoga clothes and headed to the Y for an afternoon class, but not today. She ate a peanut butter rice cake in the kitchen while she thought about the past weekend and Flo's words. When she headed down the hall, intending to change into jeans and a T-shirt, she hesitated at her doorway and instead turned toward Geoff's room.

She stood on the threshold for a few minutes, prevaricating. They mostly respected one another's privacy. Since they took turns doing laundry, it was perfectly acceptable for her to come into either man's room to put away clothes. Because of that, she knew Chris wore roomy flannel or plaid cotton boxers, mostly in blues, browns and greens. Geoff wore brief shorts in dark colors.

Every once in a while, Chris would slouch through the kitchen in his flannel boxers to get his coffee, his thick brown hair tousled and the wall of his muscled chest and abs greeting her as she turned from the counter where she'd be making her own breakfast. He'd normally touch her face or shoulder, give her hair a playful pull before he grunted pleasantly, picked up the coffee and headed back down the hallway. She'd be treated to an equally appealing rear view of the shifting muscles in his back as he lifted the coffee to his lips.

That image would stay on her mind most of the day. The same way it would when Geoff would breeze through in the morning in his slacks, his dress shirt still open, a look that never failed to make her want to curl her fists in both sides of the shirt and put her open mouth on his flesh to taste and bite. Chris was pleasing male fur and bunched muscle. Geoff had tight, hard pectorals and a stomach ridged with lean muscle. His long-fingered hands as he set up his coffee fascinated her.

She moved to his bed now, running her fingertips over the tan-and-white comforter. What would it be like to share his bed? She imagined herself in his arms like she'd been yesterday. She imagined Chris there, too, the two men sandwiching her between them as the three of them dreamed the night away. Sometime during the night, someone's hand would start moving, caressing. Lips would find another mouth, and they'd all be twined together another way.

Standing in the hushed coolness of Geoff's bedroom, she could see it vividly. Her eyes closed, body swaying at the thought of so much sensual input. Their hands all over one another, chuckles and small gasps as they figured out how to move together. Heat building, her body getting slick, ready for either or both of them. She wanted to be taken over by their strength, their demands on her and each other.

It was just her in the house right now, no one to see. Not giving herself much time to think about it, she went into her room and retrieved her vibrator from the nightstand drawer. It had a quiet motor, but when she used it at night, when the men were home, she muffled it beneath a pillow between her legs, self-conscious about them hearing her, particularly Chris on the other side of the wall. But usually she used it at a late-afternoon time like this, when she had the house to herself.

Ever since she'd decided she wanted to take their relationship to the next level, masturbating had practically become a daily ritual, her body on a constant needy hum. Taking Geoff and Chris to Naughty Bits had only made it worse.

She also always did it in her own room, but not today. She retrieved a pillow from Chris's mattress, and returned to Geoff's bed. Slipping out of her heels, she stretched out on the king-sized expanse. She wasn't in here much when he was sleeping, but she remembered he slept in the middle, the sign of a man who'd never shared a bed. She adjusted herself there, inhaling his scent. She still had on her office attire; a pale yellow blouse tucked into a knee-length brown plaid skirt, thigh-high stockings beneath the skirt. Opening several buttons of her blouse, she closed her eyes as she slipped her hand inside of it, fingers tracing the curve of her breast. He'd do it like that. Start with light touches, slowly undressing her, teasing her, taking his time.

She imagined strong hands curling around her ankles, slowly spreading her legs. Chris, standing at the end of the bed, would be watching as Geoff reclined on one hip beside her, his fingertips playing over her quivering breasts.

"Please . . ." she whispered.

Geoff's eyes would get that spark, his mouth setting in a thin line that told her he wanted to make her suffer, beg. He wanted her so hot a single touch would catapult her to screaming orgasm. Only then would he thrust into her, filling her as her pussy convulsed on his length, as her hips lifted off the bed to take him deeper. When he was done, he would shift off of her, grip her jaw, begin kissing her with deep, tongue-swirling, teeth-nipping kisses. She'd moan into his mouth as Chris's hands left her ankles. He'd settle between her thighs, brace himself over her, because he was going to take her next, both men spilling their seed into her, making her theirs.

She was theirs. Florence was right. That decision had been made long ago. She also thought she understood a little better what Flo had been trying to explain. There was a difference between trying to push a Dom around and making him understand that she was here, she was his, she was eagerly waiting on his desires. She wanted the lead dog of their pack to snap his self-imposed tether. Doing things that would convince him it was time to do that might straddle the line between begging and demanding, but Flo had hinted that the proper blend would have the desired results for all of them.

Plus, yanking at him scared and thrilled her. Scared her because it could go bad, thrilled her because she sensed that he could be a little bit dangerous when pushed too far. The way he'd taken command and spanked her seemed like the tip of a very large iceberg.

She ran the vibrator over the crotch panel of her panties. She'd set it on a rhythm that went from low to high and back to low again. The pattern engorged her clit to near orgasm, then pulled her back from that edge. If she used that one first, instead of the instant gratification of the maximum setting, her orgasm was more satisfying. A rolling, building wave that carried her to shore gasping, heart thundering and body trembling. Denial could build sensation and need to an incredible height, so that the fall was that much more thrilling. She bet sex with Geoff would be like diving off a skyscraper. He'd liked her being helpless, dependent on him setting the pace. She'd seen it, felt it. Reveled in it.

Pinching her nipple, she swallowed a moan as the rhythm of the vibrator brought her hips off the bed, seeking that final step, but no . . . it receded again. She visualized Geoff holding it, watching her intently as she became more frantic, as she moistened her lips, held his gaze. He'd be wearing nothing but his shorts, the size of his erection against the stretched cotton making the need between her legs an insistent, pounding throb even beneath the vibration.

She rolled her nipple between her fingers, feeling the pressure of Chris's mouth. Geoff would tell Chris to suckle her while he held the vibrator between her legs. Chris's fingers would tangle in her hair as he kissed her throat, her sternum. As his heated mouth closed over one aching peak, Geoff would delve into Chris's thick dark hair with his own hand and tug on it, adding to the movement and pressure of Chris's mouth upon her. His grip would slip over Chris's shoulder, conveying his need to touch and possess both of them.

She could see Chris lifting his head and meeting Geoff's eyes. Chris's own gaze would be glowing with fire, the heat of lust, all his gentle power transformed into something else. "Make her come, Geoff," he'd growl. "I want to hear her come."

"There will be a price," her Master would say. "You come for us next."

A flash went through her mind, Chris's large body stretched out naked on Geoff's bed, Geoff leaning over him, kissing Chris as thoroughly and with as much demand as he'd kissed Sam. While he did that, he'd reach down, find her hand and close it around Chris's stiff cock, guiding her to stroke that shaft as Geoff merely kissed him, his hand drifting back up to pinch a nipple, grip Chris's throat and tighten. Chris would close his hand over Geoff's wrist, but Geoff would turn the grip over, tangle fingers palm to palm. He'd push Chris's hand back to the bed as Geoff shifted halfway over him, his chest against Chris's, holding him there as Sam brought him to climax.

Come up here, Sam. Come be with us.

Geoff would bring her up beside them, guide her to kiss Chris as Geoff held both of them, Chris's arms tangled around them as well. Their bodies would strain against one another, and she'd know they'd take one another in every possible way before dawn, and still not be sated.

Sam arched off the bed as she found the button on the vibrator that took it to maximum rhythm, her body ready to channel all that pressure into an explosive climax. She gripped Chris's pillow, covering her face and chest with it. As she inhaled his scent along with Geoff's all around her, the cotton slid against her face and breasts, exposed by the lace bra. Geoff's mattress gave beneath her as her hips rose, fell.

"Yes . . . yes . . . please . . ." She went over the edge begging to give them anything they wanted from her. She just needed to be taken, overwhelmed, loved so completely by them that she'd never want anything more.

As the climax ebbed away, that vague sense of shame that always seemed to accompany the self-indulgence of an electronic climax dug its claws into her. This time it brought an extra twinge, since she'd done it on Geoff's bed and screamed her release into Chris's pillow. She'd put a towel beneath herself, so she wasn't worried about the honey trickling down her labia and between her thighs, but a part of her wished she hadn't used a towel, that she'd put Chris's pillow between her legs instead, so her scent could be on their bedding.

Now she was being fanciful. Men weren't German shepherds, able to separate the scent of a woman's arousal from that of laundry detergent and their own bodies. Still, she wondered if either of them would subconsciously recognize it and have erotic dreams about her like she was having about them.

Once she recovered her breath, she reluctantly left Geoff's bed, straightening the comforter. Going into the bathroom she and Chris shared, she cleaned the vibrator and tucked it away in her bedroom. That should hold her for about half an hour.

Rolling her eyes at herself, she changed into her yoga clothes. She wasn't going to hang around here for the next couple of hours losing her mind. Yoga would center her. She hoped.

She picked up the grocery list on the way out the door. She'd hit Whole Foods and Harris Teeter on her way home. Life went on, no matter her hormones, or the stubbornness of one particular Type A, sexy-as-hell lawyer.

~

When she returned, she saw Geoff's car in the driveway. Her stomach made a little leap. Since he was home at a reasonable hour, they might be able to talk about this weekend . . . or not talk at all, in the right kind of way. If he didn't have work to do tonight.

He was sitting at the table with his laptop, but she didn't take that as a bad sign. He tended to check on details when he first arrived home, even if he wasn't planning to work through the evening. However, his dark-cloud expression wasn't encouraging.

"Hey," she said, putting the groceries down on the counter. "I'd ask how your day was, but . . ."

He shot her a look full of irritation. "Sarah's son was having an *I'm winning an award for being totally mediocre* ceremony today, probably the fifth one this year. But of course she couldn't miss it, for fear she'd permanently damage the little mutant's self-esteem. So she took care of the senior partners' stuff and blew mine off. She didn't assign it to another admin, and I didn't know until I was heading out the door. I have about three things to review tonight, and now I have to type up my brief, because it has to be ready first thing in the morning, and we all know I'm a crappy typist."

He paused for a breath, glaring. Sam tried not to smile, but he targeted the twitch of her lips in an instant. "Don't you dare snicker."

"I can't help it. 'Little mutant'? It's safe to say they're not putting you in charge of HR policy anytime soon."

"No, we couldn't have that. People actually doing their jobs instead of personal bullshit on the company's dime. Being deathly sick or having a close relative die, like a mother or spouse, are the *only* acceptable reasons to not have your ass at your job. And attending the funeral is only permitted if you had a documented, proven close relationship with said mother or spouse. Stop laughing."

"I will. Let me just imagine something to compose myself. Um . . . mucus, pus. Starving children in Africa."

His lips gave a telltale quiver. "I'm going to beat you," he said.

Promise? She barely managed to bite back the word, but his expression reflected something less definable and more intriguing than work-related annoyance, suggesting it had shown on her face.

Clearing her throat, she turned her attention to putting away the groceries. "I'm pretty open tonight. I'll type up your brief while you review the other stuff, and then maybe you'll have some time to relax." *Please, God.*

"I'm not asking you to do my work, Sam. You've already put in a full day."

"You're not asking. I'm volunteering. Let me just go get changed and I'll get started."

She went down the hallway to strip off her yoga clothes and clean up, smiling a little as she heard him muttering to himself, still venting. Nothing bugged Geoff like unprofessionalism, but his sarcastic wit made his rants as entertaining as stand-up.

Professionalism . . . She stopped in the middle of pulling out jeans and a T-shirt. If the three things he had to review weren't that long, and she typed up his brief fast enough, it wouldn't take until bedtime. Why not give him a little push, or yank, whatever, as part of his work? Nothing was likely to get his attention faster.

She went to her closet. As she made her decision, her cheeks heated and anticipation curled in her belly. Did she dare?

A few minutes later, she tapped back up the hallway. Geoff had already started to read one of his files, but he'd placed his recorder and the earbuds by her laptop on its portable computer table, so he'd quickly reconciled himself to her help. Typical man. She hid a smile.

The sound of her shoes was enough to have him lifting his head. A tiny ripple of panic, a quaking in her lower extremities, had her wondering if she was about to act like a complete fool, making things awkward for them both, but that all depended on how she played this, didn't it? Madison, the Naughty Bits proprietress, had talked to her about role-playing, about how much fun that could be, and both men had perked up when Sam had considered a naughty version of a schoolgirl uniform. She hadn't bought it, but the interest had definitely been there.

The stilettos she was wearing gave her hips a sultry sway as she moved from the hallway to the kitchen. The extremely short black microskirt was one she hadn't worn since college, when she'd gone out to dance clubs with friends, and even then she usually put a pair of tights beneath it for modesty. She hadn't done that tonight. She hadn't put anything under it at all.

She also hadn't worn a bra under the pale yellow blouse she'd worn to work today. She had the top two buttons undone, which would give him a glimpse of the curve of her breast almost to the nipple if she sat in profile to him, which she fully intended to do.

Meeting his blank gaze, she took advantage of that brief moment of shock. "Sarah had to take her little mutant to his Mediocrity Ceremony, Mr. Tywin," she said smoothly. "But she said I would be able to meet your needs. I'll just be over here, typing up your brief. Let me know if there's anything else I can do for you."

"Sam . . ." It was gratifying to see how much trouble he was having pulling his gaze up to her face, but he wasn't the only one who knew how to taunt and tease a person to distraction. She didn't linger in front of him, at least no longer than necessary for him to realize she had nothing on beneath the yellow blouse. From standing in front of her mirror, she knew the smudges of her nipples were unmistakable beneath the nearly transparent silk.

She took her seat in the chair, her back straight, the skirt barely covering her ass when she sat down. Modestly, she crossed her ankles and tucked her legs at an angle beneath the chair. If he'd been directly in front of her, the small open triangle where the fabric stretched over her thighs would give him a shadowed view of her bare pubic mound. She expected he was already wondering what was under the skirt. She'd see how long it would take before curiosity inspired action.

She respected Geoff's work, but he'd been working pretty much nonstop since Sunday. She and Chris both knew sometimes he needed forced breaks to give him balance. Normally, that was when she and Chris would gang up on him, drag him off for a bike ride or to see a concert in the park. Maybe go out to dinner at a new place.

She wasn't under any illusions she was being motivated by such selfless concerns right now, but if it served both purposes, all the better.

She fitted the buds into her ears. She'd put up her hair with two sticks, letting some of it fall and tease her nape, the sides of her face. She wondered if he'd pull it all the way down. She wanted him to do that.

She had to be impairing his focus, but that was a two-way street. In order to type up his brief correctly, she had to get past the way the sexy clothes and his hot gaze were making her feel. It helped to realize that true absorption in the task, acting oblivious to his regard or her provocative appearance, was a good way to drive him to even further distraction. She pressed play on the recorder.

She loved listening to his voice. Geoff tended to dictate as if he were presenting information to the judge or a jury, his tone alternating between humor, patience, instruction, and—her favorite—stern reproof.

On tape or in person, it was obvious he had such passion for learning and understanding how the law worked. He wasn't the least bit idealistic about the legal system, but he believed in the law and its purity even when it was twisted to ill purpose, as it so often was. For a man who seemed like a no-nonsense cynic, he was actually quite a romantic.

She and Chris had attended a couple of his trials. She'd learned the lawyer was usually required to stand in one specific spot, not allowed to wander around for dramatic effect as they did on TV shows. Even with that restriction, Geoff was mesmerizing to her, an orator who could have stood in the center of the Roman Senate and swayed minds to his way of thinking.

She finished the brief, read it through twice for any corrections and sent it to his computer to be reviewed by him before he printed or submitted it. Throughout, she'd been aware of the slow turn of pages at the kitchen table, mixed with the heat of his regard. He was watching her and, though it had taken an effort more strenuous than running uphill with a backpack of rocks, she'd made sure she hadn't looked at him once, focusing only on getting the job done.

Now, as she rewarded herself by finally glancing his way, she realized he was done. He had his laptop lid pushed halfway closed and was sitting back in his chair watching her, fingers templed, elbows braced on the arms of his chair. He had his legs in a casual sprawl. He'd shed his coat when he got home but was still in what she not-so-teasingly called his "power wear": slacks, shined shoes and dress shirt. He'd loosened his tie and rolled up the sleeves of the shirt and, because of his agitation with the admin, his hair was spiked over his forehead. His eyes were filled with such intensity that when she met them, it felt like she was standing close to a fire burning dangerously hot. Pressing her lips together to cover an erratic breath, she rose and stood before him, cocking a hip and giving him a light smile.

"Brief should be in your inbox, sir. Is there anything else I can do for you? I've been trained in several ways to relieve stress." Not letting herself chicken out, she let her gaze slide boldly down his body to linger between his sprawled legs. The slacks couldn't disguise how much he approved of her outfit. She wet her lips at the sight, as aroused by how he made no move to conceal it as the evidence of the erection itself. "You look stressed. Sir."

His gaze didn't leave her face. Would he play along? She thought the whole world spun once on its axis before he finally spoke, a slow drawl that made her heart leap. "Are you wearing anything under that skirt, Miss Gerard?"

She shivered at the address. "No sir."

"Turn around, bend over and show me. You look like someone who does yoga. I'm betting you could grab your ankles and fold yourself in half."

She pivoted, heat sliding down her neck, over her back and hips as she complied, slowly bending forward and then clasping her ankles. As the skirt adjusted, it inched up over her buttocks, telling her he was getting a view of those and the folds of her pussy, framed by the curves of her thighs. As the seconds ticked away with her face pressed to her shins, her legs began to tremble.

"Stand up, turn around and face me again."

She did. He was leaning forward with his hands clasped loosely between his spread knees. He cocked his head, eying her from head to toe. "Miss Gerard, you dress inappropriately for an office environment. Someone probably needs to take you in hand and teach you better behavior."

"Well, Mr. Cade has offered. And you know, he's so authoritative and in charge. I'm sure he'd be a good mentor."

She squealed as he lunged for her, caught her wrist and tugged her forward until she had to straddle his knees. Putting his hands on her hips to hold her there, he flashed a dangerous grin at her, but his hot gaze returned to her breasts, the tips pressing up high against the fabric. He slipped another button, then another, spreading the blouse open.

"I want a massage, Miss Gerard."

When she started to move back to circle around him, he shook his head. "You'll do it on my lap. Take off the skirt so you can spread your legs. Leave the shoes on."

He let her step back to shimmy out of the skirt. "And the blouse," he added. "I want you in nothing but those fuck-me shoes."

God, what did it say about her that she loved the rough sound of his voice when he spoke like that? She was quivering all over as she let the silk float to the floor. When she was done, she stood before him in nothing but a pair of high heels, her tiny diamond stud earrings and her navel piercing. His attention slid over her once again, slow, taking his time. She didn't think she could ever get tired of him looking at her like this, absorbing her into his gold-and-green gaze.

"Geoff." She had to say his name, couldn't play anymore. His eyes lifted to her, broody, unfathomable.

"Do you know what you're doing, Sam?"

She nodded, shook her head. His mouth quirked at the dual response. "Good to know we're in the same boat. Take off the shoes and come here." He extended his hand. She took it, grateful for the firm pressure of his fingers, and he slid her back into a straddle of his lap, guiding her legs so she could brace her heels on the slats of his chair for support. He enclosed her hips in his arms, holding her there. When he leaned forward, she expected him to go right for her quivering breasts, but instead, his mouth found the pocket of her throat. She dropped her head back, eyes closing, fingers clamped on his forearms.

"Miss Gerard," he murmured. "Take down your hair."

She did, shaking it loose so the brown straight strands fell down her back and into his waiting hands. "Very good. Now give me that massage."

With pleasure. She ran her hands over his shoulders, indulging herself with their feel and shape. "May I unbutton your shirt, sir? To be more thorough."

"Not this time. Work with what you're given."

Well, she'd had to try. Touching him, even through the cloth of his shirt, was still a sensual gift. As she did that, he moved one hand from her hip and toyed with the navel piercing, sending a lovely swirl of feeling radiating from that point. His knuckles were brushing her mound, reminding her that her legs were spread, her bare cunt just above the seam of his thighs. "Chris gave you the little bear, didn't he?"

"Yes sir."

His attention went to her face at the address. She kept her focus on his shoulders. He had such good muscle tone there, but he was tense. All those hours at a desk, reading, reviewing.

"You should go to yoga with me," she said.

"Men don't do yoga."

"They certainly do. We have several men in our class, and yes, heterosexual men. One of them is really hot. Like you. You could wear bike shorts like he does so I can see everything ripple and flex."

"Really?" His brow lifted. "Does he notice everything ripple and flex on you?"

"I wouldn't know. I don't pay attention to that," she said primly, but with a hint of a smile. "Come to the class to find out. Seriously, you should consider it. You need to figure out ways to relax. You're too tense."

She was sitting in his lap naked, babbling at him, because being there, in this situation at long last, was just too much to take in. But he'd decided he wanted to build them up again, because he wrapped one hand in her hair, focusing her attention.

"Be quiet, Miss Gerard. I'll let you know if I want to hear you talk."

"Yes sir. My mouth is willing to be occupied by anything you wish."

She could feel her cheeks heat as she said it. She kept her attention on the movement of her hands as if her life depended on it. He touched her face, though, gripping her jaw to make her meet his gaze. She expected she was turning deep rose.

"What do you mean by that, Miss Gerard?"

"I think it was pretty clear. Sir." She wet her lips, and the next word came out as a soft rasp. "Please."

"Christ," he muttered. "Chris would kick my ass."

Her brow creased, and she searched his hazel gaze. "Why?"

"It's . . . We shouldn't be doing this." His grip on her hair eased, both hands going back to her waist. She could feel him withdrawing, and she was still sitting on his lap. Naked. Freaking naked.

A shiver of cold went across her skin. "Really? Why is that?"

Geoff gave her a torn look. Whatever was going through his head was tying up his tongue, but she wasn't in the mood to wait for an answer. She slid her hands down the front of his shirt and backed off his lap, sinking down between his knees before he could move away from her. When she hooked her fingers in his belt, the heel of her hand rubbing against the head of his erection, he grabbed her wrists, his expression hardening.

That reaction was what Flo had warned her about. Doms didn't like to be pushed, the sub trying to call the shots. But she'd prefer his anger about that over whatever the hell he'd been about to do or say. Unfortunately, he refused to close that door.

"I'm not going to use you like that," he said. "You deserve better."

"I deserve better," she said slowly. "You want me on a pedestal, Geoff? Is that what you were thinking when you were spanking me, when you had me begging? I know what you want. You want to order me to go down on you. You want your cock in my mouth. You want me on my knees. That's where I want to be. On my knees to you."

She was fucking this up, because things were twisting into a hard knot inside of her. She was freaking *telling* him what he wanted. She'd made herself too vulnerable and he wasn't responding as she'd hoped. When he said nothing, obviously still struggling with the right words, the right response, she snapped.

"Forget it," she said, sliding back to her feet and picking up her clothes. She would have been better off striding bare-assed back to her room, because the moment she pressed the fabric against her, the shame of being so exposed gripped her. The ache in her throat was what tore it, though. She was not going to cry. If she did, he'd be sure it was all a mistake. At the moment, he might be right, but she knew that was just her fear of rejection talking. If he could just unbend one fucking moment, let go of control, of the idea that he had to keep everything in their world ordered the way he thought it was supposed to go, rather than how they all wanted . . .

"Things have to get messy sometimes," she snapped. "Not being in control of everything isn't the end of the world. Sometimes it can be just the beginning. If it gets fucked up some along the way, it's not the end of the world, either. It doesn't have to be."

Though unfortunately, this kind of hurt made it feel that way.

"Sam . . ."

"No," she said, dashing by him. She hurried down the hall, her movements so uncontrolled that she closed her door harder than she'd intended. She locked it, probably the first time she'd ever done that, and leaned against the panel, holding the clothes against the ache under her breastbone. She couldn't stick her neck out more than that, could she? Had she gone down the wrong path, been too blatant, too contrived? Up until she'd brought up giving him oral, he'd seemed to be getting into it. She shivered again as she replayed it in her head. Miss Gerard . . . God, if she worked for him in truth, hearing him address her so formally would get her aroused every time.

But this was about more than getting off. If that was all she was risking, she'd have stuck with her vibrator and her fantasies.

Oh hell. Maybe he'd been right all along. Maybe she'd been too impatient and they should have waited for Chris. He had a way of balancing things among the three of them, making their curves and edges complement one another. She couldn't deny that Geoff's forte was his intelligence, knowing the best approach or timing for things. Which meant she'd pushed all this, fucked it up. Maybe not irretrievably, but if she'd set them back, if Geoff would now take months before he was willing to even talk about this again, let alone act on it, she might just lose her mind.

What was her forte? What did she bring to all of this? Other than being the one with an aching need to submit to them. And the one with girly parts. A painful half smile crossed her face. She didn't have Geoff's brains or Chris's penchant for creating harmony. She'd thought of *harmony* as a fluffy greeting-card kind of word until she'd met him, but he was the true, deep spiritual meaning of it. There was nothing so amazing, so perfect, as a touch of harmony.

The door vibrated against her back at Geoff's light knock. "Sam, are you okay?"

She cleared her throat. "Yeah, I'm fine. Listen . . . you were right. We should have waited for Chris. It's okay. Don't worry about it, all right? I'm good. I'm sorry I . . . I'm sorry I rushed things. Let's just . . . We can talk about it later this week when he gets back, just like you said."

A long pause. She didn't hear his feet move away. She laid her cheek on the door. She needed to get dressed, but her heart felt too heavy to move. It would pass. It would be okay. They weren't children, to believe that a moment's stumble was a complete loss. She was supposed to have the maturity to step back, know that they'd have other chances, other approaches. As Florence had said, their relationship could weather a stumble or two. She just hadn't expected a stumble to hurt so much. It told her she'd invested more of her feelings in this one moment than she should have.

"I want to see you," he said firmly. "Open the door."

"I said I'm okay. It's all right. I—"

"Samantha Beth." His tone made the words stop in her throat. "It wasn't a request. Open the door, or I'll open it myself."

She'd left a terry-cloth robe on the bed, so she rose, slid into it and belted it tightly. Putting the clothes behind the door so they couldn't be seen as an embarrassing reminder to either one of them, she unlocked the door, turned the knob and stepped back, crossing her arms over herself.

Geoff pushed the panel open, his eyes immediately going to her face. She adjusted her gaze to the space left of his shoulder. "See? I'm okay. No biggie."

He came to her. She had the bed behind her and couldn't retreat, though she shrank back. He stopped in front of her. "You're not afraid of me, Sam. Are you?"

She shook her head. "No, of course not. I'm . . . I don't know what I am."

"Look at me."

She shook her head again, her mouth set, and he sighed. Tugging one resisting hand from her body, he closed his own around it. "Sam, this is hard for me to admit, but I'm as worried about doing the wrong thing as you are. Maybe more, because . . . I *want* to be in charge." He paused, his voice getting rougher. "I fucking ache . . . to take control of you."

Her gaze snapped up to his face. When he was worked up about something, the green in his eyes became more pronounced, like emerald sparks. She saw them now. "I want to do everything you said, and way more. I have no idea how you'll react to all the things I want. And Chris . . ."

"Chris is the one who knows if we're on track," she said softly. "I was just thinking that. Thinking I screwed up by rushing this when he should be here."

Just like that, things were better, connected. She still felt fragile, but now it was the type of vulnerability that made her want to stay close to him, not pull away.

"No." Geoff shook his head, squeezing her hand. He repeated it more forcefully, touching her chin for emphasis. "Absolutely not. You pretty much melted my brain in that outfit. For all I know, those three files I reviewed might be arguments to throw out the judicial system and go back to trial by combat."

"I wouldn't mind seeing you in gladiator wear. Russell Crowe style." She gave him a tentative smile.

"Come here," he said abruptly, unfolding her arms.

He didn't draw her to him right away. He slipped the loop of her robe first and opened up the panels so when he brought her against him, her naked body was pressed against the fabric of his slacks and shirt, but she could feel the warm, firm male beneath. Dropping one hand to her ass, he hiked her up his body in a forceful move he underlined by cupping her jaw and planting his mouth on hers.

A small moan broke from her lips at the unexpected gesture, the intimacy. The heat and demand that he injected into that one kiss was enough to burn away every uncomfortable second of the past few moments. His lips parted hers and his tongue swept in, tangling with hers, his fingers tightening on her ass and the side of her neck. The kiss, the hold, told her she'd stirred him up considerably. When he finally lifted his head, he kept holding her, which was a good thing, because her knees were weak, just like the romance stories said they should be. As she pressed her lips together, she felt the moisture his had left upon them. His eyes were hot with desire, his gorgeous mouth firm. She wanted it all over her.

"I masturbated on your bed today," she whispered. "And thought of you and Chris there with me."

"Bad, bad girl," he murmured, bending his head again. "Next time you wait until I order you to do it in front of me. Otherwise, I'll take a belt to your ass."

She clung to his shirtsleeves, her fingers making fervent caresses of his bunched muscles beneath them, her body straining against every inch of his. His short groan of need told her he liked her aroused reaction to the threat. She'd liked the spanking. She thought she'd like even more things like that. A belt would be incredible. Or a paddle. The flat, wide wooden cooking spoon in the kitchen . . .

When Geoff nipped her lips, finally taking the kiss into a more playful place, she was smiling. He looked down at her. "Why did you initiate this while Chris was gone?"

"Because you're both tiptoeing around each other about it. You think it's a contest between you, about who I want to be with. I want you both. I thought maybe if I could get you to see that first, it would help, because, like you said . . . you're the one in charge."

She dropped her gaze and toyed with a button on his shirt when she said that. Though she thought these things easily enough, saying them aloud could fluster her. Touching her chin, he made her look up at him.

"It wasn't just that," he said. "We wanted you to make choices based on what you want, not what's safe. We're safe. You haven't had a date in a while."

After that demanding, brain-scrambling kiss, *safe* wasn't the word she'd use to describe Geoff. Maybe that explained why she didn't think before she spoke. "I have a date."

"Excuse me?"

In a blink, Geoff switched from reasonable lawyer to a hostile-looking male with testosterone loaded and ready to fire. A bull about to charge a china shop might have the same expression. While it thrilled her a little too much to see that reaction, she hastened to correct the assumption.

"I was thinking about that very issue this week, so I thought I should test it, you know, while you and Chris were still stalling on the whole thing. But I was wrong. This tells me I don't need to do that. I'll cancel it."

"No." Geoff folded her robe over her again and tied the sash, though she caught her breath as he cinched it more forcefully than perhaps he'd intended. Holding the ends in tight fists, his knuckles pressed against her abdomen, he stared down at her, a million indecipherable thoughts flickering over his features. But before she could react or reach for him, he stepped back from her. "You're right. You should give it a chance. Since Anthony, you've stayed pretty close to us, and that hasn't been fair."

She blinked in confusion, but irritation replaced it pretty fast. "You act like I just handed you an escape clause. Something to keep you from having to face any of this."

"No," he said. "It's not that." But his body language was stiff, his expression now wooden. "I'm just trying to be fair to you. Go on the date. Who's the guy?"

"Mark in the Records department. It's just drinks at a bar, a group thing. Not really a date." Sort of. "This is crazy. I'm going to call it off." After that kiss, she was sure she knew her mind on it, but Geoff was suddenly as far away as the moon.

"No. Don't. Go on the damn date." He pivoted and moved toward the door.

"Geoff, what the hell . . ." She heard a hint of desperation in her tone, which kind of disgusted her with herself. Her gut was roiling with confusion, hurt and anger.

"It's all right, Sam." He turned at the doorway, met her gaze. "I'm not saying any of what just happened was a mistake. You were beautiful. Perfect."

If he'd sounded patronizing, she would have hit him with a blunt object, but he didn't. He sounded conflicted. But she wasn't in the mood to be kind.

"It's not me, it's you?" she said frostily.

His expression cooled. "I need to think about this, just like I said. And so do you."

She wanted to tell him he couldn't tell her what to do, but that would sound a little fucked up, wouldn't it? Given that she was pushing him to take charge of her. She literally didn't know what to say, but he took care of that.

He cleared his throat. "I'm going to reread those three files and then head to bed. Good night."

He closed her door behind him, an external manifestation of the internal doors he'd just closed against her. She didn't know whether to spit, hiss or cry. She wondered what he'd do if she whipped out her vibrator and turned it up on maximum setting so it would vibrate through the walls like a jackhammer. She'd scream out her climax like a banshee. Let him deal with that.

The anger wasn't enough to keep the other, deeper emotions at bay. Sinking down on the bed, she played with the ends of the robe's sash and wiped impatiently at frustrated tears. Damn it, damn it, damn it. That set look on his face said the round was over for tonight. She wouldn't whip out her vibrator. She'd get a glass of wine, settle in here with a book and ignore him the rest of the night. Or relive every single moment of the past couple of hours, when she'd gotten so very close to the place she wanted to go with him.

Goddamn stubborn men.

Geoff paused in front of the Naughty Bits erotica store. Most days, he ate lunch at his desk, unless he had to meet a client or have a powwow with coworkers, but today the problem he faced took priority over his work schedule. He'd told Sarah he should be back in ninety minutes. If she could take a whole afternoon for her kid's award ceremony, he could take ninety minutes to resolve a sexual dilemma about his roommate.

Despite all the arousing things about that scene in the kitchen with Sam, what he kept remembering was how she'd looked when she teased him about Mr. Cade. With her gray eyes dancing, she'd put her hand up to her mouth to hide her smile. Her hair was baby soft, so straight and silky. The strands sometimes caught in the corner of her mouth or on her eyelashes.

It made him think of the night she'd drunk too much at a New Year's Eve party. She wasn't a drinker, but in the spirit of the holiday, she'd unwisely downed three tall, fruity drinks with tinsel sparkler garnishes. When he'd heard her throwing up in the bathroom early that next morning, he'd slid out of bed fast, but Chris had beat him there, of course. He was kneeling behind her, holding back her hair as she hunched over the toilet.

"Oh God," she'd said weakly when she saw him there. "Now my humiliation is complete. Both of you get to see me vomit."

Chris rubbed her back as another convulsion took her. Geoff estimated about a third of the alcohol, plus the pizza and snacks she'd had at the party, evacuated. "I'm never drinking again," she moaned. "Or eating."

He ran a washcloth under the sink faucet, dropped to one knee and wiped her mouth, then a trembling hand that had gotten in the path of the rapid expulsion. Despite her misery, it was clear she was embarrassed. She was a private girl when it came to anything that happened in a bathroom, but neither he nor Chris gave that a second thought. Caring for her was as automatic as breathing to them.

In the small space, he was pressed hip to thigh with the other man, but casual contact between them wasn't something they thought about, either. Well, Geoff did, a lot more lately, but it wasn't from a desire to avoid it.

He watched Chris tease her gently as he held back her hair with one hand, stroking it lightly with the other. Geoff expected Chris didn't mind having an excuse to enjoy those strands of silk threading through his fingers.

She'd worn jersey cloth shorts to bed. Since she was kneeling on the bathroom floor, hunched over, they were stretched out low on her hips. Geoff could see the pink elastic band of her panties and a hint of the cleft between her buttocks.

Since then, he'd thought about that tempting spot quite a bit. Slipping his finger down to trace the sensitive tailbone and going lower, he'd massage her anal rim and make her writhe. He'd oil up his finger and slide it into that tight passage. He wondered if Sam had ever done any anal play.

In short, at this point, he had an anthology of fantasies about her the size of *War and Peace*. He hated that he might have left her last night thinking she was alone in fighting those kinds of feelings. He'd kept his own under wraps, but her drawing Chris and him into Naughty Bits had broken that seal, or at least damaged it enough that he wanted to stop fantasizing and start doing. Badly enough he'd given in and made a move in that direction yesterday.

And what had happened? He'd second-guessed himself and screwed things up. She'd barely been speaking to him this morning, and didn't waste any time getting out of the house for work, though usually she left after he did. He should have taken control of that situation, made her sit down and talk it out with him, but if he didn't get it straight in his own head, he was going to take them right back to the place where he'd hurt her and made her angry. He'd rather have cut off his arm than cause her pain, but what was done was done. When things went the wrong way in a trial, he didn't waste time chasing the mistakes, but instead focused on how to push it back in a winning direction. Though he had an ache like a punch in the gut and wanted to do anything to bring a smile back to her face, he had to figure out how to fix it, the right way.

Christ, he wished Chris was home. He was better at the touchy-feely stuff with Sam.

"Geoff?"

He'd been made. He tried not to jump like a guilty shoplifter as Madison, the owner of Naughty Bits, peered at him through her half-open door. "Are you coming in to see me? Or just window-shopping? We storeowners love it when you come in, though. We can talk you into all sorts of unlikely things."

"You could have done that on our last visit and you didn't," he pointed out.

"Well, maybe I've come to my senses and I'm ready to empty your wallet. Run while you can."

He smiled. Her long brown hair was tied back loosely with a ribbon, and she wore a corset-style lace top over jeans and boots that made the most of her curvy figure. She was an attractive woman, but today she looked . . . prettier. If he had to guess, he'd say something was going on in her life that was making her happy. Maybe she was falling in love.

He'd been in love for a while, and the feelings grew stronger every day. But so did other feelings, and that was what worried him and held him back. How would this impact his friendships with Sam and Chris? He'd always sensed Sam shared some of those reservations, and that had helped him keep things status quo, but it appeared she'd worked past that and was going full steam ahead. Jesus.

When she'd walked into the kitchen in that outfit designed to give him a lifetime hard-on, he hadn't even known where to start. All the things he'd ever wanted to do to her flooded into his head. Serious, things that went beyond a little spanking. Did she really understand that? Could she? What if that wasn't what she wanted and he opened

46

that can of worms, making her feel like he couldn't be happy with less?

He had no idea what the hell he was doing and, for some reason, that had brought him back here. But he wasn't sure how to broach it with Madison. She had her Dungeon Room and had shown him a few things, but he didn't necessarily get a Domme vibe off her. Actually, she had more of Sam's kind of vibe. But she could still be knowledgeable about both sides of the fence. He wasn't really looking for a discussion of the mechanics, though.

"Geoff?"

Shit, he was still standing there like a statue. Before he could snap out of it, make some lame excuse and hurry onward, Madison hung her clock sign on the door, indicating she'd be back in ten minutes, and stepped out, locking the door. "Come with me next door. I think I can help you with whatever you're thinking so hard about. Well, in a way."

She took his arm with a friendly smile. Before he could say anything else, they were headed into the hardware store. Troy, the guy he remembered from the last time they were there, was setting up a pyramid of bug spray. The guy had excellent upper-body definition, the kind that suggested the job he did here required a lot of physical labor. Chris was like that. He'd never seen the inside of a gym, but he'd never needed to lift weights, not when his job was all about strength and stamina. It was the turtle-versus-hare kind of strength. He and Geoff had run together before, and Chris would get winded long before Geoff, but if they did yard work together, Geoff would hit the exhaustion point days before Chris did. They had different skill sets, different approaches.

Chris being Chris, he hadn't hesitated to note why Geoff was a good runner, even though Geoff was gratified that he had to make his snarky observation while he was bent over, wheezing from their four-mile run. "You were one of those skinny kids who couldn't keep his mouth shut, so you had to do a lot of running," Chris pointed out. "I was easygoing. No one picked fights with me."

"No one picked fights with you because you look like a tank," Geoff had retorted. Chris's response to that had been to tackle and pin him in a wrestling hold. Geoff had thrown a few punches against his radial motor points to get him to let go, which Chris claimed verified his theory that he'd had to fight off bullies. Then Sam had broken up the friendly argument by suggesting they get Chinese for dinner.

Geoff remembered something else about that wrestling match. When Chris had pinned him, there'd been a moment when Geoff noticed Chris studying his mouth in a distracted way, his hands flexing on Geoff's hip and biceps. "Let go of me," Geoff had said.

Instead of it coming out the way it would if two guys were wrestling one another for fun, there was another note to it that had caused a spark in Chris's eye. As if he was about to say, *Make me.* Then the moment was gone. He'd sat back on his heels and helped Geoff up with a firm hand clasp, his other hand steadying Geoff briefly against his back. The touch was a near caress, a quick grip of his shirt, but when Geoff turned to look at him, Chris had already released him and was striding to the house.

As complicated as things might be with Sam right now, he and Chris were a quagmire in comparison. They both seemed to prefer to focus on Sam, a mutually unspoken agreement that gave them an indirect way to address what simmered between them. No matter what happened with Sam, they could always leave that part of things right there.

But that thought just left Geoff with another layer of dissatisfaction. He knew where Sam wanted to take them all, but what people wanted wasn't always the best thing. That was what worried him most. He didn't trust his own impulses, because they were too damn strong, and Sam was trying her hardest to tear loose any restraint he had. If he let that happen, those impulses could consume him, Sam and Chris, override his judgment and destroy everything he valued.

"I should probably go." He came to a stop with Madison inside the hardware store. "This maybe isn't—"

"Is Logan here, Troy?" Madison asked.

"He's in his workshop," the young man responded. "It's been pretty quiet this morning, and he has a customer picking up a piece at the end of the week. He wanted to put one more coat of finish on it." When Troy's attention shifted to him, Geoff was surprised to see recognition there. Troy nodded, a friendly greeting.

"Just go on back," he added to Madison.

"Good. Okay." Madison glanced up at Geoff. "I'm sorry, I didn't mean to interrupt you. What were you saying?"

Geoff shook his head, brushing it off. Giving him a smile, Madison proceeded to the back of the store, passing through a curtained area to bring him into a storage area. As she guided him along the narrow alley flanked by stocked shelves, Geoff heard an eighties radio station playing, the sound filtering through a door at the opposite end of the storeroom. Madison drew him through that door, bringing him into Logan's workshop.

From the sawdust smell, he'd deduced Logan was doing woodwork, but his current project wasn't a birdhouse or bookcase. Geoff had visited enough BDSM clubs on his travels and surfed enough websites to know what a spanking bench looked like. This was a custom-made one, with some intriguing additions that, if his mind wasn't focused on another priority, would have captured his attention far more thoroughly.

Instead, he focused on the man who'd built it. A rugged, powerful-looking forty-something, Logan had thick, long brown hair bound back in a thick tail that fell between his shoulder blades. While most men over forty couldn't rock that look, Logan did. Geoff didn't consider himself a romantic, but he could easily see the man in boots, breeches and an unlaced shirt on the bridge of a pirate ship, doing the Tyrone Powers thing. His mother had watched *The Black Swan* a hundred times.

Geoff's own love of black-and-white movies had come from watching those kinds of flicks at his mother's side. Hell, he'd received his first guidance about lines between right and wrong in those romantic mediums. Which was painfully ironic, considering his current relationship with his nuclear family.

This was so not the moment for that. Pushing away those thoughts, he planted himself firmly in the present.

The cushions for the bench were propped off to the side while Logan painted a cherrywood finish on the frame. He glanced up, pleased surprise in his warm, brandy-colored eyes as Madison entered. Since he followed that up with a leisurely perusal of her from head to toe, Geoff wondered if the spark in Madison was glowing brighter because of her next-door neighbor. Given that her cheeks pinkened a little under his regard, Geoff expected the answer to that was a resounding yes.

"Logan, I'm sorry to bother you, but do you remember Geoff? He was in your store not too long ago."

"His face is familiar." Logan set the can and brush aside and extended a hand. "Geoff."

He had a strong grip, strong as Chris's. During their earlier visit, Sam had come into the hardware store with Geoff and Chris briefly before going next door to Madison's shop. When Logan had asked her if she was looking for anything in particular, she'd gotten a little tongue-tied. Chris had teased her later about getting all flustered by a handsome older man, but based on the events of the past few days, and what Geoff read from the guy pretty clearly now, he thought there was another reason Logan's steady regard had flustered her. The same reason Geoff could fluster her when he looked at her a certain way.

If she was even now berating herself for reacting like that, he'd feel even more like shit. He'd tried to make sure she'd feel no shame about it, but she'd shot down his comment about her being beautiful and perfect as the lame bullshit it was. If she could only see and feel what happened inside him—heart, head, cock and soul—when she looked at him as her Dom, she wouldn't feel any dismay. Hell, she'd probably have a valid reason to gloat, because he'd never reacted so strongly to a sub. But he hadn't shown her that, had he?

Some, but not enough. He had to figure this out. Either be all in or all out, but not this limbo state, which confused her and made him want to tear his heart out and hand it to her.

"Geoff, I apologize if I'm being presumptuous," Madison said, "but I think maybe you have some questions that Logan can answer better than I can. He mentors other Doms. I'm going to leave you two to talk. If that's okay with you?"

She looked toward Logan then, with an expression that said she hoped she hadn't been presumptuous toward him, either. Geoff knew a lot of people in the lifestyle were pretty careful about their identities. Either Logan didn't need to do that, or Madison and he already had enough of a rapport that she'd known he'd be okay with this.

"I'm here to help you with whatever you need, Madison," Logan said. "You know that."

That resulted in a deeper flush. Geoff had no interest in any woman other than Sam, but as a man and a Dom, he could definitely appreciate that lovely reaction. Geoff deduced that she wasn't entirely comfortable with her responses to Logan yet, because she made a noncommittal noise and then hurried out, leaving Geoff with a cordial nod and warm smile. "Come by before you leave and get a cookie," she said. "I made peanut butter blossoms. You can take a couple home for Sam and Chris. Maybe a half dozen for Chris."

Geoff turned back to Logan as the man bumped a Van Halen tune on his radio down a few notches. "She took me by surprise," Geoff admitted. "I'm not sure if I should be talking about this, or what I should be saying."

Logan picked up the finish and brush again, squatting on his heels next to the bench. "Don't have to say anything, son," he said comfortably. "Not if you don't want to. But if she thought you looked like you had questions I could answer, she's probably right. She's starting to get a good sense of what her customers need. Are you new to exploring the Dom side?"

He didn't sound derogatory, just matter-of-fact. "Seems like I've always felt like that's what I wanted . . . what I am," Geoff said slowly. "But I've never really pursued it too much. School and work haven't left a lot of time until recently. I've gone to a few clubs and parties and hooked up with one or two subs there for sessions, to get a feel for it, but nothing turned into an ongoing thing." Nothing that resulted in even a tenth of the response he had when Sam merely called him *sir*.

"So tell me what the questions are and we'll figure it out from there." When Logan gestured at a stool, Geoff slid a hip onto it. What the hell. He found himself explaining in fits and starts, where it had begun and where it was now. Logan asked a few directed questions that helped him focus. Once he felt more comfortable, Geoff laid it out like he did a case, with all the necessary information. Only since he was far more personally connected to this, he found himself correcting himself, backtracking and figuring out things as he went along, in a way he usually didn't have to do for work.

He sighed, rubbing a hand over his face. "I've always known she's a sub. God, it's like living with the biggest temptation in the world. But as long as she didn't hit on it directly, I thought it was better to keep it under wraps, so as not to force it with her. She brought us to Naughty Bits, though, and since then . . . she's starting to get pretty direct about it."

"So what's holding you back with her, if it's obvious she's a sub? Is it Chris? He wants her for himself and you don't want to trample the friendship?"

Geoff shook his head. "I think we were both worried she would want to make a choice, but she's made it clear that's not a problem." He had no idea how that amazing truth would play out. But it also wasn't the only important reason why neither of them had moved on it. "We met her under difficult circumstances. She had this guy giving her a hard time. We asked her to move in with us to protect her."

"So you see yourself as her protector. It's hard to transition from there to wanting to leave marks on her skin and make her cry. In the right way."

Geoff lifted his head. To hear it said straight out like that, with no sense of shame, was almost a revelation, a reassuring one. He searched Logan's expression for condemnation, and saw none. The man bent back to his task.

"Say you have Sam tied up and you're spanking her," he said casually. "You can tell she's wanting it rougher, harder. What's your first reaction?"

Damn, the guy didn't mince around. For some weird reason, Geoff didn't want him saying Sam's name, as if somehow that exposed her to another man in a way he didn't like. On the other hand, having the opportunity to talk about it so directly, with a guy putting off vibes that said he knew what being a Master was all about, brought a relief stronger than Geoff had expected to feel.

"It's all right, son." Logan's gaze met his. "We were all new at this at one time. You seeking help and guidance about it, to work through your feelings and figure it out, is the right thing to do. And I have nothing but respect for another Dom's sub, so even if I talk about her in an intimate way, it's not to get overly familiar about her. I'm just helping you figure out what you want. So what's your reaction, if she wants things rougher, harder?"

Some people were good at putting out the authoritative, knowledgeable vibes, even when they didn't know shit. As a lawyer, Geoff knew all about high-level bullshitting. He wasn't getting that vibe from Logan. So he answered his question.

"To give her that. But how do I know that's her wanting it and not something inside of me, wanting to give her that even if she doesn't really understand what it means?"

"Would you ever hurt Sam?"

"No. Of course not."

"Would you like to spank her?"

Christ, he'd loved it. And damn, the guy could read faces too well. "Okay, you've already been there," Logan said. "Good. But a spanking can hurt, right?"

"That's different."

"Yeah, it is. Did she get excited by it?"

"Yes. It made me want to do it more."

"Until she's bruised and bleeding and she's afraid of you, begging you to stop?"

"No." He recoiled. "Christ no. I'd kill anyone who'd treat her like that."

Logan's brown eyes glowed with approval. "See? There's a difference. To someone who's never had these inclinations, they might not see a difference. But you do. And she does. That's all that matters."

Logan put aside the can of finish and leaned against his workbench, crossing his arms over his broad chest. "Geoff, you know the reason BDSM gets such a bad rep? It's extremely hard to explain in a politically correct way just how intense and right a healthy power exchange feels to the people involved in it. I expect Sam is a pretty independent woman. She's not looking for someone to wipe her ass and forbid her from pursuing her career, having friends and being an accomplished individual."

"Wow. No. She'd hit you for even suggesting it."

"Right. So how does that kind of woman say, 'I fantasize about having the man I love restrain me so I can't move, because when he does that, I feel helpless, like I have no choice but to relinquish control to him.' Which in turn can get her so aroused that she wants you to do all sorts of things to her when she's helpless. Not just spank her, but mark her with a whip, with a strike brand, with a violet wand, with your teeth. Maybe she even wants you to treat her like your property in a scene, like she has to ask your permission to even breathe. Everything that's the exact opposite of what she embraces in her day-to-day life."

Geoff realized he'd gone still, all his muscles tense. Logan's gaze rested on him, his expression saying he understood all too well the feelings rolling through him. "And while you're doing all that, you're also wanting to hold and kiss her, talk to her, show her in every damn way possible just how much you cherish her. The two go together. Your urge to dominate, to control and care for her, is as strong as her desire to submit, to trust you to take her for a journey, keep her flying, but make her yours as well."

Geoff could imagine it, so vividly he was afraid he was going to embarrass himself by getting an erection here and now.

"Not going to see that written up in *Modern Woman* magazine anytime soon, right?" Logan continued, his eyes glinting. "But a world scared of its own shadow won't take a close look at what's really going on there. They won't realize it can be a healthy, damn near spiritual form of sexual expression to people who enjoy or need it. If I hit your girl or hurt her feelings, made her cry, what would you do?"

"I'd kill you."

Logan's lips curved. "Yeah, it's automatic, isn't it? You'd protect her from the wrong kind of harm with everything you are. What you do in session is different. You flog her until she cries, and yet she's not calling out a safe word. You put your hand between her legs and find she's seconds away from climaxing like she's never climaxed before. What does that tell you?"

"That kind of pain releases other emotions, good ones."

"Yeah. Women have a different relationship with crying than we do. They have a hundred different languages when it comes to tears."

Geoff tightened his jaw. "I should have sought more guidance earlier. I didn't connect with anyone at the clubs or parties and, since it seemed too difficult to get into the right space with anyone, I was worried that if I pursued it with Sam . . . Sam really matters. But she's set things in motion."

"You want to make her happy." Logan grinned. "Selfless guy that you are."

Geoff found himself grinning back. He also experienced a guilty twinge, because he'd second-guessed her on the damn date thing, assuming he knew better than her what was best for her. Wow. Talk about being an arrogant asshole. And on top of that, it wasn't him being selfless. He'd been pissed at the idea of her dating another guy and had gone with a knee-jerk reaction. Which meant now he'd have to honor it and let her go through with it, even though he'd much rather ask for a do-over on that bad judgment call.

He glanced at his watch regretfully and extended his hand. "I've got to get back. Would it be okay if I needed to talk again?"

"Absolutely." Logan clasped his hand. "I encourage you to do so. If you decide you want to join the local BDSM group, I do demos at a lot of their events, and you'll find other experienced Doms there, men and women. Any one of them worth anything is willing to answer questions from a Dom learning his path."

Logan paused. "That's something else I want to mention. You're a natural Dom. And since Sam is a natural submissive, she picked up on it. But instincts are one thing; experience is another. If you don't want to hurt her, don't do this half-assed. If you decide to do anything with her more than the light stuff like spanking, make sure you understand the risks."

Turning to open the drawer of the bench, Logan withdrew a sheet of paper off a short stack of them. "Here's the handout I give out at my demos. It has some good sources and BDSM 101 safety-type stuff, some of the most common bullet points. You may already know some of it, maybe not. Better to hear it twice than not at all."

He grimaced. "It's easy to fall into the trap of thinking we have to act like we know what we're doing when we don't. Sam has to learn to be your partner in that, and that's not always easy for someone with a submissive nature. Best way to help a sub to do that is to set up the opportunity, give her a structure. For instance, make her talk over a scene with you before and after. Command her to give you feedback. That tells her she's not topping; she's just communicating and helping you honor the priority that's above every other priority, even your pride. You know what it is already."

"To keep her safe. To protect her."

Logan nodded, satisfied. "And to love her. Don't forget that one, because sometimes when you're new at this, you talk yourself out of stuff, thinking somehow you're protecting her when what you're doing is depriving you both of a journey of discovery together. She may be your submissive, but in your case, she's also your lover. You're not alone in this."

"When she let me spank her . . . I thought, I could get lost in this, never stop, never want to stop. And then I thought, I might get carried away and really hurt her, emotionally or physically. Or do something that makes her afraid of me."

It was the first time he'd said it aloud, which told Geoff that Logan was right. He didn't like being seen as anything less than cocksure in front of the woman he loved. He supposed that didn't differ from how most men felt in front of their women, but if he wanted to explore the Dom/sub stuff with her, he was going to have to get past that. Having a restaurant reject a credit card during a romantic dinner was a far cry from a misstep during a BDSM session where Sam's emotional and physical well-being was entirely in his hands. "I don't want to harm her, not for anything in the world."

She was so important. But it was more than that. She and Chris . . . he wasn't sure what he would be without them. That was the part he couldn't talk about with Logan, that kept eating at him when he got close to what Sam wanted, to what they both wanted. What if he screwed up and lost her? Chris loved Sam with all his heart and soul. Geoff would lose them both.

"So don't," Logan said placidly. His shrewd gaze was watching Geoff's face in a way that told Geoff he might be picking up on some of those deeper issues. "You seem like a careful guy to me. You'll find the balance together. You're going to be fine, son."

Logan picked up his stain brush once more. "I'm here every day except Monday, and the occasional weekend day off when I trust Troy to run the place. Call the store if you need a quick question answered or if you want to drop by for a face-to-face. If it's urgent and I'm not here, Troy will give you my cell."

"You should charge for this."

Logan shook his head, smiled. "It's a pay-it-forward thing. Someone did it for me, so I do it for others. When you gain experience, you'll run into someone who needs guidance, too. It's how the Wheel works. That's what Alice used to say, the woman who ran Naughty Bits before Madison. Capital *W* for *Wheel*. She was one of those new age, crunchy-granola hippie types." Logan winked. "I teased her about that, but she was a smart woman. A lot like her sister."

"Sam's smart, too. Smarter than me, when it comes to emotions and things like that. Maybe that's why I keep hesitating."

"Her being smarter than you is actually a pretty good thing. Trust me on that." Logan offered him another grin, a look of man-to-man wisdom. "The fascinating thing about women, especially submissives, is how they'll make themselves vulnerable in a manner that opens us up the same way. It lets us see a little clearer the things we want and truly need."

Geoff had other questions and thoughts, but he had more than enough to digest for now. "Thanks," he said, and meant it. "I'm going to pick up a few things in your store before I go."

Normally he'd buy from the lower-priced stock in a Lowe's or Home Depot, but he doubted he'd have gotten this kind of Dom-to-Dom advice there. Though it might have been interesting to see how they'd page someone for that. *Attention, Dom advice needed in Electrical, aisle 11. Customer waiting.*

Amusement crossed Logan's face. "Appreciate that, sir. I know you've got to get back to work, so ask Troy to show you some of the more popular items for our Dom visitors. He's a submissive with a very demanding Mistress, so he's fully informed on the lifestyle."

Geoff had been thinking about functional household items, like a four-foot aluminum stepladder for the kitchen. Sam had a harrowing habit of clambering from a chair onto the granite countertop to reach the cookbooks they kept over the cabinets. They also needed some lightbulbs and a switch plate to replace the cracked one in the garage, but Logan's comment had intrigued him. He'd looked at the possibilities in hardware stores before and imagined, but never bought for that purpose.

As he stepped out of the back room, he emerged on the fastener and rope aisle, which he could only interpret as the hand of fate. He texted Sarah that he'd be about a half hour longer, his gaze coursing over the different types of rope. Nylon, twine, cotton. D-hooks, connectors.

"Can I help you find anything, sir?"

Troy had reappeared at his elbow. Along with the compelling physique, he had hair like golden beach sand and direct Carolina sky-blue eyes. Geoff expected Logan had straight women and gay men who stopped by just for the pleasure of looking at him. Geoff appreciated such features. He certainly appreciated Chris's physique often enough, even though he kept that tamped down almost as well as he'd restrained himself from pursuing Sam's submissive nature. Until now.

Maybe both of those things were about to change, though he had no idea how Chris would react to the Dom/sub stuff. He'd definitely seen Chris checking out his ass on occasion, but that was a far cry from wanting to be topped. As far as he knew, Chris had never sought out male company for sex, so even that was a bit of an unknown.

His lips tugged up ruefully. Maybe Sam was right, that it was best to deal with one person at a time and work from there. Still, Geoff took a second, harder look at Troy. He was a submissive who belonged to a Mistress, but it wasn't obvious, was it? Of course, he of all people shouldn't be making assumptions about what a male sub did and didn't act like.

Chris was in no way as obviously submissive as Sam, but that *Make me* challenge had sent a charge to Geoff's Dom-dar. Maybe women were easier to recognize as submissives, because so often it was more acceptable for them to take a submissive role with a man. But Geoff had seen men at the private parties or in clubs who wanted the full subjugation treatment, following their high-heeled Mistresses around on hands and knees with a collar and leash attached to their dicks. Humiliation could be a fetish, and he didn't pass judgment on it. But he couldn't see Chris doing that and, when he thought of doing it to Sam or Chris, he knew it wasn't his thing, either.

But there were as many types of submissive inclinations out there as there were Dom preferences, weren't there? When Logan had talked about him tying Sam up, flogging her until she cried, until her pussy wept, Geoff's breath had caught. He wanted her to call him Master in such a moment. He wanted to put a collar around her throat, a brand on her ass. Jesus. What would Chris think of that?

Realizing that Troy was waiting for some kind of indication he wasn't talking to a zombie, Geoff shoved himself out of his head. "Your boss said you might be able to show me some of the more popular items for . . . Doms." He'd said it aloud. Jesus.

"Absolutely, sir." Troy straightened. "You'll pay less for it at a hardware store. Plus, when you DIY it, it's usually better-quality materials, unless you're dealing with a craftsman like Logan. You're already looking at the rope. I typically recommend the cottons because they don't slip and they don't chafe, but it depends on how you're going to use it. You have any sense of that yet? Are you interested in doing suspension stuff?"

"Not yet. I'm figuring this stuff out."

Troy's expression warmed even further. "That's cool, man. I've dealt with new Doms who try to pretend they know it all, and don't ask the questions they really want and need to ask. I want to punch them in the head, because they aren't doing themselves or their subs any favors."

Geoff blinked. "Not very submissive behavior."

"If you have someone in mind for this rope, I'm guessing you already know subs aren't doormats. A lot of us can be giant pains in the ass." Troy flashed a grin at him. "So cotton would be a good start, though if you go for aesthetics, like different colors, you might look at a couple of online sites for Japanese rope bondage I can recommend. In a hardware store, typically your colored ropes are the more slippery nylon. Now, when it comes to fasteners . . ."

Geoff found himself listening intently. Intuiting that Geoff was learning as much as seeking shopping direction, Troy kept offering insights as they moved through the aisles and looked at hooks and chain, and rectangles of flexible rubber that could be cut into paddles to the size and shape preferred. When they stopped at the stepladders, Troy put his hand on one of the four-foot ones Geoff wanted to keep Sam off the counters.

"A lot of people prefer to have things in their home that can't be readily identified as BDSM toys or equipment. A ladder can take the place of a St. Andrew's cross or other type of frame in a heartbeat. You just embed a few hooks into the wall of your garage to mount it, and then tie someone up against it in a variety of ways. If you choose one of these heavier, eight-foot folding stepladders, it gives you even more options."

Troy directed his attention to it. "My Mistress has me thread my arms between two of the steps and hold the cross piece on the opposite side. Then she ties my ankles to the bottom part. It won't be as stable as one that's mounted to the wall, but a way to deal with that is to command the sub to stay perfectly still no matter what, though you still want to stay close enough to make sure they don't topple it, especially if you're doing things that are making it hard for them not to move." Another grin. "Which is usually the case with you sadistic types. This one weighs quite a bit more than an aluminum ladder, and makes the sub feel more stable and secure."

And so on and so forth. Once or twice, other customers came into the store, but their needs were quickly met. Geoff browsed while Troy took care of them, letting his mind wander through the possibilities until Troy returned to him. When the store was empty, Troy's descriptions were far more visual, planting all sorts of images of what he could do to Sam . . . or to Chris.

When his do-it-yourself bondage tour was over, Geoff had narrowed down his purchase options. Chris already had a heavy ten-foot stepladder, so Geoff bought the four-foot one, a couple of lengths of cotton rope, strong mounting hooks, and that switch plate.

He'd be back for more, but there were far more important things to resolve first. Like how he was going to get Sam to speak to him again. Logan had said not to be half-assed. Was letting her go out with this guy instead of saying *Hell no* doing that? If he was being absolutely truthful, the only choice he wanted to give her was to belong to him and Chris.

Sitting in his car, he grimaced. He'd fucked up; he had to take his lumps. If she went through with the date, which she was probably going to do just to show how much he'd pissed her off, he wasn't going to stand in her way. He'd grin and bear it, let her go out with Mr. Asshole without making a peep about it. Even if every minute she was with the guy, Geoff would visualize burying him up to his neck in sand and dumping fire ants on his screaming face.

If she came home from the date and said she'd found the love of her life, he'd impale himself on a railroad spike. But if she didn't, he'd make his feelings clear then. Make things right.

It still felt fucked up. Christ, he wished Chris were home.

Sam put the finishing touches on her makeup. Why was she doing this? She should have canceled, no matter what Geoff had said. But he'd been so adamant. And such a horse's ass about it. *"Go on the damn date."* So fine, she'd go on the damn date. If Mark from Records ended up being the Dom of her hottest, wildest dreams, Geoff would have no one to blame but himself.

Yeah, she wasn't seeing that. Mark had some nice qualities and was handsome enough, but he didn't give her that Dom sense Geoff did. Was that a deal breaker for a relationship with her now? After one almost-there session with Geoff, was she that deep in her fantasies and desires that she couldn't adjust them back to mainstream relation-ship dynamics?

No, it was more than that. When she fantasized while using her vibrator, it was all about commands and restraints, spankings and more than spankings. It wasn't a sudden whim. Usually when a girl hadn't dated anyone in a long while, all she could think about when it came to sex was finding someone with whom she could have a halfway decent experience. One that would come with a good emotional connection that "might" lead to an in-love relationship.

In contrast, all she could think about was Geoff and Chris, and things that were far beyond that. She wanted sex that involved kneeling at their feet and exploring the deepest levels of surrendering her soul to another...

But Geoff wanted proof she hadn't let some weird thing happen during the Anthony disaster where she thought Geoff and Chris were her only options, the only men she could ever trust again. Which was bullshit. She knew what her feelings were and she should have said them straight out to Geoff. She'd been set back on her heels and reac-tionary, instead of saying what she should have said. Adamantly. *It has nothing to do with Anthony, and everything in the world to do with the two of you.*

"*Go on the damn date,*" she mimicked at the mirror. "He can be such an ass."

Because she was mad, she knew she might have overdone her outfit for a casual date. Rather than the jeans and pretty top she would have worn to hang out in a trendy bar with coworkers, she was wearing a short lavender dress with a fitted bodice that had a scoop neckline. The point of the bodice stopped at the abdomen and scal-loped over her hips, framing them before it gave way to the skirt, a romantic fall of soft lavender gauze pleats with a flirty hem that stopped just above the knee. The back of the dress had faux lacings like a corset.

She'd put it with strappy heels and some simple silver jewelry. Because she'd needed a touch of whimsy, she'd added the sparkling Tinker Bell pendant Chris had given her after he and Esteban's crew had spent a couple of weeks down in the Orlando area. He hadn't gone to Disney World, but he'd seen the castle at a distance, and he'd been excited about all of them going sometime. Even though Geoff looked at him like he thought his roommate had lost his mind, she thought it would be tremendous fun to visit the park with them.

Stop it. Think of Mark. She turned in a circle. The dress was fine for a date. She looked pretty but not slutty, though any man's eyes would be drawn to the gentle swell of her breasts over the scoop top and the hint of her legs through the gauzy skirt. Because of her height and metabolism, she tended to be on the thin side, so the style pumped up the breasts a bit, and the skirt gave her hips more of a flare. Geoff hadn't ever behaved like he thought she had a boyish figure, though. She'd been teased about being a scarecrow at school, so the first time Chris had looked at her and said she was like Liv Tyler's Tolkien elf, the beautiful Arwen, he'd won a million points in her mind.

Good grief. Mark, Mark, Mark. Tonight was about *Mark*. She was going out on a date with Mark, who had a nice smile, green eyes and thick dark hair. He went to the gym and did the CrossFit stuff, so all the bank ladies said he had a hot body. She might get up close and personal with it tonight. Who knew?

Pushing down any thoughts to the contrary, no matter that there were enough of them to overflow a mini-storage unit, she put her lipstick into her small evening bag, spritzed some fragrance in the air in front of her and walked through it as she left the bathroom.

Geoff was sitting on the couch, working on his laptop as usual, though he had the news on the TV. He kept his gaze moving between both screens. *Fine.*

"I'll see you later."

"Yeah, okay. Have a good time."

She'd put her lipstick in the bag without putting any on her lips, so she took it out, uncapped it. She took her time, applying it delicately to her mouth, using her compact mirror to make sure she didn't draw outside the lines. She coated it with gloss, spreading it with a finger, then cleaned her fingertip on a napkin. Pursing her lips, she wetted them further. When she glanced left and saw him looking, *finally*, she turned on her heel so she was halfway facing him. He looked back at his computer before she could meet his eyes, though.

Fine. Be an asshole.

She put her gloss into her purse. "I'll text if I'm going to be out later than expected. Or not back until morning."

"What?" That got his attention. She glanced at him, all casual-like.

"It's the twenty-first century, Geoff. Men and women on first dates sometimes hit it off and decide to have no-strings-attached sex. Kind of a trial run before the relationship goes any further."

"It would be that easy for you?" His eyes fired up. "Just screw him as a test drive?"

"No, it would not be that easy. No easier than it is for me to walk out this door when I know what you feel about me and I feel about you, but you said go on the damn date. So fine, I'm going on the damn date. And fuck you, by the way, for being a prick about it."

He tossed the laptop next to him on the couch and straightened, spreading his hands out in an angry gesture. "I was just trying to look out for your best interests."

"Oh, don't even." She shot him a stormy look. "You're worried about what you want from me, Geoff, and whether or not I can handle it. Whether or not it will destroy our friendship. Well, I think we're strong enough to take the risk, all three of us. So don't you put this on me. You're the holdup. Until you green-light, we can't. Yes, I get that that's more pressure on you, but, hell, you thrive on pressure. You're so revved when you work a case you practically glow like a lightbulb. I don't understand why this decision has you cowering."

He surged up from the couch, the look on his face making her take a step back, but he stopped there, fists clenching, hazel eyes narrowed.

"Whether the case goes good or bad, I come home to you and Chris," he said in a measured, tight tone. "You're what makes the rest of it work. I'm not willing to risk that as much as you are. Maybe it isn't as important to you."

Hurt speared her, taking her breath so that she couldn't respond right away. His gaze flickered with regret, but she spoke again before he could say anything more, since she was pretty sure if his next words were along the same vein, she wouldn't be able to bear it.

"I'd forgotten you can be mean when you get scared," she said softly. "Maybe because I've never been the one who's scared you. I'm always what you need me to be. I'm going out. If you truly don't think I value this relationship as much as you do, if you don't get that's *why* I've been pushing this, then I don't know what else to do."

She was close to tears that would ruin her carefully applied makeup, so she fled, sliding out the door. She got into her car, fumbled with her keys and stuck them in the ignition. She'd worn a pretty dress, but she knew she'd worn it for Geoff. Geoff really liked it when she wore girly things, evidence of that romantic streak he tried to hide. If he had the choice of seeing her in a crotchless teddy or a clingy satin peignoir like the starlets wore in the black-and-white movies, he'd choose the latter. He'd push the thin straps off her shoulders, let the gown pool around her feet...

Oh God. She knew him and Chris so well. Too well. She wanted to take it all off, put on flannel pajamas and hide in her bed. So she wasn't going to do that. She was going to . . .

She sighed. She was going to be fair to Mark. It was a group thing, after all. Florence and several other people from work, including Mark, were meeting at the bar. There'd been some implication that they might go from dinner there to a dance club. Any other time, it would have been fun, whether or not she and Mark hit it off. It proved how sensitive her potential date was, suggesting a good, low-pressure environment to make a decision about each other. He was obviously a nice guy, and she wasn't going to dick him around, using him as a pawn in a situation that didn't involve him.

She sent Mark and Flo a text, indicating she'd had something come up and couldn't be there, but she hoped they had a good time.

After she hit send, she closed her eyes. The car was humming. Maybe she'd go to a movie, pick up some dinner, whatever would keep her away from the house for the next several hours. She wished Chris was here. Then again, maybe she wasn't ready to talk to him about this, either.

She put the car in drive, but her door opened before she could press the accelerator. Geoff reached over her, put the car back in park. Switching off the ignition, he pulled out the key and pocketed it. Then he eyed her with a set jaw and resolute expression. "You're not going on a damn date," he said.

She crossed her arms over her breasts and shot him a mutinous look. "Sorry, it's what we insensitive sluts do."

His firm lips pressed together. Squatting next to the car, he put his hand on her knee, fingers incidentally sliding beneath the gauzy pleats. The warm strength was too welcome. She told herself to jerk away, tell him to let go and give her the damn keys.

"Come in the house, Samantha Beth," he said quietly.

"You'll say you're sorry first. That was a really, really horrible thing to say."

"Yes, it was." He sighed, surprising her by kissing her shoulder before he pressed his forehead against it and the side of her breast. "Forgive me. Sometimes I need to have my tongue cut out."

"It'd be really hard for you to be a trial lawyer that way," she said. She wanted to touch his head, run her fingers through his hair in comfort, but she steeled herself to stay motionless. She refused to go backward again, and a simple apology with no indication that anything would be different wasn't something she was going to accept this time.

He lifted his head, his eyes thoughtful. "Someone told me earlier in the week that submissives are braver than Doms," he said. "Maybe because a sub's mentality is all about reaching a point of vulnerability where you can surrender and let go. Doms don't have that, Sam." He grimaced. "We're all about control, beginning to end. He told me to think of you as a partner in this, and I'm trying, but there's this pounding drum in my head that says I'm in charge of all of it, that if it crashes and burns, it's me who will make that happen. I think I could forgive anything you or Chris did to me. But I couldn't forgive myself if I pushed us away from one another. And look, Christ, isn't that what I just did, in there? I said things that made you bolt."

Something else entered his gaze, something vulnerable that she wasn't sure he meant her to see. "You're my family," he said. He stopped, cleared the break from his voice, but kept his eyes fastened on hers. "Do you understand that, Sam? I need you to understand it, to help me . . . get us where we both want to go."

She could feel the tension strumming through his body, as if he was willing her to understand things that were too hard for him to say. She realized then why what he'd said had hurt so much. Hadn't she harbored that exact worry, that she was so trapped in her own desires she might mess something up, which was what someone who didn't value their relationship as much might do? She *did* value it, just as she'd said.

Because Geoff was so good at being in control, it was easy to forget really important details about him. He wasn't being sentimental. She and Chris *were* Geoff's only family. His dad had screwed around on his mother and Geoff had ended his relationship with his father. That could have turned out okay, except his mother had returned to his father, even though it was widely known he was still philandering. Geoff's mother had told Geoff she could overlook his father's infidelities as long as he took care of her, and his other siblings had supported her wish. Geoff couldn't, so he'd walked away from them and the family money, which had been considerable.

That was what so many people didn't get about Geoff, but she and Chris did. A lot of people became attorneys for the money or the prestige that came with saying, *I'm an attorney*. Or just to have a career path. Even if the legal system dealt with a lot of shades of gray, Geoff believed in clear lines of right and wrong. Though he worked for a corporate firm to pay for his student loans, she knew what he really wanted was to be on the front lines, trying to see those lines honored. He'd told Sam once that even if that happened only once out of every hundred cases, there was value in being one of the guys who helped make that one time happen, and who at least tried get the other ninety-nine as close to that state as possible.

She put her hand down on his. "I do get it," she said gently. "But you really hurt my feelings. Why would you strike out at me like that?"

"Exactly why you said." A muscle in his cheek flexed. "Because I'm an asshole when I'm cornered. If Chris had been here, he'd be sitting on me in the living room right now, turning my face into mashed potatoes and breaking my ribs like matchsticks."

She couldn't help a small smile at that. "I was just thinking I wish Chris were here. I wasn't wishing for him to do that. Though, now that you mention it, that would have been nice."

"Thanks." His look was wry, but after a moment's reflection, he removed the keys from his pocket and put them back in her hand. "It's your choice, but I'm asking you. Don't go on the date, Sam. I know what I said, and maybe it's true, you should give some other guy a chance, but I don't want you to do it. Since I've already been an asshole tonight, I might as well be a selfish bastard while I'm at it."

"You know what I was thinking when I was putting on my lipstick?"

"That you were going to torture my dick as much as possible before you left?"

She colored a little bit at the crude language. Geoff was regaining his composure. With it came that direct look that could swirl things in a lovely way down through her chest, to her lower abdomen and even farther. His gaze swept her. "Like this dress. You know it's the kind I particularly like to see you wear. Don't you?"

She nodded and his lips tightened. "What are you wearing under it? Tell me." His palm slid up a few more inches, his thumb on the seam between her thighs, and her legs loosened under that touch.

"Geoff . . . the neighbors—"

"Can't see anything. It's dark, we're in our driveway and I'm in front of you. I won't let anyone see you, Sam. I don't share, in case I wasn't clear on that topic."

"Not with anyone?" Her lips quivered in a near smile, a tight one because her pulse was speeding up. He'd dropped to one knee so he could lean farther into the doorway, his energy pressing in around her.

"You know the answer to that. Chris is different." His gaze softened. "I know where I want to take this tonight, Sam. As soon as you give me the answer to one question, I'm going to start down that road, and I'm not going to stop until we get where we both want to go."

Thank God. As she processed all the titillating possibilities, he touched her lips with his thumb, his other fingers caressing her jaw, her throat. "There are no wrong answers. No matter what you say, I'm still going down that road. You have a problem with that?"

She shook her head. "Is . . . is that the question?"

"No. This is." A smile touched his lips, though his gaze remained serious. "Am I forgiven? Don't lie to me." A quick flare of heat in his expression accompanied that admonition, twirling a feather of sensation in her chest. She would have put a white lie out there, just to make things go more smoothly, but he was right. Raw honesty was what made this moment all the more potent. And real.

"No, not yet," she said. "I . . . It hurt, and I'm still a little mad."

He nodded, simple acceptance. "I'm still sorry." His gaze passed over her again, taking even more time, lingering on her mouth, the quick rise and fall of her breasts. "How would you feel about Chris and me sharing you, Sam? Over and over, all night long, making you serve our needs?"

She'd tell him, as soon as her vocal cords unlocked. Fortunately, he wasn't done. "I'm sure he's had as many fantasies about you as I have."

"You don't talk about them . . . together?"

"No. Until now, until you set this in motion, I think we both figured it was better not to put it out there, in case one or the other of us had more exclusive designs on you. Which Chris still might."

"You don't believe that. You've both always been so worried that you'd be stepping on the other's toes, but I think you've always realized that wasn't how it needed to be. As long as I felt the same." She bit her lip. "I do."

"You still haven't told me what you're wearing under this dress. Don't make me ask you again. Be detailed. Tell me what Mark was going to get to see."

"He wasn't."

"No? But you wore it for someone. Someone who wasn't me."

He'd just acknowledged that she'd picked out an outfit to deliberately torment him, but the glint in his eye helped her figure out what he was doing. Tossing her hair back, she offered him an indifferent look, difficult as that was. "String bikini panties in lavender. Pretty see-through." She moistened her lips. "I shaved, so I'm all smooth and pink. The bra matches the panties. It's transparent at the top, almost to the nipples, then satin cups for the rest. It's the push-up kind so the neckline would show off some curves."

His fingers slid higher as she spoke, making her stammer. He leaned in the doorway, pressed his lips to her throat. As he moved to her sternum, his hair brushed her chin. She tilted her head back against the headrest. "Spread your legs, Samantha Beth."

She did, and then whimpered as he explored the silky, translucent panties, finding the small blotches of dampness he was inciting. She quivered as he passed a knuckle over her clit, traced her labia, then made that circuit again, a slow massage. Bracing his elbow against the seat at her shoulder, he let his hand drop down over her breasts, fingertips teasing those curves, playing in the valley of her cleavage.

"So you would have let Mark touch you like this?"

She shook her head.

"I expect to hear words come out of your mouth when I ask you a question." His tone was silk over a blade's edge, and she shivered as his hands continued to stroke, torment.

"No. No, I wouldn't have."

"Why not?" His eyes were close enough to lock her in place.

"Because." She inhaled him through all her senses. "I don't want him."

"Good, but not good enough. That's about you. Why wouldn't you let him touch you? Did I mention the selfish-bastard part?"

He found his way beneath the panties, and one finger slid inside her, then another. "Geoff . . ." she said with a touch of scattered desperation.

"Answer me."

"Because I'm . . . yours."

"That's correct, Samantha Beth. You're mine. Ours." A tight smile touched his lips. "You're right about us worrying we'd step on each other getting to you, but I realized tonight I've always thought of you as ours. Mine and Chris's, never just mine. But no one else's."

She shook her head in emphatic agreement as his fingers did a slow thrust and retreat. "Oh . . ."

His gaze stayed fastened on her face as she fought to breathe. "Do you forgive me, Sam?" he asked again.

With the arousal came a tangled knot of other emotions, ones that captured her throat and wouldn't let her utter anything less than the truth. "I'd forgive you anything. Which was why it hurt so much." She took a breath at his shuttered look, was afraid it meant he was withdrawing from her again, no matter what he'd said. "I think part of what a family is . . . what it should be, are people who can take risks with you and who will be here, no matter what. If not, we weren't ever really family. Staying away from the stuff we think will test that isn't a way to make it truth, right?"

His eyes darkened. He pressed his mouth to hers, and her lips trembled under his as he spoke. "If I could take the words back and never say them, I would. But I'll try to make it up to you by not being a coward from here forward. By not being afraid anymore to show you just how much I want you. Deal?"

As restitution went, she couldn't come up with anything better. He broke the kiss to nuzzle her nose, her cheek. When he slowly withdrew his fingers from inside her, he brought them to her mouth, painting her response over her lip gloss. "Who are you so wet for?"

"You," she whispered.

"Good." He rose to his feet and extended his hand. "Come back inside with me."

She put trembling fingers in his grasp, and he helped her out of the car. As he escorted her back inside, he had his hand on her lower back, curved over her hip. Once they stepped inside, he held her in place while he closed and locked the door. She could hear her heart beating. He'd turned off the TV so the house was still except for the hum of the refrigerator.

Gently turning her away from him, he unzipped the dress, guiding it over her head. She lifted her arms to help him remove it.

"Stay like that," he commanded, low, as he set the dress aside. He slid his hands down the length of her arms, palms molding under her armpits, the frame of her rib cage, down to her waist. Learning her body, possessing it, marking every inch with his touch. She shivered.

"All right, lower them now."

Taking her hand, he guided her to the center of the living room and adjusted her so she was facing the couch. "Stand there," he said. He took a seat, stretching his arm out along the back, hooking his ankle over a knee as if he were preparing to watch something on TV. Only he was watching her instead.

Straight men liked to look at women, quick glances that focused briefly on hip or breast, legs. This was the first time in her life she'd been looked at the way a man might look at a pinup, one he could hold in his hands and peruse as intently and as long as he wished. Geoff started at her feet, working his way up. It felt as intimate as if he were learning her with hands or mouth. It made her self-conscious, but he made a quelling noise when she twitched uncertainly.

"Your Master is looking at you, Samantha Beth. Your posture should show how proud you are of that, because he finds you perfect in every way. Your long, slim legs. Your pale, soft skin. Your gorgeous breasts, nipples already so tight your bra can't hide them. Your pussy is wet, your panties stained with that response. And then there's that gorgeous mouth." He gave her a lazy look. "Do you want to tell me what you were imagining when you put on your lip gloss?"

"You remembered."

"There's very little I forget, when it comes to you."

She blushed, and his lips curved, but there was no humor in the gesture. Only heat, and barely leashed demand. She could feel it waiting, and she wondered if he knew how it heightened the anticipation, to make her aware of it even as he held back until he was ready to release it. Whether by instinct or premeditation, it affected her, took away any of the conflict she'd had earlier.

"Yes, I'd like to tell you. May I?"

Those same instincts had her asking permission, and she earned a reward for it, his body noticeably tightening, increasing that sexual tension between them. He gave a short nod.

"Do you remember *The Matrix*, when Persephone told the Merovingian the lipstick she meant wasn't on his face? I noticed both you and Chris shifted during that scene. Like you were getting aroused, and didn't want me to see how the thought of that girl giving him oral sex made you both hard. I fantasize about you treating me like a submissive, Geoff. I have for so long . . ."

She took a deep breath, encouraged when he followed how the movement lifted her breasts. "So I would like to ask . . . what I hoped you'd command me to do the other night. I want to be on my knees to you. I want you to make me put my mouth on you. Please . . . sir."

Had he realized she'd wanted to say something far more dramatic than that? She'd wanted to call him Master, but just the thought of it and her face had colored, because it didn't feel entirely right, not when so many things were up in the air. But she couldn't resist the *sir*. She'd loved using it during her secretary role-playing with him.

As he continued to stare at her, she reached behind her, fingering the clasp of her bra. "Would you like me to take this off?"

"Yes. But leave the panties on."

She unhooked the bra, letting it slide down her arms. Dropping it to the side, she waited. Remembering what he'd said, she straightened, making her small breasts tilt proudly under his gaze.

"Run your fingers through your hair. Pile it up on your head with one hand, and slide your other hand into your panties. I want to see you play with yourself."

She complied. Molten heat coursed through every artery, down to pool between her legs. When she put her fingers there, his attention was on everything she was doing. How her arm was lifted to hold her hair in place, how her fingers moved beneath the fabric of the panties, how stiff her nipples were. She swayed at the sensation of being at the center of his attention. He was letting her pleasure herself for his pleasure, which just made her hotter. She bit her lip as a spasm from between her legs made her hips jerk, her shoulders twitch.

JOEY W. HILL

Geoff opened his jeans, reached in and gripped himself, starting to stroke. She made a tiny noise of protest, her gaze clinging to the movement of his hand beneath his shorts, which offered her a glimpse of the head of his cock as his hand slid upward, covered himself, then stroked down again. She licked her lips.

"Ask me again, Sam."

"Please . . . I want to suck you to climax."

"You want to act like my submissive, service my cock, be on your knees to me?"

"No." She shook her head. "I want to be your submissive, not *act* like it."

"Then get your pretty ass over here and prove it to me."

She hurried and didn't watch where she was going. She hooked her high heel on the coffee table. Quick as a flash, he was on his feet and caught her against him. The speed of his reflexes took her breath away. As did the press of his body. His jeans were still open, the zipper scratching against her abdomen. The head of his cock pressed against her navel, but despite those temptations, it was the strength of his hands holding her, how he tipped up her face, that made her knees tremble.

"Clumsy girl," he said gently. "That's why you have to have two of us. So there's always one around to catch you."

He and Chris teased her about her propensity for tripping over her own feet, saying she'd never really grown into her long, coltish legs, but they never meant it in a mean way. She smiled up at him. "I guess you'll just have to do double shifts on that until Chris comes back."

"I guess I will." He sank back down on the couch, holding her hand, and then he tugged. She went to her knees between his spread thighs, hands gripping his knees. Her gaze riveted on his thick, erect shaft, the cotton of his shorts barely containing it. But when she reached for him, he put his hands on her wrists and held her. "No," he said. "Not yet."

"But . . ."

"Hush." Rising, he tucked himself back in and stepped around her before scooping her off the carpet. As he moved toward the bedroom, he held her securely in his arms and she wrapped hers around him. Her hip pressed against his abdomen, feeling the shift of muscle groups there. Despite her height, there was no awkwardness in how

72

he carried her. She always thought of Chris as the brawn of the two, but Geoff and Chris were pretty evenly matched when they wrestled. Chris claimed Geoff was a dirty fighter and able to twist out of holds more easily, but no one could hold their own with Chris for more than a second unless they also had some real strength.

Geoff laid her down on his bed, switching on the bedside lamp. "We're doing this right," he said. "Before you do any of those other things, before we take this further, I want to be inside you. Chris will have his turn, but I'll be first." His eyes gleamed emerald and gold at her. "There's a pecking order to these things."

"And he's not around to argue."

"No, he's not. But I'll win this one either way." From the look in his eyes, she believed it. There was only one alpha dog in the house, though she thought if he ever ceded leadership to anyone, it would be to Chris. Imagining what might happen when and if he did made her shiver.

Taking off his shirt, Geoff bent to remove shoes and socks before skinning off his jeans. When he straightened and moved toward her again, only wearing his dark brief shorts, she made a noise, lifting her hand. He raised an eyebrow in question. Sam wet her lips and gave him a shy look. "Would you mind just standing there, as I did for you?"

"Exactly as you did for me?"

As a submissive, waiting on the Master to give the next direction. She colored at his expression. "No. Definitely no. I just . . . I've always wanted to look at you in your underwear. I saw you once, sort of. You had your door cracked and you were on the phone with someone while you were getting dressed for work. You'd stopped at the end of your bed and were telling that person what you needed for a meeting. You should have looked funny, sounding so authoritative while standing in nothing but your underwear, but . . . you didn't. Then you turned your head and I rabbited up the hall. I wasn't sure if you saw me . . ."

"I did." His eyes sparkled. "When I realized you'd been standing there deliberately looking at me, it gave me a lot of distracting thoughts that day. So . . ." He took a measured step back. "Look your fill."

It was probably a pretty unusual request for a sub to make of her

Master. One he might not normally indulge, because, as she'd discovered in the living room, it was a bit unsettling to simply stand still under someone's concentrated regard. But maybe it was different for a Dom. She didn't see any self-consciousness in Geoff's expression as she savored the moment with avid gratitude, poring over his shoulders, the expanse of his chest, the gleaming dark hairs that arrowed down his fit stomach to the waistband of the charcoal-gray shorts that stopped high on his corded thighs.

His arousal seemed to have gotten fuller, longer, and when she flicked a surprised glance at his face, he cocked his head. "Yeah, watching my sub stare at me with that hungry look makes me think of all the ways I'm going to please myself with her. Which gets me even harder. So keep looking, Sam. I'll tell you when you're done."

He kept making her heart trip. She noticed a damp spot on his shorts where the head would be, evidence of his desire that made things pull between her legs in restless response. He had elegant feet and long-fingered hands. Even his neck tempted touch. She wanted to feel the intricate layering of tendons, veins and arteries.

"You're beautiful," she said in a hushed voice. "I've always thought so."

He grimaced at that and she smiled. "In the most manly way," she added. "Like Chris Pine beautiful, as Captain Kirk."

"You didn't even get interested in *Star Trek* until he started playing that role."

She lifted a shoulder. "I'm sure that's just coincidence. I've been very busy for the past couple of decades."

"Mm-hmm." His eyes lit with amusement. God, she needed, wanted him. Some part of her couldn't believe this was finally happening. She didn't want to rush anything, yet another part of her was sure she was going to explode if he didn't get on with it right now. She let herself be held in stasis by that tangled morass of desire and his gaze.

"Sam, I want you to spread your legs. Bend your knees so your feet are flat on the bed. Stroke yourself again."

She did, her knees wide, and he shifted so he was framed between her bent knees, watching her. She drank in the sight of him as he removed the underwear. His arousal was so stiff, and the weight of his testicles was framed by his thighs. She wanted to run her hands down his chest, tangle in the hair there, feel him pressing her legs apart with the weight of his body. It had been so long since she'd had sex, but if it had been yesterday, it would be a distant shadow. The actual act with those past lovers wasn't as intense as her anticipation of it now, with him.

Geoff might be learning how he wanted to express himself as a Dom, but she had no doubt he was a skilled lover. She and Chris both knew he never had to be told anything more than once, and he strove for perfection in all that he did. Sometimes that could be a pain in the ass but, when it came to this, she had a feeling she was going to be thanking all the divine powers for that personality trait.

She rubbed herself over the panties, under the panties, her lips parting at the sensations through her core, along the insides of her thighs. Standing there, impressively virile, he crossed his arms over his chest, shifting his weight to one hip. Heavens above, she could come just from his regard alone as she pinched and fondled her clit, teased the wet crotch of the panties. Her other hand drifted to her breast, intending to caress the curve, but he made a negative noise.

"I didn't tell you that you could touch yourself there. Those pretty tits are mine. Just like that cunt you're stroking is mine. Right?"

She jerked her head in assent, too spun up to question or argue, to debate it in any way. Besides, it was true. He stayed motionless, though his eyes were as alive as a sunrise, changing color and heat second by second. When she was making little gasping pleas, her body lifting and falling under those tides of sensation, he finally spoke again.

"Stop. Put both hands up above your head and hold on to the pillow."

She obeyed, her glazed eyes on him as he took a condom from his nightstand, tore it open and rolled it on. Then he put a knee on the bed. Hooking his thumbs in the panties, he brought her knees together to slide the garment off her legs, then parted her thighs again. The pressure of his hands said he wanted her to keep her knees spread and bent, her feet flat on the bed as he'd ordered. He slid his hands under her ass, lifting her hips off the bed, holding her there, thumbs caressing her buttocks.

"I like it when you have that sexy, pleading look in your eye. It makes me want to do all sorts of things to you, Sam. Terrible, rough things that will have you screaming in ecstasy. Gentle, soft things that will make you beg. There's no end to the things I want, and it over-whelms me, how deep it runs." His gaze locked with hers again. "Don't let me hurt you."

"I don't mind if you hurt me," she whispered, the first thing that came to her mind. "Just promise me you won't turn back. That we'll see this all the way through, whatever happens."

He answered her with his body. Easing forward, he teased her with the head of his cock between her legs until she was gasping. Just when she was prepared to beg to be fucked, he backed off and stretched out between her legs. Pressing his abdomen against her core, he framed her breasts in his hands and gave them his undivided attention. His heated mouth covered one tip and began to suckle, swirling liquid warmth in her belly like vanilla-fragranced batter in a mixing bowl. She writhed in reaction, but he kept her pinned, licking and sucking on the nipple until it was hard and aching. He didn't ignore the area around it, kissing and tracing that with his tongue, squeezing her hard in his strong hands so a guttural sound came from her throat. She nearly came off the bed when he moved to the other nipple to give it the same treatment.

"Geoff . . . please. Oh God . . ." Her knees quivered, her thighs shaking from the bent-legged position he was making her maintain. He didn't need restraints like she'd seen on the websites. He'd told her to stay like this, and she had, only requiring his command to hold her in place, even though everything in her strained for more.

He lifted off her when she was nothing but electric impulses from head to toe that made her twitch and jerk. "Do you want me to fuck you, Samantha Beth?"

"Yes. Please. *Please.*"

He shifted back, sliding his hands underneath her hips again, tilting her up for his penetration. She shuddered from head to toe as he breached that gateway with the head of his cock. He paused, still cradling her ass to keep her at the right angle. "Say it again." His voice was strained, his eyes burning into hers.

"*Please.* Please fuck me."

He sank into her wetness in one sure thrust, taking himself to the hilt. His testicles pressed against her buttocks, the weight of his body holding her fast. The sensations were incredible, powerful. Little spasms shot through her. If he so much as moved, she thought she might start to have a hundred mini climaxes like starlight.

He withdrew slowly, letting her feel the friction of his corona at the mouth of her sex, then reversed and pressed back in, just as slow. She swallowed gulps of air with parted, wet lips. His gaze fixed on them as he did it again. And again. Her body was being swept with fire.

"Geoff."

"Keep your feet flat on the mattress." His pace picked up, the thrusts becoming deeper, more powerful. He made her keep her legs in the position he'd ordered, and the clutching sensations that gripped her clit, that rippled deep in her womb, told her she was right, that he knew exactly how to satisfy a woman sexually. Stretching the long length of his body over her, he adjusted so his upper chest and shoulders were in her field of vision and he could grasp the headboard with one hand. Gripping her buttock with the other, he braced a knee between her legs to drive into her more deeply, change the angle so a cry broke from her lips. It was as powerful a sensation as a climax, but still, astoundingly, not the actual thing.

Had she believed she'd had an orgasm before this? That was like comparing a bite of cheap novelty chocolate, the kind used to make holiday shapes like bats and witches or reindeer and snowflakes, to a chocolate whose only purpose was to be the best chocolate possible. This was Ghirardelli, Dove, Hershey's and Lindt all rolled into one sweet, thick waterfall.

He'd told her to keep her hands above her head, but she so desperately wanted to touch him, to wind her arms and legs around him. It might change the sensations, but this was about far more than just the physical. There was an emotional component she needed just as desperately. The orgasm was so close . . .

"Geoff," she gasped. "Please . . . I want to hold you. Please."

He met her gaze. There was something there, something more he wanted, but maybe he thought, like she had, that it was too soon. Yet in this moment, with everything else swirling around her, she knew it wasn't time that defined when something was right; it was the heart and soul.

"Please, Master. Please let me hold you."

It was worth everything to see the reaction on his face, as if by calling him that she'd just given him the answer to everything he was and wanted to be to her. No matter how many missteps they might have on the way, it didn't change what he was to her, or her to him.

He nodded. His expression was so concentrated, the muscles in his arms and chest so defined, she realized he was holding on to control by a thread. Wrapping her arms around his shoulders, she brought him down closer. The sensation of having him pressed against her aching breasts, feeling their hearts beat together, elicited a cry of delight from her. His arm changed position, banding around her waist, palm pressed to her hip. His breath against her ear, his chest pressed against her breasts, the friction of her nipples against his chest hair, was pure bliss. She rocked her hips up, took him even deeper, and another cry broke from her lips.

"God . . . sir . . . Master, I'm going to come. Please . . . let me . . . come."

He said nothing and kept thrusting into her, but his gaze was on her face, watching her frantic eyes, her mouth opening wider, taking in more air as she tried to hold on to control. "Please . . ." she wailed, the climax starting to take her.

"Now," he muttered, putting his cheek down against hers, the sandpaper rasp of his stubbled jaw abrading her tender flesh, another welcome sensation. His hand stayed on her knee, though, keeping her legs in place even when she so desperately wanted to wrap them around him too. Yet, as the climax rolled through her, it became clear why he had kept her in this position. It was a mind-boggling overload of sensation, more so than anything she'd ever experienced. She was straining up from the bed like she was possessed, raking his back with her nails. Maybe she *was* possessed, because she was in the grip of something that wouldn't let her go. That she didn't want to ever let her go.

He came at that pinnacle, adding to the unforgettable pleasure of it. She closed her eyes, holding on to him, riding that wave together, wishing he hadn't had to wear the condom so she could feel his seed jetting inside her, marking her. His strong arm held her, his hips still thrusting, taut buttocks flexing against the inside of her thighs.

"Oh . . . oh God." She was chanting it as he slowed, as they hummed to a stop like race cars passing the finish line, not really wanting to let go of the sense of exhilarating speed. Not wanting to let go, period. She pressed her mouth against his throat, his crashing pulse, and when he turned his face to hers, it was the most natural thing in the world to meet him mouth to mouth. He took a slow, penetrating kiss even deeper, framing her face with his hands as he controlled the pacing, dueling with her tongue, bringing wet heat against her lips.

He put pressure on her thigh, letting her know she could finally straighten her legs. Her feet slid over the backs of his knees, coming to rest on his calves as she cradled him between her thighs. The change of position sent another aftershock through her and she whimpered against his lips. He thrust a little deeper. When she was at last able to open her eyes, he was studying her face with a gaze alight with desire, making her think of what he'd said, that there was no end to the things he wanted to do to her. It was a scary, scary thought. But it was the good kind of fear.

"How did you learn to do that?" she said.

His look of male satisfaction amused her. "I read a lot of letters to *Penthouse*. They're far more educational than you'd expect. And *Men's Health* always has great sex tips."

She chuckled and closed her eyes, pressing her face to his. "Oh God. Geoff." She held him so tight, and received the same gift in return as he banded both arms around her, pressing a kiss to her throat, her shoulder. Threading her fingers through his dark blond hair, she caressed the nape of his neck, finding the strength to run her foot along the back of his thigh, cross her legs over his hips and squeeze them over his gorgeous naked ass.

"You didn't say it. Please promise me. Promise me you won't back away from this again. Please."

"I won't. I promise. Shh. It's all right. I'm here."

How did he know the glorious moment of delight was mixed with a weird kind of downward swoop, where she desperately needed his comfort and strength to be sure everything was okay? She'd worked toward this goal, and she'd definitely, finally, gotten them past the starting gate and on their way down the track. But that meant the race would now have a life of its own, beyond her control if a crash was imminent. Yet if Geoff told her it would be okay, that he and Chris would be right there with her, all the way, she'd know it was okay.

JOEY W. HILL

Opening her eyes, she realized her thought about shattering into starlight wasn't entirely random. Over his shoulders, she could see the glow-in-the-dark stars, constellations and planets she and Chris had stuck to Geoff's ceiling as a prank. He hadn't noticed them right away, since he often worked at the dining room table so late that, when he came to bed, he fell face forward into the pillows and was out like a light. A week later, when she'd been getting ready for work, she'd heard him snort with laughter. "All right," he'd called out. "Who put this shit on my ceiling? What's next, a *Star Trek* bed?"

But he hadn't removed them. She'd recently found some *Star Trek* sheets on sale and tucked them away, she and Chris conspiring to put them on Geoff's bed for his birthday. She'd also found a stencil of the various phrases the *Star Trek* captains used to order the ship in motion and intended to paint those on the wall while he was at work that day. She'd put them in a whimsical arc: *Make it so*, *Engage*, and Chris's favorite—given that it would be over Geoff's bed—*Punch it.*

"Once those are up, he sure as hell won't be bringing any girls back to our place," Chris had observed. "Not that he ever has."

It was a joke, but when she thought of it now, her fingertips slid over Geoff's shoulder, down to his biceps. "So . . . do you have to use the condom?"

Geoff lifted his head. As if suddenly realizing he was still fully on top of her and might be getting heavy, he shifted, pulling out with a regretful look she appreciated, given that her own body protested the loss of connection. Stripping off the condom, he dumped it in the trash can by the nightstand, then he turned on his side next to her and gathered her close. As she pillowed her head on his biceps, she wasn't sure if he'd answer or make her repeat herself, but he touched her face, running his fingertips along her cheek and jaw.

"You're the one who has to answer that," he said. "While Chris believes my insistence on keeping the kitchen so clean is evidence of an overabundance of estrogen, I'm fairly sure you're the only one in the house who can get pregnant."

She smiled. She was making little whorls in his chest hair with one tentative fingertip. When he didn't object to her touching him, she started threading through the light mat of gleaming strands. She pressed her palm over his pectoral, feeling the steady heartbeat beneath his firm flesh. "He had to revise that idea when he saw what a slob I was."

"You are not a slob. You're a clutter bug, as my mother used to say. You collect things and refuse to give them away. And you forget to pick up after yourself. The day I tripped over your heels in the living room was the first time I gave serious thought to spanking you."

He squeezed her buttock hard enough that she realized—with a tiny thrill—he intended it to be uncomfortable. She saw him watching her carefully to gauge her reaction to it. Wondering whether it was too much, just enough, or if she wanted more.

Just call her Oliver. *More, sir. Please, I want some more.*

"I take birth control," she said. While she was open about most things with them, she believed in certain courtesies. Like not leaving her feminine products or birth control compact out with her deodorant and toothbrush. Either in reaction or because they were naturally that way, Chris and Geoff were equally courteous about such things. She'd never seen a condom packet left on a dresser, or a pair of dirty underwear on the floor. "But there are other reasons . . . for protection."

"You're fishing," he said mildly.

She didn't deny it. She also kept her eyes on his chest, following her hand down as she traced his hair to where it narrowed into a tight arrow that cut between his abdominal muscles. His cock was at rest on his thigh, a very different animal from the turgid shaft that had her tissues still vibrating with gratifying soreness. But she had a feeling it could rouse to that thickness and length again in no time. She needed the answer to her question.

"I don't have to wear it," he said at last. "The last time I . . . Christ, it's bad when you can't remember the last time . . . ah. Okay. Yeah. Then."

"When?" she asked, with just enough demand to earn an amused glance.

"It was a weak moment with an attorney visiting from our New York office. She needed to let off some steam, and so did I. I don't do unprotected sex anyway, but that was also well before my last physical."

Tally Winters. She knew it had to be. She'd hoped Tally had been his last lover, and hearing it was reassured her, even if it still didn't feel great. She reminded herself it was months ago. To a twenty-something single male, that probably seemed a lifetime ago. Whereas she hadn't had sex with anyone since Anthony. And what about Chris? He'd dated a nurse a couple of times. How long ago had that been? About a year, she realized. But he might have had a hookup here or there that she didn't know about.

"Hey." Geoff tapped her forehead. "Come back out of there. You've got the frowny face happening."

"Do not." But her lips quivered as he deliberately traced their downward curve.

"How long have you thought of the three of us as together?" His shrewd eyes drew the answer from her silence. "Yeah. So it feels crappy to you, to think any one of us might have been doing something, or someone, since that time."

"Chris could be doing someone right now, down in the Gulf. Some FEMA worker or Red Cross nurse."

"No, he couldn't. Sam, whatever's gone on before, when you took us to Naughty Bits that day, you were sending us a pretty clear message. Neither one of us would act on anything outside of this relationship until we had time to address that, see if we wanted to take it deeper together." His gaze swept their two naked bodies. "I'm thinking you pretty much got a resounding *yes* out of me. I'm not seeing Chris giving you a different answer, though only Chris can answer for Chris."

All reminders that this was just the beginning, and sex could make things seem so easy. He pushed her hair away from her face. "Stop it," he said sternly. "Don't do that overthinking thing you do, or I swear to God, I will start all over again."

She grinned at that; she couldn't help it. "Promise? Like right now?"

"Like right after I have a nap," he grumbled, adjusting the blanket over her as she shivered. He rolled away from her, stretching in an intriguing way toward the floor and coming back with his underwear. At her disappointed look, he shook his head.

"If I go to sleep without putting on underwear, I might get attached to the sheets in an unpleasant way. Bodily fluids are Elmer's glue, not Post-it note adhesive."

He brought the covers over them as she giggled. When he drew her close once more, she twined her arms around him, resting her head on his bent arm. She was in Geoff's bed, being held by him, and he wanted her to stay and sleep with him.

Her mind was buzzing with a million possibilities and future plans, but inside his arms, as she curled her arm over his back, tucking her other one against herself, she let out a little sigh and with it some of that energy. Right now was a time to shut it all off and just enjoy the moment. Follow him into dreams.

His other hand slid down her waist to her hip, fingers stroking her flank in a casually intimate way. He moved his palm over both her buttocks to cup them, his middle finger pressing between the seam to rub against her rim, a peculiar and not unpleasant sensation that pushed sleep back again, especially when he spoke against her temple.

"I want to be here first, Sam. Has any other man done that?"

"No. I've been a pretty vanilla girl. I haven't really been with anyone who had an interest in that or, you know, who I trusted that way. I've played with toys some. It felt good when I did it."

"Hmm. A pretty vanilla girl with very unvanilla thoughts. You pushed me about as hard as any sub could without getting herself into the wrong kind of trouble with her Dom." His lips pulled into a smile against her.

"It was worth it," she whispered.

He grunted at that. A few moments later, his breath started to even out. Geoff never got as much sleep as he needed, so when it came to postcoital effect, he was obviously a goner. Letting her fingertips glide up and down his back, she nestled her face against his chest, gratified when his arms tightened around her even in sleep.

He was right. She couldn't hold the New York skank from months ago against him. But he was hers. She thought of him that way, him and Chris, but . . . oh God, she'd gone with the divide-and-conquer idea, but what if Chris wasn't on board? Was this a package deal for her, for all of them? Both of them or nothing?

No. Yes. She didn't know. It was clear both men were attracted to her, in a way that was strong yet not competitive, not in the usual way. In light of what had just happened between her and Geoff, she thought she had a better sense of what the nature of the competition was. It wasn't *She belongs to you or me* but *She belongs to us both, but I take the lead.* Which meant any tension had more to do with Geoff's Dom nature and Chris's undefined one. Up until now, whenever she'd felt any hint of the usual competitiveness between two men interested in the same woman, the two of them were quick to back off in deference to each other.

She'd been surprised by what Geoff had said about how he and Chris had interpreted the trip to Naughty Bits as a halt to any plans to date others until the issue was pursued. They'd been far more in tune with her feelings on all this than she'd given them credit for. Which meant she probably could and should have waited until Chris returned.

Christ, Sam, it's a little too late for second thoughts. Don't chicken out now. Let it happen, like Geoff said. Just see how it unfolds.

"If you don't stop thinking so loud, I'm going to gag your mind," Geoff muttered against her. "Go to sleep, Samantha Beth."

With a little quiver at the tone to his voice, even sleep slurred, she nestled deeper into him, held on and tried to obey, slowing the wheels of her mind so she could fall into slumber with him. She'd be waking up with his arms around her. One-half of her waking dream had been realized.

She'd be crazy to cut and run now, just for fear things wouldn't work out. Right?

When she woke, she was alone in the bed. It brought a groggy ripple of unease, then she realized she wasn't going to have to worry about a lover bailing on her. Not when he lived in the same house. Her sleepy smile disappeared as she realized there were other ways Geoff could bail. Maybe he'd woken up and decided this was a bad idea, and was even now concocting ways to put her at arms' length again. He'd promised he wouldn't, but that was last night, during the aftermath, when things had seemed far more dreamlike and possible.

How many times would she have to break through? The first two times had been hard enough. The results had been incredible, which should enhance her confidence and courage to coax him to that same edge, as often as it took. But the plain fact was she embraced a submissive orientation. She didn't really enjoy forcing a Dom's hand. Her Dom's hand. Sure, once things got rolling, he took the reins, but if she was always having to get him onto the horse, it would start to feel like she was pushing him into it. Not a great feeling.

Rolling out of bed, she shivered in the cool morning air. When she saw her robe lying at the end of the bed, it both helped and added to her worries. She'd slept naked in Geoff's arms, his warmth keeping her company throughout the night, but when he left, he'd left her another way to get warm. He and Chris always watched after her.

When she detected the pleasantly reassuring scent of coffee, she smiled. Geoff had a cup before he went for his morning run, and the time suggested he'd be well into his third of six daily miles by now. She'd get cleaned up while he did that, because anything was possible after a good hot shower.

Donning the robe, she made herself leave the sanctuary of his room and the cocoon of memories they'd created there. Once in the bathroom, she turned on the shower to get the water hot and put toothpaste on her toothbrush, taking it into the shower with her. The heated water cleared her mind and soothed sore muscles, though she kind of liked feeling that strain. Geoff was a powerful lover, demanding a lot from her physically, even if she'd thought at the time that all she was doing was just hanging on for the ride. She thought of him thrusting into her, the grip of his hands, that intent look in his gaze.

When they had sex, a lot of guys turned inward, their focus on getting off, even if they were still being reasonably generous and making sure she was headed the same way. Geoff's focus had never left her. It was as if controlling and directing her climax, her responses, was as much a component of his release as the proper friction on his cock. For a Dom like him, maybe it was.

She slicked the soap over her neck and shoulders, down over her breasts, imagining his hands there, sliding over her nipples. She moved from there to her sex, fingers gently rubbing the crevices. Her nostrils flared, taking in the musky postsex smell. She'd told him she was protected from pregnancy, and he'd said he didn't have to use a condom going forward. She thought of him taking her like he had last night, only his release would go into her, jetting deep inside her cunt, instead of being trapped by latex. She leaned against the wall of the shower, the water pattering around her fingers. She should take the shower head out of its bracket and let the pounding water pressure push her through a quick climax while she imagined being with Geoff again.

"What are you doing?"

She yelped, eyes springing open to see the object of her masturbation fantasy standing outside the shower. The water running down the shower door blurred his features like an Impressionist painting, but did nothing to dilute the impact of his tall, imposing figure. "Don't sneak up on a woman in a shower," she said emphatically. "Haven't you seen *Psycho*? Or any other horror movie, for that matter? The person opens their eyes and there's the axe murderer, just watching and ready to cut them up."

"Which never made much sense," the blurry image of her Dom replied. "Why would a killer wait until the person opened their eyes? Wouldn't it make far more sense to jump in there and kill them while you had the element of surprise?"

"If that was all the killer was after, sure, but they want to see the fear. It's not just about the kill." She rinsed the shampoo out of her hair. Even with the door closed between them, she could feel him watching her. Would he be looking at the arch of her body, the thrust of her breasts? Even if the profile wasn't all that clear, the hint of something could sometimes be even more titillating than the actual experience. Or a great appetizer, like looking at Geoff in jeans or Chris in his favored camo pants. Their nicely shaped asses shifting beneath the fabric, the snug hold in the groin area.

"Right." Geoff brought her out of her prurient musings with his dry tone. "I forgot I was talking to the *Criminal Minds* addict. Has the Behavioral Analysis Unit accepted your employment application yet?"

"They say I'm overqualified, since I've watched every prime-time criminal procedure show that's ever been written. And don't make a face—I can tell you just did. Remember, I was the one who told you about that episode that helped you with one of your cases."

"It was a total fluke," he said, taking another sip of coffee as he leaned against the tile wall. "I'm not going to be out-lawyered by Sam Waterston."

"But he has that sexy silver hair thing going on," she said, with a chuckle. "You have a few years before you get that advantage."

"Uh-huh."

Setting his coffee on the counter, he opened the shower door. As the steam billowed out around him, she saw his T-shirt was sweat-stained over his Nike running shorts. Geoff pushed himself hard when he ran. Too hard. Chris told him he was destroying his knees, but Sam knew it wouldn't change anything. Geoff didn't know how to do anything less than a hundred and fifty percent. Looking at the damp hair clinging to his nape, the light sheen of perspiration on his muscled arms, her routine concerns were nudged aside by vivid memories from last night. She wondered what he'd do if she leaned against the shower wall to start pleasuring herself again. Would his hand close over her wrist, twist it behind her back as he stepped into the shower and made it clear her pleasure was his to demand?

"Want me to show you why it works better for the killer the way I suggested?" he asked. "Close your eyes and tilt your head back under the spray like you just did. Stay that way so you can't hear or see anything."

Obediently, she did as he ordered. She anticipated his touch, her body tense and eager, but it didn't come. She couldn't hear anything with the drumming of the water around her, so she didn't know if he was still watching her or . . .

She gasped as he twisted her face-first against the shower wall, pinning his now fully naked body against hers. He had his hand on her wrist just like she'd imagined, bending her arm behind her back to hold her there as he dipped his head and pressed a kiss with the sharp cut of his teeth against her throat. His cock slid between her thighs as he bent his knees to insinuate it there, rub it against her pussy.

"I better not *ever* come back and catch you touching what's mine without permission," he growled against her throat. "Your climaxes belong to me, Samantha Beth. Every damn one of them."

Wow. No hesitation about pushing the Dom card this morning. A moment ago she couldn't have guessed how she'd react to Geoff telling her she couldn't masturbate unless he said so, but with that intimidating growl in her ear, she only had one response.

"Yes sir."

"Totally defenseless in this shower. At my mercy, aren't you?"

"Yes . . ." She swallowed a moan as he flipped her around and lifted her in one effortless motion. Once he parted her labia to get him past the non-lubricating effect of the shower water, he found what she already knew: that her cunt was slippery for him. He impaled her on his unsheathed cock in a slow slide down the wall, one arm cinched around her hips, the other cradling her head, fingers tangled tight in her hair. She contracted on him tightly. He hadn't let her wipe the water out of her eyes, so she had to keep them closed as if she were blindfolded.

"I was just thinking about you being inside me without a condom," she said hoarsely.

"All I did on my run was think about fucking you just that way. I thought about you, so sweet and soft in my bed. Thought about waking you with my mouth between your legs, getting you nice and slick for my cock. Thought about tying you down and fucking you a couple of different times before feeding you breakfast and starting all over again." He thrusted, punctuating the idea, and she gripped his shoulders.

"You'd be late for work."

"It'd be worth it. You left some scratches on me last night. I liked it, but I guess I'll have to punish you for that. Abusing your Master."

She almost smiled, but more urgent things were taking precedence. Immediate precedence. "Geoff . . ." It came out as a helpless gasp. She dropped her head back as the climax roared up on her. It was as if her dreams had built her back up to this point even before she woke, so the needs and feelings were just as strong as they had been last night.

"Yeah, I'm there, too. Come for me, Sam."

She went over clinging to his shoulders, her arms wrapped tight around them as he hammered her against the tile, all while keeping his arm at her waist and hand at her head to protect her from the hard wall behind her. It was a mix of physical demand and emotional care that undid her entirely, especially when he released inside her, bathing her channel with hot streams of semen. She moaned, pushed into additional aftershocks, and he uttered a reverent curse against her ear. Dipping his head, he set his teeth to the cord in her shoulder, clamping tightly on it as he finished, holding her fast. She'd never had a man do something like that, his claim upon her attention and flesh almost more fierce when he finished than when he'd started, as if the coupling only spurred his need to possess, to keep her so close that their hearts thudded together.

Eventually, he pulled out and let her slide back down to stand on her own feet, but he kept a steadying grip on her as he braced an arm against the shower wall. Wiping the water from her eyes, she looked up at him. His hair was wet and tousled around his face, droplets of water hitting his shoulders and bouncing, other rivulets streaming down his chest and arms. She traced his lips and jaw, and lifted on to her toes to ask for a kiss. Granting her wish, he pressed her back against the wall and captured her mouth in hungry response. Her hands slid down his back and came to rest on the rise of his buttocks, her fingers itching to knead and squeeze.

"May I . . . touch you?" With her fingers stroking where they were stroking, it was clear what she was asking. She'd never thought to ask a lover such a question, but what she needed from Geoff was different. She let intuition guide her.

He gazed down at her, looking bemused. When he nodded, she molded her hands over his backside, fingers following the seam, pressing into muscled flesh. "You have a gorgeous ass," she said, and earned a flash of those teeth.

"I like yours way better than mine."

She slid her hands back to his hips and curled her fingers there. "You looked pensive when I asked you if I could touch you. Have you ever had a lover who was like me? A submissive?"

She held her breath, releasing it when he shook his head. Seeing it, he touched her face in amused reproof.

"Fishing again, and possessive." He ducked his head under the water to slick his hair down fully, and she let her hands roam over his chest, his sides, up over his armpits to his biceps and back down again. When he opened his eyes again, he settled his arms around her and pressed her against the corner, brushing his lips against her cheekbone, nudging her chin to the left so he could kiss her neck, give her a quick nip before he raised his head, studying her with the water drumming against his back, the steam and heat of his body keeping her warm.

"I've had Dom cravings most my life. Took me a while to figure out what they were, learn how to speak and act on them in the right way. I've gone to a few parties, visited a couple of clubs and done a session or two, but the spontaneity of the occasional hookup isn't really set up for deeper stuff. You can do a little spanking or tie someone up, but what you just did, Sam . . ."

The look in his eyes sharpened, making her breath catch as his lips firmed, pressing drops of water between them. He bent his head to apply that moisture to her throat, the rush of the water forming an even more private bubble around them. "The way you hold so still when I do that, pressing your cheek to the tile, exposing your throat, the way you tremble in my arms . . . Fuck, I have no idea how I managed to wait this long to do this. Maybe because I didn't let myself imagine it would work this way between us so easily. If I had, this might have happened way too soon."

In her current position, she thought the second they'd met wouldn't have been soon enough. Just toss Anthony out of her building and get right to it.

"So . . . you didn't do this kind of thing on those occasional hookups?"

He lifted his head to pin her with his gaze. Yes, she was unabashedly fishing, but he was obviously in a mood to indulge her. "There are some things that come without any instruction when it's natural to you. Like asking your Master for permission to touch him the way you just did. Right?"

She nodded.

"Trying to teach a partner that kind of intuitive thing, versus her doing it because it's in her as well? There's no comparison." His voice echoed off the tile, tingling along her flesh like his hands upon her. "You reach for those things without thought, Sam, and maybe I always knew you would, which made you an even stronger temptation."

"I'm glad you said that," she admitted. "I think part of it is me anticipating what you want, but another part of me voicing it is . . . telling you how I'd like it to be with you." She lifted her gaze to his attentive face, but for the next part, she focused on his throat and shoulder, her fingers sliding along that slick terrain. "I know I've been pushy these past few days, but that didn't feel right for me. The things I want and need, that I say now . . . I'm hoping like hell I won't embarrass myself, going too far or doing something that doesn't work for you."

"You haven't yet." Touching her cheek, he made her look up at him. "But if you do, and I say so, I don't want you to be embarrassed. I may ask for more than works for you. If that happens, we talk about it and figure out a compromise. Your feelings are more important to me than anything I want to do to you, Sam."

His fingers closed on her chin, holding her in place. "I'm not throwing out some feel-good bullshit. I mean it. You do something that makes you afraid or uncomfortable just to please me, that doesn't work. Got it?"

"Yes."

His jaw tightened. "Yes, what?"

She pressed her lips together, wondering if she'd always feel that little adrenaline spike when he used that tone with her. She sure hoped so. "Yes sir."

"Good."

His countenance eased. "So, do you still need to wash stuff or are you done?"

She still had things to wash, and he needed a shower after his run. For the next few moments, things were more playful as they worked around each other, helping and hindering in ways that had Geoff chuckling and Sam smiling. She started teasing him, rubbing her soap-slick body against places he'd already rinsed. Taking down the shower-head, he sprayed it in her face until she called out for mercy, flailing at him. He angled the spray lower, backing her into the corner, and then abruptly the playful tone disappeared. Closing a hand over her throat, he held her in place, a gesture that stilled things inside her. His hazel eyes glittered, mouth firm with carnal purpose once more.

"Palms on the tile on either side of you," he ordered. "Spread your legs and keep your ass against the wall."

They might not ever get out of this shower. Since she didn't mind risking a lifetime of pruny toes and fingers for this, she complied, swallowing under his grip as he ran the sprayer over her breasts. He aimed the force of the water on her nipples as they contoured into aroused points. Then he lowered the shower head and changed the adjustment from the needle spray to the massage setting.

As the first triple shot of that concentrated setting hit between her legs, she jumped. Mindful of his order, though, she did her best to keep her backside against the wall, her legs spread. His hand constricted on her throat as he moved the shower head spray over her pussy in short passes, random, up and down, back and across, then centered it on her clit, an overwhelming sensation after such a recent climax. She gasped, twitched until he moved it away. At which point her sex throbbed, begging for it to come back.

He obliged after spending a little time on her breasts again, getting her moaning in a constant hum from that stimulation before he took the spray between her legs again. His thumb idly rubbed against her collarbone as he held her in place, working her up until she was crying out, near climax once more. She blinked, disoriented as he took the spray away, putting it back in its mount.

"Last night you said you wanted to serve your Master on your knees," he said. "Do it now, do it well, and I'll finish what I just started."

She went down on her knees, and not just because of the promise of a climax. As the shower spray slid down her back, keeping her warm, she braced herself against his thighs and got up close and personal with the shaft jutting out over his thighs. His erection had returned in full force with their shower play.

Pressing her open mouth against the side of his cock, she played her lips over it, nuzzling and teasing him with the tip of her tongue as she curled her fingers around the base, the side of her hand pressing into his testicles. Opening her mouth, she took him in, slid down and down, far as she could go without gagging herself. She wanted to take all of him so badly, but he was too much. So instead she reached around him to pull some soap from the shower caddy. She made her hands nice and slippery and gripped him at the base with one and cupped his balls with the other, sliding the soap over them and around his shaft, rubbing her thumb over that pulsing vein. She could still recall the demanding grip of his hand on her throat, and the bliss of total obeisance took her over, all of her centered on this. Giving him pleasure at his command.

His hand fell on her head, the clutch of his fingers in her hair showing her he enjoyed her ingenuity, but he apparently had a different demand in mind. He slid her back off him to rinse his cock and then directed her mouth back onto it. Pushing her down on him in ruthless demand, he challenged her gag reflex, helping her learn how to relax it and take more of him. Was he testing her, seeing what worked or didn't for her? Or showing her what kind of Dom he was, determining how demanding she wanted him to be? So far he was doing great.

Her teasing of his cock with mouth and soapy fingers had made him stiffer, thicker, but now he wanted her to get down to business and suck him off. Since her pussy was still throbbing, aching for that climax he'd held out of reach, she was more than eager to prove how dedicated she could be.

She clung to his thighs, nails digging in as she sucked, licked, rose and fell on her knees, gripped him, stroked, squeezed and worked his balls in her eager fingers. A glance up through her lashes showed her he had his head tipped back against the shower wall, his hips jacking up into her mouth so she could hardly keep up. She worked her ass off for it, even as her jaw tired. He'd come only a little while ago, so it would take extra time, and she was determined to prove her stamina.

He made her stop, his cock still deep in her mouth. "Stay just like that," he said, his voice reverberating with fierce command in the small space. Pulling the showerhead from its mount, he dropped it down to dangle against her leg. "Put the head against your pussy. Hold it there so the water is hammering your clit, and then get back to sucking me off."

His hand tangled in her hair again as she complied, jerking at the stimulation. "Your sweet ass better not come before I do," he warned. "Or you'll be in big trouble."

The idea of that trouble was almost as stimulating as the spray itself. She went back to work. He'd cracked the shower door to be sure she had oxygen in her kneeling position, and that trickle of cool air along her spine was just one more sensation among many. The shower-head trapped between her thighs adjusted with her movements as she rose and fell, such that the spray slid over her labia, her clit, her thighs. Sometimes a straight, random powerful shot hit right under her clit hood, making her jerk and moan against his shaft. But she struggled to keep her focus on bringing him to climax, even as the water pressure made her crazy, until everything was pure physical response. Throbbing cunt, aching jaw, the taste of him, stretching and filling her mouth, his hand in her hair, her fingers digging into his thigh.

God . . . oh God, she was going to come. Blissfully, though, he thrust harder into her mouth then, hand spasming on the back of her neck as the first shot of his seed hit her throat and bathed her tongue.

Thick fluid filled her mouth. She couldn't contain all of it, but she swallowed as much as she could.

He'd fucked her cunt, her mouth . . . Though she knew she was having crazy, sentimental, sex-driven thoughts, she wanted him to do it to her ass, too. Leave no area unclaimed.

She totally belonged to him.

~

As the pummeling water pushed Sam into climax, her cry of release became a scream that sent a hard shove of pleasure up the base of Geoff's spine, through his chest and definitely through his cock, flooding his own response into her vibrating throat.

He gripped her shoulders, holding her in place so she couldn't get away from what crashed over her, through her. He wanted her to fly like she'd never flown before, so when she fell to earth he could catch her.

"Oh fuck . . ." He choked out the words, more fervent than a curse. What he'd told her was so incredibly true. He'd imagined such an intuitive interaction with a submissive, but he'd always been too practical to believe it could happen like this. But the freaking remarkable thing was this was just the beginning, the tip of all the things he wanted to do for her, with her, to her.

She was thorough, of course. He had to stifle a half-pained chuckle as she kept working him in her mouth, not willing to ease up until he stopped her, drew her back. She was so eager to please and, though he was the Dom, he was amazed at how much her generosity spurred his own to the point he knew he'd do anything for her.

Even now, she kept her head pressed to his leg, her arms wound around him as he reeled the showerhead back up and returned it to the mount. Lifting her to her feet, he settled her in his arms, holding her against his chest and letting them both lean against the wall.

"I'm done," she mumbled. "I'm going back to bed for the rest of the day."

Geoff couldn't think of anything he'd enjoy more than spending the rest of the day in bed with her. But the only reason he could indulge their shower play was because he had an off-site meeting this morning that wasn't until nine o'clock, which had given him an advantageous extra hour at home. He was glad to be able to give her that much more time, to reinforce what had started the night before. He was sure she'd woken up worried he might renege on his promise. He wouldn't. If he backed away, leaving her alone with these feelings like she'd done something wrong, he was not only an idiot, he'd deserve every bit of the thrashing Chris could and would dish out.

He kissed her brow tenderly. "Sure, you say you're exhausted. Now. But if you're like most women, your batteries will recharge in the next hour. I'm the one who will nod off in the middle of the client meeting. Which, by the way—and I say this with total regret—I better get my ass in gear so I can be on time for it."

"Boo," she complained, but she smiled up at him. Shutting off the shower water, he shifted her in his arms and pushed the door open. She stepped out, his hand on her elbow steadying her.

Which meant he felt her freeze, as abruptly as if she'd been shot through with ice.

Chris was standing in the doorway of the bathroom, watching them. Because of the damn steam and water on the wavy glass of the shower door, Geoff had no idea how long he'd been there. His face was unreadable, but the second Geoff's gaze met those cold brown eyes, Chris was gone, pivoting on his heel.

"Chris," Sam said urgently, but Geoff knew he wouldn't respond. *Damn it.* He grabbed a towel and handed one to Sam, giving her a hard second look to make sure she was steady on her feet. "I'm fine," she said, understanding. "Go after him."

He strode out of the bathroom, the towel held around his hips, water beading off him and leaving a trail on the carpet. "Chris," he said sharply. "Damn it, don't you fucking leave."

He heard the heavy tread of Chris's work shoes hit the kitchen before Geoff even reached the living room. When he came into the kitchen, he didn't see him, but he didn't have to wonder if Chris had beat him out the door. He walked right into his fist.

The son of a bitch cold-cocked him at the kitchen threshold, the power of the punch knocking Geoff back against the frame. When someone hit him, Geoff's first response was normally retaliation. Over the years, he and Chris had had enough fights they practically had a scripted choreography. One hit first, the other hit back, and there was usually an exchange of three punches before they hit the ground and turned it into a down-and-dirty wrestling match that sometimes went Geoff's way, sometimes Chris's. In the end, it always ended up with them sitting together, bloody and bruised, sharing a beer.

Somehow he had a feeling this wasn't going to end as amicably, especially since Chris didn't seem interested in further physical contact. Of any kind. He'd stepped back and was dominating their modest-sized kitchen. They were of like height, though Chris had a more muscular bulk, and his skin was bronzed by outdoor work, blending the scattering of freckles he'd had across his nose and cheeks since he was a kid. His dark hair was tousled over the frosty brown eyes.

"Chris, it's not like that, man."

"Sure it is," the other man said, lip curling in a sneer. He wore camo pants and a T-shirt. When he came straight from work, he was usually in one of the dark blue Cortez Landscaping shirts Esteban had his employees wear. Since Chris was wearing one of his eclectic, off-the-wall T-shirts instead, it told Geoff they'd probably driven through the night, stopping at a truck stop for a quick cleanup. This T-shirt had a drawing of a brontosaurus wearing sunshades, with "Dinosaurs are Cool" printed around the long body. It had been a gift from Sam.

Sam slipped past Geoff's elbow. Without thought, Geoff reached out and caught her arm so she wasn't in between them. Right on the heels of her startled glance was Chris's incredulous expression, making Geoff wish he could recall the gesture.

"Really?" his friend said, his voice tight. "You really think I'd ever raise a hand against her?"

No. He wouldn't. Maybe it was the power of the things rolling off Chris that had made Geoff grab her, as if he knew other ways Chris could hurt her right now. This was his fault. He should have waited, no matter what Sam had thought. No matter that he'd found her eagerness to embrace her submissive side too irresistible. He'd been weak.

Sam was wearing the robe he'd left on the end of her bed, a silky thing that clung to her in patches because she'd dried off hastily. It was barely tied, so the neckline was revealing the curves of her breasts. She looked irresistible still, especially if he thought of where she'd been moments ago, how he'd taken her in the shower and then on her knees.

But she wasn't aware of her appeal. When either of them told her she was beautiful or hot, it flustered and pleased her in a surprised way that wasn't artifice. So it wasn't vanity that made her do what she did next. Far from it. Maybe it was all those feelings that had been bouncing between them too long, the braveness of her submissive nature, or her womanly intuition, but whatever combination it was made her risk herself now, in a way he didn't anticipate until the move was made.

Chris was still staring daggers at Geoff, so when Sam moved her hand to the tie of her robe, neither of them was overtly focused on what she was doing. She loosened the tie and opened the garment, sliding it off her shoulders so it whispered to the floor in a pool of thin fabric.

Chris's gaze snapped to her. With her back to him, Geoff saw the quick rise and fall of Sam's shoulders, her slim fingers curling next to her thighs, all signs of nerves as she stood before their roommate, letting him have a good, long look.

Geoff had meant what he'd said last night, about how he thought of her as theirs, not just his. However, if he'd ever needed direct proof of it, he had it now. As she stood naked between them, he wasn't jealous. Instead, he wanted Chris to feel everything he'd felt last night, an experience he wanted to share with Chris as much as Sam did.

She said nothing at first, and he wondered if she was building on what they'd done last night, giving Chris a chance to look his fill without interruption. For Geoff's part, he couldn't take his eyes off the lingering impression of his teeth on her shoulder, evidence of how he'd claimed her last night. It was probably good her hair was spilling forward over that side, because seeing that might be a little over-the-top for all the emotions Chris was handling right now.

Though it was difficult not to interfere, Geoff stayed motionless, watching the two people he cared about most in the world face each other.

"This is yours," Sam said to Chris. "I belong to both of you. You understand that. You know it." Her voice broke, a little tremor, and she moved a step forward. Then another.

He and Chris were both taller than Sam, though Chris's burlier build dwarfed her. When she reached him, she hesitated before she put her hands on his chest. Once the contact was made, she slid her arms around his neck, fingers briefly outlining his shoulders before she stretched up even higher, pressing herself full against him. Geoff well knew the bliss of that. His cock twitched, recalling how her small breasts and slim thighs felt against him, her sex rubbing against his length.

Chris's arms moved, stiff, undecided, a reflection of the conflict on his rugged face. When he put his hands on her hips, fingers closing over pale skin, she lifted higher on her toes, tugging on his hair to bring his head down to her, to her mouth.

They almost made it. But a breath before the distance would have closed into a kiss, Chris drew back. He stared down at her, then he gently clasped her wrists and slid them off his neck, pushing her back a step. From the flicker in his eyes, the tensing of her shoulders, Geoff could only imagine the hurt in her face. He wanted to move forward, to intervene, but something held him where he was.

Clearing his throat, Chris stepped around her and picked up her robe. He returned to face her as he threaded her hands through it and belted it securely. He wouldn't leave her standing there naked, vulnerable. A hard knife of guilt twisted through Geoff's chest. If he'd been in Chris's shoes, he wasn't sure he would have thought past his feelings on the matter to hers. But in the same breath he realized this wasn't about Sam. Not to Chris. This was about him and Geoff.

He'd wanted Chris to feel everything he'd felt with Sam last night. Which he could have, if he'd been there. Yet Geoff had acted on his feelings. He hadn't waited. How would he have felt if Chris had been the one here instead of himself? He might have not only punched him in the face, but gotten in a few kicks while he was on the ground.

"No," Chris told her, not unkindly. Geoff knew the pain in his friend's face would still tear her heart to shreds. Chris lifted his gaze to Geoff, and his expression became far cooler. "Not like this."

Turning away, he opened the kitchen door and left the house.

HEART

Part II

*G*eoff knew he couldn't miss his client meeting. Yet if he thought it would help Chris's state of mind, he'd say to hell with it and stay. The problem was, he knew it wouldn't.

Geoff latched on to Sam's arm, keeping her from following Chris when he stormed out of the kitchen and went into the backyard. Her body was vibrating with tension, the need to soothe, to fix. She was good at those things, but Geoff knew Chris in this mood better than she did. It didn't tear his heart out of his chest any less than it did hers, but Chris had to have his space when he was dealing with a surfeit of emotional shit. Finding the two of them naked and in the shower together qualified as a dump truck load.

"He needs some time to settle, Sam," Geoff told her. He put both hands on her shoulders so she had to face him square and pay attention to what he was saying. "Give him some breathing room, then we can talk it out."

She wasn't going to do that. Her gray eyes were filled with pain, her mouth taut with worry. He bit back a sigh. "You're not scheduled to work today. Why don't you come with me? The client meet is at a restaurant near Southpark Mall. You can go wander around there, and come back to my office after. Read a book on my couch, whatever. If it gets late, you can take my car home and I'll catch the bus."

She shook her head. "I won't leave him alone, even if he doesn't want to talk. One of us needs to be here."

Geoff's fingers tightened on her. "Don't push him, Sam."

"I'll just follow my intuition," she said. "Like I did with you."

"And that worked out so well, didn't it?"

Shit, had he really just said that? He grabbed her hand when she recoiled, and gathered her to him as she started to struggle. "Stop. Ow." She slapped at him and hit his jaw, which was still sore thanks to Chris's much larger fist. He caught her wrist and gave her a little shake.

"That's not what I meant, and you know it. What happened between you and me wasn't wrong. It was everything I imagined, Sam. And a whole lot more than that."

She stopped struggling but glared at him out of steely gray eyes. "Why do you have to be so mean sometimes?"

"Because I open my damn mouth before I think about what's coming out of it," he said wearily.

At home, not at work. At work, doing the right thing at the right moment was second nature to him, but with her and Chris, he wasn't always as sure of his way. He could become the best orator in the history of the legal profession, and he still wouldn't know how to put together the right words to tell them exactly how much they meant to him. Case in point: he was pretty sure Chris had an altogether different impression of how much Geoff valued their friendship at the moment.

She was watching his face and seeing too much. "You meant we should have waited," she said brokenly. "*I* should have waited."

"No." He cupped her jaw. "Sam, this is on me. Yeah, maybe we should have, but you weren't wrong. We've been dragging our feet for months, even knowing we all felt something, and you were the one who realized something had to give."

"But you told me from the beginning, just wait until he gets back . . ."

"Yes, I did. But I didn't, either, did I?" The consequences of that speared him through the chest as much as he was sure they did her, but hell if he was going to let her shoulder them. From that parting cold look Chris had given him, his friend wasn't putting it on her, either. On that, at least, they were in agreement.

Despite the ache in his chest, he pulled his shit together. "Sam, I told you, this is new for me," he said steadily. "Not the wanting-to-be-a-Dom part, but doing that, and this, all of it, with someone as close to me as you are? You're my first."

Truth, he felt like she was the only one he wanted that way, now or forever, but he wasn't sure if this was the best time to tell her that. Some great and powerful Dom he was. He felt like a complete idiot. He needed to go to work, where he felt on far more solid ground, but that wasn't the answer, either. Fuck it. If he was late, he was late. Mike was going to be at the meeting, and Geoff could text and tell him to get it started.

Sam was still staring a hole in his chest, her body stiff. Geoff ran his hands over her thin, silky robe, feeling the slim bones of her shoulders. He moved down to her elbows and back again. "I know it hurt like hell, him pulling away. But trust me, he just has to think it through. He wouldn't have reacted that way if he weren't so crazy about you he can't walk a straight line. He walks in on that, he's not sure where he fits. And then you put your arms around him, offer yourself to him. *Oh well, look, Chris is here, let's just throw him into the mix.*"

She parted her lips on a protest, but he shook his head. "I know it's not that way. We both do. The timing just went screwy on us. If he'd gotten home later today, we could have sat down and talked about it, fully clothed. It would have gone better." He hoped.

His fucking phone buzzed on the kitchen table—probably fucking Mike trying to see if he was on his fucking way.

"You have to go," Sam said.

"I know. I don't want to. Not unless you come with me so I know I'm not leaving you in the middle of this."

"No, I really feel I need to stay. Don't worry, we'll figure it out." She put on a far-too-bright smile. "It's going to be okay. Go to work. I'm going to get dressed."

"Sam, this isn't on you to fix. You get that, right?"

Of course she didn't. She was a Type A personality and a submissive, and thought every damn thing in the world that went wrong was either her fault, or her responsibility to fix. She was a smart woman, but she was also a creature of the heart. Between heart and mind, her heart usually won. Maybe that was how he needed to approach it.

Taking her hand, he drew her over to the kitchen table and took a seat in one of the chairs, pulling her to stand between his knees. Her brow furrowed. "You need to go—"

"I'll go when I'm done here." He slipped the tie of her robe, letting it fall open so her lovely torso was visible to him, the pink-tipped breasts, the pale skin, the shaved mound and slim thighs. As he returned his attention to her face, he shifted both hands to her waist inside the robe, and gripped her firmly. He liked the way his hands looked pressed against her skin and, from the little tremor of reaction, he knew she liked how they felt.

"You can't imagine what it does to a man, to see you open yourself to him like this. He may be out in the yard fuming, but I guarantee what's branded in his brain is you standing before him naked, your mouth soft and your eyes asking for everything from him. I can't stop you from trying to talk with him while I'm gone, but I am going to tell you this: Put aside any strategies to solve this and go with your heart. Only your heart. There's nothing you need to fix. Nothing. Say it."

He pinned her with a hard look, and tried not to let the light tinge that came to her cheeks, the shift of her gaze and nervous moistening of her lips, all classic signs of submission, distract him from his purpose.

"I don't know . . ."

"You say it and mean it, or you go to work with me. I'll throw you over my shoulder to do it if I have to. I won't let you stay here and punish yourself for something that's not your fault, or set yourself up that way in front of Chris. He's not at the point he'd know how to deal with that the right way."

"And how is that?" At her mutinous look, he almost smiled, because it was the reaction he wanted.

"Cut a switch and beat your ass with it until you were saying you were sorry for the right things."

"He'd have to catch me first," she said decisively, but he was watching her pulse rate increase in her lovely throat. Pain for pleasure didn't turn her off, and Christ, that was way too much of a turn-on for him.

He drew her closer and kissed a nipple, giving it the edge of his teeth and a swirl of tongue that had her shivering again. "I could catch you," he promised. "You'd like that, wouldn't you? Chris punishing you while I watched."

"Stop it," she said, trying halfheartedly to pull away. "I don't want to get all . . . you know . . . while he's upset."

"I know." He softened his tone. "I have no problem with you reassuring him on how you feel about him, Sam." Geoff met her gaze, making sure she was listening closely to what he was saying. How he was saying it. "But you won't accept any blame. That's going to be between him and me."

"But I . . ."

"Do you trust me?"

She fidgeted. "On most things."

He suppressed the desire to shake her. "If you want me to be your Master, you have to figure out which areas are yours and which are mine to handle."

"And how will I know that?"

"Because I'll tell you." Dropping his hand to her ass, he squeezed it hard enough to make her jump. "Anything related to vacuuming or washing dishes is totally your area. My area is to stand around, issue orders and look commanding."

He saw her move from worry to exasperation and amusement. Though it looked like an uphill battle, he thought he'd made her feel a little better. She spread her hands out in a helpless gesture. "Geoff, the last thing I wanted to do was hurt him. It's killing me that he's out there, mad and unhappy, and somehow thinking he's outside of this."

"I know. We'll figure it out." He pursed his lips. "Hand me a Sharpie."

They kept assorted notepads, pens and markers in a big fruit bowl on the table. She reached over to it to get a marker, the robe sliding away from her naked body in a way that had him stifling a groan. Without her saying it, he knew she hadn't made any move to cover herself because he was the one who'd opened the robe, and it was up to him to decide when he wanted her covered.

Forcing himself to focus, he turned her around. "Drop the robe off your shoulders. Don't take it all the way off."

She complied. It was unspeakably provocative, the baring of her shoulders at his command, him standing behind her, his breath stirring her hair. He slid the straight brown strands over her shoulder so they tumbled over her right breast. She stood, a bemused look to her profile as he began to write between her shoulder blades. He blew on the print, making sure it was dry before he pulled the robe back up on her shoulders. Turning her around, he overlapped the panels of her robe and tied it, wrapping the ends around his hands to hold her to him.

"You're not allowed to see what I wrote until after he sees it. If he pulls a single tear out of you, you show it to him. You hear me?"

"Chris won't make me cry."

He gave her a patient look. "Not on purpose, but if he does, promise me."

"I promise."

He touched her nose. "You were brave enough to kick me in the ass to get this moving. Now I need you to throttle back. Focus on what you do best for us."

"What's that? And if you say ironing your shirts or cleaning toilets, I will kick you in the balls."

He chuckled at that, at the flash in her gray eyes, and folded her against him. She let out a frustrated little sigh, but looped her arms around his waist and back and pressed her cheek to his chest. He leaned down and spoke in her ear, giving her the truth in two words.

"Loving us."

Sam tried to give Chris breathing space, but by early afternoon, she was the one who couldn't breathe. Chris hadn't come back into the house, but he hadn't left. He'd been working out of the garden shed and in the yard. One of the projects had involved digging a sizeable hole, and she wondered if he intended to put Geoff into it after he brained him with the shovel. However, after watching him out the window through the morning, she surmised he was working on the man-made pond he'd been talking about creating for some time. Which was fine, except he was doing that after having driven through the night to get home to them.

He hadn't come in for food or water, despite his shirt getting soaked with enough sweat he'd eventually stripped it off. She'd had enough.

She marched out into the backyard armed with Gatorade. The

waistband of the camo pants he wore was also damp, his upper body gleaming with sweat. After he'd finished with the hole for the pond, he'd moved to edging out a border for another natural area near the aviary. She remembered him mentioning a desire to arrange bird feeders and other landscape features there when he had time. Or when he needed to work off a mad, apparently.

"I brought you something to drink."

"Thanks. Just set it over there." Chris kept grinding the edger into the red clay of the yard. Setting her jaw, Sam stepped in his path so he had to check his movement. He missed the tips of her sneakers with the edger by an inch. "Damn it, Sam."

"Can you just take a break? Stop and take a moment."

"I will in a while. I need to work right now."

When she put out a hand, he stepped back from her. She masked the hurt as best she could. "Chris. Please."

"It's okay, Sam. Just . . . leave it alone. Leave me alone." He sidled around her with a painfully stiff courtesy, but when he put his head down to focus on what he was doing, she pivoted to watch his back, the ripple of muscles along his shoulders, the tension he was carrying there.

"It doesn't feel okay."

"Well, I'm sorry it doesn't feel okay to you." He snapped it out, but then straightened, rubbing a hand over his face. "See what I'm trying to tell you? What I'm feeling now, I don't want it to spill out on you, okay? It doesn't matter if you can handle it or not; if that happens, I'm just going to feel worse. I assume you don't want me to feel worse."

He said that last part caustically enough that she flinched, but when his expression darkened, she knew he'd just made his point. His brown eyes could be as sweet and placid as a bull at rest in his pasture, but they could also hold fire, like now. Making a monumental effort to try and respect his desires, she reined back a dozen responses and went with the one that seemed most likely to let her remain.

"Okay. But drink something for me. You've been out here a long time and I'm worried." She stepped closer. Holding up the Gatorade, she gave him an expectant look.

He eyed her and sighed. Leaning on the yard tool, he took the bottle from her hands. There was dirt creased between the folds of his knuckles. He always smelled like the earth, even after he washed at the end of a workday. He liked feeling whatever he was touching, so he rarely used work gloves. Every night, when relaxing in front of the TV, he cleaned his nails and trimmed the cuticles. Even so, he had the hands of a man who embraced manual labor. Big and callused, and always warm.

Tipping his head back, he emptied the container, telling her she'd been right to bring some out to him. She wanted to reach up and let her fingers trail over the movement of his throat. She wanted to press against his body and caress the damp hair at his nape, inhale the combination of earth and male scents that meant Chris to her. But whether she was genuinely trying to respect what Geoff and now Chris himself had told her, or because his rebuff was too recent and she didn't have the courage, she didn't.

When he handed the bottle back to her with a stiff nod, she retreated, but she didn't leave. She sat down on a stump. At his look, she set her chin. "You said leave it alone. You didn't tell me to leave *you* alone. Do you want me to?"

"There's a loaded female question if ever I heard one. Right up there with *Does this make me look fat?*"

The touch of wryness offered her hope, but his eyes remained shuttered, his mouth tight. He went back to edging. Silence reigned for the next quarter hour. It wasn't the first time she'd sat outside on a pretty day to watch Chris work in the yard. Usually she brought a book and lay in the outdoor hammock he'd strung between two maples, or sat in a resin chair on the patio, all to be near him. The two of them would talk in comfortable snippets, as natural as the comings and goings of a breeze. If Geoff was home and working, he'd be sitting at the dining room table. When the weather was nice, he'd shut off the air and open up the screened windows flanking the picture window so he could hear them, occasionally calling out a comment or two.

Chris leaned on the edger. His gaze was on the aviary. Harry was preening his feathers while Hermione hopped from branch to branch. Ron was doing the same, chasing her, a game that couldn't help but make Sam smile a little.

Harry was a mockingbird with a crooked right wing; Hermione, a dove with a missing right eye and left foot. Ron, a glossy brown bird twice their size, liked to perch in the center of the aviary as he clacked and fluffed his wings.

Nothing was wrong with Ron. He'd been dumped out of a nest as a baby when his tree was cut down, and Chris had hand-fed him until he was strong enough to forage for himself. However, he'd formed an attachment to the aviary and to Harry and Hermione, and kept coming back. Chris still let him out several times a week, to make sure he hadn't changed his mind. So far he hadn't. At night, the three of them roosted together, three unlikely friends who would have merely tolerated one another in the wild. But different circumstances had called for a redrawing of boundaries. Ron had found something with Harry and Hermione he couldn't find out in the great big world.

She knew how he felt.

"I thought you guys would wait for me."

Her gaze snapped back to Chris. The careful neutrality of his quiet tone concealed as much as it revealed.

"It's not like that." She didn't think so. "I wanted something to happen after the visit to Naughty Bits, and it didn't. It felt like I needed to try something else."

"We went there less than a couple of weeks ago, Sam." His gaze shifted to hers, sparked. "You say it's the three of us, but you two didn't seem to think I needed to be a part of it. Maybe I've thought a bunch of shit about this, too. Maybe I hoped, the first time, it would be the three of us."

Guilt swamped her, taking her breath away. Knowing that he'd imagined things as she had, perhaps in just as much detail, was a hard thing to hear. She'd thought he was simply avoiding or preventing it for the same reasons as Geoff, and maybe that was true. But it didn't change the fact that her impatience had taken an opportunity away from him. She tried to push past that and think about why she'd done it. It hadn't just been hormones. She needed to grasp the potential of what was, rather than what should have been.

"It felt like it needed to be in bite-sized pieces," she said. "Do you know how this will impact your relationship with Geoff? Do you want a Dom, Chris?"

She hadn't been sure if Chris knew about that part of Geoff, but it wasn't a surprise to her to see the tightening of the mouth that told her he did. "Do you want to submit to him? Is this two straight guys wanting to share a girl, or two semistraight guys who are kind of interested in each other as well?"

She was curious about the answer to that herself, since she had her own theories. He looked away, not answering, and she rose, closing her hand over his where it gripped the wooden handle. "See? The one thing I figured you both understood was how you feel about me. Girl parts and stuff, those things are good. Right?"

His lips tugged at the corners, and she stroked his fingers. "I don't know if you have the same . . . urges toward me that Geoff does, or if you're a different animal, but I know you want me. Or you did."

When he shifted his hand out of reach and didn't respond to that, still not looking at her, she did her best to mask another sharp pain. She'd thought long and hard about what Geoff had said, about following her heart on this. The way he'd said it, that look he'd given her, had pinged something inside her. It was like her submissive side had an under layer she could only access by feeling, not thinking. So though she couldn't put into words what he'd meant, she felt his intent. And decided to act on it.

"Do you know what Geoff asked me? Whether it would turn me on, you punishing me while he watched. Spanking me . . . Well, he said you might cut a switch in the yard . . ."

"I'm not like that. That's not my thing." He said it so brusquely, she swallowed her words midsentence. Wrong tactic, and he'd shut her down sharply enough she wasn't sure where else to go with it. Geoff was right. Maybe she needed to leave this alone.

"Okay. Well, I'll go inside and change into some work clothes so I can help you with this."

"I don't want your help right now, Sam." He tossed the edger aside and picked up the shovel. As he straightened, he pushed several unruly locks of brown hair out of his eyes. "I get it, all right? You feel bad and you want to make me feel better about things so you don't have to feel so bad about it."

She set her jaw. "Maybe I'm sorry and want to make you feel better because you're my friend."

"Friend? Yeah. Great."

Damn it, she was going to take the shovel and brain him with it. Instead she stepped closer. "Don't back away from me," she said ominously as he looked like he was going to shrug her off. She put her hands at his waist, her fingers curling in the fabric belt of the camos, knuckles pressed against the impressive muscle groups at his abdomen and hips. He stood rigid as she looked up at him.

"I get it," she said quietly. "We should have waited. But I didn't want to wait anymore, Chris. Whether or not you want to hear it, I felt like I had to get Geoff on board first, because he's . . . what he is. You may be that, or something else I don't yet understand, but we both know what he is, right?"

Chris lifted an irritated shoulder, and she reached up to his face. He clasped her wrist, stopping her. "I don't want this right now," he said, though his grip and the look in her eye told her otherwise. "Just . . . I don't want to be harsh, Sam, but I really need you to leave me the hell alone. Okay? You can't fix this."

She tried to push the ache in her throat back, to stop it from happening, but damn if tears didn't well up. She should turn around, march back into the house, but a promise was a promise. "I told Geoff I would do this if . . . I just told him I'd do it."

Taking a breath, she turned away from him. Since where Geoff had written between her shoulder blades necessitated taking her T-shirt off to reveal it, she did. She hadn't worn a bra, because she didn't know if it would obscure what he wrote. The aviary screened her from the neighboring house she faced, and they had woods behind them, their house on her right. Even so, she heard Chris mutter a "Jeez, Sam . . ." but then he fell silent.

She stood there for interminable minutes, waiting. She watched the birds in the aviary, felt the sun on her shoulders, the light flirt of the wind that tightened her nipples and skittered across her skin. If Chris told her to go away once more, she would bolt. She could only handle so much rejection at once. Maybe that was what Geoff had meant about her not trying to fix things. Probably exactly what he'd meant.

Geoff really had looked like he was a breath away from taking her decision to stay at the house out of her hands, by physical intimidation if necessary. Ninety percent of the time, Geoff and Chris were as enlightened about women as she could wish, but when their protective instincts were goaded, they reverted to the behavior of men two or three centuries ago. Honorable men, but it could frustrate her, as it would any woman with a brain. On the flip side, sometimes that aspect of their personalities made emotions and needs well up in her she couldn't explain. She wanted to be as protective of them as they were of her.

She should leave Chris alone, but she couldn't. He was hurting, and she couldn't be okay with that. Not for another minute.

She quivered as his fingers whispered over her bare shoulder, then slid down. It felt like he was tracing the words. "What does it say?"

"None of your business."

Coming from Chris, it was an unexpected response, but his tone was mild, his touch a quest, exploring her as much as outlining what Geoff had written on her. She closed her eyes to better absorb the sensation. Up and down, in looping circles between her shoulder blades, then down along her spine to her jeans, finger sliding along her waistband. Back up again. Her nipples now had another reason for tightening, because the more he touched her, the more she wanted to be touched by him.

"Don't talk, Sam. Close your eyes."

She already had them closed, but she'd parted her lips to say something, she wasn't sure what. Since her back was to him, she wasn't sure how he'd known she was about to speak, unless her shoulders lifted from the preparatory breath. If so, it proved how closely he was studying every inch of her, which overwhelmed her enough to keep her silent even without the command. A tremor ran through the fingers she curled uncertainly at her sides.

He turned her around to face him. His body was wide enough to block the neighbors' view. He'd make sure of it. She trusted him to do that. Thinking of what Geoff had said about how he felt when he looked at her fully naked, how it would be the same for Chris, she wished she weren't wearing her jeans and sneakers. She wanted to stand before Chris that way again.

His hair brushed her brow, and she realized he'd leaned in toward her. His lips, warm and firm, came against hers, and she sighed in delight at the unexpected contact. He slid his big hands along her bare waist, drawing her in until she was pressed against him and he was tasting her, tracing her lips, touching her tongue with his. When she emitted a needy little moan, her fists now tight balls to keep her from climbing up and into him for more, he broke. Crushing her against him, he delved deep into her mouth, his other hand coming up to twist in her hair, hold her fast as he gave her his anger and frustration, his lust and even deeper emotions, the most important ones. Her hands opened, slid up to his shoulders and clung. She couldn't imagine comparing Chris and Geoff's kisses and rating one over the other. It was the mountain and the lightning, both bringing something incomparable to the mix.

Her breasts were pressed against his chest, against the rough layer of hair there, the damp sweat and dirt, but she didn't care about those. It was Chris. She melted into him, held up by the strength of his arms, overwhelmed by the harsh male need in the kiss. When he finally broke it, her heart was pounding crazily, whirling butterflies in her stomach.

"He had me thinking about it. Or you did." As he lifted his head, his accusing look had a glimmer of raw humor in it. It eased some of her tension.

"About what?"

"About spanking you to feel better."

"Is that what he wrote?"

"No. And don't ask me to tell you what he did." He framed her face, thumbs on her lips, his eyes roving over her face. She was still trembling and he noticed, his hands beginning to slide away. She grabbed his wrists.

"Please don't stop."

"You're cold. I'm getting your shirt."

"I'm not cold."

His eyes came back to her face. He left one hand on her cheek, but he bent and picked up the shirt. Putting it back on her, he guided her hands to the sleeves. There were plenty of incidental touches as he did it, steadying her as she found the armholes. When he pulled the T-shirt back down over her body and smoothed it, he molded his hands over her taut nipples so her small curves pressed into his palms. He didn't pause there, but he didn't rush it, either. At her waist, he curled his fingers in her belt loops, holding her.

"It's time for you to go inside, Sam. Really. Let me think things through, all right?" He lifted one hand and touched her cheek. "I'm getting you dirty. Smudges on your face."

"That's okay." She wanted to say she was sorry, but she couldn't truly be sorry for a minute of what had happened with Geoff. She tried for the next best thing. "Can I make you some lunch? I picked up some Boar's Head at the grocery and that fresh sourdough bread you like. I could make you one of my world-class sandwiches. There are fresh tomatoes and kettle chips."

His eyebrows, thickets of copper and brown hairs, lifted now. "You think food will help?"

"My mother told me that when it comes to men, food always helps."

"I am hungry."

"When are you not?" She smiled, but when he managed only a halfhearted smile in return, she pushed past his defenses and wrapped her arms around his waist, putting her cheek on his broad chest. "I love you, you know that, right? I'm in love with you. With both of you."

His hands had tightened on her shoulders, maybe to ease her back, but at that, they stopped, got even tighter. He muttered an oath. "It doesn't work that way."

"Yeah, it does. It does for us." She slipped away and moved toward the house, forcing herself not to look back. She'd done what she could . . . without fixing anything.

Once inside, she remembered what Geoff had said about what he'd written on her back. *Until after he sees it.* She hurried to the bathroom. The smudges Chris had left on her cheeks made her smile. Pulling the shirt off her arms again, she let it collar her neck so she could twist around and see the reflection in the mirror. A smile spread across her face as she read the words backward.

She's ours, dumbass. Kiss her, and you'll see. I dare you.

Chris might have told her to leave him alone for now, but something in his eyes said he might not want to be left alone indefinitely. There were overlapping qualities to Chris and Geoff, things that complemented each other as well as her own needs. But they were also very different men.

When she brought him his sandwich, she forced herself to go back inside, but she watched through the window as he sat on the concrete bench by the aviary and ate. If Geoff was eating, he was multitasking; reading, watching TV or typing on his laptop. Whereas Chris gave his full attention to digestion, chewing slowly, his gaze following what the birds were doing in the aviary, or the movement of the clouds overhead. He had a tendency to stretch out right after a meal and take a fifteen-minute nap, which he did today.

Lying back on the stone bench, one work shoe braced on the ground, the other on the bench, he bent his arm over his face to shade his eyes as he closed them. She drew her feet up on the window seat, linking her arms around her knees as she watched him. His other hand curled in a relaxed position on his stomach, the breeze riffling his dark brown hair across his brow. His skin was tan even in winter, because his job had baked it into his flesh. The sun never disappeared for long in North Carolina.

He always had a scattering of cuts and scrapes, because pruning back overgrown holly bushes or pulling weeds and maintaining equipment with his bare hands would leave marks. She'd given him some vegetarian ingredient udder balm ointment, informing him it was what farmers and other laborers used to keep their hands healthy. He'd finally started using it, so the cuts healed more quickly, though a few were deep enough the scars remained.

Simple things, simple thoughts. She should get up and do something. She had some bills to pay, a book to read, a tear in a pair of slacks that needed mending. But she usually did that kind of thing near Chris when he was home. She did that because she loved his company, not because she had to do so. She was a well-rounded person. She had her yoga and took classes and workshops to expand her mind. Since she'd been living with Chris and Geoff, those educational experiences had covered everything from stained glass creation to using essential oils for better health. She went out with Flo and other friends. She wasn't dependent on Chris or Geoff's presence to entertain herself.

But today she was like Chris. She only wanted to focus on one thing. Only wanted to do one thing. Suppressing a tight smile at the double entendre, she rose. She'd go get the slacks and mend them by the window.

When she returned, he'd woken from his nap and was working in the yard again. She mended the slacks, read her book and did her bills, all where she could watch him. She ventured out a couple of times to bring him more water and snacks and retrieve the sandwich plate. She'd hoped their short interlude might have eased his mind, yet he was still working at a much more grueling pace than he usually set for himself.

He'd used the dirt from the pond hole to create a berm by their small vegetable garden. At the base he'd inserted several cinder blocks so they looked like the openings to small caves. When she bent to examine them, she saw he'd sealed the back openings so the square spaces would remain dirt free.

She liked frog houses and had talked about creating a fairy garden. He'd told her about a month ago he'd build her a berm under the sheltered canopy of one of the older trees that would accommodate both. Once he had that set up, she could start designing it how she liked.

She straightened to see him watching her, but as she started to smile and say how she liked the results of his work, he put his head down and went back to it. Trying to ignore the painful twist of reaction in her chest, she made herself go back into the house. Left him to his thinking.

She'd had several texts from Geoff through the day, checking in with her. He must be busy, because they were short things. Raspberry-blowing emoticons, and aliens with antennae zooming across the screen. However, as if he could sense her mounting frustration—or maybe he'd finally had a lull in his work—the one she found on her phone now included words.

How's it going, Miss Fix-It?

Narrowing her eyes, she punched in a response. *Middle East peace, lower cable bills and which came first, the chicken or the egg, all solved.* She paused. *He looked at my back and kissed me. But that's all.*

Her phone chirped again. *So which was it, chicken or egg?*

She shook her head. *Chicken. Can't have an egg without having a chicken first.*

Just like you can't get to the finish line unless you run the course. Don't worry. Be home soon, I hope.

She sent back a couple of Xs and Os to that, and put her phone on the counter. Okay, what pointless thing could she do next so she wouldn't lose her mind? She could have gone out for a couple of hours, but she was determined to be here when Chris came back into the house. She was certain if she left, he'd take that opportunity to duck in, take a shower and disappear into his room. She wanted to respect his alone time, but she refused to be avoided.

When the day started to ebb toward late afternoon, he at last reached a stopping point. She judged that he'd completed a couple of months' worth of projects in a single day. Even with his level of fitness, he was going to be aching tomorrow.

After he put away his tools, he didn't come back toward the house as she'd hoped. Instead, he headed for the trees. For Chris, the back-flanking forest had been one of the big draws of their rental house. He'd built a tree house just inside the tree line, big enough she could glimpse it from the rear of the house, since she knew where to look. Otherwise, the weathered wood blended into the canopy.

This was his home. She wasn't going to let anything drive him from it, even her or his own thoughts. She'd given him a whole day of space. If the mountain wouldn't come to Mohammed, Mohammed was going to the mountain.

She packed up a tote with snacks, a gallon jug of cold water and a small container of ice. Leaving the house, she crossed the backyard and chirped a greeting at the aviary birds before she went through the rear gate and into the woods. Technically the property wasn't theirs, but it was undeveloped land. Kids made bike trails through it and built dams in the creek, doing what kids had done throughout time, transforming wild places into their own imaginary world. She'd wondered if Chris had built a tree house goaded by that same impulse. He liked to build as well as plant, and had a knack for seeing what would integrate the best with his surroundings, rather than strip it of its natural beauty. The tree house was no exception.

The wide platform had four thru-holes for the trunks of the trees that supported it. The tree house itself was a box structure with geometric cutouts for windows. A hexagon, a star, a crescent moon. It had a roof, but he'd threaded thin branches into the treehouse under it, interlacing them along the ceiling and stringing them with a thicket of lights that ran on batteries and could be switched on and off. At night, in pitch dark, they could lie on their backs on the wooden floor and turn on those lights. It was as if they were looking up at the stars.

She paused at the base of the tree house. "Do I need the secret password?" she asked.

"Probably."

She pursed her lips. "Naked girls."

His half chuckle heartened her. "You know, guys aren't as easy as you think we are."

"Does that mean I didn't get the password right?"

"Didn't say that." She looked up into his face, peering down at her through the trapdoor. "Looks like you also brought provisions," he said.

"I did. I have Little Debbie oatmeal cookies, cold Pepsi and a few other things. Can I come up?"

At his nod, she handed up the items, and came up herself. He was there with a helping hand, ensuring she made the transition safely from the bolt hole onto the platform. The late-afternoon sun gave the interior a plush yellow light, reflecting off the golden pine. She'd hung some glittering silver stars from the ceiling branches and a couple of chimes. They made music from the breeze wafting in through the geometric cutouts.

Chris rarely looked tired. He looked a step away from exhaustion now, which concerned her. After he helped her inside, he took a seat on the boards, his back pressed against the wall between the hexagon and the star. He'd put his shirt back on. His knees were bent and splayed, his forearms resting on them, hands loose. His hair appeared as if he'd raked his hands through it numerable times, leaving the thick locks spiked. The late afternoon still held warmth, so he had sweat beads on his brow and neck. His brown eyes studied her.

Taking a seat across from him, she drew up her knees and clasped her arms around them, studying him right back.

She reminded herself she'd been brave enough to push Geoff, and he could be intimidating as hell. Chris wasn't the intimidating sort, not to her. Her hesitation had to do with being rejected, but even more than that, she didn't want to hurt him any more than she already had. After a long moment, she shifted onto her knees, closing the yard of space between them to slide between his large work shoes. She brought the container of ice closer to them.

Folding her legs beneath her, she touched his shirt, spreading her fingers over his chest. The cloth was damp from sweat. Rising on her knees, she grasped the hem, telling him with her body language she wanted to help him take it off. He didn't immediately comply, that intriguingly hard-to-read gaze resting on her face. Then he straightened, his hands brushing hers away, not unkindly, so he could pull the shirt over his head.

The sinuous ripple of muscle so close to the heat of her own body made her want to swallow, hard. But she took the shirt, folded it and put it to the side. After pulling open the container of ice, she withdrew a bowl from her tote, as well as a cotton washcloth. She poured some of the water from the gallon jug into the bowl, but she set that aside, instead reaching for the ice.

She was proud that her hand was steady as she put the cube against his collarbone. She slid it in a slow arc along that line, watching it make a sleek track through the dirt on his skin. He had gleaming dark hair on his chest, and she combed her fingers through the rough-soft feel of it, sliding the ice along the same path. His skin shuddered under the touch of the ice, even though his hands had returned to rest on his splayed knees as he watched her closely.

She'd used sexual triggers to motivate Geoff to action, but even with that she wasn't the type of woman who believed a man could be led by his cock. Nor would she want to treat either man that way. With Geoff it had been the right timing, a sincere message sent, and his response hadn't been mindless in the least. Sex could soothe, heal and open communication, if both parties were willing to let it. When they were, it wasn't manipulative or wrong. Which was why she was taking her time, letting Chris decide what he would welcome or rebuff. As she continued to move the ice against his body, his heat and energy pulled her in, so the nervousness receded in favor of pure joy at touching him.

Taking the ice down his pectoral to the nipple, she watched it bead under the cold. His fingers flexed. In this position, the camo pants were stretched across his groin so she could see the intimate shape of the man beneath. When he reached beneath his waistband and grasped his growing erection, adjusting it to a more comfortable position, the blatant eroticism of his doing it in front of her with no self-consciousness spiked her blood pressure, making her fingers twitch on him. He returned his hand to that dangling position on his knee, his eyes still fastened on her as she moistened her lips in involuntary response.

Geoff was sleek and polished, a dangerous Dom lover like a leopard, whereas Chris was all earthy sensuality, basic and primal. Sexual tension hummed off him like the distant thunder behind a mountain range.

The ice was melting against the heat of his skin, drops of water rolling down his chest and the sectioned muscles of his stomach. She picked up another piece, running it over his shoulders and behind his neck. To do that she had to stand on her knees, and his breath touched her breasts through her thin T-shirt. He still hadn't moved his hands.

"Touch me," she murmured. Could she command him? She'd sensed something between him and Geoff, a deference that had made her wonder if Chris nursed some submissive tendencies, but she'd only seen it come out around Geoff, in ways so fleeting she wasn't sure if she'd imagined it. But she could test it now, couldn't she? It wasn't her thing, but she wasn't necessarily averse to the idea of having a big, strong man at her command for a short interlude.

She moved the ice down his arm out to his hand, then back up under the arm, teasing the armpit. Then—

He captured her wrist with the opposite hand, holding it up between them. Dipping his own hand in the container, he came out with a handful of ice and put it in her palm, closing her hand over it. As she felt the burn of the ice, he met her gaze. "Think you can order me around, Sam?"

She saw licks of flame in his brown eyes. "I don't know," she said. "Can I?"

"No. You can't." He opened her fingers, letting the ice drop with a clatter to the wood planks. Bringing her cold palm against the heat of his body, he warmed it without flinching, without moving his attention from her face. The man was arousing her with nothing more than how he was looking at her. With hunger, with a need to take, held back only by his own restraint, by whatever thoughts were moving through his mind. "Tell me what you want," he said.

"I want to wash you."

Surprise flitted through his gaze. He'd need a full shower to be clean, but she had a different purpose from cleaning. All she needed was his acquiescence. "May I?"

He didn't agree or disagree, but he didn't stop her. After a weighted moment, she sank back to her heels and untied his work shoes, removing them and his socks, fingers caressing his arches before she rose to her feet. "Will you stand for me?" she asked.

He did so, a big man in a small space, though he'd made the sloped roof so he could stand up straight, even with the interlaced branches above him. Hooking her fingers in the rings of the canvas belt of his camo pants, she pulled it free and unbuttoned the top of the pants. She left them that way as she bent and retrieved the washcloth. As she did, she stilled, for his hands slid over her hips, catching her belt loops as he did earlier, only now his touch slid lower, cupping one buttock. When she straightened, his hand stayed on her hip, fingertips curved into her back pocket. The other captured her breast, thumbing her nipple through the thin T-shirt.

Her reaction to his touch spiraled out, sending electric tingles throughout her upper torso. She made herself focus, though, sliding the washcloth over his shoulder. The excess water rolled down his chest, his back and arm. She moved the terry cloth in slow glides over that same terrain, and when she moved closer to him to run it behind his neck to get the sweat and grime there, he obligingly dipped his head. His large hand descended even lower, his firm hold pressing into the seam of her jeans at the base of her ass. A tiny breath escaped, a shudder going through her. As he curved over her, she ran the cloth over the widest part of his back and he shifted his grip to clasp her buttocks in both hands.

The way he was looking at her made the space much smaller and more charged with heat in a blink. She thought he might finally have a few more things on his mind than being mad at Geoff or her. It made her dare to ask him the next question.

"Do you want me to take anything off?" Her voice wasn't much over a squeak.

After three long heartbeats, he reached out to finger the hem of her T-shirt and tug on her jeans waistband. "Everything but the panties," he said roughly. "I want to watch you wash me in just those."

His manner wasn't as overt as Geoff's, yet he took her over just as powerfully. Chris was more like a strong undercurrent that ran below the surface, arousing her with how it teased and tugged at her submissive side, while giving her more freedom to play around him and explore.

"Like a slave girl washing her Master," she said, though her lips couldn't quite curve in a smile, especially when he didn't smile back. He waited.

She pulled off the shirt and shimmied out of the jeans, shoes and socks. She was wearing thin white panties with a touch of lace, and she was sure the front panel was as damp with her arousal as his shirt had been with sweat. His gaze slid there, then back over her stomach, her quivering breasts. His arousal was growing thicker and more insistent beneath the camo pants. The pants were now half-unzipped because of the strain being put on the fly.

Bending, she dipped the washcloth into the bowl again. She ran it over his chest and arms, moving around him to do his back. Rivulets of water slipped down his lower back and beneath his waistband. After rubbing the cloth over his arms and down to his hands, she rewet the cloth so she could do an even better job cleaning the dirt from his palms. She pulled out a fresh washcloth and dipped it into the ice container, enough water there to dampen the cloth. Back on her toes again, she wiped his face, passing it over his eyes as they closed for her. Then the bridge of his nose, his lips and cheeks, the strong jaw.

A higher stretch let her reach the back of his neck once more, and his broad shoulders. His arms slid around her, hands taking possession of her ass again, though this time there was nothing between the heat of his palms and her flesh except the thinnest barrier of silk. He fondled her with obvious male enjoyment as she swayed, her lips parting.

Taking the cloth from her, he dropped it on the floor and leaned back against the wall, bringing her closer so her breasts pressed against his chest, her cheek to his shoulder. He held her that way, his hand holding her skull and his other hand stroking, rubbing and fondling her ass. The position put her mound against his thigh, his erection against her abdomen, and she wanted to rub, to entice.

She expanded the fantasy in her mind. Maybe he wasn't her Master the prince, but the royal gardener who loved the slave girl. The gardener would tell her he wanted her to wash him the way she'd wash her Master. He wanted her to show him it wasn't money or royal power that commanded her obedience, but the nature of the man.

When Chris split her legs open by insinuating one of his muscled thighs in between them, he seated her right against that flexing muscle. She grabbed his biceps for balance as he began to work her against him, creating explosive friction.

"Chris," she gasped. His hand tightened.

"I want to hear you come, Sam. I want to hear you come without that vibrator you use. No pillow to muffle those sexy moans you make."

Her gaze snapped up to him, color suffusing her cheeks. His jaw set. "I've jerked off listening to you, the bumps and creaks of your bed," he said roughly. "I want to hear you come for me, because of what I'm doing to you, how I'm touching you. Not because of . . . anything else."

"Anything else, or any*one* else?"

She meant it as a gentle tease, because his hesitation implied the word as clearly as speaking it. A blink later, she wished she'd let the powerful arousal gripping her keep her from speaking at all, because apparently it was the wrong thing to say if she'd wanted them to keep going in the direction they were headed.

For just a second his grip constricted on her hard enough to bruise, then he released her and straightened. He moved her off of him decisively enough it sliced into her heart. Bending, he scooped up her clothes and handed them to her. He fastened his pants, retrieved his T-shirt and pulled it back on before he gave her an even look, his expression wooden.

"I told you it was better to leave me alone," he said gruffly. He picked up the bowl, dumped the water out the window and stuffed it and the washcloths back into the tote. "Put your clothes back on and come back to the house."

He didn't wait for her, though he took everything she'd brought with her so she didn't have to navigate them down the ladder. When she was alone, watching him stride back toward the house, the tote on his shoulder, Sam stood there, holding her clothes against her tingling skin despite the chill settling over her. She wouldn't cry. She wouldn't.

This was just a bump in the road. She wouldn't turn it into a huge life-or-death drama, no matter the size of the jagged lump in her throat.

Even so, it took her a half hour to find the courage to return to the house. When she entered, she hoped he was there as much as a craven part of her wished he wasn't. The shower in their shared bathroom was steamed up, telling her he'd used it, but he was in his room, the door shut, his TV on. She didn't bother knocking or trying the door, knowing it would be locked.

She should have gone to work with Geoff.

~

"Not all Doms are obvious alpha males, and many alpha males are *not* Doms."

Her friend Flo had told her that. Flo was a Domme herself, so she'd know. Lying on her bed in the dark, Sam thought that through. Geoff was alpha with a capital *A*, automatically assuming leadership of any situation. A strong overachiever in college, he'd finished at the top of his class.

But Chris was no less resolute than Geoff on the things that mattered to him. When he'd told her to strip for him, the look in his eye told her he wasn't necessarily acting on whatever understanding he had of Sam's submissive desires, but pursuing interests of his own. Chris was always his own man.

Several years ago, a string of hurricanes had hit the coast. Chris had come home with enough money to start his own landscaping company. Yet as usual, he banked it and went back to tending yards in Charlotte as part of Esteban's crew. He wasn't lazy, not in the least, and he was entirely self-sufficient. He just seemed to prefer working for someone.

Esteban was really good to him, because the company owner was no fool. Chris was a rare find. A twenty-something who worked hard, had a natural talent for landscape design and could be trusted with any task, large or small. Chris was smart enough to run all aspects of the operation when Esteban took a vacation, but he had no obvious desire to make that situation permanent.

The only time he and Esteban had had a disagreement of any seriousness had been when a new homeowner wanted a tree taken down because she didn't want the sprawling maple blocking the street view of her house. She felt the tree detracted from the house's curb appeal. Chris had explained it was nesting season for a great many animals and birds. If the owner insisted on killing a perfectly healthy tree, she should at least hold off until later. The customer disagreed.

The tree came down while Chris was on a lunch break, but when he returned and found Esteban and the crew about to cut up the branches and trunk, he shouldered them aside and fished through the branches until he found three nests. Two of them still had live birds. He gathered up the tiny bodies of three that had been thrown from the nest and hadn't survived the tree's fall. He also found a nest with squirrel babies.

The customer's eight-year-old daughter had been playing in the yard, and Chris's discoveries horrified her to tears. Chris had comforted her, letting her help him carry the nests to a neighbor's house, who'd agreed to let them put the nests back up in his trees, where the babies would be close enough their calls might bring the parents. Chris camped out in his truck on the street until he verified the parents returned to all but one of the nests. That one he brought home and hand-fed the babies until they could be released.

Esteban never again agreed to take down a healthy tree so readily, and never during the spring. The attention Chris's actions drew from surrounding neighbors, as well as the embarrassment of the homeowner when she had to deal with her daughter's dismay over the dislodged nests, even inspired Esteban to change his company's brand. Cortez Landscaping was now promoted as an environmentally conscious and wildlife-friendly operation. Chris was his "expert" advisor to the homeowners on the best way to live in harmony with nature and still have a beautiful yard.

She smiled a little. Even during that incident, Chris had never once said anything in anger about Esteban. It wasn't his way to rant or trash talk. He simply made his point and pressed forward, not letting anything deter him from his intent, until he brought everyone else on board.

At home, Chris was always cognizant of her or Geoff's states of mind. If Geoff was in a bad mood, Chris was the one most likely to coax him out of it. They'd been friends since middle school. According to Chris, they'd met when Geoff had been getting his ass kicked by three other boys for running his way-too-smart mouth. Chris had jumped into the fray. Geoff insisted he'd had everything under control. Nevertheless, they'd been friends ever since.

When Geoff had walked away from his family, he'd literally had nothing, his entire education and housing having been funded by his parents. He'd moved in with Chris. Though he'd eventually secured the jobs and loans he needed to finish his education, Chris was the one who'd given him a place to stay and food to eat until that happened.

She sighed, turning on her side. Chris never said what he didn't mean, so when he'd said this wasn't about her, she understood that the two of them had to work it out. But patience wasn't her strong suit. Not when she'd already opened Pandora's box.

She put her hand on the wall. Even by herself in the dark, she flushed as she thought of what Chris had said. He'd heard her mastur-bate, despite how quiet she thought she'd been. And he said he'd done the same, listening to her. While thinking about that heightened the arousal she'd been able to choke back down to simmering since the tree house, she wanted something more than the physical from him right now. As selfish as it might be, she needed some type of acknowl-edgement that they were still friends. That it was going to be okay.

She tapped the first few notes of "Itsy Bitsy Spider" on the wall, waited, and hoped. It was their usual bedtime good night, but she told herself it didn't mean anything if he didn't respond. After the day he'd had, he could well be asleep. She closed her eyes, swallowing the lump in her throat.

. . . *went up the water spout.* The taps came a few minutes later, when she'd resigned herself to falling asleep with only her own thoughts for company. Her heavy heart thumped with hope as she did the next few notes. He finished it, then did the two taps he always did at the end to say good night.

She did the same, two taps, but tonight she added three. *I love you.*

It soothed her enough to send her into a fitful sleep, but she woke around midnight to hear Geoff moving quietly down the hall. She was surprised to hear him open Chris's door. She couldn't determine from the murmur of male voices what was being said or the tone of the conversation, but then they both quieted and the house was still once more.

Whereas her mind was now spinning like a top. It took her another hour to get back to sleep.

Since Esteban's crew went to work at dawn, usually Chris was in the bathroom first in the morning. However, from his closed door, it appeared he was sleeping in today. Esteban had probably given them a day off after their nonstop work in Mississippi. Geoff's door was closed as well. She suspected he'd be working from home after such a late night at the office, unless there was a meeting or trial.

She took her shower. When she got out, she tucked the towel around her and cracked the bathroom door to let the steam out as she always did, since the bathroom didn't have a vent. She was putting moisturizer on her face when she looked in the mirror and saw Chris peering around the door at her. "Mind if I come in and keep you company?"

She felt like the sun had come out from behind clouds. "I can't think of anything I'd like better."

Pursing his lips, he lifted a Krispy Kreme bag. "So I get to keep all these for myself?"

"You're evil," she informed him, and he grinned. There were still shadows in his eyes, but he was obviously making an effort, and she'd do the same. She'd sit on every compulsion she had and try not to force a thing between any of them. At least not today.

Chris took a seat on the edge of the tub, straddling the wall as he pulled out her favorite, a raspberry-filled glazed donut with powdered sugar on top. He handed it to her with wax paper wrapped around the base. He also had a flat of coffee, and he offered her one of the three cups, which she wasn't surprised to find had been mixed to her preference. As she leaned against the counter, sipping on it and inhaling that intoxicating Krispy Kreme smell that even clung to their coffee cups, she was aware of his gaze drifting up her bare knees to mid-thigh. The towel was the only barrier concealing her from him. Was he as hyperaware of that as she was?

Drink your coffee, Sam. Let him decide.

"I'm sorry about yesterday, Sam," he said quietly. "You know none of that had anything to do with you, right?"

"I started all this."

"So it's your fault?" His brown eyes clouded. "That's bullshit."

"It's not Geoff's fault, either," she responded. "It's just . . . It's growing pains. Our growing pains."

"Smart woman."

Geoff was in the doorway, wearing his running shorts and T-shirt. He looked toward the other man. "Did you get a lemon-filled one?" His personal favorite.

Chris pulled one out of the bag, again in the wax wrap, and passed it over with a cup of coffee. Geoff took a bite of the donut, studying her in the mirror's reflection. The steam in the bathroom had left a mist on the clear shower door and the mirror, but having the door open was evaporating it. Putting down the donut, Geoff stepped closer to her. She had her hair up in a twist until she could dry it, and her skin tingled as he slid his finger over her shoulder blades. "That permanent marker's holding pretty well."

She hadn't scrubbed it. Hadn't wanted it to go away just yet, in case she'd ruined it for all of them and yesterday was the closest she'd get to what she wanted for the foreseeable future.

She was cognizant of how close Chris was to her, his foot within a few inches of her toes. They were both close to her in this small space, and she didn't know where to take it. Or if it was even her job to take it anywhere now. Geoff answered the question for her.

Removing the donut from her hand, he held it to her mouth. His other hand on her lower back kept her facing the mirror. "Take a bite."

She did. Geoff watched her chew and swallow, then turned the donut toward him so he could run his finger along the bite area, collecting some of the raspberry filling on his fingers. He spread that over her lips. "Lick it off."

She obeyed, her body starting to throb. She couldn't gauge Chris's response to what they were doing, but she hoped he wasn't about to surge up from the tub and leave the room. Geoff stepped back and took a seat on the tub edge. He straddled it and leaned against the bathroom wall, a mirror position to how Chris was leaning against the shower wall.

"Take off the towel," Geoff said, low.

Had they talked to one another? Arranged for this? Chris's jaw was tight, studiously avoiding looking at Geoff, but she noticed his eyes were trained on her as if he couldn't look away, no matter what conflicting thoughts he might be harboring.

Yesterday she'd broken the mood between her and him by bringing the shadow of Geoff between them, a poorly-timed attempt to resolve the conflict between the two men. She didn't have to do that now, because Geoff was here. She was going to try and trust the truth: that he'd been Chris's friend longer than he'd known her, and so he might have a better idea of how to make this work. She'd also ignore every TV show or movie that said lifelong male friendships were sure to be destroyed by a conflict over a woman. What did they know? They didn't know these two men, or herself.

She let the towel fall. Mindful of the lesson Geoff had taught her, she stood up straight and proud, no matter the frisson of nerves that went through her stomach. Geoff hadn't told her to turn away from the mirror, so she watched their eyes course over her in the glass's reflection. All the pale flesh of her limbs and abdomen, her breasts and sex. Her neck, where the pulse was jumping like a small bird beneath her jaw.

"I'll be right back. Don't move." Rising, Geoff left the bathroom and moved across the hallway into her room. Her brow creased as she heard him open a drawer, maybe to her nightstand. What was he doing? Chris's gaze stayed on her, and a blink later Geoff was back, holding her vibrator. How had he known exactly where to find it? His gaze met hers in the mirror, his lips curving as he enjoyed the erotic humiliation staining her cheeks.

"Looks like her clit is already swollen," Geoff said conversationally, glancing toward Chris. Taking a seat on the tub wall again, he extended the vibrator to the other man. "You're better with power tools than I am. Want to see if you can make her scream? I know we've both imagined doing it, controlling it so she has to depend on us to make her come, rather than making the choice herself."

Chris gave Geoff an unfathomable look, but he took the vibrator from him, turning it over in his hands. Sam swallowed. It was a standard rabbit design, the clitoral stimulator shaped like a rabbit's head, the long ears and pointed nose both capable of transmitting a variety of arousing patterns against her sensitive flesh. The dildo part was shaped realistically like a man's cock, the rubber sheath like human flesh.

Geoff's gaze lifted to meet hers in the mirror again. "Spread your legs to shoulder width and hold on to the edge of the sink with both hands. Don't let go unless one of us tells you to do it."

That beat in her throat became even more frenetic, matched by a throbbing between her legs. But she obeyed. In this position, she was slightly bent forward. With her legs spread, she'd be showing them the folds of her sex. Their eyes both swiveled in that direction, with such heat and deliberation it felt like they'd touched her there. Her fingers tightened on the sink.

Geoff retrieved his donut and took a bite. "It's Chris's fault I know about your vibrator," he said. "He told me if I'd shut off the TV instead of falling asleep to it, I'd hear you when you use it. It's very faint, but once you know the sound, you listen for it."

"I mostly do it when you're not home," she said weakly. Though lately she'd been having to do an encore at night, because of the direction of her thoughts and the two of them being so close.

"Not anymore." Geoff's gaze met hers, held. "Not unless you ask."

She wasn't sure if she could comply with that as long as the two of them were capable of sexually frustrating her to the point of insanity. His gaze gleamed, registering her recalcitrance.

"Do you just use this part"—Chris tapped the rabbit's head—"or do you put it inside you?"

"Both," she managed. The whole conversation was surreal. "It depends. If it's a quick stress release, I'll just use the stimulator. If I'm . . . fantasizing more, I'll use the rest." Actually she had a pretty rich fantasy life no matter which part of it she used, but she was feeling self-conscious and overwhelmed by the abundance of testosterone in the room, so she was sticking to short answers.

"Do you need lube for it?"

Geoff answered that one for her. "All the lubrication you need is between her legs. Rub the head gently just inside her pussy to coat it and get it started. You can also use your fingers to be sure, before you put it inside her. Just like you'd do before you fuck her."

Sam couldn't imagine what unspoken messages were passing in their exchanged look. Knowing Chris was less sexually experienced than Geoff wasn't a surprise. Nor was seeing him be more concerned about doing it right than pretending he knew what he doing. That was so Chris. It made her heart tighten, even as her body tightened for different reasons when he rose.

She stayed as Geoff had ordered her, her hands gripping the edge of the sink, legs spread to shoulder width. When Chris's hand settled on her shoulder, her quiet whimper had his eyes sharpening with his own desires. Setting the vibrator on the counter, he held her steady as he dropped his other hand over her buttock and then between her legs from behind. His fingers stroked, probed, making her quiver. Geoff's gaze was on what Chris was doing with his hand, yet Chris's didn't leave hers in the mirror. It reinforced that this was between her and Chris in a singular way, even as Geoff's presence added an explosive level of heat to the mix.

It was so close to her ultimate desires, having them both here, watching her, touching her. Yet there was that precarious barrier between them, an edge she could feel all three of them walking, seeing where this would go.

"Oh . . ." She bit her lip as Chris eased his large finger into her. She tensed at first, no help for it, because one never knew if a man would move too fast, trying to thrust before he knew the shape of her channel, but this was Chris, who handled baby birds in his palm. He found his way slowly, his expression concentrated as he put another finger in and explored. Her lips were parted, her eyes glazing with her response, her cheeks flushed, all things she saw in the mirror as she watched him as well.

"Does that hurt?"

She shook her head.

"He's right," Chris murmured. "You're wet as you can be. Is that for us?"

She nodded emphatically. A faint smile touched his lips and approval flashed in Geoff's eyes, drawing the web of heated lust around her. She was held between the two of them, and they were pulling those threads ever tighter around her body.

Chris slowly withdrew his hand. He switched the vibrator on its lowest setting before sliding it between her legs, caressing her with the pink head. The vibration rippled along her petals, up inside her, along her clit, and her hold on the sink edge constricted once more. He didn't put it inside her, but instead moved it between her spread legs so she was watching the head rub against her clit as the rabbit's ears teased her labia.

Her breath caught as his hand on her shoulder shifted to curl around her throat, tipping her chin up. His palm was wide enough to collar her from her chin to the base of her neck, his fingers wrapping around to her nape. His strength and the size of his hand reminded her how fragile she was. But she felt no fear when Chris was holding her life in his one big hand. Just the opposite. Now he looped his arm around her so he could insert the vibrator between her legs from the front, tickling her clit with those potent ears.

"What speed gets you the closest without making you come?" he asked.

"It's the fourth one . . . It's like rain pattering, followed by a quick surge, then it goes back to the other."

He pressed the button to get there, his expression morphing into fascination at the results. Each time the rain pattern intensified, her body would arch, a moan breaking from her lips. He crowded her at the sink, holding her against his body, and her response escalated. Geoff leaned against the wall watching them, a still, dense energy.

Another patter, surge, patter, patter, surge. She was rising up on her toes on each surge, that same sound breaking from her lips and becoming louder when Chris wrapped her hand around the toy to make her hold it there. It freed him to reach across her, cup one breast as his forearm pressed against the other. His aroused cock was against her buttocks, a steel bar beneath his clothes. She jerked and writhed against it.

Up, up, so close, then down. The two men watched her cries grow more helpless, more pleading. Chris caressed her throat as his other hand constricted on her breast to hold her still, allowing her only small movements to absorb the powerful waves that took her ever nearer to climax.

"Please." She spoke in a strained whisper. "I want . . . you to hold it. To choose . . . when I can come." She wanted her orgasm totally under his control. She wanted to feel the press of his knuckles against her thighs, wanted him to choose the pattern and rhythm he liked, testing and experimenting.

When he closed his hand on the toy, taking over again, she was so close she thought she'd waited too late to make her request. Yet instead of sending her over, he switched the toy off and set it aside. She swallowed her cry of protest as he gave her something even better —direct contact. He rubbed her pussy with his knuckles, light brushes that rocketed through her. She quivered, strained, her hips working, rubbing her ass against his cock at the same time she moved herself against the rough pads of his fingers.

"Chris . . ."

"Scream for me," he said, his eyes fiery and intent. He pushed his fingers back inside her, thumb worrying her clit as he took her over that edge. She bowed back against him, legs still spread as Geoff had commanded, as Chris had reinforced with the press of his body. When her knees buckled, Chris had her, pushing her over the counter, holding her against his braced thighs as he kept playing and stroking, as he supported her with that gentle hand against her throat, his expression far less gentle. He looked like he wanted to plow his cock into her like a rutting bull, and she was all for that.

She screamed out her climax, and he kept her riding it to the very end, until she had her cheek pressed to the mirror, her body canted over the sink. Only then did he slide his fingers from her, pressing his palm against her still-spasming flesh, sealing in a satisfying ripple. Bending, he pressed a kiss between her shoulder blades. After he helped her straighten slowly, he picked up her towel and tucked it around her hips, leaving her bare to the waist. Her lips quirked at the obvious male preference, even as it took her back to her slave-girl fantasy.

He was still aroused, she could see it in his face, in the tension of his body, in the obvious erection pressing against his pants. Yet he wasn't demanding anything further from her, instead staring at her in the mirror as if she were a mystery he wasn't sure how to pursue next.

Geoff rose. In the small bathroom, he was close enough to touch her, but he didn't. His expression told her that he wished to do so, but was holding back for reasons of his own, many of them probably connecting to Chris. He nudged him with an elbow.

"She needs you inside her, your mouth on her. She doesn't look like she slept well last night. One more orgasm, and she'll sleep like a baby. In your arms."

Chris met his gaze. A muscle twitched in Geoff's jaw, but he inclined his head, spoke even more softly. "Take her to bed, Chris. Make her ours."

～

Geoff left the bathroom then, carrying the Krispy Kreme bag and coffee cups with him. His footsteps told Sam he was headed for the kitchen. It was unexpected, his leaving them like that, but the post-climactic numbness of her brain didn't allow her to think about it right now. Chris was still watching her in the mirror. She parted her lips, feeling like she needed to say something, but he shook his head. Curling his fingers in the front of the towel, he got rid of it once more, letting it drop.

The heat that expanded in his gaze, the primal tension of his body, took any words she might have said. Her stomach tilted as he lifted her off her feet to carry her naked in his arms. It was a breathtaking feeling, being carried by a man who obviously intended to have her body in whatever way he desired when he put her down.

He took her to her room. She hadn't been sure which he'd choose, his space or hers. "Why here?" she asked quietly, hoping not to disturb the mood but wanting to know.

Laying her down on the bed, he leaned over her. "Because I want you to remember me here, even if I'm sometimes on the other side of the wall."

He left her there to go to the door. For a distressing moment, she thought he'd changed his mind and was going to leave, but he stopped. When he put his hand on the panel, Sam understood what he was debating. Closed or not closed? In the end, he pushed it open, looking back at her. She smiled, agreeing with him, and lifted her arms.

He pulled off his shirt as he came across the floor. He was wearing painter's pants today, a secondhand pair he considered his run-out-early-and-get-donuts wear. Because of his size, his muscled thighs and heavy bone structure, most jeans didn't fit him comfortably and well unless he bought the more expensive brands. With his job he didn't see any point in buying pricey clothes, except for a few items in his closet when he needed to dress up more. She had no objections. His camo pants and the painter's trousers fit his ass nice and snug and made the groin area, particularly when aroused, all the more noticeable.

He unhooked the top button. She remembered how the zipper had pulled loose yesterday because of the size of the erection beneath. A strategically located damp spot on the trouser fabric made her real-ize, with a suddenly dry mouth, he wasn't wearing any underwear.

When she lifted her gaze to his face, his expression made every-thing inside her yearn and go still at once. Dropping to one knee beside the bed, he grasped her bare foot and bent his head, kissing her insole with lingering tenderness. Then he kissed her ankle. His gaze swept down her body like a meandering breeze. Everywhere his gaze touched tingled with its passage.

"Stay there," he said. He left, and she heard him in his room, opening a drawer. As he came back, she saw he carried the canvas belt he'd worn with the camo pants yesterday. Leaning over her, he held out a hand, palm up. She laid hers in it, mystified by the almost courtly gesture. He waited, and she realized he wanted both her hands. When she complied, he wrapped the belt around her wrists, threading the end through the rings. He pressed her arms up above her head, looping the end on her headboard, cinching it so her arms were lifted even farther, her elbows by her temples. She forgot how to breathe, especially when he sat a hip on the edge of the bed and continued to stare at her.

"You're trembling," he said. "Are you afraid?"

"In a way." She moistened her lips. "The good way."

"It's kind of Geoff's thing."

"Is it your thing?" She didn't want him doing things in imitation of Geoff, thinking that was what he had to do to please her. But his thoughtful expression and response reduced her concerns.

"Don't know. Think I have some of it inside me, because I sure like how you're shaking. Maybe it's how you respond to it that works for me. When you took off your clothes because I told you to do it, it twisted something hard inside me. Bringing me water and ice to clean me up because you wanted to do it, wanted to care for me like that, opened up something inside me, too. In a good way."

As he handed her words back to her, his fingertips slid down her abdomen, played with the tiny pewter bear in her navel piercing. "I almost didn't give you this," he continued. The sexy timbre of his voice, the manner in which his eyes kept coursing over her bound and stretched body, were playing havoc on her senses. She was restless, hot, needy, even though she'd just climaxed. She also wanted to cling to every word he spoke.

"I thought it might be too sexual and intimate," he said. "But you were so pleased with it. You took off the one you were wearing right away and put this one on. When you were playing with it, stroking your skin, holding the hem of your shirt up, your jeans low on your hips, you gave me a hard-on that took half a day to get down. I about blacked out, I jerked off so hard in my room that night."

Her breath was erratic, noticeable in the quiet of the room. "I wish my hearing were as good as yours. I would have snuck into your room and watched you." She couldn't speak over a whisper.

"I'll bet." He smiled wryly. It was the kind of expression that made her see his vulnerability and strength both, because with Chris one was inseparable from the other. Then the strength took over, his gaze shifting to hers, mouth firming. "I don't want you to talk for the next bit. Just feel, okay? I want you to feel what I'm feeling."

She nodded, her fingers curling in the belt. Moving back down to her feet, he placed his mouth there. A surfeit of emotion filled her as his hand forged a path ahead of his mouth, exploring her skin as if he was discovering a woman for the first time. The ceiling fan turned, moving currents of warm air over her, his heated mouth adding to the sensation. He worked his way up over her knee, to her thigh. His hands slipped under it and her calf, and he adjusted her leg outward.

When he lifted his head, met her gaze, she understood what he wanted. She shifted the other leg so they were spread equally, and the shivering came back. Geoff could say *Spread your legs* and make her cream instantly. Whereas when a look from Chris demanded the same thing, her reaction was just as intense.

A strangled moan came from her as he bent and pressed his lips against her cunt. Not teasing or licking. He tasted her as an explorer would, learning her body, the secrets it held. Secrets she didn't even know, because her reaction now was new to her as well. He lifted his head again, lips pressed together and moving, obviously savoring her taste.

"You look so aroused and hungry, so hot. I want to make you come over and over, even as I want to keep you just this way, because it makes me so fucking crazy to see you like this. All tied up, waiting for me. Maybe Geoff isn't the only one who likes that."

That seemed to bemuse him. She thought she might start whining if he didn't go back to kissing her again. Fortunately, he obliged her before she embarrassed herself. He spread kisses over her hipbones, over ticklish spots that made her squirm and him chuckle. He traced the curves of her breasts with his tongue, played over the nipples until she was lifting off the bed toward him. Then he moved to her neck.

"Turn your cheek to the pillow and keep it there."

She did, and he spent endless moments kissing her throat, setting his teeth to the delicate combination of tendons, veins and muscles there. Nuzzling beneath her ear, he kissed the tender spot between her collarbones. Cupping her face, he turned the opposite cheek toward the pillow and did the same to the other side of her neck.

As he broke her mind into fragments with that, he slid his other hand up her arm and clasped both her wrists, digging his fingers into the belt and reinforcing the bond holding her. Her legs were still spread as he'd left them, and her tied state tilted her breasts up. Everything about her position suggested a desire to be taken, but Chris wasn't a man who let himself be rushed. She'd never been so frustrated and aroused at once.

"Please . . . Chris."

As he lifted his head, inches between their faces, her gaze latched on his mouth, wet from kissing her, from tasting her pussy. "Please, what, Sam?"

"I need you."

"How?" At her discomfiture, he closed his fingers around her jaw. Though he didn't hurt her, he made sure she felt the strength in his grip. She couldn't move her face at all.

"I don't consider them dirty words, Sam. There's nothing pure and real as the earth. Damp, rich soil tumbling between my fingers always reminds me of a woman's cunt. I want to bury myself in yours, Sam, but I want to hear you say that's what you want as well. I want to hear it come from your mouth. What do you want me to do to you?"

"I want . . . you inside me. Fuck me. Make me yours. Please. I think I'll die if you don't do that, right now." Yes, it was ridiculously dramatic, but every throbbing cell wanted her to be dramatic, over-the-top. No room for misinterpretation.

He stood, opened his pants and pushed them off his hips. Her gaze slid down the heavy layers of muscle. Chris had the burly bulk of a deep-sea fisherman, a construction worker, a bricklayer. Muscle layered tight and hard on large bones was molded by firm, tanned flesh. She'd seen him shirtless and in shorts in the summer, but it was the first time she'd had the gift of seeing him naked and aroused.

The skin below his hips was lighter. His cock matched his size. It was thick and curved up against his belly, the tip glistening with more fluid. His testicles were a heavy sac against the cradle of his thighs, and bore a light layer of fur, like the rest of him. He was a sexy male animal, one with liquid brown eyes that bore the colors of flame and earth and a young man's lust, powerful enough to fill her with a thrilling fear.

Not a fear that he would hurt her, not that way, but that he would take what he wanted, fuck her beyond exhaustion into euphoria, her link to him the only way to come out on the other side without losing herself. But she'd willingly cut herself loose inside that euphoria, willing to trust everything she knew and loved about him.

"Chris," she repeated. "I need you."

He put his knee between her legs, paused, then slid back off the bed, bending to search in the pocket of his pants. Apparently the belt wasn't the only thing he'd retrieved from his room.

"If you haven't . . . in a while, you won't need that."

She knew she should probably let him wear it to avoid disrupting this with a revelation of a meaningless, or not-so-meaningless, hookup he might have had. But the words were out before she could take them back.

In the semidarkness of the room, the morning light filtering through her blinds, his face was shadowed, though his eyes found hers and pierced deep. "You know," he said with deceptive mildness, "the last time you had a date, Geoff and I played a drinking game where we had to come up with last-letter insults about the guy."

She blinked. In her aroused state, it was hard to switch gears, to follow his meaning and how it connected to this. "What?"

"If I said he had a little dick, Geoff had to come up with the next insult starting with the letter *k*. If he couldn't come up with something we both agreed wasn't lame, he had to drink. And vice versa."

She coughed over a half chuckle. "Bet it was hard to beat him. He has a pretty extensive vocabulary."

"But I work around contractors all day." Chris's teeth flashed. He deliberately set the condom down on the nightstand and gazed down at her. "Do you remember who that guy was?"

She stared up at him. "I don't even remember his name."

"We do. John Howard. We remember every one of them."

She swallowed. "Who won the drinking game?"

Meditatively, he slid his fingers over her breast as he stood there, naked and erect, less than a foot from her. She gasped as he shifted his grip back to her throat, his hold strong enough to push her jaw up, make her look into his suddenly impassive face, his mouth set in a line.

"I drank him under the table," he said. "Geoff's more civilized than I am, sometimes. I'm just now realizing that."

Her eyes fluttered closed as he bent and put his mouth over hers. His touch on her legs, her breasts, her cunt and her stomach had been questing, sensual. This started that way, but his fingers tightened further, stealing her breath as he parted her lips and invaded, tongue tangling around hers. She whimpered into his mouth, and he growled in answer, shifting so his knee was between her legs and then all of him was, his other hand sliding beneath her buttock to lift her as his cock found her wet entrance.

He didn't thrust into her like a jackhammer. Chris might be less civilized, but he wasn't a beast, and she'd never felt anything from him but care for every cell of her being. Even now, when it was clear he'd shifted from explorer to conqueror, he pushed into her slowly, stretching her, giving her the chance to work her hips over him, help them find their way to the right fit. Yet the moment it was evident they'd achieved that, he took the last several inches with determination, purpose and an impact that told her he was putting his claim right there with Geoff's.

Make her ours. The words resounded in her head as she emitted a little cry against his lips. She turned her face into his hand as he tunneled his fingers through her hair, palm against the side of her face. She set her teeth to the heel of his callused hand as he began to work her, hips rising and falling, her own lifting to his. Her body caught fire instantly, because he'd already brought her up to the point where she couldn't control a single response. He had all the control.

"Chris . . ."

"Scream for me again, Sam. Scream for us. You know he's listening."

She had no choice. The shriek wrenched from her throat as the orgasm hit her like a lightning strike, jolting her body against the power and weight of his. He was able to pin her down, increase the intensity, keep her shooting toward the moon as his thrusts intensified. His face was tight, eyes locked on hers, watching her lose herself in what he could do to her. He gave her the same pleasure, because as her cries escalated, he shot over that edge with her, his seed jetting into her, her legs locked over his pumping muscular ass, her body open and straining to give him every ounce of ecstasy he was giving her. They rode that ride well past the climax, both wanting to milk every ounce of sensation out of it, such that when they came to a stop, they were both breathing heavily.

She pulled against her bonds. "Chris . . . I want to hold you. Please. Don't move yet."

"I'm too heavy." But he stayed where he was and loosened the belt from her wrists, letting her slide free. Her hands immediately found his broad shoulders, the sides of his throat as she stared up at him.

"Please . . . let me hold you. Just for a minute. Please. I've wanted to, for a really long time."

"Ah, Sam." Blowing out a breath, he put his forehead on hers and curled his arms around her as she wrapped hers over his back. They'd done it. Made the first steps. The problem would be where and how to go from here. Sex was the least of it, she was sure. But as he let himself rest on her, that didn't matter. This was everything.

She ran her fingertips down the valley of his spine and out into the corrugations of muscle, up to his nape and the dark hair that curled over her knuckles. With as much time as he spent in the sun, his hair should have been coarse, but it was always thick and silky, burnished like it had captured sunlight in the brown strands.

Though he was softening, she still felt enough of his presence inside her that she could constrict her internal muscles on him, earn another push from his hips as he responded to the aftereffect, a ripple that went through them both.

"That's enough. I'm going to crush you." He withdrew, but he kept her securely in his arms as he rolled. She shifted to his side so she could lie on her hip and prop herself on her elbow. Indulging herself, she ran her fingers through the hair on his chest, teased his nipples, moving down to his navel and skating through the trimmed hair at his cock. It surprised her that he groomed himself there, rather than letting his pubic hair be an unruly, bushy tangle, but maybe that was Geoff's influence. There was no telling what men did or didn't talk about.

Her fingertips grazed the damp head of his cock, the folds along the shaft as it returned to its resting state. She moved onward to the crease between thigh and hip and back up his side. It was easy and natural to touch him. While he'd proven irrefutably he did have some topping qualities, he didn't have that clear Dom vibe Geoff had that would have made her hesitate to touch him without permission.

"You're so different, yet some things are the same," she murmured.

"They always are. No matter what most guys claim."

She smiled at the drawled response that hadn't come from Chris. Lifting her attention to the doorway, she met Geoff's gaze. He was leaning against the frame. Her heart thudded at the look in his eyes. How long had he been standing there? Had he watched the flex of Chris's body as he thrust into her? He hadn't been there when Chris restrained her hands, because she'd been able to see the door at that point. Maybe he'd given Chris *quid pro quo* by making this first time a private moment, as it had been for her and Geoff.

Yet it wasn't a surprise to see him there now. What held her motionless was how his gaze moved over both of them. Thoroughly and possessively. His attention lighted on her thighs and breasts, her expression, the hand she had on Chris's chest. He moved from there to a perusal of Chris's big body, to the relaxed thighs and genitalia between them. Despite the intensity of the climax she'd just experienced, additional sensation pulsed between her legs when she saw no abatement in desire as Geoff's focus shifted between her and Chris. She'd told Madison, the owner of Naughty Bits, that she thought Geoff wanted to top them both, but she hadn't been sure. Seeing the look in his eyes now, she was.

While Geoff was more sexually experienced, she didn't think he was any more experienced when it came to relationships than Chris was. Neither of them gave their heart lightly. She had a private theory that the reason they'd never had a meaningful romantic relationship outside the bounds of their friendship was because that friendship had always been stronger than the pull of anyone else. Until now.

She wouldn't have pursued this if she hadn't been sure they both felt more than friendship for her, so that revelation wasn't ego driven. If anything, it summoned uneasiness. The direction this could take might be miraculous or catastrophic. But it was too late to turn back now. She thought of what Flo, her friend, coworker and a Mistress, had asked her when she'd gone after Geoff so aggressively.

"Can you live with it staying how it is? The three of you just 'friends' who are fantasizing about one another but not doing anything about it?"

No, she couldn't. She'd decided she couldn't let friendship be the door that kept her heart's desires shut away.

However, if this didn't turn out as she hoped, she vowed she'd do whatever was necessary to make sure Geoff and Chris could still be friends when it was over. Even if she lost them both over this, she couldn't bear the guilt of them losing each other for the same reason.

"Sam, can you call in a personal day?" Geoff asked, pulling her back into the here and now.

Chris was stroking his hand along her back, teasing her snarled hair. It had been damp when he'd brought her in here, so it was likely a mess now. She'd have to wet it back down to get it to behave, but with his fingers combing through the strands, she didn't want to move away from that touch anytime in the next century. When Geoff spoke, Chris didn't stop, telling her he'd been aware of the other man's presence. But looking into Chris's face, she did see a slight tension, an anticipatory awareness. Was he thinking about Geoff standing there, staring at them both, at Chris sprawled out naked and replete? Chris was gazing absently at the ceiling, though, as if he wasn't yet ready to acknowledge what a Dom standing in the doorway looking at them like candy might mean.

"Yes, I think I could take a personal day." She brought herself back to the question with effort. "Do you have the day off?" She realized he'd showered and changed into one of her favorite pair of jeans on him, stressed and clinging in the right places. His Nike T-shirt stretched over his shoulders.

"I can shuffle some things. Chris, you're off today, right?"

"Yeah. Esteban said not to worry about showing up until tomorrow morning." Chris wound his fingers around Sam's hair, lifting himself up as he spoke. She closed her eyes as he nudged beneath her chin and put his mouth on her throat to tease her with tongue and lips. Her hand fell to his biceps to grip. She needed the anchor, because when his other hand slid over her hip to curve over her ass, the ground just fell away. Chris was kissing her body, her naked body, while Geoff watched. For all she'd fantasized about being with them like this, the reality was overwhelming.

"She's all I want to do today," Chris said against her flesh. "Come taste her, Geoff. She gets sweeter with every lick."

Geoff circled to the other side of the bed. Sam let out a shuddering sigh as he stretched out behind her, his hand molding over her thigh as he dropped a kiss on her shoulder, her upper arm. The soft material of his shirt brushed her shoulder blades as he straightened, and the firm heat of his chest beneath pressed against her. When he slid his fingers over her thigh and down between her legs, dipping into the mix of fluids she and Chris had left there, she dropped her head back on his shoulder, giving Chris better access to her throat. He moved lower, closing his mouth over one nipple and the flesh around it, pulling on her in a warm, swirling way.

She was in her bed, with Geoff and Chris. With both of them. It was like waking up in Willy Wonka's chocolate factory and getting a private tour, surreal and delicious, every moment too freaking precious to waste.

Geoff lifted his hand from her pussy and curved his long fingers over Chris's shoulder and neck, fingertips burying in his friend's dark hair as Chris suckled her.

Chris's big body tightened, and he drew back slowly. Not jerking away from Geoff's touch exactly, but making it clear that was an intimacy he wasn't prepared to accept. She couldn't read what was in his expression, but it brought the clock to a sudden halt as the two men considered each other over her. She put her hand on Chris's chest, her other on Geoff's thigh behind hers, fingers constricting on them as if the physical act could prevent a mental withdrawal. Chris put his hand over hers and caressed her fingers, while Geoff lifted her other hand off his leg, bringing it to his mouth to kiss. Yet when she glanced up, she saw he was still studying Chris with speculation in his sharp gaze. In this light, the hazel color was muted gold. His eye color seemed to change like his moods.

"I was thinking we could go back to Naughty Bits today," he said abruptly. "It's time to buy some things. Things she'd like. We could get some lunch while we're out. Go to Reedy Creek Park. You know Sam likes watching the dogs in the dog park. As nice as it would be to stay in bed all day"—his lips curved—"we need to work some things out. Right?"

Between work and schedule conflicts, it had been a while since they'd been able to spend most of a day together. Because of that, Sam would have been excited about the prospect, even if everything that had happened in the past couple of days hadn't happened. But knowing it had, knowing she'd had both men inside her and it was more likely than not to happen again, made the idea of a day with the two of them even more wonderful.

"All right." Chris glanced down at her. "That work for you?"

"Okay," she said, but she held on to them an extra moment. She wanted to ask them for promises, promises that if this didn't work, it wouldn't change things between the three of them, but that was a child's wish. "Okay," she said, and scrambled out from between them before they anticipated her. She hopped off the end of the bed and bounced on the balls of her feet, giving them both a radiant smile. "We could pick up sandwiches from Jersey Mike's and have a picnic. I'll bring a ball to the dog park area for Chris to chase."

"I see something I'd rather chase," Chris said, with a lazy look. "Do that bouncy thing again."

She hadn't thought about the intriguing side effect of her exuberance. She almost blushed, then instead decided to embrace the moment. Linking her hands behind her back and assuming an expression of feigned innocence, she rocked left and right, amusing herself by watching both men's eyes follow the movement. "You're like one of those cat or owl clocks," she teased them. "What is it about breasts?"

"It's where we start as babies," Geoff informed her. "And we never get over the attachment. Now quit being a tease. Or we'll each take a turn at spanking you."

Seeing the flicker in Chris's eyes, she remembered how he said he wasn't built that way, at least not using something as extreme as a switch cut from a branch in the yard. But spanking . . . She didn't necessarily see rejection in his eyes, and anticipation spiraled through her.

"Christ. Go get dressed," Geoff ordered.

As she moved toward the door with a grin, she saw Chris rolling off one side of the bed and Geoff rising from the other. "Sam."

She turned to meet Geoff's now sober expression. "I meant what I said earlier. From here forward, if you want to get off with your vibrator, you bring it to me and ask. Or you ask Chris, if I'm not here. If neither of us is here, you wait." He glanced toward Chris. "Agreed?"

A delicate power play. Geoff had taken the lead, as he naturally did. However, he'd acknowledged the unresolved nature of what his and Chris's relationship was in all of this, by asking for accord on how the two of them would top her. While all the possibilities of such a dynamic could make her light-headed, it brought tension as well. Until that element was resolved between them, it was going to be a sensitive area. But it wasn't going to be solved in a day. She'd do better to immerse herself in watching it happen than worrying about it crashing and burning.

Chris had pulled on his pants, leaving them unhooked at the waist. He didn't answer Geoff right away, instead looking toward her. She could almost see him considering all the angles of it, and wondered if he was imagining watching her use her vibrator to climax again. The sparks in his eyes sent another rocket launch effect through her brain.

A draft from the hallway made her shiver, and the men shifted gears. As quickly as they could arouse her libido, they could melt her heart just as quickly with their care for her. Geoff picked Chris's T-shirt off the bed almost at the same moment Chris reached for it. Geoff passed it to him with a neutral nod and Chris brought it to her, sliding it over her head and letting it fall down over her body.

"Agreed," he said. A glance up into his brown eyes, kindling with a heart-stopping heat, told her he was answering Geoff's question.

"Sam?" Geoff drew her attention to him. "Do you understand?"

"Yes sir." Calling him that was automatic when he used that tone. Chris's expression shuttered, holding so much she didn't yet understand. She could only hope it meant good things.

"I'll go finish up in the bathroom so you can get showered and dressed, too," she told Chris. Then she dashed off, leaving the two men alone in her room.

It was both lovely and bemusing, how the relaxed banter among the three of them while they prepared for their outing was the same as it always was. What was different was that the sexual undercurrent that had vibrated below the surface for so long was now right up top.

Geoff's hand slid along her lower back and lingered on her buttock as he moved past her in the kitchen. When he reached over her head to pull down a cup, Chris sandwiched her playfully against the counter, but then wound his arm around her waist so he could kiss her throat before he released her.

When Geoff put on the TV news and started getting worked up over the politics as usual, Sam gave Chris a subtle look and he snapped it off before Geoff could get too far along. Geoff of course complained, and Chris pointed at her as the guilty party. A moment later, she yelped when Geoff pinched her ass, hard, as he put his coffee cup in the dishwasher. Chris, packing up the cooler with drinks and snacks, followed up Geoff's punitive measure by leaning over to give the offended cheek a soothing pat.

"If he gets too mean, you let me know and I'll beat him up."

"You can try," Geoff said dryly. He'd parked himself on a stool at the counter and eyed the man in challenge. Chris shrugged with another hard-to-read look, and then disappeared down the hall to retrieve something else from his room.

She watched him go. Geoff was so in charge, she didn't worry as much about what he might be thinking and feeling, but it was second nature for her to worry about Chris, because he could be so quiet about his feelings. She didn't think he could be pushed into doing things he didn't want to do, but his comment made her wonder if he really thought Geoff was being mean to her. Maybe she should . . .

She jumped as Geoff cinched an arm around her from behind, drawing her back against him with a decided thump. She hadn't even heard him move. "Stop worrying, Sam. He'll work it out. Just give him space. I swear, you're like a terrier."

"Did you bring a ball to throw for me at the dog park too?" she asked tartly.

"No, but a collar might not be amiss."

She had a rude response for that, but she couldn't hold on to it because her mind was invaded by the thought of Geoff putting a slender collar on her throat. She thought of how Chris had gripped her there. At Naughty Bits, there'd been a wealth of collars . . . What would Chris think of that? Or Geoff?

Geoff tipped up her chin and locked gazes with her. "Sam, I'm going to make this easy for you. I'm not asking you, I'm telling you. Leave it alone. Just because he isn't as up front about it as I am, doesn't mean that it's okay to push. Respect him. You understand?"

"I do respect him. I—"

"Not what I meant, and you know it."

Chris returned and Geoff broke off the conversation. As they finished their preparations, Sam considered his words. Geoff had put both of them over the "vibrator permission" clause, sending a not-so-subtle message that Geoff viewed both of them as her tops. He was telling her to trust them, and to let go. Let them take the lead on this.

There were plenty of things she did better than either of them, and they deferred to her lead on that. She was a better driver, Geoff too much of a road rage troll and Chris too absentminded to pay attention to things like stoplights or when he was meandering along at fifteen miles below the speed limit merely because he was enjoying a sunny day. She had a better head for numbers, so she tracked the house expenses for all three of them, and she'd prepared all their tax returns.

But the subtle things on which she deferred to them were significant. It was hard to quantify them in a manner anyone else would understand. She'd automatically bring Geoff a cup of coffee when it was empty at his elbow, or give each of them her full attention if either man was speaking to her, listening carefully to what it was they were trying to tell her so she'd know the best response to please or help, because that was what gave her joy.

If she was napping on the couch and one of them came home, she'd start to get up, even if they hadn't asked her to do anything. Interestingly, the men responded in similar ways to that ritual. A touch on her shoulder, a murmured command for her to stay where she was, that they were fine, that they didn't need anything right now.

On the surface they were supposed to be three roommates, equals sharing household chores and conducting separate lives, so there was no reason she needed to get up and do anything for them. Yet she hadn't ever questioned why they said it that way, any more than she challenged her compulsion to try to get up. Both responses complemented her nature.

She doubted Geoff had ever questioned it, either, for the same reason, but maybe Chris wasn't aware of it. Which meant both of them might be responding to her in an intuitive way, playing on her nature as well as respecting their own, even if it might be unconscious.

"I like to watch you sleep," Chris had told her one time when she'd

woken that way. He'd then sat down in a chair to do just that. Though it should have made her self-conscious, it hadn't. She'd fallen asleep under his gaze. *"I want you to rest,"* Geoff had told her another time. *"Taking care of the whole universe is hard work."* He'd tugged her hair and gone to the table to work, but she'd sensed his eyes on her while she dozed.

She did defer to them in subtle ways that Geoff understood and she couldn't deny. So she'd listen to him. At least for today.

It was about a thirty-minute drive to Naughty Bits. They took Sam's car, Chris in the passenger seat, Geoff's handsome face in her rearview mirror as he tied up some loose ends at the office on his tablet. Chris fiddled with the radio, she and Geoff giving their usual opinions of the different musical selections. With matching groans, the guys vetoed the Taylor Swift song she wanted to hear, but Chris left it on that channel until the finish while she sang along. When it was over, he flipped it forward and found "Take It Easy" by the Little River Band. Chris cranked it up and they both sang along. Geoff tapped his fingers, accompanying the beat, though he had a frown line between his eyes as he read his email.

Seeing it, Chris shot her a look. Sam nodded. He reached in the back and copped the tablet, fending off Geoff's attempts to get it back with a patient look as he held him at bay with one long arm. "Asshole," Geoff said. "All right, I'll shut it down. Just let me finish that one email."

Chris grinned at her and handed it back. "We're timing you," Sam said. "One minute."

"Yeah, yeah."

Chris stayed half-turned in the seat, keeping an eye on Geoff, though Geoff shot him a look. "Do that again, I'll break off a few fingers."

"Big talk." Chris yawned. He had his hand propped against the seat, but now dropped it onto Sam's thigh. When she shot a quick look his way, she found Chris studying her profile, that scrutiny increasing as he slid his hand up her thigh to the hem of her knit shirt, tunneling under it to trace her side and abdomen. He insinuated a finger into the waistband of her jeans, finding the band of her panties. He traced that, caressing her hipbone. While she could focus on her driving safely enough, his attention was undeniably diverting.

Removing his touch from her jeans, he lifted his hand to her shoulder, one knuckle following the line of her throat. "Your pulse is jumping," he noted. He played with the dip at her collarbone and teased her bra strap, finding it beneath the shirt. When he twisted a finger in the strap so the cup tightened over her breast, her hands flexed on the wheel. The stoplight ahead went to yellow, and she pressed the brake, her Honda and the cars ahead of her coming to a stop on red.

"Geoff," Chris said. "Tell us when the light changes."

It was a busy intersection where there was a full round of light changes for protected left turns and through traffic. Sam didn't hear Geoff's reply. Maybe he'd looked up, realized why Chris had made the request and given him a silent acknowledgment. Or maybe the thundering response in her ears had masked his answer. Chris cupped his hand under the back of her neck, pulling her toward him as much as the belt allowed so he could crush his mouth over hers. Sam let out a whimper of pure delight as he parted her lips and dove, his tongue taking hers over, his lips teasing and caressing her mouth, nipping, sucking on her lips, then rubbing them in a sensual give-and-take.

His heated palm moved up her thigh to the crease between leg and hip, so close to her core the pad of his thumb was pressing against her outer labia through denim. It sent a flash of sensation through her. His grip on the back of her head tightened, holding her steady as he kept kissing her. He bit her lip, then moved to her throat, right behind her ear. When his teeth clamped there, his lips sucking hard, she realized he was intending to leave a mark.

"It's about to change," Geoff said. He was leaning forward and to her left, for his breath stroked over her other ear, her neck.

Chris broke the kiss. Sunlight turned his brown eyes to bright copper. His mouth was wet from hers. She could feel the faint tingle of the abraded skin at her throat.

Muffled sounds penetrated her window glass, causing Chris to look past her. He grinned. Turning her head, she saw a group of college girls were in the car next to them, and they were giving thumbs-ups and clapping. One of them had scribbled "10" on a pad of paper and was holding it up.

She thought the rating was a little low. "Go," Geoff said, chuckling. "Light's green, sweetheart."

She cleared her throat and accelerated when the car in front of her did. Chris went back to tuning the radio. She stole quick glances at him, the silken fall of dark hair over his brow, the shape of his mouth, which he'd just had on her. When she looked in the rearview mirror, Geoff had stretched his arms out over the back of the seat, the tablet put away as he watched them both with his multicolored gaze. Now the forest green of his eyes had a blue tinge when the sunlight flickered across the back.

"I'll have my loans paid off by the end of the year," he said conversationally. "I thought I might keep working for Payne & Greenway for about six more months to bank up some cash and then look at some other possibilities."

"Really?" Chris met her surprised gaze, then looked back at him. "What possibilities?"

Geoff shrugged. "When I got out of school, Patricia Levine told me they could use me in the DA's office. I've been thinking about it. The hours would be less, fifty or sixty a week as the norm versus eighty to a hundred, and it would be more along the lines of what I want to do with my degree. There'd be a certain amount of bullshit, but there is in anything. I probably wouldn't get rich unless I hit politics and decided to try for the DA job. Or I could become a public defender."

"You don't care about getting rich. Plus, just watching the news makes you want to shoot people. I'm thinking politics isn't your field." Chris stopped on a station playing a Bruno Mars and Mark Ronson song. He shot his friend a grin. "You don't want a job, you want a life."

"Yeah, Bruno and Mark don't seem to realize one is pretty much dependent on the other," Geoff said dryly.

"I think you should do it," Sam said. "I think you'd be happier. You're getting sick of helping businesses fight one another over minutiae that doesn't mean a thing."

Geoff pursed his lips. "You'd probably end up being the top breadwinner in the house. Especially when they promote you to manager, which they will. Of course, Chris spends so little beyond bills, he's probably already a millionaire."

"I'm planning on getting a diamond-encrusted bulldog hood ornament for my truck any day now." Chris glanced at Sam. "Though my financial manager is insisting I contribute that amount to the Roth IRA she set up for me instead."

"Long term financial planning is important," Sam said primly.

They pulled into the parking space in front of Naughty Bits a few minutes later. Though Chris was joking with Geoff and tossing her comments, when his gaze met hers, it was as if all that died away. She saw his lips moving, Geoff's lips moving, knew the world was turning around her how it always did, but she was still caught up in Chris's embrace, back at the traffic light. While it had been casually executed, there was nothing else casual about it.

Meeting Geoff's gaze in the mirror, she also saw his full awareness of just how much it had stirred her up. It planted a pleasant anxiety in her, because she suspected he was considering ways to stir her up further. Apparently her arousal could set off a chain reaction between both men. Since she wanted to do all sorts of things for them as well, she wasn't at all immune to the same effect. She could foresee it becoming a circular thing, like a spiral of sexual anticipation that could be reset again and again.

As they left the car and headed for the entrance to Naughty Bits, Chris held the door for her, Geoff and him filing in behind her as Madison greeted them. Today she was wearing an open tunic printed with cherry blossoms over a formfitting black body suit. A belt made up of links that looked like handcuffs rode low on her hips. She had her long brown hair twisted up on her head.

"It's great to see the three of you again." She covered the mouth of her store phone. "I'm handling a problem with a shipping company, my apologies, but go ahead and wander around. Get yourself a cup of coffee and a scone from the Dungeon Room. I'll be off in just a few minutes."

The first time they'd come here together, the two men had stuck close to Sam, demonstrating typical male wariness of a lingerie store, but Madison had helped alleviate that. She'd drawn Geoff over to the Dungeon Room selections and left Sam and Chris to examine role-playing choices and lingerie. Sam wasn't sure how they'd behave this time, but she received an answer quickly enough. Geoff moved straight toward the Dungeon Room and Chris to the wall of lingerie and open display jewelry offerings, as if both men had specific ideas in mind.

Wow. Well, then.

For perhaps the first time, she let herself believe how thrilling it might be to wait and see where their minds were taking them. She could let them control their direction.

She knew what she wanted to look at, but she drifted in that direction instead of making a beeline there, though she was unsure why she was self-conscious about it. Functional collars, black straps in varying thicknesses and embedded with D-rings for attachments, were hung on the wall. More expensive ones were under glass. She saw choker-style necklaces in pewter or with rhinestones, iron bands with pin locking mechanisms, and delicate braids of silver and gold. She studied one that looked like a buckled collar. Instead of leather or fabric, it was stainless steel, a silver circlet.

"That one would look beautiful on you. And I'm betting it's the right size, though it can be custom ordered." Madison had finished her call. Moving to the opposite side of the display, she unlocked the back of the cabinet and put her hand on the piece. Sam shook her head.

"I can't afford it. Not even close."

"That's why it's fun to put it on. Just promise me you won't make a dash for the door." Madison winked and held out a foot encased in a strappy heel. "I didn't wear my chase-down-shoplifter shoes today."

Sam chuckled, but before she could tell Madison not to do so, she'd moved back around the case with the silver band. Madison took her hand in her friendly shopkeeper way and drew her over to the mirror. "Here we go. I'll just slide your hair over this way so I don't snag it. You have such beautiful hair."

"It's too fine and straight."

"Perfect for Southern humidity. Yours looks lovely and silky all the time, whereas us thick-haired folk look like we stuck our fingers in a light socket and made it worse by dragging ourselves backward through a hedge." Madison fitted the collar around her throat, keeping her fingers beneath the hinge so it couldn't pinch Sam's skin as she hooked the decorative buckle in the front. "You fit the peg into the buckle to hold it. This one is actually a very good fit on you. You have a swan's neck."

A finger's width could still get beneath, but it was snug enough that things quieted inside Sam, the effect of its hold. She imagined Geoff or Chris putting it on her when they wanted her to go into full submissive mode, so they could explore their desires for her, together or separately. She was fine with both scenarios, as long as it wasn't an either or proposition. Each man had proven capable of immersing her in pleasure, but when the three of them had been on her bed, her in between them, she knew she would never be content with separate only.

Chris's reaction to Geoff's touch made it a grim possibility, yet she also remembered Chris was the one who'd invited Geoff to come taste her with him.

"So how is it going?" Madison asked in a low voice. The just-between-us-girls tone told her what she meant. Sam had opened up to Madison first about her secret desires for both her roommates, and Madison was giving her the opening if she needed more help and guidance.

"A work in process. But progress has been made."

"Looks like it." Madison glanced over her shoulder. "They didn't even go for the food and coffee first."

"I'm sure you'll be light a few scones before we leave." Sam chuckled. She looked at herself in the mirror, putting her hand up to touch the collar, slide her fingers along it. She thought about either man touching it, tugging so she felt its hold even more keenly. She knew she'd love that, just from how she'd reacted to Geoff or Chris gripping her throat.

As Geoff appeared behind her, Madison stepped discreetly out of range.

"What do you think?" Sam asked, a little nervous. The man had too good of a poker face, giving nothing away. Chris had been looking over a selection of electronic toys, but now he joined them, standing at her other side, the two of them studying the collar and her.

"Madison had me try it on," she said, realizing Chris might think Geoff had put it there, and finding herself worried that might bother him. "Geoff?"

"I'm thinking about it." His gaze stayed on the circlet. She had a little trouble breathing when he was studying her with that weird detachment that wasn't detached at all. Like being surrounded by a ring of fire while a sex demon stood just on the outside, considering his plans for her. "Chris found something for you," he added absently.

She saw a sparkle before Chris closed his fingers over the bauble. "No. It's nothing."

"What do you have?"

He shook his head, but she turned toward him, her shoulder pressing into Geoff's chest so she could lean there. Between them like this, she could feel their merged heat on her skin and was glad neither moved back. Capturing Chris's hand, she pried open his fingers. If he'd really not wanted her to see it he could have simply held it over her head or retreated, but he let her see. Her heart tilted. "It's lovely."

It was a ring, the design a little cat whose twirling whiskers and tail made up the silver wire band. The eyes winked with rhinestones like her pewter bear navel jewelry.

"You're always talking about getting a cat," Chris said.

"Hmm." Geoff's eyes twinkled as he drew their attention to the designer tag. "My Sweet Pussy Designs."

Sam giggled. "Well, it's appropriate." She stuck out her hand. "Will you put it on me, Chris?"

Chris slipped it on her ring finger. It was too big for that, so he switched it to her middle finger and she flexed her hand in the grip of his, letting the sparkling eyes catch the light. "I love it. And this I can probably afford."

Chris slid his hands into his jeans pockets. Today he'd worn one of his few pairs, the fabric dark blue and snug in the right way. "I'm buying it for you, so yeah."

From the beginning, they'd agreed that everyone would pay their fair share of everything. She'd insisted, already feeling the two men were doing more than their part, giving her a safe place to live. When they'd come to Charlotte, her resolve to enforce that policy was even more emphatic, because having to find a place with private spaces for three single adults meant they had to have a three-bedroom place instead of two, a considerable jump in rent rates.

Chris had chivalrously told her he was the one who'd tipped up the rent, because he'd wanted a rental house with a yard. Geoff had suggested in that case they could have bought a big doghouse and a hammock for Chris and stayed with a two-bedroom.

Birthdays and Christmas gifts had a set budget. Over time, as her salary increased and Geoff paid off more of his loans, she knew they could splurge on bigger gifts, but she liked keeping it within a range. The ceiling on what they could spend meant creativity, not ostentation, drove the purchase decisions.

This wasn't Christmas or a birthday. It was a special occasion, for certain, but she didn't know if she wanted to view it that way, because that might mean treating it like a holiday, here then gone for another year. But as she parted her lips to speak, Chris closed his hand over hers. "I'm buying it. No arguments, Sam. This doesn't fall under the budget stuff."

It was a prime example of what she'd been trying to puzzle out in her mind earlier, how to explain what each man did and how he did it to incite this sudden stillness in her. A stillness that focused all her attention on him, on what he wanted or needed. It was as if there was a crackling energy between her and the man speaking that held her entranced, made her feel wild and reckless and docile and quiet, all at the same time.

"Okay," she said, and realized her voice had cracked. She cleared her throat, but they weren't done pushing her off balance. Geoff took her other hand.

"What did you mean, Sam? About the name of the company being appropriate?"

This was why she shouldn't say the first thing that popped in her head. She didn't usually, not around anyone else other than these two. Color rose in her cheeks. "Um . . . it didn't mean . . . I wasn't thinking. It was silly. Nothing."

"She's such an awful liar," Chris observed.

"The worst," Geoff agreed. "Spit it out. You're only going to be more embarrassed if you wait until Madison comes back and you have to say it in front of her."

"You wouldn't . . ." She trailed off at his arched brow and piercing look. He surely would. He'd enjoyed her initial discomfiture when he'd brought the vibrator into the bathroom. She'd responded enough to that that she knew certain types of erotic humiliation pushed some of her own buttons. Proof of how much she'd be willing to submit to him, given time and trust. Scary but titillating.

"Because My Sweet Pussy . . . well, I'm yours. Both of yours. Including that part of me." She was going to turn scarlet and match the lace-trimmed teddy she saw hanging on a rack behind them.

Geoff leaned in, brushed his lips across her cheek and spoke against it. "So you're telling us your cunt belongs to us both. No one else? Not John Howard, or Mark in Records?"

Chris's nostrils flared, his eyes getting a caveman glint in them that should dismay her, not thrill her like she'd been handed a lit sparkler at a July Fourth celebration. "Who the hell is Mark in Records?" he demanded.

"No one. And yes," she said hastily. "To no one else."

Geoff had implied part of today's outing was going to be about pulling back, talking things out. Maybe they shouldn't have scheduled a stop at Naughty Bits first, because Sam was having a hard time imagining that she could settle down and have a rational conversation after they'd stirred her up like this.

Geoff traced his finger along the collar, then tugged on it again, harder this time, so he pulled her a step toward him, just as she'd imagined. She put her hand out for balance and Chris captured it, so they were holding her between them. Geoff's eyes became a deeper, richer green and gold. Though he did it reluctantly, he removed the collar, putting it back on the counter for Madison to replace when she returned from her current task, which appeared to be straightening one of the toy displays. He kept one hand on the juncture between Sam's shoulder and neck, though, running his thumb between her collarbone and throat, pressing against the gentle beat there.

"Chris saw some things he liked in the lingerie section," he said. "Would you like to see?"

"Yes." Her voice sounded breathy.

As Chris drew her toward the wall, they had to pass the rounders of role playing costumes. When Geoff fingered one that looked like a harem girl outfit, Sam slanted a smile his way. "Did you have a favorite teenage fantasy?"

"Scarlett O'Hara. And pretty much any of the old movies where the heroine got spanked. There were a lot."

"His mom got him hooked on movies pre-1960s," Chris said, with a smile. "I went for the *Sports Illustrated* bikini issue and Victoria's Secret catalog choices. The Dallas Cowboy cheerleaders. Never has been a better cheerleader outfit than that one. Oh, and Trinity in *The Matrix*. That latex she wore, her double firearm skills . . ."

"In short, you wouldn't have wanted to put a black light in his bedroom as a teenager."

"I think you could say that about any teenage boy." She gave Geoff a quizzical look. "Rhett never spanked Scarlett."

"No, but he really wanted to. I kept hoping he would. Might have solved a lot of issues for them."

As she was chuckling, Chris drew her to a wall display and showed her a bra-and-panty set of sheer black lace with tiny blue forget-me-not flowers at the joining point of the straps. The panties were low-rise and also sheer black.

Geoff shifted behind her, putting both hands on her shoulders, continuing his caresses. With the weight of his hands taking its place, the collar felt like it was still there.

"I like this, too." Chris pointed to a silver-colored bra where the cups had only a two-inch-wide satin cup above the underwiring, the garment intended to lift the breasts but not cover the nipples. The matching underwear was merely a latex waistband with lace strips dangling from the sides. The strips tied around the thighs, forming the "legs" of the panties, if they could be called that. A fringe of beads ran along the band, longer in the front and sculpted so they fell in a point that would stop above the bare sex. The tag showed a sexy blond model wearing it. The outfit would make every inch of her accessible to a lover, without having to remove a bit of the provocative outfit.

"Geoff?" Chris cocked his head.

"Can't wait to fuck her wearing that," Geoff observed, hands sliding around her waist, holding her against him. "I'll bet when she walks in it the beads tease her clit. I like that silver-gray corset and thong over there as well." He bent, kissed her throat. "Chris would like lacing you in a corset, Sam. Cinch you up tight in it."

Sam wondered if she should remind them they were in a public place. She didn't want to, though. Geoff gripped her jaw, turning her head to press her cheek to his shoulder so he could bite her neck where Chris had left his mark. Geoff didn't do it as aggressively, but the intent was in the forceful clamp of his jaw, as well as what he whispered in her ear.

"When we're alone again, I'll put the kind of mark Chris left on your neck on your ass, Sam. I like biting you."

He pulled back, though he kept his hold on her until he was sure she was steady. She was grateful for the consideration and less self-conscious than she'd expected. While some of it could be their surroundings, an erotica shop instead of the local Walmart, she didn't

155

want to mask how much they affected her. She had no desire to play those kinds of games. Not with them.

"I'm going to go get a few things from the Dungeon Room." Geoff's smile was pure sin. Then he was gone, leaving her in Chris's care. Chris ran a hand down her back.

"What size would you wear in these things?"

She picked them out for him, but she wasn't sure about the corset, so she turned to find Madison. The shopkeeper was sitting on her high stool at the cash register counter, waving an elegant silk fan in front of her in a butterfly-like way so her hair moved in a gentle rhythm against her amused face. Sam bit back a smile. Yeah, she guessed they had been getting a little combustible. It made her like Madison all the more that the woman hadn't done a thing to defuse the situation, but instead had stayed quiet as a mouse to encourage it.

"Um, we're not sure about the corset sizes."

Madison set the fan aside and grabbed her measuring tape. "I can help with that. Even if you know your clothing sizes, it's better to measure to be sure the style corset you're getting is the best one for your body shape."

From pleasant voyeur to efficient shopkeeper in a blink. Sam was thinking about putting her on her Christmas card list.

"Hey, Madison?" Troy, the sandy-haired twenty-something who worked next door at the hardware store and looked like he could model for swimwear ads, poked his head out of the back storeroom. "I'm doing a sandwich run. Logan asked if you want your usual."

"If he lets me buy this time. Fair is fair."

"He told me to tell you he'd take it out in trade." Troy grinned. Madison pressed her lips against a smile, but from the spark in her eye, Sam thought she didn't mind that trade at all.

"Tell him I have some discount thongs that might look very pretty on him. I'll let him have two for the price of three."

Sam bit back a chuckle and Troy glanced her way. "Hey there," he said, recognizing her. Which was impressive, because she'd spent far less time in the hardware store last time than her two roommates had. "Good to see you again. If you're into gardening, we're having a sale on women's gloves today. Some fancy lady designer name brand, so they're usually overpriced."

It was impossible not to respond to that charming grin and those sky-blue eyes. When Chris shifted to stand closer to her, Troy's attention moved to him. "Oh, hey, man. We got that gravel in stock you were asking about."

"Cool. I'll come check it out."

Though Chris's tone was friendly, Sam noticed there was a subtle reserve to it she wasn't used to hearing. The last time she'd noted it was when John Howard came to pick her up for that date Chris had forever replaced in her mind with a vision of his and Geoff's drinking game. She hadn't remembered the date all that well until they brought it up, but since then it had been coming back in more detail. They'd both been there when John picked her up. Chris's reaction to Troy was a more toned-down version of how they'd acted toward John, which was good, since they'd made a not pleasantly memorable impression on John.

"Have you ever been involved with either of them? Or both?" John had asked, shooting a nervous look at the house as they pulled away, as if he expected those two sets of measuring eyes to still be pinned on him.

"No," she'd said. "They're just protective. Like big brothers."

Wow, what a lie that had been, but at the time she'd been trying to accept that as the limits of their relationship. Now she wondered why she'd ever made an effort toward something so ridiculous. Poor John.

Troy spoke to Madison. "I'll go get the sandwiches at the usual time."

Madison returned to measuring Sam for the corset. Chris moved out of the way to let her do that, wandering off toward the Dungeon Room. He didn't go into it, instead perusing a display of violet wand options, tucking his hands in his back jeans pocket as he studied them, his size and presence making him seem like the center of the room. Or maybe that was just because he felt like the center of the room to Sam.

"Yep, definitely some progress made," Madison whispered to her. "Another minute and I think he would have whipped it out to mark a circle around you."

As Sam put her hand over her mouth to stifle a giggle, Madison shifted in front of her, flipping the tape around her waist. "You could tell them Troy has a Mistress and is very devoted to her," she continued, "but what fun would that be?"

Sam's eyes widened. She hadn't realized Troy was part of a Dom/sub dynamic and, with his confidence and overt masculinity, she wouldn't have guessed he was a submissive. But then she wondered why. She was a confident, independent woman who craved submission like the best kind of chocolate. Only the misguided media, who offered controversial images of Dominance and submission out of context, depicted a submissive as a pathetically cringing caricature. From the things Chris had said, she thought he'd struggled with that same issue in addressing her desire for submission, concerned about the lines between abuse and pleasure.

"Troy's so handsome, he can't help but stir up the right kind of trouble," Madison continued. "I try to take a coffee break whenever the soil or seed trucks arrive so I can watch him unload them, get all sweaty and flexy."

"Flexy?" Sam muffled another snort. "I don't blame you a bit."

"It covers both areas. Flexing and sexy. Okay, I think the best match for you will be the 'Willow' body type range in this size for height and build." Madison indicated the right one, pulling it off the rack. "It should do the trick, but if you ever have the chance to have a professional corsetiere fit you for one, it's well worth it. These are nice enough for the price, though, and lots of fun to play with."

Geoff emerged then, a book in hand. Sam glimpsed the title, *Build-It-Yourself Bondage,* before he drew Chris over so the two of them could study it. She didn't realize she'd closed her hands in a knot under her breasts until Madison's hand closed over them. "It's a crazy feeling, isn't it, when it's all starting?" she murmured. "I'm still not sure quite how to get a grip on it myself."

Sam looked at her, surprised, but as if the woman felt she'd revealed too much, she stepped back, the warm but professional shopkeeper's smile back in place. "How about you? They're picking out things they like, but anything you'd like to see them try? Cock-and-ball harness, maybe?"

Sam couldn't quell her bark of startled laughter, and the two men glanced her way. She shook her head, waving them off. Madison linked arms with her and strolled past a wall full of chains and straps obviously intended to bind a man's member in many creative ways. "I think they'd both turn as white as sheets and run," Sam said. Then she sobered. "No, most of what I want right now . . . has to do with what they want. I mean, I'm fantasizing like crazy . . ."

"About?" Madison had somehow managed to maneuver her over toward the Dungeon Room, sliding past Chris and Geoff. As they passed, Sam heard a snippet of their conversation, something about garage space and power tools. She had a feeling she was going to get the chance to see those garden gloves next door.

This was her first time in the Dungeon Room section of Madison's shop. The smell of coffee and baked goods, the pale yellow walls, made it a comfortable space, and Madison's arrangement of the BDSM toys was tasteful and provocative, the same way she arranged all her inventory. When Sam slowed down in front of a display of paddles and floggers, Madison slowed with her, though she stepped out of visual range. It allowed Sam to be in her own private world as she threaded her fingers through the silky ends of a soft black flogger.

She moved on to the impact toys, classified as "thumpers" by the sign above them, which included an amusing rendering of the Disney rabbit of the same name. Her practical mind said a kitchen spoon or spatula would work as well as a paddle at far less of a cost, but one held her attention. The polished cherrywood framed a padded crimson vinyl center. "I've been bad" was stitched on it in a heavily knotted, thick thread she suspected would add to the impact when used.

She wanted to be really bad for Geoff and Chris. She also wanted to be oh-so-very-good for them. As she traced the edge of the paddle, Madison nudged Sam's shoulder with her own. "I'm going to leave you in here to look around. You're being watched, just so you know."

"I can feel them," Sam murmured. Madison squeezed her arm and retreated. Growing ever more fascinated, Sam moved along the wall and floor displays. Wrist restraints came in everything from iron shackles to padded Velcro. Geoff would choose something padded, she knew that. In the heat of the moment, he'd implied he was inter-ested in rougher things, but as much as he had enjoyed spanking her, turning her ass red, the only one she knew more protective of her well-being than him was Chris. But what would Geoff do if he realized she was curious enough to explore what "rougher" might mean? She didn't know how much of that she'd enjoy in reality, but she'd really thought about some of it.

She was now in the sensory deprivation area, over which was a compelling erotic black-and-white print of a woman in a lace black teddy and a full head mask. The eyes and ears were sealed, depriving her of those senses. All that showed of her face was her moist red lips, parted to take a chocolate from her Master's hand as she knelt at his feet. As Sam's gaze coursed down to the head masks on display, she landed on one crafted of overlapping gray feathers, tightly sewn against the mold so they looked smooth as a dove's breast.

Several gag options were arranged around it that could cover the mouth opening and match the colors and style of the rest of the mask. One was a short phallic-shaped plug. Another was larger and thicker. She could imagine it filling her mouth, holding down her tongue so that her loudest cries would be muffled. Where the eyes would be, the mask's designer had painted a pair of eyes in shades of gray and black, rounded and lit like a dove's eyes.

Looking closer, Sam saw the black pupils were Velcro patches. When she pulled one away the eye hole was no bigger than a pencil eraser. A sub could be allowed to see, but only in a very limited way, and in the direction her Master desired. An additional accessory could be purchased with the mask—a silver collar designed to look like the band put around a bird's leg, to indicate where the bird belonged.

As she petted the smooth feathers covering the mask, Sam read the card that went along with it. The artist guaranteed the feathers were gathered from ripe-plucking, meaning she'd acquired the feathers after they'd been dropped naturally by chickens after molting. As Sam had been an ethical vegan since she'd done a project about Gandhi in middle school, that made the mask all the more tempting, but she saw the price. While she was certain the mask was worth it, it was way beyond her budget. Beyond that, it felt presumptuous of her to buy it, as if she was trying to tell Geoff or Chris what to do. Still, she couldn't help imagining how that mask would look with the items her two men had picked out for her, particularly that gray corset.

She made herself move onward, to the whip display. She learned that a dragon tail was a whip that looked like a triangle of velvet cloth attached to a wooden handle. The bull whip made her think of Indiana Jones. This one was made of kangaroo hide. She wouldn't feel right about buying something like that, but she had no problem integrating an animal-free version into her fantasies. She wondered what it would be like to be tied up and feel one of those whips snap over her flesh. If it hurt a lot, she probably wouldn't like it, but trusting Geoff to take her on that journey, help her learn how much she could take, was something she would like.

Truth, her fascination with it probably had more to do with its psychological impact. She thought of Indiana Jones snaking his whip around Winnie's waist to jerk her back to him in an overwhelmingly dominant way in Temple of Doom. She thought of Geoff trailing the fall over her breasts, looping it around her throat, letting it caress her there, wrapping it over her arms to hold them to her sides . . .

She let out an unsteady breath. When she shifted back, her buttock pressed against a wall of flesh behind her. A glance showed her Geoff on her right, Chris on the left. "Finding anything you can't live without?" Geoff asked.

She looked up into his hazel eyes, then shifted her attention to Chris's brown ones. "Yeah," she said in a throaty voice.

And the stuff on the walls is pretty nice, too.

She didn't purchase anything for herself, but Chris bought the ring, which she left on her finger. Geoff bought a handful of Velcro cuffs, the soft flogger she'd touched, and the *Build-It-Yourself Bondage* book. Just as she expected, he and Chris said they needed to go next door and pick up a few things. Madison gave her a smile, a scone and a to-go cup of coffee. "If you get tired of all the manly shopping, come back over and we can chat between customers."

Sam nodded. Chris and Geoff had already gone on ahead of her, so she paused in the door. "How long do you think it takes to get your mind wrapped around it?" she ventured. Since Madison had changed the subject after making that personal comment, Sam wasn't sure if she'd get an answer, but she had to ask.

A shadow crossed Madison's expression. "Sometimes the hardest thing to do is get out of your own way," Madison said slowly. Looking up, she gave Sam a reassuring smile. "But honestly, I think that's more my problem. It seems to me you've already wrapped your mind around it. The unknown is the two of them. Your biggest challenge may be helping them do what Logan is helping me do. I mean, the guy I'm . . ."

She blew out a breath at Sam's grin and shook her head. "He's helping me get out of my own way, but I expect that's an affliction a Dom can feel as much as a sub. Especially if the Dom or man in question is already insanely in love with you, as your two are."

Sam flushed but Madison waved a hand. "It's pretty obvious," she said amiably, the shadows disappearing from her expression. "Watching the three of you could jump-start a corpse's libido. In fact . . ." She considered Sam. "I'm considering starting an erotic performance theater. I have a friend up in New York who runs a community theater, but she's been talking about making a change. I might coax her down here to help me get something like that going."

"That would be amazing."

"I've already been researching different forms of erotic performance and how I can integrate some of my artisan-quality pieces here as part of the sets. Like that dove mask, which would look gorgeous on you." Madison gave her a knowing look. "Anyway, if it comes to life, I'll send you an invitation. Then I'll see if I can talk you three into getting up onstage."

"Oh hell no." The words were out before Sam could bite them back. Madison laughed.

"We'll see," the shopkeeper said. "Always keep your options open."

Sam left her with a grin and a wave. When she moved down the sidewalk to the propped-open front door of the hardware store and stepped inside, she saw it was moderately busy. Mid-mornings were obviously a more active time for hardware shopping than lingerie. She saw the gloves Troy had mentioned and picked out a bright green pair with a pattern of ladybugs on them. She could hear Geoff's voice a few aisles over and Chris responding. Knowing where they were contented her. Since the main reason she wanted to be here had to do with that and not so much with shopping, she wandered over to a patio set.

While a sign noted that it was a display, with stock available in the back, she expected it was also there to accommodate patient wives or girlfriends, due to the amusing selection of women's magazines and secondhand paperback romances, as well as a dish of wrapped chocolates. Groupings of potted flowers, plants and lawn ornamentation likely to catch a female gardener's eye were arranged around the same area, as well as a terra-cotta planter full of the brightly colored gloves. It looked like a fabric bouquet.

By closing her eyes, she was able to hear Geoff and Chris better. She only heard the occasional word, but it was their voices that mattered. They were talking to Troy, because she heard his voice in the mix. Geoff was asking most of the questions, but Chris interjected a key sentence here or there that she could tell altered the direction and focus, helping to shape whatever they were trying to accomplish. She'd watched Chris and Geoff cook dinner together plenty of times, and the same dynamic happened there as well. Geoff would have the master plan for the meal, but Chris's improvisations would sculpt the end result. She wondered if it would be the same when they finally took her body at the same time, both of them inside her.

The power of positive thinking. She'd thought "when," not "if."

Since getting herself worked up like a furnace wasn't immediately productive, she turned her mind to a more amusing memory of them making dinner together. That night, she'd been told she had to stay out of the way, that they wanted her to do nothing but relax. So she'd sat on the couch and pretended to read a book, all while watching how the two of them worked with each other, listening to the things they talked about. Geoff had been discussing a case.

". . . this guy is a complete nutbag. But because he's allowed to represent himself, the judge gives him twice as much time. Today he brought in one of those little cymbal-clapping monkeys to explain something about his constitutional rights. So when we recessed for lunch, I picked up a handful of wind-up hopping penises at Spencer's."

"Now you're shitting me." Chris chuckled. "The judge would have busted your ass."

"Yes, she would have. But she tends to be late, so we were seated a good ten minutes before she returned. I kept one bouncing in circles on the desk. Jennings pulled out the second one and we got into it, racing them from one end of the desk to the other. I asked Mr. Nutbag if he wanted to lay odds on who hit the end of the desk first, and told him I had a third one if he wanted to play, too. If looks could kill . . ."

"Jesus, man."

"The court reporter was losing it. I put them away as the judge came out, but nothing gets by Judge Roberts. She gives me a look and says, 'Mr. Tywin, I can assure you that I have confiscated more than one penis in this room. I will not hesitate to take yours.'"

Chris roared with laughter. "Man, the last time I stopped in to hear you try a case, it was some boring crap about a bunch of paperwork that was filed incorrectly. You have to give me a heads-up on this stuff."

"I can't predict my moments of genius."

Returning to the present, she smiled to herself. Having a chance to listen to or watch them when she wasn't an active part of the interaction was a particular indulgence. Even if, like now, she could only hear a word or two of their conversation, because they were a couple of aisles away from her.

When overhearing a conversation between strangers, there was a tendency to be discreet about it, to pretend one wasn't listening. But she had a right to listen to them, to be an intimate part of their lives. She was still part of the conversation, even without being there. And she liked this, not being distracted by the need to contribute. She could absorb them through her senses—hearing, sight, smell—and embrace the simple joy of just that.

They came into view then. Chris was listening to what Troy was telling them, his gaze periodically flicking to Geoff as they exchanged silent cues of agreement or marked the significance of something they were being told. Geoff had his back to her, but his arms were crossed over his chest, feet planted shoulder width. Chris had one hand on the top of a display rack, his other hooked into his pants pocket as he stood in a similar cocked-hip stance, listening. His gaze shifted briefly, found her, and she smiled.

He didn't smile back. His gaze stayed on her, though. She sensed he was still listening to the conversation, but he apparently wanted his eyes directed right where they were. A little self-conscious, she smoothed her jeans over her knees. Now a serious smile did touch his lips.

She'd been surer of her footing with Geoff, though her fantasies had fallen short of all the possibilities, a thrilling thought. Chris's expression as he looked at her now was an intriguing mix. He wanted to take her again, wanted her naked and under him. She could read that clearly enough, and it made her hands curl on her knees. Yet she also thought he wanted to scoop her up and keep her safe, tend to her in all the ways that defined the word *cherish*.

Geoff said something and Chris turned his attention back to him. She'd been holding her breath again, she realized. It made her chuckle at herself. Taking a sip of her coffee, she picked up one of the paperback romances. It was an older historical, with the clench pose on the front. A woman whose heaving breasts were barely contained by her bodice was being held by a virile-looking male whose look said he planned to do away with that bodice and the rest of her clothing quite immediately.

She volunteered for a humane society that had a thrift shop with an extensive paperback book collection, so she was very familiar with those poses. She preferred them to the modern-day ones that would use a hint of a body behind a flower or a bit of lace. They were as romantic and sexy as a doorknob, whereas this . . . It didn't matter that it was overly dramatic. She could close her eyes and imagine being that heroine, her knees already giving way because she knew he was strong enough to hold her, that she could surrender everything to him . . .

She wasn't stupid. She knew that was fantasy, that no one could surrender everything to anyone full-time. She could and would take care of herself. Because of that, she knew her feelings for Chris and Geoff weren't rooted in how they'd appeared at the right moment in her life, stopping Anthony, her stalker ex-boyfriend, from whatever terrible plan he'd had for her. It was everything else they'd done since, in her day-to-day life. Things that had won her trust. That trust would allow her to give them control when the moment called for it, when surrender was an option that could free her soul, without fear of abdicating her right to run her own life.

"It's funny. When I initially put a copy of *Newsweek* or the *New Yorker* over here, I could tell a lot of women felt like they *had* to pick those up and completely ignore the *People* magazine or the romance novels. But by only having those choices, pretty much all of them will page through them while waiting for their husbands or boyfriends. At least once or twice I'll see them smile, like you're doing now."

She opened her eyes, and her heart rate bumped up in an altogether pleasant way. She'd only met Logan Scott briefly, when she was in the hardware store last time, but Sam could completely understand why he was the one changing Madison's life. She'd even felt a vicarious thrill on Madison's behalf when the shop owner let Logan's name slip.

The hardware store owner was hitting a sexy and rugged forty. With broad shoulders and a strong-boned frame, the whole package was displayed well in jeans, work shoes and a chamois shirt that outlined his powerful upper body. But it was the energy around him, and the measuring look in his molasses-colored eyes, a darker brown than Chris's, which elevated her heart rate.

Maybe it was because Sam was getting more in touch with her submissive side that she recognized Logan as a Dom right off. One who'd completely embraced that identity and made it a vital part of who he was. This was very likely what Geoff would be when he grew up, so to speak. Since Geoff could overwhelm Sam now, she understood why Madison had looked a little overcome when talking about Logan.

She'd met some tops on her visits to private BDSM parties with Flo, men who wore their sexual Dominance like a hat they took off when they left the club or bedroom. That worked for them and their partners. However, she expected being a Master was like breathing for Logan Scott. Something he was and did without conscious thought. Geoff gave off those vibes as well.

"Hello," she said. "Sorry, I was just daydreaming."

"No need for a beautiful woman to apologize for that, especially if who she's daydreaming about will benefit from it." He winked. "The ladybug gloves are a good choice for you. You might consider a second pair. They're on sale individually, but if you buy two, I'll knock twenty percent off the second pair in addition to the sale price. I have an overstock."

"I liked the lavender ones with the butterflies. I'll get those as well."

He waved her off as she started to get up. "No rush. Just wanted to mention it to you and make sure you didn't have any other questions. Troy and I are here to help you if there's anything you need."

"Okay. Um . . ."

He'd started to ease back, a considerate shop owner, but stopped at her hesitation. His shrewd eyes studied her, then followed her gaze to Geoff and Chris and back. "Madison sometimes has me talk to her clients about their interests," he said carefully. "So I'm also available for non-hardware-related questions, if you have one you think I can answer."

Yeah, the man definitely had well-tuned radar. "I was wondering . . ."

If she'd read the signals wrong from both him and Madison, she was about to mortally embarrass herself, but she was on a roll lately on asserting herself in risky ways, so why should she stop now? "One of them is like you, without a doubt. The other one, I can't tell. I think the key to Chris is Geoff, but they're circling each other like wolves who are crossing paths for the first time. Yet they've known each other forever. It makes me worry that I'm going to . . ."

She paused, struggling with it. Logan sat down in the chair across from her. He didn't prompt her, didn't seem impatient. He was just waiting, listening with senses that she thought went far beyond his ears. It flustered her even as it gave her the courage to continue.

"Geoff says there's nothing I need to do, that I can't push. That they have to work it out, that Chris has to work it out. I sort of get that, but it's not my thing to sit back and wait to see if something is going to go the right way or crash and burn. If it crashes and burns, how do I know that my not doing anything didn't contribute to that? I love them, and I'm so afraid of hurting them, but I tell myself that's pointless, because the gate's wide-open now, the horses all out of the barn. I might as well just let them run, right? Or should I try to chase them down and get them going in the right direction?"

A smile had slowly grown on Logan's face as the words spilled out. Now she took a breath. "Talk about the gate being wide-open," she said lamely. "I'm sorry."

"For what?" He leaned forward, knees spread and wrists loosely resting on them. He had long, thick brown hair tied back off his shoulders. It reminded her of Adrian Paul's in the Highlander series. "Sometimes we answer questions just by saying them out loud," he said. "But it probably is going to crash and burn. Not just once, but quite a few times."

Gee, thanks. I feel loads better. He shook his head and touched her knee in reassurance. "Sometimes that's how you figure out what will work," he said. "You love them. It's the love that will keep you working toward it. While love can sometimes be about maintaining status quo, overall, love isn't a stagnant force. If it's real, it grows and changes with the people involved."

His look was thoughtful. "Geoff told you to let it be. Am I right?"

"Yes sir—I mean, yes." She turned scarlet. His expression and tone had shifted, steady and even in a way that she recognized all too well. It was merely a Southern courtesy to address someone as *sir* or *ma'am*, and he was probably about fifteen years older than her, but that wasn't what had prompted it.

Help, I've found out I'm a sub and I can't turn it off.

Logan moved on smoothly. "So if he's told you to let it be, and the two of them have a long history, trust your Master."

Hearing someone else call Geoff that gave her a delightful little flutter, but her tart response was out before she could bite it back.

"That's just what I'd expect another Master to say."

Logan's sexy smile would scatter any breathing woman's brain cells. "You may be right about that. But it doesn't mean I'm not right. Trust your instincts, not your fears. The trick is knowing which is which."

"Logan?" Troy approached, giving her a courteous nod. "These two guys have a question I think you're the better one to answer. It's about building . . . furniture."

Logan glanced at him, then over his shoulder at Geoff and Chris. Geoff looked Sam's way with a *Doing okay?* smile. The smile she sent back had extra wattage, not only answering the question but reacting to Logan and Geoff's expressions side by side. The Dom quality was as evident as a brand stamp, though the models were deliciously different.

"All right," Logan told his employee. Then he looked at her. "All good here?"

"Yes," she said, though she was wondering what furniture Geoff and Chris were considering in that book. "Thank you," she said.

"Good luck." He touched her knee again. "Have fun with it. That's almost as important as anything else when you're getting started. Love has more room to figure things out when we don't take ourselves too seriously. Learning to let go is tough. For particularly stubborn subs, the only way to do that is to tie them up and teach them to let go. I might share that tidbit with these gentlemen, see what they can do with it."

At that outrageous statement, he winked and rose. When he left them, Troy's eyes danced. "It completely blows your concentration when they say things like that, doesn't it?"

She blew out an exaggerated breath in agreement and earned his chuckle, which left her grinning as he retreated to help other customers. It was fun to play—and commiserate—with another sub, another new experience for her. Okay. Worry less and have fun with it. Maybe she should tattoo that on her hands so she'd remember it.

She blanched as she saw Logan talking to Geoff and Chris and motioning to something on the wall. An old-fashioned buggy whip. While Geoff and Chris discussed whatever Logan had just told them, the store owner tossed her a look over his shoulder, full of mischief. She narrowed her gaze at him, even as her heart pounded a little faster and her hands got damp. Surely he hadn't suggested . . . but what if he had?

She bought her gloves. When Chris and Geoff came to make their purchase, they were empty-handed, but Chris took her arm, guiding her out the front door into the late-morning sunshine hitting the front sidewalk. Geoff was taking out his wallet and waiting for Logan to ring up whatever he'd been writing out on a piece of notepaper.

"So what are you buying?" she demanded.

"Something." Chris slid an arm around her waist, hooking his fingers in the waistband of her jeans.

"You're not going to tell me what it is."

"Nope." His eyes twinkled at her, though his mouth remained serious, as if part of his mind was still mulling over whatever he'd been thinking when he'd been staring at her so intently in the store. Pinching her lightly, he withdrew his hand and ambled along the sidewalk displays. He studied a flat of yard plants, but something in his face told her he wasn't even seeing them.

"Chris . . ."

He lifted his head, his brow arched. "Okay," she said. "I'm going to say it straight out. If any of this is making you uncomfortable, I don't want you to feel like you have to . . . like we can't go back . . ."

"Yeah, a lot of it's making me uncomfortable." He slid his hands in his back pockets like he had when studying the violet wands, only now he was studying the selection of wheelbarrows Logan had lined up on display out front. He stood that way a long moment. Anyone else she'd have prompted with more questions, but she knew Chris's cadence. He'd think it through before he spoke, and you had to give him a few extra seconds to do it. Not because he was slow, but because he believed in being honest and thorough. As a result, often his response would have weight and impact far beyond what was expected. This time was no exception.

"You know how many times I've thought about coming into your room at night, Sam?" he said at last. He kept his eyes on the wheelbarrows. "Getting into your bed and putting my hands on you. Wrapping my hands in your hair, tasting every inch of your skin. Burying my face between your legs until you came with those little bird cries, your body trembling . . ."

It was a good thing no one else was out sidewalk shopping, but she wasn't sure she would have noticed them if they were. She was frozen, staring at him.

"At first, it was every once in a while, harmless fantasy. Then you went on the first date you've had since Anthony. That sign that you were ready to start being with someone again flipped a switch. Ever since, the more time I've spent around you, the more I think about it."

He turned his brown eyes to her then, darker than usual in the shade of the striped store awning. "Now I think about it every night. Usually right before I tap out 'Itsy Bitsy Spider' on your wall. So no, I don't feel like I *have* to do anything. I don't want to go back."

"What stopped you from acting on it? When that switch flipped, I mean." Her skin felt stretched tight over her bones, the sunshine making her aware of every inch of it. From here forward, when he tapped that good-night ritual on her wall, she'd be thinking of the words he'd just spoken.

"Same reason it took you a while, and Geoff. Three isn't the usual thing, is it? We didn't say it to each other, though we were both thinking it. But for that to happen, you had to be on board before either of us. I didn't know that had happened, until you took us to Naughty Bits. Then, you know, it takes me a while to move forward, even with the green light. I think it through from all angles. But coming home and finding you and Geoff pretty much expedited that, big-time."

As he turned to contemplate the wheelbarrows again, she had to bite back another apology. Chris had something specific on his mind. She waited.

"Geoff has a dinner meeting with clients tonight," he said slowly. "We're going to do the picnic in the park. After that, we'll go home and he'll get his shower, head out for that. Then he wants me to take you to bed again. Which is good, because that's what I planned to do."

"Oh." Her mouth was dry. "You worked this out, the both of you?"

"Yep. But there are a couple of things you need to realize, too." He turned to face her. "Geoff said to make sure I was looking at you when I say this, so you understand we both mean it. He didn't need to tell me that, but he's a control freak, like you. On different sides of the fence."

A wry twist of his lips. She had to bite her own to keep from saying anything, which would only prove his point. Her heart thudded at his steady look.

"Rule number one. You don't have to do anything you don't want to do. You got it? You don't want to do something, that's not going to change a thing for either of us. But you do something you don't want to do just so you feel like we're happy, that won't make us happy. Geoff will be ticked, and I'll just be plain pissed. We're not mind readers, Sam. Don't let us hurt you, because neither of us can imagine anything worse in the whole world than living with the guilt of that. Got it?"

"Got it. I felt that way . . . when you walked in on me and Geoff. It was the worst feeling I've ever felt."

Her voice came out as a whisper, which tightened his jaw, made him step closer. She had to tilt her head to look up into his face. He wasn't touching her, but she was starting to tremble as if he was. He was saying these intimate, important things out in bright sunshine, on a public sidewalk, but none of that mattered. It was just them in the whole world.

"Okay," he said. "Rule number two. You do what we tell you to do. Unless rule one applies."

She'd have expected Geoff to say such a thing. The jolt of hearing it from Chris, seeing him say it because he felt it, meant it, was a shock to the system.

Chris handled what needed to be handled, not by issuing orders and commanding men, but by taking care of it himself, one-on-one, whether it was a force of nature or one of Esteban's customers. He was like Hercules or Atlas, whereas Geoff was Caesar or Captain America. The unique way each took control weakened her knees. It was a new revelation, a good one.

"Final point," he continued. "Being uncomfortable isn't a bad thing. We like it when you're this kind of uncomfortable. Where your heart gets to racing, and you breathe funny, and your eyes get a look in them like you can't really focus on anything but what we're telling you."

A woman had come out of the store and was browsing the bedding plants. Chris leaned in, spoke quietly. "It's making you wet, me talking to you like this, isn't it?"

When she gave him a look of helpless agreement, he put his lips on her cheek, his arm sliding around her waist to bend her like a reed against him as his voice became a husky whisper. "When you get aroused, your brain gets all scattered, but you don't fight it. I like that, because it says you trust us."

She swiped a tongue over her lips and made a little noise as he followed the movement with his own mouth, taking his fill of her lips before he lifted his head and drew back, tucking his hands in his back pockets again. He didn't move back, though, and she was tempted to spread her fingers out like wings on his chest, feel the man beneath the cloth.

Instead, she kept her hands still, not trusting herself. "So . . . you said Geoff suggested you tell me this?"

"Yeah. He said you weren't going to relax until you had half an idea of my mind on it. Else you'd think I was being tugged along like a dog going into the vet's office."

She blinked. "I never . . . I just . . ."

"I know what you were worried about, because you worry about us, always. Me specifically, in ways you don't worry about Geoff." He slid his arm around her again. His gaze on her face, he spread out his fingers, taking a firm grip on her ass in front of the whole world. She didn't dare look over her shoulder at the other shoppers. There were three women browsing the sidewalk displays now, because she could hear their muted comfortable chatter.

"Chris."

He gave her an immovable look. "I appreciate you caring about me, but when it comes to this, you're going to stop worrying. And you're going to tell me you understand and agree, right now, or I'll turn this public display of affection into something even more blatant."

When she struggled with what she could say to that, his hand shifted as if he intended to slide all the way under her ass to cup her between her legs. She put her hands on his chest and pushed, her glare mixed with a half-exasperated smile.

"Okay, I get it. I get it." She repeated it more softly, then shook her head. "Big jerk."

This was a side of Chris she wasn't used to handling. Correction—he'd just made it clear he wasn't going to be handled.

"So do you think we can use a new wheelbarrow?" Letting her go with a light squeeze, he turned to look at a few models out on display. "Our old one is about rusted out."

He stirred her up like a cake mix and left her to bake, her arousal rising and steaming off her skin. Those scones had made her think of too many cooking metaphors. Before she could untie her tongue to reply, Geoff emerged from the store, pushing his wallet into his back jeans pocket. "Let's go get Jersey Mike's. I'm ready for a picnic."

"I guess you're not going to tell me what the two of you bought, either," she said. Geoff took her elbow in firm fingers.

"Absolutely not. You also don't get to ask. Patience is a virtue."

"A saying made up by smirking people who already know the answers the impatient person wants to know."

"Master Po never smirked."

"*Kung Fu*," Chris supplied at her confused look, taking her arm on the other side. "Kwai Chang Caine's mentor. She's not infected with geek."

"Seriously? She has the complete Ron Perlman and Linda Hamilton *Beauty and the Beast* series on DVD."

"That's romance, not geek stuff," Chris said.

"There is some overlap," she admitted, and chuckled at Geoff's smile. "And I bet Master Po was always smirking. He just did it off camera."

They headed to Jersey Mike's to pick up subs and went from there to Reedy Creek Park as planned. She squelched her curiosity about their purchase while polishing off lunch at a picnic table and watching other people's dogs play in the dog park.

Conversation gravitated toward their usual debate about when they thought they could adopt a dog, and what kind they'd adopt. When Chris suggested a St. Bernard, Geoff pointed out they didn't need two large, furry behemoths in the house. His vote was for a man-eating Chihuahua. Sam told them it wouldn't matter; when the time came and they went to the shelter, the proper dog would pick them.

The three of them bantered back and forth on that for awhile, then drifted among the usual topics of politics, family and friends, work. Part of why moving in with Geoff and Chris had been an uncomplicated decision was how easily they could talk to one another about most things, whether it was the three of them together or one-on-one.

While Sam didn't enjoy all their interests or they hers, they still had fun talking about them together, and she'd never found either Chris or Geoff an overbearing conversationalist. For one thing, Geoff often liked being able to listen more than talk after a long day of having to do the latter at work. Chris's work, mostly being a silent communion with nature, meant he was equally comfortable chatting or remaining quiet, depending on their mood.

Reedy Creek Park had plenty of hiking trails and an open lawn overlooking a natural pond and a fishing pier. Locating a good shade tree on the lawn, they spread a blanket on the grass.

Geoff sat down, propping his back against a tree, and Chris directed her to sit there, between his spread and bent knees, her shoulder blades against Geoff's chest. For his part, Chris stretched out on the blanket to rest his head in her lap. Geoff had wrapped his hand around her waist, his knuckles brushing the crown of Chris's head.

"Comfortable?" Geoff murmured after they settled. She nodded. She was sleepy, the usual effect of a good lunch and a bath of sunlight, and though their proximity stirred her up in expected ways, she couldn't think of a more favorable position for an afternoon nap.

"Nothing better than an afternoon siesta between the thighs of a beautiful woman," Chris said, reading her mind. Turning his face to her thigh, he kissed it through the denim, chuckling when she flicked the side of his head.

"Any beautiful woman?"

"There is only one beautiful woman in the entire world, and we are with her," Geoff intoned, the words vibrating through his chest against her back. "So said because we are smart men who live in the same house with her and she has access to cooking knives."

She *hmphed* at that and let her gaze drift over the lawn. A small group of college kids were playing touch football. A woman was reading on her own blanket, her head pillowed on her chocolate Labrador. His head was up, eyes trained on the movement of the football. The woman reached up, rubbed his ears and spoke a calming word, the light smile on her face saying she knew he wanted to play and would probably give in to his desire soon with the can of tennis balls she'd brought.

"You're humming." Geoff's arm tightened on her. "What song is that?"

She had a tendency to do that, but when Sam realized the song she'd been humming, she felt a little embarrassed. Chris opened his eyes and looked up at her. "One of those romantic chick songs," he said. "Best not to ask."

He'd watched *Hello, Dolly!* with her, and he had a great memory for music. "It Only Takes a Moment" was what she'd been humming. It was probably a little over-the-top, but nevertheless, it was what had come to mind. Maybe because this was a precious moment—the first time they'd acknowledged in public the attraction among the three of them.

It hadn't gone unnoticed. There was a group of women sitting at a nearby picnic table, playing a card game and chatting as women did. The rhythm of their conversation was part of the music around her, so it caught her attention when the note changed, from casual chatter to lowered voices.

She noticed a couple of them glancing her way, probably prompted by the woman who'd just spoken to them in an undertone. It was obvious from how Geoff and Chris held her that she was intimate with them both. What was curious to her was that she was more intrigued by her own reaction than the women's speculation. Instead of feeling worried about the latter, Sam felt satisfaction curl in her belly. She became even more aware of Geoff's hand, spread over her hipbone, stroking her upper thigh in an intimate but not indecent way. Chris had his head still turned toward her upper thigh, his breath heating her flesh through her thin clothing.

Maybe she had some exhibitionist tendencies that had been dormant until now. Thinking of Madison's comments about performance art, Sam understood what the woman had meant about keeping herself open to the possibilities.

Geoff took her hair out of its barrette, combing his fingers through it and tugging so she laid her head back on his shoulder and looked up at him. "You liked the mask at Naughty Bits, didn't you?"

"It was beautiful."

"It was. But you liked the idea of wearing a full head mask. Why?"

She wondered if Chris felt the thrum of awareness that went through her when Geoff shifted to a Master's tone, posing a question he expected to have answered. In her peripheral vision, she saw Chris's gaze lift back to her face. Geoff didn't break eye contact.

"I'm not sure," she said. "I think it's having all my senses muted like that. Sight and sound, the ability to talk. I'd have to rely on you for guidance, my only focus . . ."

"On what we want from you?"

She nodded, and he touched her mouth. "I want you to say it."

"Yes. I like that. The idea of all my focus being on that... If you like it." She lifted a shoulder. "They kind of go together."

"Same for us." Chris spoke. Geoff's touch had created a silken fall of her hair over her right shoulder. It was over her breast, so when Chris reached up to play with them, his knuckles rubbed her nipple. It peaked and tightened against the stimulation. Chris registered it, making slower passes. It still looked like he was just playing with her hair, but as her nipple sculpted into a tighter point, he squeezed it between his knuckles. She drew in a breath.

"She's so responsive, isn't she?" Geoff murmured. "We could keep her hot and wet all the time, ready for either of us to fuck."

"She's that way now," Chris responded. When he lifted his gaze to Geoff, she wasn't expecting that gesture of male accord to intensify her response, but it did. As her lips parted, swallowing air to manage her reaction, Chris kept playing with her nipple in that disguised way. He watched her mounting desire with ruthless fascination. Still holding her, Geoff unzipped the tote of snacks she'd brought and withdrew a glossy cherry tomato from a container.

"Open up, Sam."

He put it on her tongue. It was the size of a smallish golf ball, but before she could chew, he made a quelling noise. "Hold it in your mouth, lips closed. Don't bite it."

He slid her T-shirt off her shoulder, the bra strap with it, and found bare flesh. "She focuses more on her own responses when she can't talk," he said casually to Chris.

Her cheeks heated. When she lowered her eyes, Chris touched her chin. "Is that so?"

He uttered the three words with a vibration of sexual demand that kept her eyes down, focused on his forearm, because if she looked up she was sure anyone looking would see she was a woman being blatantly stimulated. She nodded.

"Hmm." Chris rubbed his nose along her inner thigh. "She always smells so good. I want to put my nose right up against her pussy. I'd stay like that so I could feel her jerk in that sexy little way she does when she wants more."

"You said you wanted more from both of us," Geoff said against her throat, scoring her with his teeth. "If Chris wants as much of you as I do, we might take it all . . . and then some."

He slid his hands down both her arms, back up. She'd never been so aware of her skin. The women at the picnic table were getting an eyeful now. There'd be no doubt at all that these men had a sexual claim on her, but despite her internal war between civilized restraint and her own surging libido, the libido won. Sam wanted them to know. She wanted the whole world to know. No matter their reaction, she'd embrace whatever Geoff and Chris wanted from her.

Geoff's words were more than a sensual threat. They were a promise. The two of them would have fantasies and desires she hadn't even contemplated, and she was eager to discover what they were. Up until these past couple of weeks, she'd explored her submission as more fantasy than fact, but finding that she trusted them enough to do her best to follow rule number two, to do what they told her to do and explore those fantasies together, only made her want to get started on that now. Now, now, now.

"I think we might be skating over the line of public decency laws,"

Geoff observed. "How about a post-lunch hike to cool this down some?"

She shook her head, but Geoff slid a hand up to her shoulder, pinching the sensitive point between her neck and shoulder. "I wasn't talking to you, Sam." That mild Dom menace shot another direct reaction between her legs, but his voice was laced with amusement that made her want to roll her eyes at him as well. She didn't, though. She had a feeling he knew temptingly cruel ways to hold her on that line of discretion like a tight wire, all while getting her so aroused her panties would soak through.

Chris pressed another kiss to her thigh and rolled over, sitting back on his heels. "Sounds good." He cocked his head. "You going to make her hold that tomato in her mouth, or let her swallow it?"

"I was just enjoying the silence," Geoff said. She tried to elbow him in the stomach and he stopped her, chuckling. Brushing a kiss along her cheek, he held there. "Give it to me, sweet girl. I want to taste what's in your mouth." He captured her lips, parting them with his own. She relinquished the tomato in a moist, heated tangle of tongues and teeth before he drew back, bit and chewed.

She slid her fingertips along his lips, collecting some of the juice that had escaped. He kissed her lips again, lightly this time, and then pushed her up into Chris's waiting arms. He accepted Chris's free hand to pull him to his own feet. "All right," Geoff said. "Let's go work up a sweat the publicly acceptable way. For now."

Though it took a while, she was ultimately glad for Geoff's suggestion to take a break. The breathers gave them the chance to explore the new intimacy of their connection, not just as sex, but as three people falling in love.

No, correct that. They'd made that step long ago. This was finally exploring and enjoying it, realizing they had time to do that. It didn't have to be rushed in a conflagration of hormones, though she was sure none of them objected to the occasional bonfire.

On their hike, they found a softball abandoned on one of the baseball fields and Geoff started a game of keep away, nominating her and him to keep it away from Chris first. She shot a ground ball between his legs and Geoff narrowly evaded Chris in a feint and dodge as he snatched it up and fired it back to her. With Chris thundering down on her, she lobbed it over his head and gasped, laughing as he seized her around the waist and dumped her over his shoulder, circling to face Geoff again and calling to him to throw the ball, which Chris neatly caught.

"That is *so* cheating," she protested.

"It's completely acceptable to tackle or carry someone to keep them from getting the ball," Chris disagreed.

"Yeah, like I'm going to be able to do that with you or Geoff." She thumped his back and then shrieked as he hefted her so she slithered further down his back. Seizing his belt, she wormed her hand down beneath the belted waistband to grab a handful of boxers and yank. It didn't work as well as it did with briefs, but even so, at his amused grunt, she knew she'd accomplished enough of a wedgie to make an impact.

He laughed and hiked her back forward over his shoulder, flipping her in a move that had her cradled in his arms. "Little brat. Geoff, come deal with this so I can pull my underwear out of my ass. She hates to be tickled, you know."

"Does she? I hadn't noticed."

"No, no, no." She started to struggle as Geoff approached. He and Chris took her to the ground together, Chris leaving her in Geoff's care as he backed up to deal with his underwear. Since to do that he unbuckled his belt and unzipped his jeans, he effectively stole her attention as he reached down in back to handle things in a sinuous, wriggling motion. Then Geoff's long fingers were under her shirt, spidering along her waist and rib cage. "Let's see, where's she the most ticklish? Here . . . or here?"

"Stop. Stop it!" She squealed and shrieked, giggling and shoving at him as he persisted, as inexorable as Chris when he was holding her over his shoulder. "No, stop." She rolled and twisted and he sat on her, straddling her hips. He kept teasing those sensitive areas until she was begging for mercy. "Help . . . Chris, *please.*"

Though he was the one who'd started the whole thing, the best part of play was that sides could change in a blink. Geoff let out an oath as Chris tackled him. They rolled off into the grass while she scrambled to her feet, flushed and giddy. Since Chris was working on getting Geoff into a headlock, she shot into the fray and tunneled her fingers under Geoff's shirt, taking her revenge on some of his more ticklish spots. He snarled at her while strangling on a laugh, he and Chris still grappling. Then he managed to break free and grab her by the waist, tumbling all three of them in a tangle of arms and limbs.

"Time. Time out," Chris called. The wrestling stopped, though she noticed both men kept her pinned, their hands overlapping at her waist and hip. Glancing down, Sam saw Chris's hand was over Geoff's at her waist. A blink later, he'd adjusted it higher so they weren't touching, but she saw one of those intriguing looks pass between the two of them, Geoff's quizzical lifted brow, Chris answering with a blank *I didn't do anything* expression that had Geoff curling a lip at him.

"You concede defeat," she told Chris, drawing their attention from one another. "You called time."

"I called time because you jumped into the middle." He pulled her hair. "Boys play too rough. I didn't want you to take an elbow in the face. Geoff likes to throw elbows."

"It's the only defense against a human python who likes the head-locks and body pins," Geoff retorted. "And you knew I wouldn't throw elbows with her in the mix, which gave you the advantage."

"So I was being fair," Chris pointed out.

"In what universe would any rational person come to that conclusion?"

"You're both sexist," Sam interjected. "I had plenty of scraped knees and busted lips growing up. I even had my nose broken once."

"By who? We'll go beat them up for you." Geoff stretched out in the grass, one arm over his head. They'd left the baseball field during their keep away and the wrestling match had occurred in a grassy spot just off the wooded trail, a roomy glade to do what they were doing now. Geoff drew her down next to him. With a little satisfied sigh, she put her head on his stomach. Chris stretched out on his hip, his large hand resting on her abdomen, fingers curling in her shirt.

"Darcy Strange," Sam said. "She was a cheerleader who was making fun of me for being skinny and awkward. It wasn't the first time someone called me 'Knobby Knees,' but when I tried to walk away, she shoved me. I fell and landed on a curb, broke my nose. In all fair-ness, I don't think she intended that to happen, but I was so mad, I got up and punched her in the face. Broke her nose, too. We became friends sitting in the nurse's office. Still exchange Christmas cards. So I'd rather you not beat her up."

"Well, hearing it was a girl fight changes thing. That's a spectator sport."

She elbowed Geoff again, then subsided, staring upward through the interlaced tree branches. Clouds were drifting across a blue sky. "I was just thinking . . . I'm pretty sure I fell in love with you both a long time ago. I can't even remember when it happened. It just seemed meant to be, you know? It took me a while to figure out how that would work, because I'd always been told it had to be one person."

"Yeah," Geoff said. He was playing with her hair, strong fingers massaging her scalp. "I think we both were in that spot as well. Until you took us to Naughty Bits, telling us it didn't have to be that way. Thinking about it as a real possibility is a different level of critical thinking."

She looked down at Chris, who'd plucked a dandelion and was rolling it in his fingers, his expression pensive. She touched his face to make him look at her. "Would it have been easier if I'd chosen only one of you?"

"Depends on who was chosen," he said. His lips quirked as if to pass it off as a joke, but she knew him too well. He'd meant to say something else, she was almost sure of it. But he curled his fingers around her wrist, gave it a little squeeze and then let her go to grasp the hem of her shirt, lifting it up to expose her navel. Since he was still twirling the dandelion, she tensed, but he shook his head. "It will tickle a different way," he said. "Okay?"

"Okay." She understood the message. *Leave it alone for now.* She didn't tilt her head to look at Geoff, but she wondered what his reaction was to Chris's odd response.

Chris moved the white puff of seeds over her flesh, tracing his way around the teddy bear navel jewelry. She reached behind her, curling her fingers in Geoff's shirt, bearing down so she could stay still under the sensual tease. His hand closed over her wrist. Her other hand was free, but Chris adjusted so his grip curled over that one, pinning it to the grass. Her toes balled up in her sneakers as he bent and blew over the same flesh, sending the dandelion seeds floating away over her head. As she watched them go, he kissed her stomach, tugging the teddy bear in his teeth.

Before she had a piercing, she'd never thought of her navel as an erogenous area, but a tug like that could twist sensation from that point and radiate it outward in heated swirls.

"I want to touch his hair," she said. Geoff's hand tightened on her.

"Ask me to let you go, Sam."

"Please . . . I'd like to touch his hair. Sir."

Chris stilled. She held her breath, waiting to see if he'd have any reaction, good or bad, to her addressing Geoff that way. Apparently he was processing it, like he had when Geoff made her hold the tomato in her mouth, because after that brief pause, he resumed what he was doing, teasing the indentation with his tongue. Geoff was still holding her. "Please, sir."

Geoff's grip loosened and she tunneled her slim fingers through Chris's thick mane, along his ears, his nape. Geoff stroked her hair as well, playing with the shell of her ears and caressing the tender skin of her throat. Chris's other hand traveled up her thigh, the heel of his palm pressing close to her pubic mound as he followed the strip of skin above the waistband of her jeans. Pushing two fingers beneath, he tugged on the elastic band of her panties. She gripped his hair in aroused response, and he made an approving noise against her. Lifting his head, he looked at her with a heated expression, shifting that look to her Master.

"I think it's time to go home, Geoff."

"It might be at that. Come here."

Geoff hauled her up his body and brought her down to kiss his mouth, a demand that made her whimper, especially when the position twisted her onto her side and Chris slid his hand from stomach to hip and captured her ass. Kneading her flesh through the thin denim, he put pressure on the seam between her buttocks with his broad thumb. When Geoff finally broke the kiss, she stared into his intent eyes, wanting that firm mouth back on her.

"That's so you don't forget me while I'm gone tonight," he said. "Just in case, I'll be leaving something with Chris to remind you."

~

When they arrived home, Geoff had an hour to shower and change before he had to leave for his client dinner. Chris flipped on the TV to do some channel surfing while Sam put away the picnic supplies. Geoff's words had a million wild possibilities dancing through her mind, so it was his fault she couldn't settle down. She listened to the faint sound of the shower running in Geoff's room. He hadn't closed the door to his bedroom, and she suspected he hadn't closed the bathroom door, either.

"What do you think he'd do if I went and watched him shower?" she asked, coming back into the living room. She leaned against the back of the occasional chair, doing a deep bend over it to stretch out her back and hips. Yoga had taught her the importance of keeping the body limber, inside and out. She had even more reasons to keep it flexible now.

Chris's attention shifted from the TV to watch her with lazy pleasure. "Since he knows what we're going to do when he's gone, he's probably jerking off so he can pay attention to whatever bullshit he's going to have to do tonight."

She was heading down the hall before she could stop herself, though Chris stopped her with one reproving word. "Sam."

She looked over her shoulder at him with a mischievous smile on her face and a tight feeling in her belly. "Come with me. Let's see if he'll let us both watch."

She was teasing—mostly. Like Chris, she knew it wasn't fair to push Geoff like that when he had to go to work. As such, it surprised her when Chris answered seriously.

"He won't let you watch. Not until it's his idea and he's calling the shots on it." He shifted his gaze back to the TV, watching the screen a little too intently.

How much of this stuff were the two of them talking about, and how much was Chris intuiting? At the park, it seemed he wasn't ready to talk too much about how he and Geoff were interacting on all of this. Yet when they were of a mind to work together regarding her, the results were enough to dissolve her brain.

Pondering that, she returned to lean against the occasional chair. She looked companionably toward the TV, but she imagined Geoff in the shower, water following the curves and angles of his body, strong arms and defined abs, the taut buttocks. He'd be clasping his erection and working it toward a climax in a loosely curled hand. He'd rock up onto the balls of his feet, his head dropping back to expose his throat, a fist tattooing against the tile as the orgasm boiled up and overtook him, his release fountaining from his cock and splashing onto the shower floor.

To keep herself from sprinting down the hallway after all, she moved to the couch and sat next to Chris. Drawing up her feet, she clasped her arms around her knees and studied him. He kept his eyes on the screen.

"If he didn't have to go to work and he would let us watch, would you do it?" she asked. "Would you get aroused by watching him?"

Chris lifted a shoulder. "It's more about you."

She wasn't so sure of that, because of the sudden tension in the shoulder she was leaning against. "Do you think you're less of a man for being attracted to him? Do you think I'd think less of you if you wanted him . . . that way?" She was going to say *if you wanted Geoff to top you*, but she had a feeling that topic was way the hell off-limits, so she stuck to the safer perimeter. Sex alone.

His lip curled. "It turns you on to think about the two of us together, doesn't it?"

"Exponentially."

Her deliberately perky expression inspired a half smile. "You look like a happy squirrel," he commented. "Why would you want to see two guys together?"

"You and Geoff both like that burger commercial where the two hot girls in bikinis are eating the hamburger at the same time, like they're almost kissing." She frowned. "Though seeing two guys eating the same hamburger would probably just be gross, because most of you have the table manners of farm animals. But kissing, or doing other things . . ." She elbowed him.

He sighed and settled deeper into the couch, stretching his arm across the back of her cushion and crossing his ankles. She cuddled closer to him, reaching up to the tense shoulder to knead. A few minutes later he dropped his arm around her and she laid her head against his shoulder. . "Sleepy?" he asked.

"A little. Too much sunshine. We never did take a nap at the park."

"Take one now."

"Don't want to. I might miss . . . things."

He touched his lips to her cheekbone, his deep voice vibrating against her skin. "I want you to take a nap because you're going to need energy for those things. Lots of energy."

She promptly closed her eyes and affected a snore. He chuckled. "I was right. You're such a brat. Doze off. I'm right here and you won't miss anything. Count on it."

"What are you going to be doing?"

"Thinking about everything I plan to do to you in my bed, soon as the door closes behind Geoff. Which is another reason he's jerking off. He knows I won't wait any longer than it takes him to get in his car and turn over the engine."

She lifted her head and met brown eyes that were no longer mild or gentle. "That makes it really difficult for me to take a nap."

"Try." Chris brushed her mouth with his own. "Lie down and I'll sing to you."

When she settled her head on his leg, he turned the TV down and stroked her hair. He began to sing by humming. He had a gravelly, rough bass that was nowhere close to a good singing voice, but she loved listening to it.

"Itsy Bitsy Spider . . ."

She smiled, closing her eyes. Though she wasn't sure it was going to work, between the slow, rhythmic caress of his large hand and the murmur of his lullaby, she did drop off for awhile. When she became aware again, the room was semidark. It was twilight outside, and since the lights in Geoff's room and the hallway were off, she knew she and Chris were alone. His hand rested on her hip. When she shifted, showing she was awake, he gripped her thigh, squeezed and picked up the remote. He turned off the TV, the oven hood light in the kitchen providing the only illumination.

"When did he leave?" she asked thickly.

"About fifteen minutes ago. Said it'd probably be eleven or so before he was home."

"Okay."

Chris was always quiet, but there was a particular immobility to him now that seemed to discourage questions or suggestions. In her logy, just-waking state, the weight of what was about to happen wrapped them in sexual tension. Arousal spread through her belly like a slow, rich syrup, ready to flow in any direction he desired.

"Come here." He slid her into his lap, cradling her as he rose. He kissed her forehead and she wound her arms around him, sighing in contentment.

He took her to his bedroom. He threaded them through the doorway, turning so her feet didn't hit the frame, and put her down, holding her around the waist. His hands found her face, tracing her cheeks, her lips, in the darkness. "You steady on your feet?"

She nodded against his touch. "All right," he said. "Stay right here."

He moved away from her to his dresser. A match struck and he touched it to several candles. They hadn't been there earlier and she wondered if Geoff had put them there for him before he left, so Chris hadn't had to disturb her slumber. It was the type of thing she'd expect them to do.

"It's like you read each other's minds, anticipate what you each want before it happens."

"Sometimes the one thing you have in common makes the rest work out." Blowing out the match, he faced her, resting his hips against the dresser. "Will you take off your shirt and bra for me, Sam?"

Removing the T-shirt, she set it aside and unhooked the bra, letting it slide down her arms. She was restless and still at once, restless with desire and yet still, waiting for him.

Her gaze coursed around the room. He collected things from and about the work he loved. Bird nests, rocks. Secondhand books on plants and landscaping were organized in wooden crates he'd stacked up as his bookcases. Her attention lifted to the ceiling. The candlelight flickered over what he had hanging there, creating interesting shadows. He liked to work twigs into shapes, using long, resilient grasses to hold them that way. As a result, he had the wooden outline of birds and butterflies hanging from the ceiling, or pegged flat against it.

Chris didn't like to be hemmed in, even by the four walls of his bedroom. *"Whichever one of us becomes the billionaire tycoon,"* Geoff had once said, *"will make sure the mansion has at least one room with a glass ceiling. That will be Chris's bedroom."* Before Chris started hanging his twig sculptures—or maybe he did it as a result—she and Geoff had painted his ceiling like a sky divided between night and day. Clouds, blue sky and the sun on the one half hosted seagulls, Canadian geese and cardinals flitting against the azure. The other half was a night sky full of stars and a crescent moon, the silhouette of an owl and a cadre of bats passing through and behind wispy, transparent gray clouds.

Where Geoff had the biggest bedroom, Chris had the one with the most windows, though right now the blinds were closed. He usually left them open, even at bedtime, because his windows faced the backyard. She knew he'd closed them to help her feel more comfortable. Or asked Geoff to do it, again so Chris wouldn't have to disturb her sleep.

It was like earlier today, when they'd called off the wrestling because she was in the middle of it. For all that they could be too protective at times, there were moments she understood what a miracle it was to have another person give such priority to her well-being. And she'd been given two people like that.

Chris was looking at her, and his expression made it hard to breathe. Such a look from Geoff made her want to kneel at his feet. Chris's expression held her still. It did amazing things to a woman, having a man look at her like she was a dessert. The kind to be savored in the ways that made the most of all its creator had intended it to be.

"Now take off the rest."

She removed jeans, socks and underwear, putting them all aside. His gaze followed the lengths of her thighs, grazed over her abdomen, her sex, dropped to her feet, then he worked his way back up again. "Chris."

His eyes lifted to hers. "What do you want, Sam?"

"You. Closer. Closer than breathing."

His lips curved and he moved toward her, stopping with a stride between them. Dropping to one knee, he closed his hands over her thighs, thumbs sliding along them until they touched the point of her sex, spreading the labia so air touched her intimately.

"I want you to put your hands behind your back. Link your fingers, hold them there."

She obeyed. His grip shifted to her waist then slid up her arms. "You tremble when I tell you to do that. Why?"

"It . . . excites me, when you or Geoff tell me to do something. I can't explain why . . . I mean, if you told me to wash the dishes just because you didn't want to do it, it wouldn't be the same." She managed a tight smile when his eyes twinkled in response to that.

"But . . . if you told me to bring you a glass of water, not because you weren't willing to do it yourself, but because you wanted me to know you were going into . . . this mode, it would get my attention."

"Yeah. I've noticed that. Geoff said he threatened to use a belt on you."

"Yes." What if Chris didn't approve of that? What if . . .

"And you liked that idea."

"Yes. But I . . ."

"You don't need to explain that to me, Sam." His touch returned to her upper thighs, thumbs parting her sex once more. When he pressed a simple, moist kiss on her clit, her fingers tightened into a knot where they rested on the rise of her buttocks. A needy sound broke from her lips when he touched her with the tip of his tongue, traced a circle. Sitting back on his heels, he studied her.

"Your nipples are tight little points." His fingers slid into her folds, found her wetness and spread that lubrication before he put his fingertips inside her. "Talk to me, Sam. I want to hear that breathy sound in your voice as I get you wetter."

She swallowed. "How did you notice . . . how I am?"

"Little things at first. Like when we were watching that *NCIS* episode where Tony tells the doctor he was dating to get behind him before they confront the drug dealer. When she asked why, and he said 'Because I tell you to,' in this really non-Tony-like commanding way, you froze up like a mouse in front of a cat." He smiled against her thigh, kissing her there. "Or when Gibbs told Abby that if he ever smacked her, it wouldn't be upside the head."

"I feel transparent." The joke fell flat, because she couldn't tell anything from his tone. Did he think that was an okay thing about her? Had he been aroused by her response? Or did he have no reaction to it at all except puzzled curiosity?

"If you know what to look for, yeah. It's there. But transparent like a creek, sparkling and showing all sorts of interesting possibilities. Most people never see anything more than the water, even though it's clear. They don't look deeper than the current, the ripples it causes on the surface. Do you notice something different about my room? Other than the candles?"

She'd thought Geoff was the sadist, but Chris was making her play twenty questions while he had his fingers inside her, his lips playing along her thighs and mons. He teased the sensitive gate of her pussy, making her move against him as much as her standing position allowed.

Her gaze skated back over the ceiling, seeking a new item hanging there. Nothing struck her as different, so she lowered her attention to the items he kept on his desk and dresser. She was pretty sure he wasn't talking about the paperwork he had scattered there or the book on organic pest control. When she'd first come into his room, the first thing she'd noticed was his mattress on the floor was made up neatly with the army blanket and couple of pillows he used. Since she'd assumed that was their ultimate destination, that explained why she'd overlooked the hammock, and how he'd adjusted it.

Rather than being strung between two corners, the hammock was hung from the ceiling, one end loose so the woven mat was vertical, gravity giving it a banana shape.

Chris withdrew his hand and rose, taking her elbow. "Keep your hands behind you," he reminded her. She thought of the cuffs Geoff had bought earlier today. It would be thrilling to have those snapped onto her wrists, but she quickly discovered that being told to keep herself restrained was equally powerful. The candlelight and darkness added to the persuasion, though it was Chris's mannerisms mostly doing it. He was holding himself somehow apart from her, staying in control yet so intimately close to her in mind and thought.

Chris brought her to the hammock, bent and lifted her, guiding her feet into two of the diamond shape openings of the webbed rope. The openings were wide enough he could push her legs through up to her thighs. He had her unlink her hands and threaded them through two higher holes, spread farther apart. When he brought the loose end of the hammock up from the floor, her feet were back on the ground, the webbing tight against her buttocks, snug around her thighs as he stepped onto a stool and hooked that end up where the other was.

Having her in the net he'd created, he modified her position to his satisfaction. He adjusted the ropes around her thighs so they pressed into the channel between her thigh and outer labia on either side, a sensation that compressed nerve endings, made them throb more. He cradled her breasts, framing each in a diamond opening. Withdrawing some single lengths of rope from his dresser, he wove them through the openings beneath her breasts and around her back, and did the same at her waist. He included her arms in the wrap so they were held at her sides.

He stepped back, pulling the stool away to study her again in that distracting, absorbed way. Her lips had parted, her teeth worrying the lower one, and he bent to put his mouth over it, bite it himself. "Got you at my mercy now, don't I?"

"Y-yes. You do. Did you . . . you and Geoff figure this out?"

He shook his head. "You don't imagine I think about this kind of thing, do you?"

"I didn't know. I . . . oh God." He cupped her breast, pinching her nipple between thumb and forefinger. With her already so stimulated from the restraint, if he kept doing that, she was pretty sure she'd come from nipple play alone. Especially since he could use his hands in ways that were . . . damn . . . near . . . perfect.

"You were saying?" he asked.

She choked on a chuckle. "I wasn't sure . . . how you felt about it. Didn't want to push . . . or assume you wanted the same things."

"I don't." His mouth firmed. "You called him *sir* earlier. That fits him. Not me. I'm just Chris. I didn't think of it, Sam. Not really. But when I saw what happens to you when he tells you what to do, the way you reacted to the TV shows, little things like that, it clicked. Sometimes you don't know how much you can enjoy something until you learn more about it."

He touched her face. "Most of the time, dating is about the games, you know. Figuring out what a girl's thinking or what she wants you to think, to say. It's different this way. I feel like you're so open to me, so raw and vulnerable, and it makes me . . . I don't want to play any games ever again. Not those kinds. I don't understand all the other stuff, so I figured, it didn't matter. I'd just follow Geoff's lead, we'd both go out with girls, and it would be good enough. But once you have this, who could settle for good enough ever again?"

"No one," she said, her voice vibrating with her need.

His gaze returned to her face, her parted lips and eyes she knew had to be feverish with wanting him. She let out a little cry as his fingers slipped through the opening of the ropes and into her, scissoring in the wetness. "God, you're so worked up. It starts with the smallest trigger. When Geoff tells you to do something, or when I told you I was taking you to bed tonight, everything else closes down for you, except this thing in the center of your soul. You lose yourself in it, Sam. A wild animal takes you over, beautiful and unconditional, no awareness of anything but instinct."

She was back to making small whimpers, her heart grown too large to allow anything but feelings to escape her throat.

"When I first saw it," he said huskily, "This part of me woke up and wanted to take you down, make you helpless and screaming, pull you into me and never let you go. Hold you fast."

She swallowed. "Chris . . . I don't have to call you *sir* to think of you as my Master."

He locked gazes with her, his lips pressing together. She couldn't tell what he thought of that, but after a moment he bent his head again, tracing the ropes along her thighs, around to her buttocks. "Seeing you helpless, wanting me this badly, drives me to my knees at your feet, Sam. It also makes me want to be a complete beast. I may not be him, but whatever it is inside him . . . maybe a part of it is inside any man who's given the gift of what you're offering."

His gaze lifted to hers again. "I want to let that beast loose and see where it takes us. All right?"

"Yes." Her voice came out a whisper. "Please."

"Do you remember the rules?"

She nodded, a quick jerk.

"All right, then." He circled behind her, using the other hand to caress, pinch. When he did it to her buttocks, she felt the imprint of the rope against her tender flesh more keenly. Dipping his fingers beneath her, he sank them into her pussy once more. She undulated in the bonds, like a caterpillar struggling in its cocoon as he thrust, scissored, withdrew. He parted her buttocks, fingers lubricated with her response pressing against her rim and easing into her. The feeling was different from a clitoral massage but just as arousing. He worked his way deeper while still stroking her rim. The two rings of muscles relaxed, letting him in.

"Sweet girl. You trust me. That means everything, Sam."

She closed her eyes as he worked his fingers back out. "You've thought about us being inside you at the same time," he said.

"Yes. A lot."

He chuckled, a tension to it that made her fingers stretch out, recurl. She wanted to touch him. He moved away from her, but only to go to the dresser, where he withdrew something he didn't let her see. When he came back, standing behind her again, she knew at least one of the things he had was lubricant. She heard it being uncapped and the tip of the tube was pressed against her rectum. As Chris put the heated ointment inside her, he spoke in a conversational voice, though the strain threaded through it suggested his reaction to having his hands on her this way.

"Geoff said he was going to make sure you remembered him while he was gone. He left this."

Withdrawing his fingers, Chris moved against her back, his arm pressing against her side as he brought his hand around to her front and showed her a lavender-colored butt plug. It had a slim tip that flared out to a medium-sized base. The flared end was embellished with a purple rhinestone the size of a quarter. Purple was her favorite color, and the gem had a thin silver border. While she'd noted things like that at Madison's shop, she hadn't expected the prettying up of that kind of toy to appeal to her. However, when she imagined it seated in her rectum, Geoff or Chris making her walk around naked so they could see how it looked, the faceted jewel with silver highlights nestled between her buttocks, she found the idea tantalizing.

"Since most days he's a walking dick in a fancy suit, I told him you wouldn't have any problem remembering him once you saw this."

She strangled out a half chuckle. "You're terrible."

"Just the truth." He began to return to his position behind her, but she tried to follow, pressing against him.

"Can you hold me a moment?"

Both arms folded over her, and the plug pressed against her side where he still had it clasped in his hand. Brushing his lips over her temple, he constricted his grip so she was held even more securely by his arms than the rope. She drew in a breath, an erotic sound as he shifted and the head of what she assumed was the plug pressed against her rear opening, all while he was still holding her. "Ever put anything in here, Sam, while fantasizing about us taking you?" he asked.

"Yes. Small things. So I'd know how to make it work."

"Good. Because it's not my usual area. I don't want to hurt you. Tell me how to do it."

"Like you did it with your fingers. Ease it in and I'll push against you and . . . there." The man was a quick study. The plug was bigger than what she'd used on her own, but he'd worked it in so easy and slow, lubed it up so well, the discomfort and burning were minimal. The response from her body was instant, nerve endings between cunt and anus starbursting. He kept his body against hers but his hand between them, playing with the toy. Her hips lifted, a moan breaking from her lips.

"Yeah, you like that. What if I did . . . this . . . too?"

The moan increased in volume and range as he moved his other hand between her legs. Her rectum contracted on the dildo, and she could imagine Geoff taking her from behind while Chris thrust into her pussy. Then they'd change places, or eventually both take her mouth. She wished she could put both of them in her mouth at once. Not really possible except in theory, but the very idea of it increased the moisture between her legs as she thought of how their thick lengths would stretch her lips . . .

"Fuck, this makes you hot. Doesn't it, baby?"

She was beyond speech. She liked that they both called her *baby* in more intense moments.

"He's going to be the first one to take you back here, but he wants me inside you when he does it."

So they had talked about this kind of thing. Like when she'd had the tomato in her mouth and she'd been unable to speak while they conversed so casually about how they wanted to use her body. "When . . . when did he say that?"

"Last thing he said before he left tonight." Chris paused as if there'd been more to it than that, but he adjusted the ropes so one was over the flare of the plug. "That should keep it in place. You can imagine that's Geoff there when I'm inside of you. Understand?"

She nodded, vehemently. "Chris, I need you inside me. Please."

He moved in front of her. As her avid gaze clung to his every movement, he pulled off his shirt, presenting a wall of heated male muscle before her, rippling with his movements. His burning gaze was locked on her face. "Keep telling me that. Tell me how much you need me. I've been on this side of the wall a long time, Sam, wanting to be balls deep inside of you, pinning you and never letting you go. Your legs wrapped around me, your breasts rubbing against my chest. Part of walking in on you two in the shower was hurt and a bunch of emotional shit, but there was a part that was just pure rage that he'd had what I'd wanted for so long."

It startled her, but he wasn't done spiking her adrenaline when neither fight nor flight was an option. His hand snaked out and clamped around her throat, making her swallow uncertainly at the look in his brown gaze, a little more animal than man. "So tell me how much you want me," he growled. "Beg."

"Please . . . need you so much. Want you now. Chris . . ." She bit back a wail as he stepped back. Putting his hand to the button of his jeans, he slipped it, pulled open the zipper. She licked her lips, a nervous gesture that curled his mouth in a lazy, dangerous way. She wanted to bite his lips, taste them. She wanted him to bite her, demand everything from her. It was a good thing the hammock was holding her up, because her legs wouldn't have.

He got rid of the jeans and the rest of his clothes, revealing his powerful, large body from head to toe, every small nick and scar, the areas of paler skin her private pleasure to enjoy. His cock was hard and high, the shaft and head flush with blood, his balls drawn up tight against his thighs. He drew closer as her gaze returned to his face.

"Chris," she whispered. He traced her parted lips, and she nipped and licked at his, little crazed movements. She thought she might come the moment he pushed into her. Hell, if he simply ordered her to do it, she might come right now. As if sensing how spun up she was, his touch gentled, slowing them down. Her throbbing body needed him, but her soul drank in the words he spoke just as greedily.

"I want it to always be like this between us. I always want you to speak to me straight from the heart. I've wanted that for so long."

"Chris . . . oh God. Please . . ."

Curling his fingers in the hammock at her hips, he lifted her and positioned himself between her spread legs. Slowly, slowly, he eased into her opening. She spoke his name again, a plea, as he worked himself all the way inside. Her hands fluttered and clenched, her body helpless and spasming from all the desire spiraling through her.

Yet there was one thing that didn't fit. "Chris . . . can you take the other out? It's like you said . . . I want it to be real."

The emotions he'd stirred inside her told her it was the right decision. As sexy as her initial thoughts had been about the plug, it had no place here. Not right now. The only way this could be any better was if

Geoff was here, too, but if he wasn't, the force of emotion between her and Chris was the only acknowledgment of their third partner needed or wanted.

He understood. He dropped his hand to grip the base of the plug and remove it. Her muscles relaxed, but her rim was stimulated by the slow removal, such that when he dropped the toy and started thrusting into her in an easy, torturous rhythm, she let out a surprised groan at the sensations that rocketed through her. His jaw tight, Chris measured her every response as he moved in and back, slow and deep. He had his arms threaded through the ropes and was lifting and lowering her as well, adding to the sensation as he controlled all of the movement. "Do you like this?" he murmured.

"Yes." Her gaze clung to his face, the tight muscles that told her he was close as well. "I never want it to end."

"Good. Let's draw it out, then."

She bit back a half laugh and a desperate protest that bordered on a shriek as he withdrew from her, but he dropped to a knee and framed her breasts in his hands, pressing the rope around them as he took one nipple in his mouth and began to suckle. She shrieked in earnest now, writhing as much as her bonds allowed. Her head dropped back on her shoulders and she was lost in a swirl of shadows, heat and candlelight, the twig-shaped butterflies and birds flitting across her vision.

He took his time, moving from one to the other, until her mind was breaking up like radio static, only fragments of words getting through. Never. Need. Love. Help. God. The restraints added to it in a way she couldn't explain. The more helpless she was to what he was doing to her, the more she felt like she was flying, all while still holding on to him with every shred of her heart.

Coming back to his feet, he reached though the ropes to grip her hair, the back of her neck, holding her head in that tipped-back position. When he shoved back into her with force, anything else she could hope to hold on to, beyond him, was lost. He covered her mouth with his, kissed her with all-consuming purpose. His cock created erotic friction, inside and out, and everything started to spiral up, fast. She could barely get the words out. "Chris, I'm so close . . ."

He wrapped his other arm around her waist, using the force of his hips and the band of his arm to maintain the momentum and power of his thrusts. Her mind shattered, carried away by the birds and butterflies. Her lips drew back in a near snarl. "Oh God . . . please . . . Chris . . ."

"Come, Sam. Come now, for us."

She had no choice. The position, the psychological impact of the rope, the friction of Chris's cock inside her, shot her off the edge, into the type of climax that was a searing knife edge, far into a realm where she'd never stop wanting or needing them to take her like this, in a dozen different ways. She screamed like a banshee, but Chris covered her mouth with his, probably saving them from a 911 call by the neighbors. She might need an emergency call, though, because the climax felt like it was pulling her apart, tearing everything loose and leaving her in a web of ropes that she never wanted to leave, even as she longed to wrap herself around him and never let go.

He came then as well, grunting hard, his brow pressed against her temple, the hammock jerking with the impact of their bodies. He held her tight through his release, and she felt so full of everything that made sense, everything that she could want.

"Chris . . . Chris . . ." She was panting his name.

"I'm here. It's all right, baby. I'm here." As he held her close, she thought his legs were shaking, but she knew he wouldn't leave her without his warmth and strength. His hand slid around to her rim and teased her there, two fingers sliding in slowly, her tissues contracting over them. The aftershock, as strong as a mini-climax, had her bound arms straining as she tried to hold onto something, a plaintive cry tearing from her throat.

"You know he'd want to have the last word," Chris said, making her choke on a laugh even through the tide of feeling.

"Oh God . . . Chris."

He pressed even closer. Her fingers could touch his thighs. "I'm here. Let's get you out of this."

He unhooked the end of the hammock and shepherded her carefully out of the ropes, shifting and supporting her body to take her down to his mattress on the floor. He joined her there, wrapping himself around her and pulling a blanket around them both. It was only when they were in that position she realized why he was suddenly being so protective. More than usual, that is.

As the climax had ebbed away, she'd begun to shake again, so hard that her teeth were actually chattering. He held her, rubbed her over the blanket, kissed her brow, her mouth, put his bare leg over her hip, surrounding her. "It's all right. Geoff said this kind of thing happens. You're fine. Just nod if you agree with me."

The concern in his voice recalled her enough she managed a quick nod. Subspace. This was like subspace. She'd felt the promising hints of it with Geoff, but the deeper the three of them moved into this, she suspected the more likely it was to happen. Flo had said some subs never really got there because it was a combination of triggers, and had a lot to do with the relationship between Dom and sub, how deep it was, how much the Dom understood about the sub. Sam didn't think anyone in the world had ever understood her the way these two did.

"Okay. Just relax. Easy there." He kept rocking her until she evened out, came back to reality. When she at last nuzzled his throat with her lips, he let out a relieved sigh. He had been worried. She loved him for that, as well as a million other things.

"You've never called me *baby* before today." Her voice was raspy.

"Yeah. I get mushy after sex. It's like the *I love you, man* beer buzz." He smiled against her brow.

"That was . . . amazing. In every way."

"Mmm. Same goes." His hand slid down her spine, fingers tracing the valley to the seam of her buttocks, playing there. "I think I'm warming up to the idea of spanking you, Sam."

The unexpected segue gave her a hitch. Not an unwelcome one.

"I thought I should tell you," he said. "In case I gave you the wrong idea about that earlier."

"You seemed . . . averse to it then."

"Yeah. I know what Geoff is, and I've thought about the things he might do with women, but for some reason I'd never applied those things to you. And when I did, at first, it felt wrong. Maybe because I wasn't entirely on board with Geoff's preferences. Yet, it's like I said. Watching how you respond, and finally turning the mirror on myself, thinking about it . . ." He gave a half chuckle. "I had this really hot dream the other morning."

Curling her fingers in his chest hair, she smiled against his flesh. "Yeah?"

"Yeah." He kept up that tantalizing rubbing motion over her ass, grazing her upper thighs and returning to her lower back.

"We were in the kitchen, and you dropped a plate. You said you were sorry and were all blushing and upset about it. I told you I'd fix it before Geoff found out, but first you had to drop your panties and bend over, because you'd been a bad girl."

He shifted, a sheepish note entering his voice. "Sounds kind of silly, but it was a dream. I couldn't control it."

"It doesn't sound silly." Far from it. "If it was never your thing, I was okay with that. Totally okay. But if you are . . . I have thought about you doing something like that as well."

"Oh yeah?" When he raised his head so he could look down at her, she tucked her head farther under his chin, making him chuckle. "So now *you're* going to be the shy one."

"Well, it's easier to talk about it when I'm not looking right at you."

"Okay." He rubbed her back some more. "So how have you imagined it?"

"Which version?" she asked, and earned another laugh.

"Tell me a current favorite."

"Well, with Geoff, I imagine a cause, kind of like how you did. I do something 'accidentally' to piss him off and he decides to punish me. He has this way about him . . . It makes me want to play it out like that." She paused. Men tended to be competitive, and she didn't want to imply that because Geoff brought out different feelings in her, they were somehow better than what Chris could inspire. But she realized she had to proceed under the assumption the men wouldn't compete that way. Because if they did, this wasn't going to work, was it? She'd be exhausted by keeping the balance.

Since Chris kept touching her and listening as if he'd had none of those disquieting thoughts, it reassured her. She took a breath. "You're different. You'd do it just because you want to do it, and that's what would get me all . . . worked up."

He put a hand beneath the seam of her buttocks to probe between her legs. They loosened and she purred helplessly as he played in the residual dampness of her climax and his.

"Tell me more," he said in a low rumble. Close enough to a

command to give her another shiver. His other arm tightened around her.

"We're out in the yard, and you're raking. I'm planting some flowers. I go into the garden shed to get something and, when I turn, you're standing there, blocking the door. I have a pitcher of water, and you tell me to pour you a glass. When I do, you drink it and I watch the beads of water gather on the glass and drip against your body, because you're shirtless."

"Of course. Voyeur."

She smiled at that, pushed at him. "Can't help that you and Geoff are both such hot, sexy guys."

Chris snorted. He didn't see himself that way. He'd probably say Geoff was the pretty one, but both her men were beautiful.

"So I'm leaning in the doorway, guzzling water."

"Drinking water. This is my fantasy," she reminded him primly. "But when you put down the glass, you're looking at me in a way that gets me all nervous, but excited, too. Like you did when we were sitting in the front room, before you took me in here." She paused. "What were you thinking then? No editing. Your words, your fantasy."

"I was thinking I needed and wanted you so badly, in so many ways, I almost couldn't trust myself to touch you, for fear I'd just rip you open to take and take and take."

He banded both arms around her again, holding her closer. "You're trembling again."

"The good kind."

"Okay." But he still rocked her, rubbed her soothingly. "I want to hear more about your fantasy. Keep talking, Sam."

"Okay . . . You set the glass aside, step forward, and grip my wrist. You sit down on that old decrepit stool we keep in there and pull me down over your knee. You don't say anything. You're just rubbing my ass, like you're staring at it, thinking all sorts of thoughts you won't share with me. Then you start spanking me. Light at first, then harder, stinging slaps that have me struggling, but you hold me down until you're done. You make me straddle your lap and kiss me. While you kiss me, you grip my backside in both hands, kind of hard so I can feel the spanking. After this endless kiss, when I can feel how hard you are, you push me gently off your lap, pat my ass and leave the shed. You go back to raking."

"So I'm an idiot in your dream?"

She giggled. "It's part of the charge. The way you do it, just because you wanted to do it, and then you go back to work, because you know whenever you're ready to . . . have me, I'll be ready for you. Because you know making me wait makes me crazier . . . and happier, all at once."

After that earth-shattering climax, she wasn't ready for another round yet, but calling her fantasy to life for Chris sent questing tendrils through her lower vitals, a promise that she could revive more quickly than expected.

He twisted a piece of her hair around his finger. "In my version, I'd make you take off your jeans and put you on my cock right then and there, with your ass still smarting. Because if my dick was hard and you're ours, I'd want you to know I expect you to take care of it then and there. That I'm not willing to wait another second to fuck you."

"Oh." She drew an unsteady breath. "Well, that works, too."

His lips pulled into a smile against her temple. "So what you're telling me is these fantasies of yours can be somewhat flexible?"

"Yes. For certain. Because when it's our fantasy, it can go in a lot more directions than when it's just mine."

"Got it." He pressed a kiss to her brow. "Okay, no more right now. My mindless dick is trying to flail back to life. It doesn't realize it needs a little longer recuperation time to keep from embarrassing itself. Don't snicker."

"I would never snicker."

"Uh-huh."

They were silent for a few moments, a companionable stillness. He caressed her hair, continued the stroke down her back and returned to her nape to repeat the motion, slow, methodical sweeps that helped her ease back from the pull of their shared fantasies and turn her mind to her own necessary recuperation time. She'd never needed sleep after sex. Like most of her gender, sex usually energized her, but apparently the emotional demands of her submissive desires were more capable of stealing her energy. A drifting postcoital doze sounded entirely appealing.

Her body was starting to melt into the angles of his, into the cradle of the mattress, when he spoke again. "We can move to your bed if you're more comfortable there."

"Your scent is on the sheets and mattress. You're all around me. I like that."

He went quiet, but his arms constricted around her, almost taking her ability to breathe, but she didn't mind. Snippets of everything they'd just shared drifted through her mind, and she wondered how long he'd been lonely, wanting this from her. From her and Geoff. Her heart broke a little, even as it also swelled with the potential for a happiness greater than she'd ever imagined. She tried to push away the thought that it was from great heights that great falls happened. She had two wonderful men who would catch her. But could they catch Chris, a big man with an even bigger heart, if he needed it?

Chris was a deep sleeper. Being sheltered in that subterranean repose had a restful effect on her, such that she stirred in the small hours of the morning without alarm, a slow slide into wakefulness that was filled with contentment. She blinked, her eyes growing accustomed to the shapes around her. Some of the candles were still lit. Since Chris's door was open, she knew Geoff was home, because his bedroom lamp was spilling dim light into the hallway. Which allowed her to see Geoff himself, standing in Chris's doorway.

He was leaning against the frame and, though he was silhouetted, she thought he was simply watching them. She'd turned on her opposite side in her sleep and Chris was spooned around her, arms folded over her waist and chest, holding her securely, but she was able to lift a hand, flutter her fingers in a gesture of silent greeting.

Geoff lifted his hand in answer, but then he straightened and pulled the door to a crack, hiding him from her view. She heard his soft footfalls return to his room and, a few minutes later, his light was doused.

She closed her eyes, drifted again. When she next woke, she estimated it was about forty-five minutes later. Her mind had been working while she slept, apparently, because she was wide-awake, with a clear purpose.

"Chris," she whispered. She twisted in his arms so she could kiss his mouth, nibbles that became deeper, more intent. She slowly brought him to wakefulness, and wondered if he had the same series of reactions she'd had when she first woke. Surprise to find her there, followed by intense contentment that she was.

Her lips parted to ask him, to tell him what other thoughts were flitting through her mind, but he took her words away. His hands slid down her body and he pushed her to her back, nudging her legs apart as he shifted over her. The look in his eyes when they latched on to hers reminded her of what he'd said when he'd thrown that curve into her fantasy.

Because if my dick was hard and you're ours, I'd want you to know I expect you to take care of it then and there. That I'm not willing to wait another second to fuck you.

He slid into her willing and ready body. She curled one hand around his neck while he tangled his fingers with her other one, holding her gaze as he set a slow, dreamlike rhythm that brought her to a gentle pinnacle, cutting her loose to spin as he released as well. She pressed her gasps into his shoulder, held him as he shuddered and finished. She was going to be so sore tomorrow for work, and Flo would tease her. She didn't mind.

As he slid off her, still holding her, she put her hand on his chest, heard the thunder of his heartbeat settling. Chris touched her face, traced it, and she pressed her mouth to the heel of his hand. "I'll be back," she whispered.

She slipped off to the bathroom naked, his come trickling down her thighs with a welcome warmth. She took care of her needs and heated a washcloth. Coming back to him, she cleaned him by touch in the darkness. While she knelt over him, his hand slid down the curve of her back in sleepy appreciation as she performed the task. Setting the washcloth aside, she leaned down to speak against his lips.

"Come with me." She found his hand and tugged as she got to her feet. She could sense his questioning look, but he didn't disturb the silence. He would follow her, because he trusted her, the way she trusted his lead.

He only paused to retrieve a pair of his flannel shorts from his drawer and put them on. She would have preferred him to be as naked as he seemed to prefer her, because he certainly didn't object to her decision not to wear any clothes, but at least he'd only donned shorts. When she took him across the hallway, into Geoff's room, his hand tightened on hers, either in question or hesitation, she didn't know, but he didn't stop her.

Geoff slept in the middle of his king-sized bed as he always did. As Sam drew closer to the edge, she could see his features. His bedroom had a small square safety light plugged into the outlet, same as in Chris's room. Chris had installed them as a way to find the bathroom or a lamp switch if needed. After his Orlando trip, he'd brought Sam a Disney princess night light to replace hers.

He'd installed the lights for safety, rather than the lingering childhood need to be able to see through the dark. Though Sam thought no one really outgrew that feeling, an adult sometimes had a need to dream their dreams in the illusion of privacy an absence of light provided. As such, sometimes she took hers out of the socket to explore her somnolent fantasies, or to indulge the womb-like comfort darkness could offer.

She was glad Geoff hadn't done the same tonight, though, because it helped her get to him without tripping over the shoes he'd left by a side chair, probably to remind himself to polish them tomorrow. It also allowed her to see his face more clearly when she came to the side of his bed, Chris's hand still firmly enclosed in hers.

There was a faint smell of fine alcohol on him, suggesting he'd had several drinks with the client. He never drank to excess, but she wondered if he'd intended it as a way to put himself to sleep more quickly when he came home, so he wouldn't have to feel left out of her and Chris's embrace. Which was stupid, because he could be part of that embrace at any time. Once he and Chris figured things out, that was.

She knew everything had to happen at its own pace. Even so, she wondered if they would be willing to twine around her and each other in this big bed. She wouldn't know unless she tried. Maybe if it was just to sleep, Chris could handle that. Which meant she probably should have worn something.

But seeing Geoff shirtless didn't inspire her to modesty or moderation. Beneath the thin sheet, he was probably wearing only his brief shorts that hid almost nothing. She bent over the bed, reaching out to touch his sculpted jaw. "He's so handsome," she whispered. Theirs to touch as much as they wanted, within the parameters of his commands. But even though they were just starting to explore how that worked, she knew she'd always eventually get to touch him, because he wouldn't deny her anything her heart truly desired.

She glanced up at Chris to see him looking between her and Geoff. His expression was hard to read in the shadows, but she didn't sense that he wanted to leave.

Geoff's hand closed over her wrist, as if he'd read her mind and surfaced from sleep as a result. His eyes opened, studying her, shifting to Chris, a quiet wall behind her.

"We'd like to sleep in here, with you," she said in the same low tone. "May we?"

She asked on her behalf and Chris's, even though she wasn't sure if she should include Chris in that sub-like etiquette. Regardless, Geoff agreed. "You may." His voice was thick with sleep, but his eyes were sharpening, coming awake.

He opened the covers, inviting her in. She put her knee on the bed and slipped under it, following his direction so she was lying facing away from him, his body cradling hers. She was right. He was only wearing the shorts. When he pressed his sleep-induced erection firmly against her ass, she wiggled against him in return. "Sleep," he admonished.

As soon as she'd lain down, she recaptured Chris's hand. She tugged, but he remained in place, looking down at the two of them. She sensed Geoff watching him, then he shifted behind her. He tossed a pillow over her, which Chris caught. He settled on the floor next to the bed, disappearing from her view.

She scooched forward, holding on to Geoff's arm. He blew a breath on the back of her neck, bit her gently, held her fast.

"I want to be able to see him," she murmured, tilting her head back so he could hear her. "Can we go to the edge?"

A multilayered question, but he chose to answer the surface of it. Geoff slid them both forward, but broke the intensity of the moment by deliberately overcompensating, tilting her over the end so she was grabbing for the mattress edge. Instead she found Chris's hand, since it was there, steadying her and helping her lean back as Geoff readjusted with a chuckle.

Now she was on the edge of the bed, where she could peer down at Chris without difficulty. She kept hold of Chris's hand, clasping it with both of hers against her chest as Geoff fitted himself behind her again, his arm banding around her waist before his hand slid up to the underside of her bare breast. He explored the curve around her and Chris's clasped hands. He had to be touching Chris by doing that, but Chris didn't withdraw. When Geoff pressed his turgid length against her ass again, she pressed back, drawing in a breath as his fingers slid down her hip, behind her buttock and probed between her legs.

"Did he leave you nice and slick for me, hmm?" Geoff's husky voice had a wicked note.

She bit her lip as Geoff adjusted his shorts and guided his cock into her, holding her in that half-curled position so the entry was tight and full of sensation, especially so soon after Chris had taken her almost the same way, surfacing from his dreams to enjoy her body. Her hand tightened on Chris's, nails digging into him. He sat up, propping one arm on the bed as he kept the other in a position where she could retain his hand. His eyes were dark pools in the night, his unshaven jaw and full mouth drawing her eye.

"Keep looking at Chris," Geoff said. "Let him see you get all frantic and helpless." His voice was heavy with lust. "Chris, when she's close to going over, kiss her. Kiss her like it's the only way you have of showing her what you feel about her. I'm going to take this nice and slow"—he dropped to a whisper—"just the way I imagined it during dinner tonight, when I thought about Chris inside you, how he'd bring you pleasure. He did, didn't he? He took care of our girl."

"Yes. Yes sir."

Geoff pressed into her a little deeper, wresting a quiet noise between ecstasy and discomfort out of her as he wrapped his hand around her throat and centered her in that takeover way he did so well, so naturally. "Did you take care of him as you know you should? Or do you have some punishment coming?"

Chris's mouth tightened in an inexplicable way. "I . . . I hope so," Sam managed. "I mean, I hope I took care of him . . ."

Geoff chuckled darkly. "Yet you also hope you earned some punishment. I wouldn't expect anything less. What do you say, Chris?"

As Chris leaned forward, the safety light reflected the earth color of his irises, the expression in them a mix of things. "She blew the top off my world. But I expect there's always room for improvement."

If she'd doubted she could have an orgasm so close after the last one, Geoff's commanding touch and Chris's opening to a veiled, sensual threat knocked things up into a zone that left doubt behind. She sighed, a sensuous sound, as her body moved restlessly against Geoff, pressing her hips deeper into the cradle of his, taking more of him. Oh God . . . He felt so good inside her, so much, filling her.

"She wants your touch, Chris. Play with her pussy while I'm fucking her. Let's see if we can blow the top off her world, hmm?"

She assumed Geoff wording the last part as question instead of command was intentional. If she could sense the warring factions inside of Chris about what was happening here, whether he was participant or subordinate, she knew Geoff definitely could.

Chris propped both elbows on the bed and pushed one hand beneath the covers, fingertips sliding along her hip and then across to find her. Geoff helped, gripping Sam's thigh and lifting so he guided her foot back over his calf, spreading her legs a few inches wider. When Chris started stroking her clit, she jerked, a lightning bolt of sensation adding to what Geoff was building within her. His hand tightened on her thigh and throat, a direct restraint as he continued to thrust inside her, smooth, deep. Relentless.

She was panting, those little incoherent pleas struggling in her chest again. They must be the utterances that came from the heart and soul, weighing too much to reach her lips. They stopped in her throat, twisting into a hum of need that could be translated and answered only by the two people she needed so much.

Chris's gaze was fastened on her face, reading that language as he plucked, pinched and rubbed. He didn't focus only on the clit. He traced the lips of her sex, stretched over Geoff's cock. In response, her body twisted and lifted, pushed and pulled between the two of them. When Geoff's breaths became harsher, she thought Chris had to be incidentally stroking him as Chris worked her pussy with his fingers and Geoff did it with his cock. Chris's gaze flicked up to her face, and she saw his awareness that this wasn't just about her in the middle, but about the three of them, what they could do for each other.

"Don't you come until I start, bad girl," Geoff said gruffly. "He has you ready to go off like a rocket, doesn't he?"

She nodded, and when his grip on her thigh constricted to an almost bruising hold, he wrested another cry from her. "Yes sir."

"Show me. Show us you can obey our desires."

The strain in his voice told her how close he was. Thank God, because she released barely a breath behind him, not because she had enough control to hold out, but because her timing was lucky. Chris closed the distance between them, capturing her mouth with intense purpose just as Geoff had demanded, as if it were the only way Chris had to show her how much he was feeling for her. Yet he kept his hand busy between her legs so she milked Geoff's cock with strong, spasming muscles, reveling in his harsh groans.

Geoff bit her shoulder, holding her as his hips pistoned against her, taking the full measure of satisfaction from their joining and then some as her cries increased. Higher and higher, Chris's touch and Geoff's cock, the pressure of their two bodies on either side of her, catapulting her to sheer ecstasy.

Only when she was limp in his arms did Geoff ease into a slower rhythm, bringing her back to earth. Chris kept working her hypersensitive tissues with light fingers, making her twitch and shudder in a way that seemed to please both men.

Chris had to be hard again and she wanted to do something for him. Of course, if they kept staggering climaxes, they might never leave the bedroom again. With a flash of desperate amusement, she realized she had no objection to that consequence.

Yet Chris drew back, pushing himself up off his knees. "Where are you going?" Sam asked groggily, reaching out. His fingers tangled with hers, but he squeezed her in a way that said he intended it to be a passing affection before he pulled away. She tightened her grip. "Stay."

"Yeah. Stay." Geoff shifted, and another pillow was tossed over her. Chris caught it by reflex. Geoff laid his head back behind Sam's again on his own pillow. "Lay your ass down on the floor. You know she's not going to sleep unless we're both here."

Was Geoff commanding him to lay on the floor as a way to underscore who the alpha dog was here? Or did he realize Chris wasn't ready to share the same bed with him? Or some of both? Regardless, she reached out again and curled her fingers over two of Chris's, clasping the pillow. "Please stay," she whispered. "We can move over and make room."

Geoff's arm tightened around her, but before she could determine if that was admonishment not to countermand him, or to help move them both over, Chris shook his head. He stretched out on the floor.

She didn't have to scoot forward much this time to look over the edge
and Geoff helped, moving with her. Chris was on his back, and his
brown eyes met hers. She dropped her hand down to graze his shoulder, sliding her touch over to play in his chest hair. He took hold of
her fingers, giving them a kiss and her a half smile. It wasn't an
entirely easy smile, but it wasn't distressed, either. She was reassured
when he held on to her fingers, their clasped hands resting on his
chest.

A surreptitious glance told her Chris was still erect under his
flannel shorts, but it was clear he had no plans to address that right
now. Closing his eyes, he tapped out Itsy Bitsy Spider on her hand,
making her smile. He wanted her to go to sleep, but he was holding on
to her. They both were. Geoff lay against her back, his arm around
her, his lips pressed to her neck.

She'd let that be enough for now. Her eyes slowly closed, her body
melting into the heat of Geoff's, and she let herself drift.

It was close to dawn when she surfaced again. She had a sense that
it was best to pretend to still be asleep, so she opened her eyes to
mere slits. She was still securely in Geoff's arms, but Chris was sitting
up. She watched his hand slide from her hand to her wrist and elbow,
then hesitate on her upper arm, where Geoff's hand was curved over
her biceps. Geoff's breath was even, suggesting he was asleep, but she
wouldn't be surprised if he wasn't, because there was a slight tension
to his body.

She felt Chris slide his hand from her to Geoff's hand and linger.
He kept it resting there as he put his head on the covers between her
chin and breasts, his breath light upon them. Geoff's hand moved, just
slightly. Though she wouldn't risk turning her head to look, she
thought maybe he'd adjusted enough to rest his thumb on Chris's
hand, a light clasp that wouldn't spook him but established
connection.

What would it take to break the barriers down between them? She
reluctantly understood this was one role she would have to play only
on the sidelines, but if it went in the direction she hoped, being a
spectator wouldn't be a bad deal.

Still, scorching male-male fantasies aside, there were deeper
considerations. The way Chris's cheek rested on the covers under her
chin, like a mute supplication regarding questions he didn't yet know

how to answer, a conflict he wasn't sure how to resolve, was too much for her to ignore. She knew what it was to be worried that her wants and needs wouldn't mesh with theirs, and that she might ruin everything. She was still wrestling with those things, but she was in a better place now than she had been, because she knew they loved her and she loved them. Anything else would be icing on the cake.

She also understood Chris had to go through his own process. Still, she'd do everything she could to help. Shifting her hand to his head, she stroked, slow, easy. Nurturing, with hope and love in every movement. As he let out a slow, deep breath, she pressed a kiss to his head, smiling a little as she inhaled the scent of earth and sunshine.

"It will be all right," she whispered. "No matter what. Sleep, baby. Just sleep."

He fell asleep that way, sitting up but leaning against the bed. When Geoff's hand moved to cover hers, both of them stroking Chris's head, she pressed her hips back into the cradle of his, an unspoken thanks and connection. Putting his lips against her temple, he breathed warm heat over her.

Whatever was coming, they would figure it out. They had to.

MIND

Part III

*C*hris fished through the box of resin figurines and pulled out a
squirrel sitting on gray haunches and holding a nut. No bigger
than his thumbnail, the creature had a steel pin in the base, which he
pushed into the earth next to a fairy. Her pale skin and slim face
reminded him of Sam. The fairy's slim legs dangled over the edge of
the bowl-sized pool he'd created. Her dress looked like it was made
out of petunia petals and her long straight hair was in a high ponytail,
the way Sam wore it when she went to yoga.

Okay, he had enough pieces in place to test the stability of the
channel he'd created. The water was supposed to meander from the
fountain at the top of the berm down through the fairy world, and
then funnel into an irrigation system for the vegetable garden. "This is
either going to be great or set off a mudslide," he muttered. Hearing a
clack-clack sound from Ron, watching him from the aviary, he shot the
bird a warning look. "No laughing," he told him.

He started up the hose, then opened the valve. Sitting back on his
haunches, he watched the rock fountain fill with water. As it spilled
over the spout, it chuckled its way into the gully he'd created,
becoming a sparkling creek. A couple of turns and it emptied into the
small pool, where the fairy and her squirrel waited. The water made it
up to her feet as he'd intended, so she could enjoy a dip of her toes.

He'd covered the liner of the pool with flat stone and outlined the
interior of the rim with a variety of multicolored polished round

stones that matched the style of the fountain. The water made them shiny, bringing out the array of colors. Before it could get higher than that, the water filtered into an exit pipe that emptied into another channel, which zigzagged down the remainder of the berm.

He watched it find its way around several rock structures and a garden of small concrete mushrooms. A stone turtle with a fairy perched on his back watched the water go by. Just below them were three frog houses with a few pansies planted around them, which served as both shade cover and "trees" for the tiny Fae figures and real world frogs that would come check out the lodgings.

Rising, he moved over to the garden, nodding in satisfaction as he saw the drip hoses begin to water the soil around the growing vegetables. It all seemed to be working. He'd add some phlox and other ground covers to fill in the dirt areas. He came back to the berm, squatting to adjust one of the frog houses.

"She'll love it."

He'd heard the screen door clap against the frame, had known Geoff was making his way toward him. The cast of his shadow said he was standing behind Chris, a little to the left. There was less than a foot between them. Chris didn't have to turn to verify it. Since Sam had left for her bank conference in Asheville yesterday, Chris had been like a GPS on Geoff's location.

"Here. Do you think she'd like this?" A paper bag rattled and then Geoff dropped to a knee next to him. He'd gone by the Fairy Cottage, which specialized in fairy gardens. Chris tended to hit less pricey places, but he and Sam liked wandering through that one, her to chatter ideas at Chris, him to watch her enjoy the miniatures and sharing garden ideas.

Geoff was careful with his money, but he seemed to know the right moments to spend more. He'd bought a pair of cats, just little bits of clay that had been hand-pressed by someone's fingers, toothpicks used to mark eyes and mouth. An artist knew how to do a lot with a little. They were the size of postage stamps, one curled up in a ball sleeping, the other curled up but head lifted.

"I thought these might work on that piece of tree limb you turned into a stump." Geoff pointed to it. Chris had three fairies dancing in a circle around it. "Cats being like cats are, I thought it would look like they were saying, *Yeah, big deal, fairies dancing around us. We're still taking our nap.*" Geoff pulled out a seed packet. "They also sold me these. The lady said they'll pop up into a good mix of wildflowers. Figured that might work as a border between this and the garden. But you're the plant guy. Did I waste my seventy-five cents?"

"No. You want to put the cats in place?"

"Hell no. I'll mess something up. Here."

Chris opened his palm and Geoff transferred the cats to them, his fingers brushing Chris's callused palm. Geoff's gaze rested on his mouth before he rose. He was wearing his office clothes, slacks, tie and dress shirt, but he'd shed the coat. Chris had a sudden urge to tackle him, roll him in the leaves and get him dirty. Tear open his shirt and watch Geoff's chest and arm muscles tighten as he tried to throw Chris off. Hand to hand, Geoff couldn't overpower Chris, but Geoff was fast and smart. He wasn't pinned too often.

Chris turned back toward the berm, tenting his fingers on the ground by his knees. He let the idea peter out in his mind. Geoff couldn't afford to replace his clothes because Chris had a crazy adolescent impulse. "You remember that time in eighth grade when you were getting the best asshole award?" he asked instead.

"It was the highest grade average, but yes."

Chris pursed his lips. "You said something to piss me off on the way to school and I shoved you into the creek. You were wearing nice clothes, like you do all the time now."

"Yeah. I remember." Geoff's shadow shifted behind him. Chris's gaze stayed trained on the shape of it. Long, because it was late afternoon. "I remember you felt bad about it," Geoff continued. "So you skipped class, jogged home and brought me new clothes. You got into trouble when you interrupted Mrs. Field's class to bring them to me."

"The next period was the awards ceremony."

"I had to cinch up my belt like a hillbilly and the shoulders of the dress shirt were so wide, the cuffs flapped over my fingers. Hadn't hit my growth spurt yet, and you were already built like a fucking tank. They took a picture of me with the Honor Society advisor, Mr. Williams. It's in the yearbook."

"Proof that you weren't always on the cutting edge of fashion. You never did hit that growth spurt," Chris added, lips curving despite his mercurial mood. "But sometimes I still get that urge to knock you into a creek."

"Like now?"

Chris nodded. Things inside him stilled as Geoff moved forward and his knee pressed against Chris's back, Geoff's shin against his hip and the buttock resting on his heel. "You get this shirt dirty," Geoff said quietly, "and I will kick your ass into next week, even if I have to use a two-by-four to do it."

Then he was gone, striding back across the yard, leaving things vibrating around Chris. With deliberate care, he placed the two cats on the stump among the fairies. He pocketed the wildflower seeds, knowing it would be better to wait another couple of weeks on those. Geoff was right, though. They'd make a good-looking border between the garden and the berm. Sam liked random groupings.

When she'd first told him she wanted to make a fairy garden, he'd told her it was a pain to mow around something like that, and the features tended to get disrupted by wind and rain. Mother Nature broke anything man-made into the shape She really wanted, but if a man knew how to work with Her, the results were worth it. Sam had known he wasn't saying *no*. It was a *Let me think about how to do it* thing. Sam was good about giving him the space to work things like that out. Up until this thing with him, her and Geoff, that is.

Ironically, it was when he'd been working off his mad about coming home from Mississippi to find Geoff and Sam together that he'd finally figured out the best place for the fairy garden. He'd built the berm near the vegetable garden, where the privacy fence gave it shelter on two sides. In that position, he could easily rig something to put over it when the weather was dicey.

It was a good feeling, thinking how Sam would react to it when she came home. She'd likely go wild, buying little things like Geoff had brought and adding onto the berm with her own competent landscaping skills. Before long, they'd have a fairy enclave across the whole back fence. Talk about a mowing nightmare. She'd want to hang things on the fence, chimes and Green Man faces, things that celebrated the fairy world.

He smiled. He was pretty sure Sam had a drop of Fae blood deep in her soul. She surely had the willowy look and fine features.

Chris straightened, cracking his back, and surveyed the yard with a critical eye. Over by the patio, the pond from which he'd obtained the berm soil was complete, a fountain gurgling in the middle, a couple of white-petaled lilies floating around in it.

While he liked spending his time outdoors, he knew that wasn't why he was lingering there now. She'd been gone less than twelve hours. He could sleep out here, in the tree house he'd built in the woods a few yards beyond the back fence. Yeah, right. He was being stupid.

He didn't know what he was avoiding. Geoff was giving him space, wasn't pushing at all. But that just made him feel twitchier, especially with Geoff right here, right now, just the two of them. Any other time, Geoff would be working until half past the ass crack of dawn, yet today he'd pulled in the driveway at half past five, better than a guy who punched a clock.

Sam's trip wasn't the first time one of them had to travel on business. Chris himself had just returned from doing some storm damage work down in the Gulf, and sometimes Geoff flew out at a moment's notice for a case. Sam traveled the least of the three of them, but she had a couple of trips a year with girlfriends or banking powwows like this one. He and Geoff always felt out of sorts when she was gone, like a three-legged stool with one leg gone, but this time there was a different quality to it. An anticipatory tension, something waiting to be resolved.

Chris went to the pond and sat down in the Adirondack chair Sam liked to use for reading. He thought about her shapely ass pressed against the boards, her knees pulled up to her chest and scarlet-painted toes curved over the edge of the seat. One Halloween she'd had a pedicure with tiny bats painted on her big toes, *B-O-O* painted on the three others of each foot, the tiny pinkie toenail done in a touch of bright orange for contrast.

He thought about her body straining against his in her bed, in his bed. Then his mind went to when they'd been in Geoff's room, her on the mattress and Chris on the floor. Her fingers had flexed in the grip of his, her lips parting and frantic eyes staring up at his face as he knelt by Geoff's bed, his hand on her clit and Geoff's cock thrusting into her from behind, bringing her to a climax.

He thought of stroking her pussy, soft as a lamb's ear. The thick base of Geoff's dick sliding in and out along Chris's fingers. He had deliberately not looked at Geoff when that happened, but he'd heard the breath clog in Geoff's throat, seen his hand on Sam's hip tighten further. Geoff had reacted to Chris's touch. Knowing that, Chris had hardened more, though his dick had already been capable of jackhammering concrete.

Since the night they'd spent in Geoff's room, they hadn't gotten that close to a three-way in the bedroom again. Throughout the workweek, however, neither he nor Geoff had restrained themselves from touching *her*. Sam herself encouraged that.

Like when they were keeping Chris company in the kitchen on the night he was in charge of dinner. She'd slid into Geoff's lap, talking and teasing them while her fingers curved over his nape, her body pressed against his, his arms loosely holding her. When Chris had come to give her a taste of the stroganoff, Geoff had dropped her backward in his arms, making her laugh as Chris tipped it into her mouth. Later, on the couch watching TV, she'd curled up next to Chris, pillowing her head on his thigh as she read. He'd laid his hand on her hip and thigh. And when it was time to go to bed, she'd come to bed with Chris. The next night, she'd gone with Geoff.

Since both men were keeping their bedroom doors open, listening to her soft gasps and breathy moans as Geoff brought her to climax on "Geoff's night" had forced Chris to put a choke hold on his own cock. He steadfastly refused to jack off while listening to that, for reasons he refused to discuss with himself.

However, the following night, when it was "his turn," he'd taken her up against the wall with animal need. She'd clung to him, her crystal eyes full of desire, love and hope. As he pushed her over into orgasm with him, that last one had haunted him. Watching, waiting, hope.

As he said, she usually provided him the space to work things out. While she was more impatient about this, he expected Geoff had exercised that Dom/sub thing he and Sam had going to compel her to give Chris even more room. So they hadn't talked further about it, not yet, but it was clear enough to Chris she was letting them all get familiar with intimacy with her, and trying her best to wait and see what the two of them might do to take that intimacy even further. She'd kept things in the "public areas" of the house affectionate but not overtly sexual.

Until right before she left on her banking trip.

Her friend Flo was driving Sam and a couple of other ladies up to the conference. When Flo's white Crown Vic pulled into the driveway, Sam waved at her friend out the side door, then stepped back inside the kitchen to get her rolling tote. Her silver-gray eyes touched both of them.

Giving them a measured look, she made a beeline to where Geoff leaned against the counter with his cup of coffee. He set it aside just in time as she twined her arms around his neck and went up on her toes to put her mouth on his. Geoff took over the kiss pretty immediately. That was the thing with Geoff. Never any confusion about who was in charge. He delved deep into her mouth, his hand dropping to her ass to hold her hard against him, so she let out a little moan.

She reached out toward Chris with fluttering fingertips, questing, and Chris couldn't refuse her. He closed the distance and squeezed her hand tighter than he probably should have. When Geoff let her down, she turned right into Chris's arms and gave him the same kind of kiss. The desire that gripped him was likely the same as what had seized Geoff. Her full-body message of *I will miss you* was impossible to answer any other way than with the same yearning.

Geoff gripped her hips below Chris's hold, the two of them sandwiching her between their bodies. When she drew back, she laid her head on Geoff's shoulder and caressed his jaw while she slid her fingertips along Chris's face. "It's like leaving the Garden of Eden," she said. The twinkle in her eye contrasted with a somber set to her mouth and a tremor in her touch that made Chris's brow crease.

"We'll be here when you get back," he promised.

"That's what makes it even harder to leave," she responded. Sliding away reluctantly, she moved back toward the door. Her tote trundled across the linoleum behind her, a poignant noise that reminded him of a little girl trudging up her driveway with a painted wagon. Though the person who stopped at the door and looked back at them was all woman, sexy and mysterious, her eyes liquid pools.

"I love you," she said, and then she was gone. Silently, he and Geoff moved to the window to watch her greet Flo and the other two ladies in the car. They chatted in that way women did, like a cheerful congregation of birds in a birdbath. Their laughter was like the fluttering of their wings, the words the bright droplets scattering about them.

"You know Flo's a Mistress?" Geoff asked casually, keeping his eyes on the women. "Sam went to a couple of parties with her. That's how she's been exploring some of this. She told me that the other night."

Chris made a noncommittal grunt. They'd talked about Geoff's Dom side several times before, Chris indulging his curiosity about it as a spectator and intrigued friend. Never in a way that would affect him, at least not consciously.

Which was maybe why he'd made some vague comment and escaped to the yard, rather than encouraging further dialogue.

Returning to the present moment, Chris closed his eyes and turned his face up to the dying sun. Sam was with both of them. Sleeping with both of them, having sex with both of them. Ever since that first night, the significance of it had hit him at unexpected moments. While working with Esteban's crew, while brushing his teeth, while lying with her in his arms, or while she was sleeping way too far away in Geoff's. No matter when or how he thought about it, it brought him a sweet, tight pleasure.

What if that was all he wanted? What if he didn't want to take it further? Sam had made it clear she would accept that, but there was an unspoken caveat. She could accept it as long as his insistence that that was all he wanted didn't trip her bullshit meter. And he couldn't even say it to himself without tripping his own.

This was just the starting gate. While there was a whole territory to explore with her, it could crash and burn as quickly as it started if he and Geoff didn't figure out how to relate to each other over it. He saw the worry about that in her face. However, unlike her, he knew he and Geoff were more worried about how a crash would impact her than the two of them. He and Geoff had had plenty of ups and downs as friends, yet there was a constancy to their relationship that would endure everything. Well, as long as they kept it in the lines where that constancy wasn't challenged to become something else.

He wasn't in the habit of lying to himself. He was good at leaving things alone that really didn't need to change for things overall to be okay. Trying to make something perfect was a pointless way to drive yourself crazy. But leaving this as is wasn't going to be an option.

Even so, he wasn't like Geoff or Sam. He didn't necessarily feel a problem needed an immediate solution. Sometimes you had to wait, give things time to play out to figure out how they wanted to work. It couldn't be rushed or forced. Maybe that wisdom came from years of gardening. What was natural and lasting should never be hurried, or forced to grow in a certain direction. You could do it, sure, but it took constant vigilance to keep it going that way, unless you convinced the plant it would be happier climbing up that trellis than across the ground. If it insisted on its own way enough, you had to respect that.

Now he was rambling off topic. On top of that, he truly was bullshitting himself. The impulse he'd just had to wrestle Geoff in the dirt hadn't been patient in the least. Rising, he went to shut off the water. He'd finish up out here, take a shower and stop being a pussy. There was no reason he and Geoff couldn't bond in mutual Sam-absence misery as they usually did. They'd grab something from the grocery store and grill out.

Geoff and Sam thought he was the most easygoing of the three of them, and he guessed he was. But maybe sometimes they overestimated his placid nature. Geoff surely did, because he came back out of the house . . . and he still hadn't changed clothes. He'd stripped the tie and opened the neck of his shirt, loosening the cuffs and rolling them up. He'd run his hands through his hair, because it was tousled. The late-afternoon sun drew Chris's gaze to the five-o'clock shadow on his jaw. He looked like a cross between a *Fortune* 500 magazine ad, and a guy with whom Ray Liotta would share his 1812 scotch in a heartbeat.

"Hey." Geoff strode across the grass. "That meat loaf Sam left us. Do you remember if she said to heat it in the oven, or can we chop off a couple of slices and nuke it? I was going to stick it in the oven while I changed if—"

Chris rose to his feet, pivoted to face him. Geoff had some of today's mail in his hand, flipping through it as he asked the question. Chris moved forward. "She said the oven makes it taste better."

"Yeah, that's what I figured. Just didn't know if I wanted to trade out taste for speed. I have to do some shit after dinner and . . ."

Geoff had acute intuition. He sensed danger before it happened.

His head came up abruptly, his expression registering that Chris was bearing down on him with only a couple of steps to spare.

"Do not, you son of a—"

Chris hit him midbody, taking him off his feet and back several yards, tumbling them into a bank of leaves he'd piled up for mulching. Geoff's snow-white shirt was a good contrast to the gray and brown tones of the dried leaves. His shiny shoes had no traction, so he couldn't get his feet underneath him to push up. Chris usually played fair with him, but he wasn't in the mood. Geoff figured that out pretty damn fast and responded accordingly.

Chris grunted as the male managed to buck, roll and slam his elbow into Chris's mouth, splitting his lip. It jarred him enough that Geoff slithered free and jumped on his back. Chris could shake most opponents like a Rottweiler, but Geoff was like a Jack Russell terrier. A Rottweiler would chase you out of his yard. A Jack Russell would pursue you to the edge of a cliff and then jump over it with you, just to make sure you ended up dead on the bottom.

He'd intended to flip Geoff on the roll, get him under him again, but instead, Geoff got his feet on the ground, clamped his hand on Chris's wrist and twisted. It was a sure pin, the pain of the angle discouraging movement. Chris was able to throw Geoff off enough to escape it, narrowly. Pain lanced up his arm. As a result, when he threw them both over backwards, he misjudged his toss.

Instead of Geoff ending up in the leaves, his friend landed on the much more unyielding ground of the yard, with a solid *thump*. From football, Chris knew the look of a person who had had his wind knocked out of him. A sudden disorientation as the abdomen slammed into the solar plexus, a quick expulsion of air, followed by panic as breathing suddenly didn't work as it should.

Geoff being Geoff, he didn't look panicked as much as confused and then pissed, but either way, Chris was instantly beside him, hand on his shoulder to keep him in place.

"Jesus. Sorry about that, man. Just relax. It'll pass in a minute."

"Fucking . . . tank. Like a circus bear . . . in a china shop . . ."

"It gets better faster if you don't try to talk."

In answer to that, Geoff grabbed his shirt and yanked him down so their faces were nearly nose to nose. "Paid . . . two hun"—wheeze, wheeze—"hundred dollars for this shirt . . ."

"Well, you're a dumbass. That's too much. It's just a freaking shirt."

Geoff's breath smelled like the cinnamon Trident he liked to chew throughout the day. If Chris touched his stubbled jaw, it would be rough like his own. Well, not exactly like that. Geoff's would be more like fine-grain sandpaper, whereas Chris's was coarser.

His mind snapped away from that as Geoff's fingers tightened in the collar of his T-shirt. Geoff was moving his fingertips over Chris's collarbone and the stray chest hairs at the base of his throat.

Geoff's breath was evening out, whereas Chris's was suddenly harder to find. Geoff's hazel eyes, which Chris had noticed one night were like ginger ale behind green glass, were fixed upon him. Because of Geoff pulling him down like this, Chris had one hand braced against the earth by his shoulder, the side of his other hand pressed up against Geoff's belt and the summer wool beneath it.

When he tried to draw back and Geoff's grip only increased, the pounding in Chris's ears grew louder. The blood from Chris's split lip had gotten smeared on Geoff's shirt. Geoff was going to murder him for that, when he noticed.

"Get off of me," Geoff said quietly.

Yeah, he'd gotten his wind back. His eyes were sharp again, the mouth tight. Chris lifted a brow, wondering if he should point out that Geoff was holding him, but since Geoff's grip eased as he spoke, Chris moved back. He really didn't know what had gotten into him, didn't know how to explain it, but . . .

He'd left himself unguarded, and that was his mistake. Geoff tackled him while he was resting on his heels, so Geoff had the benefit of balance. When he knocked Chris down, he had his knee planted between Chris's legs, enough weight resting on Chris's balls to keep him there, and his hand was partially wrapped around Chris's thick throat. Before Chris could think to struggle, Geoff stroked two fingers along the carotid, a firm pressure that was oddly arousing and then started to change the world, making Chris's head swim.

Geoff's gaze locked on him as he kept up those tiny movements. The light-headedness made all of this feel really weird to Chris, but okay, too. It took him a while to realize when Geoff had changed the pressure of his touch so that he was now tracing Chris's throat lightly with his knuckles, his other hand resting on his chest. When Chris tried to move, Geoff mashed his balls and cock harder beneath his knee. He let out a soft curse. Geoff tilted his head.

"Yeah, hurts some, doesn't it? If you're feeling a little dizzy, that's the carotid massage I just gave you. Learned it from a Dom in San Francisco one night. It can kill someone if it's done wrong. He said I was about as precise and focused a Dom as he'd ever met, so he knew he could trust me with it. Done right, it can give a sub a lovely sense of euphoria, float some of them right into subspace."

He could shake him. He could. But despite Chris's jaw being clenched, a reflection of the tension in the rest of his body, it was as if his mind was in stasis, waiting. Geoff leaned closer, visibly studying his reaction. His mouth was so close Chris pressed his lips together, resisting a compulsion he didn't want to face.

"My mouth wouldn't be soft and tender like hers, would it?" Geoff observed. "When I kiss you, you'll feel the heat, but it won't be sweet or female. I'd lick that blood off your lip, then bite you again. When my tongue's in your mouth, your ass will clench, because you'll think about my tongue there, as well as curling around your cock. Sam's all sweet, all female. Can't kiss her mouth without thinking about her pussy, because it's the same slick heat. You like fucking Sam, don't you, Chris? You love being inside her. You can't wait to do it again."

Chris snarled as Geoff shifted, sending a shot of pain through his balls with that knee. "You remember what I told you that day when you and I were standing in her bedroom?"

Sam had dashed off to the bathroom. Geoff had looked at him, then spoken in a low voice, full of lust and promise. *The first time I take her ass, I want you inside her cunt.*

Geoff's eyes bored into Chris's. "Next time you sink your cock into her, I'm going to be balls deep in *your* ass."

"Get off me," Chris said, repeating Geoff's own words.

"In a minute." His knee shifted, trailing over Chris's length. "You're hard. No surprise there. When you're thinking about sex with me, you pick a fight."

Chris shook his head, shutting his eyes. Though it only made Geoff's point, he threw Geoff off. He paid for it, gritting his teeth through the agony of Geoff's kneecap rolling over his dick as he flipped him. They both had fast reflexes, so they were on their feet facing each other in an instant. The problem was that surge of adrenaline coupled with the carotid thing made Chris react like a drunk. Hell. He couldn't stand up.

He managed to drop to his knees rather than crashing like a cut tree, but only because Geoff caught and took him to that position.

"Easy, man. Fuck, we're a pair of idiots, aren't we?" Geoff ran a hand over Chris's hair, because he had his head lowered as he tried to even out. He used Geoff's touch and voice to steady himself. "Time-out, I promise. Forgot one of the most important things about that technique. Making sure whoever you're doing it to doesn't freak out. You okay? Just nod."

Chris nodded, realizing he was gripping Geoff's forearm across his chest.

"Okay. Okay." Geoff's forehead touched the back of his head, his breath a sigh across Chris's neck. "Crap. Sorry about that. How about a truce, big guy? Ice for your lip and we eat some meat loaf."

Since staying out in the backyard and trying to kill each other for reasons Chris couldn't articulate wasn't as appealing an option, Chris offered an agreeable grunt. As he steadied, he didn't want Geoff to help him up, so he pushed him away. The brief flash of hurt on Geoff's face was like a screwdriver twisting in his gut. He got that tight look, the set to his jaw that said Geoff was thinking he should have cold-cocked Chris and left him sprawled in the yard. That might have been preferable. But Sam's meat loaf was good. If Chris was unconscious, Geoff would eat it all just to spite him.

Chris ate his in front of the TV, Geoff at the table. Geoff should have opened his laptop and handled that work he needed to do, but he didn't feel like it. Chris had the TV on *Mike & Molly* reruns, which they all enjoyed, but when some of their favorite punch lines happened, Chris didn't register them. Geoff couldn't say he was hanging on every word of it, either.

Instead, he kept replaying every step of what had happened in the backyard. Once he'd been sure Chris truly was steady on his feet, Geoff left his shirt in the laundry room and went to his room to change. When he came back through in a T-shirt and jeans, he'd seen Chris squirting some of the OxiClean on the shirt. Sam said the stuff worked for almost all stains, but Geoff knew it was pointless. There was a jagged tear in the back, because a branch hidden in the mulch had punched through the fabric.

"I'll pay you for your shirt," Chris said suddenly, bringing him back to the present.

Geoff pushed aside his plate and turned his chair around to face him. Putting his ankle on his knee, he took a sip of his beer. "Damn straight you will."

His casual tone seemed to relax Chris a little. Maybe Geoff should leave it alone tonight, but his gut suggested otherwise. "We've avoided talking about it long enough. Spit it out. What's on your mind?"

Chris's gaze flicked to him, then away. He didn't say anything for several long minutes, such that anyone else other than Geoff or Sam might think Chris wasn't going to say anything. Geoff just waited until his friend gathered his thoughts and finally spoke.

"The first time, how did you know I'd take her in her room instead of mine?"

"Besides the fact you have no proper bed? It's like taking a team down on their home turf."

"You're the competitive one."

"It's not about competition. It's about territory." Geoff drew on his beer, studying Chris. "You're not competitive, Chris. But it doesn't change the fact you feel like she belongs to you, and you have some definite topping qualities. Along with a few non-topping qualities."

He didn't call it *bottoming*, because Geoff already knew it wasn't that straightforward with Chris. He had an intriguing area that would give way, like a mighty oak for the wind, yet that didn't stop him from being an oak. He just respected the laws of the wind.

Geoff wanted to be the wind.

He'd gone back and forth on it a hundred times this week. He still wasn't fully decided on how his Dom nature would fit with Chris, about how far he could take it between them, but the wrestling match in the backyard had given him a big clue that Chris had been thinking about it just as hard. Quite a bit, whether he acknowledged it consciously or not. And while Chris might be feeling messed up some about it right now, Chris's reaction to everything Geoff was doing when he was on top of him had left Geoff feeling as honed as a lethal knife.

They'd both shied away from it until now, far more than either one of them had in their imaginings about Sam. There were more walls here, more tricky areas. But Sam's desires had reached the point where she'd made the leap. Maybe it was because feelings and hormones had taken her to a *Fuck it, it's worth a shot* point, but Geoff knew she was no more willing to risk their friendship on a whim than Chris or he was. Yet perhaps her initiative had been the key to helping them feel their way toward one another.

"She belongs to us," Chris corrected him.

Geoff smiled. Chris's declaration had circled his own thoughts. He lifted the bottle in a salute. "She belongs to us."

They'd both accepted it, though Geoff expected they'd always enjoy some friendly rivalry over it. "And to each one of us. Just as we belong to her, together and separate. Heart and soul, mind and cock."

Chris sent him a curious look, then his mouth eased into a smile. "Yeah, there's that. Does it seem weird to you? I mean, most guys aren't into sharing a woman."

"Does it seem weird to you?"

Chris shook his head. "I just wonder if it's supposed to seem weird for us not to be that way about her. Like you say, there's some competition, but it's not about that."

"Yeah." Geoff studied him. "We could share her, simple as that. Stay friends who happen to be in love with the same woman, and who happen to have the unique situation of not making it a competition, because she loves us both. That'd probably work out for a while, though we might have to set up a schedule so we don't wear her out. She didn't say so, but I think she was hobbling a little bit toward the end of the week. I told her it was your fault."

"Uh-huh." Chris's chuckle was humorless, though. "She has a lot of fantasies about having the two of us with her . . . at the same time. We could do more of that."

"Yeah. And I expect we'll all enjoy the hell out of it. But there's more than one way to do that. You want me to repeat what I said in the yard, in case your memory is failing you?"

Chris's brown eyes sparked. "Don't be a dick."

Geoff pulled back from that sharp edge, though it took an effort. "I'm just saying. You want me to spell out the obvious?"

Chris's gaze shifted back to the TV, an involuntary response to the elephant in the room. Chris had always known and accepted Geoff's flexible bisexual nature, so it wasn't that. And if Chris wasn't wired to get a hard-on for a guy, there'd be no elephant now. The problem was, Geoff knew they responded to each other, though they'd often channeled it other ways. There were a variety of reasons for that, most never spoken, but all boiling down to one thing. Their friendship was as vital to each of them as the air they breathed, and sometimes you bypassed certain roads if you thought the oxygen might get too thin there.

Then Sam had come into their lives, and she'd let them see that sometimes the air was just fine down those roads—better, even. So now they were facing the wall they'd built in front of that line they'd never crossed, and Geoff was pretty sure they were both seeking a door.

Everything was always timing. Sam would say the timing was here and now, no more excuses, no more waiting. But Geoff liked to have a handle on a problem before he jumped in with both feet, and he couldn't quite grasp the shape of that problem for Chris.

"You remember that day when you found Sam and me together in the shower? You punched me." He tried to keep his tone casual.

"Fond memories." Chris tossed him a neutral *Can we talk about anything else?* look.

"Yeah. Asshole. You were pissed and hurt." Geoff's tone softened, and Chris shifted uncomfortably on the couch. "I'm sorry for that. You stepped back from me after the punch, sending out this *Don't touch me* vibe as big as a football field. But I've thought a lot about that since then. For just a blink, you looked at me like you were wanting just the opposite."

Geoff had chased him from the shower to the kitchen, where the punch had happened. He'd managed, barely, to hold on to the towel he'd hastily grabbed. Chris's heated look, brief as it had been, had slid over his bare shoulders, the water beaded on him, the precarious hold of the towel low on his hips. Whenever Geoff had thought about it since then, it never failed to get him hard. "I think you were torn between wanting to punch me and wanting something else. You're a fighter, Chris, but that fight isn't always about wanting to be on top."

"I'm not like Sam."

"I know that, Chris. Look at me."

He sharpened his tone just enough to walk that fine line he was talking about. Because he managed it, he earned a glance out of Chris's brooding brown eyes. "Keep looking at me when I ask you this next question. Have you thought about my mouth being on you? On your mouth, on any other part of your body? On all of it? When I told you out in the yard that I want to be inside you next time you're inside her, I could tell it wasn't the first time you've thought about me fucking you. And how it would feel."

Christ, just saying it aloud had his jeans biting into his dick. Chris's jaw firmed. He was white-knuckling his beer.

"Chris, I know you're not fighting some bullshit sexual identity crisis. So what the hell is it? Talk to me."

Chris's look could have seared paint off of metal. He drained his own beer, set it aside and got up. "Don't push it. I'm going to bed," he said. He flipped off the TV, tossed the remote aside and moved around the coffee table, headed for the hallway.

"Gonna lock your door?" Geoff asked caustically.

Chris stopped and eyed him. "Do I need to?"

Despite the turmoil in his gut, Geoff shot him an even expression. "When it's time, you'll come to me, Chris. Not the other way around."

He shouldn't have said that. But hell, he was frustrated. Over the years, he and Chris had reached a point they could practically communicate without words, so the brick-wall routine was pissing him off. And worrying him. His friend could be as deep as a cave that went right to the middle of the earth. When he was like that, it was usually about the things that mattered the most.

Sam had been so worried *her* actions were what would ruin the friendship between the two men. Since Geoff was self-admittedly the most aggressive, and yeah, he'd concede being the one with the lion's share of arrogance, he was far more likely to derail the train. Not just derail it, but send it off a cliff and exploding with a big pyrotechnic *foom* at the bottom of a canyon. Wasn't that a cheerful thought?

He spent a couple of hours debating the pros and cons of how to proceed, but when push came to shove, what mattered to him was serving the best interests of the client. If he didn't have the skills or information to do that, he found them. It applied to home even more than to work, and he was pretty damn intense about work.

When Logan Scott had given Geoff his cell number, Geoff had programmed it into his phone, even though he wasn't sure he'd ever use it. But the owner of the hardware store next to Naughty Bits—the erotica store into which Sam had pulled them to get all this started—was also an experienced Dom, and Geoff wasn't going to let pride stand in the way of his doing this right.

Logan answered on the third ring. Never one to mince words, Geoff offered a brief greeting and a briefer explanation. He didn't realize how tightly wound he was until Logan responded warmly, loosening that coil in Geoff's gut.

"Yeah, now's a great time. I'm at a private party tonight doing a whip demo, but the host says you're welcome to come on over. By the time you're here, I should be done."

When Geoff left the house, Chris's door was still closed. Through it, Geoff heard the murmur of his small TV. Chris usually set it at low volume when he was using it to fall asleep. Geoff was tempted to try the knob, just to see if it was locked, but he'd meant what he said. Chris might be a balanced bastard, with top, middle and bottom qualities, but Geoff was pretty clear on who and what he was. Though up until now he'd only pursued his Dom side in more of a passive, watch-and-learn mode rather than seeking out a Dom/sub relationship, he'd known what he was since he'd hit puberty. Yet now that he'd finally found the partners to inspire him to grasp that side of himself with both hands and launch it into play, he was lacking some key information.

Well, that was why he was going to go see Logan. If Logan had nothing useful to offer, he'd just come back, brain Chris with a blunt object, fuck him and let him wake in Geoff's arms, the deed done. Yeah, that would work, because putting tab A into slot B was the only hurdle here. *Not.*

Despite his preoccupation with resolving things with violence, he took the time to leave a note. Neither of them used to do that, but Sam had gotten them into the habit, mainly because she'd only do it if they agreed to do so.

"Boys can get into as much trouble as girls," she'd pointed out. *"I need to know where to come rescue you if you need it."*

The thought made him smile. He scrawled the note out on the back of a bill envelope. *Went out. Have cell if you need me.* That last part was kind of superfluous. He frowned at himself for writing it, but then he shrugged, popped the envelope under the *Despicable Me* bug-eyed Kyle fridge magnet Chris had brought back from his Orlando landscaping trip. As he pulled out of the driveway, Geoff thought he saw a movement at the living room window, but it could have been the shadows.

Logan's private party was happening in a warehouse down near the NC Music Factory complex. The turn-of-the-century textile mill that had been turned into an amalgamation of trendy restaurants, clubs and entertainment venues wasn't big on parking, so everything nearby was full up. It took Geoff a few minutes to find a spot, and another few minutes to discover the warehouse entrance. A thirty-something male with dreadlocks and a trim black suit was watching the door, but when Geoff gave his name and referenced Logan, he was let through with a nod. "Take the lift to the second level," the man said. "The loud stuff's on the top level, dancing and such, but session play and demos are on the second floor. That's where you'll find Logan."

When the lift opened up on the second level, Geoff was greeted by a woman in a pink corset and thong, carrying a clipboard. "I'm Daisy," she said. "Can you sign in and show me some ID, please?"

All pretty standard fare. Despite the wild reputation BDSM had, thanks to TV crime dramas and misinformation, real lifestylers were careful and highly protective of one another. He signed in, showed his license and was told he could find Logan in the whip playroom, which was apparently at the back end of the floor. As he moved through different stations, people spoke in conversational voices but not raucously, respecting the scenes going on between Doms and their subs. He saw some impressive suspension work and a couple of electric play sessions in progress. As he passed a woman in a forced orgasm tower with a Hitachi wand buzzing between her thighs, her face contorted with the strain of the impending climax.

Geoff paused. Her eyes were streaming with tears as her Dom held her from behind, his hand under her chin, keeping it up so those watching could see her expression as she climbed toward orgasm. Her hands were bound to her sides, but Geoff noted one set of her fingers was curled in the leg of her Master's pants, holding on to him. Subtle signs of surrender, consent, of need and devotion. Geoff thought of Sam, how she had looked at him. He thought of Chris in the yard today, a different look on his face.

He really did have to be arrogant as hell to think he could provide what they both needed. But didn't that work in either direction? Sam probably worried about being enough for him and Chris over the long haul. And Chris . . . well, if he knew nothing else, Geoff knew that Chris would do anything for either one of them. Truthfully, it was why he was here. Geoff might be frustrated, but he also loved the guy. The issue wasn't just being whatever they both needed, but realizing he needed them and putting himself out there to see where it went from there.

His lips twisted wryly. Sam had figured that one out far quicker, but she was better at being vulnerable, the curse and blessing of being female. Whereas guys sometimes seemed encased in emotional armor, locked into it until it strangled them.

He paused by a man doing a hot wax and mummification scene. His male sub had been wrapped in pallet wrap from shoulders to ankles, and the Dom was ladling wax over him. He was explaining to his audience that it would create a heavy, additional blanket that would have a cocooning effect on the submissive. It would also increase the restraint in case the Dom wanted to up the edge play with nipple or genital clamping where he'd cut holes in the wrap in those areas.

The Dom had a male slave assisting him, watching the temperature of the wax in the Crock-Pots. When he wasn't doing that, he was using a flexible rod to do a little bastinado on the bottoms of the sub's feet. Geoff watched their subject's toes curl and uncurl in reaction. Mixed expressions of ecstasy and pain suffused the submissive's countenance. But when his Master bent over him, speaking softly to him, his tone obviously one of crooning praise, the sub's expression was easy to read. He was flying, his eyes dazed but adoring.

Geoff thought of having Chris in such a position. Nerves rippled through him at the idea of his friend trusting him that much. Geoff wasn't as much into the hardcore pain stuff like the bastinado, the caning or clamping, but he liked the idea of Chris letting him create a warm cocoon around him, giving him that sense of protection and safety. There were times in Geoff's life that Chris had been a cocoon of strength around him. He might like to give him the same thing, Dom style.

As to his sadistic side, it ran along a more sensual gamut. He could imagine cutting a hole in the plastic for Chris's cock and commanding Sam to wrap her lips around it to bring Chris to a climax. He might apply a switch to her pretty butt to focus her on the task, because Sam enjoyed playing more on that edge. But after she was working Chris's cock in her mouth, sliding up and down his rigid length, Geoff would lay a hand on Chris's forehead, make him stare up into his attentive face as pleasure took over, Chris giving it all to him and Sam.

Geoff moved onward, to the back, where the whip demo was being held. It appeared to have been concluded only a few minutes before, because Logan was answering some questions and people were still milling about, examining the whips he'd left out on display. Even dressed casually in jeans and button-down, the forty-something Dom, his long brown hair tied back on his broad shoulders, emanated authority and a calm in-charge vibe. It was obvious the people asking him questions and listening intently to his answers trusted his expertise, which made Geoff feel calling him had been the right move.

His demo bottom was still grounding. The young blonde woman with a light blanket wrapped over her bare shoulders was sipping a Coke, sitting on a chair. Logan's attention was clearly divided between her and the questions he was answering. When he finally broke it off with the group, he moved back to her side. She checked her watch, said something that obviously meant she had to go. Logan drew her to her feet. When he set the blanket away from her, Geoff saw she was wearing only a pair of panties, displaying a lithe body with small breasts and a tattoo of roses around her navel. Logan made her step away from him, walk, turn, and prove she was steady.

She shot him a playful look and spun in a circle, then tumbled back against him, laughing. Rolling his eyes, he slapped her ass, but after that he folded his arms around her, offering a bolstering hug. From the sigh that lifted her shoulders, Geoff deduced she was taking a last little draught of aftercare from his arms.

Then he gently pushed her back, said something. Geoff noticed they didn't kiss, and nothing in their affection suggested they were lovers. If anything, Logan's behavior toward her was paternal, and not in a Daddy Dom way. Many people sought outlets in Dom/sub play that didn't involve actual sex. Though they needed the special type of connection and intimacy that could be found in kink, their hearts might be committed to significant others in the non-BDSM world.

Based on what he'd felt from Sam so far, Geoff doubted her need for submission was going to wane. She seemed as eager to embrace that side of herself as he was his own Dom side. But Chris was a different matter. If this wasn't Chris's thing, but Sam still wanted both of them—and Geoff really wasn't seeing this working any way other than as a three-point relationship—how would they figure that out?

When the blonde moved away with an enticingly innocent sway of hips, Logan saw him. He waved him over and pointed to a chair, sliding a hip onto a stool behind him while he picked up a bottle of water and took a healthy swig. "Geoff. Good to see you."

"I appreciate you meeting me."

"Timing was good. So what's up? Things okay with Sam?" Logan gave him a more thorough look, noting the bruise on Geoff's face that had welled up after the earlier wrestling match. "She do that?"

"No." Geoff touched the spot and winced because it was still sore. "Chris and I had . . . I'd say it was an argument, but it was more like veiled foreplay that turned a little violent. Sam and I, though, we're good." Geoff hesitated. "My question has to do with Chris."

A smile touched Logan's mouth. "Yeah. I was surprised you didn't bring him up the first time, but figured you were a linear kind of guy. One complicated issue at a time."

"Yeah." On the way over, Geoff had thought of presenting the information just that way, but he decided maybe linear wasn't the best way for this. "Sam did something the other night."

Geoff explained the night she'd brought herself and Chris into Geoff's bedroom. "It seemed like a mutual thing at the end, Chris wanting to lie on the floor instead of in the bed with us. But when I told him to stay, to lie down, I realized I wanted him on the floor. Not because I didn't want him. I'm not explaining this well."

"You're doing just fine." Logan's steady eyes never wavered from his face. Geoff thought he'd be a great choice for a court-ordered mediator. "You know what was going on there. On some level, Chris probably did, too, and a part of him was open to it. Else he wouldn't have stayed. I think he would have made his excuses to Sam to spare her feelings and slipped out. He seems like he's pretty much his own man."

"Yeah. He is. In a quiet way. Most people miss it until they try to treat him like a doormat. He'll even let them get away with that for a while, if it's nothing that aggravates him. You know the way a parent's patient with a kid's weaknesses? Chris is like that with the whole world. But once you push him, he either becomes a turtle until you go away, or he simply picks you up and sets you out of his way. You have to get pretty deep inside to provoke him."

"Looks like you drew that winning straw." Logan grinned at the bruise again, but then he lifted a shoulder. "Sam is easy. First off, your relationship to her has always been more defined. And she clearly wants to submit. Chris is the unknown. You know he wants to submit, but he's not as easy as Sam. You're having to prove Dominance, because he's another male and he's got his own alpha thing happening."

Geoff thought of their wrestling match. He could have left it alone when Chris backed off, but something in him had retaliated, not willing to let it end without taking his own pound of flesh. Though the wry truth was he'd been able to pull that off because Chris hadn't been expecting it. The effort to overcome Chris in a fight always reminded Geoff of the line from the movie *A Knight's Tale*: "*How would you beat him?*" "*With a stick. While he slept!*"

"Mistresses sometimes have the same issue when dealing with a male sub, especially one who defines himself as an alpha," Logan continued. "Do you think Chris is a true sub? No editing, just say it straight out."

"No. Yes. Sometimes. To me. When it fits the moment." Geoff's brow furrowed. "But that sounds like 'gay for you.'"

"It's not out of the realm of possibility. Many of us fall hard for one person, Geoff. No one thinks that's unusual, because it's what society has romanticized. A man being attracted to other men, consistently and exclusively, is what we call gay. The opposite is heterosexual, and those who are open to being attracted to either sex, bi. But a man who simply falls in love with someone, regardless of gender, regardless of labels, is something different."

"What?"

"Enlightened." Logan smiled. "Based on the brief time he was in my store, and what Madison has told me about the three of you, that's my impression of Chris. I think out of all three of you, he's the one most open to possibilities, in a 'Standing Outside the Fire,' Garth Brooks kind of way. He can be hurt, badly, because he doesn't have any shields. Not with you two. Keep that in mind."

Logan straightened off the stool and began packing up his whips. "But you need to keep something else in mind, too. You're new to this, learning your way, but there's a core to what you are that's as old as time itself. Don't doubt that part. Your desire is as much a component of this as theirs. They're all tangled together, if it's meant to be."

It might be Zen-sounding garbage, but it resonated with Geoff. It actually made sense, and since most things today hadn't made sense, he welcomed the change. Seeing it, Logan gave Geoff a grin.

"I don't think you're on the wrong track, Geoff. You just haven't spent as much time working out your desires about Chris as you have Sam. When a good Dom stumbles, he tends to be harder on himself than a loving sub would ever be. They're forgiving, and they're willing to help us figure things out, as long as they trust that we want what's best for them above all else. If your sub feels cherished, he or she will handle a few harmless missteps. If you love her . . . and him, and that love is mutual, there's no difference between that and a vanilla relationship. Someone who loves you doesn't expect you to be perfect. They just expect you to be there with them every step of the way as you figure it out together."

Geoff looked in the direction of the blonde. She was now in street clothes, saying good-bye to other friends. "If you don't mind me asking, is she a love or cherish situation?"

"Cherish, for certain." Logan smiled fondly at the woman. "*Missive* is her scene name. Multiple meanings, multiple layers. When I'm in session with a sub, even for a demo, she becomes the center of my universe. Everything is about her, about her reactions, my responses. Keeping her safe, giving her pleasure and finding what level of sadism will add to her arousal, even if she doesn't know that herself until it happens, is part of what turns me on as a Dom. So much so it's oddly self-serving."

Logan shot him a wolfish grin, which Geoff found himself returning. He understood it, a hundred percent. "But being in a D/s session is very much an in-the-moment experience. When you step back and let that moment go, it's done. As beautiful as it was, it's transient." Logan's brown eyes kindled with a different light then, his mouth setting in a firm curve. "On the other hand, when you do it with the love of your life, the person with whom you want to share every moment, not just a D/s session, you've found Nirvana. That pure connection will be like nothing else."

"Yeah. But not everyone can have that."

"No. You're right about that." A shadow passed over Logan's features. "And it's a shame when someone wants that and can't find it, but it's no different from looking for love in the non-BDSM world. It doesn't always happen how we want it. In our world, we might have to settle for splitting it. We love outside of this, and meet our needs inside in a way that allows that outside relationship to still thrive."

He paused, considering Geoff. "But some of us won't settle for less than having the full package. If it ever comes our way, we better damn well make the most of it, because the gods aren't going to throw it our way that often."

"Like you and Madison."

Logan's eyes gleamed, appreciating him. "Careful, boy."

Geoff spread his hands out in amused conciliation. "Just calling it like I see it. Oh, and thanks for the lack of pressure. *Not.* You just said that it's okay to make mistakes. Unless one of those mistakes loses me that choice."

"If the love is there and real, a mistake won't destroy it," Logan said seriously. "That's the hardest thing for a Dom to understand. You can't control all of it and, in the end, it's the sub's heart that leads you where you need to go."

Logan closed his suitcase and hefted it off the table. "A Master may be in charge in a lot of ways, but when we fall in love, we're the ones on our knees. The sub who loves you back knows that, even if she . . . or he . . . doesn't consciously acknowledge it."

In Geoff's job, it was imperative he not only review information pertinent to a case, but know it well enough that he could respond to unexpected twists and turns. He'd always enjoyed that challenge, pushing himself to anticipate and comprehend two steps ahead of anyone else. It was a skill a Dominant used. So on the drive home, he reviewed everything that had happened over the past several weeks, picking up clues and information that would help him with Chris.

He thought about his and Chris's wrestling match in the backyard. Chris's expression right before he'd tackled Geoff had been an echo of that same heated look he'd swept over every inch of Geoff's bare skin after he'd punched him in the kitchen. Angry, hungry, confused.

Then there was the day the three of them had decided to go back to Naughty Bits. They'd been in Sam's bedroom, right after she and Chris had first had sex. Geoff had ordered Sam to go get dressed, but when she reached the door, he'd called her to a halt.

"Sam."

She'd turned, hair tousled and body naked as the day she was born. Only now she had long, slim legs, pleasing curves and a woman's heart that shone through her soft gray eyes. His own heart had beat faster at the sight, at the miracle of her. He'd had to clear his throat, so the words would come out as a Master's command, instead of the undignified rasp of a desperate man falling head over heels. *"From here forward, if you want to get off with your vibrator, you bring it to me and ask. Or you ask Chris, if I'm not here. If neither of us is here, you wait."*

He'd looked toward Chris for agreement. *"Agreed,"* Chris said at last. Then Chris went to the door and put his shirt on her, since he'd seen her shiver and knew she was cold. When she dashed off to the bathroom for her shower, the hem of Chris's T-shirt rippled off her bare ass in a delightful tease.

Chris hadn't left the room right away. Instead, he'd pivoted to square off with Geoff. Now Geoff slowed the memory to frame by frame. He needed to pick up every detail, understand the slightest nuances of what had happened next.

As Chris studied him, Geoff crossed his arms and leaned against Sam's dresser. Neither broke the silence right away. When Chris turned his head toward the sound of the shower starting, Geoff's gaze was drawn to the corded line of his throat, the bare upper body. Chris had a fine, gleaming pelt of chest hair that dwindled into a line down his stomach, disappearing into his camo pants, which he'd left unhooked at the waist. The pants were even better than jeans at molding a guy's package, drawing the eye.

Geoff thought about closing the distance between them, shoving his hand down that loose waistband and curling his fingers around Chris. He'd grip the weight of his balls, work his cock back up to the same turgid state it had been when it had plunged into Sam. Her release, the scent and residue of it, would be on him. That made Geoff want to do it all the more.

Chris looked back at him. Geoff didn't change his expression, curious to see how Chris would react to the unguarded desire in his face. Would he ignore it, duck for cover? Or would he give Geoff the green light to do exactly as he wanted? When Geoff detected desire in Chris's brown eyes, a tightening of his sensual mouth, he wanted to hit the accelerator, but he knew that wasn't enough. He held his ground and waited.

Chris's expression was suddenly hooded and harder. "Do you know what you're doing with her?" he said.

"Do you?" Geoff nodded toward the mussed bed. "Or do you want to claim I started this? If we're going to go that way, she's the one who started it all by dragging us into that store."

"Really? Going to lay that on her?"

"Yeah, but not in the way you think. I'm saying she's the bravest of the three of us. You wanted what she had to offer."

"Don't." Chris shook his head. "Don't make it like that."

While the ripple of muscle and the shift of hip in the formfitting camo was distracting, Chris's feelings kept Geoff's mind mostly out of his hormones. He straightened. "I'm not, Chris. Christ. You think I'd want to spoil anything about what you just shared with her? Look at me."

Chris turned confused and frustrated eyes to him. "We both want Sam," Geoff said quietly. "We always have, haven't we? We're all finding our way here. Not only with her, but with each other."

A muscle jumped in Chris's jaw, and he lifted a shoulder.

"C'mon, let's get dressed," Geoff said, though the last thing he wanted to do was get dressed. Chris's underwear was still on the floor, so there was nothing under those pants but Chris. But while Geoff wasn't the most patient of the three of them, he understood a house of cards required it, unless he wanted to see the whole thing collapse.

As Chris moved to the door, so did Geoff. Once they reached it, Geoff gestured with a flourish. "Brawn before brains."

"Assholes always bring up the rear," Chris retorted. Geoff left his hand out there, but adjusted it to the traditional handshake offering. Chris's lips twisted as he recalled the middle school memory, as Geoff had intended. He clasped Geoff's hand and spoke the Ashanti quote they'd learned in history class.

"'In our land only the bravest of the brave shake hands with the left hand, because to do so we must drop our shields and our protection.'"

Chris deepened his voice as they'd done it as kids, to sound like superheroes. Only Chris actually did have a deep voice now. Geoff wondered if he realized that. Deepening his voice now only made Superman sound like he had a cold.

Geoff flipped the clasp up into the upright brotherhood move, then they automatically moved in and bumped shoulders in gangsta fashion, the version of the male hug that wasn't hugging. It made them both grin.

"Sam would say we're goofballs," Chris said, but his expression was easier.

"She'd be right. But she's a girl. She doesn't get the secret hand-shake thing."

Chris smelled faintly of sweat and sex, and that ever-present aroma of earth and green things. Geoff took a deep breath of it and stepped back, releasing Chris's callused hand. Was it because of all that had happened these past few days that his attraction to the man was sharper, more intense? If Chris didn't stop studying him like that, his eyes lingering on Geoff's mouth, dropping to follow the line of his body under his Nike T-shirt and jeans, for fuck's sake . . .

Geoff cleared his throat. "We better get dressed. After you."

Chris sent him an odd look but nodded. As he passed in front of Geoff, Geoff didn't deprive himself of a good, lingering look at the muscular ass shifting under the camo pants.

"There are benefits to bringing up the rear, Dr. Banner," he said.

During their sophomore year, some of the kids had started calling Chris "The Hulk." It was Geoff who called him Dr. Banner, seeing the mild manner, gentle nature and intelligence behind the intimidating appearance.

"Oh yeah? Like what?"

"Means I can always watch your back," Geoff said. "View doesn't suck."

Chris glanced back at him, visibly surprised. No matter what had simmered between them for God knew how long, Geoff had never overtly dropped that card. Well, he was dropping it now. It was about damn time he did.

~

Amen to that. Coming back to the present, Geoff slowed down for a light. During high school, Chris had figured out that Geoff swung both ways. Geoff had been hesitant to drop those clues at first, but for reasons he didn't examine too closely, he eventually lost that reservation. When he started visiting BDSM clubs on his work trips, Chris knew about that as well. Chris had even visited one or two with him, though he'd get a drink and merely watch what Geoff was doing.

However, awareness wasn't communication. Well, nix that. It was what Sam would call typical male communication—the lack thereof—with a roll of her lovely gray eyes that would make him want to smack her ass, no matter how right she was. They never talked about it. Not directly.

They hadn't been ready to do that, because when they did, the vital current that ran between them, that connected and held their friendship, would be tested and changed. If Sam had never come into their lives, would the catalyst pushing them toward that test ever have occurred? Or would they have been forever content to find sexual release elsewhere and yet remain monogamous emotionally?

No escaping the truth now, because that was exactly what they'd been doing through and past college. It probably helped that neither of them had had trouble finding women for occasional hookups—God bless the sexual empowerment of women.

Yet Geoff was all too aware that the few male hookups he'd had over the years were things he didn't mention to Chris. Not lying, just not talking about them. He expected Chris had guessed about a couple of them, because he was typically a little distant from Geoff a few days after one had happened.

He wasn't sure if Chris had ever had sex with a guy. Even when

Chris found a woman, most of the time it took the form of double dates with Geoff. Yet Geoff knew Chris was bisexual, just not as comfortable and open about it as Geoff was. He remembered a time in college when he and Chris were studying for midterms on the bleachers by the track. He'd noticed Chris doing the same thing he was, lazily perusing the fit and form of the male track team. Chris's eyes had come back to Geoff, held there with an unfathomable expression before he'd turned his attention to his studying again.

Always before, Geoff's focus on that memory had been on the pleasing realization that Chris wasn't a hundred percent straight. Now he zeroed in on Chris's expression when he'd looked away from the athletes and toward Geoff. Maybe at the time he'd just been too chickenshit to translate it, but the meaning was clear as a mirror right now.

They're not you.

Considering the implications of that, all the possibilities, a picture formed that almost made Geoff miss the next light change. He stomped on the brake and brought his car to an abrupt stop. He stared sightlessly through the red light.

Chris had seemingly limitless patience. He could sit still for an hour, waiting for an injured animal to trust him enough to offer aid. He was loyal, faithful. If he gave his heart to someone, he wouldn't ever fuck around on them.

Geoff swallowed. Shit. Was it possible Chris had never been with a guy because . . . he thought that would betray what he had with Geoff? Yet he'd never come right out with his feelings? What the hell?

That had to be wrong, because Geoff sure as shit knew he wasn't worth that kind of devotion. But if he thought of it that way, the wall he'd kept hitting with Chris these past few days started making more sense.

Chris was patient, but more than that, he was cautious with what he held dear. Hell, he barely let Sam get on a step stool when he was in the house. Maybe he'd settled for a friendship that Geoff himself had valued more than anything, enough that they'd put anything less certain and more volatile on hold. Until Sam came into their lives and showed them that friendship was worth risking . . . if what it could become would expand and surpass it.

Okay, proceeding under the outrageous but strangely fitting

hypothesis that Chris had been saving his virgin ass for Geoff, he flipped the mirror on himself. How would he have felt if Chris had ever actually gone after a guy, even for just some down-and-dirty, nasty, pound-him-in-the-ass, no-commitment kind of sex, which was basically all that Geoff had done with a guy? He imagined male hands touching Chris, gripping his fine ass, parting his buttocks to tease him with a tongue, or closing a hot, wet mouth over his cock. Geoff's hackles rose, his lip curling in a near snarl. That answered it, didn't it? Yes. He was a fucking hypocrite, but it didn't change his reaction one bit.

A honk behind him indicated the green light. He lifted a hand in impatient acknowledgment of his distraction and accelerated. Logan had turned him in the right direction. Now he needed to figure out what he was going to do with the information. He'd go home and get some sleep, because he often did his best strategizing when he was under, where his subconscious could toss out the bullshit. He might need a drink to settle his spinning mind, though. Or a whack with the type of blunt object he'd considered using on Chris.

It was near eleven when he came back into the house. He locked the door, activated the security panel and dropped his keys in the stupendously ugly, brightly colored fruit bowl in the kitchen. Sam had found it at a yard sale, and it had become the collection point for things needed when walking out the door. Spare change, extra keys to their vehicles, pens picked up here and there, many of them with the logo of Sam's bank. Clothespins clipped on the edges of the bowl held reminder notes, like the one Sam had left before she departed on her trip. "Pick up organic milk. Happy cow logo." Chris had added "oatmeal" in his large scrawl beneath it.

Geoff slipped open the buttons of the shirt he'd donned to meet Logan and loosened the cuffs as he moved down the hallway. Chris's TV was still on that low drone. Either he hadn't hit the sleep setting or he'd woken up again and reset it. Even on weekends, Chris tended to go to bed earlier than Geoff did, since his system was programmed to be up with the sun, the pathological need for coffee to kick-start him notwithstanding. There was very little chance he was still awake.

Even so, Geoff slowed to a stop. Something had changed. The bedroom door was open. Not cracked or closed. The large rectangle of darkness flickered with the blue-gray light of the TV.

He'd told Chris—rather emphatically, with pretty Dom-like panache, if he did say so himself—that he'd wait until Chris came to him. But that had to do with other things, the undefined Dom/sub nuances between them, how that power exchange would play out. His revelation in the car made this a different kind of moment. You had to learn how to walk before you could run. Or, as the first Master he'd ever met had told him: "Learn how to fuck; then learn how to top."

Chris was the only man who'd ever seen Geoff cry. When Geoff's mother told him she was staying with his father, despite his blatant and continuous infidelity, she'd given her son a look so distant, it was as if she were someone he didn't know, had never known. "If you can't treat your father with respect, Geoff," she'd said stiffly, "you aren't welcome in our home." Geoff had packed and left.

To this day he didn't really remember making a conscious decision to go to Chris's place. He'd just somehow found himself back at college. The guy lived in an eight-hundred-square-foot box with a postage-stamp-sized patio—one step up from a storage building, but it was adjacent to the organic garden the botany students had started. Chris was allowed to room there because he watered the plants.

Chris sat him down on the patio in a sturdy lounge chair next to a huge pot of white, purple and red flowers, then went inside to get him a beer.

Geoff looked past the patio boundary, at rows of some kind of vegetable he didn't know. It didn't matter, because he didn't see them. He was staring at nothing, and it felt like someone had shot him. His heart seized, his throat closed up and his shoulders were hunched against the pain. When Chris came back to the patio door, he could have retreated without being seen, or done the awkward shoulder-pat thing, but he hadn't done any of that.

He'd come out and set the beer down. As the pain got worse and Geoff started shaking, he'd wrapped his big arms around Geoff from behind, leaning over him and pressing his head on top of his, holding Geoff tight while Geoff let his childhood and his family go with those tears.

When he was done, Chris had given him a light pat, a hard squeeze of his shoulder, and said, *"Hey, let's splurge on Luigi's. You know their lasagna cures everything. We might get that waitress with the great smile and the double Ds."*

241

JOEY W. HILL

Chris was his best friend. The man he loved. Thinking about how quickly they'd integrated Sam into their lives, how easily they'd fallen in love with her, Geoff wasn't as surprised at it as he'd expected to be. They'd shared so much together; why not love for the same woman? Sam said he was a romantic, and he always denied it, but he couldn't help feeling as if another reason he and Chris had waited on what was between them was because she needed to be part of it all coming together. Maybe he and Chris had so quickly recognized her as the missing part of their three-part puzzle because they'd had nearly fifteen years to learn what love truly was—from each other.

When Sam had stood before him the first time naked, her beautiful eyes fixed on him, her expression and soft mouth had told him everything he needed to know. He'd felt her arousal down to his soul, her craving for submission. Submission to him. His heart had locked up, everything good and perfect about the world right there in front of him. People who cherished a once-in-a-lifetime love didn't realize it could be doubly powerful when it was twice in a lifetime. And at the same time and place. What made it even more of a miracle was when there was no choice to be made between the two of them. Only whether or not Geoff would open himself up to love them both, with everything he had to offer and more.

Thinking about what Logan had said about loving and cherishing, Geoff thought he'd dig down past his soul to China to find whatever Chris or Sam needed from him. And impatience had its place. Sometimes it was needed to get shit done that probably should have been done a long time ago.

Geoff pushed Chris's door inward and stood in the threshold, letting his eyes acclimate to the dimness. Chris was looking at the TV through half-closed eyes, one hand behind his head, the other lying loosely on the covers. He was on the mattress on the floor instead of in his hammock. He liked having two options for sleeping. The covers were pushed to his waist, showing the waistband of his worn boxers that fell low on his hips. The TV light limned the lines of his firm abdomen, the roll of his biceps bunched behind his head, the tousled hair over his brow. He'd either been sleeping or scraping his hands through it, like he did when he was worrying over something.

When Geoff moved into the doorway, his friend's head turned. Chris's brown eyes were dark and compelling. His mouth was firm,

242

tense in a way that had Geoff's body tightening in response. Chris's large hand curled on the covers as his gaze skated down from Geoff's face over his chest, exposed by the open shirt.

"Turn off the TV," Geoff said. His voice was husky, strange to him.

Chris lifted his gaze back to his face. After a weighted space of time, he picked up the remote and switched off the TV. The safety light plugged in behind the dresser gave Geoff enough illumination to see where he was going, but he thought he could find his way blind. He moved to the side of the mattress. Chris had gone even more still, if that was possible, the energy around him knitting into tighter coils. Geoff knew he might be punched in the next few seconds. Chris could hit like a hammer. But no guts, no glory.

Dropping to his heels by the mattress, Geoff reached out and laid his hand flat on Chris's stomach. All that physical labor, he didn't have an ounce of fat, but with those large bones, he was built like a brick wall. Chris stared at him. He could have been a statue, except no statue had ever vibrated with so much life. Time stretched out like a wire, and Geoff found himself waiting, just as motionless. He wasn't sure if he was breathing.

Chris shifted then, sliding up onto his elbows. Holding Geoff's gaze, he closed his hand on Geoff's wrist and slid Geoff's hand into the loose waistband of his shorts.

Holy God. He'd seen Chris naked before. In the locker room in high school, plenty of times, or that crazy night in Myrtle Beach when they'd picked a couple of cheerleaders up off the beach and had sex with them in separate beds but the same room. When Chris had stripped off his clothes and put his knee on the bed, his eyes on the pretty blonde whose eager arms were reaching for him, Geoff remembered his thick, stiff member rising above the slope of his thigh.

It had been a while since he'd had a close-up impression of it, and he'd never had direct tactile experience. Chris was hard and smooth, that typical velvet over steel that coaxed the fingers to stroke, squeeze. It was his size and the rigidity that impressed Geoff. When Geoff tightened his grip on a surge of pure greed, Chris's lips parted. They were red, moist, and Geoff could imagine their taste.

"You were looking earlier," Chris said, a rasp to his voice. "Looking at it like you were already touching it."

"This better be all for me." Geoff put enough of an edge in his voice to get an answering spark from Chris's gaze. Yeah, it was different from interacting with Sam. Her submission had pleasant spikes of misbehavior. With Chris, the challenge was more constant, at a higher level. Both responses fit the individuals, giving Geoff a delightful variety to enjoy.

"*Fantastic Four* just went off." Chris lifted a shoulder. "Jessica Alba in a bodysuit. Can't help that."

Geoff snorted. "Yeah, I'll give you that one." He gave Chris's cock a firm pump and Chris drew in a breath. He curled a hand around one side of Geoff's open shirt, not drawing him forward, but holding him in that same stasis. Reluctantly, Geoff released him, put his hand over Chris's wrist and removed his hand so he could straighten to his feet. Moving to the end of the mattress, he stared down at Chris's body, ranged so temptingly below him. "I want to see you naked. Handling yourself."

As Geoff stood, legs planted shoulder width apart, hands loose at his sides, Chris's eyes slid over his bare chest and down.

"Get rid of the shirt," Chris responded.

"Give me incentive." It was like playing poker. Knowing how to bluff and how to draw your opponent out. Though his opponent's responses couldn't be predicted, Geoff usually had sure footing on this field. But for Chris, he'd give ground if needed to win the war.

As Chris held his gaze, he kicked off the covers in a fluid movement so he could remove the shorts. For such a big man, he did it gracefully, lifting his hips up off the mattress, shoving the underwear down and then pushing them off. Geoff studied the burly chest, the structure of his hips, his upper thighs, and spiraled around to the center, Chris's erection. Thick and tall, looming over heavy testicles that were a dark rose color and layered with a light covering of the same type of gleaming hair on his chest. As Geoff watched, a drop of pre-come oozed out of the slit, giving it a pearlescent sheen that made him want to lick his lips.

"Waiting," he said in a voice that was close to a growl. A reminder he'd told Chris to do two things.

Chris fanned out his fingers, sliding his palm down the ridges of his abdomen to find his cock and curl his hand around it. Geoff forced himself not to do a hard swallow. The room was so heavy with erotic tension, everything was moving in slow motion. Chris's breath clogged in his throat as he manipulated the skin over that steel shaft.

"You ever been fucked up the ass, Chris? Had anything up there at all?"

"You know the answer to that."

Geoff closed his eyes briefly. With a man, he was used to this being all about sex. He didn't expect more from it than that, not usually. This was a whole different level. He hadn't been entirely sure if he was right, about him being Chris's first male experience, but having it pretty damn close to being confirmed affected him unexpectedly.

He told himself to get a grip, opened his eyes and let his lips spread in a feral smile. "I want to hear it."

"No. I haven't." Chris's brown gaze held a trace of sullen fire now, his lips firming. Geoff understood the fire, because if Chris's answer had been anything different, he would have responded the same way, no matter how illogical it was.

"Good thing for you one of us knows what we're doing," he said mildly. He dropped to his heels, closed his hand on Chris's ankle. The intimate gesture had Chris pausing and Geoff let him see the truth in his own eyes, hear it in his voice. "Because I'd rather cut off my own dick than hurt you in the wrong way."

Chris's mouth tightened, but Geoff rose again, taking it back a notch. "It's better if you've done stuff with it, toys or fingers, to loosen it up," he said casually. "But I like the idea of taking your ass completely virginal."

Geoff stripped off his shirt and slid the tongue of his belt free. He wondered if Chris would ever submit to letting his ass be striped, because the idea of applying his belt to those twin muscular lobes had his cock stiffening up even more. As he let the strap dangle from one hand, Chris's gaze followed it before coming back to Geoff's face. Geoff was reminded of a mastiff, that inscrutable face that gave nothing away until you got close enough to lose a hand. But the key was not showing fear.

Geoff slid the strap through his fingers contemplatively. Chris was still slowly squeezing and stroking his dick. "Roll over on your hands and knees. I've got to get something from my room."

He left the belt by the mattress and slid out into the relative coolness of the hallway. Crossing to his bedroom, he fished the lube and a condom out of his nightstand drawer. He kept both there, a long-standing habit for potential bed partners, male or female, though they hadn't seen use here until he'd taken Sam.

When he came back, Chris was sitting up on his knees, ass resting on his heels as he faced the wall, but that was as far as he'd gotten. It was quite a view, the wide back and tense shoulders, his buttocks pressed into his heels, his bowed head exposing the vulnerable nape. But he lifted his head and shot Geoff a glance that said the mastiff was thinking about going for the throat rather than wasting the time on a hand.

Geoff showed him the lube, pocketed it, and dropped to a knee beside him. Chris's expression was wary. Reaching out, Geoff threaded his fingers through his hair, a soothing touch. Chris kept his eyes on him, not saying anything, but Geoff noticed his hands relaxed on his thighs.

"Thought I was just going to shove you down and do a hammer-and-nail job on you?" he asked lightly.

Chris snorted, a self-conscious sound. "Yeah, good luck with that." He glanced at the condom. "Um...you don't have to, you know. For me. And I know you're always careful."

Geoff set the condom aside, his pulse thudding at the quiet declaration. He summoned a smile. "Sam had a lot of fantasies about us. You and her, me and her, you and me with her. I expect you've given it some thought yourself. Have you only fantasized about her?"

There was a significant pause, Chris seeking the truthful answer. He was a pretty honest guy, all in all. Yet when he nodded, Geoff admitted it was a punch in the gut, but he pressed on, not letting that derail him.

"Based on present context, I'm thinking that wasn't because you didn't have any interest in fantasizing about us. Maybe you weren't sure how to make it play out in your fantasies. Or maybe you didn't want to take it in your head where you thought we might not be able to take it in real life, ever, without risking what we already have. Why tempt yourself with what could never be?"

The flicker in Chris's gaze confirmed the truth and soothed the impact in Geoff's gut. "Let's just take it one step at a time, then." Geoff slid his hand from Chris's hair to his neck. It was an incredible contrast. Sam was silk and cream, all soft woman. Chris was tanned, firm heat. Geoff wanted to touch them both endlessly. He thought of restraining them side by side on two tables. He'd blindfold them, lock them down so they couldn't move, but when he restrained their arms, he'd cuff their nearer wrists together so they could hold hands. As he enjoyed every inch of their different textures, scents, curves, softness and hardness, he'd watch their grip on each other tighten, scrape, caress and claw.

"You know what I am, right, Chris? Know the things I like?"

"Yeah." Chris's face was like carved marble, all those expressive emotions in compelling stasis.

"Anything you can't do, you just say, okay? Show me you understand." Geoff nudged him. "And breathe. You stopped."

Chris's lips tugged in a rueful smile and Geoff passed his thumb over them. Chris's eyes went deep gold and Geoff had to force himself to take his touch away. "Stay still," he ordered. "Like when you were watching that coyote and her kits in the Smiths' yard last month. Remember that? You said you didn't move for fifteen minutes, not wanting to spook her."

In this case, Chris was the animal Geoff didn't want to send crashing away into the forest, or charging him with teeth bared. Geoff molded his palm over the rounded expanse of his shoulder. The damn thing was the size of a large grapefruit. From there he drifted to his biceps, which were contracting then releasing. A glance down showed Chris was flexing his hand in a fist, nerves and tension.

"I want to try something. You'll be able to get out of it if you really want to." Geoff straightened and moved behind him. He didn't intend to take a detour from his plan, but when he trailed his hand along Chris's shoulder, he had to bury his fingers in the dark, thick hair for a blissful moment. Hunger overcame him and he pulled on it so Chris's head dropped back on his shoulders. The unwitting submissive response sent a hard shot of longing through him that tightened his fingers further. He saw the muscle in Chris's jaw flex, and his brown eyes were back to fire again.

Geoff forced himself to release him and stepped back, out of range of Chris's sight. The hot-as-hell view of him sitting bare-assed on his heels had only gotten better. When he dropped his head forward again, the layers of muscles down his back and in his tight buttocks flexed. Geoff wasn't sure where to start, because he wanted to start everywhere.

Picking up the belt again, he threaded the tongue through the buckle. As he knelt behind Chris, Chris's head turned, chin tucked toward his shoulder to watch what Geoff was doing. Geoff slid the loop over one of Chris's hands, tightened it on his wrist. Then he reached for the other. Chris quivered, one hard shudder that made Geoff pause, his own heart thudding up high in his throat. He carefully closed his hand on the free wrist, brought it behind Chris's back and worked the belt end around both of them. A belt was a good beginning restraint, because if secured loosely around both wrists, a person could work their way out of it, since it was too thick and rigid to be an unshakable binding. But if someone needed the sense of being restrained to let other things go, it was an optimal choice.

"I'm thinking maybe you did fantasize about us, but you didn't give yourself pictures. You didn't shine any light on it. Close your eyes, Chris."

Chris's lips set in a firm line as he stared at the wall, his fingers twitching under Geoff's grip. Geoff tilted his head enough to see his eyes were still open. Submissives were all different. Chris wasn't at Sam's level, plus he had some intriguing switch qualities. Yet he had desires and needs that Geoff's instincts recognized. He reacted accordingly.

"Close them, you hardheaded bastard," he said, tone as silky as a glide up Chris's cock, which was still sitting up high and mouthwateringly tight between his legs. "Else I'll blindfold you with my shirt."

Chris's lips twisted, but he complied, eyes shutting. He had thick, long lashes that fanned his tanned cheeks. Geoff gave the belt an extra cinch, putting his other hand flat on Chris's back so he felt his heart jump. His own did the same.

"So you're in darkness," he said, steadying his voice. "Total, pitch darkness. Where you're not Chris, you're not really anyone. Just pure need and want, no thought or judgment. You're on your stomach, the way you normally sleep." Geoff lowered him into that position, putting him flat, making sure his cock got pressed to the mattress in the right direction. Nothing could break a moment like having your dick at the wrong angle . . . unless the discomfort had erotic purpose.

He thought of the sub he'd seen at the warehouse, trussed in pallet wrap and under a coating of heated wax.

He couldn't let his head get trapped in that space right now. His feelings for the man under his care was a bigger demand than ruminating on future possibilities. Chris's needs became his own, because every sense was focused on standing inside Chris, understanding where he was at, taking a journey with him.

As Geoff put him down on the mattress, he kept his hand curled over his shoulder, the other at his side to control the descent. Christ, the boy was heavy. Next time he'd have him lower himself first, then deny him the use of his hands. Good planning resulted in more pleasure for them both. But once he had him there, the view was worth it. The mound of his ass, the valley of his back, the expanse of shoulders, pulled back, arms bound and knuckles resting on the rise of his ass. His cheek was pressed to the pillow, lips set in that tense line, hair falling over his brow. Geoff's gaze slid down over the powerful columns of his thighs, and muscled calves. His legs were spread enough Geoff could see the ripe plums of his balls. His cock would be like a steel pipe against his belly.

Geoff trailed a hand over his ass, down one thigh. "So you're in the dark," he continued, rising to push the door shut and draw the blinds, putting them in darkness in actuality, especially when he pulled the safety light out of the wall. "Even if you open your eyes, you don't see me anywhere. But you feel me."

He finished stripping off the rest of his clothes as he spoke, knowing Chris was hearing the zipper come down, the rustle of clothing. He expected his friend had opened his eyes at his implied permission. All he'd be able to see was Geoff's silhouette. "You know I'm here, and you wonder when I'm going to do something. Whether you should fight, how you can submit. That feels like the wrong thing to do, but it also feels right, too. The good thing is, you don't have to worry about it, not really. You can't fight the dark. It simply is. Slips around you, holds you, keeps you as long as it wants to."

He centered himself, drawing what he wanted and what he could feel from Chris into the same breath, deep into his lungs. Dropping to the mattress, he planted one knee between Chris's legs as he took a firm grip on his balls. Ah, fucking heaven. Chris's thighs quivered, his ass making a delectable twitch as Geoff fondled and squeezed.

"You don't have to worry about anything, because I'm the one making choices. Taking them. I want you, Chris." Geoff paused. "I've wanted you for a long time. But not as a casual fuck. Somehow, I knew when this moment came, it would be like this. As important as what we've started with Sam. Not a *Let's see where this will go*. This is permanent, forever, nobody getting out of it alive. This is it for us. Right?"

Another quiver. He'd wanted Chris to know he wasn't playing Dom games or just lonely for a piece of ass. He expected Chris knew, but Geoff needed to say it, because he was painfully aware there was one of them in this room who needed that to be clear. "Answer me," he demanded roughly.

Keeping his hold on Chris's testicles, he dipped his thumb between his buttocks and found the crinkled opening of his rim. Fine hairs curled around it. As he rubbed, Chris jerked in his grip, letting out a hoarse breath.

"Not hearing anything, Chris. Maybe something's got your tongue."

Geoff changed positions, letting go of his balls to grip his hair instead, turning Chris's face up to his roughly enough to stoke the fire. He stopped an inch from his mouth, teased him with his breath, his other thumb coursing over his lips. He could sense Chris's gaze on him, like being close to flame.

"You had fantasies like this, but you ignored them, shoved them down. Because you just weren't sure what it meant about you. You know me, Chris. You know me down to the soul, and so you know all my corners of dark and light. If you've wanted me, if your dick's gotten hard imagining us like this, then me taking over was part of it." He curled his hands around the belt and tugged on it, letting Chris feel the binding. "Because you know it's part of me."

Chris didn't respond, but his breath remained uneven, those eyes seeking Geoff's in the darkness. Geoff came even closer.

"That sweet mouth," he whispered. "I've thought about ramming my dick into it more times than I can count. Putting you on your knees in the kitchen and thrusting until I come so hard it spills out of your mouth."

"Fuck." A bare whisper of sound, but Geoff's lips drew back in dangerous satisfaction. The big shoulder flexed under his hand as Chris tested the bonds in involuntary reaction. "If your hands were free," he said, low, "you'd try to pull me down, because you wonder what my mouth tastes like. You wonder what a kiss from a man feels like. Or do you? Has any other man ever tasted your mouth, Chris? What bastard had the balls to taste what was mine?"

Chris trembled again, his arms still flexing, straining. He didn't speak again. Geoff wondered if he could. To have a fantasy—or in Chris's case maybe it was better to call it a hope, humbling as it was to realize he had considered this moment that way—that lived only in shadows brought to life, even in darkness, might steal words, and leave only a tumble of emotions too strong to contain except through violence or sex. Or violent sex. But this was where being a Dom came in handy. Geoff knew he couldn't let it go that way.

Easing his hold on Chris's shoulder, he moved to trace Chris's face, gentle as a mother's touch. Geoff thought he could hear the crash of Chris's heart like thunder. Leaning down, Geoff found Chris's mouth with his own. Easy, rubbing, caressing, a tracing of the tongue between the parted lips. Chris's breath touched his flesh, erratic. Geoff curved his hand around his nape, increasing the firmness of the grip as he deepened the kiss.

He slid his other hand down Chris's shoulder, over the biceps, enjoying the strength and beauty of the powerful arm, then down to release the belt from his wrists. He sat back, out of range. God. He knew how he'd felt when he'd first kissed Sam. Now, when he kissed Chris, he compared those two first kisses to all the others he'd ever had and realized Chris was smarter than he'd ever be. There was no comparison. Quantity could never hold its own against quality that pure.

"Put your arms above your head," he said.

A long pause, and Chris did it, another shot of pure adrenaline. Geoff rode it, straddling his shoulders, sitting his bare ass between Chris's shoulder blades as he rebound his hands with the belt. He wished his friend had a bed so he could wrap the tongue around a headboard, but he didn't need it. Not really. Chris's arms flexed against the binding, but he didn't try to get away. Sliding back, Geoff ran his hand over one buttock, giving it a healthy, bruising squeeze. "You could bounce quarters off that thing, man," he muttered.

Chris let out a strained half chuckle. Geoff moved farther down to sit on his thighs and take a handful of buttock in each hot palm, squeezing, learning every inch of him. Talk about delayed gratification. He had to force himself to focus. This wasn't just about him.

"So I come to you in the dark. Maybe you don't even acknowledge it's me. But you know. You know the touch of my hands, the way I want to use you. Maybe you've already had Sam that night, fucked her, spilled yourself inside her. But it's not enough. You bring her to sweet climax again by licking her cunt and sucking on her pretty nipples. You remember how tight they were after you put your mouth on them? You give her satisfaction but you leave yourself hurting for it. First, because you know she's exhausted, and you don't want to be a brute. When you leave her sleeping, you tell yourself you're done. But you know you aren't. Not until you've been fucked by me. Your second climax belongs to me."

He pressed his erection against Chris's ass. "Maybe you haven't let yourself fantasize about it, Chris, but I have. I'll loan you that fantasy and about a dozen more until you can think up some on your own. As much as I've loved thinking about every inch of your body, I've spent as much time thinking about what you say to me, how you respond, how close we've gotten—way closer than just fucking. And when I go to bed with those kind of fantasies, I wake up hurting. Needing."

Chris made a noise, one Geoff wasn't sure how to interpret, but it wasn't rejection. More like some of the same kind of primal hunger. He slid down to the backs of Chris's knees and found the lubricant where he'd left it. "No talking now," he said in a gruff voice. "You just feel. Feel what I'm doing. How I'm making you ready for me."

"Geoff."

"Yeah, bud?" He curved over him, a hand braced by his shoulder. The position trailed the head of his cock over Chris's buttocks, the small of his back. Geoff suppressed the desire to push it more firmly against him and rub like a damn cat in heat. Or a male marking territory.

"You meant it, right? I'm not some casual fuck. Not like the others." Chris tensed. "I'm not being a fucking girl, either. I'm just saying . . ."

"First off, there weren't that many 'others,'" Geoff said with a lightness he didn't feel. "But I get it. You're saying if I didn't mean what I just said, that this is something more, I need to get the fuck off of you and get the hell out of your room. Right?"

Chris nodded.

"Okay. Pay attention, then, since I thought I made that way clear the first time."

Geoff gripped his hair and slammed his mouth down on his. This time he unleashed everything that was surging through him below the waist, as well as through his heart and every blood cell.

Chris groaned, and the sound became the rumble of a waking bear. The muscles beneath Geoff bunched, gathered, but before he could counter, Chris tossed him, spinning over in the dark to grab at him. *Fuck.* He had about a second to remember the other thing that first Dom mentor had told him.

Never underestimate a sub's physical reaction to stimuli.

He'd definitely miscalculated this one's. With Chris's hands bound, he had less control over the maneuver. Geoff's head cracked into the wooden crate Chris used as a side table. Whatever was on it toppled and, when Geoff slid to a stop, half on and half off the mattress, he was pretty sure a couple of books were stabbing him between the shoulder blades. A beer bottle had prevented his head from bouncing off the much more forgiving carpeted floor.

"*Geoff.*" Chris was on his knees over him, breath harsh. "I can't . . . I've got the belt knotted, or something. Are you okay?" He was moving, scrambling away. "Fuck. I'll get the light . . ."

Summoning a quick snapshot of what was in the room and gauging Chris's direction, Geoff rolled and caught his ankle and knee in two strong hands. It felled Chris like a tree, vibrating the house on its foundation. However, unlike Geoff's, Chris's landing pad was all carpet. Geoff didn't give him time to recover, scrambling to pin him on his stomach, a knee between his legs and hand on the back of his neck.

"Easy," he said sharply. "Easy. We're still in the dark here, Chris. It's all about what's happening in the dark. Take a breath."

But Chris was rigid. "Did I hurt you?"

"Yeah, you did. But it was my fault. Shut up. Just be quiet." Geoff slid his hands over Chris's shoulders, down the flat of his back and over the tempting rise of his ass. Then back up to check the the belt. He'd only twisted it in his panic, so Geoff figured it out, loosened the strap and pulled it away to chafe at his friend's wrists. "Okay on circulation?"

"Yeah. It was fine. It wasn't too tight. I just couldn't get it loose."

"Good."

"But where did I—"

"Shut up. Keep your hands up by your head." Geoff adjusted so he was kneeling between Chris's spread thighs. He slid his palm over the round shape of Chris's buttock, bent closer and bit.

"Ow . . ." Chris jerked in response, letting out another strangled chuckle. "What the hell . . ."

Geoff gripped the other ass cheek to keep him still and tightened the clamp of his jaws, tasting Chris's flesh with tongue and teeth, digging in harder.

Chris drew in another one of those unsteady breaths. Geoff was flooded with fierce joy as he felt Chris's surprise, his discovery of arousal in pain. He wanted to take him right then and there. Heaven. He'd stumbled onto heaven with these two, because Sam responded like a flower to sunlight to the same thing.

Easy. Chris getting the first glimmer of understanding was nowhere near Sam's full embrace of the same. Geoff made himself relax his jaw and swirled his tongue over the offended flesh.

"Been wanting to take a bite out of your ass for a while," he said, lifting his head.

Chris went quiet for a moment. "I didn't put it in pictures," he responded. "Just like you said. But you have. In those pictures . . . what did you want, Geoff? What did you want from me? From us?"

Everything. I want to demand everything, and have you trust me to take you hell and gone from your comfort zone. But even then, out in that abyss, all I want is whatever you're willing to give me.

Geoff stayed silent, though. Some things could only be expressed with action, learned with time. He lubed up a couple of fingers before he parted Chris's buttocks, pushing the tip of one against him, stroking the rim. That nice little quiver went through Chris once more. Geoff saw him shift, and realized he was digging his fingers into the carpet.

"Your dick still hard, bud?"

"You know it is."

"A simple yes or no is all the jury requires." Geoff reached down between his legs, captured his balls and gave them an idle twist. Chris jerked, but quickly realized how vulnerable a position he was in. "Yes or no?"

A muttered oath came first, but Chris managed the response Geoff demanded. "Yes."

"Good boy."

Geoff suspected Chris's erect cock still had pre-come oozing out of the slit, wetting the carpet. He put his fingers inside Chris along with the tip of the lubricant to help slick up Chris's sphincter, caressing it enough that those muscles let him in, wanting more of that feeling. Chris's breathing went to a harsh rasp again.

"Feels good, doesn't it?"

"Yeah." The edgy quality of his voice made Geoff grin in a feral way.

"You're kneading the carpet like a cat, aren't you?"

"Shut up."

Geoff drew out the anticipation, tracing the curve of Chris's ass and his upper thigh, playing a single fingertip over his balls and perineum as Chris groaned, his hips flexing. Watching the show pushed Geoff's own arousal up another notch.

He lubed his own cock then. It might be overkill, but he was going to make this as comfortable as he could. At least this first time. He savored the stillness that descended upon his mount as Chris figured out what he was doing. Geoff could almost feel his mind assigning action to those slight shifts of his body, Geoff's hand working over himself, up then down, up then down.

"Going to jack off there, or do something with that?"

Satisfaction surged through him at the impatient challenge. "Keep shooting off your mouth, that's just what I'll do. Jerk off on your back and get my spunk in your pretty hair."

This time he anticipated. When Chris tried to buck him off, he shifted back, gripped his hips and yanked him up onto his elbows. The motion put his cock firmly against Chris's ass. His head was down, the pale silhouette of his back like the graceful wing movements of a stingray, expanding and lowering with his breath. Geoff ran a soothing hand over him.

"You're just big all over. Nice big ass, like a left tackle. Tight as a drum."

"Lucky I'm not a girl, else you'd be getting nothing for calling my ass big."

"I'll get what I want, because you want me to have that big, tight ass." Geoff gave him a far more possessive stroke and let him feel the firm command in it, reinforcing what was in his voice. "Stay on your elbows. There isn't anything to this. You just push out and let me ease in."

"Figured you'd ram yourself in like a jackhammer, like you said."

"That how you imagined it, without pictures?"

Chris nodded, a quick jerk Geoff felt through his body since he couldn't see it. "It's a nice fantasy, but it would hurt like a son of a bitch, especially to a virgin ass. There'll be time for that as you get more used to it. Easy now, man. Just let me in." Working the head of his cock against the tight opening, he felt the lube opening things up. He had his thumb in there too, rubbing, teasing, and he added some vocal stimulation to it.

"I want it all, Chris. You asked me what I thought about, and that's what I imagined. Everything you and Sam are, everything you want to be, I want it all to be part of me, belonging to me. But right now, I want only one thing. To have your ass. I want to be balls deep inside of you. I want to feel you give it all up to me."

Chris groaned as Geoff passed through the first ring of muscles, a glorious constriction that made him want to groan. He dug his fingers into Chris's hips. "Fuck, you're tight. I love it." He bent, pressing his mouth against Chris's spine and teasing the ridges with his tongue. Chris lifted up into him in reaction, which impaled him even deeper. The feeling was indescribable. He wanted his balls resting against Chris's, wanted to feel that friction and impact when he thrust into him with a smooth rhythm, made possible by Chris's surrender and the slickness of their joining.

Yeah, they might have unresolved issues, but the beauty of fucking a man was that conversation at a certain point was no longer a priority, even if the fate of the universe depended on it. The only thing Geoff could imagine stopping them right now was Samantha herself. She was the one who'd made this happen. The thought inspired him to say one more thing before they reached that point of no return.

"So that you never question it," he rasped, "understand that she's ours, Chris. This proves it, you get me? It's not a competition between us. Not over her."

Chris shook his head, an agreement, and Geoff slid home. Blessed fucking heaven. He pushed against Chris, a deeper angle.

"Say it, Chris. Tell me you've always wanted me to fuck you. In the dark, in the light, even when we were fucking other girls."

Chris's big body convulsed, rocked, and Geoff reached below him, grasping the base of his cock in a hard clamp. "You don't come until you say it. Say it."

"I can't . . . can't do that. Yet."

It twisted like a knife in Geoff's chest, but he got it. He understood. But, fuck, it changed where they could go tonight. It shouldn't. He should just ignore it, just let it go. He drew back and slid in home again, a long, sizzling line of friction that had Chris's body gathering again. He worked Chris the way he needed. In, out. The feeling was incredible. With the few brain cells he had left, he thought to grab a corner of Chris's bedding and work it underneath him. Chris, understanding, shifted his hands to pull it under his palms, but he was panting. "Close . . . fucking close."

"Come, then, you stubborn bastard."

Chris let out a strangled cry, his hips jacking back and forth. Geoff moved with him, making sure he hit right where he needed to hit on each impact. Being squeezed by all those incredible muscles was sexual bliss. He might have killed someone for the privilege of releasing into Chris's fine ass, but for some reason he pushed it aside, instead reveling in taking Chris all the way home, knowing that when he climaxed it was because Geoff was inside him, because he was responding to what Geoff could give him.

Once that gateway was open, it never took a guy long to make it to the finish line. Geoff remembered Sam picking up a *Cosmopolitan* when they were at the grocery store and solemnly informing him that a woman's climax was usually three times longer than a man's. What they lost in time, they could recoup in intensity, though, if it was done right. Geoff was determined to do it right.

When Chris came to a shuddering halt, head down, his wide chest moving in and out like a bellows, he thought he'd hit his mark. But Chris started moving against him, realizing Geoff hadn't yet come. Chris had a generous heart. Why that made Geoff hurt a little bit more, he didn't want to think about right now. He needed to wrap this up before he screwed things up entirely.

Gripping Chris's hips, Geoff eased back until he freed his rigid dick. Just that friction alone was almost enough to send him over. He tried thinking of fungus, his grandmother or random *Sesame Street* episodes. Anything to calm it down.

"What . . ." Chris tried to twist around. Geoff nipped out of range, barely, snagging his brief shorts and pulling them back on in a blink so he could be back beside Chris and not leave him feeling abandoned. He grabbed his arm where he was flailing in the dark, ran a hand over his face, his hair, those thick locks, settling him. "Easy. Come back to the bed. Stretch out."

Chris complied after a hesitation, probably thinking Geoff was going to go about it another way. Once he was settled, Geoff knelt over him and put a palm on his chest, holding him there. He'd stepped on the TV remote while finding his shorts, so he picked it up and clicked the TV back on. A dim light filled the room, along with the low murmur of the late night newscast. Chris was sprawled on the mattress, cock lying against his thigh, legs spread, his eyes confused but mouth slack from his climax. The view alone made Geoff bite back a shudder. His cock was well and truly pissed at him, and he couldn't say he blamed it a bit.

"Geoff." Chris pushed up on his elbows, brown eyes meeting his. "What's going on?"

Geoff shook his head. "We're not in the dark anymore, Chris. Look at me."

"I am looking at you."

Are you? The words beat on the inside of Geoff's chest, harder blows than he'd expected. But he managed a tight smile and brushed his knuckles over Chris's chest, tugging on the hair. "All right, then. I want to leave it there for tonight."

He straightened, all too aware he stopped looking at Chris as he pulled on his slacks and shrugged back into his shirt. He couldn't handle looking at Chris, his naked, muscular body, his puzzled expression.

Fuck, had he truly just denied himself the chance to come in Chris's ass because he got caught up in some dysfunctional bullshit about family rejection? He'd fucked plenty of people in defiance of that crap. People who weren't anything more than a one-night stand. That was the problem. He couldn't do it here.

"Is this some kind of Dom/sub bullshit?" Chris asked. He didn't sound angry, but he was getting close.

Geoff bit back the nasty reply that sprang to his lips. He could say yes, because maybe a small part of it was. But lying would probably be worse than the truth. Probably.

"This is enough for now," Geoff said. He wasn't punishing anyone, wasn't trying to be a dick, though he was probably accomplishing both. "We'll figure the rest out tomorrow. Maybe we'll get started on that project we were going to build for Sam."

"Geoff." Chris got up off the bed, but Geoff stepped back, raising a hand. He met Chris's eyes, and whatever Chris saw stilled him. Anger gave way to compassion in Chris's face as he obviously put two and two together. Damn it, there were times Chris's intuition was a pain in the ass. Chagrin would really piss Geoff off and make him lash out. Which would be the entirely wrong tactic, since the one he despised the most at the moment wasn't Chris. Not even close.

"No," he said firmly. "Don't do that, Chris. You feel what you feel." *Or don't feel, rather.* "No apologies. Leave it for now."

Thank God, Chris's phone began to ring, and it was Sam. Chris's ringtone for her was "Just the Way You Are" by Bruno Mars, which had made her smile from ear to ear when he'd played it for her. He used the Darth Vader theme for Geoff. Smartass.

Scooping the phone off the floor where he'd knocked it when his head had hit the crate, Geoff tossed it onto Chris's bed. "Tell her to call me after she talks to you," he said casually. "If she wants to talk to both of us. I'm headed to my room. See you in the morning."

Chris stared after him as Geoff left him standing naked and slack-jawed in the middle of the room. Damn it all to hell and back. The guy thought he was playing it all casual and relaxed, but Chris had seen more relaxed-looking telephone poles. His stiff back and set shoulders were the last Chris saw of him before he disappeared into his room.

"See you in the morning, my ass," he muttered. Chris snatched up his shorts. As Bruno's song continued to play, he thought about not answering, about going after Geoff and making it right, but charging into that without thinking it through was a great way to disturb a nest of snakes.

Dissatisfied regardless, he put the phone to his ear and tried to clear his head. The climax had been over-the-top, but still somehow lacking. He'd fucked it up, yeah. No doubt on that. All of the feelings had swamped him, threatening to cut him adrift. When Geoff demanded he admit he'd always wanted this, Chris hadn't been ready to completely let go of the shore. Yet Geoff had pulled back when he couldn't have everything he wanted all at once. So some of that blame had to be on him.

"Chris? Are you there?"

"Yeah, I'm here. Sorry about that."

"No, I'm sorry. I did try Geoff's first, because I know he's more of the night owl, but he didn't answer. Since that meant the universe is ending or he's dead, I thought I'd better wake you up and see which one is happening."

"I wasn't asleep, promise. And you know he'd answer even if the universe were ending. But no, he's not dead."

"Good." She paused. "Okay, what's going on?"

Um . . . let's see. Geoff fucked me and took off. It wasn't like Chris had wanted pillow talk or cuddling, right? Actually, that would have been kind of nice. At least share a postcoital beer. But that wasn't the problem.

"You and Geoff haven't been fighting, have you? Were any bones broken? Blood spilled?"

"Not much." He assumed Geoff didn't have a life-threatening skull fracture, though his head had hit the corner of the crate pretty hard. "He bumped his head just now and I have a busted lip from earlier today. He also face-planted in the yard. All of that was his fault."

"I'm sure. What am I going to do with the two of you?" She sounded tenderly amused, but she was too smart, and knew too much about them, to believe he was merely teasing her. "Are you okay, Chris? Has he hurt you?"

"No . . . I think I hurt him." But fuck it, it wasn't as easy as it was with Sam. The things Geoff wanted, how those unspoken things made Chris feel, were things he couldn't voice. Only by not saying things did he manage sometimes to say what he really needed to say. Which sounded fucked up, even in his own head.

"Well, say you're sorry." She drew in a breath, letting it out in a rush of words. "So-has-anyone-had-sex-in-the-house-with-anyone-else-while-I've-been-gone?"

She stuck an iron pipe in the spokes of his state of mind. He couldn't help it, he laughed. "You are such a fucking brat."

"That was not a no. Oh my God, you did, didn't you? Or he . . . or you both . . ."

"We invited the UNC-Charlotte women's basketball team over and did three of them at a time. Twice."

"Yeah, right." She snorted, but then quieted. "Chris."

He ran a hand over his face. Unbidden, he remembered that moment Geoff had demanded a yes-or-no answer from him. Some strange feeling had spiked in his belly, and he'd spoken the one word. "Yes. We did. But it's in a weird place right now, Sam. We're trying to figure this out, and you acting part cheerleader and part like the coach telling us the whole game is riding on us, it's too much pressure."

"Oh. Yeah, I can see that. I'm sorry." She sounded genuinely chagrined, but hurt was under that. He cursed himself.

"Hey, you're okay." He gentled his tone. "It's just . . . it just happened, and it ended on a kind of crappy note. I'm being kind of an asshole because it's bugging me. You didn't deserve that, and you're not acting that way."

"Maybe I was, a little bit. Sometimes the truth has to hurt, I guess. You can't pretend it doesn't, just to make the other person feel better. Otherwise nothing else will really be true." Letting that settle between them, her tone changed and became more teasing. "Maybe you should go tell Geoff that if you gave it up for him, you expect cuddling. And pillow talk."

"Maybe you should mind your busy little nose before someone cuts it off."

"Men are so dumb." There was a smile back in her voice, which made him feel better. He'd rather not alienate both of his best friends tonight. "So . . ." She cleared her throat. "Are you lying on your bed naked and sweaty? You're still a bit breathless. I can hear that part."

"You really are a brat. How's your thing going?"

"Boring, as always, but Flo and I went out to a dance club tonight with some of the girls. It was fun."

"Lesbian club? No men in sight?"

"Absolutely," she lied cheerfully. "I'll take you and Geoff there sometime and do a lap dance with a hot stranger to turn you both on." Her voice turned into a throaty little purr. "So . . . is anything sore?"

"You fishing for details?"

"Yes," she said. "I'm imagining so many things, but the reality . . . I want to hear about the reality. I'd like to watch the two of you."

He blinked. "Why would you want to do that?"

"Did you forget our girl-on-girl burger commercial conversation? Why do you want to see me give a lap dance to another woman? Seeing you two touching each other, your gorgeous bodies rubbing up against each other, your . . ." She paused. "I don't think I'm drunk enough for phone sex. But I keep thinking about the way you look now, how things feel . . ."

His cock tried to stir back to life at her intrigued tone. It gave him an idea. Maybe a bad one, but sometimes a guy had to risk the nest of snakes so he didn't miss seeing something really cool happen on the other side of them.

"He made me spew like a teenager and, when I move, I can feel the lube still in my ass." He glanced toward the cheap mirror he had up on the wall. The TV light provided just enough illumination to confirm his next words. "And there are red spots on my face where he rubbed his jaw against me."

"Oh . . ." Her voice dwindled.

Maybe it was a crutch, but the idea of commanding her made him feel more in charge of what was going on. "Did you take your vibrator with you?"

"No. I was afraid I might . . . be too tempted."

"Uh-huh. We'd have to punish you when you got home." This was new for him, but he heard the little catch in her breath and pressed onward. "Are you in your room? By yourself?"

"Yes."

"Put your hand between your legs and play with yourself. I want your fingers inside you. Are you wet and hot?"

A pause, a sound as if she bobbled the phone. His cock definitely reacted as she let out a quiet moan. "Yes."

"Good. Keep your hand in there and call Geoff. Tell him what you're doing and ask him if you can keep going."

He cut the connection and moved into the hallway, listening for the sound of Geoff's phone ringing. When he heard Geoff answer, Chris put his hand on Geoff's bedroom door and slowly pushed it inward.

Geoff was stretched out on his bed in his pajama pants, no shirt, and had the TV on the news. He muted it when he answered his phone. Looking at Chris, he switched the phone to speaker mode. All the better.

"So your fingers are in your pussy?" Geoff's slightly stern voice made Chris's cock twitch another step toward a full erection.

"Yes." Sam had that breathy sound to her voice.

"And Chris told you to do that."

"Yes sir."

Geoff's lips pressed together and Chris felt an odd leap at the address. He moved to the end of the bed and around the corner. Geoff's eyes were focused on him with a neutral expression. Chris wasn't interested in neutral. He wanted to see those sensual lips stretched back from his teeth, allowing Geoff to draw in much-needed air.

"Do we want to hear her come?" Geoff asked Chris, raising his voice so Sam heard the exchange.

"Yeah. Fast and hard. Calling both our names."

Approval surged in Geoff's expression. "You heard him, Sam."

"Yes."

"Good. You tell us what you're doing."

"I'm lying back on the bed . . ."

"Are your legs spread out nice and wide?"

"Yes."

"Spread them wider. Makes your clit and pussy more sensitive when you're touching them. Pretend Chris is holding your ankles, keeping you spread for us."

They both heard her response, an incoherent sound between moan and plea. Chris could see her writhing on the hotel bed. Pale skin, round curves, slick flesh. He paused, standing at Geoff's thigh. The other man raised a questioning brow, but Chris wasn't ready to explain himself. "Are you naked?" Geoff said into the phone.

"Um . . . panties and T-shirt. The one I stole from Chris's closet. The one with the dragon on it."

"If you call us from a hotel room and you're by yourself, we expect you to be naked. Take it all off."

"Play with the bear I gave you," Chris added. Discovering the manipulation of the tiny teddy bear shaped jewel at her navel piercing excited her was an unexpected turn-on to him. Geoff sent Chris another approving look as the throaty moans became little whimpers. Chris tilted his head, holding Geoff's gaze. Curling his fingers in the waistband of the pajama bottoms and brief shorts, he lifted both over Geoff's erection and pulled them to his thighs.

Geoff moved his hand to block him and Chris intercepted, curling an iron hand around his wrist. As he bent, he took Geoff's hand with him, twisted it around, up and over, so Geoff's palm was now resting on the back of Chris's head. Meeting Geoff's bemused gaze, he lowered his head farther. He curled his fingers around Geoff's cock, straightening it up so he could cover it with his mouth and slide down it, slow and easy, to the root.

Smelling that familiar scent of male arousal up close and personal was another turn-on, as was touching a cock he'd thought about almost more than his own. But the real charge was Geoff's reaction. His thighs tightened up like rubber bands, his eyes became jeweled slits, lips firm and totally edible.

Guy had a decent stick, about the same size as Chris's, though a bit longer. Like their body types. Both of them big enough not to get pushed around, but Chris had more girth and Geoff had more height. He'd never given a guy head, but he pretty much knew how he himself liked it done. He'd thought of it plenty of times, usually with Sam doing the honors in his fantasies. He slid himself off of Geoff, slow, working his tongue over the base of the shaft, curling around the corona. Geoff's hand was staying where he'd offered, on the back of his head, and a hard shiver of reaction went through him when his friend's long fingers constricted on Chris's hair, pushing him back down on his cock.

Sam was making little sighs and moans. It was like listening to the rise and fall of the ocean. On his own next stroke up Geoff's shaft, Chris lifted his mouth from him. "Sam, have you gone down on

Geoff? Has he put you on your knees and made you bring him to climax with your mouth?"

"Yes . . . God, yes. I loved it. I loved how he looked while I was doing that. The way he responded...oh..."

Yeah. Chris met Geoff's heated gaze, and went down on him again. Geoff's grip was going to yank hair from his scalp, but premature baldness was a sacrifice Chris was prepared to make. Reaching between Geoff's slightly spread thighs, he cupped his balls as he tugged on him with his mouth. Geoff's hold slid to the side of his neck, and Chris could feel his pulse pounding against the heated palm. "So how did you like it when Geoff was inside you?" he asked Sam. "Was he too rough? Do I need to be rough with him now?" He curled his tongue around Geoff's glans, giving it a teasing lick followed by another nip that had Geoff shuddering.

"Oh . . ." That idea had seized her imagination, though she rallied enough self-preservation not to put her Dom at his mercy. "No . . . yes. It felt good . . . and hurt, but in the good way. Like he was taking every part of me, fucking every part of me. I want both of you inside of me in every way." Her voice was breathless again, and Chris imagined her hips lifting and lowering against her fingers, her knuckles glistening with her sweet honey.

Chris swirled his tongue over the head of Geoff's cock and probed the slit. Geoff's hips bucked up.

"Bastard," Geoff muttered. He pinched Chris's nape, hard.

"That would be my response." There was laughter in Sam's voice, and a whole lot of sex, her voice pouring over Chris like warm oil. "What are you two doing?"

"Mind your own business," Geoff said. "Chris, we shouldn't let her come. Let's keep her so hot that the moment she steps into the house, we can just strip her down and fuck the ever-living shit out of her. And make her beg for more."

Geoff's eyes were firebrands now, his mouth tight as Chris slid up and down, slow. He tasted as Chris had expected. Heat and male, the salted musk of semen, and below that, something important. The flavor of a male who was uniquely his. The way Chris had hoped he would taste.

"Oh . . ." Sam implored. "Please . . . I want both."

Both of them? Or she wanted both things, permission to come in the hotel room and having them fuck her half to death when she got home?

"Yeah. I think Geoff's right." Before Geoff could respond, Chris had his mouth back over his cock. The man drew his lips back in a feral snarl as Chris started to work him in earnest, drawing him deep, sucking in his cheeks, working his way up the thick shaft. Shoving his hand between Geoff's legs, Chris captured his balls once more, cradling them, working them in his fingers as Geoff's hips lifted and lowered further. Geoff kept one hand on the back of Chris's head, the other looking for purchase next to him, gripping the sheets near the cell phone.

"What are you . . . two . . . doing? Please tell me . . ." Sam was obviously still stimulating herself as they'd required, but the desperation in her voice said she was close enough she was having to concentrate to obey, to not come unless they gave her permission.

"Chris . . . is sucking on my dick," Geoff said in a growl. Chris shot him a look, bit him, and earned a hard pull of his hair. "I had the pleasure of taking his ass earlier in the night and he has an overdeveloped sense of noblesse oblige."

Chris scored him with his teeth, even harder this time. In response, Geoff reached around Chris's body, keeping his grip on his hair with the one hand as he yanked down his shorts with the other so he bared his ass. Geoff clamped down onto the meat of one buttock. The guy was always stronger than Chris expected, using that grip to tug him closer, shift his hand so his fingers were deep in the crevice, playing over the still-slick rim of Chris's ass. His cock shifted into overdrive, erect enough to bounce off his abdomen as he worked Geoff's dick in his mouth.

"Oh . . . God . . . please . . ." A feminine sigh, tremulous and needy, came through the phone.

"Take your hand from yourself," Geoff ordered, though Chris heard the strain in his voice. "I agree with Chris. You're going to hold on to it for us. Just for us. Tell me you understand."

"Yes . . ." There was petulance in the tone, telling them exactly how close she'd been.

"Yes, what?"

Chris's own heart skipped a beat at that sharp tone.

He had to admire Geoff's ability to multitask. Because there was no doubt he was having an effect on Geoff's concentration. He was fucking Chris's mouth aggressively, pushing toward the back of his throat with rough demand.

"Suck me harder, you bastard," he whispered, pinning Chris with a gaze of molten fire, browns, greens and golds all swirling together.

Chris obliged, and Sam's voice came through the phone, laden with emotions so heavy they infused what was swirling between the two of them with additional tension.

"Yes, Master," Sam managed.

Geoff jerked, and Chris got a weird charge out of it himself, hearing her use that word instead of *sir*. She hadn't meant it in a mocking manner. Not at all. "You put your hands above you, leave your legs spread wide and listen to us," Geoff said.

Chris raised his head. Geoff's hand slid to his throat, holding him there. "You should see him, Sam. His lips are slick from going down on me, and his cock is so big his shorts can't hide his erection."

"Maybe he needs to take them off, Master. To be more comfortable."

"She's always thinking of our well-being," Geoff said, eyes glittering. "Do it."

He'd already pulled them down over his ass, so Chris finished the job, kicking them away. But as he bent back to his self-appointed task, he had a demand of his own.

"Don't you hold back on me this time," he said in a low tone. "Trust me the way you want me to trust you."

Geoff stilled at that, but Chris wasn't waiting for it to become a debate. He wrapped his fingers around his dick, and put his mouth on him again, heated breath, a teasing swirl of tongue all along the velvet shaft. He wanted that orgasm to spill, and then they'd work out the other shit.

Geoff shuddered, bucked, and Chris moved with him. He knew Geoff had been hurting for it when he left Chris's room, and Chris took full advantage of that, pushing him past the point of no return and who-the-fuck-cares-about-hurt-feelings. Maybe he was learning from Geoff. Learning that when you held the reins, it made it easier for the guy to let it all go and trust that things would work out. Just as he'd said.

Geoff let out a tearing, grunting sound of male lust. Chris heard the soft hum of Sam's encouragement through the cell phone. Geoff's fingers dug into his ass like pincers, telling Chris they'd leave bruises. That was okay.

Sam's moan came through the phone. "Please," she begged.

He didn't consider himself a sadist, but when he'd said *"You need the reminder,"* he'd been thinking of Sam in some hot little dress at a club, with guys ogling her. Even if she hadn't flirted or anything like that, Chris wanted to keep her climax out of reach. Her wanted her focus to be on getting back to them so they could take care of her needs in ways no one else could. In ways that would make it hard for her to walk, if they had anything to say about it.

Christ, where was all that coming from? The surge of testosterone made his dick jump against his stomach again. It caught Geoff's eye like a raptor spotting prey. A blink later, his fingers wrapped around it. But he couldn't do anything with that hold except hang on when Chris sucked in his cheeks and pushed him into release. The vein pumped beneath the clamp of his lips, and Geoff's body tightened up all over. When Geoff started to come, he lost his grip on Chris's cock, fingers sliding along his thigh as his focus was sucked into the orgasm.

The first flood of seed in his mouth, Geoff's come, was a rush. Chris took some of it down, letting the rest of it spill out over his fingers so he could grease Geoff up further, slick it over his balls, work him in his hand while Geoff bucked and thrust. Yeah, it made Chris harder, but Geoff had already taken him over that ledge once. He could always go back to his room and jack off.

He wasn't a sub like Sam. He wasn't going to be looking for permission to give himself release. Yet Chris knew he likely wouldn't jack off on his own, any more than he'd think about why he wouldn't. He was a guy. He had every right to avoid self-analysis. He had the broken chromosome to prove it, to validate that decision. Plus he had better things to contemplate right now.

He lifted his head to look at Geoff, the closed eyes, parted lips, the rise and fall of his beautiful chest. Geoff had been a skinny adolescent who hadn't grown into his limbs and filled out with muscle until his senior year, but it had been worth the wait, because he was all rangy power and grace now. His fingers were still grazing Chris's thigh and buttock, little random caresses. When his gaze slowly lifted, his eyes were mere slits. The inscrutable look he'd used on him a couple of times tonight could scramble Chris's brain, but this expression, where heart, mind and soul were all tangled up in his gaze, made Chris feel like Geoff stood inside him.

"Sam?" Chris said quietly.

"Yes." She sounded so temptingly desperate. Geoff's lips curved.

"I want you to stroke your fingers lightly over your pussy," Chris said. "Like it's a flower I've handed you. Just gentle and slow. Light, so very light. No more than a brush of butterfly wings."

He could imagine her doing it, her moistening her lips with her tongue, the quivering strain of her naked body, her pale long limbs. Geoff pushed himself up on his elbows. He drew one knee up, making a space so Chris sat down, Geoff's calf against his hip. He laid a hand on Geoff's bent knee, his gaze sliding down over the guy's softening cock. The natural repose did nothing to make it less distracting. He'd had that thing in Chris's ass, and God help him, Chris wanted it there again.

He had a feeling Geoff wouldn't be asking him when that moment came. Chris thought of all the ways he could fight him, and how Geoff might prevail anyway . . . because that was what they both wanted.

"Oh . . . oh . . ." Quiet moans came through the phone as Sam . . . obeyed him.

"So light," Chris murmured. "We could keep you doing that for hours, keeping you so close to the edge. Couldn't we?"

"Yes." She sounded close to tears now, a state sure to twist his own heart. But holding the unyielding gaze of the Dom lying on his elbows, his legs casually sprawled, the cock Chris had sucked to climax within touching distance, held him back.

Geoff spoke then, his voice thick.

"I think you pissed off our boy here, Sam. I think we both did tonight. Brought out an interesting side to him. What did you do?"

"I don't know. Please, Chris . . ."

"Keep doing it," Chris said. "And you know what you did."

"I . . . I went to a dance club."

"What did you wear?"

"A . . . uh . . . that red dress. The one with the spaghetti straps . . ."

Geoff's lips twisted in understanding. "The one that clings to your tits and ass and is about four inches south of legal. Did you wear heels with it?"

"Yes, but I—"

"Showing off your body. Those shoes give your hips that *I want to be fucked* sway, don't they? Yeah, you're going to have to be hurting for it, baby. He's possessive, our boy."

Geoff's glance went to Chris's hand, resting on his knee now, his fingers curved over Geoff's flesh like he wasn't planning to let go anytime soon.

She blew out a breath. Geoff tilted his head toward Chris, a silent *Your play*. Chris picked up the phone and murmured into it. "If you really don't want to wait, I'll let you come, Sam. Because I love you."

Quiet ensued. Geoff's expression changed, becoming more thoughtful. He sat up, crooking his leg on the spread and letting the other dangle over the edge. It put his knee against Chris's hip. Chris glanced down at the floor, his two braced bare feet next to Geoff's dangling one. He laid his hand on Geoff's knee again, held it the way he held Geoff's gaze, as they both waited for her answer.

It didn't surprise him, though it made him love her all the more. "I . . . I'd rather wait until I can be with you. That feels right. Horrible, but right."

Chris smiled at the resolve in her voice, mixed with a *What the fuck am I thinking?* surge of hormones he understood all too well. "Come home to us soon, then. And Sam? Wear something that you don't mind having shredded when you come through the door."

He tilted his head toward Geoff, a quizzical look to see if he had anything left to say. "No panties," Geoff said. "We don't want to wait that long. Got it?"

"I hate you both. Yes sir. Sirs."

Chris blinked at that, and Geoff grinned. Taking the phone, he clicked off, but he sent a quick text first, turning it toward Chris so he could see what it said.

Travel safe. We love you.

"She said you owed me pillow talk," Chris said after a moment. "Cuddling."

Geoff shuddered. "Women."

"Hmm." Chris studied him, his fingers tightening on Geoff's knee. He knew when his expression changed the tone between them, because the vague amusement died out of Geoff's face. "You don't get to check out on me because I hurt your feelings with the truth," Chris said evenly. "You don't get to act like you're in control when you know it's not that straightforward. So don't play bullshit games with me and draw back to teach me a lesson. It's not going to work that way for me."

Geoff tossed him a narrow look. "Because you're such an open book. You answered my question, but you didn't add anything to it, anything that helps me understand what you *are* feeling. Would you care to draw me a fucking road map? Or is this like one of those twenty-question games? Is it here or there? Not there, not here, somewhere in between, and I have to wait until I hit it dead square to get a clear answer from you? Fuck you, and I do not mean that literally."

Chris rose then, pulling his shorts back on so he wasn't standing there naked. "You know how I think, how I figure things out. You want me to lie to you to make you feel better, I can't do that. I can't feel what I don't feel."

Geoff's expression was hurt, pure and simple. Damn it. Chris stepped toward him, but Geoff shook his head. "I get it, all right? Leave it there. Let's go to bed."

Chris stepped back, frustrated. He couldn't say what he needed to say without getting into the areas he simply wasn't ready to talk about. Geoff usually understood that better. Maybe he did and he was insisting anyway. He moved to the door, knowing that Geoff was right, they needed to let it rest for now, but he stopped at the threshold, turning to look at him. He glimpsed frustrated misery on Geoff's face before it was gone, wiped away into that neutral look.

"You hoping for a kiss good night?" he asked Chris.

"No, asshole." Though the minute he said it, he remembered the heat of Geoff's mouth on his. "Have you ever let anyone do to you what you did to me tonight?" Not that he really wanted to talk about other guys with Geoff, any more than he did with Sam. Why Geoff's male lovers bugged him in a way the female ones didn't was another mystery, but there it was.

He couldn't tell if Geoff was going to answer, but he waited him out and finally got a response. "I've usually done the pitching. And I've never let someone else be on top...so to speak." He spoke slow, staring at the wall now instead of Chris. "Might be interesting to feel the other side of things . . . with a person I trusted."

Chris's heart beat a little faster. "Am I in that group?"

"Do you want to be?" Geoff arched a brow at him, eyes becoming cool.

Chris set his teeth. "You do get that we're not your damn family, right? We're not the ones who turned their backs on you. You treating me with the same mistrust isn't the way to figure this out."

Geoff's expression turned into a torn flag, reflecting the war he'd lost with his family. "I trust you, Chris." He said it seriously enough Chris knew he meant it. "You and Sam, more than anything. But this is a new area for me. I have to figure out how to navigate it."

"Right." Maybe Geoff was right. Something he'd done tonight had dug up a lot of stuff in Chris. All that holding back, waiting, not thinking about the things Chris wanted, in order to preserve the treasure he already had, had stirred a lot of shit that had built up around that treasure. "Well, here's a big tip. If you want me to open up to you, tell you what's going on, it goes both ways. If you go all honest with me, and I'm not ready to respond in kind, don't draw back and bullshit like that. Don't do the Dom-poser thing where you hold on to all the reins, try to make me and Sam rip our guts open for you while you give us nothing."

Geoff's gaze fired up at that. "You think it's all an act?"

"No, I don't. I just know how it's supposed to be. You think I haven't watched and listened, when we went to those parties and clubs together? You can feed me a line that the deprivation is part of the Dom thing, but that kind of deprivation is what we just did with Sam, getting her hotter, making her the focus, making her eager to be with us. What you did in my room? That was just an excuse to keep your feelings locked away, to not risk yourself. I deserve better than that. And I didn't think you were that kind of coward."

Geoff whitened. Chris pivoted before he could let the recoil hit him in the chest and make him apologize, soothe. He was right—he knew he was. But it didn't make him feel any less like shit. He knew the guy's most vulnerable spots, and he'd just taken a deliberate shot at one.

He returned to his room and flopped into the hammock, rubbing his face with both hands. Shit, shit, shit. How long had they known each other? Why would Geoff think they needed to play mind games like this, when they knew each other in and out?

Because they didn't know this area. Geoff was right. Hell, the sex alone was plenty to wrap his mind around. The potential had been there for some time, waiting, but it had been unexplored up until now. Maybe that was the deal. When Geoff was deep inside of his body, Chris had held on to that shore, refusing to be cut loose, because his reaction to the Dom thing had hit him out of left field.

Before it started he'd have said it wasn't his thing. Yet it had been so easy to work side by side with Geoff just now, embracing that Dom stuff toward Sam. It had startled yet pleased him, how much he'd suddenly enjoyed playing that game with her and Geoff. And yeah, that caveman reaction he had, and how he'd picked up the reins so fast to top her, had been this side of *What the fuck?* But what had rocked him on his foundation, what had turned that little disagreement of a few moments ago into something uglier, was how he'd responded to Geoff's orders himself.

Yet he couldn't say everything wasn't *quid pro quo*. A couple of hours away, Sam was wet, hot and willing for the both of them. Geoff had fucked Chris into near oblivion, and in return he'd compelled Geoff to spill his release in Chris's mouth. During that short, blissful time, Geoff had given himself over into Chris's hands fully. Suddenly, it made him feel more like a dick for taking a shot at Geoff.

When Chris's dad had walked out on his mom when Chris was nine, it had left Chris with two things. One, a determination that he'd never let anyone he loved down that way, would never abandon them. It had also left him a virulent nest of anger way down deep in his gut, which conveniently filled the hole his dad had left. That trigger could be tripped by the strangest shit, like someone wanting him to lay it all out there, make himself completely vulnerable. Like Geoff's question had.

Tell me you've always wanted me to fuck you. In the dark, in the light, even when we were fucking other girls . . . The question was far more than what had been on the surface. Geoff had been asking for everything. Or had he?

Chris scowled. The problem was, he had so much feedback coming from so many directions he wasn't sure how to process it all. He didn't do much of anything fast. That wasn't his style. He liked to take his time, get his head wrapped around things. This was like having to stuff a whole meal in his mouth in one bite. Whereas Geoff had a rapier-fast mind that could evaluate and act in a blink.

Or was he just throwing up a smoke screen of bullshit, avoiding the real reasons he hadn't reacted to Geoff the way Geoff had hoped he would?

"It's like playing one of those damn game shows."

Chris looked over to see Geoff silhouetted in his door again. That was how this had started, less than a couple of hours ago. Now, just like with Sam's actions of a few days ago, things had changed again. Irrevocably.

"That one where you have to risk the winnings you've already got to answer the million-dollar question," Geoff continued. "If you get it wrong, you lose it all; if you get it right, well, you win everything. If you choose not to answer, you get to keep what you already have, no risk." Geoff shrugged uncomfortably. "I get it, because what we have, that's already so much to me. But then . . . what you said, I thought you meant you didn't feel the same way."

"No, Geoff. Shit no." Chris realized then Geoff hadn't separated it out in his mind as he had. "It's not that at all, man. I love you, plain and simple. I don't want anyone but Sam or me to be with you, ever. It's the other stuff I can't figure out and, because they seem like a package deal with you, it felt like if I said yes to one thing, I was agreeing to all of it."

As Geoff digested that, his eyes became a little less hooded. "No line item veto."

"Yeah." Chris shrugged. "We started as friends, and I never questioned how you and I seemed even closer than a lot of guys were. How I preferred going out on dates together. And, fuck, that night when we were having sex with those two cheerleaders in the same room . . . It felt so close to what I really wanted, but I couldn't quite get it straight in my mind, so I left it there . . ."

He swallowed as Geoff's eyes took on a different expression and he stepped closer. "Then there was the night I brought Rhonda Hammond back to our place . . ."

Geoff grinned. "You took her to the movies, but you came back to the house right after to drink beer. She French-kissed both of us. Rhonda was an adventurous girl, God bless her."

"Yeah." Chris met his gaze and the smile faded from Geoff's face. "When we were on the couch, both up against her, for a blink, I let myself think about what it would be like if she wasn't there."

"Chris."

Chris shook his head. He had to get it out, work through it the way he did. Geoff understood. He fell silent, waiting him out, but Chris couldn't miss the laser focus of his gaze, the taut muscles of his face.

"She was nice, but she didn't matter. Not like that sounds. I mean, in terms of my being in love with her, or wanting to fall in love with her. It has to matter. Really matter. That's why it was always hard for me to make it work unless you were in the room. Then Sam came along, and it was like this whole new level . . . I felt, yeah, this is the way it was meant to be all along." He shook his head. "I'm making no fucking sense."

"No. Everything you're saying makes perfect sense. You're the type of guy who sees something way before any of the rest of us. But you don't act on it until we catch up. Until someone who matters takes the lead." Geoff's gaze burned into him. "Keep going."

Chris set his jaw. "You came home one night, before we met Sam, and I knew you'd been with another guy. Just a hookup, because you never mentioned him, but that was when I knew. It hit me in the chest like a battering ram. As long as you were with girls, you were still . . . we were still the two of us. And that was okay, though something about it felt off. Until Sam. She put a balance into it I haven't exactly figured out, but she did."

Chris took a breath. "You've been standing inside me for so long, Geoff, I forget sometimes you're a separate person. I expected you to understand what I meant, when I couldn't say what you wanted me to."

He saw the moment it clicked. Geoff's spine straightened, and the energy that came off of him was the same kind he'd had when he'd stood in Chris's door the first time. It made things do a nice somersault in Chris's belly. But Geoff gave a self-deprecating chuckle and shook his head. "Christ, I'm an idiot. A fucked-up idiot."

"No, you're not," Chris said, sobering. "You're a guy who was fucked over by his blood family. And I'm a guy who doesn't believe in promising you more than I can give, so I got wrapped up in that other stuff you might want from me and didn't think of how it would sound to you."

"I shouldn't have been that sensitive."

"Yeah, but I already know you're a pussy."

Geoff shot him the bird and Chris grinned. Geoff took another step closer. "My mother used to have a saying. It doesn't really mean shit when you apply it to the decisions she's made in her life, but wisdom out of the mouth of a fool is still wisdom. It's just harder to believe."

"What did she say?"

"It's hardly original. *'In the end, all that matters is kindness.'*" Geoff's gaze darkened. "Yeah, I want to torment the two of you, make you beg for things, leave marks on your skin. And I want to kiss all those marks, take care of you and keep you safe from everything always. But even though that's only the tip of the iceberg, it doesn't have to be all or nothing. All I really want to know is that your hearts belong to me."

Chris swallowed, hard, and Geoff nodded at his expression. "You asked if you were in the group of people I'd trust to . . ." He lifted a shoulder, and the poignancy of it twisted in Chris's chest, Geoff's inability to say *top me.*

Geoff cleared his throat, the TV light flickering over his face. "You are. And since the membership of that group is exactly one person, if you weren't part of it, the group wouldn't exist."

Chris stared at him. "Come here."

Geoff shifted. "Giving me orders?"

"Just shut up and come closer."

Geoff sauntered across the room. Since he wore only the pajama bottoms, the sensual movement couldn't help but draw the eye to every fine inch of bare flesh. But that wasn't Chris's top priority. Chris reached up, curling his fingers around Geoff's neck, his thumb rubbing the line of collarbone. "Come here," he repeated in a murmur.

Geoff bent. When he brought his mouth over Chris's, this time Chris felt the rightness of it on both sides. He'd never really thought of himself as gay or straight. He was just who he was, with a heart that often felt too big for his chest, because it would hurt when he saw things that didn't strike him as right. Or things that were perfectly right. Like Sam out in the sunlight, laughing, her hair touched by the heat. Geoff, sitting back on the couch at the end of a long day, one foot propped on the coffee table, a Corona with lime in hand as he and Chris talked about everything and nothing.

Geoff kept the kiss light, yet there was a lingering feel to it that made Chris want to pull him down with him, keep him there. Maybe if he were on the mattress instead of in the hammock, he would have had half a chance of getting him to join him. But Geoff drew back, though he stayed close enough Chris could see the faint quirk on his serious mouth.

"Since you look a breath away from trying to drag me into this hammock for cuddling, I'm headed back to my room before we both embarrass ourselves."

"You're only retreating because you know you love a good cuddle," Chris teased him, but his grip tightened.

"You wore me out. You have a mouth like a damn siphon." Geoff ducked free, giving the hammock a push to send it rocking. He followed it up with a quick stroke of his fingertips along Chris's face, though. "Let's leave it here for tonight. Okay?"

"You all right?"

"Yeah. Just need to think."

"Yeah." Though Chris wished Geoff didn't have to think about it at all, that he could just let it happen. But Geoff was pretty good at seeing the potholes Chris or Sam might miss and planning a route around them. He had to trust in that. "Okay."

Giving him a steady look, Geoff moved back toward the door.

"I see what you mean about that rear view thing," Chris added. "Might have been better without the pajama bottoms, though."

Geoff snorted. "Stop staring at my ass."

"Yes sir." Chris offered a one-bird salute again, intending the words as a mocking tease, but when Geoff's gaze turned back to him, Chris got that odd feeling in his chest again. His smile died away under Geoff's intent regard.

"Good night, Chris."

As Geoff's door shut, Chris moved with the boat-on-the-ocean movement of his hammock, keeping it going. He lifted his hand over his head, tangled his fingers in the rope and sighed. A smile, albeit a tired and wistful one, crossed his features. He understood what Geoff was saying. Time to go to sleep and see what would happen tomorrow.

～

Geoff had been serious about working on that project for Sam. After a Hardee's breakfast that he picked up on his morning run, they set up in the garage, leaving the door up since the day was sunny with lots of blue sky. Chris reflected that it made the darker parts of what had happened last night feel better, and the over-the-top moments feel all the more intense in recollection.

When Geoff had bought the *Build-It-Yourself Bondage* book at Naughty Bits, the item that he and Chris decided they wanted to build was a modified spanking bench. Chris had picked up a long cushion from a weight bench at a secondhand store, and the lumber and hardware they'd ordered had arrived, stacked in Chris's garden shed so Sam wouldn't notice it. Since they were both proficient carpenters, they had all they needed to work on it while Sam was on her trip.

"The plans recommend the medium measurements if the piece is for a woman." Geoff examined the drawing that looked a lot like a picnic bench, though the seat portions were closer to the table part, and the whole thing was shorter, four feet. "If she's lying on her stomach on the bench portion, these parallel places where she places her bent knees will support her shins."

"Yeah, but it doesn't indicate any kind of finishing for the ends, like a rubber foot or cushion."

Geoff consulted an attachment. "It does mention it, but leaves it open in the plans. One person folded gel shoe inserts over the corners. Comfortable, but I doubt it's attractive. I'm thinking a smooth plastic fitting, a shoe."

Chris studied the diagram shoulder to shoulder with him. Neither of them had done more than a quick wash-up and toothbrushing this morning, so Chris still felt some of the effects of Geoff's taking him last night. Whereas the slightly sweaty smell on Geoff's skin from his morning run, a familiar pleasure, made Chris think about how his friend's dick would still have the scent of his release on it, since Chris had let Geoff's semen spill over the shaft as he was sucking him off.

They were guys; they couldn't help thinking about sex all the time. It didn't mean he had to act on it. But maybe all that waiting he'd told Geoff he'd done had him short on patience now. He'd touched Geoff, tasted him . . . and he wanted more.

He cleared his throat. "We should add the ergonomic modification for people with bad necks. She has that problem with her shoulder."

"We'll need to add a restraint piece. Hey, what about this?" Geoff put the drawing down on the workbench and sketched on it. "This protects her neck. The immobilization adds to the psychological impact, but it would also keep her from jerking it out of whack. Plus, in this vertical mode, she'll be in the perfect position to take a cock right between her pretty lips while the other one of us is fucking her."

It was so easy for Geoff to say these things, so straightforward. When he turned his head, meeting Chris's gaze, they were close enough that Chris's attention was on his mouth—he couldn't help it. The faint scent of coffee and mint toothpaste was on Geoff's breath. "Think we can get it done before she gets back?"

"Should. The wood's already finished, but we can add a coat of stain to make it pretty and sealer to keep it from giving her splinters. The rest is cutting and assembly."

Chris passed his hand over the bench portion they'd already put together, pressing down on the cushion. The plans called for straps over the ankles, backs of the knees, thighs, waist, shoulders and nape. When they did all that, she'd be helpless. He imagined her pale, quivering body there, her eyes full of the dazed arousal that happened when Geoff pressed that submissive trigger inside her. Her lips would part as he fed his cock between them. Then Geoff's gaze would meet Chris's, an unspoken order and encouragement to Chris to grip her delicate buttocks and ease into her pussy. He imagined her moaning over Geoff's steel flesh.

"So you think she'll like this," he said slowly. "Really like it. It's not more for us than her?"

"It's for all of us. That's the way it works. We let her desires lead, and figure out how ours fit with them, and the result is a hell of a good time for all of us."

"Yeah." A good time.

With a searching look, Geoff set the plans aside and shifted a hip onto the bench, picking up his coffee. "How about we take a seat for a minute?" He pointed to the stool across from him.

Chris's look was quizzical, but he straddled the stool, picking up his own coffee. Geoff swiped at the dark blond hair over his brow, something he did when he was considering how to say something. He didn't take long.

"I said this to Sam and I guess, with you having known about me for so long, I forgot to say it to you, though I probably made it pretty damn obvious last night." Geoff shifted. Seeing Geoff unsettled was a rare, fascinating occurrence.

"I've thought about this stuff for a long time, Chris. Even done some of it at the parties and such, with people who are experienced. I didn't have to put a lot of effort into making sure we were communicating clearly beyond function, because it was limited, temporary. It's like you said last night. Pursuing it with people who matter to me the way you and Sam do . . . I'm not always going to be right on target. Keeping you in the loop, keeping you safe emotionally, physically, that's what's most important to me, no matter that sometimes I let my pride get in the way, or my sheer damn desire to go after what I've been wanting from you both for so long."

Chris blinked at the raw passion in Geoff's face, his voice. His foot was braced only a couple of inches to the left of Geoff's, so they were close enough to touch, if one of them reached out.

"I was thinking about some of the things you said last night," Geoff said carefully. "You've watched, and you pick up things pretty fast, but we really haven't set aside time to talk, you and me, about how Sam is. Submission is pretty intuitive for her, and I'm clear on what I am, so what she is can be easier for me to figure out. If there's anything else you want to ask, anything making you feel uncomfortable . . ."

He trailed off, leaving it open for Chris. He knew what Geoff was saying about Sam was right, because hadn't he just acknowledged seeing those triggers in her? More than acknowledged; he'd pressed on them himself last night. Yet Chris was also remembering the first time they'd met Sam, when she'd been attacked by her ex-boyfriend. "Do you think how she is . . . that's why she let someone like Anthony past her guard? She wanted to please him, the way she wants to please us . . ."

Geoff's eyes flashed, his usual reaction to Anthony's name. Chris had a similar loathing for the male. "No. And yes. I think guys like Anthony can latch on to someone who has more submissive instincts, who's a pleaser. But there's a line between that and someone who gets screwed up in the head and stays in an abusive situation. Remember, she turned her back on him. She was strong enough to walk away. A healthy submissive knows her first responsibility is to take care of herself. Which might sound strange when she also craves some pain or erotic humiliation, but once you're inside it, you can tell the difference."

Geoff ran his hand over the bench again. "Like this. We want it to be soft and comfortable, even though when she's on it, fully restrained, she's going to want to get spanked. Maybe more than that. Maybe she'll want to be caned, switched, flogged, whipped."

Chris set his jaw. "I can't . . . I wouldn't do that."

"Could you handle me doing it, if it's what she wants?" When Chris didn't immediately respond, Geoff nodded. "You might surprise yourself. You liked the idea of spanking her, making her gorgeous ass red, and initially you thought you wouldn't. But then you saw how she reacted to it. That's the key, Chris. She might want to try out some higher levels of pain. A lot of subs do, after they first get introduced to it, though I suspect Sam is mostly about restraint, low-impact play and psychological domination."

"I don't want to talk about her like a lab rat." At Geoff's sharp glance, Chris lifted a shoulder. "I mean, it sounds so detached and clinical."

"You think I'm detached about this? About wanting to make her helpless, give her climax after climax, give her the chance to explore every room inside her that wants this?"

Chris shook his head. "I get it, but . . . it's still not second nature for me, at least not like it is for you. When we bought the plans for this, and I saw her wondering what we might be thinking about doing, it felt right, the vibes I got from her. But when we're doing it . . . it feels more impersonal. This is Sam. Our Sam."

"You bet your ass she is," Geoff said. "I'm glad you mentioned that. You remember the first wild animal you ever rescued? When we were ten?"

"The squirrel Joel Tanner hit with his BB gun. Knocked him out of a tree and he fell wrong."

"Yeah. You read everything you could about how to take care of that squirrel. You visited the Raptor Center, talked to the wildlife rehab people. That was how you learned all the mechanics, right?

What they needed to eat, how often, how to rehab them back into the wild. But over time, there was the other side of it. When you knew what to do, what they needed to live, you followed your instincts and went beyond how to treat an injury to how to heal it. Two different things, but both were necessary. Right?"

Geoff reached out, closed a hand on his forearm and squeezed. It was the reassurance of a friend, but there was another element to it, too, from someone who knew way more about this than Chris. The gesture, Geoff taking the time to talk this out, reminded Chris he did trust Geoff more than anyone. And Geoff loved Sam, just as much as he did.

"We learn how to make this work, all the mechanics. But the reason we do all that is so we know how to get beyond that, how to care for her, enjoy her, love her on the deepest levels, way beyond mechanics. No one's detached from any of this. We're all in it together." Geoff nudged him. "We're all on the yellow brick road together, Tin Man."

Chris snorted at that, picking up the measuring tape. "Okay. But if I keep asking you questions, you're not going to start acting like a know-it-all, are you?"

Geoff grinned at him. "I thought you said I already act that way."

"Yeah, you do. I just don't want it to get any worse, or I'll have to kill you and grind you up for fertilizer."

"Fair enough."

They went back to work then. Measuring and cutting, switching back and forth between favorite radio stations. Drinking coffee. They'd been friends so long, they could talk or not talk and still be comfortable with each other. Topics were random. Work stuff, the mower the neighbor down the street was using. They grinned about the cashier at Hardee's who Geoff said was still nursing a hangover from the previous night.

It was their usual kind of banter, but as they moved through the tasks of building the bench, Chris noticed the personal space boundary wasn't nearly as routine. Geoff's body brushed his several times and, when Chris leaned over the workbench to measure something, Geoff's hand passed over his back and the curve of his flank before he moved on, leaving Chris with a distracted mind and a pencil mark a good inch off of where it needed to be.

When he caught Geoff's grin, he scowled and redrew the mark. Geoff picked up the skill saw and Chris backed off to let him do the cut. He watched Geoff focus on what he was doing through the safety glasses, the sure and steady progression of the blade. They'd worked construction jobs in college together, and Geoff was as handy as Chris with the tools of the trade. "Shame you're a lawyer," Chris commented as Geoff set the saw aside. "You'd be a hell of a framer."

"Yeah, because that pays so much better," Geoff said dryly.

"If you'd become a framer, you wouldn't have a butt load of school loans to pay off and you'd work way more flexible hours." Chris sat on a stool and took a drink from the bottled water he'd brought out. At the time, Geoff had said he didn't want one, but Chris still wiped the top and offered it. As he'd expected, Geoff took it, but after a single swallow, he set it aside.

Screwing his hand in the front of Chris's shirt, he yanked him forward on the stool to put his mouth on his. Chris's hands landed on his waist, digging in as Geoff's tongue slid between Chris's lips to tease and tangle. Geoff held him fast, hand wrapped around the back of his skull. He kept the kiss going until Chris's head was swimming. Only then did he pull back and hand Chris the bottle.

Chris managed to rally, despite the surge of blood to his groin. "Gross. Now I have your germs."

"In a couple of different orifices," Geoff confirmed. He stayed close, his hand sliding down Chris's side and back, covering his buttock and taking a good handful of ass. "I'm thinking I'd like to test how sturdy the bench is. Hammer myself into you over it."

"Yeah?" Chris had a mix of feelings about that. Some of it was inexplicable uneasiness, but his cock could care less. It jumped at the tone in Geoff's voice and was ready to go for it now, now, and oh, by the way—now.

"Yeah. You're wearing jeans today. An old pair. All faded, creased and with a bunch of tears and holes in them. Didn't even think you still had that pair anymore. So used to you wearing your camos and painter pants to get dirty."

"I dug them out of the back of the drawer. Need to do laundry."

"Hmm." Moving to the wall, Geoff hit the button that lowered the garage door. As the engine engaged and the door trundled down, shutting them away from the rest of the world, Chris felt suddenly like he was on a cliff ledge, hanging there by his fingernails.

"Think I'm just your fuck toy, whenever, however?"

"Nope. You're a hell of a lot more than that." When the door reached the concrete pad, sealing them in, Geoff didn't bother to conceal the lust in his expression, and swept that look over Chris. "But it's a definite side benefit. You've been looking at me all morning like you want to eat me, but I'm going to take the first bite."

How did he do that? He made Chris feel naked with those searing hazel eyes, as if they'd already peeled off his clothes and the top layer of skin, exposing everything beneath. Was that a Dom thing? And what did it say about Chris, that it disturbed him as it did, giving him anxiety and a hard-on at once?

As if knowing Chris was teetering, Geoff took a seat on another stool, stretching his long legs out in front of him. "I've watched you build things before," Geoff noted, "But not like this. Your mouth sets in a line when you're concentrating. And you handle everything with such care. You connect to everything you do, whether it's planting or washing dishes, or listening to me or Sam. You don't do anything casually. You're fully in the moment."

His hazel eyes became more vivid, so the gold, green and brown reminded Chris of bright moss on a tree wearing golden fall colors. "It makes me think if I touch you, get inside you, I'll be fully in that moment."

Chris wet his lips and Geoff picked up the water bottle again, extending it with a half smile. Not mocking, just . . . understanding. Chris's fingers slipped off the ledge a little more. When he closed his hand on the bottle and took it, Geoff caught Chris's belt loops, bringing him a step closer with inexorable pressure.

"Do you remember Larry Featherwood?" Geoff asked, taking the bottle and setting it aside when Chris was done. Chris wasn't sure where to put his hands or how to stand, when he was standing between Geoff's splayed knees.

"You can touch me, Chris," Geoff said. "Just don't go for my dick yet, because I want to get this out, and if you touch me like that, I won't."

He was used to Geoff being a master of clever words. Geoff didn't lie, but he often wrapped the truth in clever striped and twisted packaging. Straight honesty put things on a different footing, but it also helped. No games. Chris slid his knuckle along Geoff's chest, traveling between the pectorals, up to his throat, where there was a dusting of wood shavings. He rubbed them off with his thumb while Geoff's multicolored eyes stayed on his face. "Yeah, I remember Larry," Chris said. He'd gone to the same middle school they had.

"You remember when he got in trouble for drinking at Megan Sower's party? That Monday, he said he'd been grounded and his dad had taken a belt to him. You remember what you told me about that?"

"I said a lot of shit when I was thirteen." Chris was watching his own hand as if it had a life of its own. It moved from Geoff's throat to his shoulder, and then came to a stop as Geoff lifted his hand to wrap his fingers around Chris's wrist, stilling him. Chris's fingers curved into the T-shirt.

"You said you wished you had a dad who cared enough to take a belt to you. Because your mom is so great and made it work as a single parent, you felt guilty as hell right after you said it."

Chris shifted. "Yeah. Kids can be dumb like that."

Geoff shook his head. "No, I got it. And your mom would have gotten it."

"Mom would have taken a belt to me herself if she hadn't figured out worse punishments." The one and only time Chris had lied to her, his conscience had tormented him until he admitted it to her. She'd thanked him for telling her the truth, but she'd told him there was nothing he could ever do that would disappoint her more than him lying to her.

"It not only disrespects me, it tells me you don't trust me to care for you, to know what's best for you." A thousand belt stripes wouldn't have affected him the way that statement had. Nothing was worse than letting her down.

"Momma Bear is the best."

Chris smiled. Geoff had always called his mom that, ever since Geoff had been pulled over for speeding—ninety in a forty-five. Chris had been in the car with him. Geoff's dad had basically brushed it off as teenage hijinks and told Geoff he'd get a lawyer to reduce the charges so he could keep his license. The next day, when Geoff came over to Chris's house, he'd faced something entirely different. Chris had been on the sidelines, wide-eyed, while his mom had torn Geoff a new one. He'd tried to deflect her, give Geoff a break, and she was having none of it.

"See him?" His mother had pointed at Chris while a teenage Geoff stood there white-faced. "That is your very best friend in the whole world. Your brother, in every way that matters. My son. The center of my world. I don't care what kind of 'I'm immortal,' riding on hormones bullshit anyone else uses to excuse a teenager acting like this, it doesn't fly with me. I know your heart, Geoff Tywin. You are smarter and better than this. You will take care of him and yourself, because if I ever lose either one of you to some act of teenage stupidity, I will dig up your bodies and kick the shit out of them in front of God and the whole world. I promise you that. And should you live through that act of stupidity and my son dies, you will wish you'd died and gone to hell rather than having to face me."

Chris could tell Geoff was recalling that same memory, because . . . well, he could usually just follow Geoff's mind the way Geoff could follow his. Maybe that was why he was suddenly uncomfortable again as Geoff rose off of the stool. Reaching out, he slipped the tongue of Chris's belt free and slowly stripped it out of his jeans. He doubled it over, threading the strap between his clasped hands. Then he pinned Chris with a steady, unflinching gaze.

Chris took a step back. Not in retreat, but to establish a perimeter, figure out what was going on. Geoff inclined his head.

"I thought about doing this last night, but here is even better. I want to strap your ass with this, and then I want to be inside you."

The thought should have set off a *Forget this shit* explosion in him. Instead Chris felt that curious stillness of breath and heart, his hands curling at his sides, his cock suddenly constricted by his fly. He imagined Geoff, his hard hand gripping Chris's shoulder as he held him, as that strap stung and struck.

"Okay." The word echoed in the silent garage. Chris pressed his lips together. "But I want something, too. Tonight, you let me inside of you. I want to make my one-man club membership official."

Geoff lifted a brow. "You're determined to keep this on an even footing."

"Yeah. We covered this last night. I'm not Sam. If you want me to be a male version of her, I can't do that." Never mind that he couldn't take his gaze off that belt. "I don't know where that leaves us."

"Right where we're at." Geoff inclined his head. "You have a deal. Drop your pants to your knees, boy, and bend over the bench. Take a good, hard grip on it."

Chris's forced half chuckle was an attempt to lighten things up, but Geoff didn't smile. He just kept threading the doubled over belt through his fingers, his gaze fixed on Chris, waiting.

"If I don't?" Chris taunted, though his hand was on the fastener of his jeans and Geoff's attention had flicked to the arousal swelling behind his fly. He could tell himself his reaction was because the belt thing was just a precursor to Geoff and him fucking, but Chris couldn't seem to get the images in his mind past that belt and Geoff's dangerous expression.

"Then I'll make you do it. And the punishment will be worse."

He could scoff at the idea of Geoff making him do anything, but he didn't. Chris slipped the button of the jeans, slid his thumbs in the elastic of his boxers and pushed both off his tense ass, taking the clothes to his knees as instructed. If Geoff weren't acting so serious, if he'd treated it like a game, Chris might have felt foolish and backed away from this. Yet nothing about how Geoff's gaze slid over him, a possessive caress, suggested a game.

Not sure what to say, or how to quantify what he was feeling, Chris turned toward the bench and closed his hands on the top edge, pressing his palms into the cushioning where Sam's body would be resting, bound. He wasn't on the bench himself, just leaning over it, which made him feel less out of control, though he suspected that was self-deception. His cock was a pulsing, taut rod between his thighs.

Geoff moved in, the silence a palpable weight between them. The radio was still on, but it was as distant as a conversation happening in China. Chris tensed as Geoff's palm slid down Chris's back then up, finding his way under his shirt to trail along his spine. His palm flattened, exerting pressure, pushing Chris over until his hands spread out wider, his chest touching the bench.

"Better," Geoff murmured. "Spread your legs. Shoulder width."

When Geoff used the position to reach between his legs and take a firm grip on his balls, Chris's cock sprang up higher. Geoff leaned over, nudging his hair to the side with his chin, and Chris closed his eyes as the man's lips found his nape.

"That was a pretty ballsy move, coming into my room last night to suck me off when I was on the phone. I'm okay with that, just as long as you're okay with me taking my due for the presumption."

"Didn't hear you complaining at the time," Chris muttered.

Whap!

Chris bit his lip as the belt slapped across his haunches, a lick of fire. Pivoting in a blink, he clamped his hand on Geoff's wrist. He and Geoff held that toe-to-toe position, though Chris was keenly aware his pants were at his knees and his dick out there, all vulnerable and hard. His heart was racing. Geoff zeroed right in on it, putting his palm flat against his chest, leaving the other wrist in Chris's tight hold, the belt dangling over Chris's forearm.

"You can't decide whether you want it or hate it. How about you take a second and work that out?" Geoff's voice was neutral, but his eyes were laser sharp.

A long pause. Then Chris let go of his wrist, one finger at a time. Geoff lifted a questioning brow. Waiting.

Chris turned around and took hold of the bench again. The fire was settling in, a coiled serpent in his belly that said he wanted more. He wanted more than more. He wanted Geoff's ferocity, needed it like a hunger for red meat and a woman's touch. "That the best you got?" he ground out.

Geoff's chuckle was nasty enough to spear need right into Chris's balls. "Just keep talking back. Chest down and keep your ass up. When I'm done, you can answer that question for yourself."

Chris set his jaw and complied, ready for Geoff to whale on him. If he'd done that, Chris could have endured it like a hard football practice, nothing touching him below the surface. But Geoff chose another, far more devastating tactic.

The strap whispered over Chris's tense flesh, a featherlike sensation that had a shiver running up his spine. He could almost feel the heat of Geoff's gaze following it, studying every inch of his back and nervously flexing ass. When Geoff slid a firm, heated palm down the line of Chris's spine to cup one buttock, fingers gripping with casual possession, Chris's heart rate went up another octave. "Geoff..."

Crack! The blow had him sucking in a breath, swallowing Geoff's name. He could tell himself the loud pop of the strap gave a false sense of how hard it was hitting him, but the sting through his nerve endings called him a liar. He put his head down and tried to breathe, trying to keep his head in a center space where he would stand apart from this. On the third strike, he failed. A churning mix of arousal, nerves and deeper, harder things gripped him, and he was grunting as much from their clamp on his mind as the force of the blows.

Geoff began alternating the strikes from side to side, coming up from beneath so that the impact sang through his perineum and balls. He made a flat crack against both cheeks, so Chris jerked and tightened. Hell, Geoff had him practically dancing, his toes curled in his work shoes, his hamstrings straining.

Then, he'd change it up again. A couple of times when Chris was ready for the sting, Geoff ran his hand over the throbbing flesh instead, a caressing, firm touch, teasing Chris's balls. His dick got harder and things higher up got even tighter. He was white-knuckling the edge of the workbench.

"Geoff . . ."

He hadn't bent all the way over when he turned back toward the bench, but Geoff took care of that now. He pushed him down to his chest again, which meant Chris had to adjust his stance, putting his ass farther out there. Geoff clamped his hand on the back of Chris's neck and landed a half dozen blows that went past sting into full burn. Chris snarled, cursed and kept his ass lifted, some part of himself he knew but didn't understand asking for more.

He was shuddering, fucking shuddering. Something in him broke. He needed to push up, he knew he did. He needed to stop Geoff, but Geoff anticipated him. He set the belt aside and dropped to his knees behind Chris. Parting Chris's buttocks, he put his mouth on Chris's rim.

Holy Christ. The sensation was incredible, Geoff's tongue provoking sensitive nerves as it stabbed inward. His hands were locked on Chris's hips, reminding Chris how strong and stubborn Geoff could be. Chris pushed his forehead into his palms, his elbows digging into the workbench when Geoff reached between his legs and took hold of his cock.

"Let go," Geoff demanded, and Chris couldn't do anything other than obey. His hips jerked, humping against the bench as Geoff kept tongue-fucking him and playing around his rim, working his cock in a sure, firm grip. When the climax grabbed him, Chris was sure he shot come halfway across the garage, but that didn't mean anything, not with his mind breaking to pieces like this.

Geoff was still teasing him with his mouth when he came down. "Stop," Chris groaned. "It's too much. Fuck . . . quit."

"Say *please*."

Really? Was he kidding? Apparently not, because he was going to keep doing that crazy thing with his tongue, and Chris's legs were shaking too much to stop him. "Please. Asshole."

"Yours is a pleasure." Geoff drew back, his thumbs passing over Chris's buttocks, making him feel the soreness of those stripes. He bit the meat of one cheek, hard enough Chris jumped and knew he'd left another mark. He'd never seen Geoff get this intimate at those clubs, using his mouth and his hands how he used them on Chris, on Sam.

Geoff straightened to his feet, leaning over Chris's body, wrapping his arm around Chris's broad chest. "Breathe, big man. Be easy."

He should be embarrassed he was this shaky, because it was only an orgasm, no big deal, but Chris knew it was far more than that. So it helped, having Geoff hold him like this after something like that. When Geoff put his lips on his shoulder, Chris dropped his head down lower. "You need to get off."

"I surely do." Geoff's position had his pelvis pressed firmly against Chris's ass, so he could feel how hard his friend was. A chuckle rose in him, strangled in other emotions.

"Yeah, but not what I meant."

"It's all right." Geoff kissed his sweaty neck, nipped at him again. "Don't think. Just relax. Because now that I'm done beating your ass, I'm going to fuck it. And you're going to take every inch of me."

He drew back, and Chris heard the sound of him opening his jeans, the pause as he lubed up, because he was probably carrying some in his pocket. Just in case.

"You like biting."

"Yeah, I do. I'd leave teeth marks all over you if I could."

Chris dropped his head back into his hands. What had he just done, and why? He thought of when they were kids, daring one another to do Indian burns. A game, the sole point of which had been to see who could take more pain. It had usually been a draw between them.

Now, though, Chris remembered one time when Geoff was

rubbing the eraser on Chris's arm. The pain had grown excruciating, but Geoff had been watching him the whole time, so closely. Somewhere along the line, it wasn't about an adolescent need to prove who had the bigger balls. The discomfort had mixed with other things and Chris became so involved in watching Geoff register his reaction that he forgot the pain. It was Geoff who called it to a stop, who realized he needed to stop before he took all the skin off Chris's arm.

"You're trying to hold on to control to prove to yourself you're in charge of both of us," Chris muttered.

"If that's true, you're trying to stop yourself from relinquishing control because you're worried about the consequences of doing so." Geoff bit his shoulder again. "Maybe the truth lies somewhere in between."

He set his hands back on Chris's hips, pushing the head of his cock against his rim, still tingling from having had Geoff's tongue there. Chris groaned, and Geoff answered with a growl in the same octave, a deep-throated sound of possession and sex. Geoff pushed all the way in, Chris's muscles giving way as if they knew who was calling the shots here. Then they clamped down on Geoff's dick like they'd never let it go. Wrapping an arm around Chris's chest, Geoff worked his hips against him in a smooth rhythm, though his breath rasped harshly against Chris's back, his other hand flat between his shoulder blades.

"I can't remember the first time . . . I knew . . . I wanted your ass. Seems like all of a sudden, it's always been . . . that way."

Chris understood what he meant. Last night, they'd talked about how Sam had become the bridge they'd needed to cross from friends to lovers. But if it had been that simple, they would have made the leap long ago. Chris wondered if they'd had to reach the point where this element could be part of it, the one that had Chris's ass cheeks smarting, that had him thinking about whether or not Geoff would do it again. And even crazier, would Chris eventually ask for it? Punishment, desire, pain. Surrender, a loss of control.

That give-and-take that Geoff kept pushing was a raw nerve that alternated between retreat and wanting to be stroked. Maybe Sam's deeper embrace of submission had helped open up something similar but different in Chris, allowing him to step across that line now. Was it part of what had drawn him to Geoff for so long? Or was it a bunch of things, and that was just one vital component?

Chris closed his eyes, shuddering hard as Geoff reached climax, his body shoving Chris against the bench, breath hot on his neck, his fingers digging into Chris's chest through the T-shirt he was wearing. They hadn't even taken off their clothes, just pushed what was necessary out of the way.

It was possible to call this simple lust. Animal reaction, no thought involved, the result of the sexual floodgate they'd opened last night. But that idea only left him hollow. Chris's back rounded as he dropped his head even lower, his fingers clinging to the bench as Geoff's release flooded him, as his pelvis smacked Chris's ass and Geoff's thighs worked against him. As he slowed, his breath deep, erratic, Chris had to keep his hands clamped on the bench so he didn't betray his need or confusion by grabbing on to Geoff's forearm across his chest, refusing to let him draw back.

Another part of him wanted to turn and put him on the ground, pin him there with his weight until he could make sense of this, why things that had felt right a breath ago suddenly felt wrong. But he didn't. For one thing, they had sawdust all of the floor. Since Geoff's cock was slick with lube, he'd end up having that stuff stuck all over him and be eminently pissed about it.

The thought twisted his lips, making Chris want to chuckle in a way that wasn't humorous. It was more like tearing paper away and finding an empty box instead of the gift he'd always wanted.

"Chris." Geoff had withdrawn, put his clothes back together. Now he slipped his hands under Chris's shirt, fingers threading through the coarse hair. "Hey, man, talk to me. Where did you go? Did I hurt you?"

In ways he couldn't describe. Or maybe he'd hurt himself and Geoff had just opened the door. But Chris shook his head and reached down awkwardly to get his jeans back up. Geoff was so close behind him his ass bumped him, and Geoff closed his hands on his hips to steady him.

"I'm good." Chris sidled away and managed to hop clear of the bench to finish the job, zip and button his jeans. "I've got it."

"Okay." Geoff's voice was neutral. Chris could feel him watching him closely.

"Uh, I'm going to go in and grab a beer. You want one?"

"Yeah. Sure."

Escaping into the house, Chris took a deep breath once he was in the kitchen. He held the refrigerator door open, the cool air wafting over him, and stared mindlessly at what was there. The door to the garage opened, closed, Geoff's footsteps stopping at the kitchen door.

"I get that you're the still-waters-run-deep kind of guy," Geoff said slowly. "Most things about you I can figure out. But you have me stumped here, Chris. You're going to have to tell me, because you're making me feel like a dick, and I can't fix it if you don't tell me where I'm going wrong."

"You're not doing anything wrong."

"Oh. So you jerking up your pants and walking away from me with all this shit vibrating off you, as if I treated you like a whore, meant I was stellar?"

Geoff's tone was the jagged edge of a rusty blade. Chris couldn't turn around, but when Geoff laid a hand on his arm, Chris yanked away. "Don't fucking touch me again unless I say it's okay first."

He didn't know where the venom came from, the rage, but it was definitely there, filling his chest and making it hard to breathe. He slammed the fridge door hard enough to rock the kitchen walls, and then he left the house, going out into the backyard.

He wasn't sure of his destination until he arrived in front of the fairy garden. He stared at it. The raccoons had visited in the night, knocking tiny figurines askew and leaving muddy footprints tracked all over everything. Some of the plants had been uprooted.

Normally he would have laughed. The creatures were adept at causing mayhem, and he'd anticipated a certain level of mischief from them. But right now, he couldn't find that lightheartedness. He dropped to his knees in front of the berm and clenched his fists, suppressing the incomprehensible desire to tear all of it apart, before what was inside him tore him apart first.

He didn't. He stayed there for a while, just breathing, not thinking. Eventually, he started to move, albeit stiffly. He dug out the fairies that had been squashed in the raccoon tracks or tumbled into the channel. He turned the water on so he could wash them off with gentle fingers. Harry was singing in the aviary, calling Hermione to him. Ron squawked. Circumstances had brought the three birds together, two of them permanently handicapped by their injuries and one who'd healed but who refused to leave the other two. Their survival stories had bound them to one another. Just like their individual paths had brought him, Geoff and Sam together. Chris rubbed a thumb over a fairy's delicate face. It was the one that reminded him of Sam.

"I'm not like you, you know," he said. "I feel things in straight lines. I live each day as it is. I'm not a big thinker."

"Yeah, I know. You feel things way deeper than most people do."

Chris turned. Geoff sat on the nearby bench. Chris had placed it there yesterday so when Sam got back, she could sit on it and look at her fairy garden while reading. "The raccoons messed it up."

"You'll put it back together."

Geoff looked older, serious. There was a haze over his eyes, a dimness to their light that Chris didn't like. "Maybe it's too fucked up."

Geoff made a poor attempt at a smile. "You've told me nothing is ever too fucked up to fix. Unless . . ."

"Unless God knows it works better broken."

"Yeah. That's what you always say."

Chris set the fairy down. There was something in Geoff's voice that made him want to draw closer, though he stayed still. Geoff looked down at his hands, spread them out.

"You know, I . . . ah . . . I never thought too much about what I am. Just always felt this way, knew I was built this way. It didn't worry me what other people thought because, you know, you've been my best friend. You went with me to those play parties or clubs, but we never really talked about how you felt about any of it, because it didn't feel like the right time. But you were there on the sidelines; you knew what I was. So what I am never felt bad or twisted. Until a few moments ago."

Chris's eyes sharpened, but Geoff was still staring at his hands. "In the kitchen, how you pulled away, it seemed like you found me repulsive. I've never wished to be different, never thought I was wired that way. But if you can't handle this part of me . . . I don't mean *handle it*—you don't have to be a part of that to be my best friend, but what I mean is, if this part of me is something that turns your stomach . . ."

Chris blinked at the break in his voice. The last time Geoff had been moved to tears had been when his mother rejected him. He'd had that same flat tone, the rug pulled out from under his world while he tried to act like it hadn't been, to prove he was strong enough to deal with it. He had been, but without understanding and support, that strength might have warped into something so different.

Just like that, the anger and isolation that had gripped Chris so hard, putting him in a vacuum, gave way to much stronger feelings. They reconnected him. This was Geoff. The person who knew him better than anyone. Chris had never thought anyone would get him as Geoff did, until he'd met Sam.

Geoff lifted his head, and his expression was wooden. Braced. "Is that what it is, Chris? Is this something you can't handle about me? About yourself?"

"No, shit. Stop." Chris moved to the bench and sat down next to Geoff, shoulder to shoulder, hip to hip. "I got lost in my head, Geoff. When you took over, it's like I became an object, or because I don't totally get what this is, and why I react the way I do, the connection was lost. I felt by myself."

The hurt in Geoff's face was replaced by a cautious understanding, followed by chagrin. "I'd never want you to feel that way, Chris. I hope you know that." His lip curled, a wry, sad little smile, and he nudged him. "I love you, man."

Chris chuckled at that. Things weren't right, but there was less constriction around his chest, less of a cold knot in his stomach. "'Yeah, you know you always be getting emotional after gunfights,'" he said, imitating Will Smith's *Bad Boys* line.

Geoff's lips curved, more genuine. He took a breath. "You're not much of a talker, Chris, and that's cool, but I hope you know you can talk to me about any of this, even if what you say doesn't feel like it makes sense. You don't have to make sense to me. It's the same for Sam. In a weird-ass way, that's what a lot of it's about. Having feelings that you can't express with words. So when you're ready, you can just throw what's on your mind out there, and I won't say anything until or unless you want me to."

It was tempting to take that *when you're ready* as an excuse to leave it alone right now, but with emotions raw between them, Chris knew it needed to be now. And he was ready, as long as Geoff wasn't needing it to make sense. That was kind of a relief.

"Okay." He laid his hand on Geoff's leg, closed his fingers over the taut column, feeling the shift of muscle as Geoff reacted to the touch. Chris slid his thumb in a windshield-wiper motion over it. The folding of the jeans around Geoff's groin, outlining what was there, was an intriguing terrain that Chris studied absently, aware of Geoff watching him, motionless as a hawk.

"I always thought I trusted you more than anyone, that I didn't hold anything back from you. But I guess I realized . . . hell, you know it connects to my dad leaving mom and me. In some weird, shitty way I realized focusing so much on caring for you, it also sort of became a shield. I didn't really know how to let you take care of me, because that would let you all the way in. Shit, I am so screwing this up . . ."

"No," Geoff said. "You're not. Keep going."

Chris pressed his lips together and met his eyes. "That belt thing, you broke something open, man. The whole universe turned on its axis in less than a week. The stuff that's there, that you do or want to do, it's stuff that a part of me wants. It's been in this closed room I knew about but kind of bypassed, if that makes sense. So now the rest of me is trying to catch up." He sighed, removing his hand. "Maybe because you *have* always gotten things about me so I didn't have to explain them, I was hoping you could explain to me what the hell is happening. Because honest to God, man, I'm not sure."

As he stared moodily at the ground, Geoff looped his arm over Chris's shoulders, his elbow pressing between Chris's shoulder blades when he lifted his hand to tousle Chris's hair. The affectionate gesture became a light grip on Chris's nape that reminded him of the heated sex they'd just had, but also told him he had Geoff's total attention, his support.

"Is this okay?" Geoff asked in a low voice. At Chris's look, he lifted a shoulder. "You said you wanted me to ask."

Chris closed his eyes. "Yeah, it's okay. And you don't always have to ask."

It was when he thought about things too hard he would think himself into silence, the layers too complicated to parse and fit into sentences that other people would understand. But Geoff had said it didn't have to make sense. So this time when Chris spoke, he tried not to bog himself down with his own head.

"I didn't think about it directly until we got to this point, with

Sam. When I watched the two of you together, all this need and desire came up so hard and strong in my chest, for both of you, and I don't know where to go with it, what to do with it. I sure as hell don't know what to do about how you are. Because I'm not like her. I know I keep saying that like you have a hearing problem, but do you know it?"

"Did it feel like I was treating you like her just now? At the workbench?"

"Yeah, somewhat. But no. I don't know. I can't tell what's you, and what's me being messed up about it. I want to hit you and I want you inside me, like you just were." Chris blew out a breath. "Now I'm having trouble saying it. I wanted you to fuck me, but I also wanted to take your head off your shoulders."

"If you let me fuck you, *then* hit me, it will go better for me, because you won't hit as hard."

Chris snorted but Geoff touched his leg. "Look at me, Chris. I want to say something, to make sure you really hear this, so you know you don't have to keep saying it. Though if you need to keep saying it to help you, I have no problem with that. Let me know when you're ready to hear it."

He went quiet and waited on Chris. Chris watched Ron fly to the top of the aviary and swoop down, ruffling Hermione's feathers as he went by. It made Harry hop up and down on his perch and fuss. When at last Chris nodded, he didn't have to look at Geoff to know he was watching Chris, waiting for that cue.

"You're a mix of things, Chris, a bloody unpredictable mix. There are parts of you that, yeah, want to follow my lead, follow orders. But not necessarily to submit. I get the difference. I have room in me to figure out how to handle both of those things if you do. You get that? You don't have to ride any ride that doesn't interest you. But I push because that's part of my makeup, especially when I sense something in you that responds to it. Right?"

Chris nodded again. He couldn't deny it. Geoff's gaze sparked with that look that made Chris aroused and uncomfortable at once, but then Geoff carefully reined it back. "In that world, there's something called a safe word. Maybe what we need is something like that, so if something doesn't feel right to you, you just say that, and it stops."

"But the problem is, it feels right but wrong. Like too much candy.

Or maybe like something else needs to happen first for the rest to work."

"What do you think that is?"

Chris knew, but he wasn't sure he could say it out loud. They'd finally hit on the root of the problem. He could say he wanted to think about it awhile longer, but it wasn't going to get easier. Plus, Geoff had opened his heart to him, made himself vulnerable, and Chris wouldn't leave him out there alone. So he said it.

"I've never given my heart to anyone," he said. "Not really. I mean, I think you're the first person beyond my mom that I loved. Really loved, and not in the roses-and-candy way. Kind of like when we watched *The Mighty* . . . that kind of thing, between Max and Kevin." Thank God they'd watched a million movies together, so they could patch in some emotional context without him having to wrangle it out. "Then there's Sam, showing up in the mix, and I realize whatever that is, I have it for her, too. Bam, two people, a man and a woman, the only people I've loved in my life. My first loves, either gender."

Geoff studied him. "And that bugs you."

Chris returned his gaze to the fairy mound, to the slim fairy sitting next to the squirrel, her tiny feet in the swirling water. "You don't get to control love. And nobody's first love is their last love, is it? It's a way to grow up, evolve. I don't know anyone who stays with their very first love." His fists clenched at the thought. Geoff, who could sometimes be a dick and way too smart, was smart enough to stay silent as the feelings kept coming, kept leaving Chris's lips.

"I don't want to evolve past the two of you, and if you evolve past me, I just . . . I'm not sure how I'd survive. I don't want you all to be my first love, crush, whatever. I want you to be *it*, and I can't handle it otherwise, because I feel so much for both of you."

"Ah, Chris. I should have known. When something bothers you, it's the kind of thing that tears the heart out." Geoff gripped his hand, and there they were, holding hands like a couple of girls, but it felt right. "No, there are no guarantees. But Sam and I have the same hopes for forever you do. If we don't try, we'll never know."

There it was, out and declared, and Geoff wasn't backing away from it. No more double talk or covering stuff up with casual words that meant nothing. Chris's hand constricted on Geoff's, and the fierceness of his friend's expression said he knew that he'd just said something that couldn't, wouldn't be taken back.

When he'd thought about his dad leaving, Chris had always focused on the anger, the betrayal, his resolve to do better, be a better man. He'd known he'd built some emotional walls. But it wasn't until these past twenty-four hours, putting it out there for the man who mattered most, that he'd realized how much he'd always longed to feel safe, emotionally safe, with another human being. His dad had taken that ability away from him. But he had two people willing to give that back to him, if he could be brave enough. If he could leave those walls behind when he was with them.

"Spill the rest of it out," Geoff said softly. "Tell me."

So Chris opened himself even further. "Last night, after you left, I did have a fantasy. This one with pictures, full color, sound, the whole bit. I thought about coming to you while you were asleep, and sliding into the bed behind you." He swallowed, shifting his gaze to Geoff's feet, aligned with his. "Being with you, wrapping around you, holding you, being inside you, like you talked about when you said that . . . about me being a group of one. About trusting only one person to do that. Me."

Now he lifted his eyes once more, met Geoff's. "Just now, you asked me what I need to have happen before the rest can work. I think if you let me inside you, all the way, you can have anything you want from me."

∽

The tide of Chris's emotions swamped Geoff, filling him beyond speech or even movement. As Chris had spoken, he realized he'd tightened his grip on his friend's hand to hold on. On the surface, Chris's words might sound like a condition, an ultimatum. Whether or not he could get into the sub stuff, he'd give Geoff that if he opened himself up fully. Yet Chris didn't set conditions. He was telling Geoff what needed to happen for them to reach the place that they both wanted to go, not just for sex but for things a whole lot deeper than that.

The Dom/sub stuff might all be new territory to Chris, but Geoff gave him full marks. Geoff had stumbled in his own insecurities, not sure if he'd been right about Chris when Chris pulled away so abruptly. But Chris had steadied him, given him this window to understand that he actually did have the capacity and, what's more, the desire, to embrace a surrender to Geoff. Yes, it would be on his own terms, but that made it as much of a priceless treasure as Sam's submission was, because each was sculpted by the nature of the person offering the gift.

"Okay," he said. Releasing Chris's hand, he ran a proprietary touch over Chris's chest, down to his upper abdomen, earning an opaque look that meant either he was getting the big guy worked up or Geoff was about to have his head knocked off his shoulders. "Why don't we take a step back? All right?"

"Yeah." Chris closed his hand around Geoff's again, holding it in place against his chest. "With Sam, she's different. With you and me . . . it's too easy to become rabbits fucking every ten minutes, and I don't like how that feels. You matter too much. You and Sam."

Geoff curled his fingers around Chris's hand, turning it into that brotherhood knot again, no teasing this time, their combined fists pressed against Chris's heart. "Okay. So we move slower. Show some control. Put our dicks on a leash."

Chris's lips quirked. "I'm not into that kind of shit, either, by the way. In case you ever get the notion to check out that corner of Naughty Bits, you'd better be considering adopting a dog with a throat that's coincidentally the size of my dick."

"Not sure they make them that small. Maybe gerbil leashes at PetSmart."

Chris punched him in the abdomen, fortunately with strength held back. But he kept hold of Geoff's hand. Glancing down at it, he looked at the ground, his mouth sliding back into a somber line. "You going to call me a girl for wanting to take things slow?"

"If I didn't, you'd think I was coddling you." Geoff slid his other hand around Chris's neck and pulled him in to plant a hard kiss on his forehead. "I love you, man. Seriously. Whatever it takes." He drew back, met him eye to eye. "So do you want to keep working on this thing for Sam, or take a break from all of it? We could go jump into a scrimmage game at Reedy Creek and do about twenty dollars' worth of Jack in the Box after. That'd be enough to cover lunch and dinner."

"Yeah, sounds good. Maybe we work on the bench later this afternoon. You think she'll really like it, don't you?"

"Yeah, I do. And I think the more you see how she embraces that surrender feeling and loves giving us that gift, the better a lot of it will feel to you." Geoff cocked a brow. "You already like topping her, don't you? You didn't expect that."

Chris nodded. "Yeah. She gets . . . wow. It's pretty hot."

Geoff grinned. "It's hellfire hot. Makes me want to spank her all day long. That's how it goes. Whatever the Powers That Be are, they're pretty smart about some things." Geoff punched him in the shoulder. "Let's go shut things down in the garage and get out of here."

At Reedy Creek they found a football scrimmage in process with half a dozen guys broken into two teams. To Geoff's amusement, they took one look at Chris and were more than happy to incorporate them into the game. They played hard, on opposite sides, and, though it was flag football, no one was averse to some rough play and the occasional tackle. When Geoff swiped blood off his elbow, he couldn't help but grin, remembering the scrapes, cuts and bruises they'd bragged about during their adolescence, the rites of boyhood.

But manhood had its own perks. When Chris brought him down on one play just short of the goal, Geoff couldn't help reacting to the feel of his body pressing him down, or thinking about what Chris had said he needed. What they'd be doing by day's end. As Geoff had told him, he preferred to do the pitching, but now that he'd agreed to it, he realized he was already thinking about how it would play out, Chris's naked, muscular body pushed against him, his cock deep in Geoff's ass, how that would feel.

Chris was right. With guys, the hormone part was too easy. But Chris seeing that he'd wounded Geoff in the kitchen, and caring enough to try to make it right and stick to the truth? Well, it underscored that it was worth it to take it slow. As Sam liked to say, the journey was all.

Speaking of which, at the next break, Geoff checked his phone and was pleased to find a text from her. She'd been sending them every several hours since she'd been gone, cheerful status notes, some with suggestive tones he'd enjoyed answering, sometimes with Chris's help.

In regulatory meeting. Kill me now! Sooooo boring.

He tapped a quick message back. *Just think about what we could do to you on the conference room table while they all watch.*

You're evil.

He grinned, and showed the exchange to Chris. Chris took the phone and typed another text, more slowly, since phones weren't fond of his bigger fingers. *Chris here. We're having Jack's for lunch and dinner. Chocolate lava cakes for dessert. How's that hotel food?*

You're just as evil as he is.

They exchanged a chuckle, sent her a couple more texts, and then she had to get back to work. She closed with several heart emoticons. *Take care of each other. Miss you.*

That feeling was mutual. They returned to the game and played hard, until they were soaked in sweat. The guys invited them to come back anytime, because they had a standing game weekly. After hitting the drive-thru at Jack in the Box, getting a few burgers and tacos, as well as the dessert Chris had teased Sam about, they headed for home and chowed down on half of it before heading back into the garage and their project.

The physical exertion, talk and food had done the trick. They figured out the adjustments, put the bench together, and it was ready for staining. Chris put on the first coat while Geoff watched. Conversation was easy and comfortable again. When they broke for dinner, they finished up the Jack and some green bean casserole Sam had left them.

Daylight was slipping from late afternoon to evening as they sat in the living room. From the looks Chris was sliding his way when he thought Geoff wasn't looking, Geoff was pretty sure Chris was thinking about where this evening was going to end as much as he was. But this was Chris's show. No matter Geoff's natural desire to take the reins and get it started, he'd let him make the move. But as he picked up his beer and sat back on the couch, stretching his legs out on the coffee table, he had to say something, because Chris's regard was starting to get him worked up. Geoff cocked a brow at him. "Something on your mind? Or are you just admiring my masculine beauty?"

Chris rolled his eyes, but then he twisted his beer in his hand. "You know earlier, the belt thing?"

"Yeah?" Geoff said it as casually as possible.

"I don't see you as a dad. Definitely not as *my* dad."

"Thank God." After Chris's dad had left them, he'd moved around and eventually fallen off the map to escape child support payments. Chris's mom frequently wished him dead after prolonged torture in a serial killer's basement, but his absence had never stopped her from doing what was needed to raise her boy.

Chris's lips twisted. "I mean, do you think the belt, my reaction to it, is about a father-son thing?"

Geoff tilted his head left and right, an ambivalent answer. "Yes and no. Some Dom/sub relationships are the Daddy–little girl or Daddy–little boy thing. But I think what you felt was just an expression of feelings we all have. Things we have or crave from our parents as kids don't go away. They translate into more adult cravings. Safety and structure for the sub can come from punishment, as well as the desire to cuddle or control on the Dom side. Somehow it wraps up into the sex thing and gives it an extra charge." He pursed his lips. "You know how you feel when you're holding a bird in your hand?"

The absorption in Chris's face as he cradled injured wildlife, as the creature quieted under his touch, was something Geoff never tired of watching. "Yeah," Chris said. "It's a good feeling."

"What I feel when Sam surrenders to me, or when you give yourself to me like you did yesterday and today . . . It's that feeling. Like, despite how crazy and brutal the world can be, you realize for just that moment you can trust me completely. To protect you, to give you pleasure, to take both of us where we want to go. You weren't off base about what we were tapping," Geoff added quietly. "The feelings your dad left you to handle, because you were abandoned by the person who's supposed to love you enough to stand behind you your whole life . . . My feelings about my mom and dad . . . When we come together, you and me, Sam, we're reclaiming those lost connections, reestablishing them. It's scary as hell, because it feels just the way we know it should. In some ways, it's better and even more intense than an orgasm. So when an orgasm comes with it, it's pretty much paradise."

Geoff shifted so he could briefly press his foot against Chris's. Chris stared at their overlapped shoes. He gripped Geoff's thigh, a quick, rough squeeze. "Yeah. Okay." His voice sounded thick. "Um . . . I think I'm going to take a shower."

Geoff rose, gathering up their dishes and the taco wrappers. "I'll do it after you. I reek."

"I would have mentioned it, but I wasn't sure if the stench was you or me."

"Fairly sure it's both. Sam would throw us out back and make us hose off like dogs."

"Girls. They're so clean and pretty. It's nice." Chris grinned, restoring them to a nice equilibrium. A gentle one, with room to let the tender ground they'd exposed settle in and get used to the touch of light and air. As Geoff made himself move toward the kitchen, Chris rose and headed for the hallway, pulling off his shirt as he went. Geoff stopped to watch the play of muscle across his back, the tight ass beneath the camos he'd worn to the park. Geoff adjusted himself as his cock pushed up at the wrong angle inside his jeans. While he was tempted to invite Chris to take a shower with him, he was still trying to do the courtesy wait thing—no matter how his Dom side was starting to chafe over it—and Chris hadn't put out the vibe that he was looking for company.

Geoff didn't take it as a rejection. Neither shower was large. Two guys their size wouldn't have a lot of maneuvering room. He and Sam had enjoyed the space, but with someone Chris's size, they would end up being in each other's way more than anything.

Since it was never a good idea to start up both showers at the same time, because someone inevitably would lose out on the hot water, he had a few minutes to kill. Sam being in the Asheville area made him think of Merry Childers, a college friend of his and Chris's. She ran a couple of rental properties up in Bat Cave, a tiny community just outside Chimney Rock.

One of Merry's cottages was new, with all the amenities. It stayed pretty heavily booked. The other was more rustic, a long rectangle built in the seventies, easily recognized as such since the interior had laminate cabinets and appliances all in the Harvest Gold color popular during that decade. The eclectic decorating was a deer and bear motif mixed with cherubs and lace, a tribute to the older couple who'd owned it before moving to an assisted living facility.

Chris had helped Merry landscape a couple of her real estate flips, and Geoff had updated her rental agreements, all in the past year. Geoff figured he could get a cheap rate for a weekend in trade, particularly since it wasn't quite high season yet. Sam had gone with Chris on his landscaping trip and he'd told Geoff she'd been enchanted with the seventies house, particularly the huge back porch that hung precariously over the scenic creek. There was a spacious private hot tub out there.

He thought of Sam and Chris in the hot tub. Sam would wear some tiny little bikini that clung to her curves. At least until they got it off of her. Private hot tub, after all, screened from the rental office next door by a nice big slab of lattice threaded with silk flowers.

Beads of water would roll over Chris's massive shoulders, slicking down the gleaming hair on his chest. Geoff would thread his fingers through it and tip his head back to set his teeth to his corded throat. Sam would twine her legs around him, her breasts pressing into his chest . . .

He typed out a text to Merry, asking if she had a couple of days' availability sooner than later, and what she'd charge. They were winding up one of Geoff's ongoing projects at work. If Merry's dates meshed with Chris and Sam's schedule, it would be a nice getaway for all of them.

So they could keep working on their own ongoing project.

He left his half-finished beer and wandered down the hall. The shower was running in Chris and Sam's bathroom, and the door was half-open. When Sam wasn't home, Chris would leave it like that so steam wouldn't collect. Now that they were all seeing one another naked, he might leave it like that all the time, a nice change to contemplate.

Geoff told himself to keep walking, but you didn't need an invitation from the store owner to window-shop, right? No harm in just looking. Leaning in the doorway, he pushed it inward even farther so he could get a better view.

The shower door was patterned with running water, coated with steam in places, but the view was enough to keep him there. Chris's tall, broad form was outlined, his arms raised and bent to wash his hair, hands scrubbing his scalp. Geoff could visualize the twitch of his bare ass as he shifted from one foot to another, his cock and testicles cradled between his big thighs. Did the belt marks still show on those muscular flanks?

Chris rinsed his hair, picked up the soap and started lathering up. Geoff told himself to go start on his own shower, but as Chris's hands descended, soaping his chest and abdomen, he didn't move. Chris reached his genitals, his feet spread and his shoulders rounded as he took himself in hand to rub and clean. It was as if Geoff could feel those strong fingers around his own cock, tugging, stroking . . .

Chris had stilled. His head was down, but his chin was cocked, tilted toward the door, marking his awareness of Geoff watching him. The water obscured his expression, but if he continued his shower without pause or threw out a casual comment, it would tell Geoff where this moment needed to go. But if he started doing what he was doing now—slowly moving his hand down over himself, back up and down again, all while saying nothing—that was a different kind of scenario.

Geoff moved into the room, pausing outside the shower door. If it had been Sam on the other side, he would have put up his hand without thought, let her press hers to it, a romantic gesture so easy to do with women. But an act of romance and the need to establish intimacy could sometimes be the same thing. He put his palm on the glass. After another pause, Chris put his on it. Geoff took his hand away and emptied his pockets, took off his watch and stepped out of his shoes. Dressed in T-shirt and jeans, he opened the shower door. As he'd thought, there wasn't a lot of room for both of them, so he left the door open and dropped to one knee on the tile outside, bracing his other foot inside the shower.

The water sliding over Chris now pattered against him, the side of his face, his hair and the shoulders of his T-shirt, wetting them down. The heated spray, the slickness on his skin, reminded him how slick the male in front of him would be.

Putting his hands on Chris's upper thighs, he wrapped his fingers over them, thumbs spread and braced below Chris's balls. When Chris reached up and angled the spray toward the back wall, so it wasn't hitting him in the face, Geoff looked up at the bemused brown eyes.

"I want to put my mouth on you, Chris," he said. "I want to suck you off here in the shower. You okay with that?"

Chris's gaze slid over him. Geoff kneeling in front of him was unexpected, Geoff could tell. But being a Dom, a Master, wasn't about body position, and Chris had told him what he needed, what would make passing over certain thresholds easier for him. A good Master listened, understood and opened up those gates by whatever means were necessary. Especially when the prize would be so damn worth it, and the means to the end were so enjoyable.

When Chris nodded, Geoff pressed his mouth against his stiff length. Chris let out a soft oath and braced a hand on the side of the shower. Yeah, he'd better hold on, because Geoff wanted to make his knees buckle. Parting his lips, he took him to the back of his throat and scored him with his teeth, reminding him he was a biter. Since he followed that up with some targeted pressure with his tongue, Chris's sucked-in breath was followed by a grab for the wall with the other hand. Closing his eyes on a surge of pure satisfaction, Geoff worked on making Chris lose his mind.

"Fuck . . ." Chris's whisper reached him even over the drumming of the water. "How in the hell do you know how to give head like this?"

Geoff grinned around his cock and set his teeth against him, a sensual threat. Reaching between Chris's legs, he fondled his testicles like he was discovering them for the first time, and slid up between his buttocks. Finding them still soapy was a blessing, because he used the slickness to play around his rim while he kept his hand around his crank and kept working it. *Crank.* That was what they'd called it in school, because it could wind you up, couldn't it? Like now.

Geoff tossed hair out of his eyes and looked up Chris's powerful body. Every rigid muscle was gleaming with the flow of water. He'd have been a hell of a gladiator. That gave Geoff a delectable vision of Chris chained in a cell, waiting to service whoever demanded access to all that physical might. He was rocking on the balls of his feet against Geoff's pull. Geoff kept his hand busy working him and Chris's gaze went to slits, looking down at him feverishly, mouth tight.

"Mouth or hand, Chris?" Geoff cocked his head. "I'm betting you like the idea of coming in my mouth. Don't you?"

Chris's jaw flexed, and he reached down to push the hair out of Geoff's eyes. The pressure of his thumb was a rough and erratic touch. His ass was quivering beneath the spread of Geoff's fingers. "I like your hand," he said hoarsely. "But your mouth . . . fuck, your mouth feels incredible."

"Lean back against the corner and take hold of the shower bars," Geoff ordered, moving him in that direction. The bars had come as part of the house, an installation from someone who'd had an elderly relative or was just particularly safety conscious. Either way, it worked. Chris looked momentarily confused, as if he wasn't sure what Geoff was trying to do, but Geoff gripped his wrist and molded his friend's hand over the steel.

"I want to keep you safe. Don't want you to fall. You start to get light-headed, you tell me right away."

"Oh." Chris swallowed. "Yeah." He rallied enough to give Geoff a half smile. "Though you could be overestimating your skill."

The taunt was tangled with an uncertain note in his voice and a haze of lust over his expression, the beads of water on his face slicked along tight cheekbones and pressed lips.

"I'm not." Shooting him a devilish look, Geoff returned to proving it. He took two firm handfuls of Chris's ass. As he sucked on him, went down on him again and again, he flexed his strong hands over his buttocks, pushing his fingertips into his rectum, taking him deeper and deeper on both ends. Somewhere along the way, pleasuring became demand, and Chris was fully in his hands, on a couple of different levels.

He was groaning, panting with Geoff's strokes, his large hands gripping those bars so hard Geoff hoped they were well anchored. His toes were curled into the tile. Geoff was soaking wet, but steam could have been coming off his flesh, he was so inflamed by Chris's response. His Chris. His boy. His brother in all ways that mattered, but thank God, not actually his brother.

Chris swore, a long breath like birds taking flight off a lake, and he thrust harder, wilder, into Geoff's mouth. The release came, flooding Geoff's tongue and throat. Despite Chris's orgasm punching up his strength, like Dr. Banner perilously close to transforming into The Hulk, Geoff held on to him.

As Chris groaned harshly, hips still bucking, Geoff sucked him off to the last drop, getting every pulsing, throbbing contraction that spilled seed into his mouth and onto the shower floor.

When Chris finally started slowing down, the heat of the shower and the climax did what Geoff had anticipated it doing. He was ready for it, on his feet and pinning Chris to the wall with his body, holding him around the waist and shoulders, keeping him upright as Chris gasped for air and pressed his head back against the tile, gulping for air. Geoff shut off the water with his elbow as he held him. Chris's heart was hammering against Geoff's chest.

"Jesus." Chris didn't take the Lord's name in vain. He didn't claim any particular religion as his own, but he did have a healthy respect for all forms of divinity, so Geoff had always suspected that any name or word that represented those powers was included in that respect. It was one of Chris's many eccentricities that he appreciated in ways he didn't even think about. They were an essential part of who Chris was.

"Sitting down."

Geoff let Chris sink to his ass on the tile. He stepped out of the shower, keeping the door wide-open so the maximum amount of oxygen filled the small space. Sitting down on the tile outside the stall, Geoff kept a proprietary hand on his knee, both in reassurance and because he wanted to keep touching him. Chris propped his wrists on his spread knees, his forearm against Geoff's hand, and turned his head toward Geoff, though he kept his temple braced against the tile wall.

"I could feel it," Chris said slowly. "You were on your knees, sucking my dick, but somehow, you were still in charge. How do you do that?"

"It wasn't tactical. Just instinct. When we had to take down the dead tree in the backyard, you were the leader then." Geoff trailed a hand down his arm, over his thigh. "When it comes to this, I am. Did that feel good?"

"No, it sucked." Chris shot him a lopsided grin, but his dark eyes were studying Geoff seriously. Reaching out, he touched Geoff's face, moving down to the collar of his T-shirt. He screwed his fingers in it, tightly enough that Geoff felt the pull over his shoulders.

"It's going to take a few minutes to get things going in the right direction," Chris said, "but I want to go to your room. I want to be in your bed tonight. And I want to be inside you . . . like we talked about."

There was a question in it, an implicit request for permission, underscoring the point Geoff had just made. Whether or not Chris recognized it, he appeared easier with the idea, though the tension in his fingers said he had other reasons for being keyed up. Since Geoff hadn't had a release, and he was finding out how uncomfortable it could be to have a hard-on in wet jeans, he was ready anytime Chris was.

"Okay," Geoff said. "Sounds like a plan. I want to run through my shower real quick so we can both be squeaky clean. Why don't you come with me to my room? For one thing, you could probably use a few minutes of horizontal."

"Yeah, maybe. But don't look so smug about it."

Geoff grinned wolfishly, but he helped Chris up and handed him a towel. "For drying. Feel free to leave it here, rather than wearing it." Stripping off his wet shirt, he left it hanging on the shower bar. "Want something to drink? Ice water?"

"Yeah. And a couple of those peanut butter cookies we picked up at the park, if you don't mind."

"Don't mind a bit. Head for my room and I'll meet you there."

He waited, making sure Chris was steady enough to manage the hallway, and he was. Fortunately he didn't look back to see Geoff mother-henning him, since he was sure his friend would have teased him, but it didn't stop Geoff from watching out for him.

When Geoff returned, Chris was in Geoff's room, though he wasn't yet lying down. He was studying the expanse of Geoff's mattress and his back was to Geoff. He'd left the towel behind, just as Geoff had hoped. He paused, savoring the sight of Chris's powerful body, naked from head to toe, dark hair tousled and damp, a few stray drops gathered in the small of his back.

Geoff touched the ice-cold side of the glass against it and snickered as Chris jumped. His friend gave him a narrow look and took the glass, but he was too thirsty to retaliate, gulping down about half of it before he set it aside. Wiping the back of his hand across his mouth, his gaze slid down Geoff's chest. "Wet jeans can't be comfortable."

"They're not. You want them off, right here and now?"

In Chris's eyes, Geoff saw careful calculation of Geoff's intent, the weighing of the delicate balance between them. "Yeah," Chris said. "If you don't mind. But I'd like to do it myself."

In answer, Geoff dipped his head. Chris didn't need to be asked twice. Despite the short break between shower and snacks, Geoff's cock was still pretty firm and noticeable against the soaked fly. Chris slipped the button and worked the zipper down carefully, but after that, he ran into a logistical issue.

As Chris tugged at the wet jeans, Geoff couldn't help it, he chuckled. Glancing at him through the fall of hair over his concentrated brow, Chris shook his head, lips tugging into a rueful smile. "Okay, wet jeans look sexy as hell, but they're superglued to your thighs. A little help here?"

Geoff obliged. When he finally managed to skin them off and tossed them to the side, he found Chris's attention on the soaked cling of his dark brief shorts. Geoff drew in a breath as Chris passed his knuckles over the pale skin of his upper thighs, then across, a featherlight brush over his cock, which made it twitch under the damp covering. Chris hooked the sides of the underwear and took them down Geoff's legs to his ankles. Geoff stepped out of them, kicking them away, and Chris was on his heels, looking up at him, both of them naked and damp.

"First time I saw you without any clothes was when we were thirteen," Chris said. "We went swimming in that pond where that copperhead was. Remember?"

"How can I forget?" Geoff said dryly. "We could have beaten an Olympic sprinter out of that hole."

"It chased us out of the water and we kept running for like another quarter mile." Chris rose and put his palm on Geoff's chest, fingertips learning his shape. Geoff had watched Chris plant and grow things, nurture countless things with his hands. He could feel all of that in them now. Strength, gentleness, the ability to understand what a living thing most needed. Geoff thought that touch could help him grow and be more than he could be on his own. It turned the moment into something more.

"We never talked about it," Chris mused, "but neither of us ran as fast as we could, because we were both trying to make sure the other stayed ahead. It's a good thing the snake gave up." Chris lifted his gaze to Geoff's. "We wanted to make sure if the snake caught one of us, it would be the one lagging behind, so the other would be okay."

"Yeah." Geoff lifted a shoulder. "If I'd known that the copperhead is one of the least venomous poisonous snakes, I would have sprinted a mile ahead of you."

"No, you wouldn't." Chris cocked his head, gaze sweeping Geoff once more. If he kept doing that, Geoff was going to put aside his honorable resolve to let this be Chris's show and just tackle him.

A muscle flexed in Chris's jaw. "Go get your shower. A fast one."

Geoff smiled, bumped his body with his shoulder, and went into his bathroom. He saw Chris sit down on the edge of the bed to watch him as he got the water hot. When he ducked under the spray, he did make it quick, though he was thorough. As he came out, toweling off, he found Chris was still in the same spot.

"Can you come here?" he asked.

"I can." Feeling an absurd tightness in his chest, Geoff set aside the towel and approached the bed.

"Some of those guys we played football with today," Chris said. "They've been friends for years, like us. They love one another, but they don't think about doing what we're doing right now. They won't ever want to take it to this level."

"Yeah, that's true. No matter what it is or isn't, do you wish we were like that?"

Chris paused, thinking. Geoff realized he was holding his breath. Chris slid a hand along Geoff's forearm and rested his palm on his hip. "If I said I did?" he asked at last.

"If you said you did, and you meant it, I'd do my best to respect it." It would be like passing kidney stones. "It's kind of a hard thing to shut off once you've opened the tap."

"Feeling this way about you makes things more complicated. Especially with Sam in the mix."

"Yeah." Geoff curled his hand around Chris's wrist. "But I'm not going to let *complicated* keep me from getting something I want. Look at it this way. Say we have Sam's gorgeous naked body between us. You think we could just shut off any overlap on wanting each other? Forever?"

Chris shook his head. "No, but . . ."

"Are we arguing the point here, or just shooting the shit? What's the real issue?"

Chris grimaced. "The lawyer, wanting to get to the root of it."

"Actually, a lawyer figures out every way in the world to circle around the root of it until the judge is like a frustrated parent who gives in to the kid because he's sick of the nagging."

Chris smiled. Somehow he'd twisted his hand so he was linking fingers with Geoff's, thumb on his wrist. "But you're not that kind of lawyer. I think you should do it, you know. What you said a few days ago about joining the DA's office after you pay off your loans. You'll like that more."

"It will be no travel, a lot less pay and the dregs of humanity will get inside my head in ways the corporate world can't imagine."

"But it will balance. What you do will feel like it matters way more. Money pays bills, but it doesn't feed the soul."

"Deep." Geoff shoved him. "Time to shut up, unless you're trying to tell me you want out of this."

"No." Chris's brown eyes kindled. "No way. I'm just making sure you're not thinking it's open-ended."

"Excuse me?"

All of a sudden Chris looked like he wished he were wearing clothes. "Tyree Fredericks. Alex Worth. And Robert Sanders."

Geoff blinked. Chris had rattled off the three men Geoff had been with sexually in the past few years. The kicker was he'd never told Chris he'd had sex with any of them. They'd been only vague references related to work, since that was how he'd crossed paths with all three of them, but Chris had known. His far-too-neutral yet penetrating expression said so.

"Tyree comes over from the French office a couple of times a year," Chris continued, as if he anticipated Geoff asking how he'd known, though Geoff would have bitten through his tongue first. "He wears a distinct aftershave. Robert and Alex were one-time things, I'm pretty sure. Right?"

The neutral expression slipped, showing a wealth of emotions behind it. Now Geoff shared Chris's discomfort about being naked during this discussion. But Chris was waiting, those earth-toned eyes measuring. That look set Geoff back on course. Yeah, Chris deserved a straight answer, but this moment wasn't about a friend-to-friend communication. Whether Chris realized it or not, the structure and reassurance he was seeking was a challenge to the Dom side of the equation. Which meant Geoff needed to respond accordingly. He backed up a few steps to lean against the wall and give his friend a close scrutiny before answering.

"So now that I'm fucking you, you want to know if I'm going to think it's okay to fuck Tyree when he's in town? Or any other guy that makes my dick sit up and pay attention?"

Chris's lips tightened, but he didn't answer.

"Do you think Sam will ask us that question about other women?" Geoff raised a brow. "Or will she just assume it's a given we'll be faithful to her, unless we'd like our genitals hacked up with a butcher knife?"

"Don't be an asshole," Chris said quietly. "I just need to know."

"Do you think I'd cheat on Sam with other women, now that things are in play with her?"

"No." Chris's answer was immediate, and relieved Geoff immensely. But he pasted on a harder look, just to get his point across, and sauntered—yes, sauntered naked—over to stand right in front of Chris again. When Chris started to get up, Geoff put a hand on his chest and shoved him, pushing him back on the bed and stretching out next to him in one deliberate move, curling his fingers in Chris's hair, the other hand spread out on his chest.

"Then why do you think I'd treat you any differently?"

A muscle ticked in Chris's jaw. "I just wanted to be clear."

"Absolutely. Let's be clear. I should have hit you a lot harder with that belt." Geoff leaned in, met him eye to eye, breath caressing his face. "You're mine, and nobody else is going to stick his dick in you unless he wants me to personally cut it off and feed it to him. I'll make you watch, just so you get the point."

Chris blinked. "I think I'd prefer you just to punch them out and try to punch me out. Less prison time and national news coverage."

"*Try* to punch you out. Yeah, right." Geoff's fingers tightened in his hair. "I've been clear, so you be clear. Say what you want to say."

Chris reached up and skimmed his fingertips along Geoff's jaw before curling his hand in a loose fist on his breastbone. He tapped Geoff, a light tattoo. "No one but me and Sam. Now and forever."

"You got it. You need it in blood, or should I draw up a formal contract?"

"Asshole." Chris was done being pushed around. He rolled over Geoff, setting off a wrestling match. Geoff gave him a run for his money, but in this position, Chris had the advantage in bulk. When he was eventually sitting on Geoff and they were fighting with hands like a couple of boxers, they were both laughing too hard to do much damage, though Chris accidentally slipped passed Geoff's guard and bumped his jaw hard enough to elicit an "Ow" and an aggrieved look from Geoff. A look that became something else as his gaze slid down Chris's body.

"Looks like we're ready for that second round you wanted."

Chris nodded, closing his eyes as Geoff wrapped his hand around his erect cock, working it in slow, easy moves. "Yeah, there you go. Getting harder for me, aren't you, big guy? Gonna put all this up my ass?"

"Yeah," Chris said hoarsely. "But I've never done that. I did the fingers-and-plug thing with Sam."

"It's pretty much the same. A round peg in a round hole." Geoff figured it was the strain in his voice that had Chris opening his eyes again and studying him. "Get the lube out of the drawer of my night-stand." Geoff eyed Chris's dick. "Make sure you use lots of it."

Chris grinned and leaned over, retrieving the lube. Seeing muscles ripple and stretch at that proximity had Geoff skimming his hands over Chris's chest, to his hips. Sitting back, Chris studied the lube. "Girls are lucky. They come with their own natural version. Not as sexy to be slapping this on when you want to be inside someone right then."

"Depends on how you do it," Geoff said. "Did you think about me rubbing it on myself when I had you bent over the bench?"

"Yeah."

Geoff raised his attention from the lube in Chris's hand, poised over his erection, to the thoughtful eyes. "I'd like to see you do it."

Squirting lube in his hand, Chris cupped it around his stiff organ and began to slick it on under Geoff's intent scrutiny. The attention worked Chris up further, but that was a two-way street. Geoff could feel his own cock hardening and thickening where Chris was sitting on it, his buttocks shifting in a friction that had Geoff gritting his teeth at the mounting sexual frustration.

Chris moistened his lips. "You said you'd usually done the pitching. Does this mean I'm the first? Like you were with me?"

Geoff had never been big on the whole virgin thing, but recalling the inexplicable delight of knowing he was the first inside Chris, he bit back chagrin. "I wish I could give you that gift," he said quietly. "But I did it a couple of times, in the beginning. I wanted to know what it felt like, to make sure I never did it too rough or the wrong way, especially if I was doing it in a session, where someone might be restrained and gagged."

It was sensible, but he could tell Chris was disappointed. Geoff closed his fingers on his forearm. "Come down here."

Chris set the lube aside and braced himself over Geoff's face. Geoff threaded his fingers through the fall of hair on his forehead and tugged lightly. It was profound, lying here beneath Chris, staring up into his face, the intimacy between them as comfortable and necessary as their friendship was. The wonder was that they'd waited this long.

"Sex is sex," Geoff said. "Nothing more, nothing less. But when the heart gets involved, it becomes way the hell more. Tyree was sex." He moved his touch to Chris's shoulders, gripped hard. "He's actually been back to the office five times in the past year, but we didn't, not after those first two times. He made the mistake of mentioning he'd gotten married. I put the brakes on immediately. He told me it didn't matter to his spouse, the usual *We have an open relationship* bullshit."

When Chris rolled his eyes, Geoff dropped his hand to the fine pelt of chest hair on Chris's broad chest. "Yeah. I told him to get his husband on the phone so he could tell me that directly. Tyree wouldn't do it, big shock, so that was the end of our arrangement."

As Chris's gaze kindled, Geoff nodded. "You know who and what I am, Chris. You know I'd never hurt you like that. I wish you were my first, but to my mind you are. You're the first I've allowed...to take control. Tyree, Robert, Alex, all that was sex. Dinner and a little entertainment. Tyree was no more inside my heart or head than anyone else. You, on the other hand, have been in my head and heart for a long time. Now you're in my bed. Okay?"

In answer, Chris bent over him and put his mouth on his. *Thank God.* Geoff slid his hand to the back of his neck, massaging as Chris explored, discovering what it was like to enjoy a man's mouth at his leisure. He was damn good at it for a novice. When Chris curled his hand around Geoff's cock, Geoff growled.

"You don't do this soon, I'm going to take over," he muttered. "Some of us haven't gotten off yet."

Chris's grin was dangerous and sexy at once. "Should I do this with you on your back, or the other way? What way works best for you?"

"It's your fantasy, big guy." Geoff passed his fingers over his lips. "How do you want me?"

"Can we do both?"

Geoff laughed. "Sure we can. Just not at the same time."

Chris thought it over in that careful, slow way he did, then he offered Geoff a hand to help him sit up. His fingers tightened on Geoff while his other hand dropped to caress Geoff's hip, exerting pressure to turn him over onto hands and knees. It wasn't entirely natural for Geoff, because the instinct to top was so strong. However, the curiosity and lust in Chris's gaze, as well as Geoff's desire to make up for the hurt of Chris not being his first, to offer him something for allowing Geoff to be *his* first, put all that aside.

"Just guide it in. There are a couple of rings of muscles there, just like it was for you. You never shove when it comes to anal sex. Take your time and wait to feel those muscles release. I'll push out, and . . ." Geoff let out a blissful curse when Chris stretched him and pushed through, so easily it was a pleasurable torment. The guy who could handle the fragile body of a bird in his hand would never be too rough when the moment called for a gentle touch. And his care in this context was erotic as hell.

"Never mind. You're doing just fine . . . Jesus." Geoff sucked in a breath at the size of him, the sensation as Chris pulled back, pushed back in, so slow and provocative Geoff's cock felt as if it was going to split its too-tight skin. Chris reached under him, gripping him with his big hand, and Geoff arched into him in reaction, impaling himself deeper on Chris's organ. "Fuck . . . need a condom . . ."

"I'll wash your sheets. I'm not pulling out now until you come."

Chris's voice was rough with a tangle of desire and emotions. Geoff knew what he was feeling as if it was his heart pounding in the other man's chest.

He'd been so focused on the mechanics or on how Chris was reacting, he'd overlooked what this could do for him. Geoff didn't spend a lot of time on sentiment. He didn't have the need to self-analyze or expound on his feelings, but the difference between Chris and any other man he'd ever had before made it unnecessary anyway. There was no analysis to this. The sex before had been fun, hot. However, just like when he'd taken Sam, this was possession, need, fulfillment, love. It was making love.

When he'd been with Sam, a well of feeling had cracked open inside him. Woman was a vessel that could take all that feeling, absorb it into her, keep a man balanced. But with Chris doing the taking in this instance, the emotions surged up from heart to throat, wrapping around his spine, shooting down through his pelvis, into his loins, taking him over in a lot of ways and forcing a loss of control he hadn't expected.

"Chris . . ."

Chris's arm banded around his chest, body linked close. "I'm here, man. It's all right. Ride the wave with me. You feel so good."

Simple words. Poetry. Chris chose that moment to be more demanding, the best tactic possible. Geoff's fingers dug into the mattress as Chris thrust, pelvis smacking against Geoff's ass. His balls drew up, his cock leaking pre-come. Chris moved them back with his easy strength, putting Geoff's feet on the floor, body bent over the bed so Chris could have more leverage without driving him face-first into the mattress. A courtesy Geoff would remember next time he was belting his ass, which would be soon. This was so much, he wanted to take and control, demand. He wanted to jack off over Chris's ass, use his seed to lubricate his tight hole and drive into him, again and again. Take him, hold him, keep him, never let him go . . .

Chris's arm circled Geoff's chest again. With his rough cheek pressed between Geoff's shoulder blades, against the damp skin on his back, Geoff let go, grunting as the orgasm came up hard and fast, making him spill himself on the bedding, against his chest, his abdomen. Chris pounded even deeper then, giving Geoff some pain with the pleasure, but he embraced all of it.

"Come for me," he demanded hoarsely. "You big bastard. Come for me."

Come for your Master. It was on the tip of his tongue. In every cell he felt Chris was as much his as Sam. But he wouldn't say it. Not until Chris did, and he might not ever. But that was okay, because even if Chris never felt comfortable acknowledging it, Geoff knew Chris was his.

Chris released then with a deep groan, followed by a series of grunts as he thrust, thrust, and one more time, harder and deeper. He held there, deep in Geoff's ass. He was breathing hard, holding on to

Geoff, trying to keep his feet. Geoff could feel the quiver against his own less-than-steady ones.

They made it back on to the bed together, Chris still mostly inside of him because he wasn't ready to come unlinked. Geoff wasn't, either. Chris curled up behind him, back to shoulder blades, hips cradling Geoff's ass, their legs tangled and pressed together. His breath was on Geoff's neck. When his hand slid over Geoff's hip to caress his cock and cradle his balls, Geoff adjusted his legs to let him do it, staring down at Chris's hand touching him, stroking him. Having just come, things were sensitive, so he quivered under his hold, but he didn't ask him to stop. Instead, when Chris finally let go and slid his hand up Geoff's abdomen, Geoff captured his fingers, so their hands were a tight knot on his chest. A tether of sorts, but he couldn't say which of them held which end. The point was they were both holding it.

"You okay?" Chris muttered.

Geoff nodded. Even in the hottest part of the past few moments, Chris would have felt that emotional struggle inside him, would understand it without Geoff having to talk about it. But Geoff would say it anyway. For Chris. And maybe for himself, too.

"I just realized what it means to have a home," he said quietly. "I knew you and Sam were my family, in all the ways that counted, but I hadn't thought about you also being my home."

Chris's fingers tightened on him. "Dumb lawyer," he murmured. "I've always known you're home when you're with me and Sam. It's the only place you really relax."

Geoff turned his head, Chris's lips sliding over his neck. Chris sighed, his even breath telling Geoff he was dozing. It sounded like a good idea, falling asleep with a friend. With family. With almost everything that meant home.

All they were missing was Sam, but somehow she was here, because she belonged with them. That was a tether, too, one that was felt even when she wasn't physically present. Geoff shut his eyes, imagining what might happen when she was, and how it would feel to be with Chris, with her, with both of them. For real at last. God bless a pushy sub. He'd have to tell Sam that sometime. While they were punishing her for it, of course.

His lips had a light smile on them as he drifted off.

Sam closed the passenger door and came around to Flo's side of the car. "Here's some money for gas," she said, passing it through the open window. Her fingers were shaking, just a little bit, but Flo noticed. Her hand closed over Sam's briefly, a firm caress. Jena and Carly, their other two coworkers, were still in the backseat, so Flo wouldn't say anything, but her eyes gleamed. "See you Monday. If you can walk."

Sam made a face at her, but as she turned toward the house, she confirmed that Chris's truck and Geoff's car were there. Normally, if they were both home when she came back from a trip, all it meant was they'd fill each other in on everything that had happened during the absence. Then they'd go about their normal day, Chris maybe reading a plant book, or Geoff inviting her to watch a movie with him, go for a run. Or the three of them deciding what they'd be having for dinner.

It was just past dark, which increased her anticipation. Trying to rein it in, she reminded herself their phone sex talk of the other night could have been just that. Even so, she'd done as Geoff had commanded. There were no panties under her dress, a silky tunic with a leafy print pattern in multiple greens and grays. The mid-thigh hem had given her some heart palpitations when they'd stopped for a restroom break and the wind had flirted precariously with the hem. Usually she'd be wearing leggings under the thin cloth, but not today.

The deep neckline showed the pretty lace edges of her push-up bra, so her breasts were round and full over it, ready to be noticed. She thought of Chris's lips on her nipple, Geoff's hands sliding over her bare ass, and her pace toward the door quickened. *Easy, girl.* They could be watching TV, sleeping, taking a shower. They hadn't known exactly when she'd be home. She'd been tempted to text them updates every quarter hour, but she'd felt a little shy about it. She didn't want to presume too much.

The kitchen door was unlocked, and she slid into semidarkness. A lamp was on in the living room, though no one was on the couch. Could they both be in their rooms?

"Chris? Geoff?"

A hand closed over hers as she reached for the light, and she yelped, but panic was fleeting, because she'd know that touch anywhere. "Chris," she breathed.

His hands were sliding up under the hem of the dress, and then one was between her legs, his other arm banding across her shoulders in front, holding her back against him as he explored and stroked, made her gasp. "She's wet, all right," he growled.

"She's been thinking about what we'll do to her."

Before her glazed eyes, Geoff came out of the shadows, his gaze filled with such fire, his face so taut, the reflection of the living room light made him seem deliciously demonic. He took in the tunic dress at a glance.

"Hope you paid attention to what we told you," he said, a second before he laid his hands on the vee neck and ripped the dress down the front with a decisive strength that stole all of it from her legs and made her heart hammer up into her throat. He reached around her to unhook the bra and strip it away. He yanked the dress off her, leaving her naked except for her sandals. As Chris lifted her off her feet, Geoff got rid of those. Now she was all naked, while they remained clothed. Her Master surveyed her with a leisurely lust that made her want to moan, especially as he cupped her breasts, thumbed an erect nipple.

"I think we should invest in some tint film for the windows. We'll get her a pretty collar so she'll know when she wears it in the house, she's not supposed to wear anything else. What do you think of that, Sam? Are you ready for how demanding we can be? Is that the kind of thing you'd want?"

"I . . . I can't think . . ."

"She can't think, Chris," Geoff said casually. "Help her with that. I'm going to fuck her ass."

She was flipped around in Chris's arms. His mouth came down on hers, demanding and hot. She melted in his grasp, but he pulled back, far too soon. His eyes burned into hers. "Are you ready for everything we want to do to you?" he said.

God help me. "No," she whispered. Lifting her hands, she gripped the front of his shirt with desperate need. "But do it anyway."

SOUL

Part IV

*T*hey'd left the lights off in the kitchen, creating an erotic dream world, moonlight streaming in through the window, the firm heat of their bodies and the rasp of their breath filling her senses. Geoff's hands were on her buttocks, parting them, his intent to take her there clear. Chris opened his own pants before lifting her with his incredible strength to accommodate both men's desires. *Oh God . . .* They'd demanded to know if she was ready for everything they wanted, and they were just taking over, moving as decisively as she'd ever seen them, an irresistible force.

Geoff slid into her ass, his cock well lubricated. Her muscles released for him, drawing him in, the friction and his size bringing her a pleasurable discomfort. Chris eased it by stroking and probing her wetness in front. She moaned, head dropping back on Geoff's shoulder. When Chris pushed into her, the sound became a harsh plea. They were both filling her up, so tight, so big. "God . . ."

"We missed you," Geoff whispered against her ear. "You're not going to wear a stitch of clothes until Monday, because one or both of us is going to be inside you, going down on you or kissing you until then. What do you think of that, Sam? Do you belong to us? Are you completely ours?"

"Yes. Yes . . ." Her voice trailed off in another moan as Chris pushed deep, withdrew and thrust again, his gaze on her face, his hands gripping her ass, keeping her spread for Geoff's penetration as

322

Chris worked her on his cock. When Geoff pushed in deeper, it brought them in even closer proximity. They were inside her so profoundly all she could do was cry out her need for more.

As if the two men had the ability to speak in each other's minds, they came to a halt, watching her helpless writhing with avid eyes.

"Should have had her wear the red dress she wore to that dance club and torn it off her." Chris grunted. "Reminding her not to wear that for anyone but us."

"This way she can still wear it for us, because it's not torn," Geoff pointed out reasonably. She would have laughed if she weren't spiraling up so high and fast.

"Geoff . . . Chris . . . I missed you . . ."

In answer, Chris's mouth was back on hers, exploring and tangling with her tongue, as Geoff's teeth closed over her shoulder, a sharp stimulant that had her arching up, everything below the waist throbbing.

"Come now," Geoff commanded. Usually she had to concentrate to come. Now she was ready to leave the runway with no direction from her brain at all. Her body spasmed in joyful obedience. Chris changed the angle of his thrusts. With him doing that and Geoff working inside her ass, it was like being shot out of a cannon, a pure rush of thrilling adrenaline. The climax seized her, her response punctuated by a high-pitched scream. They followed her over that edge almost as quickly, pushing against her with demanding male strength, flexing, thrusting bodies, heated breath. The grunts of release, their combined scents filling her senses, made all of it even more overpowering.

Oh God . . . She realized she was mumbling it when Geoff chuckled softly in her ear, brushing a kiss along her jaw.

"I assume you mean me."

She coughed over a laugh, but Chris spoke before she could. "Just because you think you're God doesn't make it so."

"I don't think I'm God. I just want *her* to think it."

She sputtered over another chuckle. Chris bent to kiss her mouth again as Geoff sampled her neck, her shoulder, turning her laughter into a long, wistful sigh. "I thank God—the actual, separate force of nature—for both of you," she said when she could form words.

She'd hoped Geoff and Chris would figure out things with each other so that the three of them could take things to a more integrated level. She hadn't recognized the impact that would have on her directly. The two of them were so in sync on a normal day, this was like a full mind meld. They'd sure as hell come to an accord in her absence, and she'd received a ravishing like she'd only read about in romances. She might need to increase her vitamins. Do lots more yoga stretches.

They withdrew from her body, but they didn't let her go. Instead, after adjusting his clothes, Geoff sank down on the kitchen floor, his back braced against the cabinet, keeping her between his legs. Chris stretched out in front of her on his hip. He laid his head on her breast, nuzzling and playing with her nipple with tongue and lips, keeping her shuddering.

Her fingers trailed down Geoff's denim-clad thigh, up to his knee, down to his shin. She had her other hand on Chris's hair, stroking gently. Her heart was thudding back to a normal rate, though as she looked toward her tattered dress and thought about how they'd greeted her, it skipped a couple of beats. The memory would keep her aroused for the next several months. That perpetual state would likely come in handy.

Geoff overlapped her hand on Chris's head so they were touching him together. She had to clear her voice again so it came out as less of a rasp. "Can I ask a favor?"

"This wasn't favor enough?" Geoff asked. "Greedy girl."

He jumped as she clamped her fingers around the ticklish spot on his knee. "Hey, quit it." He grabbed her wrist, pulled it back to him. "You want to play it that way? You're helpless here—you know it."

"No, no . . ." She squealed and squirmed as he feathered his fingers under her armpit, tickling her mercilessly. "Stop, I'm sorry . . . Mercy . . ."

"Master," he growled in her ear. "I'm sorry, *Master*."

"I'm sorry, Master," she wailed, still shrieking. He stopped and put his mouth to her neck, biting hard enough she was sure he left teeth marks in her tender skin. She drew in a humming breath. Chris, unperturbed by their antics, captured both breasts in his large hands, so he could suckle and play with them with more focused intent. "Oh . . . I may not survive this . . ."

Geoff smiled against her throat. "We'll take care of you," he promised. "Bring you back to life. Again and again . . . and again."

"Okay," she said faintly. Chris lifted his head. She put both her hands on his face, cradling it, molding her fingers over his jaw. "I'm so happy," she said. "And you look happy, too."

He smiled. "Geoff doesn't look happy?"

She sniffed over the tickling. "I'm less concerned about his happiness."

"Ouch." Geoff chuckled but banded an arm around her chest. She reveled in his strength as he held her close. "What was the favor, brat?"

"I'd like to see you kiss each other," she said. At his lifted brow, she flushed a little. "It's sort of a fantasy of mine. I've been wanting to see you kiss Chris for a long time. I just wasn't sure until now if it worked for you two."

"How can you tell it does now?"

She shot him a *Duh* look. "Seriously?"

She'd seen it not only in their easy synchronization since she'd crossed the threshold, but in whatever unspoken message passed between them right now. It was overwhelming, seeing the chemistry of deep friendship, their intuitive knowledge of each other, taken to the level of sexual intimacy. She couldn't help wishing that she'd left up webcams everywhere so she could watch firsthand what had happened during her absence. But a kiss would help her imaginings considerably.

Reaching over her, Geoff grabbed Chris's head and brought him up to his level to plant an exaggerated kiss on his forehead. She pushed at him, sighing in mock exasperation, but Geoff wrapped her hair around his hand and held her fast.

"Ask nicely, Samantha Beth. Then maybe we'll give you what you want."

She swallowed, staring into his steady gaze. She didn't know how he switched into that Dom mode so effectively, but she added it to her list of things she was thankful for. "Please, sir. Sirs. I'd like to see you kiss each other."

Geoff kept her locked in place but turned his head toward Chris. Sam held her breath as Chris moved onto his knees. His eyes were on Geoff's, but as he leaned in, his attention slid down to Sam. She closed her eyes as Chris cradled her face and pressed a kiss to her forehead. Slow, lingering, a quiet blessing. Geoff's firm grip on her hair constricted as Chris moved to her mouth, tasting it slow, deep, but keeping it gentle, an act of love. He raised his head, and there was a burning fire in his eyes that reflected what she was sure was kindling in his heart.

She'd yearned for this moment, this complete connection among all of them, but she hadn't been alone in that desire.

Chris leaned over her. As Geoff relaxed his hold, she dropped her head back on his shoulder, surprised to see Chris do to him the same as he'd done for her. Touching Geoff's face, he straightened to press a kiss on Geoff's forehead. He wasn't teasing her like Geoff had been. He was sending them both a message, acknowledging this was truly the starting gate. It was a benediction for the journey ahead.

She touched his shoulder. When Chris turned his attention to her, she reached up, held his head in both hands and brought it down so she could give him the same gift. Pressing her lips against his forehead, she breathed in the shampoo smell of his hair, the strands tickling her nose as she lay back so her head was once again against Geoff's shoulder.

Chris's intent look made her toes curl, but then he turned to Geoff. She held her breath, a different feeling taking over as, in one decisive move, he covered Geoff's mouth with his own.

It pressed his body closer to hers, so she curled an arm around Chris's back and her palm pressed against the flex of muscle and shift of smooth skin. Chris deepened the kiss, the two men's tongues obviously tangling. She pressed her cheek to Chris's shoulder as she stared at the way they tasted and teased one another. Geoff let out a sound that was part groan, part growl, while his hand came up to hold the back of Chris's head. He dug his fingers into Chris's scalp, tugging his hair like he had hers.

Sam used her free hand to let her fingers play along their throats, their jaws. She let out a little gasp as Chris broke the kiss enough to nip her fingers, invite her into a more intimate exploration of their joined mouths, the slick heat of their lips. Geoff's tongue caught her fingertip as he played with Chris's tongue. The ball of heat kindling in her belly went up a few hundred degrees, making her wonder how long they could survive if the three of them stayed in the house forever to do just this, hour after hour, day after day.

Chris broke the kiss to seize her mouth next while Geoff moved his own lips to Chris's throat and shoulder. When Chris finally raised his head, he studied her face as if seeing it for the very first time. But he often looked at her that way, as if she were a new discovery to him. He'd taught her to do that about so many things in her life. Applying that lesson to what was happening to them now told her just how amazing an adventure this would be.

Geoff propped his head against the cabinets to give them a lazy, dangerous look. "I think we should move this to the bed. What do you think?"

"I pilfered a dozen cookies from the conference," Sam managed. "They're the size of saucers. If we can grab some bottles of water from the fridge, we'll be fortified for a while."

At the glint in Geoff's eyes and Chris's slow grin, a little smile crept over her lips. "I got a strategic planning award. They gave me a certificate."

"Sounds like it was well deserved." Geoff glanced at Chris. "Bring extra water. I'll bring her."

As Chris got to his feet, Geoff scooped her off the linoleum while he was getting up, making it seem effortless to carry her. She coiled her arms around his shoulders, and he pressed a kiss to her temple as he turned to get her through the kitchen door and head down the hallway.

"By the way," he said, "until further notice, you're banned from the garage. We're working on something there, and you don't get to see it until it's ready."

So they were building whatever they'd been poring over that day in the hardware store, in the *Build-It-Yourself Bondage* book. Her interest was piqued but, beyond that, she was privately delighted at direct evidence that she was no longer solely responsible for moving things forward. It also strengthened her faith that this would continue to evolve as it should.

While all those ponderings were lovely to her heart and soul, her body and mind had more immediate reasons to celebrate. She was pretty sure what was going to happen next in the bedroom would exceed her wildest dreams, despite what had just happened in the kitchen nearly blowing off the top of her head.

"I was worried it would end up a one-and-one-times-two thing," she murmured.

"Meaning?" Geoff laid her down on his bed and stood back. He had this way of looking at her that made her feel stripped inside and out. And he was still standing there fully dressed. She thought of what he'd said about the collar—*"We'll get her a pretty collar so she'll know when she wears it in the house, she's not supposed to wear anything else"*—and her skin flushed all over, just thinking about it.

His gaze coursed over her with hot appreciation but also as if he was indulging his right to see every inch of her, inside and out. He'd let her play with him in the kitchen, but she had a feeling here in his lair, so to speak, he wasn't going to be so indulgent. Even the one-word query he'd just issued had the ring of command.

"You know, you and Chris sharing me but not being together with one another."

"A lot of women would love that fantasy. Being the center of two men's attention all the time." His hazel eyes gleamed again. "Worried we'll wear you out?"

Not worried. Certain of it, and hoping to be nothing more than liquefied bone and muscle when you're all done. She kept that to herself, though. She was having a hard enough time staying focused.

"It's a nice fantasy. But I like the idea of it being about the three of us, giving and taking in all different directions. I think it will last longer that way."

His brow creased, and he stretched out next to her on his hip. Pushing her hair away from her cheek, he curled a lock around his finger. "That sounds like you think it will end, Samantha Beth."

"No. Yes. Hoping it won't, but knowing how these things can happen. I just want . . . as long as it lasts, to be as much as it can be. You know?"

Geoff considered that. "Chris doesn't think I listen to his Zen philosophy," he said. "That living-in-the-moment BS, but actually I do."

He lifted his head as Chris came in bearing half a dozen bottles of cold water in an ice bucket, which he set next to the bed. He'd found the cookies in Sam's tote, and put the container on the nightstand. He didn't interrupt their conversation, but joined them in the bed. Sliding in on her other side, he put a hand on her leg, his fingers exploring the crease between hip and thigh, skating up her hip and over to her navel to toy with her tiny pewter bear piercing. His other fingers fanned out over her stomach.

Geoff continued to play with her hair. "Chris says, if you learn to live in every moment fully, then you'll make the most of a lifetime. The things that are important, you'll never lose them, because you appreciate them to the point you never let them go, and their joy never dims."

Sam's gaze slid back to Chris. "You said that?"

"Not quite that pretty. Geoff tends to pick up my words and smooth them out. Lawyer."

"I can translate laconic Southern male." Geoff touched her mouth with his and tilted his head toward Chris. "Ready to live fully in the moment?"

"I never stopped." Chris held his gaze, then turned it to Sam, catching her in mid-yawn. His eyes twinkled. "But we might want to give our hardworking girl a little sleep first."

In the morning, Chris joined her in the shower first thing, taking her up against the wall and leaving her blood humming. She started her day almost maniacally happy. She even volunteered to take care of the brunch dishes, despite it being Geoff's day for the chore. While Geoff took his post-meal shower, she scraped egg off the plates at the sink and sang a favorite song in fits and starts while doing a little hip-shaking standing-in-place dance over the suds.

Chris had gone out to the work shed to fix a bent tool. The way he was hammering it against a stump, she imagined him as a blacksmith hundreds of years ago. Maybe he made swords for knights and shoes for horses. His large hands would handle the animal gently as he lifted one of the horse's legs and nailed the shoe onto the hoof to protect it.

In the current-day real world, Chris finished working the dents out of what looked like some kind of hoe. Then he retrieved the rake to clean up leaves under the Japanese cherry. Chris didn't care anything for fashion, but he liked his T-shirts. Today's was a colorful print advertising an alehouse in Germany somewhere. The graphic looked like a Viking taking a hefty swallow from a giant mug of beer. The Viking had his arm slung around a tipsy dragon. Chris did most of his shopping for unusual T-shirts at the thrift stores, so she expected he'd picked it up from one of them.

Since the day was warming up, it wasn't long before he stripped off the shirt, tossing it over a branch and continuing to work in a pair of old jeans with a couple of frayed holes and worn soft to crease in the right places. It was one of the few pairs he had for yardwork, since he usually preferred camos or painter's pants for that. He was so beautiful, she couldn't think of a better view as she washed dishes.

Geoff's arm slid around her waist, his body pressing against her. "What are you doing?"

"Cleaning up after two pigs." She purred as he teased her neck with his lips. It turned her legs to spaghetti, not that they weren't close to that already, thanks to the activities of the past twelve hours.

"Pigs, hmm?" He snorted against her ear, an *oink, oink* sound that had her giggling. Pressing her forward with the shift of his body, he reached both arms around her to push open the window, letting the breeze touch her face before wrapping one arm across her, forearm pressed above her breasts. He kept his lips close to her ear, so his voice could stay a silky murmur.

"Do you remember that fantasy Madison talked about the first time we went to Naughty Bits? About Chris being the yard boy who couldn't stop looking at you in an inappropriate way?"

Everything in her started pulsing, the sore tissues between her legs throbbing and her breasts feeling fuller, tighter under his touch.

"Yes."

He tugged the elastic scoop neck of her peasant-style dress down below her breasts, framing them in both hands.

"You didn't wear a bra on purpose," he said mildly.

"You told me not to wear any underwear—" She swallowed a gasp as he pinched her nipples. "Yes sir. I didn't wear one on purpose."

"Because you wanted the yard boy to look at you. You wanted him to know there was nothing under here but you. You knew he wouldn't be able to keep his eyes off your breasts, the way they quiver when you move, how your nipples look."

"Yes . . ."

"Despite your Master telling you that you weren't permitted to tease the help." He growled the accusation.

Even with that curl of sensual anxiety that went along with

shifting into a submissive mind-set, Sam couldn't prevent a tiny smile. She'd always been pretty sure she'd like role-playing. She hadn't been sure how well the practical Geoff would do with initiating it, though. Apparently he was diving in headfirst with no trouble.

"Put your head back on my shoulder. Keep your hands in the dish-water, holding the dish you're cleaning."

When she did that, Geoff whistled between his teeth, a short blast that caught Chris's attention, pulling him out of wherever his mind had been. There was no screen on the window, so it took only a few steps for him to determine what Geoff was doing. Geoff forced her chin up so she was staring into his eyes, unable to see Chris's reaction as he drew closer, his shoes crunching across the ground.

"You like how he looks at you when he knows he has to keep his dick on a leash. You want to make him strain against that leash because you're a sweet little tease, aren't you?" He bit her ear.

"Yes, Master," she breathed. She could sense Chris on the other side of the window, listening.

"So here we are," Geoff said, his voice deceptively mild again. "I've told you not to tease the yard boy, and yet I find you wearing this thin, short dress with nothing under it, pretending to wash dishes while you stare at him, all shirtless and sweaty. I think you need a reminder about proper behavior."

Releasing her chin, he captured her breasts in his hands again. She lowered her chin and saw Chris had his gaze trained on her breasts, watching Geoff stroke the curves. Those long fingers plucked at her nipples and she gasped again, her hips jerking against Geoff's body. She couldn't seem to stop licking her lips, her eyes devouring Chris's bare chest, expanding from the rise and fall of his breath. The beauty of that motion drew her gaze to the waistband of his jeans as Chris's stomach contracted and he shifted to one hip.

"Yeah, he's like you. Built head to toe to be fucked." As Chris's gaze flickered at that, a spark of answering fire, Geoff set his teeth against her neck once more. "Your nipples are all hard from watching him. I bet your cunt is wet, too, isn't it, bad girl?"

As he gave her ass a sharp slap, Sam jumped and Chris's eyes darkened. "I can't help it, Master," she managed. "He's so very . . . handsome."

"Uh-huh. What's so handsome about him?" Geoff pushed the

dress past her hips and took it to the floor, leaving her naked. Chris's attention slid down to see as far as he could see before the rest of her body disappeared below the sink level.

"He has all those muscles . . . all over. And . . . oh . . ." The one-syllable word multiplied into several as Geoff tweaked her nipples harder. She pushed her hips against his cock, hard and insistent against her bare ass. She could feel the weight of it through his jeans. "When he bends over, his pants tighten over his backside, and I can't seem to stop wanting . . ." She couldn't stop wanting, period, and she really couldn't think. The avid look in Chris's eyes, as if he couldn't wait to do everything Geoff was doing to her, had her making a needy whimper.

"Why aren't you washing the dishes?" Geoff said coldly. "I didn't say you could stop doing that."

"Yes sir." Groping for the washcloth, she tried to wash the egg off a plate in the soapy water as Geoff's hands moved behind her, exploring her buttocks.

"Spread your legs, Samantha Beth. You always keep your legs open for us, telling us you're ready whenever we want you."

"Yes sir. Um . . ."

She really didn't want reality to intrude on this, but Flo's earlier warnings came to mind. *"Nothing pisses us off like a sub enduring the wrong kind of pain or, worse, risking harm because they're afraid speaking up or using a safe word will make us end the session altogether . . ."*

At the time, Sam had fully agreed with the sensibility of it, but in the heat of the moment, she wasn't as sure. Though it was role-playing, there was something about Geoff in this mode that brought to life the mirror image in her that wasn't about playing at all, for either of them. She wanted to embrace it as reality. The consequences she had to face afterward were distant and unimportant.

Chris made a quiet noise that had Geoff's head lifting. Geoff moved his hand back up her body to fondle her breasts. Now he caressed them instead of tweaking her nipples so forcefully, which destroyed her focus even more. She'd be hard-pressed to form coherent sentences, but her Master was demanding them.

"You need to say something to me, Samantha Beth?"

"No sir. I . . ." She closed her eyes. "I'm kind of sore. But I want you inside me. I don't want you not to do it because you think I can't handle it . . ."

"You're worried I might be too demanding," Geoff said smoothly. "And it would hurt, because you're sore. Your body has been overused by a couple of beasts."

"I'm sorry. I shouldn't have——"

Geoff slid his hand around her throat and squeezed, silencing her. "What's a Master's first responsibility, Sam? Do you know it? Every sub should."

She wet her lips. Chris's eyes pierced her to the soul. Geoff's grip on her throat kept her in a dark, dreamlike well.

"To take care of his submissive," she whispered. "To protect her."

"That's right. But since we're not as smart as we like to think we are, we need your help to do that. You have to tell us when we might be about to hurt you in the wrong way."

"There's a right way to hurt me?" Her heart was so full of them both she needed to tease so she didn't cry instead. The tears would be the right kind of tears, but they might not understand that.

"You bet your sweet ass. You'll know it when I use my belt on it later today for forgetting the first rule. Then Chris will take a turn with it. He says that kind of punishment isn't his thing, but I think he might be expanding his horizons, don't you? Especially when he sees how crazy it makes you." Geoff bit her ear and she quivered under his hold. "You'll get some domestic discipline from both of us to remember you're supposed to help us protect you. Always. Got it?"

"Yes sir."

"Good. Now . . . where were we? So you like looking at our yard boy, at his fine ass and all his muscles. I'll bet when you're looking at him, he's been looking back at you, and he's gotten a really uncomfortable hard-on, because he's a big guy all over, isn't he? Nice big dick to go with the body. He rakes the yard, suffering that hard-on in his pants, wondering when I'll be off at work and he can make an excuse to come in the house. Maybe to get a glass of water. Maybe to talk you into letting him do this."

Geoff squeezed her breasts again and she moaned. "Or maybe he won't ask. If you tease him enough, he'll decide to take instead of being polite. You'd like that, wouldn't you?"

She nodded before the flaming heat of Chris's unwavering gaze.

His lips tightened, his corded throat rippling as he swallowed. Her fingers curled in the washcloth.

"Before you play, you have to finish your chores," Geoff reminded her. His voice was back to that growl against her skin. She wanted his teeth there. As if he read her mind, he bit, making her cry out softly as he increased the grip, letting her feel the sharpness of his canines before he lifted his head again. "You can't come until every dish is in the drainer, scrubbed clean," he said sternly. "Not a bit of food on them. So you keep working on that while I taste your pussy."

She wondered if it was possible for her brain to melt like candle wax from too much sexual stimulation. Softened candle wax felt warm and velvety under the fingertips, coating the skin, hardening on it . . . Her brain was rolling in sensory stimulation, no interest in connecting the dots of her thoughts.

"Wash the dishes, Samantha Beth. I won't tell you again."

He smacked her ass—a blow powerful enough to make her yelp—and she forced her hands into motion. Meanwhile, Geoff dropped to a knee behind her, hands sliding along her bare legs, back up to grip her ass with enough pressure to tip her forward. "Bend over, your elbows on the edge of the sink, but keep your head up and your eyes on your yard boy. Don't you look away from his face. He's going to be getting a lot harder for you, starting right now."

The position put the tips of her breasts almost into the soap suds. It also lifted her hips, that and her spread legs making it easier for Geoff to carry out his next step toward fragmenting her mind. Sam clutched the plate she'd been cleaning as Geoff's tongue and lips found her pussy. He started with gentle licks, a balm on her sore tissues that helped them swell and moisten, bringing them back to aroused ripeness without discomfort. As he swirled his tongue in a slow, artful track, she barely managed to hang on to the plate and her washcloth.

Chris was less than two feet away, him outside, her inside. It was as if he was the yard boy in truth, gazing at her with hot eyes through a window as her Master went down on her, knowing he was watching, reinforcing for another male whose she was in this primal way. Knowing the truth of it beyond the role-playing, she trembled at the look in Chris's eyes as Geoff worked her up for him, for both of them.

Washing the dishes required brief looks down to transfer a rinsed dish from the washing side of the double sink to the dish drainer side. She struggled through an erratic rhythm of looking up, looking down, while Geoff's mouth stayed busy between her legs. He slid his fingers into her pussy to collect her slick wetness and worked his digits into her rectum, adding another level of torture that wrested a cry from her lips. Chris's hand landed on the windowsill, his knuckles white as he gripped it. It was too much, maybe for both of them. *Oh God . . .* She had five dishes left to go.

"Geoff . . . Master, I'm too close."

"Yeah, you are." He stood and drew her up against him, his arms coming around to flank her as he washed his hands. Then he clasped hers, guiding and steadying them through washing the last items, water and juice glasses. He took each from her shaking fingers to rinse and place it in the drainer, protecting them from breakage and her from injuring herself. His chest was warm against her bare back, his jeans a rougher friction against her sensitive buttocks. The dress was still at her ankles, him standing clothed behind her and Chris in front as she did the domestic task naked. She was drowning in all of it without the desire for rescue, as long as the two of them were with her.

As Geoff put the last dish away, she moistened her lips. "Master, may I make a request?" Her voice was shaking.

"You may." He pushed her hair to the side and kissed her throat.

"I know I'm sore, but I really, really want you inside me. Can I come for you that way?"

"Not this time, baby. We've used you hard, and it's time to give your sweet pussy a break. Don't want to break our toy just when we've first started to play with it."

She understood his logic, but still . . . He dropped his hand, squeezing her buttock. "No arguing."

She hadn't even opened her mouth, but he'd known she was about to do so. A quirk of Chris's firm mouth told her he'd known it also. Sometimes the two of them knew her a little too well. She'd have to figure out a way to counter that. Some other time.

Geoff stepped back. "Back down on your elbows and ass lifted into the air. Like before."

She complied, trembling, and he dropped to one knee again and parted her buttocks. His thumbs played on her rim and he put his lips gently on her ass, a tender tease. "It's time for you to come for your yard boy, Samantha Beth."

As Geoff dipped his head and went to work on her cunt again, she looked up and was captured by Chris's expression. When Geoff's head pushed between her legs, widening them further so he could take her clit in his mouth and start sucking on it, playing his tongue over it and her labia, she shattered.

The climax shot her up and took her hard, cries tearing from her throat. It was one heavy wave followed by another, and another. She'd always heard that women were capable of plenty of orgasms, with very little recuperation time needed, but she'd never had lovers with the skill to make that happen. Discovering it now, this way, had been worth the wait.

She didn't take her eyes off Chris, just as Geoff had ordered. As she became wilder, her body undulating so Geoff gripped her hips, holding her fast, Chris became more still, a potent, explosive energy. His lips moved, a husky murmur. She couldn't make out the words, but it wasn't necessary. She knew he was encouraging her to come even harder and longer, and she obeyed him as instinctively as she did Geoff, going as long, far and hard as she could, knowing if her heart gave out, they'd be there to catch her.

Her body stopped flying over those waves at last, coming to rest in more gentle swells. Geoff helped take her through those last rises and falls, the incredible movements of his tongue and lips easing into light, lingering kisses over her quivering flesh, mixed with the occasional tease of his tongue, collecting her climax, consuming her.

Chris was so absorbed by her response, it was as if he'd been locked into it and never wanted the clock to start again. Or maybe that was her thought.

Geoff straightened behind her, his arm snaking around her waist. Lifting her off her feet, he tipped her forward over the sink so Chris could lean through the window and slide his lips over hers. Her mouth trembled beneath his. Caressing her face, he stared at her as he drew back. "You're so beautiful, Sam." His touch was urgent, tense. She felt the same thrum of need in Geoff's hold on her waist.

"I can take care of both of you," she said. "With my mouth. Please."

She wanted to kneel on the cool kitchen floor and take Geoff's cock in her mouth. He'd push deep into her throat as Chris stood next to her, stroking his own erection while watching her service Geoff. She'd slide off Geoff and put her mouth on Chris, bringing him so close, yet Geoff's hand would wind into her hair, tugging her away and putting her back to work on him again. Back and forth, until eventually each one would come in her mouth. In the last moment, Chris might pull free and let his seed spill over her breasts. Both men would watch as she rubbed that cream into them . . .

This had to be some weird reaction to suppressing her fantasies for so long, because she should be easing back now, slowing down. Instead, she wanted to push herself so far beyond the burn she wouldn't know the difference between pleasure and pain. It would be all about being with them. They wouldn't be able to resist her, not like this.

Geoff tilted her head up to look at him. She knew he was weighing her offer, making a decision. So she kept quiet, but when his lips pursed and she knew he was going to let things play out, a frenzied sense of victory surged through her. His attention sharpened, as if he was seeing something else in her expression, something that injected uneasiness into her crazy swirl of need. She had to do this for them, with them. He might think something was off, but she was fine. It was all good. He had to let her do this. She would lose her mind if he didn't. She'd just had a bone-dissolving climax, but she was so revved up she had to do something. Now.

"If I weren't home," Geoff said casually, "you'd invite the yard man in for a drink of water, wouldn't you? He looks all sweaty and tired, so you're just being kind, offering to let him come in and sit down, take a little rest. Course, he's not expecting to come into the kitchen and see you all naked, is he? That'd be quite a shock, wouldn't it?"

"Y-yes." With unsteady hands, she bent to pick the dress up and spread it over her breasts as if she were still wearing it, never mind that it was a two-dimensional façade, her naked ass still pressed against Geoff.

"Would you like to come in and get a drink? It's a warm day, and I just made up some lemonade." She swept her gaze downward, which would draw Chris's eyes to her breasts, the nipples barely covered by the dress. "Freshly squeezed."

Geoff's snort gave her a tiny smile, but she continued. "You've been working so hard. And you look *really* hot."

She let her gaze travel deliberately over Chris's shoulders, down his chest. She loved the layer of brown hair over his pectorals and abdomen and wanted to thread her fingers through it and tug. Caress the hollow of his throat, kiss and taste the salt of his perspiration there. She'd drawn out the comment to exaggerate the double entendre, but her playfulness disappeared into a coil of relentless need. She wanted Chris within touching distance.

Chris picked up on the shift, the humor dancing in his gaze fading away. His expression suggested he was more hungry than thirsty, and she was the main course . . . *and* dessert. "Yes ma'am. That's very kind of you. I'll be right in. Just need to put away my tools and wash up."

"Oh . . . don't." She moistened her lips. "I mean, about the washing up. I prefer you dirty."

His heavy-lidded gaze would have done Cary Elwes proud. "As you wish."

"God, he knows that line makes my knees weak," she muttered as he left the window.

Geoff dropped a kiss on her shoulder. "Yet now he understands why."

As Geoff drew away from her, she stayed at the sink, watching Chris pick up the rake and hoe, returning them to the toolshed. Whatever was going to happen in the kitchen, he understood he wasn't likely to be outside for a while, and Chris took meticulous care of his tools.

Geoff placed a glass of lemonade on the counter in front of her, bringing her attention back to him. He gave her a serious wink, turned and put the pitcher back in the refrigerator.

Instead of coming back to her side, he moved to the kitchen doorway and stepped out into the hallway to lean a shoulder against the frame, a key player exiting stage left to make way for the next act. Only in this case, he also became the director, providing her fragmented mind much-needed focus.

"You're feeling the anticipation," he said in a low voice. "He doesn't know he's going to walk into the kitchen and find you naked. Drop the dress, Sam."

At the direct order, the cloth slipped from her hand to the ground.

"Got butterflies in your stomach, as if he's the yard guy in truth?"

She nodded, a nervous smile on her face. In Geoff's countenance she saw a combination of ruthless Dom, understanding friend and new lover, all of which initiated another surge of butterflies.

"Strike a pose for him. Something to make his jaw drop on the floor."

Picking up the glass, she held it in one hand, bracing her other on the sink so she could shift to one hip. Tossing her hair back over one shoulder, she adopted a casually provocative stance. Geoff's heated approval, his lazy head-to-toe appraisal, bolstered her confidence. And made her more nervous, in a good way. "Christ," he murmured. "You're every man's fantasy."

Her stomach leaped when Chris knocked. He actually knocked. But he would, wouldn't he, if the woman of the house invited him in? She wondered if any of his customers had ever tried this on him before. He'd never reveal such a thing to her or Geoff, not in casual conversation. Chris was a gentleman. But had any of those women succeeded at what she was about to do? She banished the unpleasant thought. It didn't matter anymore. He was hers now. Truly hers.

"Come in," she said. Was it crazy that her voice was thick, her pulse thudding as if he really was a relative stranger, coming in to sip her lemonade with the potential of seduction dancing between them? Or ravishment. Whether or not it was twisted of her, she got a definite charge from that idea. A forced seduction took choices away and let her get lost in the pure dark joy of it.

When the yard boy came to do the weekly mowing, weeding and cutting, she saw how he watched her. She was a sexually mature woman. The look in his serious, intent eyes, the russet color of an animal's, the set of his firm mouth, told her what he was thinking and wanting.

Since the best fantasies were an overlap of fantasy and reality, Sam could recall a hundred instances where she'd seen that look in Chris's eye. Because she now knew what it had meant, her heart tightened as much as her pulse leaped. This was what Chris had always wanted and what she could now have in reality. Not just in play or fantasy.

He opened the door, coming to a halt at the sight of her standing in front of him without wearing a stitch.

"It was such a hot day . . ." she said. Her voice trailed away, abandoning the silly line. He stood in her kitchen in just his work shoes and jeans, his cock a thick bar sculpted by the straining fabric. The rise and fall of his breath, the fix of his glittering eyes, the strands of hair scattered over his brow, the light curl of his hands at his sides, took the playfulness right out of her. But she tried to stick with her role and her intent—to wrap her lips around that engorged organ fighting to get free of his pants.

"Why don't you sit there?" She pointed to the kitchen chair.

"No," he said, and moved toward her. Her grip tightened on the glass. She felt inexplicably jumpy as he stopped in front of her. He was so much bigger. Hot, sweaty, vibrating with life and male energy. He ran his fingers along the glass, collecting the condensation off the side, and brought it to her lips, painting the wetness there. Tilting his head to study her breasts, he touched the tip of one, a kiss of cool, wet sensation.

"What do you want?" she asked, her voice barely over a whisper. She was aware of Geoff watching them, a potent, silent regard.

Taking the glass from her hand, Chris raised it to his lips and drank a few swallows. She reached up to glide her fingers down his throat, but his hand closed over her wrist before she could touch him. He kept that hold on her until he'd emptied half the glass and set it aside on the counter.

Stretching out his other long arm, he opened the drawer where they kept the kitchen towels. He pulled out two and dropped them on the floor, one overlapping the other. Then he put downward pressure on her arm, telling her what he wanted, his brown eyes holding hers in a lock.

Sam sank to her knees on the cushion he'd provided, wondering if he realized his act of caring, providing her a cushion for her knees, combined with the demanding clamp on her wrist, sent her the very arousing message that he was in control. Had it been driven by his own desires as much as her own? She hoped so.

Opening his pants, he reached inside them and adjusted himself before pushing the jeans and boxers to his thighs so his heavy cock could spring free. She inhaled the salt-and-sweat male scent of him.

Threading his fingers deeper into the fine strands of her hair, he twisted them into a tail. Gripping it in one hand against the back of her skull, he brought her forward, directing her to put her mouth over the ruddy head of his cock.

She parted her lips, sliding her fingers around him as she tasted the tip and slid down even farther. She smelled earth, heat and Chris, a heady combination.

A scrape told her Geoff had come into the kitchen. Chris had thought of her knees and Geoff had thought of Chris. He'd brought one of the chairs closer so Chris would be able to sink into it if he decided he wanted that support. She spread her fingers over Chris's pubic area, the unexpectedly soft skin below the layer of hair. Curling her fingers around his base again, she tightened, released and stroked.

If he sat down in the chair, would he eventually bring her to her feet, turn her around and impale her on his cock? Geoff had forbidden actual sex to give her sensitive tissues time to recuperate, and Chris would hold to that, no matter how aroused her mouth made him. But maybe another time. She shivered, thinking of herself on his lap, her pussy full of his cock while he used a flat palm between her shoulder blades to fold her over her knees. He'd grip her hip in his other big hand and work her on him. Geoff would stand in front of her, curl his fingers in her hair and feed his cock between her lips.

For all her fantasies, Geoff and Chris didn't really need any input to bring her to an insane level of ecstasy. Geoff shifted behind her, his feet planted on either side of her ankles. His fingertips slid over her shoulder and she heard him opening his jeans. A slow, measured breath, followed by a slight, rhythmic rock of his feet against hers, made her realize he was masturbating while watching the two of them. Arousal bolted through her core, and it affected Chris as well. A glance up showed him divided between looking at her going down on his cock, and at the man behind her, stroking his own.

Geoff moved closer, straddling her calves. With Chris still holding her hair in a twist on the back of her head, Geoff slid his cock along the line of her spine, leaving a thin track of wetness from the slit. She whimpered against Chris's cock, digging the fingers of her free hand into his thigh. It was already quivering, thanks to her ministrations and how worked up he'd been before they even started. Chris sat down in the chair and readjusted, which pushed him into the back of her throat in an even more demanding way.

She curled herself over him, sucking and licking, all while gripping him with her hand.

"All pretty and soft," Chris muttered. "So clean and sweet."

She played her tongue along the sensitive corona. His hand convulsed against her skull.

"All ours, hmm?" Geoff prompted in the same low voice.

"Hell yeah." Chris's hand convulsed, either in reaction to the words or the stimulation, or some of both. "Fuck . . . oh fuck . . ."

Triumph roared through her at how quickly she'd been able to bring him to that crest, though it had probably been expedited by all the stimulation that had started at the sink and built from there. Chris's hips lifted off the chair, his cock shoving deeper into her mouth. He pulled her hair hard against her scalp, his powerful body rocking the chair and making it squeak in protest against the joints. She could still feel the heat and shift of Geoff's body behind her as he masturbated, watching them both.

She swallowed the salty taste and kept moving with Chris, trying to anticipate everything that would make the experience even better for him. Since his hand kept flexing on her head, his own tipped back, body trembling with multiple waves of release, she thought she was succeeding. She continued to lick at him greedily, suck and nip, as he groaned again. His soft, reverent curses included her name. She loved it. She loved him.

When at last Chris finished, Geoff took her back to her heels, stroking her head with approval. In her current euphoric state, she went with impulse, dipping her head to press her lips against his knuckles before he drew away. "Sweet girl," Geoff murmured. "Good sub. You did good. Up off your heels, Samantha Beth. Put your hands on Chris's thighs."

Despite the praise, when she dared a glance at him, his expression was stern and unyielding, matching the tone of the command. She obeyed, catching her lip in her teeth as he dropped to a squat and reached between her legs to push his fingers into her still-wet cunt. Chris curled his hands around her biceps to steady her as Geoff explored. He moved with care, yet did a thorough caress of her channel before he withdrew.

Turning her head, she saw him rubbing his glistening fingers over his erection again. She quivered as he met her gaze and pushed his fingers inside her to do it again. Then a third time. Chris was watching, his mouth slack and sexy, brown eyes a little dazed from his own climax.

After the third time, Geoff extended his hand to Chris. "Get up."

Wow, Geoff didn't believe in waiting. He was going to take Chris's place in the chair and have her go down on him right away. Chris sent him an odd look, but he lifted a shoulder, a *Fair is fair* kind of gesture. Geoff had graciously allowed him to go first, after all.

Chris clasped Geoff's hand and let himself be pulled to his feet. He started to hike up his pants and move away from the chair so Geoff could take it. That was when Geoff showed he had something else in mind.

She gasped as Geoff hooked Chris's ankle and spun him toward and down onto the table. The smooth, decisive move left Chris with his chest flat against the surface, one arm curved behind his back in Geoff's sure grasp, his pants and underwear still bunched at his thighs. As Chris reflexively began to push up with his other hand, the wrist hold kept him right where Geoff wanted him.

"Grab the edge of the table with your free hand," Geoff ordered. His hazel eyes met Sam's. "You think you're the only one who's stared at the yard boy and wanted his ass?"

"No sir."

Geoff's eyes went warrior fierce, responding to the address. Chris looked suddenly tense, his gaze moving from her face back to the tabletop. She thought he wasn't sure about Geoff taking him over like this, how it looked in front of her. He didn't seem entirely averse to it, just uncertain if he *should* be struggling against it. That told her what to do.

Scooting around the table, still on her knees, she put her fingertips on the edge of the table where she guessed his would end up if he decided to obey Geoff. She gave him a hopeful look, and he brought his arm forward slowly, overlapping one of her hands with his own.

"Let him grip the table, Sam," Geoff said. "He's going to need to hold on to something stronger than your delicate fingers."

Chris opened his mouth to retort, but Geoff reached between his legs and gave his testicles a healthy twist. Chris snarled, then his eyes became more opaque as she noticed Geoff's grip easing to a fondling touch.

"Did you like handling his balls, Sam?" Geoff asked conversationally.

She nodded and Geoff flashed her a dangerous grin. "They're a nice size, aren't they? All firm and ripe, even after he's come. Grip the table, Chris. Don't be stubborn. She wants to watch, but I'm not doing a damn thing until you listen."

"You're using her to make me to obey you," Chris said darkly.

"You bet your ass I am." Geoff slid a palm over said ass and gave it a healthy, hard smack that had Chris jumping in surprise and Sam's lips parting, thinking of Geoff's handprint there. Just like on her backside. "Now fucking do it," Geoff growled. "You're already in deep shit, yard boy. It'll go easier on you if you listen. But maybe you prefer it harder. Or maybe . . ."

Geoff slid his hand down Chris's taut back. Perhaps it was the strain in those bunched muscles that made him draw back, though he kept Chris's wrist in a pin. "Or maybe you want me to let you up, yard boy. What's it going to be?"

No. She really didn't want them to stop what they were doing. Her savage desire to see the two of them together overrode everything, except Geoff's clear intent to make sure Chris was okay with this. She could help with that.

Sam drew her hand from beneath Chris's and molded his fingers over the edge. As he let her guide him, his attention fixed on her face. If every thought and emotion had an energy vibration as some people thought, she expected there was an amazing pattern happening around Chris, tangling with hers and Geoff's in a way that was thrilling, unpredictable and arousing, all at once.

She slid her fingertips over his callused knuckles, the many tiny scars he'd accumulated from what he did for a living. Putting his hand inside a thicket of roses, or stripping out thorny vines so other things could breathe and live. Rising on her knees, she pressed her lips against his fingers, laving those small scars with her tongue. Chris let out a choked breath.

Geoff leaned over him, pushing Chris's hair off his neck to put his open mouth on it as his other hand slid down over Chris's ass once more. "I'm going to let your other hand go, but you give it to Sam."

As he released Chris's wrist from the twisted hold, she saw Geoff was ready if Chris chose to be combative. Why the idea of that made her so hot, she didn't know, but she was getting an idea of why people liked to watch underground fights. They might get far more female attendees if the two men in question ended up like this instead of bloody.

"When you were working in our yard and staring at her, thinking about what it would be like to taste her skin, touch her breasts, feast on her cunt, fuck it, you didn't know you'd end up having to take care of my needs, too, did you?" Geoff's tone went sinister, pulling Sam deeper into the fantasy they were weaving. "But now that I'm handling you, you get it. If she hadn't drained your cock dry, it would be sitting up for me, wouldn't it?"

Chris let out an oath as Geoff's knee shifted again against his vulnerable testicles. "Yeah."

That one rough word was coupled with a flick of his lashes as he stared at the table again. He wouldn't meet Sam's gaze. Sam trailed her knuckles down his face, bringing his attention back to her. "Say it again," she whispered. "Please. Let us know you're okay."

Geoff's gaze glittered in approval, a reaction she registered without lifting her eyes from Chris. His brown eyes were like bright pennies in a fire.

Chris's expression eased as he focused on her face, saw what she hoped he'd see. Love, passion, arousal. "Yeah," he repeated. "Yes."

"Hmm," Geoff grunted. "Not as pretty as her *Yes sir*, but I'll take it. The way you'll take this."

Gripping his cock, Geoff adjusted in a way that told her he was guiding himself into Chris's ass. Sam watched wide-eyed as Chris's body rippled, the muscles of his face tightening in reaction. The first time she'd seen them kiss had been explosive enough. To see them fuck in front of her made her go quiet as a mouse, as if one tiny movement might deprive her of the opportunity.

"I'd already lubed up while Sam was going down on you, but I think her come makes me even more slippery. And you like knowing my cock has her juices on it. Right, Chris?"

Chris's gaze came back to her. "Yeah." She heard different nuances every time he uttered the single word, and she clung to each meaning, cherishing all of it.

"There's my boy. Christ, I love being inside you." Geoff's voice softened. He pressed in deep, putting both hands on Chris's hips, and

Chris groaned. Geoff's eyes closed at the sensation, both men suddenly like statues, caught in the center of a volatile whirlpool, emotions and arousal churning in a vortex caused by the joining of their bodies.

Leaning down, Geoff spoke into Chris's ear, his tone a rough threat. "Next time you're out in the yard, and you see her in one of her pretty, thin dresses, no panties and no bra, so all you can think about is sucking on those cherry nipples or eating her pussy, are you going to stare at her like you did today? Let your dick get disgracefully hard, even though you know she belongs to me?"

Chris drew in a breath as Geoff punctuated the comment with a deeper thrust. "Hell yeah," he muttered. "Every damn time."

Geoff grinned, a baring of teeth. "That's what I thought. Your head's as hard as your dick." He seized Chris's hair and jerked his head back, startling Sam. Chris snarled another oath, fingers whitening on the table edge. "And why will you do that, Chris?" Geoff demanded.

Chris's gaze met Sam's. "Because she's mine, too."

"That's right." Geoff's fingers relaxed. "Exactly right."

As Sam let out an unconsciously held breath, Geoff stroked Chris's hair, moving down the valley of his spine. He pressed his mouth between Chris's shoulder blades as his hips lifted and fell. The rhythm moved the table beneath her touch, causing a scraping noise against the linoleum. Chris's fingers flexed again, responding to every thrust.

She couldn't help herself. She was up off her heels, pressing soft kisses to his parted lips, capturing his panting breaths, her lips moving to his eyes, his cheeks, fingers sliding into his hair over Geoff's.

Geoff closed his eyes then as if turning his focus inward, slowing things down. He settled into an even slower in-and-out motion. It looked as if he was pressing in deep as he could on each thrust, holding a beat before slowly pulling back and then doing the same thing over again. Sam wished they had a mirror on the wall of the kitchen. She'd like to be behind Geoff, watching his ass flex and pump as he thrust into Chris. But she was equally mesmerized by the look on Chris's face. His arousal had gone subterranean, deep inside him, and she understood that soul-level response, a reaction far beyond words.

Role-playing was done. Kissing Chris's hand again, she played her tongue over each of his fingers. She lifted off her heels, intending once again to lean over the table between his spread hands and put her lips against his, swallow those appealing quiet grunts. Several inches from her goal, she stopped and looked up at Geoff, remembering herself.

"May I kiss him?"

Chris's expression suggested he had a mixed reaction to her decision to defer to Geoff, but disagreement wasn't part of that response.

"You may. If you apologize for not asking the first time."

Despite his admonishment, Geoff showed his approval for her taking that initiative. It shot warmth through her core. Perhaps one of the best things about all of this was that they were exploring it together, so many moments new for each of them.

"Yes sir. I'm sorry for not asking before."

"Apology accepted."

She stretched out over the table, her breasts pressing between Chris's elbows, and touched her mouth to his. Lifting one hand from the table edge, Chris gripped the side of her head, fingers overlapping jaw, nape and throat to hold her fast. He might be under Geoff's command, but he left no doubt she was under both of theirs. He parted her lips and invaded her mouth with his lashing tongue, letting her feel the storm Geoff was creating inside him. She became part of their rise-and-fall movement as he held her, the table trembling and squeaking beneath them. She felt Geoff's every thrust in her own womb.

Chris broke the kiss, moving to her throat, her shoulder, and put his teeth there, an erotic claiming as Geoff reached under him to work Chris's cock. "God, you feel so fucking good . . ." Geoff muttered.

When Geoff started to come, Chris's teeth dug into her shoulder, his breath rasping against her as she wound her arms over his taut shoulders. Then harsh groans spilled from him, along with his seed. His climax was so violent it splattered on the linoleum, some of it baptizing her knees. She laid her head on Chris's shoulder, holding on to both of them by holding on to one.

Geoff kept emphasizing she was theirs, which she loved, but in truth, it worked in every direction. They were all hers as well.

Geoff slowed, breathing deep. He put his palm on Chris's back, then moved his touch to Sam's head, a caress for them both. "Let's move into the living room. Someone call nine-one-one to get us there," he added.

"You know, there may be a logical reason that threesomes are not the norm," Chris said, his voice muffled in Sam's shoulder. "Like the limits of physical endurance."

Geoff chuckled and helped him up. Sam reluctantly slid her arms from around Chris's shoulders. Geoff wrapped his own around the broader man, steadying them both. "I'm looking at it as a new exercise regimen," Geoff said. "It takes time to build up to it, but once you do, you'll just want more."

"You're the running addict. Like a rabbit," Chris pointed out. "I'm the manual laborer, the turtle. Slow and steady wins the race."

"Slow and steady has no cardio endurance."

"Only for sprinting. You whine like a girl whenever you pitch in with Esteban's crew for extra money and do half a day's work."

"Like a girl?" Sam protested. Chris tossed her a logy look.

"Give me a break. I don't have the brain cells for a PC analogy." Chris sobered then, his gaze coursing over her. She had her arms crossed on the surface of the table, her chin propped on them as she watched their every move together with fascinated eyes. "Did you like watching that?" he asked roughly.

"Yes. I've fantasized about a whole lot more than just you two kissing."

It was clear he'd worried she'd think him weak, letting Geoff take him like that. The power exchange between them was still a work in process.

She didn't mind having a front-row seat to seeing that happen, but she had some worries about it. That Geoff was a Dom, there was no question. Chris could exercise Dom tendencies, but he wasn't a Master like Geoff was. He also wasn't a submissive like her, eager to surrender to the two men she loved and trusted.

As Geoff let the need to dominate seize him, would he pull Chris into the same submissive mix indiscriminately? If he did, would that cause problems between the two men? When he first put Chris down on the table, she'd sensed that possibility. She wasn't sure if it had fit Chris's desires entirely, but he hadn't resisted Geoff too strenuously, either. He might have, except for her putting her hands on him. So had she helped or hindered Chris's true desires by doing that?

She had no immediate answers, so she had to put her faith in two truths. Geoff cared for them both, enough that he would draw back if needed. And Chris had a far more stubborn will than most people realized, until they ran up against it.

"See? It's her fault, her and her fantasies." Geoff brought her back with the outrageous comment. He squeezed Chris's shoulder. "Her active female imagination is going to kill us. Living room. My knees aren't going to hold me up much longer."

"Want me to carry you?" Chris tipped his head, his expression a little easier now.

"As if you could." Geoff bent, picked up Chris's pants and tossed them at him as he pulled his own jeans back up. He gave Chris the room to do the same, though Sam noticed Geoff stayed close enough he could steady his friend if needed. Once he was sure Chris had his balance, Geoff came around the table, offered her a hand to help her off her knees. As he ran a light hand down her hair and her back, her Master gave her an assessing *Are you okay?* look.

She smiled to reassure both him and herself. No matter how sappy it was, she did believe love was strong enough to work its way through anything. Since she was fiercely in love with both of them, she was armed and ready for whatever came their way.

As soon as they all had another nap. And some form of carbs. Preferably those cookies she'd been too worn-out to eat last night. If Chris had left her any.

~

"Here. Take these." Flo put two Aleve and a Dove dark chocolate bite in its bright red wrapper on Sam's desk, next to her open can of Diet Coke. "You're moving like you're ninety."

"I think I wept during Downward Dog at yoga this morning," Sam confessed. She wagged a finger at Flo. "Do not smirk."

"Don't give me orders, little sub." Flo flicked Sam's ear with her long nails, but she softened it with a light touch on Sam's hair. Then she smirked. "So things went as planned after I dropped you off?"

"Yes. But I'm having to rethink the plan. I wanted to get them on the same page, feeling comfortable with all of us . . . being together." Out of habit, Sam glanced toward her office door, making sure none of their other coworkers were wandering by to hear their assistant manager discussing her sex life. "Apparently, them being on the same page means they're happy doing it one-on-one *and* as a threesome. They're insatiable."

"They're men. Handsome, powerful young men at their sexual peak." Flo shuddered. "You poor thing."

"Your sympathy is bringing tears to my eyes. Again. I think the plan is out of my hands now."

"Then all is as it should be," Flo intoned, and dodged her jabbing elbow. "I've got to get back to my desk. Take the painkiller and chocolate to get you through the rest of Monday."

As Flo retreated, chuckling, Sam tossed back the Aleve and chased them with a swallow of Diet Coke. Unwrapping the Dove bite, she placed the smooth chocolate on her tongue, her lips curving slightly at the taste and . . . well, everything. Despite Flo's teasing and her own complaints, she wouldn't have traded a moment of her weekend. And yet...

She stared sightlessly at the screen as her mind dove backward into all the amazing experiences they'd shared over the past forty-eight hours. Geoff's intent gaze, Chris's hands sliding over her skin, them inside her, around her . . . It had been the erotic bliss she'd fantasized about for months. Glancing down at her hands, she turned them upward, staring at her palms. They looked so empty, as if she needed to be holding onto Geoff and Chris physically to be . . . right. She shook her head, trying to get rid of the feeling. She'd had it several times this past weekend, but it kept coming back. She thought Geoff had picked up on it once or twice, giving her odd looks, but he'd left it alone and she hadn't wanted to talk about it. She hadn't wanted to ruin anything with some weirdness she couldn't define.

Today, when they'd had to turn their attention back to work and real-world demands, she'd expected the feeling to vanish, but as the morning progressed and she struggled with her reports, it came and went more frequently, an urgency that pricked at her until she couldn't sit still. The uncomfortable tides of emotion and physical agitation made her feel slightly hysterical one moment, close to tears another. But since when it passed, everything else was a humming euphoria, it had to be a temporary thing.

When it had happened during the weekend, all she'd wanted to do was jump whichever one of them was available. Pounding, insistent sex appeased it for a time. She should have talked about it to Flo, and couldn't pinpoint why she hadn't.

Stop it. You have to work. You remember work, right? That thing that allows you to pay your bills.

She shook it off, but compromised. For every fifteen minutes she worked, she indulged in a two minute fantasy flashback. As soon as it gave way to that strange, less comfortable feeling, she forced her attention back to the job. It didn't result in a terribly productive day, but she supposed the silly grin Flo kept seeing on her face for the fantasy part of things provided her co-worker some Monday morning levity. And kept her from noticing the other, darker feeling Sam was unable to comprehend.

At least by quitting time, Flo's Aleve and chocolate had helped restore her energy and flexibility. As she pulled into the driveway and got the mail from the box, Sam was moving more easily. She flipped through the mail, mostly bills and junk, and found a hand-addressed lavender envelope from Naughty Bits. Opening it up, she smelled a hint of jasmine. Reading through the contents, she smiled, making a note to share the invitation with her men.

Her men. She liked thinking of them that way. Curiously, though, when she thought of Geoff alone, she simply thought *Master*. She'd even doodled it on her notepad while on the phone resolving an account problem today. *Sir* came more easily to her in front of Chris, though she wasn't sure why she was self-conscious about calling Geoff *Master* with Chris watching.

She paused in the kitchen, clutching the mail to her chest, overcome with a longing for the two of them so hard it almost made her lightheaded. "Stop it," she whispered. She knew there was something wrong with the strength and tone of that feeling. It was like the exuberance of a child confronted with pounds of candy and no parent to supervise how much was consumed. Over time, that ebullience would give way to uncertainty and unbalance, as well as a weird, unsettling panic, as if tipping over an edge with nothing to hold. A blind search for the structure, safety and control needed would be accompanied by a serious sugar crash.

She wanted to keep consuming the candy, but she was an adult. She knew how to tell herself no, right? Yet she resisted that idea like a child, resentful that too much candy could make her sick. She was going to keep eating it until someone told her no . . .

Well, someone had said *no*, hadn't they? She wondered if that was the root of what was bugging her. At the end of the weekend, Geoff had suggested no sex or sexual activity for the next several days, giving them a mental breather to wrap their minds around what had happened thus far. Which she'd agreed to, in theory, though her assent had felt hollow to her. They needed to keep pushing this. Didn't they see that, feel that, the way she did?

She shook her head. Even if she had talked to Flo about it, she wasn't sure how she would have presented it. Her mind was cycling like an engine caught in a higher gear, with no way to downshift. Then suddenly it switched off again, leaving her achy and uncertain. Strangely empty.

Fortunately her phone distracted her from the dilemma, with a beep tone that told her she'd received a text from Chris or Geoff.

When she opened it, she saw Geoff had sent one to them both. *Hey, Merry's got a free overnight for us at her Bat Cave place. The one with the crazy decorating and hot tub. Fri-Sat, just the three of us. Sound good?*

Chris had sent a thumbs-up emoticon, and she did the same. They'd gone up to Bat Cave before. The quaint little North Carolina town was in the shadow of Chimney Rock. However, on their previous trips they'd been there with Merry and her husband. This would be the first time they'd have the place to themselves, under their new circumstances.

She frowned. *Circumstances.* When people talked about a three-some, they thought of something temporary, a fling or fantasy come to life. She thought of what Chris had said, joking about the unrelenting demands of three-way sex. But that wasn't the main obstacle to thinking of a threesome as . . . a relationship. A permanent one. Society, emotions, jealousy . . . hell, tax returns. Things weren't set up for three people to be bonded, were they?

Going into her bedroom with a fruit snack, she sat down at her computer and pulled up the FetLife website, one of the more reputable lifestyle forums. She typed in *polyamory*. That was the term Flo's friends used, the ones Sam had met when Flo took her to their private parties.

From listening to their discussions, she knew swinging was categorized differently from polyamory. Yet polyamory had its own subcate-gories. Three or more polyamorous partners whose connections were primarily sexual were still considered different from swinging because the connections were long-term and consistent, though it appeared the lines could be blurred. Then there was further overlap with three or more partners who shared lives as married couples did, which could include child care, living together and providing emotional support as well as physical intimacy. While it reassured Sam to know her ques-tions weren't unique, the different opinions offered on the forum thread made her head spin.

Throw in the BDSM elements, and it became even more complex. There were plenty of permutations of Masters, subs, slaves, domestic discipline households and the like. As she read through different postings, she found some of it matched what she knew about her, Geoff and Chris, and some of it didn't. Did it have to fit, or was it like an ocean, with all different types of life and ecosystems that worked as a part of the whole? She liked thinking of it that way.

The funny thing was, she was a traditional girl. She'd always thought of a relationship as falling in love, getting married, maybe having kids. How did that work if she was in love with two men? What would her parents and siblings think? She wouldn't spend her life hiding who she loved. She was part of a practical, up-front family, and she couldn't see herself pretending to be something she wasn't with them, no matter their initial disapproval or negative reactions. They loved her and she loved them; hence, they'd work around to acceptance or at least tolerance in time. They all knew Geoff and Chris, and her parents liked them both a lot. Even though they'd initially had mixed feelings about her living with two men, they'd seemed okay with it when they understood it was a roommates situa-tion. Though her mother had nudged her in Chris's direction. Then Geoff's. Or maybe both?

Sam grinned, remembering the conversation she'd had with her mother on the Fourth of July. They'd been at Sam's parents' house for their annual picnic, and she and her mother were replenishing bowls of food her dad, her brothers, Chris and Geoff had demolished like locusts.

"That Chris is one nice young man," her mother said, filling up the

potato salad bowl anew. *"A hard worker, and kind. Kind is important."* She gave Sam a significant look.

"So's a really nice butt." Sam elbowed her mom with a grin. *"Both he and Geoff have that."*

"That's true enough." Her mother sniffed. *"But you already know love is more than a nice body."*

"Maybe, but if I agree, you'll go into full-blown matchmaking. You don't like Geoff?"

"I like them both. There's just . . . Geoff can be a little intimidating at times. I'm not sure if he'd be the best long-term partner." Her mother had paused thoughtfully. *"But he's smart, and I'm sure he'll be successful. And there's a sharpness to him that says he'd always take being the head of a family very seriously. Sometimes Chris is a little too . . . unfocused. Not in a bad way. I think he'll just need people in his life to give him direction and purpose."* She sighed. *"Too bad you can't just put the best parts of both of them together. Then you'd be all set. If you were interested in either one of them, that is."*

"Mom," Sam said with mock severity. *"No matchmaking."*

"Can't help it. It's a mother's right."

~

Her mother had inadvertently pointed to the exact solution Sam had reached herself. The two men together filled all her empty spaces and corners, and she thought maybe it worked the same for them. She hoped so.

Jace, her oldest brother, would probably be the first one to accept it. That thought took her to another get-together, this time a cookout they'd had at their own house, within the past couple of months. They'd invited a few friends and, since her brother only lived thirty miles away when he was home on leave, she'd invited him and his current flavor of the month.

It wasn't as derogatory as it sounded. She usually liked the girls Jace dated; it was merely obvious that he was with them for sexual companionship, rather than a long-term relationship. With Jace's looks and personality, he never lacked for female company to warm his bed when he was home.

Maybe Sam was overly romantic, but she believed it was never too early to find the love of your life, and she wanted that for him. She understood he was pretty dedicated to his military career and didn't feel there was yet room in it to start a family. He was always honest with and kind to the women, so she didn't have to go after him for being a dick. However, given his attitude toward his own relationships, he'd shown a surprising level of insight into her own situation.

At the cookout, she'd left off her teasing of Chris about his grilling style when Geoff had chased her away with a spatula, telling her outdoor cooking was serious man business. Jace was already eating one of the first round of burgers, so she came over to sit with him at their picnic table. As she leaned against him companionably, he gave her a bemused look. "You involved with either of them?" he'd asked in a neutral voice. "Or both?"

She was glad she wasn't eating anything, else she would have choked. Her knee-jerk reaction was to deny, to elbow her brother as if he was making a joke, but since he wasn't playing, suddenly she didn't want to do so, either. She hadn't broached anything with Geoff or Chris yet, though she'd been percolating on it more and more.

Out of all her siblings, she was closest to Jace, so it made sense that he'd picked up on what she hadn't yet voiced to anyone else.

"No and yes. It's complicated."

"Hmm. Can't choose?"

"Don't want to. Not sure . . . if I need to." She stole a glance at him, uncertain what she'd see in his expression.

Jace took a few more bites before he said anything else. "Well, it sounds strange saying this, but you three look good . . . as a unit. And you're happier than I've ever seen you. So whatever's happening or going on, as long as you stay that way, I'd say follow your heart. They're good men. Both of them. But if they fuck you over, I'll kick their asses. You know that, right?"

She put her arms around him. He was wearing his Captain America T-shirt, a gift she'd given him after he finished his first tour in Iraq. He'd worn it so much it was thin and fading. She loved him for that, despite the ribbing she knew friends in his unit gave him about it. "They watch after me as well as you do," she promised him. "They'd never hurt me on purpose. Whatever happens, whatever I decide . . . We'll make our stumbles together, if that makes sense."

"Yeah. Not like me and Traci. She's not all that much into the stumbling." He smiled at the pretty blonde he'd brought with him.

She was chatting with one of the wives of Esteban's landscaping crew. "Think she's mostly about hooking up with a hot military guy. When she realizes I'm no different from any other jerk who leaves his underwear on the floor—except I know how to deactivate bombs—she'll split. But it'll be fun while it lasts. I'm not where you are yet, little sis. That could be good, though. If you trip all the land mines first, you can put me on course when I find the right woman."

"Gee, thanks," she said. "Not that you'd listen anyway, you and your dumbass hard head. It's all about boobs and long legs for you."

"Hey, whoever I marry, it will be about way more than that, so it's best to take my fill of the shallow stuff while I can." He winked and pushed his plate at her. "Got any more of those burgers?"

Coming back to the present once again, Sam said her usual daily prayer for Jace, back overseas now, and studied the computer screen. She couldn't read any more of this. She wanted Geoff and Chris. That needy feeling was rising, capturing not only her body but her mind, disturbing her anew. Focusing on her reflection in the computer screen, she could tell she was too wound up. Maybe she should use her vibrator. Maybe more than once. Was it possible to get stuck in an "on" setting when it came to physical arousal? But these waves of agitation were more than being horny, a word she particularly despised for its crudity, so she wasn't sure why she was using it now.

To follow Geoff's rules, she'd need to text or call one of them to use the vibrator. Or she could say to hell with that, do it and not tell them at all. Or ask for forgiveness. She shifted. That wasn't what she wanted, either, damn it. A power exchange was a willing thing. It wasn't like Geoff could force her to ask permission to get off. But the point was she was giving him that control, right? That was what turned her on, as much as it did him.

She shoved away the chaotic roar of her hormones and whatever else was going on in her head and brought herself back to the more important topic at hand—whether this would work long-term. Was she naive to think the word *forever* when it came to the two of them? She wasn't a teenager anymore.

Maybe it was possible to integrate all of the possibilities and lock them in place with Chris's philosophy of slow living. Soak up the experience rather than worrying it away, all while remembering who and what was important. If they could do that, if she could do that, maybe they'd stumble into the right way to make a go of this.

"Sam, you home? Where are you, crazy girl?"

Things leaped up inside her, like swallowing a chocolate bar down whole. The surge of adrenaline was overpowering, the kind that came with doing something wrong that didn't have immediate consequences.

Stop it. Settle down, take a breath.

Shutting down the computer, she left her room and came into the kitchen. Chris was setting his lunch tote on the counter. He looked hot, tired and sweaty, as he usually did after a full day. He had a dirty bandage wrapped around his arm—also not unusual, since he often came home with scrapes. She went right to him, winding her arms around his neck and pressing her body insistently against him as she rose on her tiptoes to bring her lips to his.

He looked a little startled, but then he figured out the same thing she had in the time it took her to get from her room to the kitchen. They could do this now, greet each other as lovers did at the end of the workday. He cradled her head in one big hand and deepened the kiss, pressing her against the counter. She curved her leg over his hip, willing him to put her up on the counter, press himself between her legs, relieve her all-over throbbing, but instead he moved her back, lips tugging in a smile.

"I'm filthy. I'll get you all dirty."

She so didn't care, but she forced herself to go back to her heels. "What happened to your arm?"

Chris rolled his eyes. "New guy on the crew. Don was swiping at a bee with his clippers and took a nice chunk out of my arm. Idiot. Think he'll work out okay, though, if he doesn't manage to kill us all first."

"Did you—"

"Yes, Nurse Nancy, I disinfected it and kept it clean. All's good. I'm going to go hit the showers. Geoff's on his way home—on time, for once. He's going to pick up some salads and fish sandwiches from Whole Foods. Pretty cool about the Bat Cave thing, right?"

"Yeah." She trailed him to the bathroom and watched him strip off the shirt. He hesitated when she was in the door.

"Oh, sorry." She started to move away, but he shook his head, offering her a half smile with enough lazy promise to uncurl warmth in her stomach.

"No, you're welcome to stay. Just getting used to it, you know. In a good way."

He stripped off his clothes, leaned in and started the shower. Her gaze slid down his back and over his bare haunches, but when he began to unwrap the bandage, she came forward and took over. She told herself to focus on his arm, not the tempting weight of his genitals, so close she could brush her thighs against them.

She grimaced. "*Chunk* is right. This is going to leave a scar."

"Won't be my first." He kissed her cheek, reached into the shower and flicked water at her, making her draw back with a mock scowl before he stepped in and closed the shower door.

His cock had started to rise at her proximity, she noted, and wondered if that was why he'd so quickly moved under the spray. Chris had agreed to Geoff's mandate about no sexual activity for the next several days. Yet Chris was aroused by her presence, so why shouldn't they take advantage of that? If she slipped into the shower, he wouldn't deny her, would he? She fingered the hem of her shirt. All she had to do was strip it off, after all . . .

Chris spoke, his deep voice echoing off the tile amid the rush of water. "Geoff said to have you make up some of your famous lemonade to go with the fish. Mr. High and Mighty said you'd better have it ready when he gets home, or else."

She did like those masterful ultimatums, though she knew when her chain was being jerked. "I can see this whole Dom thing is going to his head."

"Yeah, I could have warned you about that. If you spit in his lemonade, I won't blame you. Just set mine apart before you do it."

She would have happily sat there and watched Chris run his capable hands over every inch of his powerful body, including all the tempting crevices, but she reluctantly left him to do as bidden. She was pretty sure she wasn't going to stay outside the shower if she remained another minute. Besides, Chris was studiously not looking at her, making it clear she was a temptation he had to avoid. It irritated her a little bit.

She needed to lighten up; she knew that. As she fixed the lemonade, she turned on her iPod and did a little disco improv around the kitchen to the Bee Gees classic "Staying Alive." Fortunately, it did lift her mood. Putting the pitcher in the fridge, she saw Geoff pull into the driveway, and those good feelings spiked further. She watched him get out and head up the walkway, handsome and serious in his suit.

As he entered the kitchen, she had the lemonade in a glass and was posed provocatively with it, like she'd done for Chris. Only today, instead of being naked, she had her T-shirt tied up under her breasts, baring her midriff and highlighting her breasts. When she was squarely in his sights, she shook down her hair in a practiced move she'd perfected in high school. She hadn't used the move since well before Anthony, the stalker ex-boyfriend Chris and Geoff had helped her banish into her past once and for all.

"Your lemonade as ordered, Master," she purred.

Geoff wasn't a 24/7-type Dom, any more than she intended to become their domestic servant, but he'd probably do things like this to tease or remind her of those moments when it would be about that. She was good with that, and teasing him back.

Geoff's lips curved, but the playful note she'd intended came out as mocking challenge, and he detected it. As her mother had said, he was sharp. A trace of puzzlement filtered through his expression. She set aside the lemonade to come to him, wanting to give him the same hello kiss she'd given Chris.

True to his nature, Geoff was even more demanding about it, setting down his briefcase and wrapping his arm around her, bringing her up on her toes as he kissed her back, scoring her bottom lip sharply.

His five-o'clock shadow was less coarse than Chris's, something she'd noticed before, but this hyperawareness of every difference, every sensation, was a delightful part of the change in their relationship. As she inhaled his aftershave, a contrast to Chris's earthy sweat, she thought she might be one of the luckiest women in the world, having the opportunity to indulge herself in those pleasurable variances with no restraint. She should have no complaints, no issues.

"Smartass," Geoff muttered, referencing her lemonade pose. He drew back and gave her a closer inspection. "Good day at work?"

"An even better end to it," she said. She'd push past this. No reason they needed to deal with her weirdly vacillating moods. "You have the food? I can get it set up if you want to change. Chris is showering."

"Sure. That'd be great." But he gave her one last penetrating look before he went down the hall.

She threw herself into the routine they all knew. Fortunately, things did level out for the next couple of hours. Maybe just having them close was all she needed. There was a lovely, different cadence to their three-way bond now, exercised in ways large and small. Lingering touches, easy affection, intimate teasing.

Geoff was looking out for all of them, right? Emotional recuperation was important. Time to breathe and think. Plus, him and Chris making the mature decision that it wouldn't be 24/7 sex should make her feel even better about her earlier thoughts. This was how a normal relationship worked. Quiet times, companionship, mixed with intimacy. Friendship. And the really hot sex. Right here at her fingertips, if she could force the issue.

She had that thought as Chris was loading the dishwasher and Geoff was settling down with his work. Her phrasing, the use of the word "force", gave her a start. Why was she trying to challenge Geoff? What was the problem, damn it?

If she could have some kind of physical release, maybe she could settle down. She just needed to feel a little more in control of what was happening inside her. Though she was eagerly embracing her submission, something was warring with it, saying that she needed to assert herself. Make sure there was a balance.

Or maybe it was the inner child poking out her lip and saying, *He can't tell me what to do.*

Shaking her head at herself, she left them to change into her pajamas. Pausing over her choices in the dresser drawer, she didn't pull out the flannels and comfortable oversized T-shirt she would have normally worn. The T-shirt was an extra large freebie Geoff had given her some time ago after he'd run a half marathon for the animal shelter charity drive.

He'd chastised her about wearing provocative outfits in front of them, but that was before they'd all been sexually intimate. Now they could act on it if they wanted to do so, right? It was fine for Geoff to act as Dom, but they hadn't agreed he could impose things on her full-time. Okay, yeah, some things, sort of. But this was still a willing thing, and ultimately they were equal partners. She could change the rules if she wanted to do so.

She withdrew a baby tee and coupled it with gray jersey shorts she donned over a hot pink pair of panties with a high Brazilian cut. The light pink T-shirt was thin, showing off the shape of her nipples. When she was curled on her hip in her favorite reading chair, the shorts would ride up the curve of her ass. Just enough to make them a little bit crazy, which seemed quid pro quo, since she was all crazy at this point.

Don't do this, Sam.

Why not?

Her mind couldn't give her the right answer. Her gaze fell on the Naughty Bits envelope she'd pulled out of the mail, and she seized the distraction it offered. Coming back into the living room holding it, she pasted a smile on her face, trying to pretend she had on nothing out of the ordinary. Their new intimacy was simply making her comfortable wearing less around them. It wasn't like she was doing it as a deliberate provocation.

Which she was.

Chris was stretched out on the floor, his feet up on the arm of her reading chair. Geoff was on the couch reading through something work-related while Chris channel surfed.

"Hey, look what we got in the mail." She waved the invitation. Her cheeks were flushed, so she kept her head down as she spoke. "Madison is doing a benefit for an erotica theater she's planning."

She placed the brochure on the coffee table where they could both see it. "She's calling it Carnival in the Round. It'll be in that old theater in downtown Matthews. There'll be performances with whip play, wax, all sorts of things. Says it's a fetish costume thing, so we can dress up however we want. Or not at all, but I think I'd like to, even if you two don't. There will be changing areas at the theater if needed. What do you think?"

She was talking in a rush of words, so she made herself shut up and backed into her reading chair, sinking down in it and curling her legs up beneath her. She dared to give Chris's bare feet propped there a quick caress, then she drew a steadying breath and raised her gaze.

She realized immediately she should have looked at Chris first. She met Geoff's cool hazel eyes, inscrutable as a sphinx's. Her cheeks flushed anew. "Hmm," he said. His gaze swept her, then Geoff put his feet down from the coffee table with a decided *thump*. She jumped, but he merely leaned forward to pick up the invitation. She looked toward Chris, trying a casual smile. He was trying to look anywhere but where it was obvious he wanted to look, at her scantily clad body, so he turned his attention to the invite when Geoff handed it to him. After Chris set it on the table, the two men exchanged a glance.

"I think it's time to give her the gifts we set aside for her birthday," Geoff said. "One in particular."

Chris's mouth tightened as if he was undecided about that, but when he glanced her way at last, his gaze latched on to her trembling breasts and bare legs. For some reason, when her nervous gaze slid back to Geoff, she felt exposed in the wrong way.

"I think you may be right," Chris said at last.

"My birthday isn't for another month," she said. "And we're supposed to buy only small things. We agreed."

"Well, in this case there was an exception clause to that agreement, supported by two of the three signing members." Geoff gave her a trace of his normal smile, which made her feel easier and, oddly, a little ashamed. She crossed her arms over her breasts. Not trying to hide them. Not exactly.

"I wasn't aware the agreement was based on popular vote," she said.

Chris took one of her hands, pulling it away from her body. "This one time it is. You know you never have to buy me anything for my birthday, anyway. Just make one of those white layer cakes with the powdered sugar on it."

"Suck-up," Geoff grumbled. Rising from the couch, he took her other hand. Her fingers were tense, but she curled them over his, absorbing the strength and heat as he brought her to her feet. "Stand up straight, Samantha Beth. You wanted us to look at you. So let us look."

She swallowed, but when she would have spoken, he touched her mouth. "Not a word. Unless you want me to take off those nonexistent panties, stick them in your mouth and keep them there with duct tape."

She stilled. His tone was velvet over steel, as was his expression, and she wasn't the only one brought up short by it, or by the shocking words. Chris's fingers had dropped to caress her ankle, and now they paused, as if he'd looked up at Geoff to see if the menacing tenor was a joke. It hadn't been, but Geoff tightened his fingers on her, caressing her pulse.

"It's all right. Come on, sweetheart."

He called her that when he wanted to reassure her, and it worked. She let out an unsteady breath. Chris rose with a warm look, which helped further. Geoff led her to his room and snapped on the light. "Your gift is in a box under the bed."

When he didn't move to get it, she moistened her lips. Chris twitched beside her, but Geoff shifted. She was pretty sure he'd motioned to Chris to let her get it. In this outfit, that would be quite a show. She started to move toward the side, so she wouldn't be sticking her ass up in front of them, but Geoff spoke.

"You'll reach it easier from the end of the bed."

She met his gaze. If he'd still had that terrifyingly cool look, she honestly might have bolted, but he gave her a wink, and a genuine smile. "You know how Chris is about watching a woman bend over. Don't deprive him of the small joys in life."

She chuckled nervously. "How about you?"

His eyes flamed, a sudden lick of fire she felt on every erogenous zone on her body. "Everything you do only makes me want you more, Sam."

He nodded toward the bed again. She hesitated as she got on her hands and knees, that sense of shame still interfering with her reaction, but then she thought of Chris in the shower, Geoff meeting her at the door. She was theirs, damn it, and she wanted them to know it, see it, push past whatever bullshit this was to get back to what she'd felt with them this weekend. Both of them in tune with her body and her mind, touching her, holding her, taking her over peak after peak.

So fine. She could make that really clear. She dropped to her knees and, with a flexibility that made her very pleased with her yoga practice, she went down on her elbows in a move that stretched out her back like a cat and lifted her ass. As she ducked her head to locate the box, her knees were spread enough they'd be seeing the crotch of her hot pink panties through the loose opening of the short shorts.

"You've got this pretty far back," she said, her voice muffled.

"I know how nosy you get."

"I would never go through your things without you saying it was okay," she said, coming out with the box and a mock-indignant look, an attempt to coax them all back to a more teasing mood. She wished she'd worn the other pajamas. "Unlike other people who knew where I keep my vibrator."

"You won't go through my things, but you'll masturbate on my bed." Geoff crossed his arms. "Want to quibble over privacy issues?"

She stuck her tongue out at him, but when he merely raised a brow, unsmiling, he chased her teasing away like a strong wind dispersing a cloud. She was on her knees at his feet, a distinct psychological disadvantage, so she turned her attention to the package. They'd already wrapped it. Despite the weird mood in the room, it touched her to see the gray-and-silver packaging with the curly ribbon. They'd probably had the store wrap it up, but even so.

"Pull the storage box out," Geoff ordered in a neutral tone. "The one that was next to it."

She did so, this time her fingers trembling, because the heat of their attention on her nearly bare haunches felt like burning flame, incinerating her stomach and lower areas, an uncomfortable mix of arousal and humiliation.

When she sat back on her heels, Geoff was right behind her. She drew in a startled breath as he gripped her breasts in the tight T-shirt and used that firm hold to bring her off her heels, standing her upon her knees as he fondled her curves, plucked at her nipples. The inexorable handling of her body made her panties wetter than they already were. He didn't let her lean up against him, straight-arming her so it was all about what he wanted to do. As if he was both rewarding and punishing her. Chris's simmering look felt like his hands were on her as well.

"Geoff . . ." she whispered.

"Open your gift, Sam," he said, moving away from her.

He must have read the incoherent plea she was feeling, for forgiveness, for something, because his expression softened. "Open the gift, sweetheart," he said. "It will be all right."

Chris stroked her hair back from her face. "If you don't like it, we can take it back."

"If you two bought it, I'll love it," she said. They'd never bought her a gift she didn't adore. Sometimes they knew what she wanted better than she herself did, though Geoff had teased her once that they rarely had the chance to prove it, since she usually printed out and circled exactly whatever it was she wanted for birthdays or Christmas. Within the strict budget they'd set.

The storage box didn't give her any clues to its contents, but the ribbon on the wrapped package was held in place with a pretty silver tag that said *Naughty Bits*. Chris sat down on the bed next to where she was kneeling, while Geoff took a seat in a chair. She looked up at him. "May I open it?"

He'd already told her she could, but their sudden intimacy made things feel . . . better, clearer. Maybe she was just looking for the additional reinforcement, offering him proof that she wanted to behave, to do the right things.

At his nod, she freed the tape at the corners and peeled back the wrapping paper. Madison, the owner of Naughty Bits, used the good, thick kind. The box was about the size of a dress box. When she pulled off the lid, her eyes widened.

"Oh, guys. You shouldn't have."

But she was amazed and thrilled that they had. It was the full-head mask she'd seen at the shop. It was designed to look like a bird's head, with silver-gray tightly overlapped feathers. It would be a perfect match for the silver-gray corset Geoff had bought for her, which they'd not yet had a chance to try out. She fingered the soft, silky mask. "It's so beautiful."

"Not as beautiful as it'll be when you're wearing it," Geoff said. Chris's fingertips whispered along her collarbone, tracing bare skin under her T-shirt. She pressed her cheek to his hand briefly as Geoff spoke, reaching out to touch her hair. "You can wear this the night we go to Madison's event."

"I hope you guys will dress up, too," she said.

"Well, now that you mention it, I got something for Chris, too. It's in the other box." He tossed a grin at Chris. "I didn't wrap yours, so no pouting."

Chris rolled his eyes. "You're so insensitive to my feelings," he complained in a girlish tone.

She chuckled but noticed Chris looked a little wary when she opened the lid of the storage box. All the things they'd bought from Naughty Bits were there in neat arrangement. Rope, Velcro cuffs, the soft flogger. The gray corset. She passed her fingers over the flogger, wondering, thinking, but took her fingers away quickly when Geoff gave her a glance. *My toys, not yours,* that look clearly said, which was kind of thrilling.

"It's in the purple bag," he told Chris. Chris picked it up and shook out the contents, a mix of latex, straps and metal. As he separated the two items and spread them out, Sam felt a little leap in her chest.

"No way," Chris said emphatically.

It was a pair of latex pants and an upper-body harness. When she touched the thin material of the pants, she could tell they were intended to fit Chris like a second skin. She thought of the fabric pasting itself to the muscular curves of his ass, clinging to the weight of his testicles and cock, which would be nice and erect. The straps would delineate every roll of biceps and pecs, like those of a barbarian warrior.

"A suitable look for a dove's guardian, I thought," Geoff said, unperturbed by Chris's abject refusal. "Sam, what do you think?"

"If he wears it, I won't be able to stop looking at him. Just thinking about him in it makes me want him a hundred different ways."

Chris blinked as a slow smile crossed Geoff's face. "Our dove is at her most irresistible when she's unfiltered. And honest."

That last word hit Sam in a way that made her eyes slide away from Geoff's again. She could feel him marking her avoidance like a brand on her cheek.

Chris grimaced. "Yeah. And you knew I couldn't say no if she wanted me to wear it."

Sam put a hand on his arm. "Don't worry. I bet there will be plenty of people dressing up. I'll call Madison and make sure. But if you feel embarrassed, you don't have to do it. Really."

Chris's expression grew troubled. "Sam, I can't say no to anything you want. Do you get that, what it means?"

She bit her lip, uncertain of how to reply. Geoff stepped in to answer for her. "Yes, she does. Without a doubt. But she's forgotten that with that power comes a pretty serious responsibility."

Sam's brow creased. "I just said he didn't—"

"Not that. Look at me, Sam." When she complied, reluctantly, Geoff spoke in an even tone. "You wore this outfit, thinking you could make me override the rules I set about these next couple of days, which were intended to give all of us time to consider what we're doing here. It was a direct challenge. You crave submission, but you're trying to push us around." He shifted his glance to Chris. "Which means she's being a brat."

"I wasn't trying to act that way," she protested.

"It was disrespectful." Geoff shot her an ominous look she wasn't sure how to interpret. She usually noticed the playful beneath the façade, but he didn't look playful at all. "If all you want is a little slap and tickle, fun in the bedroom, that's a whole different ball of wax from what we did this weekend. Is that what you're wanting?"

He took a step forward. She suppressed an irrational desire to scoot backward on her knees. So far, she'd experienced flashes of the pure, undiluted version of the type of Dom Geoff could be, enough to know his particular blend of domination and sadism called to the kind of submissive she was. However, the manner in which she was starting to tremble now, with a mix of anticipation and anxious fear that coiled into a tight ball of sexual and emotional need, told her just how good a match it was.

She could stand up, tell him to piss off. If she did only want the slap and tickle he'd just described, that's exactly what she would have done. Instead she held her spot on her knees, tilting her head as he took another step toward her. She could almost hear the click as the give-and-take sharpened, coming into better focus for both of them.

"No, I don't think so." She was barely whispering.

"You don't *think* so. You're not sure, because instead of thinking about what's really happening here, you've been fucking with our heads."

"Geoff," Chris said, low.

"It's okay, Chris," her Master said. "Trust me."

She noticed his tone changed when he talked to Chris. Still in control, but more peer to peer, asking Chris to trust his lead based on the friendship they shared. Chris said nothing further, though she could feel his tension and uncertainty, a different form of her own. A muscle flexed in Geoff's jaw, but his hazel eyes never left hers.

"There's nothing we take more seriously than your well-being, Sam. That requires your respect. As Chris said, there's nothing we won't do for you, and when you give us conflicting desires and push it, that's moving right into brat territory."

Her gaze darted to Chris. In a blink, Geoff closed the distance between them and jerked her face back up to look at him. "Looking over at him to see if he can protect you, because he has the softer heart or is less experienced in dealing with a submissive like you, is not the way to go. Unless you want the punishment to be worse."

"No sir," she stammered. As his expression hardened, she amended that. "No, *Master*."

Just like that, things started to level out. That itchy-in-her-own-skin feeling receded, her heart emerging from the confusing thicket of emotions with its sharp barbs. Geoff took such uncertainty away when he took full command. Had that been the problem all along? This weekend had opened a whole tangle of things for her and, as soon as things returned to a normal routine, she'd been floundering. Had putting on the outfit, teasing them like this, been like a call for help, not wanting to have to exercise her own self-control? She wasn't that kind of person. Yet she wanted to be sure Chris and Geoff would hold the reins when she needed leveling out. Was that wrong? Inexplicably, tears stabbed at her eyes. Why couldn't she figure this out for herself?

"I'm sorry," she said. "I'd never treat you guys like that. Not . . . if I'd been thinking."

Geoff still held her chin, making her look at him. While she was flushed, under that she felt pale, shaky. He was waiting, quiet now, just watching her. When he lifted the hand at his side, a small twitch, she expected it was a signal for patience to Chris, and his quiet words toward the other man confirmed it.

"She's different from you, Chris," he said, a cryptic warning. "She needs a stronger hand. *Wants* a stronger hand."

He was waiting for her to find it, to figure it out. And she did. Something locked down, centered. Though she was nervous about being so blatant in front of Chris, she lowered her eyes. She knew Geoff was finding his center in all of this, learning how to be the right kind of Master for her, and they were having to trust each other along that new path. She had to admit he'd hit the right trigger this time, because the words came to her lips practically without thought.

"Yes sir. I was wrong. Please forgive me."

"Will punishment help you forgive yourself?"

The relief that spread through her chest answered that. Wondering at it, she nodded, and his grip tightened. "Yes, Master."

"All right, then. Stand up and take off everything you're wearing. Those clothes are intended to tempt your Masters. Naked, you have nothing to use for guile. You're simply ours, serving our will. When you've done that, pull two sets of Velcro cuffs out of the box and hand them to me."

She could say this was too much, game over, but Chris's watching silence and something else swirling in her breast told her that this wasn't too much. She swallowed, a silent assent. When Geoff stepped back, she removed her clothes under their intent regard, folded and set them aside. Then she bent and removed the cuffs from the box. She brought them to Geoff and his fingers brushed hers. She shivered.

"Are you cold?" he asked.

She shook her head. "No sir. Just nervous. And unsettled. But right, too, for the first time all day."

Geoff swept her hair off her brow, and she welcomed the caressing touch like water for thirst. "We love you, Sam. You understand that? If there's anything you can't handle, that feels wrong to you, you tell me. And we won't be angry with you. Do you understand I'm not angry with you now?"

She nodded.

"I don't think Chris is as sure," he said. "He looks ready to whisk you away from me. Which is why he's going to be the one punishing you."

In her peripheral vision, Chris started. While she wondered if he'd go along with that, Sam understood her Master's decision. He and Chris would do anything she truly desired, but Geoff exercised a certain level of intuition and judgment to figure out what those desires truly were. Chris would simply take at face value what she said she desired, because that was the kind of heart he had: open and generous, no guile to him.

She'd tested Geoff, knowing subconsciously he'd react just as he had, tolerating that shit only so far. Whereas Chris was her safety net, the definition of home, a place of unconditional acceptance. Which made him a treasure she should never take for granted, and Geoff was going to make sure she didn't. Her punishment had to come from Chris, because her infraction against him was worse.

She expected to be told to kneel again or to stretch out on the bed. Instead, Geoff clasped her elbow and guided her out of the room. Taking her down the hallway, he turned left and went through the laundry room to pass through the door to the garage, Chris following behind them with his heavy tread.

Since they'd told her she couldn't go into the garage, she'd imagined a lot of things, but it was still a crazy, arousing shock to find a spanking bench, with polished cherry-colored wood and a blue cushion. Geoff propelled her toward it as her stomach somersaulted. "What do you think?" he asked. "It could use another coat of finish, and we're still making some modifications, but it's close to being all done."

"I . . . I love it." She was also a little terrified, realizing they could restrain her on it, making her truly helpless. She suspected Geoff planned to prove that to her right now.

Taking the cuffs from her hand, he clasped her wrists and guided her fingertips to the bench, permitting her to explore the way it felt.

"When it's all done, we'll put you on your stomach on the bench, and bend your legs so your shins are flat on these side pieces," he said. "It's like that Child's Pose you do for yoga, which keeps you accessible for spanking, switching, fucking your ass or cunt . . . whatever we want to do."

Her fingers trembled and his grip on her wrist tightened, moving her hand to the cushion, trailing her fingers along that edge. "When we need it, there will be an adjustable chin piece to hold your head up, so we can see every reaction on your beautiful face to what we're doing to you. It will also support your neck when you take either of us in your mouth. Do you like your gift?"

"Yes," she said, her voice hoarse. "Very much." There were rings at different places along the sides that would hold straps or cuffs or whatever else he'd use to restrain her.

"Good. We'll look forward to using it that way, at another time. But this is about punishment, isn't it? A punishment you need."

"Yes sir."

Geoff put his palm on her back, applying pressure so she was perpendicular to the bench, bending over it. The lower piece he'd described as being there to support her shin pressed like a bar against her hipbones.

"Stay like that," Geoff ordered. She couldn't see Chris, but she knew he was there, standing outside her line of vision, watching.

Removing a tie-down strap from the drawer of a toolbox, Geoff attached it to the short end of the bench. He ran the strap over the back of her neck and fixed it to the other end, ratcheting it down so she was held in her bent-over position. He used the cuffs to stretch her arms out across the bench and hook them to the same ring. The tops of her breasts pressed against the cushion. Her legs started to quake as he fixed the second set of cuffs to her ankles and hooked them to the wooden legs so her thighs were spread apart. Geoff smoothed a hand down her back, played with the ends of her hair.

"She's beautiful this way, Chris. She's gotten wet as I've bound her, because that's how she reacts to restraint. Come feel."

Chris's fingers slid down her buttock and between her legs. She let out a soft moan and twitched against his touch.

"She knows she needs a punishment, Chris. It arouses her, even as it feeds something inside her, makes her feel better." Geoff dipped his fingers into her pussy and she whimpered as he collected her reaction there. "You think you can't do it, because you're standing outside this moment, believing this is about a man abusing a woman, striking someone you love. But holding her when she cries brings her comfort. So does this, in an entirely different way. It will release the negative feelings that have built up inside her, that have made her act so oddly tonight. Those tears you saw in her eyes a little while ago that she didn't shed? They're burning her from the inside, and she needs to let them out."

God yes. As Geoff spoke the words she hadn't known how to voice, those tears were thickening in her throat. Sam's fingers curled in her bonds.

"How do you know that?" Chris asked, his voice low. She wanted to answer it, but she wasn't sure if she could. Geoff did, though.

"It's something a Dom just gets sometimes, especially if he knows the sub well enough. Sam and I . . . well, we haven't done anything actively before this weekend, but we've picked up things from each other, the same way you and I have, the way the two of you have. It's harder for you, Chris, because being a Dom isn't your natural thing, but most of us have some topping desires. She brings those out in you. You're just wondering if they're right or wrong feelings."

Sam bit her lip as Chris's hand passed over her labia again, so deliberately she wondered if Geoff had guided his hand. "Does that feel right? Does her body language, those soft whimpers, the feverish look in her eye, tell you that you're right? You follow leads she gives you. Most times they don't involve words. You're a master at picking up subtle cues, Chris. Better than me."

She was sure that captured Chris's attention, because while she knew Geoff respected and admired Chris, he often played the arrogant know-it-all to tease his friend. But now he was being honest, keeping it all real and grounded, helping all of them.

"Look at the things your eyes and heart tell you about how she's feeling right now, what she's wanting. Talk to her, touch her. What I said to her goes for you. If it doesn't feel right, then you step back, and I'll do it for her, no shame. But I think you should try it."

"I don't want to hit her with anything."

Geoff paused. "How about your hand? You have large, powerful hands, Chris. See how her thighs trembled just now, and she lifted up some, thinking about you spanking her?" Geoff rubbed his own hand across both her buttocks, earning an aroused note from her working throat. "Talk to her, Chris."

He stepped back, and she waited. She could sense Chris thinking, struggling. Then her Master gave her the go-ahead to speak.

"Tell him, Sam. Tell him what's in your heart."

"Chris," she said, a raw plea. "I need you."

Geoff was right, about the difference between how she'd felt earlier and this. Giving them a simple, honest request from her soul, versus trying to push them into doing something, felt so much better. The results were far better, too.

Chris came to her side and dropped to his heels so they were eye to eye. If she'd seen only misery in his gaze, she would have exhorted Geoff to let him out of it, to step away from this, but she saw a different kind of conflict.

"You're such a gentle soul," she said softly. Her voice was breaking from nerves, but that was okay. "Yet you're fierce, protective. A fighter. I've also seen you get pissed, not in a mean way, when I've teased you too much or played pranks on you when you're tired and grumpy." A little smile crossed her face. "This is for every time you've wanted to paddle my butt, and I know you have, because when I've seen it in your eyes, it's made me hot all over."

His face tightened. The emotions passing through his gaze suggested he might be as swamped by them right now as she was by her own feelings. She had to look away and speak to the wall. "I'm telling you it's okay, something I want. But I can't talk about it much. I need you to understand without words, so that it's not my idea, if that makes sense. I need it to be something you want to do as much as I need you to do it. That's what Geoff is trying to say."

Chris skimmed a thumb over her bottom lip, drawing her eyes back to him. He tested the strap over her neck and ran his fingers beneath it, seeing how much pressure it was exerting. His care added a poignant element to his attention upon her. She teased his thumb with her tongue, and a muscle flexed in his strong jaw.

"Geoff was right," she said. "I wanted you both to take me over and use me however you wanted, not caring about the consequences. Not thinking about how you would both feel if you rushed this or hurt me in the wrong way, trying to do what I was demanding rather than what I really need." Those unshed tears Geoff had mentioned were scalding her throat. "It was a betrayal of what I value most about all of us . . ."

Geoff put his hand on her hip, the pressure of his fingers stopping her. "No. You don't get to be that harsh on yourself, Samantha Beth. You're just dealing with a lot of crazy feelings. You'd cut off a leg before you betrayed either of us. We know that."

She accepted that gentle reproof for the gift it was. Chris's brown eyes were reading everything she said and didn't say. She wouldn't be surprised if he knew the exact count of the tears on the brink of that dam of need she was barely containing.

"It's hard to understand, to explain all this, but you already under-stand so many things without words, Chris. This is one of those things. The more you think about it, the harder it is to justify or understand. So you've just got to decide if it feels right inside you. And whatever you want to do . . . Geoff is right. It's all okay."

She was running out of words, her heart pumping faster, the restraint making thought processes more difficult. "Chris . . ." But she stopped there. Everything she wanted was in how she said his name.

She let out a thready sigh as his lips touched the corner of her mouth and held there. "You do look incredibly hot like this," Chris murmured against her mouth. "You're right. I can't explain the why of it. Makes me uncomfortable. But not too uncomfortable."

She moistened her lips and he kissed them again, playing with her tongue with his own. Sliding his hands along her stretched arms, he reached her bound wrists. He caressed them, sending tendrils of sensation questing up her arms and into her breasts before he came back to her nape. When he broke the kiss, he studied her a long moment. Then he rose.

As he moved behind her, Geoff stepped back. Not being able to see either of them made her pulse accelerate. She wondered what thoughts were passing between them, what they were planning.

She jumped as Chris touched her, but settled as he began to rub her ass, making wide, firm circles, so wide the heel of his hand teased her labia. She lifted her hips up, begging for more, but he kept making those circles, taking his time, indulging himself. He'd figured out having her tied up like this allowed him to play with her as much as he wanted. And of course the flip side of her trying to tease them past their self-imposed restraint was that she was now riding a knife edge of sexual frustration. Yet she sensed Geoff's ultimate intent was to take care of that in a way she wouldn't soon forget. She didn't mean that in a good way. After all, sexual frustration could be a form of torture, too.

Whap! Chris struck his first blow. He came from below, hitting the meatiest part of her buttock. Was Geoff using hand signals to show him the best way to do it, or had they discussed it while building the bench? Either idea worked her up more.

Chris being Chris, he wasn't going to need much instruction. He stuck with that side for a couple more strikes, as she strangled on a moan and strained on her toes, lifting her ass even higher. His muttered expletive told her he didn't disapprove of her reaction. When he struck the other buttock, she cried out at the new burst of sensation. That seemed to intrigue him. He took advantage of the breadth of his palm and hit both at once.

"Oh God..." She couldn't stop making sounds of pleasure and need. He swept a palm up her back, tightened his fingers in her hair, pulling, and her pussy spasmed when he combined that firm hold with another set of blows.

Back and forth, then across both. She was dancing on her toes, and he started hitting harder, making the sting last longer. Punishment, as Geoff had said. She hadn't realized a hand spanking could become this painful, but if Geoff was guiding him, he obviously knew how to take it in that direction. Her reaction was only encouraging Chris to make it rougher. She held back a few curses of her own, yet she couldn't stop straining for more.

By the time Chris finally stopped, she was gasping and biting back a plea for mercy. It felt bad and good, so she didn't really want him to stop, even though she was flinching at every blow.

"I'm standing behind him and have my hand on his cock, Sam," Geoff said conversationally. "He's figured out there's an upside to spanking your ass. I think he should jerk off in front of you and deny you a single taste, because you've been such a bad girl. Would you like that?"

She shook her head. Words escaped her for a moment, because she was imagining Geoff pressed up against Chris behind her, fondling his cock out of her view. "No," she said plaintively. "Please. I want to—"

"This isn't about what you want. Is it, Sam?" Geoff's snap cut across her plea. She bit back another of those sobs that rose up to try and choke her. "Answer me."

"No sir," she said in a small voice.

"That's right. Chris, it's up to you. Decision's in your hands. Quite literally." Geoff's grim humor did nothing to alleviate Sam's sensual misery. "My turn with her ass. You've warmed it up good and made it tender for what's coming next."

Maybe Geoff's suggestion to Chris had been intended to distract her from that deliberate threat. Thank God, Chris cooperated, moving in front of her. Geoff was right. He was impressively aroused against the fly of his camo pants. Her attention climbed to his face, finding so many raging, unspoken responses there, it stole her voice once again. Keeping his gaze on her, Chris unzipped his pants, reaching in to scoop out his cock. The shaft was thick and tall, the broad head baptized with glistening pre-come that made her want to taste. She licked her lips, communicating that desire, and he registered it with a glimmer of primal male satisfaction.

She cried out as Geoff struck her with something that felt like a square of flat rubber, the flexibility giving it a hard sting. She saw Chris's momentary pause, his check that her reaction was mixed with as much arousal as pain. She couldn't hide anything from him, from either of them, and she was glad of it, because it meant Chris started to stroke himself.

Geoff wrested a feminine grunt from her with each blow, and she pulled against her bonds, lifting up for more. She clung hungrily to what Chris was doing. Her pussy was throbbing, her nipples tight peaks below the press of the side piece of the bench. Her entire body was tingling, and her heart was so full of emotions she was afraid it might break her ribs. When Chris paused again, studying her, she realized tears had spilled from her eyes, and her lips were drawn back in a grimace of total frustration. Oh God, how could she want and not want something so aggressively at the same time, so it felt like she was in danger of being ripped apart?

Chris pushed his cock back into his pants, zipped them and dropped to his heels, fingers tented on the ground, his face close. She let out a strangled noise as the rubber item landed again, vibrating through every needy nerve. Chris traced the tracks of her tears, and she burrowed her cheek into his hand, kissing, biting. With each hit, an excruciating arrow of arousal stabbed between her legs, all her limbs stretched and straining, her stomach muscles quivering. Yet maybe because of how Chris was touching her face, on the next blow, what was pressing inside her rib cage cracked through.

Physical desire was yanked back to a place where it hummed and heated, while her emotions shot her to another kind of precipice.

"Please . . ." She wailed it, and Geoff hit her again.

"Please what, Samantha Beth?"

"I'm sorry. I won't tease my Masters again. Not like that."

"It's impossible for you not to tease your Masters. Your very scent teases us, the way your body moves, the parting of your lips when you talk, the hint of your tongue. Chris is even now imagining it curling around his cock, while all I want to do is take mine out and shove it into this wet, pink cunt of yours."

"Please . . ." She would endure any amount of strikes from whatever horrible thing he was using for that.

"That's what you want us to do? Even though I said we weren't going to do that for the next few days?"

She shook her head, then nodded, and then started crying in earnest. There it was. The dam breaking. The erotic intensity of the moment was a contrasting rush of fire.

"But I want you both so much, all the time," she sobbed. "I can't stop. I've wanted you for so long, and now I have you, and . . . it's never enough . . . I need you so much and I don't know how to be kind, or smart, or slow, or right about it . . . I'm scared . . . scared it's going to be gone before I can hold on to it. I don't care how much it hurts, or how right or wrong it is . . . ever . . . just please . . ."

The incomprehensible words came so fast she started choking on them, her head pounding with the force of her emotions, her fingers clawing for purchase on something, anything. She'd been given a gift so large, she hadn't known what to do with it or where to start, only that she wanted to claw her way to the center of it and never come out.

Ever since the very first moment she'd met them, it had been here, waiting, deep inside her soul. These were the two men who would love her in the for-a-lifetime way she needed and wanted. It was such an unbelievably rare treasure that, only by burrowing as deep inside that love as she could, would she feel safe and balanced with it. If she stayed on the periphery, gave herself a respite from the feeling, she feared she'd accidentally wander outside that boundary. It would slip away and leave her, a dream gone in a blink, too good to be true. Being captured and bound by these two was the security blanket she wanted, now and forever. But it wasn't the restraints that held her; it was the two men themselves.

As if emphasizing that, Chris released the strap behind her neck and her wrist cuffs, while Geoff did the same to her ankles. "No . . . don't. I can . . ."

"Hush. It's all right. You got to the bottom of it, Sam. It's all good." When Geoff straightened her with a steadying hand on her elbow, she burrowed into his body, curling up against him. He lifted her in his arms. "Here you go, baby. We've got you. We're here. Punishment's done. All done."

He carried her out of the humid garage back into the house. Down the hall and into his bedroom. When he pulled back the covers to slide her into the bed, Chris had stripped off his shirt and was getting into the other side in pants alone, so Geoff put her directly into his arms. Geoff removed his own shirt and joined them, the two men holding her so closely they had to have their hands on each other. Their solid bodies offered her warmth and reassurance, as did the low words they spoke to her as she cried. Geoff shifted to run his fingers over Chris's hair and shoulder, another reassurance. He would need to know that they hadn't done anything wrong.

Far from it. As things quieted enough inside her that she could draw an even breath and speak through her sniffles, she had her hands wrapped over Chris's hand where it curled against her breasts. Her lower body, her sore ass, was pressed into the cradle of Geoff's thighs and pelvis.

"I've seen that kind of breakdown happen when I was with Flo, at parties, but I've never experienced it," she said at last. Her voice was thick, raspy. Her skin was vibrating wherever either of them touched her. "I didn't realize how much I needed it until it happened."

"It was a little scary," Chris said, studying her closely. "But okay, too. Good. It was as if you opened yourself up all the way to the soul or something. The scary part was seeing how vulnerable you were."

"But the two of you took me to shelter." She managed a soft smile that made her heart hurt in the right ways. "I don't think I could want to be anywhere as much as I want to be where I am now." She tipped her head back onto Geoff's shoulder. "How did you know? Did you see it happen at a club or party?"

He shook his head. "I heard stories about it from other Doms, because that kind of thing is more of a one-on-one, private scene kind of thing. They told me when a sub compresses emotions like that, such that she or he can't figure out what's going on enough even to talk about it, you have to know the best approach to crack them open. Sometimes it's to take them to climax. Sometimes it's this, the punishment thing. But a lot of it was just knowing. Feeling it. Reading your cues, the challenges. Some of the response, I thought through. But some of it was just instinct. Which was why it was a little unnerving. I'm sorry if I pushed too hard, Sam, too fast."

"You didn't. I don't think you did. Is it okay . . . Can I touch you?"

In answer, he curled his fingers around her wrist and drew her hand up to his face, letting her slide her fingertips along it as she wished. Geoff was an awesome lawyer because he knew how to project confidence in court and bullshit when needed to bluff his way into the right decision, but when he made a mistake, he learned from it. It was more important to him to actually be right than to appear to be right, especially when it truly mattered. And she mattered to him.

As much as she loved his stern Dom side, seeing the worry in his eyes now, him wanting to be sure she truly was okay, made her love the man even more. She shifted partly to her back, her shoulder pressing into Chris's chest, her hand resting on Geoff's hip, fingers curling in the pocket of his jeans to give each of them a shy caress.

"I know it's not a good idea for us to be having wild monkey sex every hour we're together, but what I really, really need right now, if you're both willing to do it and think it's okay . . ." She took a breath. "I'd like to feel each of you inside me, on top of me, one at a time. I'd like for you each to come, because I want you both . . . to leave part of yourself inside me, if that makes sense. I won't be upset if you say no, but will you consider it?"

Geoff glanced over her head at Chris. Whatever he saw decided it. He brought her fingers up to his mouth to kiss them, telling her they were going to agree to her request. She sighed in relief and quiet joy. "Thank you," she whispered.

Geoff squeezed her hand and left the bed to strip off the remainder of his clothes. She absorbed the lean strength and grace of his body as he set jeans and underwear aside. He came back under the covers to hold her against his warmth, Chris waiting on him to do that before sliding out of the bed and undressing. She wasn't left without the warmth of one of their bodies for even a second.

As Geoff pushed her onto her back, Chris stretched out next to her on his hip, head propped on his hand as he watched. His bare foot slid against hers under the covers before he made way for Geoff. A hundred emotions and physical sensations rolled through her as Geoff moved on top of her, her thighs adjusting to cradle him between her legs. Reaching down, he teased the wetness, making sure she was ready for him, then he slid an arm around her waist, holding her steady as he guided himself into her. Slow and gentle, to the hilt. Chris leaned in, nuzzling her temple. His hand moved under the covers, sliding along Geoff's back, she thought, establishing connection as

Geoff began to move, a slow rhythm that dissolved her into pure pleasure.

"Kiss him, Sam," Geoff murmured. It was natural as breathing to turn her face toward Chris, his hand coming back to capture her jaw, caress her throat. As he sipped from her lips, Geoff bent to nuzzle her breast. He began to suckle, and reaction spiraled down to her womb. She was going to climax from this, from both of them. That hadn't been her primary goal, but still, it fit the moment.

"Yours," she whispered, looking between them. "I'm yours. And I'm still sorry."

"You're forgiven for everything you could ever do to us, now and forever." Chris spoke against her ear. That brought more tears squeezing from her eyes, but Chris caught them with his lips. Geoff began to release in an intense, nearly motionless way, the climax flooding her pussy so that she moaned and arched up into his body. She tried her best to keep things easy, slow, to honor the spirit of her request. As such, her own climax, following right on the heels of his, had a different power to it, one that gripped and rolled her, made her light-headed and euphoric at once. By the time they'd both given her the gift of their seed inside her, she expected she might be little more than a boneless vessel of gratitude and love.

Geoff bent, kissing her, and she wound her arms around his shoulders, clinging to him and deepening the kiss, trying to express everything she was feeling in the one gesture. When he at last drew back, his eyes were alive with the aftereffects of his release, yet also molten with a contentment she wasn't sure she'd ever remembered seeing there before. It was as if he knew, as she did, they were standing at the doorway of the kind of happiness people always hoped to find but most never did.

As he slid from her, he trailed his lips over her sternum, each breast. He made her squirm and smile as he kissed her navel, tugging on the piercing there. She drew in a shuddering breath as he closed his mouth on her pussy, giving the petals a few soft, swirling licks and a gentle kiss, before he moved away and slid to his hip on the other side of her, his gaze now fixed on Chris.

Chris leaned over her, his broad shoulder the perfect spot to rest her hand as he kissed her deep, long. He didn't move to cover her body with his own until she thought she was floating on a cloud, captured by that kiss, held there spinning and drifting. When he did, her arms slid around him, legs curling up over his hips like she had Geoff's. As always, the enchanting differences of their body types filled her senses to overflowing. Chris slid into her, again slow and measured. He lifted his head and watched her face, his brown eyes serious.

"You tell me to stop if it hurts," he said.

The tissues in that area were remarkably resilient. Even the soreness of the past weekend had passed relatively quickly, the muscle aches the only thing lingering, a welcome reminder of the exertion.

She pressed her face into Chris's neck when he curled his arms around her head and held her even closer. Her hips tilted up to the smooth motion of his body, like the rock of a boat. "It's nice this way," he said. She agreed. It was nice every way, but this, no urgency, every move flavored by love and care, was the most unforgettable experience yet. Since all of their joinings had been pretty amazing, that was saying something.

Geoff's hand slid down Chris's torso, passing over the arms she had clasped around Chris's back and waist. She imagined Geoff stroking Chris's buttocks as the muscles in them tensed and released with his slow thrusts inside her. Chris's eyes were on her and Geoff's were on both of them. He leaned in, gave her a kiss as Chris had done when Geoff had been inside of her, connecting the three of them. His hand overlapped Chris's by her head and for a brief moment the men's hands tangled, tightened, sending a message between them that felt like it included her. She pressed her head against their joined hands and breathed their names.

When Chris started to come, Geoff's biceps flexed. She suspected he'd tightened his grip on Chris's ass, encouraging his release, experiencing it with the two of them. She shuddered in Chris's arms, riding the aftershocks from her last climax spurred back to life by his response. Her soft cries died into a contented purr as Chris slowly came down. She turned her cheek to the men's joined hands again, putting her lips against their intertwined fingers.

"I love you," she said.

Some things didn't need more than those three words to say it all.

$\backsim$

"I love you both. I really do. But I swear to God, the way you drag your asses when we're leaving for a trip makes me want to kill you." Sam put her hands on her hips and glared at Geoff.

"Did you know, if you're murdered, there's a fifty-fifty chance the perp will be someone you love, or who thinks they love you? So love is as much a source of violence as hate. Something to ponder." Geoff scrolled through the messages on his phone. Again. Seeing Sam's ominous look, he tucked the device away and held up his hands, backpedaling toward his room with a grin. "Getting my stuff now."

"If either of you did the driving on trips, you'd be a lot more concerned about getting out of town before Friday rush hour," she muttered.

"Driving is your choice," Chris pointed out. He passed Geoff in the hallway, a friendly brush of bodies, and dropped his duffel on the kitchen floor. "Geoff's road rage breaks you out in hives and my lack of attention gives you a nervous breakdown. Want to check and make sure I brought enough underwear and my toothbrush, Mom?"

She crossed her arms. "I'm going out to the car in exactly ten minutes. Whoever is not with me will be left here. I'll go to Bat Cave by myself and have a wonderful weekend wandering through all the antique shops and reading by the creek. I won't miss either of you."

"Liar," Geoff said, coming back up the hall with his rolling tote. She suspected he'd had it ready all along, and had wanted to yank her chain by making her think he hadn't yet started to pack. "But I need something clarified. Was that ten minutes from now, or ten minutes from when you get in the car?" He clucked as she shot him the bird. "That's just rude. Do we have snacks?"

She rolled her eyes. "Jordan Almonds for me, trail mix for you and Chris has two peanut butter and jelly sandwiches. It's only a ninety-minute drive and we're getting dinner once we're there. I doubt we'll starve."

Geoff's brow creased. "Crap. We're missing something."

"What?" Sam said impatiently. "It's only an overnight. Whatever it is, we can live without it."

"No, I don't think so." Geoff looked around the living room and glanced over his shoulder at the hallway, lips firming as he apparently tried to remember. "Oh, that was it." He looked toward Chris. "Did you get the thing? The most important thing we have to do this weekend?"

"We don't have to *do* anything," Sam snapped. "That's the point. You said relaxation—"

"Shit, no." Chris ignored her, shaking his head. "Don't worry. I'll get it. Grab my bag." He turned away to go back down the hall while Sam seriously considered a scream of frustration. Instead, she yelped, because Chris pivoted abruptly, ducked down and tossed her over his shoulder, head down and legs kicking. "Okay, got it," he said.

"You jerks," she said, but she was laughing, and then shrieking as Geoff tickled her nose. She grabbed Chris's belt as he carried her through the kitchen. Geoff followed him with bag and tote, grinning.

"Hey, wait a second," he said. "We're going to shock the neighbors."

She was wearing a light skirt, and it was in peril of slipping down to her waist. When Chris obliged by coming to a halt, Geoff grabbed the hem, but instead of adjusting it for modesty, he pulled it down to her shoulder blades. Pushing her panties out of the way, he gave her ass a couple of healthy smacks, hard enough to have her writhing and things going a very different way in her mind. Only then did he pull the skirt back down over her thighs, tucking the fabric in between them and under Chris's hand so she wouldn't be exposed. He'd left the panties where they were, though, so she'd have to adjust them in the car over her stinging buttocks.

"Meanie," she said, and he bent, kissing her snarling mouth.

"Don't you forget it," he said, a glint in the hazel eyes.

Despite her bitching, she was so pleased about having the two men to herself for a weekend that, once on the road, she didn't mind the traffic. They were out of Charlotte before the worst of it hit, regardless, so they didn't get delayed by many snarls. Plus there were plenty of distractions in the car to keep her mind off traffic headaches.

Like Chris sliding up behind her seat to trail his knuckles down her upper arm, bared by her knit tank top, and Geoff laying his hand on her thigh with casual possessiveness as they talked. It made her think about what might happen when they had the cottage to themselves with its six-person hot tub. They'd planned on doing dinner and dancing tonight. Logically she knew they could have stayed home if all they wanted to do was stay in the cottage, but it didn't make the idea any less tempting. She was in the company of two men she loved and wanted so much her mind and heart were overflowing, her body vibrating with the need to be as close to them as possible.

They reached the house in just over an hour and a half, as planned. The little cabin was perched over a creek, right off the meandering two-lane highway through Bat Cave. Once they put their suitcases in the bedrooms, Sam wandered into the kitchen, toward the sliding doors that led to the deck. "I think we should do takeout instead," she said, dipping her head meaningfully toward the covered hot tub visible through the glass.

"Nope," Geoff said mercilessly, drawing her away from the view. "You said you wanted to go out for dinner and dancing."

When she parted her lips on a protest, he gave her a look, part humor, but part Dom, too, reminding her who was boss. For certain things. She subsided with a mischievous smile that had his eyes doing that sexy gleam again, even as he pointed a stern finger at her. "Anticipation is everything," he reminded her.

"Think of all the people on the *Titanic* who didn't eat dessert that last night," she retorted.

"If the defense can give me a compelling argument," he intoned, "proving that flood or earthquake is going to cause a catastrophe commensurate with the *Titanic*'s in the next few hours, then we'll stay here and copulate until our private parts go numb. Otherwise, I expect you changed into your dancing shoes and your ass back in the car in fifteen minutes."

Chris came to the door of one of the bedrooms, clean shirt in hand. "He'll be a judge one day, Sam, just watch. But I'm with you. You know I don't like crowds. If I'm being given a vote about whether we stay or go—"

"You're not," Geoff said. "You spend your days surrounded by a million bugs, an army of earthworms under your feet, and talking to more birds and squirrels than a Disney princess. Compared to that, a couple hundred people in a dance club is an intimate family gathering." He gave Chris an appraising look. "And you can stand there all shirtless and sexy as long as you want . . . I'm not changing my mind. Neither is Sam. Are you, Sam?"

"Hunh? What? Well, he does look pretty drool worthy."

Chris grinned and Geoff rolled his eyes. "Go get dressed, woman."

She made a face at him, then retreated with a shriek as he picked up a kitchen towel and snapped it at her, expertly enough that the tip stung her thigh. Chris winked at her as she went past him toward the master bedroom. She paused long enough to trail a hand over his chest and curve it over his biceps, but then she had to double-time it, because Geoff went after her with the towel again. Chris intercepted him and she left them wrestling in the hallway while she escaped to the safety of her room, laughing at Chris's affronted comment.

"I know you didn't call me a princess . . ."

Truth, she did like dancing. What was interesting was how she and Chris were deferring to Geoff on the pacing for this.

On most things it had always been Chris who taught them the right speed to experience things. Like taking time out to enjoy a sunny day, knowing the best balance between play and work. Geoff's grasp of how best to savor the new intimacy between the three of them made sense, though. While it seemed to serve his own personal desires as a Master, the anticipation made things edgier. It pushed her past thinking, analyzing and inhibition into pure response mode, yearning to satisfy whatever he wanted and needed. Which took them both where they wanted to go.

She wondered what the anticipation did for Chris. Since his desires seemed to straddle both top and bottom, it would likely work for him as well.

She passed her hand over the thin blue quilt on the king-sized bed. On their past trip, Chris and Geoff had shared the room with two double beds, giving her this one with the king-sized bed, since Merry and her husband had taken the rental office apartment next door. This time she was pretty sure the bedroom with the two double beds where Chris had changed his shirt would be only a place to leave clothes and toiletries. They'd all three share this bed tonight.

She opened her suitcase. Where they were going for dinner was a pretty casual place, but dance clubs always gave a girl the excuse to razzle-dazzle it up a bit. She donned a snug purple-and-gray-striped miniskirt and a sleeveless top. The shirt was partially transparent, a sheer panel in a matching shade of purple revealing her shoulders, the tops of her breasts and her entire back, while a satin liner in silky gray covered her breasts to midriff. Geoff had given her a pair of silver earrings shaped like wings on her last birthday, and Chris had provided a matching necklace. The pendant was a silver dove with wings spread and head dipped in graceful profile. The length of the chain positioned the bird against the shadow of her cleavage. Slipping on a pair of gray wedge heels gave her a couple of inches of height. She brushed out her hair and touched up her makeup, and was ready to go within Geoff's proscribed fifteen minutes.

When she returned to the living room, her companions were ready, of course. All men had to do was change into a clean shirt, brush their hair, touch up with a razor, and they achieved the same thing that took a woman twice the time. She didn't object to the results, though. Geoff had changed to a dark blue button-down loose over stressed jeans, and Chris was wearing one of his obscure rock band T-shirts over black jeans. Handsome and rough at once was a good look for her men. "I have the best-looking dates tonight," she said, taking their hands and squeezing them. "And it thrills me to be able to say *dates* and mean it," she added.

Geoff gave her a thorough assessment, making her turn in a full circle before reclaiming her hand. "If I weren't sure you'd learned your lesson the other night," he said, "I'd say you were trying to make us stay here."

A genuine smile on Geoff Tywin's face could arrest the healthiest woman's heart. She further mortified herself by blushing, but seeing the same appreciation on Chris's face only deepened it. He slid a finger over the sheer panel, down to the silver dove pendant. Playing with it meant he also gave the valley between her breasts an intimate caress. "Glad you're wearing it," he said.

Geoff tugged her closer and touched his lips to hers. She closed her eyes as Chris stroked her side, her hip. Geoff lifted his head. "Glad you're ours," he said softly.

She curved her arms around them as much as she could reach, and they enveloped her between their two bodies. This was so much more right than how she'd felt earlier in the week, when she hadn't realized it was fear of losing them that was keeping her from slowing down, savoring. She took a nice, deep inhale of them both and tilted her head back.

"If they play the *Macarena*, you guys have to do it with me," she declared.

"Hey, I know the steps to that one." Chris brightened.

"Sad," Geoff said. "Your lack of coolness is just sad."

"You just wish you looked as good doing it as I do," Chris said, beginning to swivel his hips through the initial steps, bouncing on his size-thirteen shoes. Laughing, Sam started to backpedal toward the door.

"I'm hungry," she said. "Food, then dancing."

"Pushy, pushy, pushy." Geoff grabbed the keys from her. "I'll drive."

"The Lord is our shepherd; we shall not want . . ." she started, while Chris obligingly crossed himself.

"Get in the car, both of you. Smartasses."

For dinner she had a berry salad with pistachios and walnuts. Chris had a slab of steak and mountain of fried potatoes, ignoring the usual admonitions from Geoff about cholesterol and Sam about the benefits of veganism. She narrowed her eyes at Geoff as he seasoned his grilled chicken and asked him sweetly if he wanted any chicken with his salt.

"I'll outlive both of you," she said, shaking her head as they were both polishing their plates.

"Gender-wise, you're already likely to do that," Chris pointed out. "Women drive men into early graves. Everyone knows that."

She tumbled several raspberries onto his plate and won a mildly horrified look. "You've contaminated my cow."

"Oh, the growth hormones and antibiotics already did that."

"Not. You like this restaurant because all the meat is supposedly organic and humanely raised."

"That, and because of the desserts," she said as her vegan cupcake arrived. The frosting was sheer heaven.

"Dairy-free baked goods." Chris shuddered.

"It's not bad. Especially if you combine it with the right flavor." Geoff took a sip of the after-dinner coffee the waitress brought him, then touched the cupcake top to collect frosting on one finger. "Don't eat this," he told Sam before she could protest, and dabbed it on her top lip.

Leaning in, he kissed her, licking the frosting off with the tip of his tongue. Sam closed her eyes as he lingered to suck on her bottom lip, just to be equitable. When he finally sat back, she had parted, moist lips and elevated breathing. "I'd try it, Chris. It's better than you'd expect."

Chris obligingly collected some frosting on his own finger, only he picked up her hand off the table edge, put the creamy spread on her wrist and brought that to his mouth. He sucked her flesh a little harder, nipping her. Beneath the table, her toes curled.

Geoff had moved his leg so it was pressed against hers. Slipping her foot out of her wedge, she played with his ankle beneath the cuff of his jeans. His look increased the heat in the pit of her stomach, especially with Chris holding on to her hand and wrist, his mouth still on her.

"If we had a pint of that frosting," Geoff murmured, "we could cover her nipples and pussy and suck all of it off, making her sticky and sweet at once."

Chris's eyes kindled like firelit molasses as Geoff spoke, and Sam's hand trembled in the grip of his. "Add that to our next grocery list," Geoff told her. "Whole Foods has vegan frosting, right?"

"Yes," she managed. Chris released her as the waitress returned, though he'd adjusted his feet below the table so they were sandwiching one of hers. Geoff took the check. When Sam started to draw her hand away from Chris's to reach for her card, since they usually did a three-way split of checks for more expensive meals, Geoff shook his head and Chris recaptured her hand.

"Not this time, Sam. Chris and I are covering this weekend. You're not just our roommate anymore."

"But that doesn't mean I want you two paying for everything."

"We know that." He touched her arm in brief reproof as Chris tightened his fingers on hers. "We'll go back to our usual bill divisions on Monday. But this weekend you're our date, and we're treating you that way. All right?" Catching her chin in his thumb and forefinger before she could argue, he met her gaze. "That was a rhetorical question, by the way."

"Okay," she said. As he waited expectantly, her nerves tingled under his hold. "Yes sir."

It was the first time he'd demanded she address him that way in public. It wasn't likely someone would overhear, but it still gave her a tiny thrill.

Geoff let her go to take Chris's card and put both on the tray for the waitress to process. Chris pressed his lips back to her wrist. "More than just our date," he said, glancing up at her through his thick lashes. "Our girl."

Geoff nodded, stroking her hair. The words sank into her like sunlight. She didn't mind helping with the check, but it flustered and pleased her that they'd thought of it as yet another way to show her how things had changed. She belonged to them.

The dance club wasn't far from the restaurant. Being Friday night, there was a good crowd. Couples in outfits similar to what they were wearing hung out on the outdoor patio, dancing and talking, laughing. Once they squeezed in the front door and paid their cover charge, Chris shouted in Sam's ear that he was going to grab a beer. "I'll cop us a place next to the dance floor and watch you guys from there until my steak digests."

She relayed the message to Geoff. They watched Chris make his way through the crowd. He got inviting smiles from the women, a double take and second glance from many of the men, thanks to his size. Chris's lips moved over the usual niceties like "Excuse me" as he wound his way around them. He was always polite.

"It's amazing how much he can eat without gaining an ounce," Geoff grumbled in her ear. "But he should cut back on the red meat."

"You should both stop eating meat," she informed him as they made their way to the dance floor, his hand firmly closed over hers to keep them together. "I've told you all the reasons why a million times."

"Yes, but if God didn't mean for us to eat animals, he wouldn't have made them out of meat," Geoff said, his standard John Boy and Billy radio show punch line. She rolled her eyes but let it drop. They ate a lot less meat since she'd started planning meals, so she contented herself with that.

For now, she prepared to enjoy dancing with Geoff. The first time they'd ever gone dancing together, it had astonished her when Geoff had hauled her out onto the floor and danced half the night away with her.

When she finally had to take a break, out of breath, Chris had entertained her with the story of how Geoff had acquired those skills, to Geoff's disgust and her delight. In college, he'd fallen in lust with a girl who loved to dance. Since most straight white males refused to dance, and Geoff was the kind of man who seized an advantage when it presented itself, he'd immersed himself in Internet tutorials. The result was he could mix and match steps, and he'd become the girl's favorite dance partner—in and out of bed. Until a month later, when she fell hard for a Latino exchange student and followed him home to Central America.

"Geoff never could completely master the rumba, and that was his downfall," Chris had said with a straight face, right before Geoff fired a balled-up napkin at him to shut him up. *"Either that, or she discovered there wasn't any truth to the rumor that the way a guy moves on the dance floor is how he moves in bed."*

Actually, Sam was finding that to be pretty accurate. Geoff was decisive and fluid on the dance floor, his grip firm and strong, his touch caressing as it slipped away on the turns, then brought her back for more. When the crowd increased so that they had to dance in closer quarters, she was all for that. In the past, when they'd danced together, they hadn't gotten too body-to-body, her trying not to be too obvious about her attraction to him, and him trying to honor that weird guy code with Chris. Tonight she didn't have to worry about any of that.

So when he turned her back toward him, she came full up against him, and was thrilled when his arm slid around her waist, low on her hips to hold her even closer, bodies brushing intimately. His hand dropped to caress her buttock, and she put her hands on his chest, spreading her fingers out over it and beneath the buttons of his shirt to explore the man beneath.

Unable to resist, she slipped the next button so she could put her whole hand on his heart. He bent and kissed her, the raw heat telling her that her Master wasn't as cool as he'd projected. She moved against him, a blatant provocation to the evidence beneath his jeans, and he chuckled against her mouth. He gave her ass a hard squeeze then eased her back, keeping them dancing.

On the turn, she glimpsed Chris sitting on a stool along the outskirts of the dance floor. She waved him over, since he seemed to be finished with his beer. He shook his head, and she insisted with a more enthusiastic wave, bouncing on her toes.

"Let's try this." Geoff brought her back against him in a decisive move that drove her breath from her and reminded her of a similar step Antonio Banderas had done in *Take the Lead*. Despite the rumba, Geoff had no problem with tango moves, for sure. Banding his arm around her waist, Geoff moved them in a sensuous rock, down and back up, and nudged her hair aside to kiss her throat. His thumb caught in the waistband of her skirt, other fingers spreading out over her hipbone. His fingers weren't between her legs, but the way they were fanned out over her pelvis was highly suggestive of it.

She suddenly wished they were at one of Flo's private parties, so he could do the things that would definitely get them thrown out of here.

"Look at him, Sam," Geoff said against her ear. "Keep your eyes on him, let him see how aroused you're getting. It will bring him to you. To us."

She did. The movement of the dancers between them and Chris gave him teasing glimpses of what Geoff was doing to her. The pressure of his hand holding her, the teasing of his lips at her throat. It kept her wits scattered and her coordination questionable. His strong arm held her up, though. Chris's eyes were fastened on them as her lips parted.

Geoff spoke against her flesh again. "All I can think about is the taste of that frosting on your lip. It makes me think about the cream between your legs, about how wet you must be now, because you're imagining everything you want tonight. And I'm going to keep you waiting, because I like the things you do when you're crazy hot and aroused, when you trust us with everything you want and feel. Tell me who I am."

"My Master," she whispered. Chris's eyes flickered, and she wondered if he'd read her lips. He rose and started in their direction. She couldn't have said what song was playing, but it had a primal drumbeat that made her flesh tingle in a million places, and the guitar riffs strummed across the nerves in her abdomen and thighs.

"Who is he?" Geoff demanded, grip tightening.

"He's my Master, too. I need both of you."

"Well, he's coming to grant that wish. I'd show him proper appreciation."

Because of how Chris came through the crowd, she had to smile a little, and she thought Geoff did, too. People tended to shift instinctively to make a path for a larger-than-normal person, but on top of that, Chris had such a laid-back way of moving, it was like watching a river flow.

When he reached them, Geoff continued to hold on to her waist, but Sam slid her hands up to Chris's shoulders, lifting on her toes to kiss him, too. He obliged, bending to meet her and curling one of his hands around hers on his T-shirt. Her other hand dropped to his belt to hold on.

He started to sway with the rhythm of the music, taking her with him. Despite his comment about crowds, Chris did enjoy the people-watching and the music, so it wasn't the first time they'd been out dancing before. He would dance if she coaxed him, though usually only a song or two. He wasn't wild and fancy, more of an adherent to the Will Smith *Hitch* technique. Step right, step left, with some hip and shoulder rhythm.

With her hands on him, she could feel the move and roll of his body. His eyes held simple enjoyment of the moment and a smoldering awareness of the sexual undercurrents between the three of them.

Knowing they belonged to each other like this, indulging it in a public venue, confirmed what had happened over the past week was real, and growing. Evolving. It also turned her on in ways she hadn't expected. Maybe she was far more of an exhibitionist than she realized. Of course, in this crush of people, it was likely their three-way dynamic wasn't really discernible, so it was probably more the idea of it happening in a public venue, rather than it being noticed, that was getting her even more aroused.

When the *Macarena* came on, she burst out laughing. Despite his rolled eyes, Geoff stayed with them as the dancers formed lines and went through the steps. She dissolved into giggles as Geoff did them by standing behind her and putting hands on her head, shoulders and hips, instead of his own. She escaped behind Chris and the two men faced each other, doing the mirror image of the dance, Chris with great, studied precision and Geoff adding a little more jazz to it, to the amused delight of others on the floor. Particularly the women.

It was a fact of life that Geoff and Chris would always receive female attention, but now that attention made Sam glow with possessive pride. They were beautiful, arresting, and they loved *her*.

After the song concluded, a slower number came up. Geoff relinquished her to Chris graciously. "I need to hit the men's room," he told her, offering her a lingering kiss. "Chris'll take good care of you."

"He always does," she rejoined, and won a smile of agreement.

She slid her arms under Chris's as he wrapped one over her shoulders, clasping the other over her hips. As she laid her head on his chest, he pressed his jaw against her temple. "Having a good time?" he asked. She liked how the louder environment required him or Geoff to speak with their mouths on her flesh.

She nodded, closed her eyes and held on. Chris's hand slid down her back, thumb teasing her bra strap under the shirt. At length she lifted her head, rising up on her toes to put her lips against his ear and press herself fully against him. "Geoff told me what he wanted to do with me tonight when we get back to the cottage," she said. "How about you?"

He tilted his head to meet her eye to eye. "I think you know. What interests me more is what you want us to do to you."

"Everything," she mouthed, trailing her fingers along his cheek. She pressed her nose into his soft, thick hair. "Doing everything is the best kind of drowning. But I also want to just hold you both and be still, so the universe won't notice how happy I am and do anything to screw with it."

He drew back and touched her face. "We won't let it," he promised.

Geoff washed his hands and did the obligatory quick check to make sure nothing was left between his teeth from dinner. Noticing his appearance was second nature when it came to his job, but this weekend it had more to do with how he wanted to look for his two . . . friends? Friends for certain. Lovers. Sub, in Sam's case.

As for Chris, he was Geoff's best friend. One whom he wanted to keep as a best friend and yet push deep into territory that encompassed even more than that. Boyfriend didn't fit, nor did submissive. There really wasn't any word but *mine* that seemed to fit. It wasn't a caveman thing; more like saying that the roots belonged to the tree, an inseparable part of it.

Mine. The moment he repeated it in his mind and bracketed it around his image of Chris, he knew that was the word he'd been seek-ing. Giving himself a rakish grin in the mirror, he left the bathroom.

The wide hallway spilled into an open area with couches and chairs where people could mill and chat. A transparent dividing wall helped mute the music while still allowing a view of the dancers. He could see Chris and Sam had moved to the edge. Sam was leaning against him in front of the low wall that surrounded the dance floor. Chris had his arm propped on the other side of her so she was in the shelter of his body, protected from being jostled by people passing behind them. If there weren't a constant flow of people around them, Geoff might have copped himself a nice view of Chris's ass in the black jeans, which, because he wore them less often, fit a little tighter. And Sam's legs were like willow stems in her short skirt. Geoff wouldn't mind working his way up them with mouth and fingers until he found the treasure between.

"Hey, dude. Hey, over here."

Geoff paused, drawn out of his thoughts by the shout, the wave of a hand. When he'd arrived at the men's room, there'd been a knot of three college guys standing at the head of the hallway, holding beers and scoping out women coming and going from the ladies' room. It was a good choke point to check out the array of potentially available females. Though they were a little too obvious about it, Geoff figured it was a decent tactic. However, from the raucous tone of their conversation and exaggerated body language, he could tell they'd already gotten their Friday-night drunk on, a less intelligent decision if they hoped to get lucky. One of them in particular was the loud and obnoxious kind of drunk who'd be better off on the dance floor, where the sound could absorb his rowdiness.

But you were only young and stupid once, and it wasn't so far in his past that he couldn't grin at their behavior and give them a moment of his time now. They'd moved to a circle of three chairs, and it was the obnoxious one hailing him. "Hey." He gestured at Geoff again, even though he was already headed over. "Hey guy, come over."

"What's up?" He gave them a nod and got a variety of friendly responses.

"I'm Dave. This here's Brad and Kent. You dance pretty good for a straight guy." They all snickered, but Dave waved his hand, showing they weren't meaning it in an offensive way. "Had some of the girls watching you, that's for damn sure."

"Dancing is a great way to get women," Geoff said. "Much better than drinking."

"Yeah. But once the girls get drunk, too, you can get them without dancing," Brad pointed out. He had a goatee and a diamond stud in one ear and wore a tank that showed off a myriad of colorful tattoos. "We become a lot less repulsive."

Geoff grinned again; he couldn't help it. "Truer words, friend," he said, and began to move off. Dave, built like a bull and enhancing the look with a brush cut and 49ers jersey, lifted a hand again. "Hey, dude. Not finished with you. What you and your buddy have going with that girl is hot. You think once you're done with her tonight, she'd give us a spin?"

Geoff came to a halt and turned back, not sure for a moment he'd heard Dave right. The man was pressing on, though, oblivious. He tilted his head toward his two companions. "We got a place up at the lake where we hang out. We could all go up there later, have some more brews. Share her, since she's into doing multiple guys. Then we can split the cost of being nice to her. You know, giving her beer and getting her home, that kind of thing. Maybe even give her some extra money for being nice to us, if you get my meaning."

Any amusement or affinity Geoff had felt for the three vanished. Even at his drunkest, he'd never have assumed such a thing about a woman. Alcohol lowered inhibitions and impaired judgment, but it didn't sever a person from his moral compass. Which was why inebriation wasn't a get-out-of-jail-free card for felonies like rape.

But the basics were still true. They were young, stupid and drunk. He should just ignore them and move on. But he couldn't help but think of how Sam would react to this asshole's assumption. It had taken her a long time to get over how Anthony had treated her. She'd struggled with whether any of it was her fault, if her behavior had encouraged him to not take *no* for an answer. If she'd worn the wrong clothes, put on too much makeup. Women often blamed themselves for such things, but with a service submissive personality, she'd shouldered even more of the guilt. For far too long, she'd thought she should have been able to do something to keep it from happening.

He and Chris had done everything they could to help her rebuild her confidence, embrace her beauty and natural sexuality again. Christ, in truth, they'd probably suppressed their desire to pursue their relationship a lot sooner because of that, not wanting to affect her negatively in any way.

But whereas Anthony was not her fault, Geoff accepted the blame for this moment. He'd been thinking of nothing but enjoying her, and had forgotten his first job was protecting her. Why wouldn't their behavior attract attention, desire, envy? Or encourage this kind of thinking.

He didn't have to resort to violence, as tempting as it was to hammer the point into them using the nearest unyielding surface. However, it was his job to set them straight on what kind of woman she was.

"No," he said tightly. "She's not a whore. She's a beautiful woman who likes to dance. And because we treat her with love and respect, she trusts us enough to express desire without worrying that we're going to interpret it as something it's not."

The conversations near them died. Perhaps he'd raised his voice more than intended. A habit in court, where he'd enunciate his words more precisely if the point was more emphatic. The word *whore* did tend to carry.

Predictably, his attitude and words had pushed the *It's time to start a fight* button in the testosterone arsenal of the drunk threesome. While admittedly Geoff felt more than ready, he knew that was the wrong play. He was a moron, but it was a late news flash as they rose out of the chairs.

"I didn't call no one a whore. But she is fucking both of you, right?"

"We're done here." Geoff shouldered past him with a sneer, only to be stopped by Kent, who was built beefy, just like Dave. Now he had one in front and one behind, one to the side. Walled in. He was usually smarter than this. Okay, Chris would probably say he wasn't, given they'd met when Geoff had been about to be pounded by a gang of kids for shooting off his mouth. What made him a good lawyer now had qualified him as a punching bag in middle school.

Where was a club bouncer when you needed one?

"Excuse me."

The men stopped and turned, blinking. Sam stood outside the tense circle, Chris behind her. Geoff cursed at her tight, pale expression, because it told him they'd arrived in time to get the gist of the argument. Despite that, she looked calm, which was more than he could say for Chris. His friend had also heard the conversation, because he had the demeanor of a bull about to gore a sparkly matador with extreme prejudice. Geoff wondered how Sam had gotten in front of him. From how resolute she looked, she must have insisted bodily.

"Yes, we share a bed. The three of us." She squared off with Dave. "I'm in love with both of them, and they're in love with me. It's taken us way too long to admit no one makes us as happy as one another. I'm not going to turn my back on that or break my heart in half by choosing just one, no matter what the world thinks of me for feeling that way."

Her gaze met Geoff's, making it clear the message was more for him and Chris than their audience. Unexpectedly, it helped settle him. She was right. Who gave two shits what the world thought?

"Atta girl." A group of girls sitting in a ring on the floor nearby raised their beer cups. The one who'd spoken had golden hair and lively blue eyes and wore a snug Appalachian State T-shirt. She wasn't quite as hammered as the three men, but her friends were riding enough of a beer buzz to cheer. While that was likely more of a response to the fantasy of a threesome than the strength of Sam's declaration, it still helped defuse the tension.

"Kent, come sit over here with us," the blonde said. "Stop being dicks."

Kent, obviously amenable to the call of a pretty face, turned his attention to the only thing that could replace a hormonal college male's desire to brawl. Unfortunately, Dave wasn't willing to let it go. He gestured with his beer, sloshing some over his hand. "What does that make you two guys? Some sword crossing happens, I'll bet." He looked at Chris belligerently, jerking his head toward Geoff. "Is this skinny prick your bitch, big guy?"

Hearing Dave refer to Chris the way Geoff often did himself unleashed an unexpected spike of possessive temper. "No," Geoff said, stepping toe to toe with Dave and staring him down. "He's an unneutered Rottweiler who'll rip out your throat if he feels like you're pissing on his territory. And she's his territory. As well as mine. So back the fuck off and learn some manners."

Chris had moved around Sam and was breathing down Dave's neck. He also shot Brad a warning look that had the slighter man looking far less certain about Dave's attitude.

"Come on, Dave," Kent called over. "Don't be an ass. You're going to get us thrown out of here."

"Whatever, man," Dave said, though his hackles were still obviously up. He sidled out from between Geoff and Chris and tossed them a glare. "Duck's a duck, no matter what you dress it up as and call it. We aren't the only ones who thought it, so no need to get pissy." He stomped over to the group, Brad trailing behind.

Chris growled, but Geoff put a hand on his chest. "Leave it," he said quietly.

Despite her excellent and emphatic delivery, Sam was looking a little too pensive for his taste now. Geoff closed his hand on hers, drawing her gaze.

"Let's go hit the floor for a couple more numbers before we call it a night," he suggested.

He wanted to call it a night right now. Sam could be a lot tougher than anyone expected, a bitch on wheels when needed. But there was a kindness to her that always seemed unprepared for someone to be mean to her. Like Anthony.

She nodded, a docile acceptance, but not the kind he liked. Shifting his grip to the back of her neck, he pulled her to him with a decisive move that made her look up at him with startled eyes. Since Chris could pick up on her change of mood as fast as he could, Geoff screwed his hand in Chris's shirtfront to hold on to him. It wouldn't take much for their Rottweiler to bare fangs and charge the men who'd upset Sam.

"They're drunk, young and stupid," Geoff repeated, low. He met Chris's fiery eyes. "Fighting with them is not the way, Chris. Making her feel better is what matters most, right? Plus, if you fight with them, I have to jump into the fray. If I get arrested, I could lose my license. We take care of each other. That's what we do. Right?"

The rage vibrating from Chris didn't turn off, but he did push it back into his gut enough to nod. He put his hand on Geoff's forearm, clasping it. It told Geoff they'd reclaimed that accord they did so well, even in their most tense moments.

"But no more dancing," Chris said. "Let's just get out of here. I don't care about making a point to a bunch of dumbass kids."

A valid observation. When Sam agreed, Geoff tightened his fingers on her waist. "All right, then. Let's go."

The car trip home was quiet. In darkness, their cottage was a small brown mushroom sitting on its pilings. The creek created whispers of sound, secret gurgles in the dark. Geoff saw Sam stop to inhale the forest scents as she stepped out of the car. But then she turned and moved through the gate to the front door without speaking.

Chris's shoulders and expression were tense. As he followed her, Geoff brought up the rear, thoughtful. Since he had the key, he touched Chris's shoulder, a tacit direction to move back so he could get past him. He caressed the small of Sam's back, reaching past her to unlock the door.

As he held it for her, he tilted his head at Chris, directing him to go in ahead of him. When Chris closed the distance between him and Sam again, Geoff noticed he touched her almost exactly where Geoff had, that universal protective reassurance, man to woman. Sam tilted her head, acknowledging it, but once inside, she left them, walking into the living room. It had deep brown paneling and eclectic hunting decorations mixed with needlepoint and lace curtains. Geoff wondered that Merry hadn't updated the place since she'd bought it as a rental investment, but he expected the decor was part of its quirky charm for renters who were looking less for typical amenities and more of an unscripted travel diary experience.

Given their own uncharted course, it was a fitting setting for the three of them. Sam stood in front of the double windows, staring through the glass. Because of the solar lights that etched the back edge of the property on the other side of the creek, there was a reflection on the water that flickered over her face.

Chris sat down on the arm of the couch, stretching out his legs and crossing his arms, patiently waiting her out, though his expression was watchful. He was probably mulling over some of the same things

Sam was. Was this a good idea, any of it? What would become of the three of them and their friendship if they kept going down this path?

Geoff allowed them one additional minute of pregnant silence, then he tossed the keys on a side table, an abrupt metallic *clank* that had them both turning.

"If this is just a fantasy we're indulging," he said, "dealing with that kind of shit should be a lot easier. We enjoy our threesome for a little while, try a lot of crazy different positions, have fun with it, let it run its course. Then, Sam, you decide which of us you want for the long haul. Maybe it will be neither of us. You'll move on, find another guy who you want to marry, set up house and have babies."

Her spine snapped straight. "Is that what you think this is? Are you saying that's all you expect or want this to be?"

He had Chris's full attention now, but Geoff didn't look toward him yet. It was all he could do to keep an impassive face before her pale expression, the pain in her voice. "I say what I mean, Sam," he said evenly. "You know that. Pay attention to what I'm saying. Think it through."

"Don't patronize me," she snapped.

"You think I'd ever do that?" He injected enough warning in his tone to startle her, to make Chris stiffen. Geoff took another step forward, holding her eyes in that lock. "I told you to think about what I just said. Exactly how I said it. You don't usually need me to repeat something, but I will, just this once. *'If this is just a fantasy we're indulging, dealing with that kind of shit should be a lot easier.'*"

She stared at him, but her face became less angry, more confused. Unfortunately, it made the hurt show more, so he had to steel his resolve.

"I'm saying a fun threesome is an easier scenario for people to accept," he continued. "If we want something more, if each of us sees this as something for the long haul, we'll deal with a lot worse than a trio of drunk assholes. The reactions of people who are far closer to home. People you can't beat up." He looked toward Chris. "Family, parents, close friends. Coworkers. And what about marriage? Kids? I'm pretty sure we all want those things. How many times has one of you said, *When I have a kid . . .*"

"Damn, Geoff, we just started," Chris said, frowning. "Ease off. It's not like we're already thinking about that kind of shit."

"Really? I am." He crossed his arms as they jerked in reaction. "When Sam took us into Naughty Bits, she pulled the curtain away from what's been going on between us all this time. This relationship may have just graduated to sex, but the rest has been building from the moment we met. How long have you been in love with her, Chris? I can tell her the day it happened, the very minute."

Chris looked like he was still wrapping his mind around where Geoff was taking this, so Geoff shifted his attention back to Sam, pleased to see she was a hundred percent in the here and now, rather than back at what had happened at the club.

"It was three weeks after you moved in with us. We'd agreed to let you help clean the apartment and it was your turn on the rotation, the first time you'd done it. You'd put on one of the paint-stained T-shirts Chris has for dirty jobs and were on your knees beneath the kitchen sink, grumbling. *'Why don't men ever do more than a surface clean?'* and *'Oh my God, there are dead cockroaches in the back corners . . .'"*

She pressed her lips against a smile as he imitated her annoyed, feminine tone. "Chris pointed out that it was better to find dead ones than live ones. You sat back on your heels and you had a smudge of grease on your cheek. You stuck your tongue out at him and pointed an imperious finger below the sink." Geoff imitated her voice once again; credibly enough he heard Chris's half chuckle and Sam's smile broke through. *"'I clean. I do not handle dead bug removal. That is men's work.'"*

Geoff took a seat on the arm of the occasional chair, stretching out his legs so his shoes weren't far from her slim foot in its wedge heel. Her toenails were painted a pretty lavender. He let his gaze travel leisurely over her, another message. He was in the here and now, the events of the club having no hold on his desire for her. She got the message, because when he reached her face, her lips had parted, her gray eyes riveted on him.

"There was nothing earth-shattering about that moment," he said. Glancing toward Chris, he found his friend's expression harder to read. "It was just one out of the thousand moments accumulating since we intercepted Anthony that day, but it was the click point. I saw it happen in his eyes. When he came to the sink to wet a paper towel to collect the bugs, he nudged you with his leg. You pushed at him, playful, but when he squatted beside you, you used his shoulder to get back on your feet. The casual intimacy was already there, easy as that. He looked toward his shoulder when you let go of him as if he was thinking about how it felt, having you touch him. And how he wanted you to do it again."

Geoff paused as Sam turned her gaze to Chris. He'd still said nothing, but his expression didn't deny it. "What you didn't see," Geoff addressed the other man, "was that was the exact moment it happened for Sam too. Even though she might not be aware of it."

Chris's attention snapped to Geoff, but swiveled just as quickly back to Sam. From how she swallowed, Geoff though she might have been aware of it after all.

"When you left the kitchen, Chris, she started putting things back under the sink." Geoff shifted on his seat. "She got an itch and rubbed her chin on her shoulder. Then she pressed her nose into the fabric so she could inhale it. Like she was smelling your scent, learning it, taking it inside her. She'd forgotten I was watching her, but when she noticed, she flushed and went back to cleaning. She could have passed it off with a joke, like the shirt smelling like paint or some such nonsense, but she didn't. She just tucked her head down and didn't say anything."

Sam sank down in the chair. Geoff stroked a lock of her hair from her face and she pressed her face into his palm. He bent over her, dropping a kiss on her crown.

Straightening, Geoff looked between them. "So, back to my original point. How many people have a relationship this long *without* starting to think about marriage and kids?" He nudged Sam. "You analyze things to death. I'm pretty sure you thought of it even before we did, so what conclusions did you reach?"

"I was trying not to go there." She lifted her chin. "The feelings might not be new, but expressing them this way . . . that *is* new. It was nice to enjoy it without making it complicated like that yet."

His heart tightened with regret, and he spoke in a gentler tone. "You're absolutely right. We don't have to rush into all of that. My point is, whatever this is, it's stronger than some stupid thing that happened at a nightclub."

"Way stronger," she said resolutely.

"Good." Geoff tugged her hair. "So we're not a fling you're having before you hook up with some rich banker."

"I don't know." She pursed her lips. "Depends on how rich he is. And if he's not too old and yucky-looking."

Geoff looked deliberately over his shoulder. "They have a wide variety of flat kitchen utensils in here. A few metal ones. They'd probably leave some nice imprints on your ass."

"You'd have to catch me first."

He gave her a look that informed her that wouldn't be a problem and was gratified to see that pretty flush on her cheeks which said she'd conjured some blatant end results of him chasing her down. It worked for him, but they weren't quite ready to shift those gears yet. Sobering, he extended a hand. When she put hers into his palm, he closed his fingers on it, and adjusted so he could look at her and Chris at the same time.

Chris was far from relaxed yet, but he'd shifted onto the sofa instead of perching on the arm, a good sign. Sam took a breath. "Geoff . . . will you tell me when it happened for you?"

"You might not appreciate it."

She studied him. "It was the night you went out with Tally Winters."

She never failed to surprise him, in so many arresting and not always comfortable ways. He did his best not to squirm as Chris gave him a look. Yeah, that gate worked both ways for them. Chris had known when it happened for Geoff as much as he had for Chris.

Geoff moved to sit on the coffee table so he was sitting in profile to Chris. He drew Sam close to plant his shoes on either side of her feet and hem her in between his knees. He gripped her hips, sliding his hands around to cup her buttocks in casual possession. "Is that right?" he said mildly.

She tried to cross her arms and look miffed, but he shook his head. "Leave your hands down at your sides and tell me why you think it was then."

Using the right words to bring forth those lovely submissive reactions of hers was a potent magic. The pulse jumping in her throat, her gaze centering on his face. The nervous little tremor that went through her body made her vibrate under his hands.

She took a breath. "You came home from the date early. Way early. You smelled like her perfume, but you went into your room and took a shower. You'd taken a shower before the date, so I thought it was peculiar, but when you came back out in your pajama bottoms, you smelled like you, not a trace of her on your skin. You sat down on the couch with me, gave me this look and asked, "Better?"

She forgot his mandate about leaving her arm at her side, her finger picking at some invisible lint on his shoulder. Reaching up, he clasped her wrist, but her words held them there. Her gray eyes slid to meet his. "I realized you'd had sex with her, which I hated. Yet you'd taken a shower before touching me. And asked me if that made things better. It confused me, but it also felt . . . wonderful. Hopeful. I nodded and you put your arm around me. We watched *Justified*, and I fell asleep with my head on your shoulder. When I woke up later, my head was in your lap and you'd put a blanket over me. Chris had come in to make a snack, and the two of you were talking. You mentioned your leg was asleep, but when Chris offered to carry me to bed you said no, you didn't mind."

She moistened her lips. "So I know when it happened, but I'd like to know how and why."

Geoff cleared his throat. Hearing all the details she'd recalled had touched him far more deeply than he'd expected. Chris leaned forward, resting his forearms on his knees, and Geoff was conscious of his hands being close enough to touch Geoff's hip.

He was reluctant to say the next words, but if he demanded honesty from her, he had to give the same in return. "Yes, we had sex at her place. While I was inside her, looking down at her, all I could see and think about was you."

Her suddenly fixed neutral expression made him wince. How many men said that kind of shit? *While I was screwing someone else, all I was thinking about was you.* She needed more than that. *You started this line of inquiry, counselor,* he reminded himself, and forged on. Chris's subtle shift was as clear as a held-up sign: *You need to do better than that, dumbass.*

"I'm not proud of it, Sam, but I realized somewhere in the middle of it that I was actually using thoughts of you to treat her properly and leave her satisfied. Yet all I wanted to do was come home to you. You and Chris. I took the shower because I didn't want to touch you until I had her scent off of me. And that was the last time I was with a woman, until you."

Sam studied him. "I'm not sure I've ever been used as an aid to—"

"Don't." He squeezed her wrist, a little harder than he'd intended. "I told you that you probably wouldn't appreciate it. But that is the true answer to when and how I knew."

She shook her head. "You know, it's weird. When I think of the three of us, it's like we each have roles that make us a whole. You're the intellectual and planner, which is why you're the one who put what happened at the club back in perspective. Whereas Chris is still working through his emotions on it, because he's all about harmony and truth." She looked toward him with a gentle smile. Chris gave her a nod. He looked more broody than Geoff would have liked, but she was right. Chris was working it out.

"I fit," she said with a sigh, "but I can't figure out what my side of the triangle is."

Geoff took both her hands. "You're Woman, capital *W*. You close the triangle. It's a quality neither Chris nor I can bring to this, but it's vital to both of us. You see the full picture, Sam. All of it. What's beyond harmony or intellect, what's important in all of it. Which is why I specifically wanted to know what your long-term thoughts about us are. I respect that you just wanted to enjoy it without getting too much into serious thoughts of the future, but share those thoughts with us anyway." He threaded his fingers through her hair, slid them along her throat to her shoulder. "Tell us. Unless I've upset you, telling you about Tally, and you need something else first."

"No. It wasn't great to hear, but . . ." She put her hand over his. "It's funny, with two people falling in love, there are already so many norms that tell you how to handle it, what to do, what the potential pitfalls are. If it had been just two of us, me and you, Chris and me or you and Chris, we probably already would have moved on those feelings long ago, right? It was this that held us back. That and the two of you thinking I needed decades to heal from one asshole."

She smirked as Geoff narrowed his eyes at her, and she tossed a smile to Chris. He shook his head at her. "Try to give a girl space and she complains. Rush her and she fusses. Damned if you do—"

"Damned if you don't," Geoff finished. She swatted him and he captured her hand. "Keep going," he encouraged her.

She lifted a shoulder. "Those norms give you a framework, time to enjoy it. If everything feels right, talking about commitment evolves gradually, because you sense that some of that is already handled, intuitive, if that makes sense. Those guys took me off guard tonight because the way I feel for both of you, it already seems like that, you know? When you're so in your head and heart with the people you love, you forget that other people maybe can't see what's so clear to you." She grimaced. "Which is just a complicated way of saying I wasn't ready to handle people's reaction to us."

"I thought you handled it pretty brilliantly," Geoff disagreed. "You were honest with them. Brutally honest. Despite Mr. Homophobe, who was obsessed with the idea that dicks are magnetized toward each other during a threesome, you defused things with the truth. And you humbled me with your feelings, Sam. You gave us both a gift there. Thank you."

Chris ran a hand down her back, a reinforcement of that truth and she gave them both a grateful look. Sinking to her knees, she put her cheek on Geoff's leg. The position gave her comfort, he knew. Whereas for him, her seeking reassurance that way steadied him as much.

Geoff reached out and touched Chris's shoulder. "You okay?"

Chris shook his head. "I hate it when people treat other people like that," he said. "But especially when someone treats either of you that way."

He pushed up off the couch, his knee hitting the coffee table with a jarring *thump* that revealed how volatile his emotions still were. Sam jumped but Geoff tightened his hand on her shoulder, keeping her in place. Chris moved out from behind the table. "I can let most things roll off. I see bullshit every day and just go along, do my thing and don't let any of it touch me. But we were having fun. You were relaxed and Sam was happy. It all felt right."

He sighed, looking out the windows into the dark. "I don't know why people have to suck so much of the time."

Pivoting, he moved toward the kitchen. Going outside was what Chris usually did when he was out of sorts, so Geoff was sure they both guessed the sliding glass doors leading out to the deck were his destination. However, when Sam met Geoff's gaze, he dipped his head in agreement. She quickly rose to intercept Chris, sliding her arms around him.

"They can be jerks all they want," she said. "I still know at the end of the day, I'm here with you."

He came to a halt as she leaned against him, framing his face in both hands. "Do you think I'm that delicate? My feelings might get hurt, but it's just a moment, like a shot at the doctor's. It's gone. Over and done with."

"I do think you're delicate. And strong. And . . ." He shook his head, and Sam's hands tightened on him.

"It doesn't matter. It really doesn't." Her expression warmed, eyes dancing. "Remember *Meatballs*? 'Even if we play so far above our heads that our noses bleed for a week to ten days, it just wouldn't matter, because . . .'"

"'All the really good-looking girls would *still* go out with the guys from Mohawk, because they've got all the money,'" Chris finished. His lips tugged in a rueful smile, and he repeated her words. "It just doesn't matter."

Curling his fingers in her hair and at her waist, he drew her up to her toes. "But you matter," he said, a fierce light in his expression. "I want to destroy anything that thinks it has the right to hurt you. You're the most beautiful woman I've ever met, inside and out."

There were plenty of perks to being in a three-way relationship, one of them being the chance to be both audience and participant. Sitting on the sidelines and seeing Sam bloom like a rose at such an unexpected and raw compliment ranked high on Geoff's list of perks. She rallied, though, giving Chris a little shove that didn't move him even a millimeter, fucking tank that he was.

"You say that because you love me. But I'm a skinny, gawky girl who's in love with two wonderful men who make me feel beautiful every time you look at me. *That's* all that matters."

Drawing a deep breath, she turned toward Geoff. "Not that I want you to get all bigheaded about it. I know just how much of a pain in the ass you both can be."

Pasting a blank look on his face, Geoff looked at Chris. " I think we're very easy to get along with."

"She's just anal," Chris observed. "OCD. Thank God she's hot, even though she doesn't realize she is."

"One of her few charms." Geoff grinned as Sam gave Chris another ineffectual shove, but Chris put his hands on her hips to hold on to her, fingers sliding along the waistband of her skirt. It turned his thoughts away from further conversation and toward the desire to share feelings in a far more intimate way. "Speaking of charms, I think Chris and I would like to see them."

Sam looked his way again, and Geoff deliberately let the smile on his face turn into something else. "We want you naked, nothing between you and us," he said softly. "Right now."

He'd chosen his timing well. Instead of seeing a hitch in her response as he would if she'd been immersed in the earlier upset, he saw a smooth change as she stepped away from that and into the zone she embraced best with them.

Chris was on board. He released Sam's hand, stepped back and took a seat on the arm of the occasional chair Geoff had vacated. Bracing his feet in a spread-knees pose, he crossed his arms over his big chest. Geoff couldn't have choreographed it any better, because Sam reacted as a woman did when two men who desired her made it clear she was the center of their attention. Her cheeks flushed again, and it seemed as if an internal radiance enhanced all her considerable charms.

Geoff gave her an additional push. "Show us how beautiful we make you feel," he said in a husky voice. "Undress for us that way."

Her gray eyes revealed so much of her heart and soul. He wondered if she realized what it did to them, seeing that kaleidoscope of response. Dipping her head so her hair fell forward over her shoulders, she freed her shirt from her skirt and slowly drew it over her head. The lace and small cups of her bra, the satin a rich purple color, barely held her quivering breasts.

She worked the skirt off her hips, offering a sexy little wriggle to make it drop to the ground. Her panties were a sheer purple mesh down to the folds of her pussy, with only a bit of purple lace over that area to screen the cotton crotch.

She straightened and tossed back her hair, sweeping it back over her bare shoulders in a ripple, posing before them in the scraps of underwear. She'd taken off the pendant and earrings, but retained Chris's ring, the little cat design he'd bought her at Naughty Bits. The pewter teddy bear with rhinestone eyes winked at the dimple of her navel.

"I'm going to have to buy you a collar," Geoff observed. "He's ahead of me in the jewelry department."

That glow from her increased. "I'd love that," she whispered.

"Yeah?" He anticipated the charge it would give them both, him putting that around her slim throat and locking it. Maybe he'd get one with a key and give that to Chris to wear on a chain around his neck, a whole other mixed statement of ownership. "What else would you love, Sam? Right now."

"I want to be with my Masters in the hot tub. With nothing between us."

Chris glanced at Geoff. Geoff kept his expression neutral, giving Chris tacit approval to do whatever inspired him. Geoff enjoyed watching them both. Was Chris aware of that and, if so, did it get him even harder, as it did Geoff? Watching Chris satisfy a woman never failed to stir Geoff.

Chris rose and moved toward her. He stroked the delicate curve of her breast and earned a tiny little indrawn breath as Sam caught her lip in her teeth. Geoff's attention narrowed down to every response between them, his own body tightening in reaction.

As Chris continued to caress the sensitive curves, Sam swayed. Sliding an arm around her waist, Chris dropped to a knee and pressed his mouth between her breasts. She curled an arm around his head to caress his hair, fingers pressing into his wide shoulders. She was cradling him against her at the same time she was submitting to him, a pleasure to watch.

Chris curled his tongue around a nipple just below the edge of the bra cup. Sam's buttocks tightened, creasing the silken fabric of the panties, and the muscles in Chris's arm bunched as he steadied her. "I can't get enough of tasting you," he murmured. "Geoff."

Geoff moved to join them. Once he was behind Sam, Chris locked gazes with him. "Lift her."

As Chris slid his hands behind her knees, Geoff understood. Banding an arm around Sam's waist, he whispered to her. "Let yourself fall backward," he said.

She did it without an instant's hesitation, trusting him. Chris slid her legs over his shoulders until her knees bent over them. As he sank to his heels, Geoff cradled her head in one palm, his other arm under her shoulders.

"Move the cups out of my way," he told her.

She exposed her breasts to him as ordered but arched up with a cry as Chris buried his face between her legs, his hands curving over her thighs to hold her open for him. Bending to put his mouth over one breast, Geoff suckled a nipple to tautness as she writhed in their hold. The position was a precarious one, leaving her unbalanced and relying on their support, but she didn't seem to doubt them for a moment.

"Oh . . . God . . . going to come," Sam said on a note of panic, and a little shock, probably at how quickly it was happening. Geoff wasn't surprised. Despite the disruption to their evening plans, they'd all been on pre-boil mode at the club. Plus, having had Chris's mouth on his dick, he knew just how capable that tongue was.

"Do it," Geoff said. "Come for us. It won't be the last time tonight, sweetheart."

She didn't have time to respond to that, a harsh cry ripping from her throat. He kept suckling her nipples, moving from one to the other. Chris held her fast, so the cry broke into a scream, a plea for mercy that wasn't likely to happen, not for this.

She was still gasping when Chris let her legs slide off his shoulders. Geoff moved back into a nearby chair, adjusting Sam so she was lying in his lap. Curving his fingers behind Chris's neck, he brought him off his heels to suck on his lips, tasting her sweet cunt and Chris's heated mouth at once. Sam's fingers teased their joined lips, dipping inside his mouth to play.

"Hot tub," Chris muttered.

"Hell yes," Geoff agreed. "I'll carry her there. You strip." He gave Chris a glittering look that Chris answered with a curled lip of challenge, but when they rose, Sam cradled in Geoff's arms, Chris was already pulling off his shirt and opening his jeans, toeing off his shoes.

The hot tub had been prepped for their arrival, so all they had to do was uncover it on the back porch and turn on the jets. The tub was screened by lattice, so they had their privacy. The night air was just cool enough to make the contrast comfortable. Chris stepped into the hot tub, already naked, and Geoff eased Sam into his arms. She was still boneless from the climax, but Chris captured her mouth in a demanding kiss that said they weren't planning on giving her a respite anytime soon. Her grip on his shoulders said she had no objections. Geoff passed a hand over Chris's hair, giving it a tug, then he stripped off his own clothes.

He ducked back inside for the practical stuff to circumvent the water's complete lack of lubrication, but he also snagged a couple of other things he thought they might enjoy. He'd noticed someone had been considerate enough to install handles along the wall of the hot tub to help with getting in and out, and that was an opportunity he didn't intend to underutilize.

As he returned, he used the shadows to cover the things he'd brought, putting them down on the corner of the tub. The creek below was a gentle music adding to the bubbling of the hot tub, and the night was punctuated by a variety of twinkling lights from distant houses, like earthbound stars. Mountain air always smelled so clean, and Geoff inhaled it as he sat on the ledge of the hot tub, letting himself get used to the temperature. It was a little hotter than he or Chris preferred, but with Sam being more cold-natured, they wouldn't change it. And there was plenty to distract their attention from the threat of boiling.

Chris brought the two of them closer to Geoff, Sam still sitting on his lap. Sam's eyes were more focused now. A safety light on the porch and the crescent moon illuminated her creamy skin, her radiant eyes. Her fingertips slid along Geoff's thigh, questing, and he closed his hand over hers. As Chris released her, she rested her knees on the lower step. Water spilled over her breasts, highlighting their shape and the nipples jutting from the small curves. She raised wet lashes to him. "May I put my mouth on you, Master?"

Would there ever be a time his whole body wouldn't surge at hearing her call him that? Or his heart leap at what it meant, what it could mean, as the love and trust between them grew? He hoped not.

At his nod, she lowered her head and covered him with her mouth. He braced his hands behind him, his eyes closing. They opened as Chris took a seat next to him on the ledge. Without a pause for warning, he dug his fingers into Geoff's hair and tipped his head back so he could set his teeth to his throat. He ran possessive fingers over Geoff's chest, teasing his nipples.

"Bastard," Geoff muttered and seized the hand, but only to put it to his face and bite the heel of Chris's hand. Leaning in, he took a deeper taste of that wide, sexy mouth. Jesus, having their lips on him in different ways was an incredible experience. Sam's pull on his cock was irresistible. He wanted to come right then and there. But instead, as he broke the kiss with Chris, he touched her shoulder and drew her off him, ignoring her pout of protest. "Stand up," he told her.

She obeyed, her eyes widening at his tone of wicked intent. Picking up the cuffs, aware of Chris's eyes on them both, he clicked them around her wrists. He'd visited Naughty Bits earlier in the week, thinking he might need something like them, in addition to the Velcro cuffs they'd already bought. They were modified police handcuffs, lined on the inside so that foam instead of metal would press against delicate bones when they were tightened, like now. He put his hand on the short chain between the cuffs, smiling a little when her fingers curved up to caress his hand as well as check out the new addition to their toy chest.

"She should still be wet from her climax, but there's lube there if you need it." He pointed Chris toward the tube on the corner. "I want to see you inside her cunt. You remember what I told you a while ago? About wanting to be balls deep in you while you're balls deep in her?"

Chris's eyes were already black in the shadows, but now they sparkled like coal, his mouth tightening. Sam trembled under Geoff's hold, the sound escaping her throat telling him she approved of their direction.

"Do you want her from the front or from the back?" Geoff said softly.

"Back," Chris said.

Geoff reached out and caught Chris's face in one hard hand. "Is that because you don't want her to see your face while I'm fucking you?"

Sam froze much the same way Chris did. Good. The lines were fluid, particularly now when they were all figuring their way, but Geoff wanted to be clear that he wasn't going to be dicked around. Chris's gaze locked with his, the muscles of his face tight, but Geoff didn't back off an inch. "No," Chris said in a low voice.

"Sure about that?" Geoff said silkily. "I happen to know you love spreading her thighs, watching the quiver of her tits as you thrust into her. You love watching her face while she gets lost in it, in what you're doing to her. Maybe she'd like the same thing. To see both of our faces."

"Yeah. Maybe. Didn't think about it like that. Okay. Front, then."

Chris pried Geoff's hand off him and brushed his mouth over Geoff's. "I don't worry about that other shit. I never have. Not really."

Seeing the truth of it in Chris's face, Geoff remembered what Logan had said when he'd sought his counsel about Chris. There were those rare few in the world who didn't worry about being gay, straight or something in between. Enlightened, he'd called it.

Responding to Chris's honesty with a short nod and a hard squeeze of his bare hip, Geoff turned his attention back to Sam. He adjusted her so she was sitting on the bench rather than kneeling, then put her into a reclining position, palming the back of her head until it met the cushioned headrest. Guiding her bound wrists over her head and behind her, he unlatched one cuff to thread it through a handle before closing it around her wrist again, holding her there. The position left her with her elbows comfortably bent but upper body arched and water-sleek. Between that and the leap of needy response in her eyes when he restrained her, he couldn't resist trailing his fingers over one glistening breast.

"What are you thinking, Samantha Beth?" he asked. A glance showed him Chris was working some lube over his dick, another distracting visual. The gentle giant, always making sure he wouldn't hurt their beautiful sub.

"I'm not thinking at all," she whispered.

"Good. If I'd left your hands free, I would have had you put lube on my cock, get me ready for him. But I think I like looking at you like this, waiting for him to slide into you. Watching the two of you is almost as good as being inside you."

Her eyes glowed. "It's a balance with him, isn't it?" she asked with that lovely shiver in her voice.

"Yeah. I might top him, but we both top you. Him taking you at the same time is a reminder of that."

Chris slid up beside him, his hand trailing along Geoff's waist, the upper curve of his buttock. "That may be true, but we're both hers, Geoff. She knows it." He gazed at Sam, his eyes covering the same hot-as-hell terrain that Geoff had been enjoying. "Or she should. Shouldn't she?"

"Yes," she said. There was a delicious plea in her tone now. "Please. I need you inside me."

413

"Never keep a lady waiting," Geoff said. "Unless, of course, she's a sub."

Sam choked on a half laugh, her face suffused with arousal. Geoff was aware of a tightness in his chest. It felt like happiness, belonging. And need. That need had a hint of violence, darkness, a lingering aftereffect from the club experience. There were better ways to channel that.

He moved back, palm sliding along Chris's wet back and down to his ass as Chris moved between her legs, guiding them up to his hips. He reached down into the water and stroked her. Geoff knew the moment he touched her pussy, because the water surged around her as her head dropped back, lips parting, body lifting to Chris's touch.

With his hand on Chris's buttock, Geoff felt that flex, the sense of give to Chris's forward motion as he sank into her heat. When he was lodged inside her, his knees were against the bench between her spread legs, his hands braced on the ledge on either side of her shoulders.

Geoff was in no particular hurry now, watching Chris begin to move in a deep rhythm. His friend bent to sip from Sam's lips and Geoff glimpsed her murmured response, the shining adoration in her eyes. Chris would move slow, drawing out her arousal until the climax shattered her mind, taking away every fear and leaving only this. They wanted to make every moment memorable for her. That was the goal.

But they each had their own individual desires as well. Geoff was okay with Chris doing those subtle things that made it clear he was as much in charge with Sam as Geoff himself was, but he couldn't help yanking the bear's chain himself. So when he shifted behind him, he dug his fingers into Chris's scalp and pulled him back by his hair to capture his mouth in a hot sucking kiss. He pushed his pelvis with intent against Chris's rhythmically pumping ass and earned a tangled groan and growl from Chris's throat, a leap of excitement in Sam's face.

Geoff took hold of his cock and funneled it between Chris's buttocks. As he hit the sweet spot in that tight, slick channel, he thanked the maker of waterproof lube. Pushing in deep, he dropped his hands to grip Chris's ass, squeeze and lift it.

"One day I'm going to do you the way you're fucking her," he said against Chris's ear, making sure that Sam's glazed eyes registered his words. She was already close to flying. Her pale body moved with the force of their combined thrusts. "I want to watch your face when I raise your legs around me and push into you, an inch at a time. Sam will kiss you, tease your nipples with her sharp little nails, and then I'll have her go down on your cock while I'm in your ass. What do you think of that?"

Sam shuddered, a whimper breaking from her lips as Chris thrust into her harder, a reaction to Geoff's taunt . . . or promise. "Sorry, did that hurt—" Chris managed and she shook her head vehemently.

"Do it again," she begged. "I want it to hurt some."

He did. Geoff tested that theory himself, pushing Chris hard. He dug his hands into his hips on each powerful thrust, loving how it felt to ram his cock deep into that delectable ass. Reaction rippled through Chris's body every damn time, the muscles tensing and releasing. Chris's breath rasped in his throat. Geoff could feel him ramping up toward a finish, so he set his teeth to his shoulder, biting hard enough he earned a curse.

"Yeah, I'm going to leave marks on you," he muttered. "Those won't be the last."

Chris let out another harsh noise. He was moving beyond words and it thrilled Geoff fiercely to know that the tight clutch of Sam's cunt, the drive of his cock, everything they were giving and taking from one another, was shooting Chris up that peak, taking Sam right along with him again.

It took a lot of effort—Geoff made sure of it—but gentleman that he was, Chris managed to wait until she fell before launching off that pinnacle. As she started to cry out, Geoff grabbed two handfuls of Chris's muscular ass, pressing the lobes tighter around his cock. "Come now," he demanded, and Chris came apart with guttural groans that Sam matched with high, thin wails.

Chris groped behind him to seize Geoff's nape, a grasp that conveyed both the force of his release, and what he wanted from Geoff. Sam's eyes, fastened on Geoff's face, reflected the same desire. They needed him to fall with them. Not a command as much as a compulsion impossible to resist.

But he wasn't ready to let go yet. Being fully erect and embedded inside Chris was almost as good as an actual orgasm. He wanted to prolong it a minute or two more. He muttered to Chris, and Chris heard him, fumbling to unfasten Sam's cuffs. They fell off the edge of the hot tub, clattering to the deck. In the aftermath of her release, Geoff knew the strain on her arms and back was starting to interfere with her comfort. He moved back, taking Chris with him so he could slide from her, let her straighten up, adjust. Now she had the freedom to slip out from beneath them.

Whereas Geoff had no intention of freeing Chris yet.

Watching Geoff take Chris on the kitchen table when she returned from her trip with Flo had been incredibly hot. Being linked together all three of them, where Geoff's every thrust into Chris was like a double penetration into her womb, had been even more intense, if that was possible. Though they took off the cuffs and gave Sam the ability to move, a courtesy, no discomfort in the world would have compelled her to move away from them. She wanted to be holding on to them when Geoff decided to come.

She slid behind Geoff, touched his back. She spread herself over him like a starfish, her arms sliding down along his arms, hips curved over his thrusting ass, her leg pressed against the back of his as he took Chris as deep and hard as Chris had taken her.

She knew or had guessed men often had rougher sex, though she suspected it could be tender between them, too. When Geoff was in Chris and Chris was in her, she'd felt some of that roughness, that male strength unhampered by concern about delicate female bones or tissues. While she appreciated that quality in them both, getting this close to what it was like between them made her long for even more of that rougher edge herself.

As Chris moved closer to the tub edge to grip it for balance, Geoff curved over him, the two of them like one creature. A creature of rippling, water-drenched muscles, sleek hair, intent, sharp eyes and taut mouths.

With a groan, Geoff released his seed into Chris, jamming himself against his back, licking and nipping at Chris's throat as his hips jerked, plunged. Chris's knuckles were white on the edge. Sam had shifted back to the wall Chris gripped, so she bent and pressed her lips to his wet fingers. Kept them there as they eventually slowed, as Chris's hold released and he touched her hair. He was in a full kneel, his head bowed and forehead almost to the handle where she'd been cuffed. Geoff had a firm grip around his chest, but he looked as if he was recuperating. Though it was a little late to be thinking about it, she had a momentary flash of worry about the heat of the water, if it might overcome one or, God help her, both of them. But Geoff hiked himself out to sit on the edge and offered Chris a hand to help him do the same. She drifted between their knees, gazing at the two naked, wet men, breaths bellowing in and out.

"Cold water?" she ventured. "To drink?"

Geoff nodded, and she left the hot tub, snagging a towel to wrap around her. She hurried into the house, retrieving two bottles of cold water from the fridge. It was chilly in the night air, so when she returned to them she stepped back into the tub. Geoff lifted a hand, stopping her there. "Don't sink back below the water yet." His voice was still hoarse from his climax, but the order was unmistakable.

Lustful sadist that he was, he kept her standing there a full minute, most of her out of the water, all shivering gooseflesh and tight nipples. Yet while her skin was cold, everything beneath it heated as they both looked at her. Theirs. It was obvious in the twin expressions and from the desire that rekindled in their eyes as they stared at her, drinking their fill of her bare flesh. God help her, they were only taking a breather. Yet her own body rippled in eager answer, ready for more.

"All right. You can get warm now."

She would have told them they'd already taken care of that in the most important way, but that hot water *was* blissful. She sank back into the water. As she moved her arms in a graceful flow around her, maybe it was just a bit calculated that she kept her breasts mostly above the surface, the nipples just below the gently lapping water, clearly visible since they hadn't turned the jets back on when they timed out. She felt like a mermaid seductively teasing a couple of pirates sitting on the rail of their ship.

"We'll take her once more tonight, won't we?" Chris commented. He kept his eyes fastened on her but spoke deliberately to Geoff, not to her, which made her stomach somersault. Yeah, he was learning the way of this whole Dom stuff. Enough that she might be the one overcome by the water's heat. Not that she really cared about that with

417

brown and hazel eyes fastened on her, a wealth of simmering demands in their depths.

Geoff lifted the bottle to his lips. "Oh fuck yeah. Maybe twice. She'll need it; we'll need it. Action is worth a whole lot more than words. After she can't walk, she'll know she doesn't need to worry about that kind of shit that happened at the club again. Not now, not ever." He shot her a dangerous grin, then bumped Chris's shoulder. "Neither do you. Come on. Let's move this inside."

There was a large shag throw rug in the living room. Its earth-toned colors were well past their most vibrant days, but it was soft and clean. That was where Geoff directed the three of them, sprawled out in a tangle of limbs as they rested. They dozed a little and, as Sam moved through that hazy, dreamlike state, she figured they'd just been teasing her about more sex to keep her on low boil until the next encounter. It was far more likely to happen sometime tomorrow, when they were capable of movement again.

She was wrong. She woke about an hour later to find Chris sitting up next to her. What had stirred her was that he'd captured her ankle in one hand and lifted it to his mouth. He was teasing her insole with his tongue. She hadn't ever thought of her feet as particularly erogenous zones, but a jolt thrummed straight along that track to arrow between her legs. He had his other hand under her knee, bending the leg, supporting it. Her heart moved into her throat as Geoff clasped the other foot and bit her ankle, following it up with a swirl of his tongue.

"You know," he said, "I don't think we're ever going to get tired of tasting your sweet pussy. *Our* sweet pussy."

Their time in the hot tub had been passionate, but there'd been a more relaxed interaction there, an organic flow. The expression he tipped toward her now was decidedly less low-key. The energy was more like what she'd felt from them at the club. While they'd put aside their stronger reactions in favor of making her feel better, that aggression hadn't entirely dissipated.

She remembered her sudden urge for rougher treatment and knew maybe she was harboring some of those unsettling feelings. As they made her more helpless with their mouths, she craved their demands, wanted them to push her far beyond what she thought she could endure or give.

Geoff guided her foot up to his shoulder, working his mouth along her ankle and calf. Both men shifted as needed, each moving at a gradual pace up the length of the limb he'd claimed, spreading her legs ever wider to give them room to scatter sucking kisses across her flesh, tease her with a tip of a tongue along the tender bones of the ankle, the back of her knee, the curve of the calf, and then to her thighs.

She drew in a breath, her hands landing on Chris's head and Geoff's shoulder, gripping, stroking, her body rising to their mouths. Chris shifted to his hip, courteously allowing Geoff first taste of the damp folds between her legs, and giving himself the indulgence of her breasts, moving up to suckle and squeeze them with his big hands as Geoff's tongue slid inside her, began to lick and swirl.

"Oh . . . God . . ."

Geoff let out a demonic chuckle against her flesh, stabbed deeper into her and wrested a scream from her throat. She was twisting, pleading. Chris clasped her wrist, pinning it as Geoff held her legs down and they did as they desired to her.

It wasn't until her body was undulating like a crashing storm wave that they shifted and changed position, smoothly as the movement of water itself, so she had the pleasure of both their mouths covering the same terrain. Each time she was close to coming, they'd draw back, switch to another part of her body, until her skin tingled all over, stimulated by every touch and kiss.

"Please . . ." She moaned for the thousandth time, her fingers sliding off a shoulder, tugging a handful of hair, nails digging into firm muscle. She knew each of them distinctly, every touch upon her unique to the man giving it, yet it was all one at the same time.

Chris gripped her waist, bringing her to her feet in an abrupt display of strength that sent her heart somersaulting and her dizzy head spinning. He gave her to Geoff, who pressed himself against her back, pushing her hair aside to claim her neck with teeth. They'd been leaving marks on her since the beginning, and she knew she'd never tire of seeing those abrasions and bruises tattooing her flesh, all administered in the name of desire. Geoff clasped her breasts in strong hands, tilting them up for Chris as he put his mouth on one nipple and started to suckle again. "Oh . . . fuck . . ."

They weren't giving her time to breathe, to do anything but ride the wild force of this testosterone surge, which she understood in some primal way was their alternative to bashing those guys' faces in. Well, if this had to be her contribution to world peace . . .

She didn't even have the room to laugh at herself. They intended to take her forcefully and well, burning away everything in her world but them and their passion for her. She'd seen the desire between them, had the fierce stimulation of watching Geoff take Chris, of them kissing, touching one another, but right now that cohesion had another form. They had one shared goal, and that was making sure she knew she was theirs. Or taking her to death's edge from an overdose of sexual release.

Either way, she was good with it.

Geoff lifted her and she wrapped her legs around Chris's hips, crying out as he thrust into her. Geoff parted her buttocks and then his slick cock was there. Torturously, he let Chris's momentum be the hammer that drove her down on him, inch by inch. She started to come when he was only halfway in, the climax ripping through her so hard and fast there was no way to stop herself. Geoff slid all the way in and she reached back blindly, grabbing at his neck as she gripped Chris's shoulder in front of her.

"Yes . . ." she breathed. "I love you . . . both . . . of . . . you."

"Same goes, baby," Geoff growled against her ear. She saw the same knowledge in Chris's gladiator savage expression as they followed her over that edge, holding on to her all the way over and down, taking the ride together.

"The CCI bank deposit was off by fifty thousand dollars. They're calling in the higher-ups, but it looks like you're going to get accused of embezzling. I suggest you get a good lawyer."

Sam chewed her sandwich, swallowed. "I guess that makes sense." She blinked and looked away from the ducks placidly paddling across the retention pond. "Hunh? What?"

Flo chuckled. They were sitting outside the bank at one of the picnic tables provided for employee lunch breaks, where the breeze filtered through the canopies of the dogwood trees above them.

"Would you like to tell me what's on your mind?" the older woman asked, taking a sip of her half-and-half tea. "Originally the suspense was driving me crazy. Now it's just making me want to slap the shit out of you."

Sam smiled. "Sorry about that. I was just thinking about something that happened this weekend." Briefly, she explained what had happened at the club, gratified when she saw Flo's lips thin in righteous annoyance on her behalf.

"I know they were off base, but it got me wondering. You're my friend, you'll be honest with me. Do you think this is an *Oh my god, two guys are sharing me and isn't it fabulous while it lasts* kind of thing?"

Flo pursed her lips. "Have you ever thought about Neanderthals?"

"Are you comparing the guys at the club to them?"

"No. I suspect Neanderthals were more polite. Anyway, I wonder what it was like to be cavemen, at a time long before social groups started forming, with rules and structure and implied expectations of behavior. What if the norm for committed relationships had been a threesome, instead of just two people? Then couples would face the questions you're asking yourself now. *Well, everyone else chooses two people to love, but I only have this one person. Will it last? What if she or he decides they want a third at some point? How will society look at us as just a two-person family?*"

"You're saying I'm worrying too much about it." Sam took another bite of her sandwich. "But it's even more than that. Geoff and Chris seem fine with it now, but what do I do if one of them ever finds someone else and it leaves just two of us? I love them both, so separately, it should still work the same, right? People have been doing fine with the idea of one-on-one forever. But it doesn't feel that way to me. I feel like if one of us died after all three of us were together forever, then the two left would still be together. That's a whole different thing. But if it's a matter of one of them walking away, it would be the end of it all. Like, hey, we *are* three people in love and I'm not settling for anything less."

"Nothing in life is guaranteed. You don't know what will happen until you get to it. But I can tell you what I do know. As with any relationship, if you want it bad enough, then you have to be willing to work your ass off for it, not just when it suits you, but every day. You also can't assume that every time Geoff mentions a handsome guy at work or Chris notices a pretty girl walking down the street, or one of them is in a bad mood, or if you fight about bills or who does what chore, that things are coming unraveled."

"We won't ever be able to be married. All of us."

"Being married on paper is a wonderful reinforcement of what's already in your hearts. A lack of paper doesn't change that. Enjoy the hell out of being with the people you love. Because the one thing we all know is none of us are given that gift forever."

The shadow that crossed Flo's eyes reminded Sam that she'd loved and lost before. She'd had to divorce an alcoholic husband who, when he cleaned up a decade later, had reconciled with Flo. He'd died two years after that. Sam nudged her friend, drawing her away from dark memories. "So are you going to the Carnival in the Round this weekend?"

"Have to go to my damn nephew's wedding," Flo grumbled. "It's a marriage doomed to failure, but I have to attend and pretend that opportunistic bitch won't wreck his life. I'll probably gain twenty pounds keeping my mouth occupied with hors d'oeuvres and wedding cake."

"Ouch." Sam winced. "We'll do extra walking when you get back. Damn, though. I hate that you're going to miss Madison's event."

"I have a feeling she'll be having another one. She's already reached her goal of two hundred and fifty attendees and had to turn another hundred or so away." Flo touched Sam's hand. "Which, circling back to the original point, says people are more open to exploring their desires and tolerating new ways of looking at them than ever before. I think people are learning *Hey, even if that's not my thing, it's okay if it's their thing, as long as wrongful harm isn't being done. And as long as they're not shoving it in my face and saying I have to throw a party in honor of their form of freakiness*." Flo arched a brow. "So I assume you're going?"

"Yes. We are. I even have something beautiful and crazy to wear to it." Sam thought of the mask and corset and imagined Chris in the pants Geoff had gotten for him. She wondered what Geoff would be wearing. "If you could go, who would you have brought? You know, to celebrate your own form of freakiness?"

"Hmm. He's a fifty-four-year-old Russian with eyes like a winter forest. He looks like a cross between a grungy biker and a wealthy mobster. He likes kissing my feet and calling me Mistress with this glint in his eyes that makes me want to tie him up and have my way with him. Since he likes that idea, too, it's win-win."

Sam's eyes widened and she scooted closer. "Why have I not heard about him before? When you talk about him, your eyes twinkle and you blush a little."

"I certainly do not," Flo said with mock horror. Sam poked at her with a potato chip and she fended her off. "Do not annoy me, subling."

"Is that anything like *duckling*? You just made that up."

"I did, but it fits."

"Don't get off topic. Tell me the first cool thing he did to attract your cold Domme heart. Details."

"You're a menace," Flo informed her, but her lips quivered, telling Sam she was going to relent and offer a couple of choice morsels of information. "The first time I was in a session with him, he put me up against a wall, my feet dangling six inches above the floor, and said, *'Are you afraid of me?'*"

"No way. Did you kick him in the balls?"

"It's not about physical force." Flo sniffed. "Though it's intriguing how often a physically dominant man will test you that way. I told him *no* in a tone that would have frozen off your eyelashes, and to put me down. He looked down at his hands and said, *'You have tiny waist. Like bird. Mockingbird, mean and sleek at once.'* Which is ridiculous, as I have an average-sized waist, but apparently he's been used to bigger women. He put me down, bent and kissed my feet to ask for forgiveness. But I think he introduced himself to me that way to prove how much stronger he was, that he could do anything he wanted to me. He knew that would excite me . . . but he also wanted to see if I'd know that wasn't what he wanted to do. He wanted me to do anything I wanted to *him*."

Sam blinked. Flo looked almost . . . dreamy. "When did you meet him?"

"Not long ago. About a month or so. I meet a lot of people when I go to the parties. He's different, though. We've been out a few times on regular dates. You've been busy. I didn't want to distract you."

"You wanted to keep him all to yourself for a while, you mean. Enjoy the feeling and not make too much of it in case it was a fling."

Flo broke off a piece of her pita, chewed. "Yes. Maybe. I'll introduce you to him sometime if you like. His name is Kirill." Her brown eyes twinkled. "It's of Greek origin, and means *master* or *lord*."

"No way."

"Yes way. But see what I mean?" Flo lifted a shoulder. "Nothing is set in stone; nothing is so predictable that it's impossible to imagine it another way. You want to be in love with two men from now until you're all old and gray, then do it. Don't worry about anything other than how you feel about one another."

"I do worry about some of that. And even though a lot of stuff is resolved, I admit sometimes I still worry about Chris when it comes to the Dom/sub stuff."

"If he wasn't interested in any of that, but he still wanted to be with the two of you, could you make it work? Does it have to be Dom/sub twenty-four/seven?"

"No. Of course not. We're not twenty-four/seven. I mean, there are these little flirty undercurrents between Geoff and me a lot of the time, but when it's not about being in that mode, we're still doing the day-to-day things. Sharing chores, expenses, me dealing with my family, that kind of thing. So it doesn't have to be all or nothing. I want to be with them more than I think I've wanted anything before, and I'm willing to figure out whatever we need to figure out to make that work."

"Then that's all you need to worry about." Flo tapped her forehead in an amusing gesture of benediction. "Go forth, child, and have your way with their gorgeous asses as long as the fates allow."

She laughed, ducking as Sam threw a crumpled napkin at her. "Come on. Lunch is over, Ms. Assistant Manager. Back to the scintillating world of financial management."

⁓

The night they were going to the Carnival, Sam's intention was to close herself in the bathroom and make a grand appearance in the gifts they'd given her, but she soon realized her best intentions were not going to give her the ability to put herself in a corset.

Poking her head out of the bathroom, she glimpsed Chris in his room. He'd finished his shower but was still shirtless, because he was putting on deodorant. He wore a pair of dress jeans open in the front, the belt unbuckled. As he applied the deodorant, he bent and used his elbow to bump up the volume on the Temptations playing through his speakers. When he put down the capped deodorant and ran a hand through his still-damp hair, she realized she was just watching. Enjoying the hell out of one of her men, just like Flo said. She finally cleared her throat and Chris turned, lowering the volume. He gave her an equally appreciative look, since she was clad only in her thin robe, loosely tied.

"I think I need some help," she said. "Want to try tying a corset?"

"I looked it up on the Internet last night, so I can probably figure it out."

She blinked. "Of course you did. Why did you do that?"

"Well, when we bought the corset from Naughty Bits, Madison mentioned how much a lot of women liked the feeling of being tied into a corset. Especially in the case of someone like you . . . by her Master." He shifted when he said that, as if he wasn't sure if she'd be comfortable hearing it that way, but he was right on target.

"She's a smart woman. And I have two Masters. You just happen to be the one in the right place at the right time."

He grinned. Fastening his pants and buckling the belt, he came across the hallway to her, stepping into the bathroom as she retreated to the sink. His hair still had that damp clean smell and the jeans were the stressed, designer kind that looked really good on him. It wouldn't be a hardship to reconcile herself to that look tonight, if he decided against putting on the pants Geoff had given him once they arrived there.

She bet he'd tried them on in his room this week when she and Geoff couldn't see. Which meant he probably had experienced another *What the fuck?* moment and was waffling on whether he'd have the courage to wear them. She was hoping he would and made a mental note to be sure he didn't leave them at home "by accident."

She didn't think he'd resort to that, though. She'd mentioned them several times this week, making it clear she would love, love, love it if he wore them. As Geoff had pointed out, neither of them could really resist doing something she truly wanted. She didn't view her pressure on him to wear them as an abuse of that power, though. Far from it. Especially since she suspected Geoff actually approved of the tactic this time.

She hid a smile at that thought, but then humor gave way to other distractions as Chris stepped up behind her. Without asking or hesitation, he unbelted her robe and slid it from her shoulders, leaving her clothed in nothing but a silver-gray thong and his regard, which roved over her with purposed pleasure. She wondered if he'd been taking lessons from Geoff, or if he was just learning to follow his own inclinations, encouraged by her obvious response to such decisive action.

She let out a pleased hum when he cupped a breast and slid his hand down to her hip, hooking the thong with his thumb before he caressed her ass and leaned over to pick up the corset.

It hooked in the front on steel pins and was already drawn snug enough he could hook it down the front and it would stay in place, though it wasn't yet tight enough to shape her properly. She bent her head, watching his capable fingers move over the hooks, then he shifted behind her again, making her face the mirror as he started adjusting the laces. Watching his intent expression, the set of his mouth and focus of his eyes while he did it, inhaling his scent, feeling his heat so close behind her as he bound her in the snug garment, kept her feeling all tingly and anxious in the right ways.

As he figured out what he was doing, anxiety was replaced with arousal, a sweet little surge of it with each pull of the laces. The boning began to etch out her waist and the flare of her hips like an hourglass, her breasts rising over the top edge. The firm mounding drew his eyes as he tied it off in back. He smoothed his large palms over her.

"Too tight?" he asked.

Yes. "No." He could cut off her breathing and she'd just ask for more. She loved how it felt. When Chris grasped her buttock with one hand, the other resting on the stiff fabric at her hip, she swayed into his touch. It wasn't just the way he'd taken off her robe, but everything he was doing. There was something different about him tonight. Quieter, more direct. In control.

Leaning down, he pressed his lips to her bare shoulder as his hand slid back up to frame her breast, thumb rubbing over the plumped-up curve and dipping into the now deep valley of her bosom. "No, what?" he murmured. His lashes lifted to capture her gaze in the mirror with his own. He held her there with an unwavering attention.

Who was this man and what had he done with Chris? Yet it was

Chris, not an act. That was what had butterflies doing triple somersaults in her stomach. "Yes sir. I mean, No sir."

He smiled, reached over and picked up her hairbrush. She quivered, wondering if she was about to get a spanking. While that would have been lovely, he surprised her with something unexpectedly as welcome. He used it as intended, brushing out her hair until it shone like silk on her shoulders. Gathering it up in his hand, he rubbed his lips and nose over it. Closed his eyes. All of it made her want to breathe his name. Meaning she wanted to use his name as a way to draw in breath and release it. As well as speak it.

"Chris."

He opened his eyes again. "Bend over the sink," he said.

Her knees almost buckled, but she managed it. He curved a hand over her right breast, kneading and playing with it, and he hit her ass with the flat back of the brush. Her fingers tightened on the sink as that breath left her in a gasp. It stung, but she only wanted more.

He gave her more. Five then ten whacks, each more stinging than the last, until her ass was throbbing and she was making a little cry in her throat at each strike. She was also getting light-headed.

"Nice marks," he said. Laying down the brush, he straightened her, holding her fast and meeting her gaze in the mirror. "I'm going to ask you again. Is it too tight?"

"A little," she admitted breathlessly.

He returned to the task. This time, when he was done, she was still snugly wrapped in it, but breathing was easier. He gave her one more whack with the brush, this one enough to earn a yelp, then gripped her throat, caressing it. Cradling her face in a hand that could easily break her neck, he tipped her head back on his shoulder to look at him. "Remember the first rule, Sam. Got it?"

She stammered her response. "Yes sir."

He kissed her and his eyes softened, more like the Chris she was used to. "Better finish getting ready. Geoff said we're out of here in about ten minutes. Are you wearing the black heels with the silver bottoms?"

At her nod, he smiled. "Good. I love the way you walk in those."

Turning, he left her there. She might have dropped her jaw on the floor if it weren't hinged properly to her face. If this was any indication of what kind of night it was going to be, she might not have any unexploded brain cells by the end of the evening.

When she finished dressing and left the bathroom, she found Geoff already dressed and waiting on them in the kitchen. He wore a fitted black dress shirt in a brushed cotton so soft it made her want to rub against him like a cat. It was open at the throat and tucked into stonewashed gray jeans, a combination that would complement her own colors. The jeans were a pair she hadn't seen before, and they fit snug over ass and groin, His black belt had a silver buckle shaped like a dragon's head. The black boots under the jeans were sleek and supple with a low heel.

His tanned forearms were visible because he'd rolled up the sleeves of the shirt to his elbows. For some reason, his silver-and-black watch only made the look even sexier. He was mouthwatering, head to toe.

She'd donned a skirt over the thong and the bottom part of the corset, and carried a gray shawl she could wrap over her shoulders. Would Geoff and Chris choose to take the wrap and skirt off her once they hit the doors at the Carnival? She was nervous about that idea, but if they were headed into the kind of environment she hoped it would be tonight, she also welcomed it. She was more than willing for Chris to act just as much like her Master as Geoff did naturally and without thought. Geoff's gaze moved over her, displaying the obvious male desire that Chris had, along with a similar possessiveness. That look fostered a sudden titillating suspicion.

Was it her being in a public venue tonight, wearing this kind of outfit, that had compelled Chris to make it clear that she belonged to them, in a way that engaged her senses in that ownership? He was certainly clever enough to figure how much that reaction would excite her, but what bemused her was how genuine it had seemed for him.

He wasn't Dom through and through, but he didn't mind mixing it into his nature when it brought him, her or Geoff satisfaction. She had no objection to that mix, for certain. Her buttocks were still smarting, and she knew the mark of that last swat might still be there if they did remove the skirt once they arrived at their destination.

Chris came into the kitchen then. Geoff glanced at the small tote she was carrying over her arm. "Is the mask in there?"

She nodded.

"Put it on now."

She set the tote on the table. Pulling out a hair band, she fixed her long hair in a flat knot at the crown of her head. The mask allowed room for such an eventuality by including a "crest" for the bird's head. Touching her hair recalled Chris brushing it. As she picked up the mask, the sleek feathers that covered it caressed her own fingers. All her senses were on erotic high volume, but particularly touch, as if every inch of her skin craved sensation and magnified the barest contact.

Under Geoff's silent scrutiny, she slid the mask over her head and drew it down to cover her face. It had discreet zippers and lacing in the back to tighten it. Chris came up behind her, once again handling the lacing part, tightening the mask, making everything fit in its intended place so her face was enclosed by the supple material. The bottom of the mask curved under her jaw and molded to her nape, leaving most of her throat bare. The opening for the mouth framed her lips, making them feel more sensitive and exposed.

She'd folded her nervous hands in front of her as Chris did the task. The eyeholes weren't covered, and Geoff stood in her line of sight, but it shifted her into a different headspace, having her key senses cocooned like that. It was as if looking at him through the mask was like being a bird in a cage, looking out at her Master, waiting for his will to free her.

When Chris was done, he rested his hand on her shoulder. She drew in the heat and strength of his body pressed behind her as Geoff picked up her hand, bringing it to his lips. He took her shawl and Chris moved back so Geoff could wrap it around her shoulders, putting the twisted ends in her hands.

"Our beautiful dove," he said. "Let's go."

Tonight Geoff drove, first because he was the one who could drive like a New York cabbie if they hit traffic snarls and second, she wasn't in any condition. DWIA, driving while insanely aroused, was definitely no safer than driving drunk. Geoff hadn't even asked if she wanted to drive, directing her firmly over to his car. As he got in the front, Chris put her in the passenger seat, taking the seat behind them.

Geoff turned over the engine but then leaned over, adjusting the tiny rolled flaps that accentuated the shape of the eyeholes like lashes when they weren't in use. When unrolled, they put her in darkness.

"You'll stay blindfolded until we get there. Spread your legs, Sam."

A needy sound came from her throat as his fingers slipped under her skirt, found the crotch of the thong and stroked her wetness, a slow, methodical rhythm that had her body moving restlessly on the seat. He drew his hand away. "Chris and I are going to talk, but you don't speak without permission first unless something's wrong. Understand?"

"Yes sir. Thank you, sir."

She added that without thinking. The silence suggested the two of them were studying her or exchanging a glance. Either way, she hoped they understood. *Thank you for all of this. Thank you both for loving me, for being willing to do all of this. For wanting to do this.*

Geoff put the car in drive and pulled out of the driveway. They did start talking, and it was incredibly arousing to have them talk about the things they might always talk about, all while she sat silently, blinded, waiting on their direction. Her body was aware of everything: the bump of the car over the asphalt, the feel of the recirculated air against her skin. Chris's hand stayed on her shoulder, and Geoff's occasionally curved over her thigh, both of them maintaining a connection with her.

It was what she'd always imagined being a submissive could be like.

Chris had asked Geoff something about the program, because Geoff was explaining it. "When I talked to Logan, he said they'll do the stage performances first, but there will be vendors and socializing afterward. They'd thought about setting up a dungeon with the local BDSM group, but they decided for this first event they'd keep it more limited. The vendors are going to be offering hands-on demos of everything from whips to sex toys, so we might see some impromptu play under the guise of shopping." Geoff chuckled.

"If we wanted to tie her up in someone's restraint system, we could?"

"Possibly. I wouldn't mind making her climax like that with some sex toy they want to promote. Did you bring that gag?"

"Yeah. It's in the tote."

Geoff's hand closed over her thigh again. "Breathe, Samantha Beth."

She gave a nervous half laugh, but did so. She was vibrating just from his command to sit here and listen, with her legs spread and her body showcased in an outfit designed to make them want her even more. She wanted to spread her legs wider, shamelessly encourage him to touch her there again.

Chris passed his hand along her neck, teasing the edge of the mask at her nape, petting the feathers. "Do you think she'd like that? Coming in front of an audience?"

"I think she won't even be aware there's an audience. Not that way. As long as it's us doing it, and we're totally in control, I think she'd love it. I think she wants to prove she loves belonging to us."

She hoped nodding in emphatic agreement wasn't against the no-talking rules. Geoff slowed the car, probably for a stoplight, and her lips parted eagerly when he traced them with a fingertip. He pressed it between her lips so she could suck on it, swirl her tongue around it with wanton implication.

"So she doesn't want anyone else touching her?" Chris slid his touch down her arm, caressing the top of her breast under the shawl.

"Not if she knows what's good for her," Geoff said with tantalizing menace. It almost made her smile, because he knew she didn't want anyone else to touch her. She might be willing to have them take her body in front of a stadium of people, as long as it was only about the three of them. People watching would be titillating, a witness to their relationship, but she didn't want anyone crossing that personal barrier between her and them.

"Here we are," Geoff said a few minutes later, turning into what she assumed was a parking lot and bringing the car to a halt.

Geoff came around and opened her door. She heard the distant sound of people talking, a flow of conversation that drifted back as they all headed in a common direction. Geoff didn't open the eyes of the mask, instead taking her arm.

"I'll let you see when we're inside," he said. "You're already getting a lot of attention."

Her lips parted, but Geoff's mouth was on hers before she could utter a syllable. Pressing her back against the car, he took her over with a kiss that was pure demand. When he was finished, he had his hands around her throat, thumbs sliding up and down her jugular, putting just a little dizzying pressure on it.

"What did I tell you, Samantha Beth?"

"No talking," she managed. "Without your permission."

"Don't forget again. I have no problem spanking you in front of a group. In fact, I was damn well hoping for the opportunity."

He dropped his touch to her waist. "I know you were about to say it's the outfit. It's not. It's the woman in it that has their attention. When you're under command, restrained, you glow. The energy around you could fuel a stadium."

"Amen to that," Chris added, curling his hand around her elbow. "You're stunning, Sam."

She moistened her lips, brushed against his body and squeezed one of Geoff's hands, the only way she was allowed to say thank you. Geoff made a noise of approval and drew her away from the side of the car, taking them toward their destination.

She'd never been led by someone while completely blind, but with Chris on one side and Geoff on the other, she was secretly thrilled with her lack of worry. She had no problem walking on her high heels as confidently as she would when she could see. Their hands never left her, honoring her trust.

They moved inside a building filled with the low rumble of noise of a gathering crowd. The theater had the pleasant combination of woodsy scents that identified it as an old yet well-tended building. There was carpet under her heels. On top of the building's olfactory imprint, she detected a variety of body perfumes and colognes, as well as the musk of wine. The *clink* of glasses verified the last. Geoff guided her to a wall, where the noise became more muted, telling her he'd taken her out of the flow of foot traffic.

He didn't open the eyes of the mask right away. Instead he took the shawl off her shoulders, letting the cool, dry air of the theater interior tickle over her bare shoulders and the tops of her breasts. He unzipped the skirt next. Chris took her other hand and Geoff guided her to step out of the garment. She was standing in front of strangers in a thong, thigh-high stockings and her corset. And the mask. Madison had told her many would be dressed in fetish wear, and she knew Geoff wouldn't have undressed her unless she would blend. Even so, she was feeling dizzy, but her men steadied her, their hands on her sure and strong.

"Okay?" Chris asked.

"Yes sirs."

"Good girl." At last Geoff lifted the eye flaps, tucking them into the slits intended for that purpose, so she could see her surroundings. Here again, the tunnel feeling of the mask made her feel protected, as if she were a bird in the cage he'd made her, detached and safe. Able to experience everything even more forcefully, because she wasn't required to talk or interact. Nothing was expected of her but to feel, hear, see, taste and smell.

The area where they stood was a large foyer open to the stage area, allowing plenty of room to mingle before the performances began. She saw plenty of leather, lace and metal mixed with fancy, sexy club wear made of silk and rhinestones. More than one Master or Mistress had their submissive on a leash, and a couple had head masks shaped like canines, submissives who enjoyed puppy play. There was also a good mix of people she could tell were new to all this but fascinated by those around them who weren't. They held their wineglasses and smiled and talked, even as their eyes darted here and there, taking it all in.

Her own eye was attracted by a Master who had a whip tucked into his boot, ready in an instant to hand out discipline to his submissive, a black woman with doe-like eyes, full moist lips and dressed in a transparent silver shift with nothing under it. She knelt at his side as he spoke to several other people.

Sam's hand crept into Geoff's on one side, into Chris's in the other. It wasn't that she was afraid . . . just somewhat overwhelmed. A quick glance at Chris suggested he might be in a similar boat, since he was looking around like some of the others who were obviously less experienced with the BDSM lifestyle. He'd said he'd gone with Geoff to some of his club visits, but she wasn't sure he'd ever been exposed to this size of a crowd or this mix of fetishes before. Geoff seemed less off balance, though from his frequent glances over the two of them, gauging their reaction, and the protective energy vibrating from him, she expected it was the first time he'd brought his own submissive.

She also saw he was right about her getting a lot of admiring looks. She still thought the main reason for it was the corset and mask, because they were a striking combination no matter who was wearing them. But she had to admit she'd never felt so sexy in her entire life.

The old building had been decorated for the event. Madison had draped the beams laced across the high ceiling in shimmering fabrics and hung erotic artwork on the cracked plaster walls. Some pieces Sam recognized from the Naughty Bits store. Heavier drapes had been hung in key places to dampen the white noise in the foyer gathering space and increase the sense of an intimate party, no matter that over two hundred people were present.

"Why don't you go change before the show starts?" Geoff said to Chris then. "You have ten minutes."

"I can do it afterward."

Since one of Chris's hands was on her other shoulder, she tilted her head in that direction, rubbing the smooth feathered front of the bird mask against Chris's knuckles and finding them with her mouth, caressing flesh with tongue and lips. He let out a muttered, amused oath as she lifted her eyes to him. "May I speak freely again, Master?" she asked.

"You may." It was Geoff who answered, probably because she'd never called Chris *Master* directly that way, and even more likely because he knew what she was going to do.

"Please," she said to Chris. "I would love to see you wear Geoff's gift. I know he would, too. Please?"

He ran his thumb over her lips, sighed and shouldered the tote. "Back in a minute," he told Geoff. "And for the record, you're both pains in my ass."

"Glad to serve a purpose," Geoff rejoined, grinning.

As she'd noted when Geoff first removed the eye coverings, the foyer was open to the performance area, where the graduated seating arranged in a crescent shape around the stage down front ensured no one's view would be blocked. Since the seating was already filling up, Geoff directed her to an aisle spot. Many of those seated nearby looked in their direction, studying Sam and her Master. In an environment like this, everyone would be curious about everyone else, and since she was looking just as intently, she couldn't feel self-conscious. Plus, Geoff's hand never left her elbow. She was sure he was gauging everything about her state of mind through that grip. Whether she was cold, afraid, nervous.

Nervous, yes, but she wasn't afraid or cold. Heat shimmered off her skin and she felt like a wild creature, ready to fly and play under his and Chris's control.

Geoff took the aisle seat, leaving one seat between them to hold a place for Chris, but he kept her hand firmly in his grip, his thumb sliding along her pulse. She could feel his eyes upon her and she lifted her own. What she saw in his face made her wet her lips. "What are you thinking?" she asked, bemused to hear that little break in her voice again.

He leaned over the empty seat to caress her masked cheek. His face was very close, and what was in his eyes infused his quiet words with a power that made her shudder. "Nothing proper. Nothing sane or civilized."

"Say it anyway," she whispered.

"I want to put collars on you both and stamp them with my name. I want to have you both kneeling at my feet, so I can just put my hands on your faces, like I'm doing with yours now, have you looking up at me and know . . . that you willingly belong to me. That you're as fully mine . . ."

She'd never seen his expression so open and raw, so savage and vulnerable at once. There was a heartbreaking beauty to it that stole her breath, stopped her heart. He paused, as if collecting himself. She tangled her fingers with his, and gave him the words that emotions had taken from him.

"As you are ours," she finished. "We are, Master. Always."

He put his mouth on hers, all demand and need. She surrendered all of herself to him through that kiss, so he'd know it wasn't the heat of the moment. It was simply truth.

He lifted his head, stared at her. "I love you so fucking much," he said. "I should have told you that the first second I met you, because I bet somewhere in my heart I already knew it was true."

"That might have been a little scary," she said with a tremulous smile. "You know, stalker stuff."

His lips curved. A smattering of applause broke into their absorption with each other. Glancing toward the stage, Geoff reluctantly drew back, though he kept her hand as if he had no intention of ever relinquishing it back to her. "They must have some pre–main performance stuff. I didn't know. Hopefully Chris will get back soon."

"Hopefully Chris will leave the bathroom before the end of the evening," she teased him. "He's probably even now standing in front of the mirror, saying, *No fucking way.*"

Geoff chuckled and squeezed her hand. Then they both turned their attention to the stage.

Two Dommes, one in a sequined white sheath and black boots, the other her mirror image in black sheath and white boots, were executing a performance with a single tail whip. As one Domme held up a board target with balloons shaped like a flower mounted on it, the other Domme burst all the balloons, one by one, with the throws of her whip. Letting her whip coil at her side, she produced another balloon, this one held up in her bare hand for the other Domme. That Mistress had a longer whip than the first Domme's, yet she was just as proficient. She broke the balloon with a sharp, dramatic pop.

They bowed and exited the stage to applause. More people wandered in from the foyer. Sam thought it had been a smart tactic on Madison's part, to offer a couple of mini-offerings onstage to bring in the foyer stragglers, getting everyone seated and quiet before the main performance.

The next to take the stage was a large man with mustache, shoulder-length brown hair and broad, handsome features that reminded her of Lee Horsley in *The Sword and the Sorcerer*. The movie was one of Geoff's classic "geek" DVD collection, as Chris called it.

This man wore a vest over his bare upper torso and pantaloons. He twirled and tossed knives with firelit blades in an impressive display. As he did the traditional fire-eating trick, an Indian woman wearing no clothing at all, her head shaved to a pearlescent gleam, came and knelt before him. She put her forehead and elbows to the ground so the brown curve of her spine created a delicate bridge. Another woman, pale and also naked except for a glittering copper collar, stood at his side with further props.

He gave the knives to the helper, and Sam drew in a breath as the fire seemed to leap to his hands. He stroked the bowing woman in swift, graceful movements with the flame as she stayed docile and trusting under his touch. Over the curve of her back, to her nape, over her bare scalp, lingering over her raised buttocks. When he spoke a one-word command in a language Sam didn't recognize, she stretched out on her back, gazing up at him.

Going to his knees beside her, he drizzled a fluid on her flesh that shaped the flame into a bluish zigzag pattern on her breasts, mons and thighs. When he stretched out on her as if he was going to take her right there onstage, the fire rippled in the space between their bodies. He quenched it by closing that gap, pressing tightly against her from breasts to hips. The crowd *oohed* and gasped; then, just as quickly and smoothly, he was next to her again, once more applying the flickering gold-and-blue heat to her skin with the bare palms of his hands.

He finished his performance with the woman coming up on her knees and pressing a kiss to either of his now doused hands, which he curved over her bare skull before kissing her forehead.

As the fire performers were exiting the stage to further applause, the house lights dimmed, indicating the main show was about to start. Geoff's hand tightened on her, drawing her attention from the stage once more. She didn't know if that was his intent, or if the flex of his fingers was purely in reaction to Chris, but after one look at Chris, she was pretty sure it was the latter. As for her, thought deserted her in favor of a pure surge of *I want that*.

Chris could have put on the pants but retained his T-shirt, keeping somewhat within his comfort zone, but he'd gratifyingly gone full out. He'd worn the upper-body harness. The straps and metal rings accentuated his impressive upper body just as she'd anticipated they would. As for the pants, they would have inspired a saint to dive right into a vat of sin and happily do the backstroke. They fit him like a second skin, his cock and balls mounded up against the fly in a way that made her fingers itch to touch. Since she had enough detail from the view to tell he was circumcised, she was sure his ass would be just as distracting.

She didn't have long to wait to confirm that. When Geoff gestured to her to do so, she moved to the middle seat so Chris could take the seat on the other side of her. Since it was clear from his smirk that Geoff wasn't relinquishing the aisle seat—probably for exactly the same reason she was thrilled to move to the middle seat—Chris had to turn sideways and sidle over Geoff and her to get to his chair.

There was no way she had the self-discipline not to take advantage of that up-close ogle of an ass so fine. Geoff didn't even try, sliding his palm smoothly over it as Chris moved past him, so she did the same. The thinness of the material let her feel the heated skin beneath.

"Lot of sexual harassment in this row," Chris muttered, making her giggle as he took the seat beside her. "You know, my legs are longer than yours," he said across her to Geoff. Geoff lifted a shoulder.

"But my dick's bigger."

That carried enough to incite a wave of chuckles from the audience members around them. A middle-aged man in front of them, wearing a collar and no shirt, rolled his eyes toward her and Chris. "Damn Doms, right?"

The comment suggested he was a submissive, but the proprietary arm the large bald-headed man next to him had along the back of his chair, and the head slap and gimlet eye he earned from him, confirmed it. "Keep that up, dog," the Master threatened with an amused twist to his lips. "I'll make you lie on my feet and miss the performance."

The sub gave Sam an affectionate, conspiratorial wink, but settled down. "Where did you get their outfits?" A woman behind them leaned forward to speak to Geoff, her long-nailed fingers curving over Sam's seat at her shoulder. "Was it at Naughty Bits?"

Madison would be pleased at the plug. Geoff confirmed it and answered her additional questions with friendly warmth. A question about clothing from a woman would usually have been addressed to the woman in their party—Sam—but they were in a different world tonight. Here, it seemed a Dom was addressed first, by those familiar enough in the lifestyle to recognize the dynamic between them.

The innate qualities that had first stamped Geoff as a Dominant to her hungry submissive nature were pretty obvious in this environment. She wondered if Chris's topping qualities not being so easily identified would bother him, but a glance at him reassured her. It didn't seem to be on his mind at all. Instead, he took her hand with a mock-annoyed look. "You owe me for this," he said. "Big-time."

The ways she could beg to repay him unfurled like a Christmas list in her head. It must have shown in her face, because Chris shook his head and lightly bit her fingers. She stretched them out to graze his mostly bare chest, coming in contact with the intriguing contrast of snug straps and metal links. He gave her another reproving look. "Brat," he muttered. As the lights started to come down, he leaned forward, looked over her at Geoff. "And you're an asshole."

She heard exasperated affection for both of them in his voice. Sam squeezed each of their hands.

A haunting flute piece filtered through the speaker system, quieting everyone and building the hushed sense of expectation. Sam's heart tripped a beat. She had a feeling the things she was about to see would feel familiar, even if she'd never seen them before, and yet those elements might be presented in ways that she'd never imagined. Thrilling, like a darkly sensual circus.

Geoff whispered in her ear. "Put your hands flat on the chair arms and leave them there. Spread your knees so they're at the corners of your seat. Stay that way unless I tell you otherwise."

Though she hated letting go of them, she complied. As if the two men could communicate telepathically, their hands settled over her wrists, holding her arms to the chair with flesh-and-blood manacles. That heart-tripping thing accelerated.

The first performers took the stage. A man clad in nothing but a snug pair of shorts backed toward the audience from between the rear stage curtains. A spotlight followed him, the rest of the stage dark. Handsome and well muscled, he had silky blond hair and a sinuous masculinity that made him an excellent choice for stage performance. He knelt.

The Mistress who came onto the stage from the side wing had lithe, athletic movements and vibrated with sexual power. She was wearing what Sam might expect a sexy biker female fantasy to wear: chaps over jeans, a tight T-shirt, riding boots. She carried a single tail whip like the other two Dommes, only Sam was pretty sure her target wasn't going to be balloons.

The woman walked around her sub, trailing the whip over his shoulders, tipping his chin up to her with the handle, holding his gaze with a still expression. Then she strode behind him and squared off, whip in hand. Sam thought she heard the crowd take in a collective breath.

Cognizant of the performance aspects of what she was doing, the woman warmed up with a few stylish swirls around herself. Sam had learned enough about using a single tail to know that it could be painful and dangerous if the user hadn't practiced enough or didn't focus as they should during a scene. She didn't think the woman would fall short in either regard. When she stopped the twirls and settled on her actual intent, Sam could almost feel her concentration narrow, cutting out the audience, the stage, everything but the connection between her and the man on his knees.

She began. The first whip throw landed high on his shoulders, the fall caressing his flesh before it came back to the Mistress, fluid as a snake's movements. It went back out again, quickly and efficiently. Her technique was smooth and rhythmic, the whip singing through the air, touching down, coming back, then returning again.

The spotlight on his back showed the faint red marks there. When the Mistress paused, speaking a low order, the man turned his face toward his shoulder. Sam recognized him, with a thrill of surprise. It was Troy, Logan's employee from the hardware store. His Mistress moved forward as another stage hand brought a wooden frame out and set it up in front of Troy. She locked his hands in the cuffs hanging from it and clamped them so his hands were spread past shoulder width, emphasizing the play of muscles across his broad back.

She slid her hand down inside the thin shorts, rubbing his buttocks with blatant familiarity before she pulled the fabric down to his thighs, revealing a beautiful, tight male ass to the appreciative response of the audience. His fingers flexed in the bonds. He turned his face up to her and she stroked it with her other hand, which was gloved. Bending down, she let him taste her lips before stepping back.

"Do you want me to touch you with my bare hand?"

"Yes, Mistress. Please. Though I don't deserve such an honor." His voice was throaty and thick, and Sam's toes curled. She understood how he felt, even though she didn't think she could put it in words, how his response resonated with her and made her feel it, too. The mirror of it was that raw moment where Geoff had showed her how much he wanted to take, to possess . . . there was a matching hunger for the same level of surrender, submission and giving inside her.

The Mistress's lips tightened. "Who decides what you deserve?" she said sharply.

He hung his head, realizing his mistake. "You do, Mistress."

"Lift your face toward me."

He did. She drew off the right glove, pulling the fingers free with unhurried precision. She slapped his cheek sharply with it. He didn't flinch or try to protect his face, even when she did it twice more, the same cheek, so redness bloomed on it. When she put her bare palm over the spot, Troy swayed toward her in his bonds, his body language conveying his devotion.

This might be a performance relationship only, but Sam doubted it. She was pretty sure this was Troy's actual Mistress.

She put the glove back on and paced away again, turning and

taking up the same stance. As the whip flew once more, she concentrated on his exposed ass. His buttocks tightened and released in a delicious way as she popped the whip over them. One time, though, she pulled up at the last moment, winking at the crowd as Troy automatically flexed his ass in preparation.

Whistles and chuckles swept the audience. The Mistress tossed back her red mane of hair and offered a little bow. Moving toward Troy again, she reached around him where the audience couldn't see, but it was obvious that she'd clasped his cock. His head dropped back on his shoulders. "Let's make it a bit challenging, shall we?" she said in a purr, the words enunciated so all could hear.

She extended her arm and another stage hand brought her a short thick wooden dowel. She placed the piece vertically between his buttocks. "Now, you hold that tight for me," she said. "You drop it, I'll be very displeased. Will you drop it?"

"Never, Mistress," Troy said, his voice strained.

Moving back, she lifted the single tail again. Troy groaned as she seemed to land a harder pop on his ass this time. The impact noise was more muffled, and when he flinched, his buttock muscles constricted even more, demonstrating his conscious effort to hold onto the dowel. And he kept holding it, though Sam wondered if it made the whipping more painful, keeping the muscles rigid beneath the lash.

At last, his Mistress came back to him, kissing his damp neck in reward, feathering her lips over his cheek, his mouth.

Sam's fingers were doing a slow, curling dance on the chair arms. Turning her hand over, Geoff loosely manacled her wrist again, fingertips flirting with hers and her palm as he restrained her anew. Chris kept moving along the back of her hand from knuckle to nail, tracing the bones and veins of her hand to her wrist and back again. She was aware of the movements of all the bodies around them, how the aisle lights and dim overheads made hair gleam like bird wings and glitter-painted skin sparkle. She felt as close to Geoff and Chris as if she'd been wrapped up against them in silken ropes. It was the perfect meshing of reality and a dream.

Troy and his Mistress left the stage to enthusiastic applause. The next two demos were equally provocative and amazing. If Madison had intended to emphasize the performance artistry that could accompany BDSM practice, she'd lined up some excellent examples of it. Three rope artists coordinated their efforts to form a breathtaking web upon which they suspended their submissives. After that, the fire artist returned, demonstrating more arousing ways to use fire, including a dramatic flogging.

Then came a nonconsensual consent performance, in which a woman was caned to the point she was begging for mercy. Sam was a little unsettled by it, but each time the Dom approached his sub and murmured to her, Sam was captivated by how the woman ended up kissing his fingertips and agreeing to do a little more. As the submissive gazed up at him with a tear-streaked face, her expression so raw and open, Sam understood what was happening. Relinquishing her right to call a stop to the session was an act of ultimate trust, building the bond between them. She wasn't sure she could be that brave, but it worked for these two.

However, she didn't think she needed to worry about it. The way Chris put an arm around her and Geoff increased the pressure of his hand on hers, the expressions on their faces, said they would never think of causing her that level of pain. It wasn't their thing, either, though she admitted it was pretty stimulating to watch people for whom it was.

With each subsequent performance, that lovely mix of dream and reality kept her engaged, spinning, alert and flushed, off balance. She could feel her Masters watching her, gauging her reaction and feeding off it. When she stole glances at their intent faces, felt their aroused reaction through the pressure of their fingers on hers, she did the same.

The next performer took that arousal and twisted it into an even tighter center, just from his appearance on the stage. Since the crowd quieted even more than courtesy dictated, she expected she wasn't alone in that feeling.

Logan wore black jeans, boots and a black shirt with several buttons undone. The last time Sam had seen him, his brown hair had been thick and long, like a pirate captain's or Viking's. Now it was short. Her first reaction was dismay, because the longer hair coupled with his rugged looks had conjured fantasies of pirate captains or Viking raiders. Yet as she studied him center stage, she found she liked how the short-cropped hair accented the strong planes of his jaw and forehead. The style also made his piercing brown eyes, intent on the quiet crowd, even more compelling.

"There are those who believe that the feelings Dominants and submissives have are unnatural." He had a presentation voice, deep and melodious. "The opposite is true. It's been a natural part of who we are since creation began, and we've found many ways to explore it. You've already seen some tonight, and will continue to see more. Fire, whip, rope. Wax, electricity. The methods are endless, but there is a root from which all of it grows."

He stepped back to the middle of the stage, and the spotlight sharpened on him. The other house lights came down further, putting the audience in full darkness. Logan turned with military precision toward the left side of the stage. He stood utterly still, taking his time looking at what was there. His singular focus on that something was a palpable energy, building the audience's anticipation. As he spoke at last, that deep voice rolled through Sam.

"Come to me."

Madison walked out of the wings. Her hair was pulled up at the sides, braided with tiny purple flowers that fell in ropes against the sable strands. She wore a filmy lavender chemise over black leggings, and her feet were bare. On her ankles and wrists were slim silver chains strung with clusters of chimes that made a faint music as she walked. Her eyes never wavered from Logan's face, until she reached him.

Sam had never attended a play so mesmerizing that she would follow the slightest facial shift on one of the actor's faces, but when Madison lowered her eyes, Sam felt the emotional impact in her lower belly. She gave him everything, right there. Sam understood that feeling, and it was doubled when the woman sank to her knees, head bowing. Geoff's fingers tightened on Sam's wrist. She suspected he knew what Logan felt, as the man on stage gazed down at the bowed head of the woman on her knees before him.

Sam realized she'd clutched Chris's fingers, which he'd shifted to rest between the spaces of hers.

Logan closed a hand on Madison's shoulder. Approval, reinforcement. From his pocket, he produced a blindfold, letting it unfurl and dangle from his grasp. He slid it along her mostly bare shoulders, over the straps of the chemise. "Close your eyes and lift your face to me."

When she did, he wrapped the blindfold over her eyes and tied it securely before stepping back. "Rise."

He put his hand under her elbow to help her and directed his next words to the crowd. "What will happen in the next few moments has not been rehearsed," he said. "I told Madison her only charge is obedience, immediate and absolute, to whatever I tell her to do." He cleared his throat, a smile crossing his face. "Something I can't get away with when it comes to our mutual business interests."

The chuckles in the audience were a faint ripple. It fell quiet again, two hundred and fifty people transfixed. Logan made a gesture toward the wings. The other performers, including Troy and his Mistress, slipped silently from the curtains, following the stairs along either side of the stage down to the main floor. They spread out along the edge, forming a perimeter in front of the stage.

"Whatever I tell you to do, you do immediately and without question." While it was a different version of what he'd just said, Logan's emphasis had changed, clearly no longer addressing the audience. That steady, implacable tone was targeted for one woman alone. "Tell me you understand, Madison."

"Yes. I do."

When Sam came to the Naughty Bits store, she was used to Madison speaking in warm welcome, with amusement or thoughtful intelligence. The three syllables, broken by that nervous pause, matched Sam's fluttering pulse, the anticipatory tautness of her body, leaning forward. She'd watched far more extreme things tonight. But this had her on the edge of her chair.

She could feel Geoff watching her every reaction. He liked seeing that submissive side of her come to full, yearning life, and the more she wanted, the more he would demand. The more he demanded, the more she'd want to give. Unconsciously, she realized she was straining against his hold on her wrist, not because she wanted to get away, but because she wanted to feel the power in his grip as he tightened it, refusing to free her.

Chris had released her hand so that he could slide his heated palm down the tense curve of her back, up to caress her bared nape. She shivered at the touch, turned and rubbed her jaw against his hand once again. She loved the bird mask, the sense of freedom it gave her to experience and react however she wished, but she also wanted it gone so her flesh could be against his.

Logan stepped behind Madison. "Turn to the right. Away from me, facing the audience."

Madison obeyed. Even as she came to a halt, the chimes made their whispering music, and Sam realized the woman was trembling. Logan slid her hair off one shoulder, bent and kissed the line of her collarbone. His hands gripped her waist. "Who am I, Madison?"

"My Master." She spoke it in a shaky voice, but there was love there, wonder, as if she was still exploring all that meant in her mind, heart, soul. Sam knew how she felt about that, too. Hell, she might as well have been standing where Madison was, with Geoff and Chris standing in Logan's place.

Logan brushed his lips over the same spot, bit lightly. "I like the sound of that. Say it again."

"My Master . . . Master."

He curled his fingers around her wrist to draw her arm behind her, obviously to guide her palm in a slow rub over his fly, though his reaction was concealed behind her body. "See what that does to me?"

She moistened her lips. "Yes, Master."

"Prove you mean it. Walk forward until I tell you to stop. Not as if you're blindfolded, but as if you trust me as much as you trust your own eyes."

She murmured something, and his expression shifted in a fascinating response. His grip slid around her waist, fingers spreading over her abdomen as he kissed her neck, a longer and harder contact. Madison tilted her head back against him, arching her throat, a breathy sigh escaping her.

"Say that again," he demanded. "Louder."

"I trust your eyes more." Her voice cracked but was clear.

He twisted her hair in his hand, dislodging some flower petals, and kissed her mouth. "Then walk how you would if you could see yourself through my eyes."

Releasing her, he stepped back, but Sam noticed his hand lingered, making sure she was steady.

Madison moved forward, and the tranquility on her face was a lovely thing to see. She did exactly as he told her, walking the way a woman walked when the man who desired her was watching. And Logan watched her as if he was only a breath away from devouring her, every sense focused on her. It made Sam hurt and rejoice at once. She wanted to cry and laugh. She wanted Geoff and Chris inside her, right now, but she settled for pulsating between them like a charged wire.

Hips swaying, head up, arms gracefully flowing with her body's movement, Madison walked forward without any hesitation. The group on the perimeter of the stage closed in on her direction silently, but a foot away from that edge, Logan spoke.

"Stop."

Madison came to a halt, lips parted, fingers slightly curled.

"Turn around and walk toward my voice."

She did. As he began to move around the stage, he spoke to her, one-word commands he would repeat if she got disoriented. She followed, at one point walking so close to the perimeter that even Sam was holding her breath. Someone else brought a chair to the middle of the platform then, and Logan brought her back toward him, bringing her to a halt when she stood before it. He took her hand. "Step up."

She stood on the chair, her back to the audience. Slipping a strap of the chemise off her left shoulder, he adjusted the garment so it was obvious he'd exposed her breast. Logan leaned forward, his hand coming up to curve around Madison's flesh. The act wasn't visible to the audience, but Sam felt a twinge through her own nipple, knowing he was giving Madison's a sweet, easy suckle that had her swaying. He gripped her hip to hold her. When he lifted his head, he slipped the strap back onto her shoulder, covering her again.

As he did that, Troy hoisted himself lithely onstage. He moved around to the other side of the chair, facing Logan. Logan met his gaze.

"Fall backward, baby," he said to Madison.

The crowd let out a collective *gasp* as she did so without hesitation, a slender tree falling in the forest. Logan caught her, Troy ready on the other side if needed, but she'd fallen directly into his grasp. Troy left the stage again. The performers on the perimeter of the stage left their posts, melting back into the shadows, leaving the audience an unimpeded view of Logan holding Madison in his arms. He shifted her and spoke low, a private communication between Master and sub. Maybe he was wearing a mic, though, because Sam was able to hear the throaty question.

"Are you still with me?"

She nodded, her head against his shoulder. He lowered her to the stage, this time putting her on her hands and knees facing the audience. "Head up," he instructed her. "Tell them why I want you to do that."

"Because I'm always proud to serve my Master. To be seen as yours." Her body shivered then, a hard jerk of reaction, as if she wasn't expecting words like that to come out of her mouth, especially right now, in front of this many people.

The other performances had been by turns arousing, intriguing . . . emotional. But this did as Logan had stated. It showed them what it all truly meant. What was really happening in the Dom's soul, in the sub's heart, through the touch of fire, drip of wax, or sting of the lash. It all connected to this. It was the essence of Geoff and Chris's connection to her, what all the Dom/sub stuff, every touch and word they exchanged, meant. Sam was still perched on her chair like a bird about to take flight. The press of their bodies, the welcome, unrelenting contact of their hands upon her, told her Chris and Geoff felt what Sam was feeling.

Logan dropped to a knee by Madison's head and leaned down. This time whatever he said was muted, perhaps because he put his hand up to his collar and covered the mic, making it just between them. Madison nodded, lips pressing together at the obvious personal reassurance, but it was clear Logan wasn't content to leave it at that. Whatever they were about to do was disrupting her focus, making her a little nervous.

He eased her back on her heels, gripping her wrist to guide her hand to his chest. Threading her fingers inside his open shirt so her palm could rest fully over his heart, he gave her skin-to-skin contact. Though Logan's broad chest, covered with a light mat of gleaming brown hair, was certainly worth an ogle, Sam realized the partly unbuttoned shirt hadn't been an act of vanity, but a vital preparation for this specific moment. He shifted his grip so his hand pressed over Madison's. When she bowed her head, he bent his over it. They held that way for a minute, and Sam could feel her own heartbeat. Thump-thump, thump-thump.

"You're doing so well, baby," he said. Though Sam wasn't sure if he'd intended that to carry, it had, and heated her from head to toe.

Yes, what was happening onstage was the epitome of all she felt and knew about herself, about the relationship between her, Geoff and Chris. But they weren't an exact copy of Madison and Logan, or any of the other Dom/sub relationships here. They were their own unique world, with a language that was different, tailored to their experiences together. She needed an expression of that here and now, her body and soul hungry for it.

Maybe Geoff wasn't as experienced a Dom as Logan, but he picked up on her desires as if they were his own, and maybe they were. He lifted her arm at last, transferring her wrist to the hold of his other hand, which stretched her arm out over his thighs. Sliding beneath her elbow, he reached between her legs. Sam drew in a breath as he pressed a finger under the elastic edge of the silky thong. He dipped and played, making her thighs tremble in their locked-and-spread condition. When he pressed in deeper, she swallowed a noise of pure carnal need. As he withdrew, he gave her inner thigh a brief stroke.

Chris had been watching, so Geoff didn't have to command his attention beyond the lifting of his fingers, glistening with her response. An offer to taste.

He'd left his fingers low enough that when Chris leaned over her, his shoulder and mostly bare side pressed against her arm, his hair brushing her breasts, pillowed high over the corset's hold. It kept their activities from disrupting the view of those behind them, but it also put Chris in a deferential pose toward Geoff. She wasn't sure if he registered that, not until he put his mouth fully over Geoff's two fingers, taking them deep in his mouth. Sam could feel the desire to take over push hard against the wall of Geoff's self-control. Chris's brown eyes gleamed with a feral look that said he relished the challenge.

Sam thought she might forget how to breathe entirely. Especially when Chris took his time licking her taste off Geoff's fingers. The shift of his body rubbed the harness and muscled flesh against her arm, the straps and metal rings cool against her in contrast. As Chris sucked on Geoff's fingers, her Master traced Chris's lips with his thumb, moving outward along his jaw. When he freed his hand and Chris started to lift his head, Geoff dropped down to capture him with a brief, hard clasp of Chris's throat that had her heart stuttering. Her Master held them in momentary stasis, his gaze lit with gold-and-green fire. She remembered what he'd said to her when Chris was changing, about wanting to take, to possess, to have them both on their knees. She saw all of that in his face, and so many other emotions, many of which spilled out of her own heart when Chris, picking up on what Geoff was emoting, turned his head to press a single, hard kiss against Geoff's forearm.

He shifted his gaze back to Geoff's face. Chris's expression was unreadable, but he didn't draw away until Geoff opened his hand. Before sitting back, Chris kissed her, letting her smell herself on his lips. She made a tiny, plaintive noise against him, and he dropped his hand back to her wrist, sliding it to the arm of the chair and holding it there once again as Geoff did the same on the opposite end. A reminder of restraint, of their ownership of her heart, mind and soul. And a way to connect them all once more.

Sam's gaze reluctantly turned back to the stage, only because Geoff directed her attention that way with an imperious nod and a squeeze of his hand. Logan had put Madison back on her hands and knees facing the audience and was rising, obviously more assured now of his sub's state of mind.

"Right now, she's at perfect rest," Logan said, low, not disrupting the hushed suspense of those watching. "She's attentive to my voice, to my desires, because they are aligned with her own. It takes time to get here. This was a simple exercise. There are far more complicated ones. As each of us explore relationships as Doms and subs, there are plenty of times it doesn't go this smoothly. It could have gone that way tonight. She could have taken one extra step and needed the human net I provided to keep her safe. But that wouldn't have ruined anything. It's a chance to adjust, to learn, to become closer." He lifted a brow, his lip quirking. "And an opportunity for me to impose direction or correction."

A small wave of laughter came from the Dominants in the audience. Geoff squeezed Sam's hand, and she remembered that night when he and Chris had punished her to bring her back on course again. It had been painful, her emotions so scattered, but she knew she'd want something like it to happen again. Maybe not for the reasons it had happened that night, but for the thrill of taking punishment, what it would give Geoff and her both. And Chris was definitely getting into it. Good thing she *did* relish punishment.

Logan stepped behind Madison and dropped to one knee again. Curling a restraining hand on her shoulder, he stretched his other arm out behind her, bringing it forward in an upward sweep. Sam jumped in her seat as he gave Madison's backside a resounding blow. Her generous breasts, partly revealed by the chemise top, quivered. Madison let out a small noise.

"What do you say, Madison?"

"Thank you, sir."

"More?"

"If it pleases my Master."

"I could spank your beautiful ass all day. Nothing would please me more."

The bells on her ankles were making that lovely, shivering music once more as her legs quivered. He gave her three more strikes, and she was taking little nervous licks of her lips by the end. He slid the leggings down, but since she was facing the audience, her nudity was implied rather than revealed. He gave her five more and, when she was curling her fingers into the wood of the stage, he dropped his hand lower behind her.

From the writhing of her hips, the sudden gasp, her moan of response, he was playing with her cunt. Geoff's hand slid back between Sam's legs again, and Chris's left the seat to drape over her shoulder, caress the top of her breast. Sam bit back a moan just like Madison's. If others in the audience were reacting the same way, it would explain the density of sexual energy closing in around all of them. It saturated the air.

"Nice and wet. When we talked about this, you thought you couldn't do it onstage, but I knew you could. Do you know why, Madison?"

"Because . . . we're alone."

"That's right. Just as I told you. Doesn't matter if we're in front of a thousand people, in front of a small group like this or at home. It's always just you and me. It's only about what I demand of you and what you surrender to me. Isn't it?"

"Yes, Master."

"Good. Because I want to hear you. No shyness now, baby. You're going to come . . . right . . . now."

Sam shuddered as Madison climaxed. Her own pussy pulsed frantically against Geoff's hand, her back arching, lifting her breast into Chris's touch. She whispered his name as he bent and pressed a kiss to her throat. When he sat back, she saw Logan had an arm around Madison's waist, his shirt pulling over his broad shoulders, his haunches and thighs tight under the hold of the jeans as he gave her stability, worked her to completion.

After she was done, her head dropped down, shoulders rising and falling to catch her breath. Logan pulled her leggings back in place, then lowered her into a fetal position onstage. Troy brought him a blanket, which Logan wrapped around her tenderly. Watching the large man curl over her, bend down on his elbows to kiss her temple, her lips, made Sam's heart melt. He put a hand on his sub, then rose, standing over her so she was curled around his feet.

He spoke with a quiet authority that reached every corner. "And that's what it's all about, isn't it?"

Single-word responses rose from the audience like random notes on a piano that connected to create a song. All in the same low tones, all fervent agreement. She even heard a couple of *Amens*.

Logan waited until it was quiet again. Then his gaze swept the audience, his expression changing. Sam thought he looked momentarily almost hesitant, then a rueful smile crossed his handsome features, as if he'd admonished himself. He straightened, his natural confidence gripping him once more.

"Whether you realize it or not, many of you have been instrumental in helping Madison and me find our way together. Once she trusts a Master, a submissive who dreams of being collared trusts him with that dream, those hopes for a permanent bond and connection. We Masters may not be as open about our hopes and dreams, but I can tell you that finding the submissive we want to collar completes our hearts just as much."

Sam looked toward Geoff, finding his expression open to her and Chris, his heart in his eyes, a full agreement. She mouthed the words *I love you*. When Chris reached behind her and gripped Geoff's shoulder hard, tears pricked her eyes. But it was Logan who pressed the trigger that had them overflowing.

"As such, I would like the privilege and honor of announcing that Miss Madison Fine, your hostess for the night, this beautiful woman at my feet, has recently agreed to become my permanent submissive, my lifelong partner. My wife."

He quickly put his fingers to his lips, raising his hand in gentle admonishment before any applause or cheers could start. He inclined his head, glancing meaningfully at his feet. "Baby's resting. Let's not disturb her. She might change her mind."

Quiet chuckles went through the audience, and he gave them all a warm smile. "We both thank you, from the bottom of our hearts. Thank you for coming tonight."

The crowd honored his request as he bent, scooped Madison off the floor and carried her offstage, cradling her in her arms. But once he did that, applause began, and built to a congratulatory cheer. Sam saw Troy whooping by the side of the stage, and he grabbed his Mistress for a kiss, who likewise looked delighted by the announcement.

Once she was willing to extricate herself from that enthusiastic embrace, she moved to the steps and mounted the stage, lifting her hands to quiet everyone down before she spoke. Troy followed her, taking up a position behind her and to the left.

"I'm Mistress Shale, for those who don't know me," she said. "And I know everyone here knows Troy. My boy is a big flirt, which is why I have to beat his ass all the damn time."

Laughter and catcalls answered that, and she grinned as Troy dropped to a knee in courtly apology. The handsomeness of the gesture so underscored Shale's point it incited another wave of mirth. Rolling her eyes at him, she turned back to the audience.

"Logan and Madison provided a very fitting end to tonight's performances," she said. "When this becomes an erotic performance theater, it will continually reinforce how we integrate erotic expression into our relationships with one another, whether it's kink, vanilla, Tantra or Baptist." She grinned at the laughter. "Yep, thought our Baptists would appreciate that. You guys know how to get your freak on like nobody's business. Now, even though the performances are over, feel free to socialize and mingle. And please, give yourself a treat and visit our sponsoring vendors for the evening. They've brought a lot of lovely things for sale and will be doing demos with any willing

Doms or subs. No hard pressure tactics. They're just as happy to give you their business cards so you can consider future purchases as they are to get a sale tonight. Of course, knowing some of you as I do, I'm sure many of you will find things you can't resist."

She winked, concluding her speech with a short bow. Troy jumped offstage and put his hands up to grasp her waist and lift her down. They exchanged another heated kiss that captivated Sam, watching the formidable Mistress melt in his arms. Troy obviously had the same knee-weakening powers in his lips that Chris and Geoff did.

Glancing at Chris under her lashes, Sam saw he was studying them with a curious expression. Was it intriguing to him that while Troy was a sub who enjoyed restraint and punishment from his Mistress's hand, it didn't stop him from lifting her down from a stage or capturing her mouth with possessive demand? Much as Chris did with her, even as Geoff was deep inside his ass, demanding the same kind of surrender from him.

"It never has to be one thing," Sam said. "Does it?"

When she looked toward Geoff, his hazel eyes were approving. People were making their way out of the theater, but as she started to get up, Geoff kept her in her seat by closing his hand on her thigh, holding her in place.

"Chris has more he wants to say to you," he advised.

She turned toward him and her vision was filled with Chris's brown eyes as he put his mouth on hers. While she made a little mewling sound of surprise against his lips, he ravished her mouth, eclipsing the heat of the kiss she'd just witnessed with Troy and Shale. Chris was kissing her in a way that told her how he was going to have her tonight. Hard, often and thoroughly.

She let out another whimper as Geoff occupied himself between her legs again, so that her thighs trembled and her toes pressed hard into the concrete floor beneath her. Waves of response rippled up her body. She was going to climax right here. Knowing the house lights were up and anyone was able to see them doing this to her just made it all the more certain. She gasped against Chris's lips, a warning, and Geoff eased up, though it immediately made her wish she'd kept quiet.

As Chris drew back, her head was lying on the back of the seat, and she was fully in surrender mode, her body open to them in all ways. Geoff threaded his hand into Chris's hair, tugging at the thick locks. Chris glanced at him, then back at her. "I get it now," he said. "I've wanted to hold you like a bird in my hand from the first day, Sam." His gaze slid over the mask, lips quirking. "I thought that was just about being protective, in love with you. It was, but these other feelings . . . aren't gentle in the least."

She didn't know where she found the ability to speak, but she did. "I'm glad. But I'm okay with however, whatever you need to be with me, with us. You loving me, that's what matters."

Chris shifted his attention back to Geoff, and she witnessed that fierce exchange of thoughts. While she still couldn't always discern what was being communicated, she picked up the feelings well enough. And she'd have time to learn their special language, as much as they were learning hers. They already answered her different needs and desires, picking up on them so easily. Evidenced now by Geoff grasping her wrist, rubbing his fingers on her pulse, a Master's demand, while Chris played with her fingertips like he was gliding his touch along meadow grass.

"Let's go see some of the vendor stuff," Geoff said.

As they helped her up and guided her back into the large foyer, they both stayed close. She was in a hazy cloud of arousal and sharp need, and hyperaware that the thong she wore had to be obviously wet with arousal. Fortunately, she saw the same evidence in other scantily clad audience members, though she wasn't entirely sure it would have mattered to her regardless. Not in this state.

Some of the vendors were craftspeople whose wares Sam recognized from Madison's shop, but there were others as well. She and Chris browsed a booth with boxes of vintage erotic postcards. The collections were sold by a wizened old man who told them stories about being part of the original Leatherman movement in the sixties. Chris bought a few he liked, adding in the several she wanted to purchase. From there, they wandered with Geoff past booths offering paraffin wax, restraint systems, handcrafted whips and impact play toys.

When they reached the table that advertised Logan's custom BDSM furniture, there were pictures on display and a couple of actual pieces people could examine hands-on. Troy was manning the booth and gave Sam a grin, coupled with an appreciative look. He'd pulled on a pair of jeans but was still shirtless, so she couldn't help but steal a reciprocating appraisal. Though she bit her lips against a smile as Chris's hand slid along her waist, giving her ass a not-so-subtle reproving pinch.

"Just looking, not buying," she muttered and stifled a yelp as Geoff gave her an even harder pinch on the other buttock.

"The mask and corset look gorgeous on you," Troy said, either actually oblivious to the exchange or trying to save her from further retaliation. He slanted a glance at Geoff. "If you don't mind me saying."

"It's only the truth," Geoff said. He examined the large cross-shaped frame. "This says it unhinges for easy storage?"

"Way easy. It stays in one piece, but folds." As Troy turned to show Geoff, Sam's gaze slid over the faint red marks on his back, fading souvenirs from Shale's whip play with him.

"Would you like to touch them?"

She turned to see Shale watching from a corner. She was sitting on a stool, sipping a canned soda. The Domme's gaze was so direct, so unflinching, it added to her both intriguing and intimidating demeanor. She rose, passing her hand over Troy's back. He instantly stilled at her touch, straightened. "It's interesting," Shale remarked to Geoff. "Subs often like to touch the marks on another sub, as if they can absorb the reaction."

Geoff met Shale's gaze, then shifted his attention to Sam. "You want to ask me for something, Sam?"

She bit her lip. Chris was a quiet presence to her left. "May I touch, Master? If it's okay with . . . both of you."

She wondered if she needed to explain that it wasn't about touching another man. Shale couldn't have described it more accurately. Her fingers were itching to touch evidence of a type of play that intrigued her, that she might want her Master to do to her.

Geoff glanced at Chris, but whatever he saw there satisfied him. He nodded. Sam slid her fingertips over the marks, just below where Shale kept her hand against Troy's nape. When Troy turned his head to look at her, Sam had to ask, "Did it hurt?"

"In all good ways. It gets bad at a certain point, and I think I'm going to safe-word, but I break through that point. It's like I'm channeling how she feels about it, which balances the pain. And then . . . I fly."

Sam took her hand away and murmured her thanks. Geoff spoke to Troy another few minutes about the cross, then they left Troy and Shale to visit the next booth. The vendor was a man whose short limbs and stature indicated dwarfism. When Sam's attention met his steady blue eyes, she was intrigued. From the quirk of his lips and gleam of appreciation in his gaze as he studied her, she was pretty sure he was a Dom. He had a square jaw and a tangled mop of dark hair, but the handsome face only contributed to the compelling attitude he projected. She wondered what his story was, and how it had brought him here.

His card read *Grant Juneau*. Grant was offering different strike-branding techniques. Electric, freeze branding, heat. Sam thought any of it would be terribly painful, but Grant explained that when being done for marking, the contact was quick. The mark would remain anywhere from six to eighteen months.

"Hurts less than tattooing," he said to Geoff. "And a lot less expensive way to put a mark of ownership on your sub or slave."

Geoff glanced at Chris quizzically. Chris lifted a shoulder. "I don't really want to mark her skin that way."

"How about me marking yours?"

Chris blinked. Geoff's hazel eyes were sharp. "You remember that blood oath we made?"

"A blood oath?" Sam asked.

Chris grimaced, with humor. But she noticed his brown eyes were bemused, showing how very aware he was of Geoff as he shifted behind Chris, stroking his back around and beneath the hold of the harness straps. He tugged on a metal link hard enough to make Chris brace himself against the pull before Geoff dropped lower, fondling the curve of Chris's ass in the formfitting pants. Chris's head tilted as Geoff tucked fingertips beneath the waistband, caressing the dip between his buttocks.

"Watch her breathing, Chris. She gets so turned on when I touch you. Think she'd get even hotter if I branded my initial into your shoulder, here?" He traced the spot as Chris's eyes moved to Sam's entranced face.

Geoff lifted his gaze to Sam. "We'd just turned twelve. The oath was a promise to never let women come between us, inspired by the sudden loss of three of our friends who'd fallen under their diabolical spell. It ruined our afternoon baseball games, because those guys wanted to hang out with icky girls instead of meeting up to play."

Sam smiled but the smile died as Geoff wrapped his fingers around the base of Chris's throat on one side. When Chris's muscles tensed, Geoff soothed him by sliding the other hand back down his arm, threading it between elbow and back to put him in a light restraint hold. Chris could throw him off, but when Geoff tightened his grip, Chris went more still.

"His pulse is hammering." Geoff pressed against Chris's back. "You feel my cock? I plan to have it in both of you tonight. I like the idea of branding your flesh, Chris. I like it a whole fucking lot. What do you think?"

Chris was silent for a moment, then Sam saw him curl the fingers behind his back into Geoff's shirt, as much as the position allowed. "I want that," Chris said. His gaze met hers, and suddenly an erotic moment opened up into something far more, bringing forth everything that had led to this moment. Chris's expression became brilliant with emotions that tied her heart up in a dozen ways, all of them connected to her two men.

"I want you both to know I'm yours," he murmured. "Every part of me. If I could figure out a way to brand it on my heart and soul, I would. You can destroy me with nothing but a word. It fucking scares me like nothing else, and it makes me happier than I've ever been in my life."

He'd mesmerized her, drawing her closer with every word. She gripped the straps of the harness as Geoff slid an arm over his chest, overlapping her tight fingers. He pressed a hard kiss on Chris's shoulder and Chris brushed his head against Geoff, a fierce gesture of tenderness.

"Sam, go pick out a *G*," Geoff ordered roughly. "And one you'd like him to have."

There was no shame and definitely no choice in her need to collect and compose herself before approaching the vendor. Grant had busied himself in his booth, but Sam knew he'd stayed tuned in to them, and not just because he was a smart man who understood when he was close to making a sale. When she stepped up to his table, his expression was warm and knowing, as if he understood just what kind of feelings she was experiencing from Chris's unexpected declaration.

"These two," she said quietly, touching a brand shaped like a bird and the *G* brand next to it.

Grant's blue eyes passed over her outfit, the bird mask, and he nodded with a faint smile. "The *G* is a freeze brand, and the bird is a heat brand." He quoted the price to her as Geoff and Chris drew closer, standing shoulder to shoulder again. Geoff handed her the money. After pocketing it, the vendor motioned to Chris to come around into his application space. Gauging Chris's height, he pulled over his taller stepping stool. "You sit on this. I'll step on the other so I can get the right angle to apply them evenly."

Chris complied. Sam shifted so she and Geoff could face him together. Geoff took her hand. "Breathe," he said. "If you pass out, I'll make fun of you."

She rolled her eyes at him. Grant had said it wasn't any worse than getting a tattoo, but she still held her breath a little bit. Sensing her trepidation, Chris grasped her other hand and smiled. It was quick, no more than a blink, and Chris didn't even flinch. She came around at Grant's gesture so she could see the new imprints.

"They look pretty widely spaced out, but that's because they'll get a lot bigger over the next few hours. You can touch it lightly, but try not to touch it too much during that period." Grant picked up her hand to rest her fingertips on the *G* representing Geoff's name. Grant's grip was surprisingly firm and strong.

"You can look at them to your heart's content, beautiful bird. He looks like he spends a lot of time in the sun. Even when they start to fade, they'll remain lighter than his natural tan, so you'll see it show up that way for quite a while."

He gave them the rundown on the safety tips to keep it uninfected, and then he was turning to another knot of customers. They'd drawn an audience, people wanting to watch Chris be branded, and several now took advantage of Grant's services.

Sam wanted to touch the brands again, but mindful of Grant's warning about overdoing it, she settled for just looking at them. "I should pay for the bird," she told Geoff. "That one was more for me."

Geoff shook his head. "No. It's proof that you're his as much as mine, something I particularly want him to remember."

Chris gave him an inscrutable look, then tilted his head to look down at her. "Like it?" he said.

She nodded and watched his lips tighten in reaction as Geoff touched the *G* with a brief fingertip. When Chris lifted his gaze to meet Geoff's, heat flashed between them.

"I think it's time to go home," Geoff said. "I want to be alone with you both."

~

They had her step back into her skirt and Geoff wrapped the shawl around her shoulders before they left the building. Chris had changed back into street clothes, though she expected they wouldn't have any problem getting him to wear that scintillating outfit again, now that he'd seen firsthand how much she and Geoff had enjoyed him in it.

Geoff or Chris always opened the car door for her before getting in their own seats. This time, when they went into the parking lot, Chris touched her arm, holding her in place as he took the backseat, pulled off his shirt so it wasn't chafing the brand and then drew her back there to sit on his lap. He pulled the belt over both of them, Geoff reaching in from the other side to help to fasten it. It pressed into the corset and against her shoulder, holding her closer to Chris's bare chest. His hands slid down her thighs, helping her adjust. She made a little noise as he pressed her against his groin, and she saw the flash of Geoff's teeth.

"Got a couple of lumps in that seat, Samantha Beth?"

"Comfort is overrated," she said, rotating her hips against Chris playfully and earning a grunt from him. Geoff undid the mask, sliding it from her face and combing his fingers through her hair to loosen it from its binding. He brought it tumbling down on her bare shoulders. Chris rubbed his face in it as he liked to do, and Sam dropped her head back against the passenger window as he removed the shawl and kissed the rise of her breasts.

"There's our girl," Geoff said. He got into the front seat and turned over the ignition. "Keep her occupied, Chris."

"Gladly." Guiding her arm around his neck, Chris speared her with a look that sent tingles from her nape to the base of her spine. "Guess I'll have to figure out ways to keep you moving like that." Wrapping his hand in her hair, he held her head back forcibly and began to feast on her throat, working his mouth along her jugular, down to the meeting point between the collarbones, along the sternum and then back to the pillow of her breasts, his tongue curling inside the corset to find her nipple.

"Oh God . . ." She clutched his shoulder. It seemed like she'd been in an edgy state of arousal for hours now, a state that surged to the forefront as he played with her nipples with his tongue, teased her skin with his mouth, all the way home. She writhed and squirmed, his damp, muscled skin pressed against her. She was panting, moaning, pleading, but neither man took mercy on her. Geoff was even humming as he was driving, something Mr. Road Rage never did. Maybe she'd recommend having her in an erotic frenzy every time he drove to keep his mind off of homicidal behavior. Another sacrifice she was willing to make.

She didn't care who might be looking in at the stoplights, trying to see what they were doing. "Please . . ."

Chris shook his head and lifted his face. "I like you like this. I'm beginning to get why it makes Geoff hard and hot. So be quiet and just take it."

Wow. He didn't say it mean, but his unrelenting tone had her shuddering in his grip. She could feel Geoff's attention, sharpening on them when Chris got tough like that. Their desires were like blades closing in on both sides, and she welcomed the edges.

They pulled into the driveway. She wasn't sure she'd make it into the house on her own, but she didn't need to worry about that. Geoff came around to open their door. Chris unbuckled the seat belt and lifted her into Geoff's grasp. Her Master steadied her on her feet and put a proprietary hand on her ass, holding her there.

"You getting all worked up with her behind my back just makes me want to kick your ass and then ram into it. You know that, don't you?"

Chris tossed him a challenging look. "Maybe I'll do it to you first. And then take her while you're figuring out how to walk."

Geoff bared his teeth, but she saw the light in his eyes, reflected in Chris's grin. "Big talk. Inside," Geoff said.

Geoff picked Sam up and carried her up the driveway as Chris preceded them, opening the door. Once inside, Geoff put her down on a chair in their living room with deliberate gentleness. He lifted her hand and kissed it. "Just one moment," he promised her.

He turned, caught Chris by the shoulders and slammed him up

against the wall, making her gasp. In the next second, he was kissing him just as ravenously as Chris had kissed her. Sam tucked her knees beneath her and pivoted on the chair so she could watch them, her fingers curled in the top cushion. All the evening's stimulation was culminating into this, charging the room with an explosive heat that radiated among all three of them, reckless, careless and radical emotions charging the air.

Chris fought and reversed their positions, pushing Geoff against the wall, his hands wandering hungrily over him, ripping the black dress shirt open as Geoff half laughed, half cursed against his mouth. He put his hand on Chris's shoulder, half covering the brand, but immediately realized where he was and shifted his touch. Sam was strangely overwhelmed, seeing that studied gesture of care inserted into the animal desire between them.

Geoff straight-armed Chris. "Get out of your clothes, all of them." Pushing him away, he moved into the kitchen, pulled out one of the sturdy chairs and pointed to it. "And sit your ass there."

Chris's gaze was all sensual fire, but he shed the jeans, underwear and shoes. Geoff had plans for her as well. "Lose the skirt and the panties, Samantha Beth. Leave the stockings, shoes and corset. Then come over here."

She came to him, every inch of her sizzling with awareness, aching for contact. Geoff unhooked the corset and unwrapped it from her body. Tossing it to the side, he left her in only the heels and thigh-high stockings.

"With the shoes or without?" He cocked a brow at Chris.

Chris had taken a seat in the chair, thighs spread, cock erect and against his belly, his arms crossed. He took his time examining her before answering Geoff, gaze sliding over the high heels, up her legs to her hips and mons, her stomach, breasts, shoulders and waiting face. "Without. She's hot as hell like that, but my favorite way of having her is just as our girl. Our Sam."

"Agreed. Take hold of yourself, stroke your dick."

Chris's gaze shifted to him. "For her or you?"

"Does it matter?" Geoff's brow lifted.

"No. Except I like to hear it's making you just as crazy as you two are making me."

"If you have any doubts about that, I'm about to clear that up in a way that you'll feel for a few days." Geoff flashed a wicked grin. Taking Sam's arm, he held her in place and waited pointedly until Chris clasped his cock and began to pump it. While doing that, Chris hooked his elbow over the back of the chair, a casual, sexy look enhanced by the kindled gaze he fixed on them.

Geoff bent to whisper in her ear. "Watching him do that, what do you want, Sam?"

"Him inside me. Now."

"Yeah. Ask me for that. And you better look at your Master when you beg."

She expected he knew just how difficult it was to tear her attention from what Chris was doing. "Please, Master. I need him."

"You sure as hell do. I can smell how aroused you are." He propelled her over to Chris. With that effortless strength they both did so well, he lifted her to straddle Chris's lap. Chris held his cock with one hand, gripping her buttock with the other, and he and Geoff together slid her down on his length in a decisive, penetrating lock that had her gasping, letting out a little cry of pleasure and discomfort at once because of his size.

"Easy there, sweetheart." Geoff helped her adjust, then left her with Chris's arms securely around her body, moving her in a slow rise and fall. Stepping back, Geoff stripped. "Bring her back, Chris."

As Chris lowered her backward, hands at her waist, Geoff took her down even farther until her upper torso formed a ninety-degree angle with Chris's. Her hands slipped from Chris's shoulders to his forearms, then his wrists. The men's grips were steady and strong as Chris kept that sliding movement in and out of her, his hips flexing on the seat. Geoff cupped her head, holding her, watching her. Then he gave her an order.

"Put your arms above your head, Samantha Beth."

She obeyed, trusting his palm on her skull to hold her up. As soon as she did it, he turned his back to Chris and straddled her, his inner thighs pressed against the sides of her breasts. The position allowed her to wrap her arms around his thighs and dig her fingers into his tight ass, so she was glad he didn't object to that, though his hand still supported her head.

Staring down at her, he used the other to guide his cock between her parted lips.

Freaking bliss. She sucked on him frantically, so close to climax as Chris kept moving inside her. "Master," she gasped around him. "Please . . ."

"You hold out until we say it's okay. Tell me you understand." He barked it, startling her into looking up into his hazel eyes, which were fevered with desire and yet cool and in control at once. Which only made this even more intense for her. Probably for all of them. She nearly lost the fight as she imagined Chris's view. Looking down at his cock pushing into her cunt; looking up merely a few inches to see Geoff's tight ass before him, flexing as he pushed himself into her mouth.

"Yes, Master," she said against his steel flesh. Geoff shoved himself deeper into her mouth, letting her feel how much he wanted from her, how much they both wanted. Oh God, it was too much. She was far too close. But she poured every bit of willpower she could into obeying him. The need swelled inside her until she had to treat it like a life-or-death decision. Even that might not be enough to hold her back, but she imagined it was Chris or Geoff's life, dependent on her willpower.

Except her mind knew it wasn't life-and-death. It was all about losing herself in the bliss of an orgasm, and if she screwed up, it just meant she might get a spanking or something even better . . . Oh hell, she was going over, she couldn't stop it.

A change of plan saved her from failing her Master. A muttered comment between Geoff and Chris and suddenly she was lifted in Geoff's arms as he eased her from Chris. She would have wailed in protest at the loss of that incredible fullness, but she was put down on the carpet and Geoff slid into her where Chris had just been. The transition was seamless, the ripple that went through her as potent as an actual climax. Her response swelled beyond all expectations as Chris knelt behind Geoff, curled his large fingers into Geoff's hips and slammed into him as Geoff bent over her.

It was a gift beyond measure, Geoff taking her and Chris inside of him, the three of them moving together like one thrusting, writhing animal, reaching a level of paradise impossible to explain and taking her to an edge incapable of being denied.

"Love you," she panted. "Love you both . . . so . . . damn . . . much. Thank you . . ."

Tears spilled out of her eyes, all of it so overwhelming and perfect. Geoff's gaze was fierce upon her, yet she felt the energy thrumming through his muscles and knew a certain amount of his focus was internal, keeping hold of what was happening between the three of them, the perfect pacing of it. It told her whatever that muttered conversation had been about, he'd permitted Chris to do this. He could open himself like that to Chris, and she loved him all the more for it.

"I can't," she moaned. "Please . . ."

"Let her go over," Chris said.

Geoff apparently squeezed down on him, because Chris let out a strangled sound. Geoff turned his head, scraping his teeth over Chris's mouth.

"Say *please*, you big bastard. You don't top me just because you're in my ass. You're the one wearing my brand."

Chris moaned as Geoff reached back with his free hand and obviously did something moan-worthy. "Say it," Geoff whispered fiercely.

"Please. Let her go, damn it. And go over for me."

"We go together." Geoff's fevered gaze locked on Sam's. "Go," he breathed.

She screamed like she was dying and being born at once, and maybe that wasn't entirely untrue. She lifted her hips off the ground, slamming Geoff even deeper inside her, and he braced himself over her, palms driving into the floor on either side of her head. Chris banded his great arm around Geoff's chest and thrust into his ass in a pummeling motion that had Geoff throwing up his head like a wolf showing his teeth. A moment later, he was uttering harsh male noises of release, flooding her pussy with his seed as Chris let go right after.

They kept moving together, all of them, well past their bodies' breaking points. Vaguely, Sam knew none of them wanted to let go, holding on to that rhythm, that choreography that wove them together even tighter with every thrust and withdrawal.

"Oh God . . ." *Oh God. Thank you, God.*

Some minutes had passed before anyone spoke or moved, the only thing punctuating the air being rasping breath and thundering hearts. Sam finally managed to open her eyes, in time to see Chris press a kiss to Geoff's shoulder and Geoff turn his head to return the favor, a brush of lips over his forehead.

Chris was the first to recover motor function, withdrawing and murmuring something about washcloths. He disappeared down the hall into the bathroom, the running water telling them he was cleaning up and heating the water to dampen the cloths. He returned with one for each of them. With a groan, Geoff slowly pulled out of her, but he didn't leave her without his body heat. He settled her into the cradle of his thighs, putting his back against the half wall that divided the kitchen from the living room. Taking a cloth from Chris, he cleaned between her thighs himself with gentle strokes.

"I could do that," she said.

"You're ours to care for, right?" He pressed the heat of the cloth against her and held it there, firmly enough she felt the blood pulse through her cunt against his touch. She nodded, her throat suddenly tight. Chris had also brought bottled water from the kitchen and now knelt on the other side of her, offering it. They cared for one another. It was intuitive for all three of them. That desire to care had been there even before sexual desire had entered into it. As such, she knew it would pervade the many ways they'd explore sexual intimacy and a life together as lovers, where they'd need to nurture one another in myriad ways, large and small.

Sam recalled what Flo had said, that the good response to an event like the Carnival showed things were changing. Even where opposition existed, there were others like her, Geoff and Sam. People who believed love had a broader definition, and it could be celebrated in all its positive forms. Remembering such a thing would help her always focus on what was most important. Not the opinions of others, but what lay in her heart, and the hearts of the two men beside her.

She put her hands on them, touching faces, chests, letting them feel the painful joy of her need. "I don't know how to say it. This feeling . . . it's like the closest thing to . . ."

"To what everything important is supposed to be about," Chris said.

She caressed his jaw. "What did you mean, that day in the park? When I asked you if it would have been easier if I'd chosen one of you?' You replied, *'Depends on who was chosen.'* You didn't want to explain that then. Can you explain it now?"

Geoff shifted behind her, an indication of his curiosity. She had to suppress a little smile as Chris's focus turned inward, thinking his answer through. Geoff pressed his lips to her limp fingers, as they both waited patiently.

At length Chris shifted his gaze to Geoff. He held there a moment, such that Geoff grew more still behind her body. "If you had chosen, Sam, it should have been Geoff. He's more of what you needed . . ."

Chris shook his head as they began to protest. "And even if that's just my bullshit insecurities about all this Dom stuff, it was more than that. I could handle having my heart broken. I couldn't handle seeing his broken again. Not after seeing what his family did to him. Or what my dad did to my mom."

Sam closed her hand on his big wrist. "Chris."

Geoff's jaw tightened against the side of her head. "He did it to you, too, man."

"Eh, yeah, but . . ." Chris shrugged. Sam expected the gesture was an echo of the boy he'd been, because suddenly she could imagine him as a serious-eyed child, taking it upon himself to be man of the house long before any other boy would have considered it. But not every boy had the makings of a wonderful man so early in life. Chris had. She was sure of it, because otherwise Geoff wouldn't have been so totally in love with him for so long.

"What mattered to me was taking care of her," Chris said. "Making sure she knew that she was enough. That I would never be like my dad. That she could always rely on me to love her and be there for her. That kind of took the place of that hole, if that makes sense. Like taking care of the two of you."

Locked in place by the weight of the emotions passing between the two men, Sam could only watch in simple, painful happiness as Geoff reached out and clamped a hand on Chris's shoulder, tightening his grip. "I guess that means Sam was always right," her Master said. "About us being a triangle. I couldn't bear hurting you that way, either. And neither of us can tolerate her unhappiness. So it's a trinity or nothing. We work best when there are no limits between the three of us."

He hauled Chris closer, roughly enough he had to put a hand on Geoff's knee to keep from toppling into Sam. Which also gave her the excuse to grip Chris's biceps. "And if it wasn't for you," Geoff said steadily, "my heart would have been screwed up forever. Maybe putting me in a place where I couldn't have seen the love you're both offering as the gift it is, or tried my damnedest to return the favor."

Chris swallowed, his eyes suspiciously moist. "If this is where you do the old-lady *Titanic* speech about how I saved you in every possible way a person can be saved . . ."

Geoff snorted and shoved him away, following it up with a head-slap that Chris blocked, grinning. "Fuck. See, you made her cry."

"Happy tears," Sam declared, wiping them away. Then, because she was delighted, and being a girl made such gestures completely acceptable, she twisted around and flung herself at both of them to hug them close. It allowed them to put their arms around each other, a three-way hug she knew would add the right kind of emotional follow-through to what they'd just told one another. Girls were good for that, too.

At length they drew back. Chris smiled, kissed her palm, then bemused Geoff by taking his hand and kissing his palm. Geoff stroked his hair.

"Sloppy romantics, both of you," he said, but there was no criticism there. "By the way, before we call it a night, I intend to have your ass myself," he told Chris. "And I expect you'd like to have her come around your cock."

"You're the Dom," Chris said, amused. "I'm not going to argue with you. Not right now."

Geoff snorted. When Chris started to get up, Geoff slid his hands under Sam's armpits and half lifted her, Chris completing the move by scooping her up off the floor. "You know, I can walk occasionally," she pointed out, dropping her head back over Chris's arm to look at Geoff upside down as he got to his feet.

"We plan to keep your knees weak until dawn," Geoff told her, bending to kiss her forehead. "Got a problem with that?"

"I'll let you know," she said, a little more faintly than she'd intended. His light smile couldn't detract from the flash of heat in his expression, which told her he wasn't teasing her about that. Chris's satisfied male expression said he was in perfect accord.

She was right, what she'd told Flo. They might kill her with their unending needs, but if being taken over and over by the men she loved until her heart gave out was her fate, who was she to argue with destiny?

~

She made them omelets for breakfast. While the coffee was brewing, she stood at the kitchen window wearing one of Chris's shirts and watching the sun rise. She brought the meal to the bedroom on a tray and sat cross-legged between them, snacking off the fruit she'd added to their plates and exchanging tidbits of conversation with Geoff as Chris sipped his coffee to wake up. Sometime during the night they'd both donned their shorts, but Chris didn't object as she ran her fingertips along his thigh and under the loose flannel leg of his to caress the curve of his testicles.

Geoff stretched out farther to lean in and press his lips to the back of Chris's shoulder. Remembering then that Grant had said they could touch the brand more freely the next day, Sam moved to look at it, run her fingers over the bird and the *G* branded into Chris's skin.

"I really like this," she said, tipping Chris's head back and adjusting so he could lay it in her lap.

He grunted, a pleased noise. Her gaze wandered over to notice how Geoff's brief shorts defined his genitals much more prominently than Chris's looser shorts, and Geoff was still in an early morning rigid state. Her fingers itched to touch him as well, but she found she was still shy about reaching for him without asking permission. It was Chris who saw her looking, gripped her hand and drew it over to press her palm against Geoff's groin. The two men watched her, Chris's eyes heavy-lidded with interest, Geoff's like a hawk's, making her think he'd probably punish her later for not asking, but he obviously had other plans first.

The next thing she knew they had her on her side, Geoff licking strawberry jelly off her nipples and Chris pushing into her cunt from behind, cupping her breasts, thrusting and retreating until he reached a powerful, shuddering morning climax. Then his arms slid around her waist and across her chest, holding her fast as Geoff took her next, bringing her and him both to release.

"Do you think it's possible for people to fuck each other to death?" she asked after another short postcoital doze.

"As long as you keep bringing us food and water, we should be okay." Geoff chuckled in a logy voice. They lay there in a tangle of

NAUGHTY WISHES

limbs, the fragrances of coffee, vegetable omelets and fresh fruit competing with the lingering scents of sex and need. "But I have an idea. Let's go lie out in the hammock together and watch the sun come up. We can bring coffee."

"Your theory being, if we're outside where the neighbors might see us, we might exercise some restraint?"

"Something like that." Chris winked at her. "Or we'll give them an eyeful and make them start their morning the same way we just did."

"I'm not sure. Mr. and Mrs. Roberts look like they haven't had sex since the seventies."

"They're probably having tons of wild jungle monkey sex behind closed doors," Geoff disagreed.

"People always say that, but when you see monkeys have sex on documentaries, it's actually pretty tame." Sam made a quick motion with her hands. "In, out, done."

"That's because they have cameras on them," Chris said. "If we ever go to a jungle on vacation, we'll see firsthand, real, live, undocumented monkey sex. It will freaking blow your mind."

Sam was giggling as they pulled her out of bed. She bent over to retrieve Chris's shirt and yelped as Geoff gave her bare ass, lifted pertly in the air, a smart strike.

"For not asking," he told her, though he tempered the stern look with a wink. "Plus your bare butt is too much of a temptation."

She made a face at him, rubbing the stinging spot, but he came around the bed, pulling on his sweatpants before he bent and kissed her offended area. "There. All better. Put some panties on under that T-shirt, you shameless girl."

She was very pleased Chris and Geoff went out into the yard as is, Chris in his flannel shorts and Geoff in the sweatpants, both bare-chested and with tousled hair, her handsome, sleepy men.

Chris immediately sprawled in the hammock and tumbled her down in it with him, so she could nestle in his arms, her cheek on his furry chest. Geoff took a seat in a patio chair he pulled over, stretching his legs out over Chris's and bracing them against Chris's calf, bare toes curling against his friend's flesh. They sat that way quietly for a while, Geoff moving them in a slow rock as he sipped coffee.

469

If pressed to do so later, Sam wouldn't have remembered most of the specifics they talked about, but the men's words were sun-jeweled raindrops to her, absorbing through her skin. Geoff's smooth timbre, Chris's deeper, rougher voice, her own like a light music weaving in among their comments. Random discussion about types of coffee, possible future trips, things they'd seen last night, the fairy garden Chris had made her. Nothing earth-shattering, but that was what made it so memorable and treasured. The men she loved, who loved her and each other, chatting and comfortable with one another and the life they were building together.

She had no illusions; there would be less-pleasant days. But they'd started out as friends and had been roommates for long enough to weather days when one or more of them wasn't in the best mood, where they lashed out about work crap, home crap. They'd locked horns on different things before, and would again.

She'd treasure all of it. Just as she treasured the casual way Chris was stroking her hair, occasionally pressing his lips to it. How she could tangle her fingers with his at her waist and caress his palm, his wrist, because he was hers. Geoff's foot, curled against Chris's calf, occasionally straightened, toes giving Chris's flesh a quick reminder of intimate contact. The way his gaze rested on Sam, she could see all sorts of titillating thoughts running through her Master's mind. Things he'd want to do, to explore, with both of them.

Glancing at Chris, she realized the worries she'd had about how he'd resolve the Dominance and submission issues for himself were exactly as Geoff had predicted. She didn't need to fully understand any of it. The only important thing was that, however it was resolving itself, it seemed to be working for the three of them.

When Geoff offered to get up and go refill Chris's coffee with his own, Sam lifted her head. "Can you bring Chris's pocketknife back out? He keeps it . . ."

"In the front right pocket of his pants," Geoff finished. "He always has."

As he disappeared into the house, she tilted her head up to Chris and smiled against his mouth as he kissed her. Chris was a toucher, a kisser, and she loved it. Loved how he did it so frequently, easily and naturally, the way he did so many things.

"Why do you want my pocketknife? I know Geoff is annoying, but there's no need to resort to stabbing."

She grinned but reached up and touched his face. "I love you."

His brown eyes warmed with a wealth of emotions. "I love you, Sam. We both do."

"I can speak for myself," Geoff said, returning, though there was humor, not reproof, in his tone. "I find her mildly tolerable. You far less so."

"Well, I'd say *fuck you*, but my dick is tired. Though not for long," Chris promised, nudging her.

"Take your time," she assured him. "A girl needs a recuperation period. And by the way, you're welcome to take turns with each other and let me watch. Works for me."

Geoff leaned over Chris, handing her the knife, and threaded his hand through Chris's hair, giving it a quick tug before capturing her nape to do the same to her. "You're so selfless. Brat. Now, why do you need the knife?"

She sat up, Chris helping her get her feet off the edge of the hammock so she could stand. "Will it hurt the tree if I carve something in it?"

She gestured toward their large Japanese cherry. At the beginning of spring it was loaded with white petals that rained down like snow as the flowers gave way to summer's green leaves. She'd lain in the hammock before, letting them fall on her. She remembered waking from a nap once and seeing Chris bent over her, smiling because she was covered in them.

"No. It shouldn't," he said, his gaze curious.

Nodding, she moved to the tree, but she found her hand strength wasn't sufficient to complete her intent, though she got the *S* carved. Chris came up on her right side, Geoff on her left. Chris took the knife from her. "What do you want it to say?"

"G+S+C," she said. "With a heart around it. Don't laugh."

He didn't. Instead, he bent to do as she'd asked. He did the +C, and handed the knife to Geoff. She liked his idea, each of them carving their own initial.

After Geoff completed the *G*, Chris outlined them in a passable heart shape and she passed her fingers over the whole design as he

471

folded the knife. "When the bark grows back over it again, it will be there, forever inside the spirit of the tree." She glanced at the two men. "It's like we've signed our names to an oath of sorts."

"A contract," Geoff agreed. Their lawyer.

"A promise," Chris said. "To have and to hold. To love, cherish and honor."

"To obey," Geoff suggested and Sam smiled at him. She took their hands, drawing them close, wrapping her arms around them.

"A promise and a contract," she agreed. "Forever."

∼

WANT ANOTHER STANDALONE STORY IN THE NAUGHTY BITS WORLD? World famous rockstar Dorian "DJ" James is a wiseass. He's also stubborn, willful, talented—and a submissive.

While falling for his client is a dangerous conflict of interest, experienced bodyguard Roy Bloodwell realizes it will take an all-in, committed Master to keep this kid safe. Especially when a tragedy tears DJ's world apart, and a nameless fan decides DJ is meant to be his.

Screw conflict of interest. Roy has a message for that fan, and anyone else who threatens DJ.

You aren't taking what's mine.

CLICK HERE TO PREORDER
NAUGHTY DREAMS

Reading this in print format?
Look for it at your favorite book vendor!

While you're waiting on that, would you like to read *Ice Queen*, a **FREE gateway** book to Joey's award-winning Nature of Desire series?

Tyler Winterman doesn't idly flirt—if he touches a woman, he has his sights set on acquisition. It's personal. And though he respects the hell out of Dommes, he knows down to his soul Mistress Marguerite is meant to be his.

CLICK HERE TO DOWNLOAD NOW
ICE QUEEN or at
https://dl.bookfunnel.com/oc9uxdowy7

[Note: Book not free at Nook; use BookFunnel link.]

ABOUT THE AUTHOR

Having penned over fifty acclaimed BDSM contemporary and paranormal titles, which includes six award-winning series, *Joey W. Hill* has been awarded the RT Book Reviews Career Achievement Award for Erotic Romance. A submissive herself, Hill brings authenticity to her intensely emotional love stories.

She is grateful for the support of a wonderful and enthusiastic readership, which allows her to live on her beloved Carolina coast with her even more beloved husband and menagerie of animals.

- On the Web: https://storywitch.com
- Twitter: https://twitter.com/JoeyWHill
- Facebook: https://facebook.com/JoeyWHillAuthor
- Facebook Fan Forum: https://facebook.com/groups/ JWHMembersOnly
- MeWe: https://mewe.com/i/joeywhill
- GoodReads: https://www.goodreads.com/author/show/ 103359.Joey_W_Hill
- BookBub: https://bookbub.com/authors/joey-w-hill
- Amazon: https://amazon.com/Joey-W-Hill/e/B001JSCIW0

ALSO BY JOEY W. HILL

Ice Queen

Mirror of My Soul

Mistress of Redemption

Rough Canvas

Branded Sanctuary

Divine Solace

Worth The Wait

Truly Helpless

In His Arms

Ignition Sequence

Naughty Bits Series

Naughty Bits

Naughty Wishes

Naughty Dreams

Vampire Queen Series

Vampire Queen's Servant

Mark of the Vampire Queen

Vampire's Claim

Beloved Vampire

Vampire Mistress *(VQS: Club Atlantis)*

Vampire Trinity *(VQS: Club Atlantis)*

Vampire Instinct

Bound by the Vampire Queen

Taken by a Vampire

The Scientific Method

Nightfall

Elusive Hero

Night's Templar

Vampire's Soul

Vampire's Embrace

Vampire Master *(VQS: Club Atlantis)*

Vampire Guardian *(VQS: Club Atlantis)*

Vampire's Choice

Non-Series Titles

Chance of a Lifetime

Choice of Masters

If Wishes Were Horses

Medusa's Heart

Make Her Dreams Come True

Snow Angel (short story)

Submissive Angel

Threads of Faith

Unrestrained

Virtual Reality